# Providence

The Providence Chronicles

# MONETA

This book is cursed.

Any errors of varying sorts found within are a direct result of this dark spell.

These are not editing mistakes. It is the Curse speaking to you through the Veil, disrupting reality as it breathes down your neck.

Read at your own risk, for this magickal malady makes its presence known beyond these pages.

You have been warned.

# Providence

## Kairos

The Providence Chronicles

ANORIN ARSSINOUS

# Providence



Cover design by: Damonza
Formatting: Enchanted Ink Publishing

ISBN: 978-1-7371862-1-2



Printed in the United States of America

WWW.ANORINARSSINOUS.COM

To the deaths we damned
and every dark we loved in.

# Chapter 1

## Mors Vivi

*October 31, 2020*
*3:25 a.m.*

Think the wrong word—let it recklessly slip from your lips at the wrong time, and the world will *burn*... I wonder who it was that said my name.

Cast out from their desperate jaw—a spell akin to sin—my name was nothing less than a *warning*; A prophecy on the tip of your tongue that breathed life into something that bleeds death.

A myth begging to burn into madness. A tempest in the eye of a tragedy.

I'm a curse, creeping in the corners of a cathedral, waiting to ignite. And you're all to suffer for it.

Especially *you*...

You'd think for a paradox as plaguing as me, Fate would've stepped in...

Fate—and *all* the titans of old weaving fables in the stars of your eyes—cannot be bothered to bend unless, every now and again, there is something to *break*.

But I can't die.

And believe me, we've *tried*...

Yet you'll still be praying to all your gods I lay myself to waste, though. Hope is funny that way.

Hope is *heavy...*

You never know what you're capable of when yours is not the only mind you keep. When the 'what was' and 'what ifs' of those around you creep into the hollows of your skull and *breed...* It's easier when I'm asleep. Your memories, your pasts, presents, and futures don't bombard my mind as if they were all my own. It's when I'm *awake* that finding myself tends to be a bit challenging. Who needs sleep—or mental health—right? Being half-immortal, the thinning line between my human side and my sanity... if you look close enough, barely a line remains.

Maybe that's why it's so easy to cross it.

If you're a Rev—if you're a creature only possible in dreams—if you pay attention, you can see it, too. The hushed violence in the broken among you, both human and supernatural folk alike. The yearning pulling at their lungs. Jagged edges peeking through flesh, dripping with the remnants of those who dared to put the pieces of one another back together. All that blood...

It's almost romantic.

Humans are beautiful that way. In how you try not to hurt each other. In how you try, with everything that you have, to protect those you love. Most humans contain their weaponry to words rather than steel.

But, then again, most humans are *shit.*

I'm relieved I'm half.

Almost...

"What are you fucking whispering? Why won't you let me go?!" Here I go again, painting you a white room. "Why the hell do you keep *staring* at the lightbulb?! What kind of a *freak* are you?!"

I smiled.

He pissed his pants.

"Do you know what fear smells like?" I hiked up my jeans and crouched down to the terribly sweaty child sex trafficker chained up to a chair of iron spikes—created by yours truly,

"Fear, Teddy—can I call you Teddy?" I grabbed his vomit-soaked shirt and yanked him to me, "after everything we've been through, I just feel *closer* to you, you know?" An itch took my attention. I reached into my bra and pulled out a couple of Teddy's teeth. "Love it when I get the roots," I muttered.

"Help! Someone help me!"

"You do realize we're in your basement, right? The one you soundproofed so that no one could hear you fuck the 7-year-old children—to death. You remember, don't you, Teddy?" I dug my fingers in his throat, his heart pounding. "Because *I* fucking do."

He gurgled on his blood, the taste of it too bland on my tongue. "Listen, someone beat you up pretty good. The bruises on your face—you're bleeding all over. I can call a guy."

"I've had a busy night—well, I suppose it's morning now. Though, you can't tell what with there being no windows in this basement. That's a building code violation."

"You crazy bitch! I don't know you!"

"No. But *I* know *you*. All I had to do was smell your *shit* on a little girl that escaped and, *poof*. Here I am." His confusion was priceless. "And honestly, man, your jaw is barely hanging on by a thread. Know when to shut up."

"The stalled shipments. The arrests…" I let him go, wiping my hands on my jeans and looked for the insurance policy he kept hidden in the closet.

"Setting free every single operation your lot have here and—" I grabbed the 5-gallon container.

"That shit back in May. With Dog's crew. Was that you too? But, *how*?" Every second in this place wrapped my skin in his…

"What can I say," I threw my blood-soaked curls over my shoulder, zipping up my jacket to hide my markings that glowed something *awful*, "I know how to get *around*." His paper bag eyes spied the plastic container and when his stomach dropped, so did mine.

"Please, don't—don't do this. I have *money*—" I sat, cross-legged, on the floor, picking some dried brain matter from the bottom of my combat boots courtesy of my last job.

"Every one of your *victims* and their families have your *money*. You won't be needing those millions." I unscrewed the cap off the container and shoved it beside him, the liquid swishing. The aroma of it filling my lungs.

"Please—" he spit, his mouth dangling by a few pieces of muscle. I stood up, dusting myself off.

"How many times did *they* say that to you? How many times did you force your sorry excuse for a *dick* down their throats as they *begged* you to stop?"

Neither of us blinked.

"There's something *wrong* with you." He spit up bile. It dribbled down his too smooth chin with every word.

"Enlighten me."

"You're—*calm*. You're—I've seen people like you. Mercenaries. Soldiers so *goddamned fucked* from war they don't know how to do anything but *murder* everything around them because they can't do it to *themselves*."

"Ah, that's where you're wrong, Teddy." I flicked the lightbulb and it swung from its wire, casting shadows and light across his placid, white face. And when he saw my coffee-colored eyes set ablaze in a bronze glow, growing brighter and brighter… "I've murdered myself. Didn't stick." I leaned in, the buzzing yellow light dilating his pupils over and over. "Someone once told me never to starts fires unless I was willing to burn. I wasn't any good at following orders. That's not the kind of soldier I am, you know? But *that*—it stuck with me."

"What—what kind of soldier are you?"

"Isn't it obvious?" I grabbed the container of diesel off the cement floor and squeezed his jaw.

"I'm the crazy bitch kind," I whispered in his bitten off ear. "Now, open up. This gasoline won't drink itself."

*October 31—Saint Helena's Cathedral—Montana*
*3:43 a.m.*

The cathedral doors trembled from my touch. My lungs filled with the scent of the water; holy only by name, not by nature. Tiny waves spilled over the edge of the stone pool as I made my way toward it down the aisle. Whether for the sake of ritual or to prove a point, I dipped my fingers into the frightened water; leaving a stream so red, it changed the color of the liquid.

Making the sign of the cross on myself, my feet moved with ease through the fevered force within the consecrated house. It tried to rid itself of the thing that made holy water boil.

I smiled.

The air crackled. The charred scent of incense lingering from morning mass strained to burn me from the inside out. It tickled. The stench lived in the pews, bibles, in the wrought iron chandeliers swaying from the gold-gilded face of a heaven that did not exist. The smell of my blood filled the cathedral; droplets dripping from dangling fingertips that couldn't choke the church fast enough.

Or is that me gasping for air?

With each step toward the altar, the stones beneath my feet *heaved*. Fractures and fault lines spread throughout the aisle, sending quivers into the skeleton of the house that made its stained glass beat in time with my heart. Only the sweet light of dead stars managed to fill the space, illuminating each painted pane.

The gaping gashes down my shoulders pulsated. The various versions of violence cracked into my skull; none of that hurts me. *That* pain I knew. It's the constant pounding from *inside* me that no amount of immortal magick could comfort.

You threw me to the lions and *laughed*...

These wounds—they'll heal because I'm not human. Not completely.

"I'm not what they did to me. I'm what they *made* of me. What you *allowed* me to become... How many more people have to die because *you* decided *I* should live? Can you even call *this* living when all I breathe is death? All I am is a static soul wrapped around a graveyard of bones housing a bleeding heart that will never stop beating. Just because I am able to sleep in the dark doesn't mean I've ended my fear of it; it doesn't mean the monsters vanish in the absence of light. It means I know what to do when they come out to play. And I *shouldn't* know what to do."

I shouldn't know...

A century's worth of choirs filled my mind. Every hymn screaming to keep me away from the cross. To drive my corpse away from the idol of *his* son. That made sitting down and leaning my bloodied back against the statue's feet all the more satisfying. "If anyone on this planet is *anything* like you, God, it's *me*." I rubbed my black and blue hands on my jeans, the fabric incapable of neither healing my immortal-marked bruises nor taking away the dirt of me.

I held my gun and made the chamber live, "Killers to the very end." My voice quivered and the entire cathedral followed suit. The tears drowning in my eyes couldn't hold their breath any longer. And as they coldly spilled down my charred cheeks that will take hours to heal from the demon attack, the pool of holy water with terror I knew better than my own name.

The water—It couldn't clean itself of my remains swimming within it.

There's no washing *this* off...

"I sure am *something*, aren't I? This place, it knows I'm—*wrong*. Everything *you've* blessed, they can't fight me off..."

You took him away from me. "Made them all fucking insane because of me." What's wrong with you? "What's wrong with me?"

The coldness of the metal against my forehead, my chin. "You so beautifully made me in your image. Be proud. I destroy everything I touch." I destroyed *him*... "You're a piece of shit. What is it, exactly you're punishing me for? How many more of your children have to suffer before you throw me back into whatever circle of Hell you plucked me out of?"

Answer me...

"Answer me!" The shattered glass, the split pews, the collapsed ceiling... "The stone pool cracking and bleeding onto your precious ground. How much longer are you going to let me walk this earth, God? How many more people do you want me to kill for you? A hundred? A thousand? Or was *he* enough?"

Don't cry, Devi. Don't you dare show weakness. Especially *here*. "A bullet to the head should work, don't you think?" I put the muzzle of my modified .45 magnum under my chin; aligning it perfectly so that brain and blood would splatter to the statue behind me, and pulled the trigger. "No? Two bullets, then." Three. Four. Five. Six. Seven. Eight. Nine. Ten. Eleven. Twelve. Thirteen…

What a beautiful sound.

No amount of bullets, immortal-piercing or not, are going to kill me dead. A girl can dream, though. I technically died thirteen times. But my body, this *shell* you've stuffed my cursed soul into, is more than capable of healing itself from each would-be death. Because that's what you wanted. At the end of the day, you *want* my heart to keep beating while Le-Mehti and DeKenna *desolate* this world until the victor leaves the battlefield with the perfect weapon. One capable of tearing out the soul of *any* creature. Living or dead. Human or—*not*… "You made me to be the thing that survives the lions. But how are *you* going to survive *me*?"

Remember that. Remember that *you* created a Killer of Gods. Your Immortal Human.

The Living Death.

Dynamite

*October 31, 2021*

Seven people within earshot of the gun fire called the police. Halloween is a good a night as any to spark the flames of chaos.

And I'm pissed.

I heard the callers. Saw their faces. Knew the contents of their stomachs. One is pregnant. While my clothes soaked up my blood, my mind channeled the soon-to-be mom Diana as she sat by her window, clutching a blanket with the name of her unborn daughter stitched into its corner. Lily gave her mother a soft kick and both our hands swept over our bellies. A smile on Diana's face, tears streaming down mine.

With the sirens minutes away, I redirected my attention to the gaping wound in the cathedral's roof. The darkened sky blanketed with the light of thousands of stars that gave their lives to reach us. I wondered for a moment if I could survive there, out in the expanse of space. I snatched some of the starlight, weaving it through my hand.

"I guess it's fitting." Hot blood splattered and dripped as I spoke. "Downright *poetic*." I had the blue hue cupped in my palm and it sparkled like snow. "Of course, *you* wouldn't be afraid to touch me," I said, sitting up, not bothering to wipe my chin. "You're *dead*, and dead things can't know fear."

Oh, but how we *should*...

Not six minutes after I killed myself, the Cathedral of Saint Helena had flashing lights crawling around her—creeping their way inside, inch by broken inch. A frenzy of discombobulation and panic spread like an incurable disease. It tasted like rotten berries and fresh plastic.

"Where the *hell* is the body?" The EMT's were mystified.

"What the—did a *bomb* go off in here?" A uniformed officer didn't get the memo.

"That's what the 911 callers said." Almost forgot. The bomb squad is here, too. I sure know how to start a party, don't I?

Arrogance—or sheer wonderment—kept me in the church. To go unnoticed, on this scale, I forewent the usual manipulation. For my current audience, a silent thought was all it took for all those around to perceive anything *but* little old me. I walked around them like a ghost in a haunted house; and, like a ghost, I couldn't touch anyone...

Not without marking them for a fate less merciful than death.

I don't know why I stayed at my murder scene. It's not as

though I didn't know what went on at these things. I think a part of me wanted to be 'in it' as they say. Us Revs—the supernatural lot—we're *so* removed from society sometimes that we forget what it's like to actually be a part of it. And though I know things—on a level that most don't, I promise you—it's always different when you're *in it.*

Always.

Full of the macabre scene, I teleported across the street in a flash.

I couldn't tell you the last time I'd been in a room with more than one person in it—when that person *wasn't* me, or something *else*—but there were too many of them. Too many emotions and lifelines, timelines, and bodily functions happening simultaneously. There's only so much I can take, especially when I'm in *this* bad of a way.

Two months' worth of memories played in my mind like a film but ended in an instant. Inside of me, time was a floating sigh. Outside of me, the passing of those two months sparked away in seconds.

The answer to why I had arrived at such a state of dereliction became crystal clear.

I had a nightmare.

And I—for the goddamned life of me—have *no* idea if I ever woke up from it.

The quiet in the cathedral brought me back. After an hour of meticulous procedure, everyone kind of... stood there.

It was almost funny.

"So, anyone want to chime in on this?"

Silence fell in the church. Even from my perch in the tree, I could see everyone's faces with immaculate precision, their confusion priceless.

"There are no shell casings, no shoe prints, no shrapnel, no *body*." The detective rested against one of the few upright pews with her notepad defeatedly cradled in her lap. Her corkscrew curls bouncing at her shoulders—more alive than I'll ever be. "It's as if the body vanished into thin air."

She took a breath through her lips as the others were

trying their best to fit the puzzle pieces together. Lucy rubbed sleep from her honey eyes. She had been asleep, warm in her bed. Now, she's in a hollow shell of a house of lies with little sticks illuminating empty clues to a mystery she'd never solve.

A part of me, an infinitesimal part—the *human* part—felt bad for what I'd done to the building. But remorse is simply collateral when it comes to confronting those that condemned you to Hell. Guilt is also useless when you're left with the dirty choices of war. The truth that many people refuse to see is that blood is spilt on all sides. The sad thing is, in *this* war, the only way to end the killing is by *more* killing. And—as luck should have it—I drop bodies like it's a fucking art.

Except for my own.

Fret not, though. I'm working on it.

The media salivated at the fringes of the yellow tape. Another news story that'll be blasted all over television screens and newspapers. More clippings that will go in a certain obsessed FBI agent's dossier.

Reporters performed in front of the white spark of cameras that burned brighter by the minute. The caved in roof of the church made for prime time viewing. The wires, cellphones, onlookers, the voices in the microphones...the *static*.

It's going to rain soon.

"Do we call them now?" Lucy's partner asked the question that both were tired of answering.

"I don't know what the FBI wants with these—what do we even call them? *Ghost* Crimes? But yeah. Call them up, Henry. I'm sure Agent McAlister is going to have a field day."

Joshua...

"You have to admit it's a bit out of our reach, Lucy. This is the *third* crime scene in Montana alone where there's been evidence of, what looks every bit like a murder, but with *no* body. No leads. No connection between scenes—I wonder how many times this happened that the *Feds* had to get their hands on it."

Agent McAlister's file-of-crazy on me is only about an

inch thick. The bulk of which is filled with crime scene photos. I tend to leave a trail of red in my wake. But don't worry. It's mostly mine.

Mostly.

The partners looked at my wreckage. They wouldn't be able to pull any information from my leftovers. I enchanted my insides to have the neat little tendency to decay immediately. Making everything utterly useless during forensics. Now, if I could only craft a spell to keep people safe from *me*...

"Do you think she's alive? The DiCaprio girl?" One of the uniforms asked the too tired Lucy Cartwright.

"Honestly? If *this* is what she's been running from the last six years..." She took a breath as her feet absently kicked a piece of marble. "If she's even alive to begin with." The words fell out of her mouth with a whisper hopeful for the contrary. Detective Cartwright would rather I were dead...

"We sure that this is the same missing person Agent McAlister is looking for?" Detective Henry Sullivan yawned. He crouched down to the crucifix. Henry is careful, more than most, not to get any of my lovely liquid on his slacks. "I fucking *hate* Halloween." He took his frustration out on his ginger beard.

"Every witness description matches the profile from the Fed." Cartwright shrugged.

"The witnesses descriptions are never consistent, Lucy." Sullivan and I both shook our heads, exhausted. I mouthed the words he spoke. "And then there's the matter of none of them ever having seen her face." They can't describe something they don't know they're seeing. Add to that some glamour magick, and no one will have ever known what you truly look like. No one will ever know the color of your eyes, the lines of your face, the curls of your hair... "This is nationwide, Henry," Cartwright and I said in unison, "that *can't* be coincidence and that *can't* be a different woman—"

"*Can't* be a different woman each time?" I mouthed the words along with Henry. Knowing what was to be said *before* it was to be said.

"No. Because *all* the witnesses say they saw a woman at or near the crime scene. Same height, same clothes."

"A tall woman with jeans and a leather jacket is not—" Cue the interruption.

"It can't be a coincidence, Henry."

"Really? Lucy, have you looked at the timelines of these crimes?" She looked away. "The ones back in May, are we supposed to believe that the *same* person was in Virginia, Florida, *and* Kansas because people saw some twenty-something wearing the same outfit?"

"I've seen the timelines, Henry."

"They were a *day* apart."

"I know."

"Virginia and Florida were—"

"*Hours* apart. I *know,* Henry."

"Something isn't right here, Lucy. Either the FBI is fucking with us or..."

"Or what, Henry?"

"Or, like you put it earlier, we're looking for a ghost."

No one here was *supposed* to be here. I'm splintering everyone's timeline. How do I know this? Because I can see every single person's *original* timeline. And now I see their *new* ones. Typically, any of my actions that end up interfering with human lives register as mere blips, little detours or delays. Other times—I do something stupid and take people *so* far off their tracks that it'll take an entirely foreign class of beings to come in and clean my very literal goddamned mess. *If* they even can. And though they're the only supernatural species I *can't* see, I *know* when they're around—and when they're angry.

"It's Halloween after all," Lucy muttered.

Lightning struck a mile away... Hundreds of millions of volts echoing in my bones. I ignored the tiny flicks of energy finding an exit through the tips of my fingers. "Unless this lady is walking around with an endless supply of blood..." A CSI tech mumbled to herself as she was starting to pack away my already rotting blood.

"What if there's a serial killer? He could be killing his victims in public but then taking the bodies with him—" Trailed off another tech. Funnily enough, the first tech's theory is absolutely on point. Funnier still, there *was* a serial killer here. Crime Scene Number 2 in Montana. That had been satisfying. Killing him, I mean. Not taking on the identity of the twelve-year-old girl he had tortured and raped for weeks.

Her memories...

*His* memories...

"What if—what if she's *not* the victim?" Henry is right to profile me as the suspect. But, tomato, to-mah-toe.

Even from up in the oak, I heard everyone's hearts beating, their insides surging. Their patience waned in me, and, if I concentrated hard enough, I could see what Detective Cartwright had dreamt of before her cellphone woke her up at 3:31 in the morning.

What I wouldn't give to close my eyes without worrying if I'd wake with a slit throat—not knowing if one of *them* did it or if I had done the honors myself.

Before I became *whatever* it is that I am, my empathic abilities were sporadic; fleeting sparks of low-intensity ESP that embedded grenades into my mind with each occurrence. After Vincent... after the Paladins trained me, my magick and psychic abilities didn't simply rush to the surface; they fucking *amplified* to full force. And if you're wondering which psychic abilities run rampant in my mind, let me save you the trouble. I have them *all*.

And when I became LeMehti...

Now, every time my Empath switch turns on, emotions aren't the only thing I channel. It's not a grenade that goes off; it's motherfucking *HMX*.

The text message in Henry's cell, the mesmerized fear in the dozens of onlookers, the spirit of the tree *aching* to be free of my body before it breaks itself. The pin drops and everything goes *boom*.

All in cacophonic synchronicity. Silent and deafening. Sweet and gagging. Sensual and numbing.

Too many people, too many visions of pasts, presents, and futures reeling in my head. I never finished learning how to control it. Not completely. I left. I had no choice…

Was I a murderer now? More than before? He had to die. What he did to those girls… He wouldn't have stopped. He'd never be caught. I've killed others. Others had died because of me and—who's screaming? Stop screaming!

It's *me…*

I have to sleep.

I'm still covered in blood.

I had to get to New Orleans. As tempting as it would be to start running there now, I couldn't. My body needs sleep. It needs water. Maybe eat something...

An immortal still governed by human needs? The biggest oxymoron fuck-you if there ever was one. I slipped down from the oak and it sighed with such a relief, I fell to my knees from dizziness.

And what happens when an object weighing nearly two *tons* hits cement from 10 feet?

A hole, for starters.

Fear not. Said hole never managed to be anything more than a crack in the sidewalk. And yes—it fucking hurt. You try taking in all that force on *your* fucking bones.

"Fucking hell…" I brushed off some dead leaves and dust. "Whatever." I gripped onto the straps of my backpack when my hands began to shake. "Start walking. One foot after the other."

I have to keep moving. I have to ignore the miscarriage happening down the street. I need rest. My body didn't just take in its own force like a magickal shock absorber; it took in small, yet effective, seismic waves that would have toppled over the rest of the cathedral.

I'm a walking tremor.

In the time it would take a heart to beat, I could be back where I've been squatting. You're already six blocks from the craptastic reject of a *Supernatural* episode. Speaking of which, I need to catch up on that. What season are they on?

Focus. Fucking *focus* for the love of Christ! You nearly phased into that car. A *parked* car. It may be three in the morning, but you know damn well there are 11 people awake on this block alone—six of whom have the probability of walking past their window and looking outside.

Is there supposed to be three of everything? It shouldn't be *this* bad. Something's wrong.

Something is very, *very*, wrong.

Think. *Think!* Where can I go?

I scanned as much of Montana as I could until I found a place desolate enough to take the beating headed its way. An abandoned train station. Perfect.

"Can you hear me? I'm *trying* to help you." What the actual fuck? "Eye contact. That's progress." Who— "The fuck are you?"

"Ok, we have a functioning voice box. Good. I'm Dr. Shereen."

"Why the attitude, Dr. Shereen? And, more importantly—" His temple met with the muzzle of my gun, "what am I doing in your house?"

What *am* I doing in his house—fifteen *miles* from Saint Helena's?

"Amelia, put the gun away. You—you banged on my door. By the time I got to you, you were half-conscious on my front porch." I can't be lied to, but I still scanned a five-mile radius, checking his fear and memories for authenticity...

I lowered my weapon.

"I'm—I'm sorry." I sat back down on the couch. "Wait. How did you get me inside?"

"What do you mean?" The doctor's hands searched for something in his medical bag. This isn't the first time Dr. Shereen helped a stranger in the dead of night. "I carried you from the porch. You were convulsing and," he recalled his memory, and by default, so did I.

"How did you stop it?" Dr. Shereen's eyes slowly set into fear. But, this time, the fear was *for* me, not *of* me.

"Stop...what?"

"The convulsions."

"Amelia..." he swallowed, I stopped breathing, "they *haven't* stopped." I saw the reflection of my eyes widen in his glasses and the room lost its focus. My mind finally allowing itself to realize that every inch of me trembling. "I'm this close to giving you horse tranquilizers, but I honestly don't think that will even make a dent. What condition you have?"

"Parkinson's." The man laughed. The sound of it—so close to me—it crackled in my chest like a fire coming to life, burning away echoes of an ache that live inside my every bone, but never the ache itself.

"You told me that already—Amelia, you're *covered* in blood—" He craftily avoided the matter of no wounds to account for all the red on me, "you need a hospital." I scoffed. Loudly.

"What I *need*, doc, is to unplug this jackhammer in me."

I had passed out. Scanned for a doctor in my concussed state and teleported my ass to him without even realizing it. I'm losing time. Again.

"The meds you gave me didn't work. Not because you're not a good physician, but because, well," I stood up, grabbed my shit and stuffed my gun into my jeans and with only slightly chattering teeth I said, "because I'm not a good patient. Thank you for—uh, helping me. It was truly kind of you."

The couch. I was on the couch. There's a stray hair on the cushion. My backpack was on the wood floor...*leaning* against the couch. The front porch... I stopped in my tracks; staring up at the stark white ceiling; seeing nothing and everything. I felt the good doctor's protests rising in our throats, so I did what I had to do.

"Doctor Shereen, it is *way* past your bedtime." I cocked my head and his knees gave out. His body now limp on the ground, fast asleep. "Trust me, doc. You do *not* want to be awake for this next bit."

A slightly illuminated wave of my hand and Dr. Shereen's

memories from the moment he heard my knocks were made into a dream.

Eyeing the big comfy couch and then the width of the front door, I knew there could only one way this thing is going to exit the building. I picked it up and threw it in the street...after fazing it through the front door. I'm not trying to demolish this man's home.

The truth of what I had to do next itched beneath my skin, but I had no idea if I could pull it off. I'm a walking earthquake that's starving to death—well, not *technically* starving to death, but semantics.

"Ok." I exhaled, put my hair in a bun, and went to work. "Oh, this is going to hurt like a bitch." I grit my teeth and set my hands on fire, crusted blood and scabs floating like embers off of my skin before effervescing. The stray hair followed suit. The spot where my backpack had lain, the sweet cherry floors now were charred black. Any other day I would repair them, but I simply didn't have the time.

My eyes followed the stairs to the bedrooms where his sleeping children and husband were. "Please let this work."

Walking backwards, every step scorched the wood, the fire doing precisely what I created it to do. Once at the porch, I shut my eyes and concentrated. Seconds later, all the air in the entire house had been emptied, burned, and expelled, taking away any evidence that I had ever taken a breath in this place.

That I ever existed...

I shut the door and locked it without touch and then—oh, son of a bitch! The fucking couch!

I stared at that godawful yellow nuisance practically heckling me from the middle of the street.

"You're coming with me." No sooner did I say the words did both my hips break. I muffled a scream in my hands that cracked my teeth instead of every window and tree on the block.

I ran to the couch and dug my fingers into the arm right as the cars around me began to crash into themselves.

I teleported and when I opened my eyes...

I ran over the tracks and fell on all fours in time for the now 2.5 quake to exit me. I lay there, following the stars, every bone in my body now pebbles and shards beneath my skin. I managed to contain the rest of the earthquake to the train station.

I heard the rain long before it left the clouds, but it's still a welcome surprise on my skin. Speaking of which—how did Shereen get the needles to penetrate? They should've broken. Weakened states *don't* make me more human.

I took a look back at the medical bag and the needles. Each one still had medicine inside. Even half-awake I manipulated his mind to make him *believe* he injecting me. Quite the defense mechanism. I left my Paladins, so I never found out *how* immortal I'd become.

If only I had stayed.

If only Vincent hadn't saved my life.

If I'd never been born...

All these goddamned 'ifs' didn't fucking matter. What's done is done. All I could do now was to keep looking for him; and, then, to do the one thing that would save everyone—even those trying to murder me.

Anyone want to hazard a guess? Here's a clue:

Click-click-BOOM.

I don't know if it was the warmth of the rain or the quiet of the ghost town—even the echoes of this place were somehow calm—whatever it was, it helped with the pain. Laughter couldn't be helped. Sometimes... sometimes I get to channel the good parts of a past. The songs sung to kids at bedtime. Lovers kissing under stark moonlight. A dog being walked, wagging her tail without a care in the fucking world.

The truth is, I can channel the bad parts of this place—an out-of-focus haze of white noise in the back of my head, scratching to come up to the surface—but my mind is putting all its energy into zeroing in on the good. A little bit of comfort. More than I deserve but what I need to survive. And I *have* to survive. Vincent is alive. He *has* to be. Please be alive...

Please be awake. *Be* awake. Be *awake*.

Go to sleep.

Twenty minutes of sleep would normally have done the trick and kept me going for a couple of months of constant consciousness but given that my mind and body were a top-shelf level shit show, my ass needed to sleep like a human. And I couldn't do that out here in the open. I could control a lot of things, but the sound of an earthquake *that* loud was not one of them. Humans and Revs alike heard it and were already on their way and I can't be here when they show up.

Let's torch this couch down to its metal frame—breathing would be nice— and let's teleport to the abandoned warehouse that's every squatter's wet dream.

I checked the perimeter of the warehouse before I walked in. Sigils and salt around each door and window for added measure.

Walking upstairs to my room, I realized I hadn't gotten myself food or water. "Fuck." Whatever. Sleep always takes precedence when it comes to nourishment. I could eat when I got back on the road.

Once in my *charming* brick studio, the ancient blood spells lit up when I walked in. The thing they were designed to protect was back. No demon or LeMehti were going to get through these forcefields. I traced the lines and curves of the illuminated magick with my finger. The memory of how so much of my blood was used to craft each mark flashed across my skin. The cold of the blade sliced into me all over again. I relived keeping my wrist from healing, until I had enough of me in the bucket.

You're going to get stuck in this memory. Get out before it's too late. Get out—

The bile slowly crept its way towards my hands; the tips of my curls already dipped in the green shit. I spit out the last of it, set the waste on fire and got myself up off the floor. "I have *got* to find a better Eject Button."

When I get stuck in a loop like that—get stuck in any god-forsaken memory—I have to do something *extreme,* even for me, to get the fuck out. Trust me when I say that you don't want to know what my Eject Button is.

Having every psychic ability is fucking grand and all, but this also means I have every way to lose my mind—Law of Equivalent Exchange and all that jazz—assuming my sanity is equal to the powers I have now.

Forgetting natural disasters take a smidge longer to recover from, when I took off my jacket, the wincing couldn't be helped.

The bruises were another story. What the demons did—"It's going to be *days* before these fade." A touch from a LeMehti or a DeKenna, it does something to my skin. Something I don't think I'll ever understand. On the same note of confusion are the bits of red under my nails. I grabbed a lock of my hair and it lay wet and clumped in my hand with brain matter. I'm a fucking mess all around.

Wait.

Didn't I sleep in the rain? Didn't I *walk* in it on the way over here? I replayed the last 45 minutes of my timeline and saw something I had simply been in too much pain to notice: It never rained.

I had seen a premonition. Fucking even *felt* it I'm such a damn good psychic. I heard the element fall before it reached the wall of windows. Rain finally kissing the glass. I traced the path of the droplets, their scent igniting a memory I kept locked away.

Shaking my head—the action taking the tears along with it—my fingers recoiled from the pane as I staggered back.

Lightning was about to strike. Not close enough for me to absorb its energy, but close enough to light up the room. To light up my face. The flash lasted three seconds, but for me, for *my* eyes, my curse allowed me to see the reflection of the beast in the glass for much longer. Its face covered in scabs and bruises, its neck displaying with perfect precision every link from the chains that had wrapped around it. The reality of my life, of a few hours ago, unfolded in the spark of a breath and the violence of it was mesmerizing…

I slid to the floor with a clear view of the storm and allowed myself to do something I normally don't have the luxury of doing.

Rest.

I wrapped up my jacket like a pillow and my head almost hit the leather when a strong scent pulled my bones back upright. Inside my bag, on top of my wig, lay a thick square of aluminum foil, a bottle of water, and apple.

I only noticed my lips quivering when my teeth had difficulty chewing the roast beef sandwich Dr. Shereen had made for me.

Cradling my bag and knees up against my chest, the light of the sun had begun to creep into the brick sanctuary. Inch by inch, the waves and particles filled the room. When the light reached the tips of my hair on the ground, you could see it flicker with hesitation. My tears were too hot as they spilled over the bumpy bridge of my nose and pooling onto my blood-crusted jacket. Hallowed ground cannot stand me. Light can't bring itself to warm me. Some days, these truths cut deeper and more jagged than others. I have magick inside of my bones and-and yet I'm dissonance. Discord. Disbelief.

An immortal that bleeds.

A paradox.

A giant fucking cosmic joke, really.

I am powerful enough to protect those that are in my path; and yet, the very thing I am protecting them from is *me*. Because I will never be refuge. I wasn't designed to be. I will never be safe. I wasn't designed to be. Because I will always be destruction. I was designed to be dynamite.

# Chapter 2

## Here

*October 31, 2021*
*Warehouse District—Montana*

Vibrations bore through concrete and into my ear. Panic opened my eyes. Lungs void of air. I lay there, unmoving as the room slowly drowned in firelight.

I overslept.

*Make sure you're awake. You're awake. Stop it. Make sure.*

The footsteps grew louder. Three demons—how did the DeKenna find me? One part of my mind surveyed the city for the mistake I made that brought motherfucking *Knights* to me while the other bore witness to the morning star flickering against my skin; never certain if it would be able to survive on my body. One check down. One to go. *Don't waste any more time. The pain will pass. Make sure you're awake.*

The shock of tearing my astral self from my body confirmed my consciousness. I'm awake...

I'm awake.

And the man who dared me kindness is in the hospital. His family in body bags...

"God damnit..." What did I miss? I found the doctor's timeline from a couple of hours ago. The Knights butchered his family and made him *watch*... The glass on the front door. I breathed on it. I didn't burn my breath off.

A snap brought me back. A crack of a twig six miles to the west. They're going to be here soon. Wait. Who the hell is *this*?

"Ellie! Come on! I keep telling you, this place *isn't* haunted."

*I'm* not supposed to be here. I should've been up five fucking *hours* ago to avoid this exact run in with the two humans.

"Very funny, Charlie. I don't know how suitable this place is for a *wedding*." Please God, no...

Why didn't I wake up? What kept me dreaming?

"This could be the space where you get ready." He's at my doorway waiting for his fiancé to catch up to him.

My magick won't let *anyone* enter or see me, but this couple has to be able to walk inside my room. To do that, I have to break my spell—the *only* thing keeping my exact position hidden from the Knights of Hell who will be here any minute.

*Fuck.*

*Stop debating and make up your mind!*

"Listen, you wanted mysterious, industrial, authentic. I'd say I delivered."

My hand wavered over the painted symbols; heart not racing nearly fast enough for the danger at my feet if the two humans came *any* closer. The soft, blue glow waiting to break the chains of my protection grew brighter.

They smiled. I gritted my teeth.

The Knights were at the abandoned train station. Nails drew blood from my palms. I know the future—I know *thousands* of futures—and I can see them all right now. But I can't focus. Nothing is concrete. Not until Ellie makes a choice.

And on days like this, days where I couldn't remember the last five hours of my life...

"I can't wait to marry you here." Each possible version of reality in my head—both theirs and mine—blinked to black, leaving only one.

He held her face in his hands with a gentleness I've only known *once* in my life. My fists relaxed and the blue light faded. I breathed and, as the lovebirds made their exit, I clung to the memory of Charlie's skin on Ellie's cheek. Warm. Safe. Then I reminded myself that my touch—that *anything* of me—kills people and I didn't feel so fucking sorry for myself. I'm not the only thing on this planet that hasn't been touched by another living being in years...

That's a lie. I *have* had a man's hand cradle my face—except, when *he* did it, he squeezed until my entire skull cracked open...

*Unmistakably* the same thing.

I shut my eyes as tight as I could to ban the images and slid out my daggers. I don't know how but they're here.

All three Knights. They somehow penetrated my forcefields and made it inside the warehouse.

Dozens of escape strategies flowed in the silence between two heartbeats. None of them showed me walking away unscathed. A wound from a fallen angel is a wound that the magick inside my veins cannot heal from.

Not fast enough, at least.

Each Knight held a position in a different area of the warehouse. There's only one way this encounter with the strongest order of Hell's army will end with me intact. And—with their chain mail echoing across the halls and their voices chattering in my mouth—that end became vividly clear.

"I don't understand. She *has* to be here," the youngest of the three spat out. Disgust and confusion dripping from his words.

"The trail died at the train station," Naphella said. Their scent—mud, cloves, and burnt wood—swirled in the back of my throat, the memories dizzying in my mind too quickly. The smell of Hell. It'd be days before it washed off my skin...

"We cannot be certain of that," the young Capheus urged, his fingers nervously tugging and tapping the metal of his coat. Capheus is afraid of me.

My sleeping ability to render LeMehti human applies to *all* immortals.

I'm an equal opportunity executioner.

"True as that may be, Caph," Naphella inspected her manicure and picked at some of the Shereen family insides from her nails, "the bitch is smart. She knows how to hide." With that, they appeared at my doorway.

This bitch not only knows how to control the minds of creatures so ancient you'll do well not to wonder your place in the cosmos, but she knows enough of their arcane magick to send her own little doppelgänger to the wilds of Alaska.

Fret not. The twin was an illusion. I'm crazy, not a sociopath. And no more third-person narrative. That didn't sit well with me either.

"Naphella's right. The witch *is* here," their leader spoke, walking into view.

"I'm not disagreeing, but Kyzza, how do you know?"

"For a reason that troubles me that you are *not* aware of, Capheus. Because this is *precisely* where *we* would come for cover."

Kyzza stared into the space I stood. The red of his irises eclipsed in a pool of black; never-ending embers crackling from the corners. Hell in their blood, on their skin, on the breath of their voices. As if the taste of Lucifer's tongue filled your mouth with every word spoken.

One more minute and my doppelgänger will be ready.

But something didn't fit right and the DeKenna Knights knew it. Their instincts told them I'd be here. Yet, for the *life* of them, they could not find the will to walk into this room. The *need* to investigate vanished along with the sight of me.

I don't know why, but I made my way to the deadly soldiers, until my toes nearly kissed the threshold that separated me from the unholy trinity. This unit didn't always grace me with its presence. So, when it did...

"Then, with all due respect, sir—where is she?" Cepheus asked and bellowing howl of wind followed.

Kyzza's lips turned up into a smile, as if a puppeteer took control of each movement. Naphella—nostrils flared, eternal heart pounding to make up for the fact that she cannot sweat—knew her fellow officer had a valid point. Her grip tightened around the hilts of her swords.

"The lady is *hiding*, Capheus. Pay attention." Before Capheus could respond to Naphella, Kyzza looked over his shoulder, sensing my twin. The soldiers vanished without a sound, the black of their uniforms lingering, leaving shadows of smoke where their bodies had stood.

Zoom out of my face cameraman. We don't need the dramatic close-up shot of my overcast eyes, yet. Save that for the *end* of this chapter. Trust me. For now, take a long shot around the room. The markings of blood magic and vandalistic art on the walls. My half-zipped backpack with my copy of *Persuasion* peeking out of it on my concrete bed. The wavering sunlight on my skin, filtering in through the splintered windows...

Why are you focusing on my hands? You're aware that this is a *book,* right? No one can actually *see* what you're doing. But, in your defense, the shot on them was a good evocative move. Especially since they're trembling.

Hands can cradle with comfort or tear with terror. The conclusion I'm sure you've come to is that I live my life fully immersed within the latter. It's a good thing I heal all super quick-like, huh? Specifically, those gosh darn times when I had a spike through the eye and, oh! That one time—at band camp—you can't see it, but I'm winking at the camera. There isn't a camera. I'm not shooting a fucking "A Day in the Life of a Really Fucked Up Half-Immortal" documentary.

What was I saying?

Ah yes. Spikes in eyes. Another time, the Devil and I—how fucking *rude* of me. No one likes spoilers. Let's get back to some proper narration. It's not here. Next paragraph, please.

The LeMehti Empire. Elegant. Enigmatic. Ancient. Pure magick and brilliant madness walking among us, living between realms. Before me, they were beautiful and sweet. Before me, they went about their lives with little surface difference from your or I. Before *me,* they would help you up if you fell, *not* dig their fists deeper into the back of your head and pound it harder and harder into the ground until blood and bone replaced a face.

But I digress.

Something must've triggered it. Maybe a spell inside of me broke them—I don't know. I don't know what curse lurked beneath my skin, if my skin itself is the curse. All I know is that my blood, my heart—my *soul*¬—poisoned *theirs.* The poison—this fight *only* response—spread to the LeMehti and what's left of Heaven's fallen angels, the DeKenna. No other Revs have been targeted. No other supernatural being has had its soul eaten away until all that remained was a hollow, twisted version of who they used to be—full of insanity and survival instincts, killing anything to protect itself from the one thing that threatens its life.

I was something a human was never meant to be—capable of something a human shouldn't be capable of. Yet, I *am.*

Except, these two ancient empires were both vying to murder me dead for something I *can't* even fucking do, yet. Logic, right? What my mere existence does done to them.... It rapes until all that's left are bullet shells housing souls void of everything except the second most lethal sense in existence.

Fear.

What we're capable of when we *fear...*

If I were them, I'd fucking kill me too. But I don't know how to *stay* dead. None of us do. I've been dragged to Hell...

Hi, there. Still kicking. But this isn't even the craziest part of the story. I mean, have you seen the *size* of this thing? We've got a ways to go. The juicy little mindfuck is the part where one of *them* saved my life.

The Paladins.

The most powerful soldiers of the LeMehti army. Immune

to the poison that drove their kind mad, they chose to help me. They trained me to survive and did *whatever* needed to be done to protect me. None did this more than the Paladin that fell for me.

Vincent.

Their defiance meant spending their immortality on the fringes of treason. It meant that they could never go back home. It meant war against their own, against Hell, and against *Fate* itself…

But when Vincent gave his life for mine…

Trust me on this, with every God-forsaken page you turn, you'll see why helping me is more dangerous than walking into the underworld. Because, you see, Hell is empty…

And *I'm* here.

# Chapter 3

## Something Wicked This Way Comes

I holstered my daggers right as the birds crashed in. Glass screamed as it hit the concrete; the fresh insides of the finches, owls, ravens, and crows slowly pooled beneath their pointlessly flapping wings. I knew they were coming, I had simply forgotten. One of the crows still breathed. Still ached to fly...I knew why they came. I *knew*, but it doesn't change the fact that I wanted to bring them back from the dead. Alas, necromancy is *not* part of my fucked up little repertoire. I knelt to the half-alive bird, touching her would only frighten her more, but what choice do I have?

She was in pain...

"Shh. It's ok." I picked her up gently, her neck barely able to support her head. Cradling her in my arms, she breathed jaggedly and her wings flailed with violent hope I recognized all too well, while her talons fought to scratch. Caught between fear and instinct—between escaping me, and killing me. "I'm so sorry, little one." Her pain was my pain. Her emotions, *my* emotions. All at once, I split. Part of me stabbing my body uncontrollably while another—the other trembled in a corner too deaf to hear from the wails bleeding my mouth.

And this was from a *bird...*

I held her cheek, soft but losing its warmth, as I hummed a song that always calmed me—a song that is magick when falling from the right lips. But the spell hardly made a change in her. I swallowed back my tears and did what I had to.

Did what I do *best...*

The cracking of her neck didn't sound any less destructive.

"You don't have to be afraid, anymore." I rested her limp body on the ground. Wiping my hands on my jeans, I made my way around the remains to the ledge—shards crunching under each step reminding me of when I was at The Court and a certain LeMehti was bored. He had to pass the time somehow.

My hands dug into the brick, anchoring me in the window. *How much time did I lose, this time? Focus. You're not in The Court. You're here. In this time. In this place...* The height still took me. Isn't that funny? I can't die for shit, I've fought all mighty immortals and yet I'm scared of falling. Nothing will happen to me, but shit—*You* jump out of an 8-story window and see how you feel...

I took one final look at what had been my so-called home for the last couple of weeks. It had been years since I stayed in one place this long... I cocked my head and all the magick combusted from the brick building, inside and out; and as I caressed the window frame, sparks escaped from my hands and set the room on fire. Every footprint that I walked went up in flames. Every fingerprint turned to ash. Every breath caved in on itself. And the aura my body emits, pieces of my soul—burned alive until nothing of me remained.

And then I jumped.

When I landed, my whole body began itching. "Fucking shit." I was still covered in blood from last night. I kept forgetting. "Where in the fuck-hole am I supposed to shower?" My eyes met the sky in exasperation.

I began my trek to the nearest working bathroom in the first uninhabited place I could find.

I walked for a long time.

As I got closer to my destination, I saw something from the corner of my eye. Well, my *third* eye. There was a fellow supernatural in our midst. This particular Rev was across the street and she was in quite the state of bewilderment.

Goldie Locks sensed the magick I used in the warehouse, and—were I *any* other person—the witch would be able to see beyond the glamour spell I had cast to cover up all the black, blue, and red bruising of me. Thing is, though, I have pixie dust that predates witchcraft. That being said, my power wasn't her only reason for housing giant question-marks quickly filling with dread in her mouth.

The Rev cannot figure out *what* I am. None of them have.

Her waif-like fingers gripped the strap of her Chanel purse, panic rising in both our chests despite the rushing cars between us—despite the little devils and pirates and superheroes running amok. Even having planned my route before the bird crash to avoid the Halloween mass, it's difficult walking down the street without bedlam in my bones.

Now parallel to the witch, I decided to examine her; I caught a mouthful of her exhaled breath and Marc Jacobs perfume in between my teeth. What was such a posh spell-caster doing in this not so post-card-worthy part of Montana? Breathing in the extensions of her helped me sus out the more relevant information about why she is about to walk into an apartment building to perform what you would know as Black Magic. Trust me when I say: you don't want to know the specifics.

Lorna Boone, 28, single, cherry hair, loves hot chocolate and surprisingly despises reality television. Fire elemental with a sixth sense strong enough to let her know—right down to the core of her horrible being—that it would be safer for her to light herself up than know me.

Because burning yourself alive is simply better than crossing the street...

It started then. On my tongue—tingly and gnawing, hot and sharp as they fought their way to come out—her words. As Lorna opened the door that would lead her to an room where the unimaginable awaited her, she parted her lips and let out sounds that we both knew I'd hear, yet the expectation didn't diminish their impact: "For the love of the Gods, kill yourself."

Lorna disappeared, breathless, into the complex and I stood across the street, staring at the metal and glass door until I didn't see anything anymore.

The crack of my fingers as they broke snapped me out of my trance. I pulled out both hands from my pockets. Appendages bent in ways bone should not be bent. I willed the pieces back together with my mind and shoved my fists back in, right as a mother and her kids witnessed me in horror.

They crossed the street.

"Momma, does the lady need a doctor? She's hurt."

"No. Keep walking. There's no helping people like *that*.."

When I arrived at the unbaptized condominium, I went around back and made my way in through the service door, picking the lock. I had lunch near the Pentagon one day. Channeling a skill like that was a natural side-effect.

Once at the top floor, I stood outside the door of the freshly painted condo. Concentrating, I shut my eyes and breathed in deep. I burned my breath as I exhaled and when I opened my eyes, I could see the entire residence as though I were inside. When I found the bathroom, I blinked myself into it.

I didn't prepare myself well enough for the immense mirror over the double vanity. The kind with the awful exposed glamor light bulbs on top? Perfect for viewing yourself with the *best* clarity. The shock of my image, even from the corner of my eye, nearly brought that roast beef back up my throat.

I turned on the water for the shower and shut off the spell that kept the concrete and fists on my face hidden. Though, enchantment or not, I can always see through my spells when I want to.

But who in their right mind would want to?

And there I am in all my chimeric glory, displayed in the looking glass like a fantastic beast in a freak show fit for gasp-worthy viewing. I'm half-human, half-immortal. An amalgamation of every psychic ability, magick older than religion… I'm capable of healing in the blink of an eye and absorbing earthquakes as easily as I create them. What am I? What do you call a thing that's died a thousand deaths wide awake? What do you call a thing that terrifies animals and evokes fear in others so profoundly, that they would rather commit suicide than risk touching it? That they would tell me to murder myself…

What am I if not a goddamned monster?

*Don't cry. Don't you fucking cry.*

Steam fogged the mirror, clouding my face. But, I can see through the mist; through fire and night. Through spells cast and lies forged. I can see through the Veil between worlds and yet I can't see, no matter how much I try, one fucking reason to live.

Not *one.*

I smudged the clouded glass and the bruises around my cheeks burst in bright technicolor. Vivid blues and perfect blacks swimming around my veins. Scabs on my eyebrows and temples... Superficial wounds didn't heal immediately but they didn't take forever, either. But fatal wounds? Now, those lovelies heal damn near as quickly as they're inflicted. Exactly why I'm still standing…

I undressed and stood there in nothing but my underwear and bra. Both arms looked as though they were dipped in scarlet nail polish—stamped with every color in between—my tattoos barely visible beneath. My hand ran over my abs, where LeMehti knees had kicked me, the force separating my stomach from my esophagus.

They were gentle that day…

The most painful injury is on my back. Two scars following the curve of my shoulder blades where enchanted DeKenna blades tore through old scar tissue and broke through my ribs to pierce my lungs; the tips nearly coming out of my chest. It took me nearly sixteen minutes to recover from those. My blood doesn't bother me. It's *their* red on *my* skin that leaves me with twisting. But, I won't lie. A part of me enjoyed slitting their throats. Maybe too much...

The weapons we use, they hurt us; delaying our instantaneous regeneration to minutes, sometimes hours for your little half-breed. The LeMehti and DeKenna are races that cannot be destroyed. Their weapons, then, were smithed to inflict as much injury as possible on one another all in the name of *balance*.

They're not fools, though. These toys don't kill. That's my job.

But fret not, for an immortal who cannot heal faster than the speed of thought is a very fucked immortal. Plus, they leave what would otherwise be a sweet remnant behind. Shining silver scars. Yes. Us *mighty* beings mar.

Lucky for me, only other supernatural eyes can see this little light show. Still, the damage displayed on my body didn't get a dent in compared to something else my eyes never fail to fixate on when I dared—and every time I do, every time I look, I break in ways a person shouldn't be capable of breaking.

But, then again, I'm not a person am I?

I quickly burned my old clothes on the tile floor. Time to shower. The water scorched at first, and I had to play with the fucking knob to get the temperature right, ignoring the too-soft glow emanating from the too inhuman birthmarks. The water was warm and—for a split second—I smiled.

My eyes shot open when I smelled iron and caught the sight of the liquid changing color. This wasn't the first time I've washed this much blood off of my body. This isn't the first time I've clawed at my ears because I can hear the dead from three different timelines in this bathroom. How many times did I die in the last 48-hours alone? Life and death swirled at the bottom of the tub; dripping from my fingertips. I could bleed for eternity and my heart would beat forever.

Focus on the water. The sound of it. Tune out the TV's. Ignore the car radios. Forget about the baby smiling inside his mother. Don't pay attention to the voices the schizophrenic is hearing 20 mother fucking *miles* away.

Forget.

Forget the ghost in the shower with you. The other one bashing his head in the mirror. The one giving herself an abortion…

Don't.

Don't waste your time listening to the song they're dancing to. Don't feel her lips on his. Don't you fucking cry when you feel him brush her hair behind her ear. It's not your hair. It's not you. It's not your baby. You're not watching your favorite tv show. It's not your body he's cradling. It's not your body you're electrocuting to snap yourself out of this empathic loop. But they are voices in my head. All of them. Everywhere. A never-ending orchestra of—everything.

Stop it. I'm not crazy.

Wake up.

You're not crazy.

You're not crazy.

Focus on the water…

Open your eyes. Wake up!

I picked my body off the shower floor and finished cleaning up. Being without a towel or toiletries—not that I need them—I conjured up a continuous gust of wind. Dry a few seconds later, I dug out some clothes from my backpack. I'm on my last set.

"Shit," I muttered.

I put on the worn-out blue jeans and black boxer briefs—though not in that order—and threw on my sports bra and black ribbed tank top to match. Shoved my Hobbit ass feet in my military boots and then started to wash out the blood from my leather jacket in the sink; making certain to boil the blood and water as it went down the drain like I did in the shower.

The shower…

Almost forgot my meltdown. Around here, you triage your personal bullshit, lest you fall to pieces. Besides—despite my lifespan—I'm without the amenity of dealing with any and all psychological maladies.

Now, back to things that matter, cameraman. Zoom out of my forced face of apathy and zero in on my black jacket in the sink. All slow and dramatic-like if you can.

We have to ground ourselves in the here and now, in the monotony of outfit changes. In the ordinary of laundry, the compartmentalization of severing three phantoms from three different timelines from this side of the Veil... Luckily, the more stubborn stains I meticulously burnt off. This is simple enough to do on leather, but to do it on my own *skin*—let's just say I need a bit more practice.

"Finally." I put on my jacket and as I combed through my damp curls with my fingers, I took one last look at myself in the mirror and teleported myself on the roof. "Thirteen minutes and forty-seven seconds. I never should've allowed myself to fall apart. You can't afford to waste time like that..."

A breeze rushed by and I detected the temperature. Cool enough to wear my favorite piece of clothing but *not* warm enough to wander about with *only* a jacket. I willed into existence a duplicate of the blue hoodie I burnt. When you're both a freak *and* on the FBI's radar, hoodies are critical in keeping a low profile—that, and the ability to psychically tamper with electronic devices. But the feds are not the ones watching me in this moment. There was someone *else*. No. Not someone.

Some*thing*.

Whatever this thing is, it's more dangerous than even *me*. And from what I can tell, it smells of iron and smoke and desperately wants another fix of tragedy. If I didn't know any better—but I do because I'm an Empath and we *can't* be lied to—the blood its craving is its *own*.

I shut my eyes for a moment. When they opened, I saw into the eyes that saw right through me. Eyes that bore into me with a hate *so* agonizing, they could only belong to one person:

Me.

And there I am in all my chimeric glory; displayed in the looking glass like a fantastic beast in a freak show fit for gasp-worthy viewing....

Fuck.

The room tilted in a Dutch angle and I gripped the sink letting out vomit and crimson. I spat and forced my image in the mirror. "This. *This* is real. This right here. It's *now*. You're in Montana. You're in a bathroom—"

*No, no, not again. Don't split!*

Half a dozen astral projections of my psyche unhinged themselves from me. Each screaming, stabbing, burning... God. You, you don't need to know... The lights flickered. The foundation shook. I nearly took out the city's grid.

Hugging myself as tightly as I could, finding my way back to my lighthouse, I put myself back together. When *we* have things like mental breakdowns, sometimes, things get literal.

I swallowed, barely breathing. My knuckles let go of their white shade and I straightened my stance. "It is Halloween Day. You are *awake*. You are *alive*. You are *not* crazy."

Every now and again, my realities—my timelines— they *blend*. I never quite know— I'm never certain whose timeline I'm in or if I'm on Earth or some other forsaken realm. The electroshock therapy I gave myself—will give—I *would* have given myself, would act as a shot of adrenaline. But, since things like adrenaline don't work on things like me, I use *pain*. It literally knocks me back into reality.

The *correct* reality.

Already having lived through this once, it helped me to avoid the emotional breakdown which spiraled into a psychic loop where my psyche split from my body—but that's neither here nor there. I'm on the roof now; hoodie and all. But, maybe you're wondering how my future-self sensed my present-self watching her. Ever have a dream *so* real, you would have bet your life you weren't asleep?

I'm connected to time in a way that you would only be able to understand if you were one of us—if you were *me*. First, you have to accept that time is a construct humans created to tether us to whatever it is that happens here. Trackable time. Calendar time. Tick tock time. That is *not* real. Thinking of it in that way simply makes living a little easier to swallow.

Think of time as a circle, instead. Everything happening all at once; together. Past. Present. Future. When I have a premonition, there's no warning, no crescendo leading up to the loudest notes. Sometimes, I see the different versions of reality *so* clearly, *so* easily, that there is no break between them. Add to that my general increasing trouble with discerning fantasy from reality, and you get me being completely convinced that I was actually living out my present, rather than having a vision of my future.

Now, maybe you're thinking why I spent a bunch of paragraphs explaining the cogs and gears of my mind. Is this shit important? Do I need to care about it later? Well, that'll be for you to decide. But, the reason I blabbed on about my five minutes of *Girl, Interrupted* is because I deemed it far more *merciful* than telling you how I ended up with a two-year-old baby girl in my arms and six dead witches at my feet. Lorna fucking Boone being one of them.

They were going to sacrifice the baby. So, I fucking killed them—*all* of them.

I dropped to my knees as gently as I could; not allowing the shock inside of me create a shock within the ground. The little girl remained quiet, but trembled—or, was that me? Why didn't I catch this earlier? Lorna must have used a spell powerful enough to elude even me. But I should've seen it.

The specifics.

When you see thousands of things every minute, you can't notice every horrifying thing. Madness has a tendency to blur the lines of perception... *Excuses. Don't fucking make excuses for yourself. You should have known. You should have known this.*

I had willed a blanket for the baby from her nursery the second before I grabbed her. I sat then—baby Nyra in my arms—a perfect circle of death in front of us and the light of a hundred candles dancing on the wooden altar from where I snatched her before slitting the throats of three witches, tearing out the hearts of two others and then setting fire to the leader. All this in six seconds flat. One precious tick of time for each piece of shit Rev.

I held Nyra as I waited for them all to die. It took longer than you would think. In the split second that I made the decision to murder them, I scanned their pasts and their futures, trying to find a reason to stay my hands. I waited for Agents of Fate to provide interventions. I waited for them to *stop* me.

Not only would the witches have killed Nyra, they would've killed *more* children; A *hundred and twenty-seven* more...

Lorna's psychotic coven—who don't deserve the name *witch*—planned to take those lives because they believed the blood that flowed in those innocent, pure veins would make their own stronger. They believed that, somehow, when they drank the blood from the bleeding throats and wrists of these *babies,* that their powers would amplify enough to take on a an evil this world has never known before.

The fucked up thing isn't little Nyra falling asleep, warm and peaceful—despite being in my arms—as I rocked us both to find calm. I didn't find strangeness in the fact that I had stolen the lives of six women with magick in them older than most cities, but whose castings held no power over *me.* I didn't even flinch at the ripples I created from their deaths. They *weren't* meant to die. Not today. And *especially* not by me.

No.

None of that made me want to set my fucking self on fire... Only *one* fact and one fact alone mattered here at my freshest crime scene. Turns out, the women here were absolutely *right*. They had visions for decades—signs of what's to come and how to prevent it. A warning whispered from winds millennia old, crossing time as fast as it could to reach who ever would listen to the words—words echoing over and over in the hopes of being found.

Fear, desperation, and psychopathy drove these women to dedicate their lives to a branch of magick *so* stained, people hardly remember its name. The fucked up part is: I think I *should* have let them kill Nyra...

I swallowed, jaw clenched, ignoring my tears, ignoring the fact that I hadn't breathed since I showered. Dismissing the thick, red blood encroaching my boots and the wafting of burnt flesh blanketing my tongue.

Nyra's body wriggled slightly; she's dreaming. Dreaming of every shit thing that happened to her up until I arrived. Waving my hand over her eyes, her tiny struggles subsided and she let out a sweet sigh. I couldn't take away her memories of being nearly murdered by her own mother, but what I *could* do for her is lead her little mind to a dream she won't be terrified to remember. With the peaceful reverie playing behind the hazel eyes of the new orphan, I knew I did the right thing in saving her and the other children. But it didn't make the truth of the situation any easier to swallow.

You see, the blood of the children *would* have made the witches stronger. To become powerful enough to be able to defend the earth from this *thing*, however, the body count would need to be much higher. A *thousand,* if we want to be precise.

Because something *was* coming. Something that drove a coven to set out a plan to sacrifice innocent children. Something that drove a mother to hold a dagger to her crying daughter's throat...

And this isn't the only coven who heard The Warning.

Earth isn't the only Realm at the mercy of a monster that drives mothers to hold daggers to their daughter's throats...

This isn't the *my* world.

*Please, God, no...*

I looked deep into Nyra's bright, teary eyes. I found her father. He's still alive but knew nothing about his daughter's existence. I hated it, but I projected everything into his mind, from Lorna's plans and death to Nyra in my lap. His nosebleed would fade. His eyesight would return in a few minutes.

I left the den of dead witches and took Nyra with me. I hopped rooftop to rooftop until I made it to her father's house five miles away. Casting the strongest protection wardings I knew on the pair, I returned daughter to father and ran.

"Wait. Come back!" Tears trailed down his eyes as Nyra did something she had never done since she's been alive—she laughed. I walked away with Ethan's crumbling voice following me, "Thank you for giving me back my daughter..."

I teleported myself back in the bathroom of the condo. "Where is the *Bridge*? How the hell did I make it back from the mirror world to *my* Earth *without* an Evenfall Bridge? I'm running out of time!"

I stared into my reflection—that familiar absence of synchronicities within. "Where are you?" I gripped the sink, the light of my markings burning through my clothes. "Where. Are. You?" My eyes sparked into an Aurora and when I finally blinked—teleported—whatever you want to call it, when I did it, I ended up with a two-year-old baby girl in my arms and six dead witches at my feet. Lorna fucking Boone being one of them.

They sacrificed the baby.

So I fucking killed them—*all* of them...

I dropped to my knees as gently as I could; not allowing the shock inside of me create a shock within the ground. The little girl quiet—her throat slit wide open; remnants of trembles still in her bones—or, was that me?

*How* did I not make it back in time? How could you let Nyra *die*?

My labored sob fractured every wall in the room. I wanted to bury my head into her shoulder and never let go, but death is not something that would deter my stain. My touch would mark her and the LeMehti and DeKenna would find Nyra and *desecrate* her remains—or worse, bring her back to life and...

I set Nyra on the ground, arm's length from me, and laid beside her. Nyra's skin was still peachy as her soul was mercifully cradled away by her angel.

The police arrived. *You need to run, Devi.* "I don't want to leave you." I reached for her hand, the lump in my throat growing beneath the ache of her little death... I recoiled my hand. "Forgive me..."

I orbed her back onto the altar—back to the crime scene—and shrouded myself in the rafters above right as the cavalry stormed in.

One of the officers *jetted* back outside to throw up the second he saw Nyra...

The words sang in my ears again. Porcelain shattering on marble—a remnant from the covens' memories. Especially Lorna's. They were the last thing that ran through her mind when I lit her up, and when they shrieked their whispers in my mind, I *knew*. I knew because I'd heard this omen before.

The police, the firefighters—they don't know what I've done. Like in the mirror world, killing the witches saved the lives of the thousand children in *my* world, too.

All but one...

But saving the children means risking all of *your* lives...

I opened my mouth and spoke The Warning, hoping that the right supernatural creature would hear it, hoping my tears would run dry already. Because, no matter how much I wished that none of this is real—that my life isn't a laughing abomination—this will remain forever true: Something *is* here.

And, God help you all—that something is *me*.

"Something wicked this way comes..."

# Chapter 4

## Mea Culpa

From my window at the condo, I watched the horde of special vehicles for a long time. Firetrucks and useless ambulances. Police cars and news vans. And, a vehicle that never seems to be too far behind me—the coroner's van.

It came as no surprise—eerie ESP or not—when Detective Cartwright and her partner arrived. What would come as a bit of a shock to *them,* however, would be Lorna Boone's wallet. A clue that would lead them to her house and then her basement. A bonified *lair* with oodles and oodles of photos of children and handwritten plans on how each kid would be bled dry and *why* their soul would be 'sacrificed to save the world from ruin', as Nyra's mother so eloquently had put it.

Cartwright will become nauseated when she sees a picture of Nyra on Lorna's desk with a beautiful note—in calligraphy, to boot—that detailed how she would murder and then drink the blood of her daughter, sharing it with the five other bitches—I mean, witches. I tried to make this easy. No evidence of me— but as a consolation prize, a lovely display of psychopaths well on their way to a murdering spree that would have quickly turned into the most abhorrent serial killings the world would have ever seen. Trust me. The cops weren't going to lose sleep over not finding the person who did these women in.

I'm far from the crime scene, but distance is irrelevant when you can see the world the way I do. While I kept a portion of my focus on the police, another part was keeping a look-out, while another was making sure the rest of the world I was channeling didn't rise above the white noise level I kept it at. My main concern at the moment was *not* falling through another realm. But with a dozen other parts of me doing a dozen other things—I should really get you a proper narrator.

The coven was desperate to save the world. For in doing so, they themselves would live. I'd kill them again, if I had to. If I had to choose between children and murdering the coven—even though that meant there would be one less force able to put me in the fucking ground—God damn it—I'd choose a world where no child died, no matter the realm.

"What's with the face?" Henry and Lucy were in their car on their way to Lorna's house. Their voices as clear in my mind as their morning sex in my—

"I don't have a face, Henry." She lied.

"Yeah, you do, Luce." I returned to the window, the hesitation of the sun palpable. "You think this is related to the DiCaprio girl. I know you, Luce. What did you see back there?" They drove for a good five minutes before Lucy could gather enough energy to speak.

"You remember the pedophile?"

"That human trafficker?"

"No, the *other* pedophile?" they exhaled, but the shit of their world didn't leave with it. "The incest case." Oh, yeah. Forgot about him.

"Right. The one that made his son and daughter—"

"Yeah, Henry." They took a moment to try and relinquish

the images from their minds. I threw up in my mouth after remembering—*reliving* being the son and daughter—and the father *watching* them…"How was he found?" He thought for only a moment then sighed.

"Dead like the rest." Lucy waited for the remainder of Henry's answer. "He had the pictures of the kids in his chopped off hands on his lap. What was *left* of it—"

"Exactly. And we *happened* to find the wallet for a Lorna Boone who was involved in some black magick, occult shit, resting *neatly* in the palm of one of the corpses?"

"You lost me." They turned on a corner. Lucy and I sighed.

"How much you wanna bet that, when we walk into Ms. Boone's house, we're going to walk into some equally disturbing paraphernalia? Beyond the run of the mill occult shit."

"There was a sacrificed baby on an altar, Lucy. How much more disturbing do you think it can get?" Lucy shrugged at Henry's words. I didn't know whether to pity Henry for his naivety or envy him… "I bet you dinner Boone was just some bored soccer mom who got too caught up in this shit. And dessert. At my place." Lucy rolled her eyes but we couldn't hide our smile. My fingers traced the shape of my mouth. It took me too long to process the expression I wore.

"You're on. And I want Italian." Their laughter choked me. "The DiCaprio girl, she's involved. I can't explain how, but I *feel* it Henry. I—I think she's taking out these bastards like some kind of vigilante." Grant it, I could practice a little more finesse, but… you don't see—you don't *feel* what *I* feel…

"This isn't a comic book, Luce. If this *is* her, she's what? Going around finding scums of the earth and then setting them on *fire*? Ripping out their *hearts*? Some of these people, Luce, the amount of violence… The dad with the incest was killed *expertly*. He was *alive* when he was dismembered. Even the M.E. said the bullet that did him in was *too* perfect a shot. In between the eyes, severing one hemisphere of the brain from the other. DiCaprio was a Psychology student and wrote *poems*."

"She is also a kidnap victim."

"*Is*, Lucy? What?" A couple crossed the street with their French Bulldog. The men's hands clasped in one another was warm. I didn't expect my hands to flinch or for Henry to drool over that puppy.

"She was kidnapped. *Twice*. God only knows what happened to her..." The things her mind trailed off too... How peaceful my life would have been. "She could have—"

"She could have become a professional *assassin*? An expert killing machine with the ability to tear into the human body? All without leaving behind *any* forensic evidence?" Well, he's *not* wrong.

"Someone is murdering these people, Henry. And yes, *without* leaving behind evidence."

"I know." His tone softened. "But why do you think this someone is *her*? It's as if you want her to be—"

"I don't want her to be any sort of killer, Henry." Her half-true words bit at him. Shaking her head with a breath almost too heavy for even *me* to breathe, Lucy stared out the window. "I want her to be *alive*."

"I know you do. I know." Henry took his fiancé's hand and wouldn't let go until they arrived at Lorna's bungalow. My hand burned and a memory crawled beneath my skin, wrapping itself around my neck... I broke my hand. There. That did the trick. Now, where were we?

Fret not. I'll keep the sweet post-traumatic flashbacks and clinically-approved self-mutilating grounding techniques to a minimum.

I'm an *excellent* multitasker. You won't even know I'm doing it.

"Hey, Nyra." You've got to be kidding me...

"Hi." Thanks to her mom's lack of, well, fucking *everything*, Nyra can't string together more than a couple of words. She never even had the chance to be raised by the television like some of us had.

"My name is—"

"Devi. I remember."

"I—" I walked over to the force of nature. Her ghost more

beautiful than her corporeal form had been. "Do you know where you are?" She nodded.

"No Nona?" Her fingers tugged on her blankie. Her dark caramel ringlets shielding her quickly misting desert storm eyes.

"No sweetheart. No Nona." Nyra had never called Lorna 'mom'. Nona was Nyra's way of pronouncing *Lorna.*

"And Papa?" I looked over her shoulder, her father patiently waited for his daughter to process what her mother had done to the both of them. Lorna had bewitched Ethan at every turn, had only used him to conceive. He hadn't even known about his daughter until a few months ago. That was when he grabbed her from her crib, wrapping her in the blue blankie that carries his scent—the only scent that calms Nyra—and nearly made it out the front door when Lorna came home early and shot him, point blank, in the head. Nyra refused to leave her father's arms. It was the safest she'd felt her entire life...

I arrived in Montana the next day.

"He's close." Ethan and I exchanged quick looks. "How did you find me, Nyra? You're supposed to be with your Papa right now." He's the angel who took her soul to Heaven. She looked down at her bare, pudgy toes then back into my eyes. And when Nyra reached her hand for mine...

"I wanted you." She ran into my arms and I welcomed the crash of peace against my chest. Nyra smiled, wrapping her hands tighter around my neck, her warm cheek snuggling into mine. Nyra was *not* afraid of me. This little baby was in the arms of a *killer* and she— "I forgive you..." Nyra kissed my forehead and swept her hand across my cheek, the tips of her tiny fingers resting at my chin. "Thank you for giving me back my Papa."

I checked in on the dynamic duo.

Both their minds reeled with the sheer level of evil they

witnessed in Lorna's basement; including the expertly-rushed skeletal remains of Ethan—whose bones were going to be used for potions, curses and your run of the mill exfoliant.

"Do you need to puke again, Luce?" Henry said, palming his own stomach.

"No. Thanks. Twice is enough." Cartwright's skin had lost a couple of shades. It never gets easier, seeing shit like this. Knowing horror exists in the world is one thing. Being knee-deep in it becomes a different animal altogether—one that isn't easily purged.

"Morris texted. The names in Boone's notebook—the one next to her instructional booklet on killing her daughter—" they both swallowed, "she's at one of their houses now." Henry took in the space and simply shook his head. A decade in Homicide and he still couldn't wrap his head around the things human did to one another. Lucy saw his 'bad day' from across the room.

"Let me guess. Basement decorated in antlers, sigils, and candles made of *unicorn* tears? Am I right? I'm right, right?" Henry chuckled and I looked over my shoulder when I heard a heartbeat racing...

"Close. Dorothy Calhoun had her 'Shrine of Death' in her attic. Identical files along with a dozen more children across *ten* different states and three countries. These women—whatever they were going to do Luce—What's wrong? Who's calling you?"

"It's McAlister." It's fucking *McAlister.*

"I swear, if he takes this case from us—" Henry muttered as Lucy took out her cell. "He doesn't even have a partner. What's he doing taking point on a case a national as DiCaprio's?" Henry took his frustration out on his coat and Lucy rolled her eyes when she finally answered on the fourth ring.

"Detective Cartwright." I could hear Joshua on the other line—not only because I could hear what Lucy could hear, or because I know the sound of his voice and could therefore track it—but because I'd been trained to locate all manner of sounds from great distances so that I could do one of three things: escape a threat, terminate it, or *become* it.

Henry's theory, no matter how laced in sarcasm, is nothing short of the truth.

"Cartwright, this is Special Agent Joshua McAlister. I'm in Helena. Can we meet?"

I now know why I didn't wake up earlier. Had I gotten up and left as I had originally planned, I *never* would have been able to kill the coven. And maybe, just *maybe*, a part of me overslept so that I would have the chance to see my friend.

Or, Door Number 3: It's getting harder and harder for me to wake up...

I can't stay. If I fall through another Bridge to another realm and Josh happens to be too close...

On the roof, I took a moment to decide where to go next. The last six years were spent searching for the Thomas—the LeMehti Paladin who *murdered* Vincent. He fueled the vendetta in my veins—and I *liked* it.

Thomas is the *only* immortal on all sides of this war capable of ending my life and—I heard the scratches of ink to parchment rush across the pages of my skin. In an instant, a murder of crows made their way above me, circling. But this flock wasn't here to attack. They'd come with an invitation to a sanctuary from someone I saw years ago outside my bedroom window on Halloween night...

A crow flew around and cawed in my face until I finally did what it asked of me. I let out my hand and she—she perched herself on my arm. Her eyes met mine, dark and cool. She cocked her head and I followed and reached for the note secured to her leg; energy surging with calm that rivaled only Nyra's touch...

"Thank you." The murder vanished into a puff of smoke. "What the hell?" Why can't I channel the person who wrote the letter? Why can't I glean where it came from? This witch—she's blocked *my* empathy. "Curious." I opened the note and read its contents.

*You will be safe here. —Keres*

When the words settled inside me, I found her. Looks like Thomas will have to wait. I'm off to New Orleans where the ancient witch—who's heard The Warning—waits. I couldn't break through her spell, which means one thing: her and I are *bound*.

I blinked myself into the street, directly across the way from Joshua...

He *bolted* to me but a van drove in between us and when it passed, Joshua was left in the middle of the street and I was in the backroads of a highway in Oklahoma.

*How did you not know he'd be on this block? Why did you let him see you? Why couldn't you tell it was his heartbeat you heard?*

He knows I'm alive. No doubt. No mystery. No question.

God help him, he *knows*...

And it's all my fault.

# Chapter 5

## One Way or Another

*Mid-July 2022*
*River Manor—New Orleans*

Fall wasn't for a few months. From up here, though, death was clearer and closer than anyone dared admit.

Time tends to forge illusions *so* powerful, we become blind to the truth. Especially when we're afraid of what it will do to us. Lucky for you, the magick trick only lasts for as long as you'd like it to. For me, however—and other Revs like me—we don't have a choice; we see right through the bullshit. We pierce through the Veil and watch its lies bleed out onto the floor as the truth stands there, naked and stark. We're so used to it, we don't even mind the mess anymore. Most of us, at least.

Red isn't a color for everyone.

Watching the Sun rise never ceases to amaze me. From the roof of the Victorian, the horizon etched the City of the Damned with a fledgling sapphire and tourmaline sky—gently spreading across its bones. And for the first time in forever, the giant star didn't have a choice. It *had* to shine on us.

*All* of us.

There is such a dense population of Revs in New Orleans—the sun can't punish the earth for a city it had no control in creating. And, if we're being fair, neither did the earth.

But then there's *me*.

In the five a.m. light, clouds bruised with color—the twilight sky a fading graveyard of constellations—I played with some rays between my fingers. Unlike starlight, the very much *alive* sunlight did *exactly* what it normally does—avoided me as much as possible.

What's interesting is that I know *why*.

It may not condemn the other Revs that live here, but the sun *does* make sure to single *me* out. Makes a girl feel *special,* you know? And that aversion to my flesh and blood holds true for everything.

And I mean *everything.*

That hushed pit in your stomach—the one tugging at your lungs? The buzzing, the headache, the prickling on the back of your neck the longer you're with me...

Some humans sense that something isn't quite right with me. Others know there is a wrongness in me so damning that they can *taste* it; a tongue dripped in whiskey, if whiskey was made with blood.

The majority have no idea what walks among them. Yet, even *they* can know that the air gasps when I breathe it. Let's not dwell on the details. We all know who waits there anyway.

You would think that I would be used to the fact that I'm some sort of anathema—in every sense of the word—in both the natural *and* supernatural worlds. You would think that pushing away the most important people in my life to save them from me would make things easier. You would think that, like my eyes, my heart would adapt to the darkness surrounding me.

The darkness *within* me...

Truth is, some things are simply incapable of acclimation. You only end up building a tolerance for the torrents of hurt and psychosis. Something doesn't *stop* hurting because you've experienced the strike a countless times before. It's another illusion—a small gift our minds construct to shield us from the world so that we can survive it. But, pain is pain. And no matter what anyone tells you, survival *hurts*.

I decided it was quiet enough for a nap. I cozied up against the belvedere and slept. I woke myself up before I shot myself in the head—the dream of Vincent and I dancing loading the gun.

I looked over the slowly rousing city behind me. I wonder sometimes, how peace can be so utterly out of reach; how beasts hide in the arms of beauty. Everyone is enchanted by the fantasy of it all; the blood beneath their feet pooling unnoticed. And if I'm not careful, this city will drown.

I took the stairs back to the second floor, ignoring the previously alive Tabitha and Dmitry going at it in the attic. At the landing, I nearly lost my footing. "It's *way* too early for this shit, you two." I gripped my t-shirt *tight*—the wall the only thing holding me upright. Dmitry's mouth slid across Tabitha's neck. A curve lead him to her shoulder—her damp skin on *my* lips—his mouth on *my* shoulder...

Istanbul flashed in my mind.

"Nope. *Hell* no. Not going down *that* mind-fuck rabbit hole." We're shoving *those* memories back in the box where they belong.

Proper rest would have to wait. Let's clean my weapons, instead. I took out my .45 and set it on the small writing desk flanking my bed. I cleaned my gun and started practicing. I disassembled the weapon and reassembled it. Once with eyes open and once with my eyes closed. Task completed in 6.24 seconds flat *without* the use of my supernatural gifts. I like to do things on both spectrums. It creates a balance between the two forces inside of me. On occasion—doing things this way—a *mortal* way, reminds me that I *am* capable of dying.

And I *have* to die. I sharpened my daggers in front of the fireplace at the foot of my bed—their sparks igniting the wood. The act was more for form than function since immortal arms don't dull. The blades sliding across one another brought with them a bit of catharsis. Purging—if only for a moment—memories of a place I'm incapable of forgetting.

I took a breath and when I exhaled, the flames effervesced. The strength I carry—I didn't mean to snuff out the fire. That's what happens, though, when I'm not in constant and complete control of my LeMehti side. That's what happens when I foolishly think I can be human.

If only for a moment.

I caught sight of something in the John William Waterhouse painting resting atop the scrolled mantle when I resurrected the flames. I shut my eyes to will the image away. When I looked again, its clarity had intensified.

The striking blues, crimsons, and jade greens had no power to deter my fixation on this object. Once I see it, it's difficult to *unsee*. I darted my eyes to the owl figurines, to the dozens of crystals meticulously placed along the mantle. But I could feel it *staring*, waiting. The hairs on the back of my neck, all standing on end because *it* demanded my attention. With a sigh, I made my way to the bathroom, knowing I'd be followed.

There it is—right where I knew it would be.

Waiting. Mocking. Taunting. Haunting.

*My* face.

My *reflection*. Proof of my wretched beating heart. It *begged*, more than anything, to be ripped out of its cage.

The question was never a matter of *if* but a simple matter of *when*. I knew it. Keres knew it. Even *Claire* knew that my death would find me in New Orleans. The blood dripping from between her legs formed a puddle on the checkered tile. She hardly noticed. I swallowed her bile.

"I don't think it's a good idea." A fly crawled out of her scabbed-over mouth and flew down to her bruised chest. "You *can't* die. I don't understand why you're going to do that to yourself." Saliva dribbled from the split of her lip, reflecting the golden hum of the gaslight scones. I watched Claire through the bathroom mirror. She rested her head of corkscrew curls—as gingerly as she could manage—against the door frame, her palms cleaving her belly. "There's no sense in it. You have to see that. Don't you?"

If I gripped the pedestal sink any harder… I inhaled and dropped my head. She'd vanish soon enough. Ghosts have a tendency of leaving you alone if you ignore them *just* the right amount. Ghosts like Claire, at least.

The scent of bergamot and sandalwood replaced the sight of Claire.

Keres is up earlier than usual making candles again. Her concoctions serve one function and one only: keep all manner of Revs—dead or alive and everything in between—away from me. Not that she required the candle to do so, but her last batch *did* keep away the more aggressive of the undead. But it's ghosts that give me the most trouble. The vampires, on the other hand, they're… Well, they gawk at me as if I'm the fucking *Sun*…

However, being what I am—I don't know. It's as if I suck the life out her spells because she always has to cast new ones; the minor ones, at least. Hence why most of the house of the timeless witch is clear. It's only *my* room that's full of activity. As for Tabitha and Leland in the attic? Every now and then, harmless Rev spirits wander in. Every now and then, I get to remember what's it's like to be touched…

Keres proved her words in the note the moment I stepped foot in Louisiana. No DeKennas or LeMehti have made it across her threshold. Not through teleportation or their ancient magick. As impossibly beautiful as that was, it still took me *weeks* to move in with her. The surrounding Revs—most of them didn't mind me—but there are those that would curse me, feed me to Cerberus; my blood on their hands their happy payment.

I found the least haunted property in New Orleans—let me rephrase that. I found the part of New Orleans with the least amount of Revs that wanted my head on a spike. St.

Vincent De Paul Cemetery was one such place. And no, the cosmic comedy of its name is not lost on me. It simply helped me close my eyes at night.

Keres's spell held. Any Revs that didn't care for me were incapable of coming near me. That made it one of the gentlest places I'd ever squatted in. And I'd never had so many conversations with so many people who *didn't* see a *disease* when they looked at me—grant it they were all *dead* and such, but semantics.

I'm a very special kind of *fucked*. So, it makes sense that one of only a handful of immortal witches would seek me out and defend me with her life. Totally sound logic there. The woman is anything if not determined and with a bond as deep as ours...

I plopped on my bed and immediately broke the bedframe and the wooden planks beneath. The entire room vibrated; candles and figurines all tumbling down. My mind is the only thing keeping the tchotchke suspended in mid-air and the bed from falling through to the living room downstairs.

"Perfect," I muttered. Down on all fours, pointlessly assessing the damage. The two front legs of the bedframe had lodged into the floor a full four inches, splintering and breaking the wood in every direction. That's actually not so bad.

Keres looked up from her cauldron when the wax and gaslight chandelier in the kitchen shook. To say that she has become accustomed to this kind of thing would be true. But, on a level she doesn't like to admit—but I know regardless because I'm inconveniently an Empath—she's also simply sad for me...

When I lifted the bed skirt, the teddy bear was unexpected. The small figure behind the stuffed animal, however, not at all a surprise. His eyes were narrow and golden as usual. The cuts on his knuckles dry and *still* infected. I finally exhaled and shook my head.

I ran my hand over the floor, repairing it in one swift motion. I sat with my back against the foot of the queen-sized, four-post bed; my fingers finding the threads in the tears of my jeans far more interesting than the ghost of the dead boy hiding under my bed from the monster he used to call 'daddy'.

"Jonah?" He whimpered at my call. "Jonah, come on now. You gotta get out from there." My hands wrapped around my thighs and dug in, *hard*. Jonah's afraid. *So* afraid that he wrapped his hands around his teddy and dug in. My heart matched his frantic tempo. For a few small moments, it was nice to feel my heart beating so slowly.

He remembered the things his father did to him, to his mother. And, by my very nature, every memory in *his* mind became memories in *my* mind. His fear, my fear. Every punch to his face, cracking on cheek. Each time his father beat him, tied him up and gagged him—locking him in the bedroom closet—I was there. I was there when Jonah watched his father rape his mother. I channeled Jonah's mother being raped by his father.

I was Jonah.

I was his mother.

And I was his *father...*

"Please make it stop." Jonah cried out. My toes curled inside my boots from his tear-filled words.

"I can't Jonah. Not unless you come out." My fingers dug into my palms, tearing skin, breaking bone.

"Do—do you promise?" I wiped off the blood from my already healed hands onto my jeans. I got down onto my stomach and wriggled my way to Jonah under the bed. I did everything in my power to keep my claustrophobia in check as Jonah cracked a small smile—the teddy and protection symbol etched into the wooden floor in gently glowing between us.

"I promise that I can get you out of here, Jonah."

"What about my momma?" Claire...

When her husband found out she was pregnant again, he took a butcher knife to the daughter whose death plays on repeat inside of Claire every time I see her. "Can you get us *both* out of here?"

"Yes." I lied. "Now, come along." What I do requires touch or else I would've been rid of him months ago. Sometimes, bending reality to save someone is worth the illusion, isn't it? His bloody hand reached out to mine and I tried to smile for him. I placed my palm on his forehead and *Poof*.

Jonah is finally severed from the living realm.

As I washed out the last of the vomit from my mouth, I heard Claire again. This time, she wept and it took all that I had *not* to cry with her.

"Thank you," she whispered with quivering lips and joy in her heart. When she vanished, I knew she followed Jonah.

Ghosts normally need help, a push to help pry them from this joke of a world most have no choice but to call home. Lucky ones like Claire—she just needed to know her baby was safe.

I stood in the doorframe and looked at my room. I don't know what it was that stood out to me. Maybe it was the 67 kaleidoscopic-colored candles competing with the iridescent lightshow dancing on the white comforter from the three stained glass windows? Maybe it was the fact that I have in my sights something that—for all intents and purposes—is actually *mine.*

A bedroom.

One with a bed big enough for *two*...

Keres—for some reason I've yet to fully grasp—wanted to protect me. With her position in the world, she was one of the few in *existence* with the power to do so. The power to know that an ancient coven from Budapest cursed me and smart enough to sit back and watch as it fell apart because

Her request to have me live with her was more of a demand. After her *5th* visit to the cemetery, she'd had enough of my bullshit.

*'You're going to live with me. I'd suggest you stop squandering away time and start choosing a room.'*

As my eyes followed the perimeter of my room, appreciating the painstakingly hand-crafted items filled with different types of craft, I had to wonder if Keres believed me to be more blessed, or cursed.

When I was human, I could see between worlds. Bearing witness to the dead one day, clawed by the roars of another the next. I'd wake up in the middle of the night with evil at my feet and my past lives in my eyes. As a human, I was a psychic that saw too much and an Empath that felt out of place. When my psychic abilities awoke to full force, when I became an immortal—a *LeMehti* immortal—my undeniable presence on the supernatural radar gave everyone pause.

But magick—magick as *atomic* as mine—it laces your tongue. *Everyone* wants a taste. Where was I going with this? Right. Hence all the protection gear from my witch.

I heard Keres set the tea tray on the wrought iron table out on the porch. "Come on. We don't want luke-warm tea." She spoke to me from the back of the house outside, in a normal, soft volume. The inhuman part of me, however, heard her as clearly as I could hear her the flow of her blood.

"I'll be right down." The words fell to her ears from my bedroom. The way she heard me was as if I were standing right beside her. I wonder what that's like sometimes. How quiet it must be...

I opened the window to let the warm summer air ebb its way into the space. I looked through my chocolate antique dresser. Changing my clothes in one motion, I blinked, I mean—I ported—shit. So many different synonyms for teleportation. When I opened my eyes, I was at the screen door downstairs in the kitchen. I walked and walked right into it.

Literally.

Keres laughed and it was adorable.

"Are you alright?"

"Not funny, Keres." Ok, it's a *little* funny. I wriggled my body and phased out the screen door. Fucking hell.

As I walked over to her and took a seat, her smile faded with such speed, it left a pounding in my cheeks.

"That was quick." Keres sighed with a raised eyebrow. She poured our Earl Grey, the steam framing her the way mist would linger in the midst of witchcraft. In the midst of *her*.

"I didn't want to make you wait." The scent of the cranberry orange muffins, warm syrup and butter made my mouth water, putting Pavlov to shame. When did I eat last? Also, she's not referring to my entrance.

"I still can't wrap my head around it." I adjusted myself, bringing my giant feet up on the bright paisley blue seat cushion.

"The fact that I can teleport?" A sugar cookie met a sweetly valiant death in my mouth. "My unrivaled knack for getting out of *tight* situations?" I smirked like an idiot. She didn't. I grabbed a muffin, buttering it and dipping it into the syrup. I know she's not referring to my ability to move through space and matter at the speed of thought.

"No. The fact that you're about to sit here and break bread with me as though the last half hour *didn't* come to pass." I swallowed.

"Ah. *That.*" I pointed with a spoon. I couldn't look at her. I took a bite of my muffin and then started fixing my cup to my liking. "Well, you get used to it after a while." I shrugged, the action making my off-the-shoulder knit slide down—well—off my shoulder. "Really, it's not as bad as you think." I lied through my teeth. Keres has been an Empath for much longer than me. If I try hard enough, I can hide the truth from her. And believe me, I have to try *hard*.

"If you say so." I could lie to her all day and she'd call me on my bullshit all fucking night.

I stirred my tea with my hand while Keres did so without the use of her bones. She shook her head with a slight sorrow, the slowing six a.m. sunlight making her deep auburn hair and the roses on her dress burn in scarlet.

She crossed her legs and took a sip of her drink. Her hazel eyes met with her lush garden that flowed right out of the pergola we were under. It took me days to fully acclimate to all the aromas in her estate. Especially the garden...

"Something else is bothering you, Keres." I sipped my tea, perfectly crafted with the right amount of honey and cream. Her gaze met with my dark, violin brown eyes. Her fingers smoothed the side of the black floral porcelain in her hands; the carnations and tulips on the cup followed the motion of her skin. "What's wrong?"

"Why is my state a sudden concern? You'll not live long enough to mind it. It's not as if you hold any admiration to anyone you're to leave behind."

"That's not true and you know it." The wind picked up. The chimes sang.

"Perhaps." The garden stole her attention again. She licked her lips and in that quick second, I recalled a memory of a European witch trial. I rubbed my eyes and the images fell out. "I only wish you would realize that you are—in every sense of the word—*good.* And you're more good to everyone *alive.*"

There were barely a few wrinkles around her eyes and hands that worked to stay alive that evidenced any aging on her body. Only those witches of the strongest bloodlines or born with Soul Magick, like Keres, become immortal. There are only two dozen witches in the world that are *this* ancient.

And every single one of them warned Keres to stay away from me.

She should've listened...

"Do you hear anything?" She looked at me quizzical; furrowing her dark, thick eyebrows. "Not energy or the wind echoes of the past." Setting down her cup, Keres shut her eyes and focused. "Well?"

"It's peaceful." She dared to smile.

"Deafening." Her face cracked as she looked at me.

"Care to elaborate?" She knew the answer. Every word of it. Let's humor her, anyway.

"Ever since I moved in, you haven't noticed how *quiet* it is? Out here, not inside." I pointed to make the distinction. "Inside can be a damn mad house." I shut my eyes in annoyance of the cacophony of insanity that's constantly in my head.

"Since you moved in, it's been simply *serene*." The sides of her lips lifted slightly. "The spirits are more active, this is true. A presence such as yourself—I would be confounded if the Revs *didn't* flock. You must understand this given that you're—"

"An Undead Magnet? A Ghost Host?" I chuckled, too animated for my own good. She didn't find me amusing. "It's not peaceful or serene." My words dropped the mood. Literally. We heard it. Kind of sounds like a stack of books hitting the floor. "The reason you don't hear anything is because I scare it all away, Keres."

"Don't be ridiculous." Her whole *body* dismissed me as she took hold of her tea again. My eyes went straight for the ink pricked into her fingers centuries ago; committing them further to memory.

"When's the last time you saw any birds on the estate? A squirrel?" I love squirrels. "Shit, a fucking *mosquito*." She swallowed her tea, contemplating eyes on the feverfew and nightshade. "Where are all the butterflies and bees to pollinate your garden, Keres?"

"Speak plainly."

"You already *know*." I huffed and leaned into my seat, nearly bending the iron.

"Say it aloud." She puffed—gracefully, might I add.

"Lorna and her coven, Helena and her *holier-than-thou* Budapest coven you saved me from all had a *damn* good reason for what they were doing."

"We've spoken our peace on—"

"I'm saying I'm going to burn the entire fucking world while you sit there and drink your fucking tea." I could barely control the tiny arcs of lightning jetting from my body. I sat there, the smell of my burnt hair and skin in our noses.

"Devi..." The wind took an order from the witch and ceased its gales. "If there is wickedness in you it is because you believe it to reside there. If you were indeed something wicked, not only would those hunting you have succeeded in ending your life," she set down her cup and straightened the Ankh around her neck, "I'd have murdered you myself." I couldn't look at her, her words settling into my skeleton with a heaviness we were both too intimate with.

"Just because no one has figured out how to kill me doesn't mean I'm not evil." I never should have come here. I should have continued searching for Thomas.

"Do you hear your insanity, azizti? The two halves are *not* mutually exclusive."

"That warning left someone's lips *centuries* ago and it left for a *reason*. Lorna wanted to murder her own fucking *daughter* for a reason. Why can't you see that? Why can't you see that *I'm* the one keeping your roses and magnolia trees alive? The only pink thing I like, by the way. The magnolias, not the roses." We both adjusted ourselves in our seats. "That calm you feel here, that thing you believe to be peace day in and day out—it's nothing. It's *literally* nothing. I create *nothing*. Now, sit there and tell me that *isn't* a warning. *The* Warning."

It's been an omen whose existence she acknowledged but refused to accept. The look on her face... God, I hate myself. *You can never pretend to be happy and keep your mouth fucking shut can you? Useless.*

We sighed and Keres allowed the wind to breathe.

The sadness in my mouth crept out and I couldn't catch it in time to hide it from her. It hit her with such force, she had to grind her teeth.

"Be that as it may, Devi, warnings, prophecies, omens—whatever you wish to name them—they are *not* determinants of murder. And this Warning—it still bears no merit to kill you. We don't even know if this is about *you*." Here we go.

"You're wrong." Hundreds of dead died inside me in a flash. When *Vincent's* death hit me, the fracture in the concrete beneath our feet shook the pergola. All the birds in the neighboring yards flew away. It's moments like this that I'm grateful I can control the elements. That little crack could have brought down the block. But, then again, it's times like this that I remember that people drop dead because of me and that makes what I want a little easier to swallow.

"Sorry," I mumbled, rubbing a tremor pulsating in my shoulder. I pushed and fused the pieces of stone and earth back together with my mind while staring blankly into the steaming liquid in my cup.

"Finish your breakfast, Devi. We have three clients before lunch." Keres has no need for money. She has more of it than most monarchies combined. So, she never charges the people who come for her *services*.

As we finished our breakfast, I deemed it safe to remind Keres of my plan. "So, to recap," she rolled her eyes. "There's a war brewing due to me being a half-breed of questionable pedigree." Keres cocked her head at me with impatience. Confusion and sheer annoyance washed over her face.

"It's *not* questionable. You are LeMehti. A psychic witch. You are a Reaper and a M—" the Persian witch rubbed her temples, "we've been over this a *hundred* times, child."

"Yes, yes. Immortal killer of—"

"Everything."

"You're not helping your case here, or theirs."

"You have no idea the power inside you, child. You've *stars* in your blood. Do what they do best: Burn. Burn until nothing of *them* remains on this earth. If they mean to fear you, give them reason..." Keres clutched her palms together. It would the closest her hands would come to holding mine.

"This *power* is what started a *war*. One that will see, at *minimum*, three Realms fall to their knees. Hell, Purgatory, and Earth. Your *home*, Keres. God knows what will happen to The Veil and Evenfall... The consequences of the violence of my life—they're *beyond* death." The sunlight shifted to the edges of the pergola and what little peaked through the leaves above us—ran for cover. "Not to mention that *fucking* omen you paid enough attention to when you offered me sanctuary from half the Revs who want to kill me, but refuse to believe it because the *other* half want me alive. You can't pick and choose what's true. Whatever I am—if I'm not stopped—" I read the quote tattooed on my forearm and took a resetting sigh, "I'm trying to do *everything* I can to protect the lives I'm risking by simply existing." Silence..."Keres—*innocent* people are dying. Whether we like it or not, whether you *believe* it or not, to end this war, I have to *die*. One way or another."

# Chapter 6

## Lovely

"Well, *he* was a *dream*," I said as Keres turned on her heel too quickly, shutting the door.

"He could've heard you!" She yelled under her breath. I chuckled making my way down the filigree-covered iron staircase. You'll find a lot of iron here. Ghosts don't like it.

"No one can hear me if I don't want them to." I cocked my head reminding her.

Keres crossed her arms and sauntered over to me. "That doesn't make your poorly crafted insults any more justified."

"First of all, ouch. My insults are *beautifully* crafted, thank you very much. And second of all," I met her at the landing as we made our way to the kitchen, "I wasn't insulting him. I was *describing* him. There's a difference." She threw me a look, her emerald lace skirt swaying with her hips.

She grabbed the kettle off the stove humming an ancient lullaby that soothed me far too quickly.

"It's nuanced, I'll give you that." Her head of black curls danced when she shook her head; holding in a laugh. She continued with her task, filling the kettle and ignoring me. "You know I'm right," I muttered, playing with an apple in the blue corundum bowl filled with fruit that trembled just the slightest at my touch. I did well to pay no mind to my reflection only *somewhat* not in sync with me in the black quartz island.

Keres had her tattooed back to me but I knew her smile grew as she looked out to her garden from the window above the hammered copper sink. I always found it funny how nearly everything in that little Eden could kill or heal, depending on the preparation.

"How did you sleep?" Keres' voice entered the space suddenly.

I raised an eyebrow. "You've been asking me that a lot lately." Suspicion. It's unlike a rope wrapping tight around your waist.

"You don't typically partake in the act. Recently, you have. I'm naturally curious." The rope tightens when the suspicion becomes more concrete.

"It's like prayer, Keres," I said, shrugging. "I don't believe much in it anymore, but every now and then, it's worth closing your eyes to have a dream. To rest."

"And did you?"

"Rest or dream?"

"Both."

"Have been for a couple of weeks now. Without much consequence. You been spiking my chai with Valerian root, Keres?"

"Oh, come now. If I fancied a peaceful slumber for you, I would not resort to child's play. Now, a *spinning wheel* on the other hand," she turned around, "that would be more on point." The crystal wind chimes laughed with us. "When is the next client scheduled?" She found something fascinating in the dreamcatcher hanging above the stained glass kitchen door. I caught a glimmer of sunlight reflect off of a speck of dust...

"Not...not for another hour."

"Are you planning on tapping the counter for the duration of that hour?" There were five impressions half an inch deep in the quartz. "Not whispering in tongues would be another thing I'd like you to do, if you can manage it." Keres tried to mask the crack in her ancient voice.

It didn't work.

"I'm sorry. I didn't realize—It's fixed." I repaired the quartz before I finished my apology.

"I don't want your contrition, Devi. I want you to be in more control of your mind."

"I'm in plenty control. Trust me." I put my focus back on the apple in my hand...I quickly checked my reflection. She checked back in sync.

"You lost time again." My eyes shot up at Keres. Her face a painting of pure concern—and something else. I exhaled, realizing what had come to pass, and dropped my head in a delicious blend of disappointment and shame.

"After I told you when the next client was coming?" She nodded. The furious tapping, the delayed reflection, the whispering... My body remained in the kitchen while my mind—"Fuck."

"Thirty-seven seconds." Gravel filled her throat. She couldn't look at me...

I backtracked both our memories. My hands cradled my face hopelessly before they reached my neck; digging into the muscles in useless efforts to relieve never-ending tension. *Where did I go?*

"These fugues—they're beginning again and lasting longer. I think perhaps a bath would set you at ease." If there were ever a more *mundane* task that I could conjure up, sitting in a bathtub and staring at a wall would be *the* most worthless use of my immortality.

Half or otherwise.

"That won't be necessary."

"Water is key to accelerating the healing of both physical and psychic injuries."

"There's no healing *this*, Keres." I felt her tears in my eyes before her body created them... I put the fruit back in the bowl. "Yes. Water is an accelerant. A *quick* shower. A *dip* in a lake. A ten-minute bath—at *most*—when I'm too jacked up or had a run in with a DeKenna. I don't see any demons around whose nasty touch delays my healing for days. You want me in that thing for a damn *hour*."

"Your point being?" She knew my point.

"What the hell am I supposed to do for an *hour*? Fucking sing kumbaya?"

"The extra time is for my potion to seep into your incredibly *stubborn* skin. You would do well to use this opportunity to work on your dahston." I hate it when she's right. "You still have not named it—your grimoire. The name will *tether* it to you and *only* you." *That cursed word...*

"Firstly, I wasn't born a LeMehti. Not my fault my skin is impervious to all things."

"*Almost* all things. There is the matter of *my* magick."

We chuckled and it was all the healing I'd ever need... "Yours is the only power I've ever known to rival that of the LeMehti, Keres."

"I should hope so." There was more she wanted to say, more I wanted to ask... And I could've discovered her thoughts by channeling her past, making sense of the emotions swirling inside her soul, but that is a boundary I would not cross. *Change the mood.*

"As for working on my spells..." I scratched my nose, "Yeah, I got nothing." The lost time. *Where did I go? What did I see?* "And third, I know the significance of 'The Naming' of my grimoire—dahston, I mean. Sorry."

"Honestly, girl! *Must* you use those air quotes? The Naming is not a trivial mat—"

"That's one of the things Shakespeare actually got *wrong*." What did *I* get wrong? Seconds passed here, but in my head... I could've been lost for *hours*.

"Enough thinking, azizti." She disappeared under the island and emerged with a bulbous beaker filled to the brim with silver and blue liquids forever swirling, never merging. "Here." The corked bottle slid across the wide island and I caught it without looking, too annoyed with my homework. "Off you go. The aroma candles are already lit. You shan't be disturbed." The sweetness of her did little to ease the pain of my assignments.

"It can wait, Keres. Desorah is a bit of a—"

"Bitch?"

"To put things mildly." We laughed.

"Be that as it may, you'll do as instructed."

"But she—"

"She is channeling her past self and the depression that came with her. That doesn't—"

"See? How can I leave you when Dr. Jekyll and Mrs. Hyde are on their way?"

"Quit your stalling, child. Upstairs. *Now*." I started to move in the direction of her demanding bejeweled pointer finger as she followed close behind.

"Ok, *ok*. But if Desorah, a.k.a. Rebecca decides to go all Clockwork Orange on you—"

"If you continue disregarding my abilities as the most powerful witch on the planet—" I stopped halfway up the staircase.

"Yes, but what if—"

Keres muttered profanities in Farsi not caring that I understood every word. "*If* Rebecca's spirit takes control of Desorah's mind, I will sort it. You *already* know the outcome of this session. Go."

"*Fine*. But I'm taking my tea with me," I willed my cup in my hand. Keres waved her hand behind her in dismissal of my juvenility and made her way back to the Victorian kitchen and her Chamomile.

The fire of the protective candles flooded the entire space; Dozens of different scents and flickering flames and shadows danced across every surface. The same warm glow flooded the black and white stones in the bathroom, reaching my skin; managing to do what the sun could not.

On the surface, to most Revs, I'd been in a state of CaElum—half in the human world, half elsewhere—for 37 seconds. To Keres and me, to the Revs that know you only see *more* monsters when you turn the lights *on*, it was CaElide. I'd been trapped in memories from The Court—the LeMehti palace.

Most of the time, I pull myself out of CaElide states and push that God awful Eject Button. Other times, times where I lose my mind to the point that I lose time, where I lose my *memory*... Where the only way I can learn what happened to me is by hijacking my own mind or someone else's—there's only one thing and one thing only that can bring you back.

And I strategically left that part out.

Putting the muzzle of my gun to my head and pulling the trigger repeatedly while Keres watches in horror—my blood splattering everywhere—the look on her face. And she went through the motions as if *nothing* happened...

You didn't need to see that. You don't need to see *any* of this.

Yet, here you are...

I cleaned up my mess the instant I made it. Perks of being a LeMehti. Our magick is, well, it's something...

CaElide is a *battle*. One that is best fought alone.

Swallowing the past, I drank my Lavender Earl Grey as I waited for the pitch black onyx claw-foot tub to fill. I'm no stranger to being frozen in past realities or future what-if's. Breathe the wrong way around me while I'm in those states and you'll likely get a dagger to your throat. Of all the tormented minds that walk through Keres's door, mortal or supernatural, *I* was the most dangerous; and she trusts me with her life.

Fancy that.

The tub filled, I undressed, and poured the bewitched concoction into the water. The interaction was immediate and the surface sparkled like a sea of stars. It glowed brighter and brighter. Painting the walls in glimmers of mercury and cobalt. The potion was not the only revolver firing starlight into the shadows.

It's *me*.

My palm met with my chest, shrouding half the space in black. I revealed my sternum, exposing the immortal marking as the cause for the lightshow. When I twisted my hair over my shoulder, the massive marking spiraling down my spine ignited. LeMehti markings glow for a few reasons, main ones being: Protection, power, and passion...

But, I'm not pure LeMehti. I'm, at best, a chimera of carnival proportions. There's something hiding at my edges. Something that brought war to armies as old as time.

Something that *breaks*.

I wept into my hands, shrouding my cries from my too trusting friend downstairs. "Tears can't erase what you've done. But blood will..." Breathing in my words, I closed my eyes and went under water.

Twenty minutes droned by and I slowly surfaced, taking in air. The potion did what it set out to do; there was newfound calm and strength in me. A focus I hadn't had all morning.

I ran my fingers through my hair and a stray one latched to my finger. I looked at that strand of hair for a long time. I twirled it. Pulled it. It took the force I would normally use to tear apart a concrete block to snap that miniscule part of me in two... I lit up both halves like matches, the fire igniting from my fingertips. The pieces of me turned to ash and vanished into thin air.

It was in that moment—that moment of realizing the scale of my inhumanity—that I understood, perhaps more so than ever before, the hopeless danger within me. And the best part? I'm only getting stronger. Faster. Unavoidable. Because that's what I was made to be. Because I am what I am.

When Vincent transformed me into a LeMehti, he knew. He *knew* I would be *this* lethal. That bit doesn't faze me.

What breaks my heart is that he knew I *needed* to be...

*Spells. We have 32 minutes left to kill. Shit.*

We're *not* trying to kill *time*. Don't do *that*.

I worked on 4 of the 5 spells. It's not particularly practical practicing portal partitioning in the nude...

Fuck. That was a mouthful of alliteration. Sorry. Byproduct of spell casting. Gotta get that pronunciation and shit all proper-like.

In the candlelight, before the mirror that shocks me every time it refuses to shatter when I look into it, I wanted to see something. Lowering the towel, I saw exactly what I spent a lot of energy trying to forget—shimmering lines and spots. My body was a map of scars; each one holding onto the magick that caused them—each one a gravestone. *My* gravestone.

My finger traced my slit throat from ear to ear. Tiny points on my carotid and jugular—a few from arrows, some from spikes, none from vampires. A constellation of bullet holes glinted across my chest and torso. A couple of stabs to the heart.

I laughed. These are the scars on the *front* of my body. Fuck, these are just the scars *they* gave me. If only you had a pair of oh-so special Reverie eyes, then you could check out the cluster of muzzle burns under my chin. My hair conveniently covers up the exit wounds...

Don't you go feeling sorry for me or some variation thereof. We *want* me to *not* regenerate. Cliff's notes: no me, no poison, no fucking war that gives birth to *Armageddon*.

My worth lies in my death.

I finished dressing as Desorah knocked on the front door. I put my daggers in their holster on my back. Wore my black 'No Place Like Nola' t-shirt and some jeans and—I'm sorry.

I'm doing it again. The mundane walk-through. Ignore me when I do that. Though, I do look pretty damn cute.

Just saying.

I crept downstairs like a super-secret agent. Literally, though. I had lunch near a CIA agent one day and learned a few things.

I waited in the guest bedroom that's adjacent to the den where Keres held her sessions. This is the norm for the Clients of Questionable Behavior. The higher the probability of them losing their shit, the closer I'd be to Keres.

She doesn't need my muscle, but that doesn't mean I'm going to keep it all to myself. Sharing is caring.

Desorah's session overflowed with tension. Her past self, Rebecca, wanted *out*. To be fair, Rebecca only wanted to understand what was happening to her. One minute she's going about her day in Elizabethan England and the next, she's catapulted in to a body of a woman she won't be for centuries to come. After a while, neither can distinguish the verity of their timelines. The curves of their faces. The sounds of their own voices. Disorientation is only natural.

And dangerous.

Psychology would call Desorah's affliction nothing short of schizophrenic and drown her with pills. Last I checked, visual hallucinations don't emerge from your body and lunge across a burning table of incense to attack our good doctor, Keres.

Keres suspended the astral projection of Rebecca in the air while I phased through the wall and put Desorah to sleep, whispering a lullaby in her ear. Keres's hand twitched in just the right way and Rebecca's wild spirit contorted, reverting into her host like a bolt of lightning.

"I did not require any assistance."

"I know *you* didn't, Keres. But *she* did." We glanced over at Desorah's sleeping body, tiny remnants of Rebecca still sparking across her skin like tiny fireworks. "No one should be conscious during *that*." I grit my teeth the moment I spoke the words, not realizing that my statement had been an extremely personal divulgence.

It did not go unnoticed.

As her words began to bubble into the back of my throat, I spat out my own. "She'll be up and ready to go in five. Parker will be here in ten." I teleported back into the guest bedroom. The witch worked on the sleeping Desorah and, once ready, walked her out with a tincture, two candles and some good old-fashioned CBT exercises. Did I fail to mention that Keres is a Clinical Psychologist?

After Parker The Mortal's session, Keres and I got comfortable on a couple of barstools in the kitchen. Parker is a sweet kid. Iraqi war vet. We had a conversation once. We all know what happens to me during a simple conversation...

"You know, you could have a session one of these days."

I stopped doodling in my nameless grimoire—taking care not to damn its origin.

"Keres, we've been over this," I replied with sing-song annoyance.

"No." She set the black iron kettle on the stove and lit the fire. Running her old bones through her hair, her silver and jade bangles jingled. The sound always soothed me. Keres exhaled then leaned over the island across from me. "*You* went over it. I actively listened. What techniques you've gleaned, absorbed, or learned—from me or from your time in school—I could help you if you'd only allow me."

I took a moment before responding. "You can't *tarot* the crazy out of me."

"That's not how it works, and you are *immensely* aware of that."

"Yeah, I am. And that's *exactly* how I know that you *can't* help me."

"You cannot know that. Not for certain. You may hide your past from me, but you cannot hide that pain of yours. Not all of it. But if you'd let me in, I could do for you what I did for Parker. For the others."

"The 'others' are nothing like me."

"I don't know what you are more: Stubborn or arrogant."

"A little bit of both. Depending of the day."

"No more of this God-awful attitude, Devi. Listen, I can—"

"I love you for wanting to help. But—"

"I hear you screaming in your sleep." She looked for something in her palms. I looked for the memories I clearly shrouded from myself... "The few times that you *do* sleep, you *scream.* I run to your room but your door doesn't always open." Keres shortened the distance between us. "You cast spells in your slumber to protect yourself from whatever it is that you're reliving." Her fingers twitched, rising towards mine, but recoiled. "Those times, I—I am resigned to sit at your door, listening to you wail... Eventually, your magick lifts and I come in."

"Did you touch me?" I said breathless. My face too full of fear for her life to know the answer before she spoke it. "Keres, did you *touch* me? When was this?"

"No. I know the rules. I only sit at the foot of your bed, helpless as you cry in your sleep. The most recent episode occurred on the last full moon." *Two weeks ago*. Keres desperately wanted to comfort me. That yearning made it difficult to breathe. I almost had to take my shirt off... I hopped off the bar stool and forced my feet off of the tiles; every step away from her simply too heavy. "You had no idea, did you, Devi?"

My hands ran over the dangling herbs and flowers from the hanging pot rack above the island until she and I had changed places completely. "I had an idea." I finally admitted.

"Why didn't you wake yourself, you think?"

"Which time?"

"Any time."

"The brain is a funny thing." I shrugged, avoiding her eyes at all cost. "I don't think even *I* know the lengths my mind will go to."

"Are you telling me your subconscious thought it safer for you to remain trapped in your *nightmares*—the loops of your past—than awaken?"

"No," my eyes flicked up, settling into her and I told Keres the truth, "it thought it safer for *you*."

Her fear, her genuine *fear* and breaking heart hit me with such power, three ribs cracked and I threw up in my mouth.

"I—I don't believe that. I'll not." She cringed at the sound of my broken bones. It was her heightened senses that told her this because I blocked as much of my injury from her empathy as possible. Like holding your breath underwater, trying with everything you have not to scream.

But when you're drowning...

"And you don't have to. But at the end of the day, the sun will set, the moon will rise, and the truth will remain. It needs not your belief to be so." Dried hemlock caught my attention from the hanging rack. I remembered the time I drank nearly two liters of the poison. The result? Incredibly floral breath.

And giggles...

"You're not the monster you think yourself to be."

"No, Keres. I'm not the *angel* you think me to be. You're smarter than that."

"You're absolutely correct. I *am* smarter. Smart enough to know that you kept yourself *locked* away in one of the greatest horrors in our realms so that you *wouldn't* hurt me." She had to take a breath and I...

I had to simply stop.

Keres crossed her arms, caressing her shoulders in search of comfort. She'd find none. "I can only imagine what you see when you close your eyes, Devi."

"And your imagination will have to suffice." The sharpness of my tongue surprised both of us.

"I know I can't help you in the way you need." My head shook with impatience. "But let me do a Cleansing for you. If anything, it will make the ache more manageable. The voices in your mind a little less crowded." The hope in her voice almost killed me.

I gave her eyes my back while I looked at the garden. The plants... they breathe easier when I'm not near them. "You *are* helping me. More than you know." When I turned around, the witch from antiquity had already begun prepping a potion.

"If we do this, when you see what I've seen..."

"I've seen my share of darkness, darling, as you are *quite* aware. I don't frighten easily."

"It's not your *fear* that concerns me."

"No? What's your reason for hesitation?"

"Your *survival*."

She stopped grinding the plants and spices. "Now you think me weak?"

"No, Keres. *Never*."

"You *do* know what I am, correct?"

I sighed. "I know *exactly* the immensity of your power. That's the problem." Rubbing the ache from my head is pointless. "I know what you're capable of. I *know* where you had your first kiss. How many children you've had. Where each of your descendants are. Right now. In this moment. I can tell you *exactly* what they're doing. How fast their heart beat is. What they fucking had for breakfast."

The look on her face... "What does my biography have *anything* to do with whether or not I endure a psychic encounter with you?"

"Everything!" The chandelier rattled. She stood her ground. "Because," I said with forced calm, "I *know* it will kill you." The lights flickered. The electrical phenomenon in the skies, however, was all her doing. Keres' eyes fell with the gravity of my words.

As realization settled into the subtle lines of her face, hopelessness bore deeper into mine. "You have seen my end..." Her words were more breath than sound.

"Yes." Keres is the type of immortal that can live forever unless otherwise killed...*hard*.

"How many possibilities of it?"

"Keres—"

"I don't want to know the manner of them. I have my own ways of discovering the answers. But, I'd rather not sacrifice a virgin." Relax. She doesn't sacrifice humans for her craft.

Not anymore...

"Six—all connected to me. The Cleansing having the highest probability of success." Today, at least.

"I see." She continued to create the potion; sparking flames from the palms of her hands and electric shocks from the tips of her fingers. "So, you don't mark people for their deaths by physical contact alone or through objects that have had physical contact with you." *Don't forget breathing on them...* "You can do so in a psychic plane, as well."

"Physical contact makes it easier for the LeMehti and De-Kenna to find you—and yes—kill you. The psychic thing... that wouldn't be *them* killing you. It would be *me*."

Her words spilled out of her mouth with such nonchalance, I wondered if she heard me at all. "But you wouldn't actually be."

"Are we seriously having this conversation right now? The shitstorm I have going on up here, it's going to ruin you in ways you can't even *conceive* of, then kill you dead. And I won't lose you, Keres. I *won't*."

We were quiet for a few moments as she finished the potion and pondered on her next words as tactfully as she could.

"There are lost souls, Devi. *You*, however, are a *shattered* soul. I haven't an *inkling* of how you keep yourself tethered." She willed my favorite tea mug into her hand and poured the magickal liquid inside. Handing it to me—careful not to make contact with my cursed skin; and me, careful not to let my breath hit hers—I took my mug.

My eyes followed the swirls of the crimson and chocolate concoction in the black porcelain. They moved on their own; their magick the source of the perpetual motion.

"How do you survive it?" There were two possibilities, and I'm sure she referred to both, but I couldn't be certain. Contrary to what I just said, I don't know *everything*. I just know nearly every *possibility* of everything. And believe me, that's quite a difference. And a lot of information overload. Sometimes I can't think let alone have complete certainty of the future.

"What?" With a crack in her heart and not a skip in her words, she answered.

"Yourself."

I smiled, hoping to conceal the quivering of my lips as my words too easily slipped out to answer hers. "I don't."

The truth was a bullet that pierced right between her eyes. But, instead of blood cascading down her face, there were tears. She finally grasped what I had been trying to explain.

If *I* can't survive the battlefield that is my own mind, how could anyone else?

"Drink your chai, azizti." Her hands trembled as they wiped away her tears. "After Mrs. Harmon's session, we have—"

"The meeting with Thing 1 and Thing 2."

"West and Sergeant LeBeau." She corrected me with a weak chuckle.

The doorbell rang and Keres went to let in little Mrs. Avery Harmon. Her beloved service dog Darcy was tied by the porch refusing, as always, to come in because I scared the shit out of him.

I took my potion and went to the roof.

The belvedere warmed my back.

I curled up my knees against my chest, trying to rid myself of the various images of Keres dead at my hands. My efforts were made in vain. Never in my life will I be able to burn away the sight of my daughter crying because I told her she would die if she ever touched me.

*Lovely*.

# Chapter 7

## Hold On

"Should we have lunch at Backspace?" Keres's words reached me from the front door that spat out Mrs. Harmon's body with a sigh. Most of the humans, like old Mrs. Harmon and Parker, know that Keres was a witch. Other clients, however, came in for the novelty of it all. A hauntingly beautiful Gothic Victorian mansion with a supposed *witch* living within its walls? Flip a few cards, serve you tea, light candles and BAM. All your woes would be vanquished.

Who could resist?

I watched as the great-grandmother walked down the stone steps and away from River Manor. Darcy looked over his shoulder right at me. I smiled. The German Shephard bared his teeth.

"Did you hear me, Devi?!" She yelled this time. Keres was my daughter in a past life centuries ago. She became immortal and I reincarnated. What struck me was that Keres genuinely has no knowledge of this.

"Yes, Keres. Super hearing. Impossible not to." I leaned against the opened French doors of her den.

"Holy Mother." She clutched the ankh dangling at her chest, nearly dropping the tarot deck she had been clearing away. "You can be so quiet sometimes. I hardly felt you move."

"Mea culpa." Every now and then, the thing that is me frightens the thing that is Keres. My arms crossed tighter, the leather of my jacket stretching across my muscles. The sound of it too reminiscent of a hand stretching across my throat...

She eyed me up and down. "It's the middle of July."

"That it is."

Her eyes found my lower extremities that housed blue jeans and combat boots.

"In *New Orleans.*" She waved her hand at the picture window that revealed nothing but green ivy and the curious eyes of a neighbor that tripped as she ran off when I met her gaze.

"Temperature doesn't have the same effect on me as it does to you."

"I'm quite aware of your physiology. However, people may give you more than a cursory glance when we step outside."

"People *already* give me more than a cursory glance. Covering up is as much for *their* safety as it is for my own."

"Not to mention your sanity."

"Come on now. We both know *that's* a lost cause." I laughed. She didn't. "Hey. Silver lining. I get a shit-load of information." She crossed her arms, shifting her weight from one leg to the other. I began counting on my fingers. "There was the librarian, the mechanical engineer, and the—" I tapped my finger to my head, "Oh! The Navy Seal! You can't tell me having *her* memories in my head is a *bad* thing. Not to mention Parker. Our sweet Army Vet." I really do have an amazing memory, but with so many *other* memories in my head...

"Do you hear yourself?" My smile fell apart. "You shouldn't have to know what a *Navy Seal* knows."

"It's not that bad, Keres." It is...

"I find that terribly difficult to believe seeing as how you *cannot* lie to me." Her patience shortened rapidly, hitting me like whiplash.

"It's not that bad."

"How so?"

"None of them know *my* memories." She broke in such a way that I had to reposition myself. "I don't know about you, but I call that a win in my book."

"I know you do. *That's* what troubles me." Her downcast eyes, all the words of a truth she couldn't bear to speak—I never should have stayed this long.

"Well, don't let it. I'm fine." If I try hard enough, some lies can be passed off as truth even to Keres. When that fails, I resort to mind control... Suffice it to say, there've been *days* I didn't speak to her to avoid bending her to my will.

I started to walk away, but just as I expected, she stayed put. I turned on my heel and made my way back to the den. "We'll be late, Keres. I don't want a lecture from Sergeant What's-his-face for being 'tardy'." My air quotes failed to make Keres budge.

"You *are* safe here. That fact has been proving itself over and over for *months*." She waited for me to agree with her—or to disagree with her. "It's a beautiful day. Why deprive yourself? You *deserve* to feel the sun, and not when I am your only witness." She smiled the kind of smile that is born of hopeless hope. When you know, with all of your being, that there is *no* point in hoping, yet you find yourself cradling that little feather in your palms as if your life depended on it.

My jaw clenched.

She noticed.

"We're back on my poor choice of dress again?" Hands went in my pockets; white-knuckling themselves in private. I'm glad I zipped up the jacket earlier. My markings are glowing something awful. If Keres were to see... "You know why I dress this way. Why I can't touch anyone. Being an Empath of

*LeMehti* fucking proportions *and* my psychometric abilities... I mean, *come on*. Are we seriously having this conversation *again*?" This time, I didn't hide my emotions from her. My irritation naked, front and center for her empathic pleasure.

"It's deeper than that and you know it." Every now and then, Keres—whether she knew it or not—made her bewitched immortality crystal clear. And its essence put you in your fucking place. "For the love of all the Goddesses, you can see the *future*. You *know* when people will move *before* they decide to do so. Devi, you can *make* them decide. Navigate accordingly."

The clock on the wall had the clearest sound in the room... next to the sound of my name in her voice...

I couldn't look at her. Not when she's trying so fucking hard to give me a life we both knew I could never have. Not the way I was—not being me. Not like this.

Not like *this*...

"Know that your exhaustion is *never* lost on me, no matter your efforts to conceal it. I still know." Her palm found a home on her chest, right above her heart. "But you cannot live what could be the very *last* days of your life a prisoner in your own body."

"You don't get it, do you? You've lived lifetime on top of lifetime, but you can't *see*."

"It isn't as though you let me *see* much of anything. Illuminate me." She rested her antique bones atop the arm of the emerald Chesterfield sofa. Both hands gingerly holding one another in her lap.

"Touch is great, really—human or otherwise. Problem is... problem is, I flinch whenever anyone comes near me." I glanced at the time, at the books in the built-in shelf, and then down to my boots. "I'm afraid."

"Afraid? What are you fearful of? Someone showing you affection?" Her sweet smile...

"No." *Yes. A hundred thousand times yes.* "Fearful that the next time someone touches me, I *won't* flinch. I'll just react naturally." *Don't remember. Don't look at the memories. Push them back down. All of them. Breathe, Devi. Breathe...*

"Devi," her hesitant voice pulled me back, "what has become your natural reaction to touch?" The clock struck twelve. I smiled in an attempt to curb the pain of the truth I'd never be able to rid myself of. I couldn't bear to look at her. Not until after I spoke the word.

"Violence."

A moment went through us. And, for beings that experience time in a way you can't really understand, those seconds took forever to end and didn't last long enough. All at once.

"Devi—"

"You may not want to accept this fact, but I'm going to tell you this once and once only: I've been a prisoner of my own body since Day One." I let her process her anger—her hurt for me. *Six seconds ought to do it.* "It's better this way. Trust me. Besides," I shrugged with quite a convincing smile, "it's not like I have any Romeo's hanging from my balcony."

"It wouldn't matter if there were." She's *so* tired of my shit.

"Nope. Not gonna be around long enough to be wooed."

"That is not what I meant."

"Yeah, I know." I could hide some things from Keres, Vincent was *not* one of them. The air shifted and cooled, filling too quickly with static.

"This isn't about love. Regardless of what happens—" she had to swallow to fight back the onslaught of tears that were now choking in the back of my throat.

"You're right. It's about protecting people. Because that's what happens when you're responsible for lives that can die *because* of you. You do what you have to do to keep them alive."

"Even if their life hammers the nails in your coffin?" she stood up and walked over to me. My entire body tensed. The fractures that ran up her walls were unavoidable...

"That's the difference between us—between me and them. I'll *always* survive. *They* won't." "You cannot save everyone and it is too heavy a burden to carry on your shoulders alone."

"You're probably right. Maybe I'll wake up one day and all of you will be dead and gone. But if you think that's going to stop me from trying—"

"Devi, you are *not* the end of the world." Keres braved a hand across the space between us, reaching for mine. I *almost* took it... "You're still *human*. Don't forget that."

"What I am is a *killer,*" every fireplace lit, the lights flickering across the tears in our eyes.... "and you're standing a little too close..."

The clouds cleared as we both grounded ourselves; Keres calmed the flames and I—I wished, more than anything, that I could be *kind*...

"You don't have many options at hand."

"Clearly." I fidgeted with my rings. One ring in particular.

"I don't think this matter is quite clear at all to you. Your options are to live the rest of your eternal life—"

"*Half* eternal," I interjected with a raised finger. What *is* half of eternity?

"You will continue to live in *hiding,* in isolation so that no one comes to harm—or you continue to fight a war that isn't—"

"You're forgetting what's behind Door Number 3. And it *is* my war to fight. It's got my name on it and everything."

"Impossible. Just impossible," Keres muttered softly to herself; chagrin all over her. "Door Number 3, as you call it, is only an option because you have deemed it such. We don't even know if it will be successful. For all we know—"

"For all we know, *you* can kill me dead. But you won't even fucking *try*. And since you've enchanted me from leaving New Orleans, I can't go find Thomas. So, I have to knock on *other* doors." Her magick did not allow the enemy *in* and it did not let *me* out. The fact that I can't teleport out of here...

"Watch your tongue, child."

"Keres, this will work. The LeMehti and DeKenna will go back to whatever they were before I turned them inside out, The Warning will fall out of existence, and everyone else *won't* drop dead—or worse—because I happened to fucking *walk* by. Problem solved. The spell will work. You'll see."

"Have you seen this future? Has the vision played within your eyes?"

"I don't need a vision to know it's the only way out."

"Does your immortality come and go as you please? Your death—if your death is *even* a possibility—cannot be the *only* end to the apocalypse."

"Ok. Give me another option. I'm listening."

"Wait with me a while longer and we *will* find another way. Elton and Leanna and I will find another way. If not, I will *create* another way." And she fucking can, too. But this way—*my* way—is a sure thing. I can't risk anything less than that. I can't risk a way where Keres dies...

"I know, Keres." The *rage* in her eyes... The house never wailed this viciously.

"You know? You *know* I can find another way to expel the poison and yet you *still* dare to force our friends to end your life?!"

"Your way will work, but it will take *time*." I shook my head, tired. "Time those bastards will use to murder as many people as possible for no other reason than just to get *off*. My way is *fast* and keeps the body count down. It saves *everyone*."

"*Not* everyone, Devi."

"It is what it is, Keres. Wouldn't you do the same? Wouldn't you sacrifice your own life if it meant countless others would live?"

She breathed in and out for a minute, staring at the ivy, before she answered what I already knew. "Yes."

"Can we stop this now, please? It's one thing to get lectured by LeBeau. It's a whole other wet sock to be at the receiving end of your former lover's death stare. West may run this city, but he has *shit* for manners."

"West appreciates rules. Traditions. Promptness."

"West needs to get *laid*." Keres almost blushed. "And he doesn't like me."

"West barely *knows* you."

"I'm doing him a favor."

"How are you so certain your plan will succeed?" Her tone rose with defeated exhaustion.

"That didn't last long. Ok." *Deep breaths...*"Because," my palm met with my tensed shoulder, "it fucking *has* to."

She took hold of the tarot deck again and placed it into a wooden box that lived on in the built-in book case that took the entirety of one wall. Her pewter-adorned fingers lingered on the enchanted box. She was hurting. She's trying to hide it from me, but for all the magick she has, truth is, blood knows blood.

Doing well to ignore one ring in particular, I glanced at my hands, again. Silver and pewter rings with opal and turquoise stones. Our proclivity for Victorian jewelry must be hereditary.

"Do you hear that, Devi?" A buzzing of voices, memories, music. Blood. The rhapsody scratched at our ears.

"Hear it? I can *taste* the damn thing." There's a Moneta in our midst. "Why don't you go and meet West and LeBeau. I'll catch up."

"Be quick about it. If a Moneta is *here...*" No Rev comes to River Manor without an invitation. "It's not for bloodshed, Devi. It's to *warn* us of it." I nodded and Keres gathered her things and left, sure to give Percival a slightly evil eye as we exited the manor. He didn't even notice, too busy playing with the branches up in his tree. "I love you,

"I'll be right behind you. Keres." I made my way to one of the *many* annoying spies Nola houses. Though some do make rather decent Private Investigators—and white chocolate macadamia cookies.

"Whaddup Percy?"

"Must you insist on calling me that?"

"Must you insist on being a fucking creeper?"

"A what?" He muttered, confused.

"Get down here, Percival. Unless you want me to—"

"No, no. *That* won't be necessary." Percy and his nervous

laugh were on the ground before he finished his sentence. With both of us under the canopy of leaves, he spoke. "How are you on this glorious summer day?"

"Cut the shit, Percy. Why are you here?" The wind blew a little too aggressively—thanks to me. They covered his Egyptian face with his bouncy desert curls.

"Why do you ask questions you have answers to?" I rolled my eyes, twirling a curly lock of my hair around my finger. He shoved his hands in his tailored black trousers. I could practically *smell* the nonchalance wafting off his skin.

"Contrary to popular belief, I'm *not* omniscient. No Le-Mehti is. Now talk."

"You *are* something, though. Aren't you?" Percival was one of the few Revs of New Orleans that basked in careful reverence of me. But not because of what I'm capable of. Percival is smart. He feared me because of the things he *doesn't* know I can do. A fact that slips many of the creatures here. "Something not quite… right." And then there's *that*.

"Are you here to kiss my ass, Percy, or do you have information?"

His broad shoulders relaxed. He smiled and he tried to charm me, literally. "Percy? Have you actually *forgotten* something? Your magick *doesn't* work on me, kid."

"I haven't. I find it fascinating." His head shook in quiet astonishment. Monetas hypnotize all manner of people when they need to gather intelligence. "The only magick that impacts you is either from the enemy or from Keres. Yet, you even evade some of her power." *Some* being the operative word.

"You wanna stop drooling. I don't have time for this."

"Do you really not know why I'm here, Devi?"

"Listen, I'll let you in on a little secret: There are 42 humans and 16 Revs on this block alone. I'm a bit crowded. I can't keep track of everything."

"I don't understand why you don't join the Delphi. You're already—"

"I'm going to give you to the count of three—"

"There's been chatter. About The Warning. Helena's coven. They're enroute here."

"And what of the covens already here?" There's something wrong. He's nauseated. His palms are sweaty. *Shit. Now, I want spaghetti.*

"You're under the protection of Keres. The Revs not on your side, they'll not *dare* break her law. None of them will touch you."

"None but *Helena's* coven." His heart's broken.

"Devi, we're on watch night and day protecting you. Even West." Where is the screaming coming from?

"I don't need protecting, Percy." He dismissed me with a wave and a grin that hid behind it the truth about my words he knew all too well. And it broke us a little.

"Everyone needs help, and you have friends here that will give it to you. No questions asked. No hesitation." No breathing. No heartbeat...

"Not me."

"*Especially* you."

"Percival, who died?" His face fell.

"Devi, you can't remember?" Not again...

"You're not here to warn me about the Budapest coven. You're here to see if I know who was killed."

"My visit was twofold, yes. But to also see if it's true."

"If what's true?"

"If you truly don't know that you k—"

"I *don't* fucking know, Percy, so why don't you—It wasn't your mother, was it?" It took all that he had *not* to hug me when the truth I hid from myself blinded me.

"No. Not *my* mother, Devi." The ground quaked. Portals to Evenfall flashed around us. The winds giving way to a storm... "Devi—you need to stop. You're going to bring the entire neighborhood down."

I scanned for her...

Lightning split the tree behind me. I have to practice my aim. I meant it to strike *me*. Percy spoke but I couldn't hear him—I didn't want to believe the lie dripping from his lips. "Devi? Are you *listening*? Only West and I know she's dead. Do you understand? But we have to find her body before the Budapest coven arrives. They know what you are. And if they find out what happened to—Devi? No, not again! Hold on!"

# Chapter 8

## In The Ground

"Devi, I can't hold them all back! Stop!"

My scream shattered every window on the block and burst Percival's ear drums. His forcefield managed to keep the fracturing bits of my psyche at bay before they completely split from me and walked off… I pulled them back into my soul and we all crumbled to the ground.

I threw up.

Percy healed. Utterly drained. Completely scared to death.

Of *me*.

"I *know* what you're planning. I've seen its outcome." The *real* reason he's here. The omen Monetas are gifted with. The good and the bad of the future. And if it's *my* future… "Please, *please* don't do this, Devi. You need to breathe. You need time to grie—"

"What I *need* is none of your concern, Percival." *Get up, Devi.*

"No good will come of this. Tell me you know that."

Wide eyes fixated on us from every house. Too furious to look away, too afraid to step outside. I opened my mouth to answer him but blood only splattered all over the sidewalk.

"Devi—"

"I'm fine." I wiped my mouth. "Going to Hell is the most good I will *ever* do."

"That's not true." I didn't expect his tears to be as cold as they were when I cried them… "You've been to Hell. It did *not* end the war. What makes you believe going back will end *you?*"

"If I'm there long enough—"

"Longer than before?!"

"Yes, Percy. A lot longer than before. I came close to finding it last time, but—"

"You can't—that gateway is a *myth*. As unbelievable as—"

"Me?" We were quiet for a moment. A tiny sliver of peace that would never repeat itself between us. "I only lived through the Circles of Hell—and wherever else I was sent off to—because of my markings, because I'm half-LeMehti. But I also made it out alive because the LeMehti and Lucifer *allowed* it. If I go there *uninvited*—Percy, I won't make it. I *will* die. No living human is meant to walk those realms and I'm still half. The longer I'm down there… it *has* to eventually tear me down."

"And if *that* doesn't kill you, you're going to waltz through the gates of Tyche." The realization of my plan did nothing less but stun him. Whether it was from anxiety, awe, or both, I honestly couldn't say. "Are you sure it's in Hell?"

"No. But once I'm there—I'll ask around." *Get up, Devi. She can't be dead. This isn't real...*

"You'll—why do I get the feeling more than torture happened when you were in that underworld?" I actually laughed. The hollow echoes made Percy's heart stop. I—I *terrified* him…

"Oh, I could write stories about what happened there... The bits I remember, at least." Percy crawled to me, making sure not to get too close.

"If you find Tyche's gates, if you're able to open them and *walk* through...You'll *never* be able to come back. No reincarnation. Nothing. There are no Evenfall Bridges connected to Tyche. No one will be able to find you."

"That's the point, Percy." You've broken him enough...

"Devi, don't cry... Think for a minute. No, don't—"

"Goodbye." With a thought, I was gone. The taste of his tears burning on my tongue. I landed on my knees in front of their shop. Percy was going to run to West to try and stop me. But, no matter how powerful a witch and shapeshifter West is, he will *not* get to me in time for one simple reason: I won't let him.

"Devi? What—oh dear. What *happened?*"

"Change of plans, Leanna. We're doing this today. Right *now.*" The bewitched couple flicked glances at one another, mouth agape but empty of words that would sway my mind. Their helpless acceptance filled to the brim in their eyes and drowned in mine... "Now that we have *that* settled, the quicker you 86 me, the quicker you can get back to your devil boxes and possessed objects. And that new one that came in this morning," I pointed to the creepier than *fuck* Georgian painting of a child, "kill it with fire. *Twice.*"

"We're not ready for the ritual, Devi. We need time to—"

"You know what? Let me just..." I snapped my fingers and burned that painting to ash and sent the demon that lived in it the last 300 hundred years to Hell. What's one more familiar face down there? "Leanna, can you remind Elton that he's talking to a lie detector? You *are* ready. Secret chamber, spell, sending my soul to the underworld, *now.* Please and thank you." I gestured to the patch of red brick adorned with a mirror of obsidian from 1888 that only giggles louder each time I pass it...

I walked by them and ignored the mirror as I phased through the brick. A moment later, the centuries old witches followed. *Push the fucking memories of them away, Devi. You don't need them where you're going.*

"Are you sure? Where's Keres?" Leanna fiddled with the

chalice in her hand. Her heterochromia eyes making every single attempt to beg me to stay. Particularly the green one.

"Keres isn't here. Where do you need to bleed me from? My throat?" Their hearts nearly burst out of their chests when I held my dagger to my neck.

"No. Your *arm* will suffice." Leanna answered, her inked hands rushing to remove my weapon.

"Fantastic." I took off my jacket as Elton made his way over to me. When he knelt at my side...

"If we follow through, once we open the Bridge, your soul—you are *Marking* your soul for Hell. There is *no* reversal. *No* spell that can bring you back." They don't know what Percy knows. They never would have helped me if they did.

"That's *literally* why I'm sitting in this here chair, sir." Beads of sweat rolled down his deep copper skin. He put his dreads into a ponytail and pissed me off.

"Devi, your sacrifice will be for naught." I opened my mouth to bite back at him but Leanna intercepted.

"What Elton means is that the ritual will rid you from the Realm of Earth, but The *Warning*—it very well may continue. As you said, you've been to Hell before and it did nothing to remove the—"

"Consequences of my existence?" Leanna muttered a curse word in Cantonese despite the fact that she knew I understood it.

"There is no guarantee this will be a success, Devi, because you cannot die, sweetheart. You can spend eternity in *any* underworld—and it would do nothing but drive you *mad*." She tucked some pink and black strands behind her ear. Fingers *too* delicate for all the chaos they'd caused over the years. *Don't remember the time she read your palm. Forget the time you baked pies together with Keres. Burn out the images.*

"Already done. Besides, the *spell* itself could be my kill-switch. My first go, I was protected. There won't be any of that now. The environment alone could be the death of me." She's not dead...

"Devi?" Focus.

"What?"

"You're tearing the Veil and—"

Me being sent *there* is the best thing for everyone. For you, your sweetly tatted husband there, the Reveries that want me dead; everyone will be safer with me gone."

"That's not entirely true. Give us time to work with Keres to make her spell—" Elton said with too much sincerity.

"Too much talking, not enough crafting." The couple looked at each other from their respective workstations. Forget the cases you worked with them in this room... "The longer I'm *alive*...the longer I'm *this*, whatever the fuck *this* is, more of you die. I can't—I can't anymore. There is *no* more time. Keres's spell—it's a solution with only *half* a life and one that will drive me mad as the centuries pass ."

"Centuries that will give us time to find a way to end this for good."

"Do you hear yourself, Elton? Her spell would not only take me but take *all* 4 of us. Over and over. How could I do that to you? How can I let her take us back in time, live out those years until we near the day before I'm conceived and then hit repeat. We could be trapped in that loop for *thousands* of years before we find a way to end The Warning. Before we cut out the poison inside of me that's causing all of this bullshit."

"It's a brilliant solution, Devi." Leanna knew I was right, but so was she...

"I didn't say it wasn't, Leanna. But it—it's too much to ask. I'd be killing you, only slowly. It's a fate worse than death. Trust me." I rubbed the ache from my cheeks when Elton spoke.

"We've already agreed, Devi. It's *not* your choice. You—you're a daughter to us. How can we stand by and not help you?" Damn you, Elton...

"There is only one way out with no casualties. If it means saving all of you from me—" A somber moment of silence moved through our veins, making our hairs stand on end, "I will do it over and over and over again. Let me do this."

"Devi? Can you hear me? Try to breathe." The crack in Leanna's voice cut me.

"What's happening?" I spat up blood as the room spun. Why am I on my knees? Why am I *alive*?

"It didn't work." Her hazel eyes were misted over.

"The fuck you mean it *didn't* work?" I stumbled back into the iron chair. "Again."

"Devi, take a minute to—"

"I said, *again*, Elton. Please." Why are they staring at me like that? "Why are you staring at me like that?"

"I can't keep doing this." Leanna ran off crying up the spiral staircase as West and Percival stormed in. Splendid....

"What is going on?" Why can't I channel anything?

"The ritual failed." The last thing I need right now is West's grating voice in my pounding head.

"Thank you, Captain Obvious. How about instead enlightening me with something novel, West?"

"Devi," Percy walked over to me like a hostage negotiator to a psycho with a gun to her temple, "what do you smell? Don't fire any bullets." Fire any bullets? When did I draw my gun out and *why* am I pointing it at Percival? I took in a deep breath.

"I smell blood." A lot of it.

"Breathe again, Devi. Whose blood is it?"

"Mine..." I'm *drenched*. There's a pool of it at my feet. I lowered my weapon. "Jesus. How many times?" my powers were coming back.

"Seven," Elton answered, rubbing the stress in his face that would only strengthen. "Some attempts your body shut down, others—your psyche split." Seven times they tried to send me to Hell and the neighboring underworlds. "The last attempts, your body vanished for a couple of seconds at a time. There is no way of knowing what Dominion—Hell or otherwise—you went or for how long you were there." Seconds on Earth can be *years* elsewhere.

"And that's how you two got through my spells." I pointed to Percy and West with my '45.

"Your defenses become null and void when your corporeal form is not on Earth."

"Your ability to state commonly known knowledge is *spectacular*, Mr. West. It's no wonder how you run this city." The glare. The crossed arms. The *ridiculous* man bun on this ancient brooding fool. "Elton, I'm sorry—"

"Your self-destruction ends now. We need to lay her body to rest. Put your selfishness aside for one Goddamned day and—" I stood up from the wet chair and walked toward West. His arms fell to his sides ever so slowly.

"I'm sorry. My *what* now?"

"Calm down, Devi." Percy and Elton flanked me. My teary-eyed Leanna returned sensing the immense mistake Keres' old flame asshole made.

"Percy, you want to give your friend a *proper* Moneta warning of the consequences his bullshit words will bring him if he keeps talking to me like that?"

"Devi," Leanna's voice... it was the calm to the storm brewing inside me, "thoughts before actions. Anchor your emotions. He doesn't know what he's saying."

"Yes, I do, Leanna. All you've done, Devi, is bring chaos to my city the *moment* you stepped foot on its soil. I understand your burden. *More* than most. But accept the truth. You are *not* innocent. You are *not* a victim. You're so far up your own ass you don't see what's right in front of you!"

"All I've done from the moment I became more powerful than every single God-forsaken thing in your precious little city *combined* is find a way to *save* everyone. From myself. Even *your* ungrateful bitch ass." The candles in the chandelier flickered. The pages of the Book of Shadows on the altar flipped uncontrollably. And the fear burning in everyone's bones..."I just tried sending myself *back* to the deepest circles of fucking *Hell*, Hades, GeHennam, take your pick—and if that didn't work, I was going to throw myself in to *Oblivion*." Percy's face when I said that. I didn't tell him that part of my plan. If I couldn't find the Gates of Tyche, I'd jump into the mouth of Oblivion. This time, however, the LeMehti wouldn't be there to pull me out.... "I did it for *you* and you have the *audacity* to stand there and call me *selfish*?!" The lamps burnt out. Candles snuffed. The only light in the chamber came from the fire in my eyes. My markings. My hands... what's happening to me?

"Let's all take a step back and take a minute to—" We ignored Elton's plea. The way Leanna held on to his arm...

"You took her from me," No..."and now I am *blood-bound* to protect you. *You.* You are an abomination." Devi, fucking *breathe*. He's lying. "You want to know what you are? The big secret? It's all around you."

"West, *enough*!" You can't be lied to...

"Both of you, stop! Devi, you're going to bring the building down on us. You'll make it out alive, but *we* won't!"

"You're the end of *every* world, not just earth.... You are the *worst* mistake God has *ever* made. No one knows why you exist. You *shouldn't* exist. There is something so *wrong* in you that the Universe *itself* spat you out like rotting meat and we're left to clean the shit."

"West, say one more word and I swear to every god, I will end you here and now!" Leanna's genuine threat hit him in the face and it left a shining red welt.

"Go right ahead. Take your husband and conjure. After what *she* did to Keres—Do you honestly think I care to live?" Mom...

Leanna pushed West back against a bookshelf with a thought. He fumed with exhaustion when the books began to tremble. Beakers cracked and windows fractured. And when the stone floors beneath our feet began to move...

"Devi, you'll split again. *Stop*." I ignored Percy's plea and ran. Ran to do the only thing left to do. "Devi, come back!" Find my mother's body.

And put her in the ground...

# Chapter 9

## Play With Fire

Not this time. Not *this* time. Those words echoed again and again with hope that the repetition would give the hollowed sounds some amount of meaning.

It did not.

I buried Keres *weeks* ago in the Atrium. The section in the woods where witches are put to rest. The same place she said would be my final resting place—whenever that were to be.

My tears watering her grave would do little to birth the willow that will grow as her tombstone. The stench of my blood and herbs from Leanna and Elton's potion almost made me vomit. Instead, my mind crazed with an emptiness I will never be rid of.

"Why didn't you tell me you were my mother? How did I think you were my daughter from a past life?" When did I kill her? How far gone am I that I can't tell apart the living from the dead anymore?

"Oh, my sweet one. You believed what I wanted you to." Her ghost sat beside me. "Your mind is a force to be reckoned with. Yet it is not without fault. I *did* tell you the truth the moment we first met. But you bear the gravity of the world inside you. Even when it is not yours to carry. When I told you who we were to one another..." she took me in her arms and I collapsed in a way I did not know was possible.

"Let me guess. I blacked out and conveniently forgot." She nodded. "That's why you switched the truth. I thought I was your mother from a thousand years ago. But it was *you*."

"Some truths are too dangerous to consume. I should've known what it would have done to you." Her touch triggered my memory.

"You were trying to help me. Help with my nightmare and I—"

"Reacted naturally to someone touching you." The fire in my soul didn't burn any less as it left my eyes.

"Mom—I'm so sorry." She held me until we both stopped crying. She held me for a long time.

"Devi, hearing you screaming. Held prisoner in whatever level of Hell the LeMehti had thrown you in. Whatever cruelty the Kuma subjected you to—I waited for your nightmare to end, but this one...*this* one had taken a different hold and it would not let you free. I was able to break through your magick, took you in my arms and—"

"Pulled me back to the present."

"Yes."

"My body was here—"

"But your consciousness was in the past. Devi, somehow you traveled back in time."

"That's not possible. I don't—I can't control time."

"With you, anything is possible. You are *my* daughter, LeMehti, a Reaper..." She looked at me in awe... "You have magick the likes the world has never known."

"And it will burn for it."

"No. It will be *saved* by it. This power that you refuse to accept, it can be your salvation if you allow it."

"How can you say that?" I tore myself away from her. "I *murdered* you. I kill everything I touch. Everything I love."

"Yes. And you do so *immaculately*. I need you to harness that skill. You are the perfect weapon, Devi. But you do *not* kill for sport. You do so to *survive*." She took my trembling hands in hers as her voice began to shake. "Those bastards ruined you but you are *not* beyond repair. You are *not* what they've done to you. You are what they *made* you. And so much more… Do you hear me, child? You did *not* murder me, daughter. You didn't even know I was there, let alone who I was. Who *you* were."

"But I *should* have."

"You suffocate and call it living. I need you to allow yourself mercy. You punish yourself too harshly for crimes that do not belong to you. Do you understand me, Devi? Enough is enough. You are more than your pain, their hate… There are constellations in your eyes. Galaxies in your blood. You're *not* the end of any world, Devi. You are the beginning…" her words blanketed me with warmth but they could never remove the truth of what I'd done.

"I cost you your *life*. Are you kidding me?"

"My life for your peace. I call that a fair trade." We had a staring contest. I lost. "River Manor, it will forever be yours. This, is *your* city. You are taking my place and the rules are bound in blood." She looked at me, worry clawing at the corners of her eyes when she caught up to my past. "You completed the ritual?"

"It failed. I never made it to Tyche. I—I don't remember anything else."

"*You* may not remember but your soul does. You know secrets you shouldn't, Devi. Lived lives that should not have been lived."

"What are you talking about?"

"That curious nature of yours. You were little and I clearly told you not to go into the woods and what did you do? Returned with a squirrel on your shoulder, skinned knees, and a tale about how you saw a shadow woman with stars for skin." She wiped our tears and straightened us up. "The ritual failed to take your life but it did not fail in sending you on *adventures*. For all we know, you *did* find Tyche's gates and it deemed you worth *saving*." I hugged my mother tighter than I ever thought I could and she returned the action. "One day, little daughter, you will remember everything. You will remember all your travels and find answers, but right now, I need you to do something I know you do not want to do. I need you to do something you are *frighteningly* good at, Devi." The wind knew before I did. The earth had known for *weeks*. And as my mother kissed her forehead to mine, she looked me dead in the eyes and spoke her last word.

"Run."

I lay there staring at the sky for far longer than I deserved. I don't know why I ran here, of all places. A train station? Planning to go back home to Chicago? Home to what? The FBI officially declared me dead six years ago. My family *buried* me and—I didn't see it coming.

Any of it.

I jumped off the building and headed to the train. It's quiet. *Too* quiet when children are on board. Too silent when I'm a thing that can hear practically *everything*. I stood still the moment I stepped inside; desperately trying to focus as all their deaths hit me in unison. Their insides dripping from the ceiling back down to their bodies and me. It's still warm. I missed the massacre by *seconds*.

The stench. It crept inside my lungs like a snake. The scent of the corpses burning the back of my mouth, nearly blurring my vision. The laughter of the LeMehti gnawing at me from behind would have to wait. Peeking out of the aisle from underneath a seat, I caught sight of something that nailed my feet into the sticky floor. A tiny curled hand soaking in a pool of scarlet; droplets of her newborn blood falling from her fingertips. The dead mother clutching her baby girl's body; tears fresh in all of our eyes...

I heard Elijah gripping the back of a seat from behind. I turned to face one of the men that made it his life's mission to hear me scream once upon a time. The LeMehti General moved into full view, utterly covered in death.

"You are one hard lady to find these days."

"I like my privacy."

"Yes. And we can see the price of that luxury." He leaned against the cracked seat cleaning some of the brain matter from his face.

"Don't pretend like you murdered all these people because you're shit at Hide and Seek. Let's skip the pretense and—"

"You, my lady, need to remember your place." Our fists tightened. His Sentinel lackey adjusted his tiny dick. You can take a guess or two of how I know its size.

"Fuck you."

"They have me doing the work of errand boys, lady." He gestured around him while dramatically rolling up his soaked sleeves.

"Aww. Is poor Elijah angry? Are you—is that *pouting* I see? My, my." Focus on them. Don't focus on the dead passengers. Block them out. Keep the train ushers away.

"You'll not leave us."

"I see. Is *that* why you killed everyone? You had a temper tantrum because you wanted me all to yourself?" The General took a step towards me while the Sentinel stood his ground; smiling like a pedophile in a schoolyard.

"We didn't want an audience." Before Elijah could say more, his Sentinel chimed in.

"A *live* one at least."

"Damn. You sound as pathetic as you look. You should really work on that." Before the Sentinel could respond to me, "And I call Bullshit. Why did you kill them?" I had been nowhere *near* any of these humans nor were they marked, which means one thing and one thing only.

"Choose your words wisely." The poison is getting worse...

"Suck my dick, General." Before, they murdered and tortured with purpose; relatively speaking of course. Now they're offing people for a far more terrifying reason.

Satisfaction.

"We don't have to take you back alive." The Sentinel spat out.

"Newsflash, asshole. Incapable of dying over here. I mean, technically. I've died a lot but I don't *stay* dead. But, semantics."

"I forgot how much that tongue of yours—"

"And since you want to use me to blink all of Hell out of existence, Elijah, you kind of totally need me breathing. Did the new guy not get the memo?" The looks on their faces. I had to choke my laugh. "And, if I'm such a *simple* errand, why, in all these years, have *none* of you managed to catch me?" Why *did* they send a General and a Sentinel? Why not Elijah and a *Paladin*? Or just send the whole brood of Paladins? Sentinels are day-to-day. Generals are for the war. Paladins are the Special Forces.

Last resort.

"Don't make this harder than it needs to be, lady."

"First off, stop calling me 'lady'. Second, why did your lovely emperor send *you* to fetch me." Any other day, I'd be able to glean that information easily. From the train, the corpses, Elijah's breathing...But there's so many people inside of me; living, dying, repeat. Keres... I saw it all. Dream-like films playing in my mind while reality played in front of me. My mind is too crowded, too many animals rattling their cages trying to get free...I can't see anything else.

"On your knees."

"Ooh." I feigned a shudder, ignoring a searing image from my past. "Going straight for dessert?" The car began to tremble. The lights flickering. "Now see, you've gone and hurt what's his face's feelings. I'm sure your friend there would *love* to fulfil that request." I pointed to Elijah's fucking *dog* licking his lips at me.

"No more of your insolence, Devi." The windows fractured. "You're coming with us. We can do it with as little or as much violence as you prefer." Elijah's daunting frame hovered over the sleeping mortals. The sun bouncing off of his stark white hair, his equally blank irises locked in to mine. "Adore your green eyes, by the way. They mask the natural shit rather elegantly. Don't you think, Denniel?" The lackey has a name.

"I think it would be more amusing if she were not as willing as you'd like, my lord. I've heard the stories." Prick.

Before Elijah or I could respond, Denniel tackled me to the ground. I tried to keep the train from being pummeled down into the earth. He broke my nose, sending the cartilage into my brain. Death Number 1. Denniel wrapped his hands around my neck and strangled me. Death Number 2. He licked the blood from my nose all the while *laughing*. All the while crushing my ribs with his knees one by one. A rib pierced my heart. Death Number 3. I'll spare you the details of Deaths 4-7...

More important than fighting back is to keep the rest of the train cars filled with people from falling over. Controlling the minds of every single human outside of this car so they don't walk into their end. Which would be a lot easier to do if I didn't have vertigo. An unusual effect. It must be the baby...

"Get off of her, you fool!" Elijah tore his dog from me. I stood up and drew my daggers. Elijah composed himself. "I told you once, I would prefer a less chaotic form of extraction. Forgive Denniel. His curiosity bested him. And he will be reminded—again—that your organs are to stay within your body as we do not yet know what wound will kill you permanently. But really, Devi. Must we do this *every* time?"

"No," I managed to say, spitting out blood while picking up my intestines off of the ground and putting into my stomach, "we don't, Elijah." I closed my eyes and traveled. The teleportation got me 20 miles from the station and I darted to a running start as soon as my feet met the ground. That distance is child's play to them, though.

So where are they?

Despite my better judgment, I stopped on the edge of the Everglades. Though it was further out than I wanted to be, I had to end my trek here because I began to realize that, though Elijah and Denniel stopped chasing me, something *else* had begun.

The sun had started its descent against the horizon and its rays cut through the thickness of the swamp; kissing the waters. The atmosphere is shifting. Air is getting heavier. Gravity is becoming painful...

There are DeKenna on Earth.

Demons.

Shit.

A Knight is making her way to me. If the LeMehti are the psychopaths tearing a newborns' throat out, the DeKenna are the ones getting off on that baby bleeding to death... I need to hide and I need to hide *now*.

Panic boiled my blood quicker than I'm used to. My stink is going to reach them so much easier now. Think Devi. Think! There's no time to burn your Aura. You have to hide. But where? The trees. I leaned against one; listening to its rhythm and the somber waves of the water. Soon, no thing with eyes could tell us apart. No thing with ears could distinguish my heart beat from the beat of the tree or my blood flow from that of the water.

I conjured the winds and blew my stench in every cardinal direction. And then she came into view.

"She was here—I know—" She spoke to another DeKenna telepathically. I couldn't hear him but I could sense him. It's Kyzza. I shifted my focus back on her. She had her pale face cloaked enough that only the crimson light and embers floating away from her charcoal eyes could be seen.

The air, the ground beneath our feet... the whole of the Everglades is trembling in the midst of me and the fallen angel sent for me. They are willing to fight this war against the LeMehti to take me back to Hell. They want me alive. Maybe for the same reasons as the LeMehti. Maybe not. But I'm not going back there...

She grit her teeth as she pulled out her katana. As she focused on tracking me by scanning, the way all immortals do; by standing still and hearing, seeing, smelling, tasting and feeling *everything* for miles in every direction that may or may not have crossed paths with me, I focused on *her*.

Saanvae.

A sadness washed over me more powerfully than I anticipated. I meant to gather information to use against her if my spell broke too soon. I never meant to have my heart break for her. This—this creature who would stop at nothing to drag me back to the place where devils sing. The place I called home for far too long.

We both heard laughter from the border of Georgia and Florida. *Elijah's* Goddamn laughter. I forced myself to purge the memories of the *angel* Saanvae. Memories I'll never be rid of.

"Change of plans. I've got company—The child will have to wait. If Elijah wants to play, I'll play." Saanvae vanished in a puff of black smoke.

I came out of my spell and witnessed the fray between the immortals from where I stood. More soldiers from either side joined the battle. I wanted to run, but experiencing the blows they received as though they were my own—I needed a moment to realign myself. But their pain wasn't the only thing that kept me prisoner. Two things anchored my alien body on Earth: the increasingly violent and terrifyingly gorgeous fight between the two irreverent forces and...

I clutched my throat; the warm blood pouring out much too fast. All I wanted to do was stay with her. I didn't want to leave her. How could I? And then I fell to my knees with my lung collapsing too slowly from the bullets lodged inside it. I held on for as long as I could, as hard as I could so that I wouldn't drop her. She's dead in my arms but I couldn't let her hit the ground. She's too small...

Not again. Detach, Devi. That's *not* you.

I lived the last moments of the mother and baby from the train. Why the delayed reaction? Maybe it's because I'll never be a mother. Or, maybe it's because channeling them—their death inside me is simply the most fitting punishment for my murdering Keres...Yes. *Them*. I didn't spare the baby's life, why should I be spared reliving her death? Didn't deem it necessary for you to know what a child knows when she's dying in her mother's arms.

I took one last look at the battle hundreds of miles in front of me and continued to run.

And this time, this time I *actually* did what my mother truly asked of me.

I ran for my life...

Despite the pause, I couldn't risk going back to Chicago. Not yet. Instead, I found myself at New York's JFK airport. I hopped on a plane to London, England. Do I know anyone there? Nope. Was it the first available flight out of the country? Sure as fuck was. Did I look like deranged asshole to make sure I didn't touch anyone on board? Of course. I could've used my magick to keep people away, but then we crossover to mind control again and, well, I did enough of that at the train station. A lady has ethics.

Some. I have *some* ethics.

In London, I found my way to a motel near the airport. It was fairly vacant, so it was quiet enough where I could block out the dreams being dreamt, various timelines playing out before my eyes, and ghosts. Always ghosts. I could hear my own voice in my mind clearly. *Too* clearly. I shook my head as I crawled in to the bed, my half-eaten dinner on the night stand, my 45 under my pillow, my daggers in their holster on my back. I stared at nothing.

It was past midnight and the stars were shining brightly beyond this box of concrete and glass. Trust me when I say I don't deserve what I'm about to do. However, I find it helps keep me sane. Seeing through the ceiling and bearing witness to the starry night above me...We gaze upon nothing but a graveyard of light and dust. Yet, the starlight finds us.

Unlike the Budapest coven.

I scanned back to New Orleans. Spied, too easily, Helena and her coven filled with anger burning in my chest as they were reminded they could not set foot onto River Manor. What is now *my* property by ancient blood rite.

"This does not end here, West."

"Yes it does, Helena. You know the law."

"There is no law that allows that *thing* to replace Keres."

"That *thing* is who you answer to now. I'd recommend you not forget that."

"And I, my lovely West, would advise you to hold fast to your sweet city. Not every Rev fawns over that anathema as Keres had. And your kindness towards her is merely blood-bound. You and I both know what that child is capable of."

"Goodbye, Helena." With pursed lips and balled fists, Helena and her coven vanished from River Manor in a flash, but her echoes dug themselves inside of West. And an echo made its way to me...

"I sense you spying, child. If you are to lead, you must learn to control your emotions and conceal yourself within The Veil, not creep at its edges."

"I'm not what you think I am. I'm trying to stop a war—"

"A war caused because you were birthed into this world and set in stone from a foolish man's love." How—how does she know about Vincent? "Do not mistake Fate's lack of action as her acceptance. You are merely tolerated by her. Nothing more. Soon enough, you will feel her wrath as Vincent did. The two of you...the unnatural bond. It sickens me. *You* sicken me."

"Say his name again. I dare you." Silence. Long, beautiful silence.

"Your threats are as empty as your soul. You've no inkling of what you are. Allow me to enlighten you: A wicked thing unlike any other. You should not exist. You cannot be *allowed* to exist. I'm certain you know how we remedy that which is not meant to be, yes? We burn it alive."

"There's only one problem with that, Helena. I've always liked to play with fire."

# Chapter 10

## Still Evil

There it is again.

Static whispers scratched at my mind. His disjointed voice pulled at the fringes of my soul. Whispers screaming for something I wouldn't give. Unable to ignore the demon that outranks the Knights at my door any longer, I opened my eyes. The somber light edging its way into the room displayed him perfect silhouettes. There's nothing of Hell coming for me. But it—it can't be...Why is a Rider watching me from the window? The breath of his mare cracking the glass. The air around me trembled. Time moved in slow motion...

You would think I'd get used to it by now. The darker souls—the ones that have violence on their tongue and madness in their hands—when *they* cross over to our Realm, time does more than slow and bend—it *suffers*. Only others like me notice this pain. Psychics, witches—people not right in the head. Or, you know, someone mounted by a faceless entity.

I can't move.

"No. No! Get off me!" My eyes grew wider. The walls fractured, the pressure in the room filling to the brim. Burning flesh wafting in my mouth as the clawing of a sword dragged against the worn floors... Metal to wood igniting sparks that sent glinting embers across the hollow of the four walls; lighting the room with a glow so mesmerizing, I almost forgot I was being strangled to death.

Almost.

The Swordsman circled the bed repeatedly. Precisely. never too close. Always out of sight. The fissures in the walls following him. Then came the knocking. Slow. Steady. Dull. Aching. Louder and louder. Losing patience with every beat when the doorknob twisted, cracking the door open. I shut my eyes and stopped my pointless fighting and spellcasting against the phantom on top of me. Stopped sweating. Stopped thinking. I. Just. *Stopped.*

One thing happened and one thing only: time ceased. And in that moment where the laws of Earth did not exist, I had the chance to send the three wretched creatures back to whatever Realms they crawled out of. I screamed without sound and its echo forced them back over the threshold—through the Veil—to their reality and *out* of mine like a hurricane. But The Rider—he remained at his post outside my room. That shouldn't be possible. Not with *that* spell. I sat up only to be thrown back into my pillow by the beast on top of me. Scanning revealed nothing but shadows. Whoever he is, he doesn't want me to know his face. *Whatever* he is, he is strong enough to evade *my* magick and pin me down with his own.

He paralyzed me and the harder I tried to move, the heavier the world became. I couldn't see him but I could feel him. The only sound in the room was of my heart pounding. My blood burning. His lungs heaving.

His breath was hot on my cheek. making me sweat; making me gasp for air...*I* don't need air. *I* don't sweat. *I'm* not bound to the rules of gravity...

I knew I shouldn't have. It would be a *massive* risk to do it, but I did it again. I stopped breathing. I stopped fighting. I stopped crying. I. Stopped. Time.

I jumped out of bed with the silver trigger ready to fire: my rib cage rattling, my bronzed eyes scanning the empty room, scanning for miles in both the human and supernatural realms. All Realms evidenced the same truth: Nothing. I took another breath, killing a scream behind my teeth and lowered my weapon. I closed my eyes, still burning with yearning for sleep, letting the nightmare fall away. At least, I'm pretty sure I'm awake now…

The Echo spell wreaked havoc in the room, but there is *no* proof of it. There are no fissure lines in the walls. No blade marks or burns in the floor. It had to be a dream because if it *was* real, the *second* spell I cast to be rid of The Rider would've sent him straight to Oblivion. And to be quite honest, the fact that I'm capable of doing anything to one of *them...*

I started a bath. My broken nose courtesy of Denniel healed, but it's the bruising on my neck that wouldn't let up. Their skin, it does something to mine. As if they *brand* me... If I looked close enough, I could see Denniel's fingerprints.

I sank into the tub full of freezing water. Despite my quick to fix body, I always endure the pain of an attack. The ache of every muscle, crack of every bone. A fair tradeoff, I suppose. Heal at practically the speed of thought, but still experience the hurt of severed spinal cords, slit throats, ripped out organs. This kind of survival—it's not without cost. Law of Equivalent Exchange and all that jazz.

I stared at the bed, needing to scan the past. See what *truly* happened. There was a Rider outside, a *Swordsman* inside, and a third mystery bachelor on top of me.

"This is gonna suck my flat ass...." I shut my eyes, and when I opened them, their soft burning amber lit up the space. The event played from beginning to end like a movie. I could see from The Rider's perspective, The Swordsman, the third entity, and the room itself. None revealed a clear face for any of the creatures. Wait. Rewind that bit—pause—well, *shit*.

There was *never* anyone on top of me. It was an astral projection of The Rider. My LeMehti warding wouldn't allow things like him to enter, so he had to improvise. In fact, no one should have been able to come near me with these wardings. Either I made a mistake, or these particular Revs cannot be touched by the Devil's magick.

I concentrated harder. "Where are you hiding?" I cracked the wall of my reality to see the door they broke in from. Reverse engineer this bitch.

In addition to a puddle of blood and bile dribbling from my lips as I gasped for air on all fours, I saw something that surprised even me. The Rider and his horse that were outside were on a mission to murder me dead. But The Swordsman inside...his mission was to *protect* me, whatever the cost.

When I wiped my mouth I noticed something behind my blurred eyes. The slightest scratch. I reached my finger to it. I knew what touching it would bring. More pureed insides. A seizure, likely. Scanning *their* kind...touch the damn thing already, Devi.

I woke up before I hit the 67-hour mark. I can't tell you what I dreamt about but I know what I saw when I rolled over and touched that scratch mark. And let me say, I *hate* being right. Not only has The Warning caught the attention of The Riders, my failed attempts of going to Hell—and its neighbors—has ruffled a few feathers. Did I see something I wasn't meant to? How dangerous am I that the agents of the apocalypse are coming for me? More importantly, why can't I see The Swordsman who deemed me worthy enough to defend?

I need a fucking break. Let's get some food, shall we? Haven't had a proper meal since New Orleans. I also need a coat. Let's shop. Shopping is a normal enough thing to do, right? As for my face—the cameras conveniently fuzzed when I came in view. I put my item onto the counter and the little onyx-haired woman flashed a big smile my way. Her bronze skin much too vulnerable now that I stood before her. I felt guilt tightening in my stomach. I smiled back, big and bright and looked the sales clerk in the eyes. Once I knew I had her under, she packed up my coat and handed the bag to me, saying some cheerful British expression as I walked out the door and to the cafe across the street.

I took what I needed from the bakery, repeating the same charm on the cashier, and turned around to start my jog to the other side of England. I'd travel but, after the shitstorm I had last night—three nights ago? Whatever, I need a little normal in my life. Instead, I bumped in to something hard as a rock, however, and nearly lost my balance.

"I wouldn't run if I were you." Thomas. *Shit.*

The vignette of the burning bodies of the customers; possibilities of the tiny massacre hit every fiber of me. I looked at the LeMehti before me but saw *hundreds* of versions of havoc playing out behind him. I tried to swallow. He sat us down at a table.

"Did you and his Majesty have a lover's quarrel, Thomas? Are you miffed that Azrael sent Elijah first to fetch me and *not* his most *trusted* Paladin?" Thomas is a very *special* kind of monster. "Unless—" I leaned in, eyes narrowed, "he didn't send you at all, did he?" Thomas is exactly like *me*.

"I don't chase what's already mine."

"Damn, that was *smooth*. You say that to all the ladies?" He ran a hand through his stark white hair, staring at anything that wasn't me. "Ok. Then why does your so-called 'possession' taste like disconnect?" Silence. "Oh, did we forget I can literally *taste* the fucking rainbow? I mean, I can *feel* it too, but this one decided to take a gustatory route."

"Tisk, tisk little one. Your table manners are shot." A sigh fell from his mouth...and right into mine. My gagging only slightly amused him. "As much as I would love to discuss the consequences my body has on your tongue—" of course he pauses for dramatic flair, "Elijah is right and you know it."

"Oh, wow! Is *this* what you're here for? *Recruitment?*" The energy in the bakery shifted; the wind chimes danced without reason. "And here I thought you took a shining to me." I scoffed, adjusting myself in my seat. "Firstly, Elijah's a piece of shit. And secondly, if you want me, you'll have to *take* me. I'm not going anywhere with you willingly, Thomas."

"I'll not leave you. So you may as well relinquish your bag before it fuses with your skin." He leaned back his massive frame and stretched. It was really comical seeing this inhumanly tall man in the teeny chair, legs man-spread and all. His eyes, on the other hand..."You think too much. You *are* capable of civilized conversation are you not?"

"I've nothing to say to you, Thomas."

"Right." He laughed with an emptiness I hate understanding beyond my Empathic abilities. Thomas rested his hands on the table and though it was miniscule, the weight of them reminded me of... everything I cannot forget.

His eyes danced down and up at me again. The furthest from calm. No one here knows how close to being torn from existence they are. Arcadian souls among neutron stars on the verge of collision. Because of *me*... "I've missed you, little one." A forced smirk drew up his lips. Why is he.... *staring* at me?

"What is it?" I prepared for another question when I finally noticed my hands trembling and the rest of my body catching on quickly. *Too* quickly.

"Stop it. *Stop.*" Thomas spat the fevered whispers at me.

He practically lunged at me; his chair screeching in his wake bringing unwanted glares to our bodies. Thomas grabbed me by the arm and we sped out of the cafe. Once at the end of the block, he turned us into an alley and he pulled me in his arms and ran.

Someone's coming.

"Stop trembling." A thousand wolves clawed to escape from under my skin. *His* skin. Thomas is *afraid*. Why does his fear have to be so fucking painful?

"What are you doing?! Let go of me, Thomas!" He's not taking me back to The Court. He's taking me *away* from them.. Don't pass out, Devi. Unconsciousness is *not* an option right now—

I don't know how long I was out. I woke beneath a tree. My eyes took a few seconds to adjust to their night vision since I lost a good nine fucking *hours*. "Son of a bitch. 'Not an option' my ass," I muttered as I stood up and took a couple of steps away from the willow.

"I'd stay right there." I whipped around and saw Thomas lounging against my tree. His silver eyes brighter than the stars. "How often do you allow yourself to run on empty like that? You know better. You're no good to anyone if you're dead." I cocked my head and crossed my arms. He rolled his eyes. "Yet."

"Spare me the small talk. What made *you* run?"

"We were to be ambushed."

"Seriously? Your buddies show up for me and you *flee*?"

"They weren't *my* buddies." The DeKenna. "The demons picked up on your trail. You were careless." The motel? What did I miss? "The bathroom in the airport. You left a partial fingerprint underneath the sink." That was *fast*.

And careless.

"Is that how you found me? And that doesn't answer my question." He took his time walking to me.

"I'll be damned, all over again, if I let anyone else take you, dollface." I'd damn Roan and the rest of the Knights to Hell, but, you know. They're demons wanting to return me to their king because—"You make them curious. It's not every day a human Reaper with the ability to render immortals mortal comes along. Or the fact that said human transformed into—"

"Is my origin story truly necessary right now? It's not

even a particularly well-articulated one." I kicked a rock. I forget the sound they make when they're in pain. I forgot rocks could feel pain...

"And yours is?"

"No. Not even a little bit. It's about 3.14 kinds of crazy in here," I pointed to my head of dark chocolate curls, "but *it*—and my story—are *mine* to tell." He stroked his plain white shirt. The motion triggering me to channel his discomfort within it. The fabric stifled him.

"Lucifer wants to use you to kill the LeMehti."

"And the *LeMehti* want to use me to kill Lucifer and wipe every demon in Hell off the map. What an inconvenience this is for all of you."

"He has other plans..." We heard the light of a star finally enter the earth's atmosphere and our head's jerked up in unison. I couldn't see the entire life of that star, but Thomas could... I shoved my hands in my back jean pockets. "What you'll be able to do to us—it's frightening." Did he *admit* that? "Your kind isn't meant to face us, let alone bring us to our knees. It throws off The Balance."

"Yeah, yeah. The Balance," I muttered. "My kind? Is that witch, human, human Reaper, half-LeMehti—"

"Everything that you are, Devi—it *is* when it should *not* be." He stared into my eyes for a second too long. Picking up a mangled twig from the forest floor, he ran it between his fingers. Those shrieks from the twig would be in my ears for days now... "I'm not going to let anyone dig their hands into that amount of raw power." His eyes couldn't be bothered to do anything but find emptiness in the ground beneath his boots.

"Anyone but *you*." I bit my lip. He licked his. "Honestly Thomas, I thought you would've picked a fight with the all-mighty Knights. They're quite charming. Sweet fashion sense, too." He ignored me. "I'm *not* going back, Thomas. Not *there*. Not *ever* again. You'd have to kill me dead first." That's the plan and it *has* to work.

"Yes. Yes, I would. But not tonight." I let out a sigh once

I remembered I wasn't breathing. See? Changed that line up for you. Thomas looked at me the way he always does when he's about to say something incredibly annoying. "You were ready to send yourself back to Hell with your coven in Nola. How is that any different than—"

"Going back to The Court? The Circles of Hell and Company *you* lot sent me to? Trust me, where I was headed was a *big* fucking difference and you *know* it. Now, why don't you be a good Boy Scout and tell me why you didn't snatch me up the moment I left Louisiana soil?" He rolled up his sleeves. I coiled my fists. The winds howled through the sylvan landscape.

"I was otherwise detained."

"Of course, you were." I shook my head, already at my wit's end.

"Would you like to tell me what a *Rider* was doing in your motel three nights ago?"

"You show me yours and I'll show you mine." We had a staring contest. "Didn't think so." I stormed off and sat down to eat my sandwich. My seizure-induced coma may have provided me the regeneration I needed but part of my body had literally starved to death. That and, Thomas's body has consequences on mine...

Very inconvenient.

Thomas remained unmoved. Eyes locked up at the sky as if there were something he were missing in it. Thomas *burns* me. This man who tormented me with an array of abuse dipped in madness that had no equal. This *thing* who had once hung me like cattle as he slit my throat; painting artwork from my blood to the tune of a Beethoven string quartet. This *wolf*... His face is *Vincent's* face, his *voice* is Vincent's voice and that has and *always* will be his sharpest weapon. Leave it to me to be held hostage by the love of my life's *twin* brother. I now know why I lost my balance at the bakery. It wasn't from the sheer force of his body. It was the sheer force of *him*...

Fate may tolerate my existence but she shows me her disdain in other ways.

I wondered if he cared that the wind breathed so rampantly because it was trying to be rid of him. To be rid of *us*, if I'm being brutally honest. Before I reached for my bottle of water, I reached for the grass. Sure enough, the blades contorted away from my fingertips. I'm not like the LeMehti, not entirely. But, I am…something. Recoiling my hand, I focused on Thomas. To the earth, the wolf and I bear no difference. If I said the elements had no reason to fear us, I'd be lying right through my clenched teeth.

They should be *terrified*.

I debated for a very short second about speaking to him. Truth be told, before New Orleans, I can count, on *one* hand, the number of times I spoke to someone. Actual, proper conversations that didn't involve me putting deranged criminals into the ground. And though I was lucky enough to have those months with Keres and my small circle of allies, I have spent years on earth severed from everyone. I go so long without speaking to people, the sound of my own voice has chords of unfamiliarity to it. Best that we practice, lest we want to lose our voice again.

"So, as long as I'm stuck here for the time being, why don't you try to have that civilized chat with me? Though you inspire self-lobotomy, I'm getting *really* bored staring at that ungodly white thing you call hair." His laughter echoed; arms crossed; the muscles of his back painted heavily against the fabric of his shirt. Thomas turned on his heel, shifting his weight from one leg to the other but not daring to near me.

"You're staring at me, are you?" We are *not* responding to that. "And what would you like to discuss, darling?"

"First of all," the burn in my heart continued and I cringed as I stood, dusting off my jeans, "*not* your *fucking* darling," I retorted with a pointed finger, walking over to him. And I assure you it was quite the task. Not only is my trepidation weighing me down heavier than gravity, the trembles in the ground, the air shivering around me, and the trees rumbling with dread made every step daunting. See, *everything* wanted to keep me from Thomas. Though they were not too thrilled about me being in their midst either, I'm very much the lesser of the two evils.

Less, but still evil.

"Debatable at the least, I'd say," he said, teeth peeking between mischievous lips.

"Doubtful," I spat back. He shrugged and I my shoulders tightened. "So, let's see? How many people have you murdered lately?" His eyes fell but his wicked grin remained drawn on his mouth. How does he wear apathy with a smile?

"No more than you, dollface. No more than you." And he sauntered backwards into the clearing.

I stood for a moment; engulfed in the soft air aching to push me back to my tree and away from the immortal yearning to set everything on fire. I took not one step when Thomas spoke.

"I know you."

"What?"

"You asked before how it was that I found you."

"Well, that's a—that's a *fine* answer. Thanks for sharing that morsel of enlightenment." We had another staring contest, and when I opened my mouth to dig deeper into his words, Thomas pulled one of his signature moves: he walked away from me.

I put my side of the woods at peace and returned to the willow; watching Thomas for far too long in the shivering space gasping for breath. Let's not waste the night. I took the opportunity to open up my grimoire and hone some minor spells; practice my glamour magick since I never finished my training on physical shapeshifting. In my defense, that shit hurts like a mother fucker.

Why aren't I stopping time so that I can escape, you may ask? I don't know how to control it. It's a defense mechanism of sorts, I gather. Besides, there's *no* running from Thomas.

Not when he's the only one who can kill me. And we want him to kill me...

A familiar intrusive thought cut into me. *Check in on your friends in Chicago. Izumi and Lennon. Hell, even the ex.* When's the last time you saw their faces? A couple of thousand miles is child's play when scanning. But, Thomas kicked a few rocks and that drew my attention back. He's playing with his own magick; taking pebbles and stones and making them dance in the palm of his hand; a turquoise glow bringing a little brightness to the mostly pitch-black evening. I'm not sure how he sees the world. For me, my night vision lets me see in perfect clarity; as if every object has its own source of illumination. Being half of what he is, our vision could very well be identical or I haven't an inkling of what hides behind his eyes.

The rocks fell victim to the laws of physics and my focus shot back to Thomas. He's bored. A bored Thomas can be a very unkind Thomas. He took a step into the clearing. Curling up my knees under my chin, I wrapped my arms around my legs and soaked in as much warm starlight piercing through the canopy of leaves above as possible. The flinch caught me off-guard. You're not being burned alive, Devi. You're not at The Court. Helena won't find you. You're in the woods. Open your eyes.

And there he stood. The moon reflecting off his stark hair, holding on to himself as if he'd implode if he were to let go. I am in the company of a devil wrapped in angel wings dipped in blood and dirt. I may exchange words with him but that is only to keep him calm. To create a semblance of sanity in the sea of lunacy I'm perpetually drowning in.

The sun wouldn't be up for another four hours. I fluffed my backpack, threw my new coat over me and tried to be comfortable; the song of the wind through the trees lulling me to sleep. As insane as it was, I didn't deem it necessary to cast a protection spell. If anyone were foolish enough to come for me with *Thomas* as my guardian, *no* incantations—ancient or otherwise—would save them.

# Chapter II

## Iron

The rain pierced my skin. When the absence of Thomas's heart became blindingly apparent, my eyes shot open. And when I couldn't sense him anywhere within the forest, I ran.

He's gone.

I stopped in the drowning woods, touching the trees. Maybe he passed by, came in to contact with something. But the barks held no memories of him. No vibrations of his trail in the ground. No sign of Thomas anywhere. With the others so close, he is my nuclear fallout bunker. I *have* to find him.

I ran again.

Faster, harder.

In circles...

I ended up back under the cover of trees behind the clearing. My breathing heavy, shallow, and too fucking *human*. Thomas is the *one* being on this *entire* planet that could protect me from the chaos that's to come. As powerful as I have become, I am only ever *half*. Half LeMehti. Half human.

Whole monster.

I heard a fallen branch break beneath the weight of something 100 yards away. When I turned around, my daggers glinting in the moonlight, darkness greeted me; floating in waves in my direction. Shadows with crimson irises and eyes soaked in coal and ember. Now would be an optimal time to run. Power walk. Really, *any* type of locomotion would be suitable.

If I could only move...

The rain pounded furiously into us; Each drop containing within it the faintest sense of the purest urge to rid its precious earth of the demons that treaded upon her. The taste of it sizzling on my tongue.

Proper mud formed beneath my feet. I thought the ground would open up and swallow the Knights of Hell whole. How are they here? Why would Thomas allow it? What purpose does this serve him?

Despite their valiant efforts, the drops of rain perished as they touched the men and resurrected as gorgeous smoke from a sleeping fire. One that would wake at any moment to eat you alive. Each step taken created cracks and ripples in the space around them evident only to Revs and the mad. The presence of the Knights, though tolerated, is terribly taxing in the human realm. The tallest man, the leader, was only a few feet from me now and he's not planning on lifting his spell from me any time soon. The fire of their eyes...it reflected too bright off my weapons; their chain mail sparking embers.

The leader, his mouth opened to speak, but the wind blew the taste of his tongue into my nose and I nearly broke through his magick and dropped from disgust. I thought I tore my feet from the ground and ran towards the forest. I thought I cast spells. I thought I did a lot of things...

"Hush now. This'll not take long." I heard his whispers despite the raging storm and he knew it. Reveled in the fear it birthed inside me. Their hands took hold of my wrists, breaking me as they forced me to my knees. I tried to control the damage of my weight to the earth. I barely managed to contain the earthquake inside of me. The Knights only smiled.

I didn't scream or yell for help or make any sort of verbal proclamation. This didn't bode well with them. This lot likes it when they hear agony. Unable to instantly heal from their touch—the leader grabbed me by the throat and squeezed. Muscles tearing and my vertebrae cracking; the shards of bone slicing through my nerves. The paralysis came and went in waves. When my voice box collapsed, the disappointment fell across his face.

I can't scream for him now.

The way his eyes lit up, lip bit, heart racing...I knew, then and there, they were going to do two things: Kill me repeatedly because they knew I'd never die completely and rape me. Rape me simply because they could.

And because they would enjoy it.

Charging up, I smiled at him, blood-soaked spit dripping from my mouth. I lit up like a lightning strike and for a few seconds, I was free of them. Free but paralyzed. Paralyzed and still containing the earthquake. I knew what I had to do then to have enough mind space left to blink away from them.

Here we go again.

I didn't realize what we heard were my bones breaking a thousand times from the earthquake. It's actually a little over a thousand. I counted. Hemorrhaging brain? Blood-filled lungs? Vomit-filled mouth? Piss-filled panties? Skeleton *so* shattered it turned to dust? All good. All good because it *worked*. I got away. I blinked to the waterfall. Barricading myself under the liquid would speed up the healing process for the damage I've done to myself. As for the rest? Demonic injuries? They take a while, even with the aid of water. And now I'm back in the crater I left behind when I ate an earthquake.

Fuckers are *fast*, I'll give them that.

The leader lifted me to my feet—why can't I channel his name? My neck in his iron grasp, my body soaking wet but not in the way they would prefer. "Try that shit again and I'll show you what we do with disobedient bitches." He smashed my body against the willow, ripping it from its roots. Before I could open my eyes, he mounted me; knees on my chest, hands around my throat, embers of his eyes falling on my lips. Singing away nearly every layer of skin.

"Devi, pay attention, *please*." He bashed my head against his own and I started to laugh, coughing up blood as he tore my shirt off. The demon may be beating the shit out of me, while the others stood in a circle-jerk watching, but *my* body, my *skeleton* is as strong as theirs. Blood dripped on to my nose from the crack in his forehead. And then, as I remembered that I am as physically strong as a thing born of the Devil, I saw him. He stood there, *watching*. Fucking *watching*.

The rage in the Knight of Hell was palpable and I fucking loved it. "Little girl, you're going to learn, sooner or later, where your place is in this world. First lesson begins now." He spoke through gritted teeth. I could feel him get hard. He stopped strangling me long enough to take out his dagger and pierce it through my heart as slowly as possible. The blade broke pieces of a rib as it penetrated. For a fleeting moment I wondered why they had stopped using their magick to keep me still. Why had there been so many of them to begin with? I may be an equal to them when it comes to physical strength, but with their touch being my kryptonite... One DeKenna would have sufficed.

Why send *five*?

He tore of his cloak, undid his britches and ripped my jeans off while the others held down my hands and feet. Please, not again...

Then my heart stopped.

The entire forest flooded with light. It blinded me. I felt no pain. No fear. It finally worked. They found my kill switch. War is over. Poison cleansed. The end.

Wishful thinking.

The electrical signals from my brain fired to my heart and then it beat. Once and then twice. Each beat more powerful than the last. My rhythm steadied and blood carried oxygen to my organs; warming my insides. The light of the sun registered in too brightly and I didn't want to open my eyes. If I did, my tears would surely escape. They could still be here. My eyes fluttered open but I closed them just as quickly. It's too bright.

Try again Devi.

It took me longer to adjust my eyes and even longer to realize I was *awake*. I began hyperventilating. They're still here. "Get your hands off of me!" I nearly beheaded whichever Knight touched my shoulder. The blood sprayed onto my eyes and lips in the same instant I saw Thomas jump back with his hand against his neck. A waterfall of red painting his chest.

"Oh dear God." My whisper—the loudest sound in the woods. I'm *awake*. It was a dream. A *vision*. What have I done?! Follow the rules of war. Never attack an un-fighting opponent. Attack *only* if you are going to be attacked. Thomas didn't hurt me. And I just murdered him...

I took a step to him but he walked away. He fell to his knees and I fell to mine. Thomas burned off his drenched shirt. Our lungs gasped for breath. We were shaking. My attack had been *precisely* what I had intended it to be.

Lethal.

"Thomas?" He motioned me to stay back. I can't breathe. He can't breathe. My heart stopped. His heart stopped. Feeling the things Thomas is feeling, with this level of purity... But his pain. He won't let me channel it. Even in this state, he wouldn't allow it. If I can do one thing it's withstand pain. I was taught by the best.

What are you hiding?

What matters is my disorientation. My out-of-focus strike. My inability to distinguish reality from fantasy. It's not that making Thomas bleed crossed a boundary. It's that I had *no* reason to do so. I fight to survive. Kill or be killed. But he *wasn't* trying to kill me so I *shouldn't* have raised my blades to him. This distinction helps to keep me different from them. I *can't* be like them...

I clasped my hands around my mouth to keep his screams locked behind my teeth. The grass around him had lost its emerald hue and had now drank up so much of him, it now wore a lovely shade of wine.

The same magick that's in my bullets is etched into my blades and it's drastically slowing his healing. A profusely bleeding immortal is a *weak* one and that's as good as *dead* in their book. And in this life, *their* life, that fleeting death gives me *just* enough time to fight my way out.

This is my one perfect moment in time to escape. And if I wanted to live, I would...

Thomas dug into the earth, holding on to gravity as much as he could. I heard his voice, then. Gurgling. Breathless.

"You were dreaming, little one. You were...dreaming." He staggered toward the frightened forest. And then he ran.

The salt of my tears lingered on his blood dripping from my lips. In the early morning glow of the sun, it dawned on me what Thomas had done. He knew of my visions. I must've been convulsing something awful from the channeled pain of my future attack. Thomas brought me into the sunlight to wake me because his calls had failed. He held me down to stabilize me; keep me from hurting myself.

Just like Keres...

One minute was all it took to strike Thomas down and have him run into the woods. It only took half a second for something else to register: How did the strongest Paladin of the LeMehti empire *not* dodge my blow?

Not even the fear of what awaited me when Thomas returns would move me. The trees spat out his body with relief. The evidence of his fatality had all but washed away. All but the slight shimmering scar across his throat that will never fade. Silver, iron, and their words etched in each blade. That's the magickal trinity that is meant to be damning.

The Dark Paladin returned with a wild bewilderment growing in his eyes. My unmoving body on the trembling ground—He knelt in front of me. His hands wavered on my own. This is it. This is where he rips my soul out of my chest. Artful vengeance could not be found in his eyes, though. This is going to be *messy*. Thomas slid my twitching hands from my mouth; the fresh blood seeping from the corners of my lips—I'd never seen him in shock before now.

"Why are you bleeding?" The second he spoke the words, we both realized the answer. Being an Empath *and* LeMehti is complicated..."Breathe. Devi, breathe." He took me by the back of the neck and pushed the air from my chest. As if that breath inside my lungs *had* to stay lodged, because if I were to part my lips and let it escape, the scream itself would end me. As if it would end us both.

And it almost did.

He held his scream prisoner inside of himself. But it broke free inside of me...

The wail traveled for miles, breaking the sound barrier far too many times. Thomas scooped me up. When I opened my eyes, we were beneath the willow. Once the forest was quiet again—as quiet as it can be after what passed—I dared open my mouth. This time to speak.

"Rahm," I said, with a surprising quiver to my voice as I wiped our blood from my mouth. Rahm. Finally found the name of the leader. The General of Hell's army sent her favorite Knights for me. The fact that Lucifer sent *them* to fetch me did not escape us. "He's coming." I looked up at Thomas but he turned away. "If, if you still want me alive, you need to get me away from here. *Far* away."

"That is *all* I want." I couldn't look away and somehow, somehow I *didn't* want to. Thomas is my *only* saving grace. I'd be no match for Roan and her Knights. If I want to live, I'm going to have to cleave to the man who's murdered me countless times. But right now—I... I can't keep my eyes open. He's making me sleep.

"Thomas don't do—" I tried with all that I had to fight against his spell. I wanted *no* part of it. I took in a jagged breath and jumped out of Thomas' arms.

I sat up in my room with music chanting in my ears. I'm fucking dreaming. But, why am I here? Thomas is the *only* poisoned immortal that can fight his way into my mind like this. Finding a way, though rarely, to walk in dreams together. Though not a perfected skill for him, he did it artfully. Another tactic to make me question my sanity.

I made a pathetic attempt to leave my bed only to fall to my knees. Blanket clutched in my hand, tears dangling on lashes. I cried. The memory of the song taunting me. Trapped in the in-between. Under a dream that I never wanted to wake from and inside the arms of a devil who—

Wake up, Devi. Wake up. I don't want this dream, Thomas! Wake up!

I woke trembling. When my eyes fluttered open, I found myself back in Thomas's hold.

"You're awake. Whatever it is that you saw," I turned to face him, rage and terror battling for my highest attention." Try and forget it." Forget. Forget? I clenched my jaw. What exactly did I see? In my room. The music. Thomas coming for me...no. There's something else in my dream. Why can't I remember?

I decided to brave moving my body away from his. I lifted myself up and out of his lap and sat myself beside him, leaning against the curve of the willow. I stretched out my legs and enjoyed my mock freedom. I looked up at the late afternoon light trickling in between the leaves. My smile lasted only a moment. His fingers made their way to my wrist and I did the only thing I knew *to* do: I moved my hand away, running my fingers through my hair as the reason and spoke. Because, I don't remember a time when I was touched by a man and not hurt. Because when *this* man touches you...

"You know what Roan is planning," I said but was met with silence. He breathed in jaggedly. We both felt the seconds fall away from us...too literally. Too painfully, if I focused enough on the process. I decided to show him the vision of the Knights in full technicolor. To do that, though, to do that with *this* type of creature, I need physical contact. They can't see what's inside my head unless I show them. Hence why he was trying to touch my hand...

With a bite of my lip, I leaned forward; building up the nerve to *willingly* touch the man who's murdered me hundreds of times. The man who murdered Vincent...

I nervously played with a few blades of grass. They played back. "I couldn't—"

"What?" Thomas pushed impatiently. I didn't realize how quiet my voice was. My fingers rubbed an invisible ache in my throat.

"When we were fighting, the Knights, they did something to me. I couldn't use my powers. Not the ones I needed, at least." No response. "Any theories?"

"On?"

"On why I was rendered practically helpless with the De-Kenna." I heard a hawk flap its wings and soar from a few miles away. The only sound. The loudest sound.

"They're Knights. They're capable of more things than lower garrisons. They're like—"

"You." Thomas looked over his shoulder to find my face. He didn't.

"Yes. They did to you what Ionnar had done." Without thought, the tuft of grass in my hand burnt to ash. "You do remember her—"

"Yes. I *remember.*" Another Paladin. Another *session* at the The Court that failed to get me to become their Royal Executioner.

I curled my knees up, then back down. Ran my fingers through my hair one too many times. I had to show him. It's not enough simply telling him. What I wouldn't give not to have to fucking *touch* his skin. A heavy sigh left my mouth. I didn't realize I was tapping my nail against my thumb ring until the sound of the pewter reverberating in the forest became more annoying than Thomas's heartbeat. I swallowed, trying my best to ignore the metal taste still lingering, rolled up my sleeves and—

"Do you enjoy making even the most *routine* event transform into a Shakespearean performance?" He scowled as a laugh fought its way out of him.

"You know, you can just say 'Hey Devi, we may live forever but we ain't got all fucking day.' Gets the job done just as well as—" He took my hand in his, ignoring my narrowing eyes and the cracking echoes in the trees around us. I stifled a laugh. He threw me a look. "Hey, don't look at *me*. That was Mother Nature giving you the stink eye for man-handling me. She doesn't take kindly to evil folk."

"I'm not the only one."

"True. But I'm the lesser of the two."

"Less, but still evil." I could feel him kicking himself for saying that to me. Either that, or I'm about to get the hiccups.

I'm not getting the hiccups.

"Yes, yes. I know. Devi. Destroyer of LeMehti. All mighty evil one. Ruiner of Realms, blah blah blah. I'm *so* scary. Got it. Can I show you the literal Knights of Hell who are going to murder me? Literally, from *Hell*. You know, where Lucifer lives?"

"It's not as though you've never been there, Devi. Get on with it." I noted his exhaustion but focused on his annoyance. Small victories. Except, of course, when I visited the first few circles of Hell...

Thomas closed his eyes first. I followed suit. I took in a breath and applied pressure to his hand and he reciprocated. The contact, the intensity of it, that's what helps make the psychic link. And marvelously enough, it only happens when *I* want it to.

Thank the damn stars.

Though we felt the vision in real time, only a few seconds passed. Even upon second viewing, I couldn't rake out anything out of the ordinary. No clues to lead me to answers. Only questions. Always questions.

Thomas didn't say anything. He removed his touch from mine. No look of surprise on his face. Except, Thomas seemed frustrated. Restless. Uneasy... I could only channel so much.

The rest I had to rely on good old fashioned human instinct. But, Thomas isn't human no matter how much he looks the part right now.

My fingers, suddenly aware of their separation of contact from another person, gravitated towards the laces on my boots. I curled in on myself. Fun fact: Humans literally need touch to survive. We go batshit if we don't and when we're babies, we die. We fucking *die* if left without skin-to-skin contact. The only time I'm ever touched is when I'm at the receiving end of a fist.

I gripped my laces tighter.

Thomas pulled out his sword from the pocket of space beside him; holding on to the hilt as hard as I held on to myself. The wind rustled the leaves, bringing a soft whisper of calm that too soon turned into a song of warning.

"I—they won't touch you. I'll be waiting for them." That's all he said. He gazed into the clearing for a long time. I could hear his heart race inside his chest and pound against my ear like a thousand wild horses running. I adjusted myself, resting my chin atop my knees. I discarded the laces and wrapped my arms around my legs. Breathing deep.

The song began to play again. My eyes opened. I am conscious. The melody had been so intertwined within me, between every beat of my heart, that it echoed from me to the outside world. Enough where it could be heard, clear as a bell, in the waves and flows of the air. It took me two seconds to understand the actual process. My molecules, my atoms, my brain waves, the whole of my being vibrated music.

I turned, for reasons unknown, to look at Thomas. Eyes closed, his lips mouthing the lyrics in real time.

"First time?" He asked softly knowing full well the answer.

"First time I've been a *radio*? Yeah, Thomas. First time." The words fell from my mouth like honey.

"Your body's gone into a protective shift. You're not simply playing music, Devi." He never opened his eyes. "Your Le-Mehti side is keeping you from—"

"Losing my mind." The effect, however, is not limited to me. Thomas is too ready to fall away into a dream. Resting against the tree trunk, I shut my eyes. The song warming us to our core.

I forced my eyes open when Thomas's grip on the hilt of his sword tightened in my hand. His eyes saw nothing but the clearing where Roan's Knights would soon attack. The wave of notes blanketed us, and under its weight, I couldn't fight myself or Thomas's predatory protection any longer. I shut my eyes and a moment later, I felt Thomas rest his.

# Chapter 12

## Hostage

I felt the deer before anything else. It took a breath and I held mine. Before I opened my eyes, I felt my backpack underneath my head, my coat draped over my body, and Thomas standing only fifty feet away from the animal. My shielding song has faded. Whatever fury in him that's been held at bay—the fire inside him has been stoking for hours.

Surprise pulled back my lids. For the most part, animals kept their distance from the monsters in their forest. So, I needed to ask why a creature as helpless as this doe is walking *towards* the apex predator. I rubbed the sleep from my face and chose to check in with the deer. I focused on her and took in a breath and let it out slowly. She's curious. She's afraid. And I'm *dreaming*. I should be looking in to the morning sky. Instead, the wrong constellations were scattered across a softly fading *night*.

Gasping for air, I woke up throwing off the coat. "Fucking hell." The words, barely audible, fell out of me with far too much exertion. I looked up at the stars then over my shoulder. Thomas's spot was empty. No sign of him in the clearing, either. I headed to the clearing, adjusting my bra, and called out to him. Out in the open, I zeroed in on a couple of things. There's a storm brewing in the midnight sky and a dead body on the other side of the woods.

A human body.

"What did you do Thomas?" I ran over to her but stopped short. He must have gone to the city. He had to kill *something*. Why not her? Kneeling beside the woman, I knew what would happen with my subsequent touch of her corpse. The air already had me nauseated with fragmented memories of her. She lay on her stomach; drenched curls hiding a too broken face already too sore on my own. I rolled her gently over and with that contact, I got a front-row seat to her life. What I couldn't understand is why there is no ghost. A murder *this* violent, you tend to stick around before you go Up or Down or In Between.

I grit my teeth and prepared my body to undergo her murder. I don't know why it took me so long to see it. To *feel* it. Brushing the curls from my face and wiping the blood from my nose and eyes. My throat had been ripped out; vocal cords dangling atop muscle, exposing my spine. Four ribs had been torn out. The bones were imbedded into the dirt with part of my lung and diaphragm peeking through the gapes. I fell back on my ass, losing balance miserably. My fingers dug into the earth. The blood, still warm, covered each appendage; drowning them. There's so much blood...

I've bled more...

I'm dreaming. Knew it the moment I saw her boots. Maybe sooner. But I didn't *realize* it. Couldn't see the nightmare. A dream within a dream. Red droplets kissed my kneecaps and cheeks. We were beneath a canopy of thousands of leaves...showered with my insides. When my laughing gave way to tears, I held my broken hand; pushing back in place some of the bones that Thomas dislocated. I laid next to her, hand-in-hand, brushing away her wet hair from her shattered eye sockets. And as the rain began to fall, I shut my eyes and wept.

My body curled in on itself. The fetal position doing absolutely nothing to soothe either of us. The wilder the storm grew, the harder I sobbed. I grabbed her, pulling her into my chest and held her as tightly as I could. I ignored the space where her spine used to be. I gave no attention to the brain matter slipping through my fingers. What *did* catch me was the fact that no matter how adamantly I held my corpse, I heard no sounds from her.

There were simply no more bones left to break...

"We're going to die. We *have* to. To save *them*." I took a breath and spoke through my quivering lips with my forehead kissing hers. "But not like this, Devi. Not. Like. This." A strike of lightning hit the forest so bright and loud, it woke me up in a craze.

But not before I saw it.

I couldn't breathe. Thomas stood in clear view of the afternoon sun. I ran my fingers through my hair and stood; taking a minute to acclimate to the real world and dissect myself from the dreamworld. When you're a Reverie—however it is that you'd classify us Penny Dreadfuls—we sense the differences between realms.

Except, of course, when we can't...

"Devi!" I flinched at the sound of my name in his mouth ringing in my ears.

"Fuck. What?! No need to yell. Super fucking hearing, remember?" He kept his back to me while a laugh stumbled from his lips down to his crossed arms.

"You zoned out. The higher volume was, therefore, a necessity. Also, it's noon." When I heard his voice, my hands curled to fists waiting to lunge at him if he made his move. He's being casual. *Too* casual. A few moments flowed by me and I used them to tame my heart. I couldn't let it get out of control. Especially not after what I saw. I *know* what I saw...

"Necessity my ass," I muttered.

"What's that?" He heard me.

"Thanks for the time. You gonna chime in with a weather forecast, too?" No response. "What the hell are you yelling my name for?" One thing, other than the mind-boggling fact that he hasn't struck me, is another matter altogether. He hadn't slept. We both fell asleep from my personal concerto, but I don't think it was strong enough to hold *him* under its hypnosis for long. Though sleep is purely recreational for them, you'd think he'd indulge even with *me* around. I found it quite peculiar. Then again, I find *everything* Thomas does strange. Enigmatic. Annoying. Strangle-worthy. The usual.

Case in point.

As I made my way towards him in the clearing, he made his way to the tree and plopped his ass down, a big relieving sigh escaping from him. My head cocked as I examined him. But I got nowhere.

"Are you going to keep analyzing?" He said with a crooked smile that exhausted us both.

"Are you going to keep giving me reason to?" Staring contest. "We have to leave. You need me *alive,* remember?" He stood up and Ported himself into the clearing. The shadows of the leaves above us rustling from relief to have the thing as far away from them as possible.

He turned to face me and I knew what the look meant.

Thomas is *beckoning* me. Don't mistake my actions as defeat. Rather, take them as carefully calculated campaign. Remember, I can see several hundred possible futures of nearly every choice I make. Grant it, Thomas and the others have the same ability and can weed out concrete futures with more ease than I can, but at the end of the day, I still *can.* So, when I decide to walk to the beast waiting for me in the woods, don't be too scared, or judgmental. After all, I am half of him. And my teeth are just as sharp.

"Whenever you're done with whatever you're doing in there," Thomas said, gesturing to his head. His voice pierced my ears and brought me back into reality. I get so lost in my thoughts sometimes. Fuck. You'd think I'm narrating a damn book. "Maybe you can join me."

When I reluctantly stood a healthy 10 feet beside him, I noticed things I hadn't earlier. The sound, for instance, was quiet and blanketed with eerie air. The smell is another factor. All I came upon though is sweet grass, more trees and more clean, crisp water. The animals were plentiful of course but, the body count was low. *Two*, to be exact. My heightened senses weren't giving me the knowledge they should and it bothered Thomas far more than I thought possible.

But then I backtracked and realized when the alteration in space occurred—the café. Yet I couldn't find a trace to explain the how or why.

"Thomas, where did you take us?" Surveying the area with my eyes this time, I moved further into the clearing. The wind gasped and tried with all it had to push me back into the safe haven of the willows, where Thomas would *not* be.

I ignored the wind.

"England's countryside." The words spilled from his mouth matter-of-factly.

"I think we're a little further away from—" This *is* England's countryside. But, where are all the people? I can't believe I didn't notice, or flinch, when Thomas's words crept into my ear from behind.

"Come now, darling. You can get those gears working a lot better than this." He tapped my head with his filthy finger as a smile formed with those words. I turned to face him but only saw my bags and the flowing emerald of the woods behind me.

"Still not fast enough, I see. You left your training far too soon, dollface." I twisted around, fuming. "Look around you. *Listen.*" He motioned to his ears. "Have you truly become *this* helpless? Don't you see it?" His arms stretched, showcasing the vast forest around us.

"So sorry to disappoint you, *dollface*. But no, I don't see *shit*. But I can sure as fuck can smell it." I sneered. He smiled. I wanted to tear out his eyes, but he *is* right. What good were my half-breed traits if I couldn't figure out what's happening?

"You're blind. You're searching for specific things rather than simply *searching*. Don't listen for cars and people and busy streets. *Listen.*" If it weren't for his gaze on my body right now, I would be on the ground in hysterics. Is he trying to *teach* me something?

"Seriously, Thomas? We don't have time for this and I'm *not* in the mood to play your mind games." I unsheathed my daggers. One still with a red edge to it. He looked at me, almost going in to hysterics himself, but stopped before he looked *too* ridiculous.

"Your guilt must be overwhelming. However, I'm presently not in any mood to battle you." My hands gripped the handles tighter and I took a step back. The one mind I *can't* get inside of. "Now put those away and pay attention." Thomas walked over to me nonchalantly and with a terror I'm still not used to after all this time.

The face of my lover and the soul of his murderer.

They had to be *identical*...

I instinctively took a step back, my blades at my sides. At least, that's what I *thought* I was doing. I heard something thud onto the grass and it was Thomas's hands that were in mine now. His breath washed over my face and it was all I could do to keep from throwing up.

"I said *pay* attention." His hands crept up to cradled my face; his skin rising in temperature . "Now focus." Don't retaliate. Don't move, Devi.

"You think I can *focus* without you fucking man-handling me?" I knew silence would be my only answer. His wretched touch on me is a teaching tool, however. A conductor. But then, the forest panicked. Anything of Thomas on me is *wrong* and even *they* know it. And yes, I'm afraid. I'm *always* afraid. But I'm also quite used to the monster staring back at me. We only fear what we don't understand. And I understand Thomas. On a level I wish I didn't.

"You're thinking about everything except what I've told you to think about." He let out a sigh, tired of my lack of, well, a lot. "The difference you're tuning into, albeit not entirely, is the date. It's October 31st." Thomas took a calculated step *away* from me. "1601." We spoke the year in unison.

"It's *when*?! What the hell is wrong with you, Thomas?" His laughter…I stared him up and down. This fucking idiot better have a *real* good reason for taking us back over 400 years in the *past*. "Mother fucker. Why would you do this? And All Hallow's Eve? This far into the past? Do you have a *death* wish?"

"Are you quite through? I can't answer you in the least if you don't *shut up*." I stood there, arms folded across my chest, gritting my teeth. "Your vision *was* about the future. Roan and her band of Merry Men *will* come looking for you tonight. When we left the café, we left because I had the *same* vision. Didn't you notice the Break?"

This future I did *not* see coming.

"If we're *here*, Devi, in *this* time, they cannot take you."

"I saw you, in the vision. You stood there. *Watching*." Why did he choose Halloween?

"You didn't deduce that you were seeing me witness the same vision?"

"Yeah, because that is a completely obvious deduction for me to come to while I'm being murdered and raped by demons." I crossed my arms across my chest. He took a second to respond.

"It should've been, Devi. Had you completed your training with your Paladin Guardians—"

"Shoulda, woulda, coulda, but fucking didn't. Ain't that a fucking shame? Can we move on, please?" There should be spirits and demons crawling *everywhere*. I'm a living haunting. So, where are they?

"The visions you have can be more complicated than they seem. You had *two* visions from two *different* timelines."

"A twofer. Grand." I rolled my eyes and scanned the forest. This time, I scanned for devils, demons, and the dead.

"Why did you choose the one night of the year that I would be the weakest? That the Veil would be more powerful than in the present?"

"You saw me watching?" His words were matter of fact. But, beneath his calm frame, a wolf waited to tear itself out through his skin.

"That *is* your thing." He flared his nostrils. I didn't look him in the eye.

"That was the *past*. You had a vision of me having a vision of you."

"Fascinating. As if I don't have enough fucking trouble—" Vincent and I never finished our lesson on that. I hate it when Thomas is right.

"I can teach you to differentiate. Navigate between the various visions." Not one wayward soul anywhere...

"When I mutter shit to myself, that's *not* an invitation for you to speak to me." He looked as though someone slapped him across the face.

"Noted," he said, almost gingerly. I went back to my willow tree. But, I forgot my blades. I turned on my heel to retrieve them when the giant prick blocked my path.

"Still forgetful as ever I see."

"Yup." I snatched my blades from him and elbowed the asshole in the gut; teleporting out of his hold. "Despite efforts to the contrary, my memory is still shit. A couple *hundred* traumatic brain injuries, and *time travel*, tend to do that." It actually shouldn't. Not with how I heal. I don't know why my otherwise perfect memory falters.

"Wouldn't have it any other way, little one." I started toward my tree when Thomas already Ported himself there. Leaning against the willow, a weak smile on his lips with a mood border-lining disgust...with himself. I gripped my stomach, my face alight with nausea.

"You know, if you're going to choose which affects—physical or emotional—I tune in to, could you please not make wanting to fucking *vomit* one of them? And while we're at it, take *all* bodily functions off the table. I don't do that shit to you. Pun intended." After a quick stare down, I rolled my eyes and took off.

I've had my fill of him for the morning.

"Where are you going?" I wouldn't have stopped but he roared with as much fire as me.

"I'm going to go find some bushes to piss in. Maybe throw up. I'll decide on the way. Do you wanna come and help?" His lips pursed and his eyes narrowed and bordered on white. We don't like white. But, he managed a wryly smile and opened his mouth again.

"I'll get us something to eat."

"Oh yeah. You know, I think I saw a Burger King on the way up here. Get me a Whopper would ya?!" I couldn't walk away fast enough.

I found a bundle of bushes amidst another heavily wooded area as far away from him as possible. I didn't need the cover of the massive branches weaving a canopy above, but it seemed a normal enough thing to do and I needed a fix of normalcy. *Bad.*

I washed my hands and drank from a stream. The coolness of the liquid did little to quell the flames in my chest. I stared at the running water and my mind went along for the ride. How on earth did Thomas get away with bringing us here? Only he and Vincent have—had the ability to Break. But, neither of them *dared* to travel through time without an order.

Without *reason...*

Azrael doesn't take kindly to disobedience—or treason. I'm not too sure of the damage Thomas has in store for himself when we get to The Court. And, despite what either of us said, we are going back to Cortem no matter what. Thomas can say one thing, and a dozen versions of reality will be layered within his words.

That aside, I am reeling through the undercurrent of how I merely *survived.* How the hell did I live through traveling through *time*?

The more my mind ran, it smashed itself into the moment where I had told Thomas of my vision. As my mind sat there, dazed in its concussion from the crash, I remembered his words. *I'll be waiting for them.* Waiting for what? If we're here, in 1601, and they're in 2022...

I ran.

I ran and crashed into a fucking tree. And, the fucking tree fell on top of me.

"Not again," I groaned. Why can't I breathe? I should be able to flick this tree off of me.

"We really need to stop meeting like this, little one." *Thomas.* I pushed him off of me as hard as I could. "You took too long, so I came after you." He spat out, laughing at me. I stood up despite the forest spinning in my head.

"You said you'd be 'waiting for them'. What does that even mean? You are *not* keeping me hostage here or any other timeline!" Thomas steadied me before I fell face first into the earth. My hand was glued to the back of my head. He pulled it away and the blood oozed down my neck and back. "Why tonight? Why Halloween of all fucking nights? The Veil's strength... You're supposed to *protect* me! The amount of spirits that'll come for me...for you. Thomas, not even *you* can withstand all of that madness. Why would you do this?"

"I won't hold you hostage here or any other time—except our own. And I said I would wait for them because I *will*. And that power that's coursing through your bones? That fire? That's *you*. You're stronger here. As am I." Thomas was level to my eyes. The truth all over him but I couldn't bear the bitter taste of it. He gripped my arms tighter, keeping me upright as I swayed too easily with the violent winds.

"Why—what's wrong with you? Why do you need—" My eyes went black. Thomas shook me and ignored my questions.

"That's why I brought us *this* far back. The dead and their like are nowhere to be found because they're *terrified*, Devi." He straightened his posture, towering over me. "Of *us*." For a moment, one full of trembling breaths in both our lungs, we were nothing but quiet. What *are* we? "Now hold *still.*" His voice was too calm. The type of calm that hid *fear*. Thomas pulled my back against his chest, brushing my hair away. The now powdered rock I landed on cracked my skull. A piece of bone pierced into the back of my brain…

Normally, no earthly thing would injure me.

Normally, I would've healed the instant my skull began to crack.

"You landed on a rock. I'm—"

"I landed on *you*! That hurts! Stop! Thomas, stop!"

"Hold still! I have to heal you since you're so keen on not doing so yourself!" I have to ignore the blurred foliage. I know what I saw. I *know* who ripped me apart in that dream. "Devi, open your eyes." My doppelgänger had *blinked*. "Devi!" And I know who did that to her because I *saw* it right as the lightning struck. A small burst of electricity went through my skeleton. Thomas's feeble attempt to bring me back to him.

"Leave me alone!" The winds gave way to the oncoming storm. The surrounding trees, however, split and fell to the earth from my scream. I finally fell to my knees. Thomas never lost his grip on me. "I *saw* it. Let me go! I know. I fucking *know!*" Eyes barely open. Mouth dry. Lips quivering. And that's when I started to shake. But the cause was far from the slow creep of Autumn air.

# Chapter 13

## Waterfall

The instant I absolutely knew which reality I was in, I jumped to my feet, daggers in each hand. My heart roaring. Dusk had begun to settle with the stars slowly rousing, taking over the blue-gray sky. Thomas walked toward me, hands hovering as if he wasn't a God damn threat all of a sudden.

I need to run, it didn't matter where. But when he spoke, his voice clear and hypnotic, I couldn't move.

"It's not what you think."

"Either kill me and be done with it, or I swear to every fucking *God,* Thomas, I will *level* this entire country and take us *both* down with it." My nails dug into my palms; little beads of scarlet dripping down the blades. "The truth. *Now.*"

"I didn't do that to you, Devi—"

"Don't. Don't you say my fucking name."

"You started to walk away from the willows. You didn't listen to me when I told you to come back. I blocked your path…you didn't see me. You phased through me." He took in a jagged breath, trying to swallow. I anchored my feet into the dirt. "You were sleepwalking. Another blackout."

"What *happened,* Thomas?"

"You killed yourself."

"Liar."

"You killed yourself because you had a psychotic break. The music only delayed—"

"Shut up." He started towards me. The air between us beginning to crackle.

"For all the immortality inside of you, you're still human. And that humanity is what was literally the death of you. No one, human or supernatural, walks away after everything you've been through. Not without consequence."

"So I tore out my own *spine* because I have PTSD?" I have PTSD...

"I don't think there is a name for what you have." Thomas took a step back, rubbing his shoulder before putting his hands in his pockets. "Your psyche broke. Your body reacted in kind. What happened—it was a perfect storm, one in which nothing could've survived."

"Don't do that. Don't try and blame my psychological maladies as the reason why you didn't stop me. You know damn well it was because you *enjoyed* watching me do that to myself." My neck hardly supported my head. My torso too much for my legs. I crumbled down to the ground, resting my head against a fallen tree trunk.

"That's not why I didn't stop you."

"Oh yeah?" I sniffled as tears slid down cool on my cheeks. "Pray tell, good sir, why the fuck *didn't* you then?" I dropped my daggers, wiping my bloody but healed palms on my jeans.

Staying put, Thomas crouched down to my level. He made an ill attempt to fix his hair as the wind tossed it around. "Because there *was* no stopping you." He let a moment fill us, allowing the words to take meaning inside me. "You were in between worlds. Trapped. Asleep. You never wake a sleepwalker. Had I tried..."

"But you *did* try." Thomas held his hands. *Tight.*

"Yes. Briefly." Silence. "Every attempt I made to stop you only served as fuel to your fury."

"I'm having trouble seeing the downside of this for you."

"After the third try, I couldn't—I couldn't *control* myself any longer." My eyes finally met his. His eyes flickered and he put the earth in his gaze instead. "There was *no* downside for me, Devi. There's *nothing* I *didn't* enjoy as I watched you." He cracked his knuckles. We both clenched our jaws.

"That's when you joined the party." I looked away when Thomas' eyes shot up at me in horror; my voice quivering. I motioned to my face with my finger. "I may be like you but *my* skin doesn't leave bruising like *that*. Plus, I can't headbutt myself, so..."

"I left."

"How noble."

"I *healed* you."

"Wait here. I'll go get you your Medic Badge Medal."

"Devi—"

"Stop saying my *fucking* name." The earth beneath shook ever so slightly...for miles. The tides rising and crashing onto the shore; waiting patiently to swallow England, and us, whole on *my* command. "Did you make me forget or was that conveniently self-inflicted, too?" Thomas stood, crossing his arms, and looked through the spaces between the leaves into the night sky.

"Neither answer will satisfy you."

"Humor me."

"Hard as it may be to believe—" laughter, filled with an emotion I couldn't identify, escaped my mouth, interrupting his voice. His voice that I could hear as if it were my own. Warm against my cheek... "I had nothing to do with that bit. You repressed the memory all on your own. And by my count, you've become quite the expert at this."

"Of course I did." My palm met my forehead; trying to smooth out an ache I knew would never subside. "How did you know I've been hiding my memories?"

"How could I not?" The leaves rustled with the force of the wind. The pause allowing us both time to breathe.

"That's not an answer." I grabbed my weapons and got up on my feet.

"Isn't it, though?"

"Just so you know, the only thing that has *any* measure of difficulty in the way of belief is the very fact that you *stopped* beating me to death." He looked at me from the corner of his eyes. "You have to admit that that's just a *wee* bit, what's the word?" I tapped one of my blades to my chin. "Right. Strange." I chuckled, twirling my blades, ignoring my tired bones. Or is that Thomas's hurt I feel inside me? "Where did you go, anyway? When you left me to my very violent devices?"

"It doesn't matter."

"The hell it does. Newsflash asshole: *Everything* your lot does matters to me. *I'm* the one who can will you out of existence yet here I am literally tearing myself apart because of every sick fucking thing *you've* done to *me*. I've done *nothing* but fight to survive *you* when all you do is bitch and moan about how it's the other way around. So when your ass runs away when I'm turning myself inside out, you better tell me why. And don't you *dare* say it's because you couldn't control yourself." The gale-force nearly lifted us both. Nearly. Calm down, Devi. Take. A. Breath. "Like you said, you healed me right back up. Made me all shiny and new again."

"You know the answer. Why do you insist on hearing it?"

"Because," I sighed, annoyed, "unlike you, I actually *need* the confirmation. It's one thing to know the sun rises, it's—"

"It's another to *see* the sun rise."

"Say it. Why did you leave?"

"I left be—" I nearly lunged toward him. My blade pointed at his truly surprised face.

"Look at me." The words slid out of my clenched teeth. I don't know whose anger raged more.

"I left because if I had stayed..." starlight pierced through the trees, playing off our skin; illuminating the darkness between us much too brightly.

"If you had stayed you would have killed—God damn you! Say *it*."

"I would have killed myself." I lowered my weapon. He swallowed. We both shook our heads knowing far too well that the whole truth would *never* fall out.

"Why?" I nearly whispered. Nearly crying.

"*Enough*."

"Answer me." The forest blurred...

"Sit down."

"It makes *no* sense." The trees tilted. Gravity increased its pull on my boots.

"What do your visions tell you?"

"Great. So we're going to ignore this topic *entirely* and start a new one. I *almost* forgot who I was talking to." A roll of my eyes and a much needed exhale to get my irritation and elements in check and then— "When I look for the answer to *that* question—you know *exactly* what they tell me. Jack fucking shit."

"That, in itself, is an answer."

"It's a warning," I spat back, digging my boots in the dirt; sharpening my blades against one another. The sparks not nearly as bright as Thomas's gunmetal eyes.

"Indeed it is. And you'd do well to listen." He started drawing closer to me with each step. My heart racing; crashing against my ribs....My blood rushed so quickly through my veins, it *boiled*. The look on his face when he smelled it...

"We both know I don't do the whole *listening* thing." I wanted to throw up. I wanted to drown. I cupped the back of my head. Thomas took another step and my feet started to gain motion away from, from all of *this*.

"Don't move. I'm *not* the enemy right now. You *have* to slow your heart." Is he fucking high? "I won't lay a hand on you. Drop the blades and sit down." I took another labored step backwards as he took two calculated ones to me.

"Stay where you are *demon*." There was more aching in my voice than malice. A slow burning in my bones that would barely let me stand.

"*Demon*? That's new. Didn't I bring you here to keep the *real* fallen angels at bay?" He paused, studying my frame. I didn't blink. His hands went in his pockets and he looked down, then towards the stars. "I'm not one of them, darling," mid-way through his words, he bore his eyes right into mine, "you *know* that."

I had to swallow before I could speak. "You're no angel, either."

"True. But, what am I then, hmmm?" His eyes widened mockingly with each suspect. "A monster? Vampire? Ghost? What scary legend do I fall under in that Grimoire of yours?" The words drenched in violence.

"All of them." I heard familiar thuds again. He held my hands behind my back. His wretched face in mine. The gunmetal of his eyes reflected off my skin.

I never saw him move.

"Listen to me and listen *well*. You hit your head on a rock. It should've left you unscathed. Instead, you bled all over us."

"I'm sorry. If you're a bit perturbed about losing your precious shirt, you can *will* yourself a new one. I'm fine with my sports bra." My words didn't even register in him. He nearly spoke over them.

"You should've healed *immediately*—you chose *not* to." I struggled in vain to break from his hold. "You didn't *want* to heal, little one." He stared at me; my heaving chest pushed up against his. That only prompted his grip around my wrists to tighten. "Hell is *no* place for you, as you so intimately know." A slight smirk nearly revealed itself on his mouth, but he bit his lip. He leaned in closer and whispered, "You are welcome to return, of course. There are many levels you've yet to discover." Thomas is *furious* with me. The silver of his eyes turned pale...

"I wasn't trying to kill myself." The lack of conviction in my voice... The glare of his now *white* eyes... "You said yourself, I was *enchanted*. Psychotic break and all. Why do you even give a shit, Tarzan?"

"If you plan on lying to me, I'll have no trouble reverting

to our *old* methods of extrapolating the truth." I stopped pointlessly struggling. "Speak."

"Will you let go of me first? It's not like I can get too far." Silence. "I don't know—" I had to draw a breath. As strong as my new body is—being in his arms like *this*... "I don't remember *not* trying to heal. I don't remember *choosing* to do anything. I just....paused." The look on his face, jaw tightening, eyes narrow... "The dissociated suicidal part of me did anyway. I, or *she*, saw an opportunity and took it. It's fucking obvious, isn't it? No me, no magickal poison infecting your souls, no *war*. If I'm dead, you and your lot, even Hell—you're all *free*."

I looked at him, straight into the white fire of his eyes and watched as the calm of the silver as it poured over his irises. He released me and backed away too quickly. My body jerked and I hunched over; choking to drink air. I rubbed my wrists, black and blue in their color.

"What the fuck do you care? I'm sure you know this isn't the first time I've tried to off myself." I wonder how many times I've done this and then made myself forget... "I know you want to keep me around to erase Hell from all of existence, which by the way, is a stupid fucking idea given the whole Balance of the Realms and all, but me dropping dead should make you all pop champagne bottles not throw hissy fits."

"You want to die? Be my goddammed guest." He flung my bags and blades and at my feet. "I'll not be your audience." For a second, the wind didn't howl and I honestly couldn't tell if it was because it was too afraid to or if it vanished altogether. "Do you want to do it here or would you rather I take you back to our time? To *them*?" His arms were stiff at his sides, hands curled up into fists. "Or," he Ported behind me. His words crashing against the curve of my neck. "Would you rather *I* finish you off? Like I used to."

Thomas twisted me around to face him. My head craned back as he leaned into me. Closer and closer until the tips of his thick, stark hair swept across my cheeks. Memories of him and I in The Court blasted across my eyes. His heart raged beneath my palms. His breath hot on my skin. My knees buckled and I nearly passed out. Thomas only held me tighter...

"Thomas... let me go."

"You ask the impossible." He breathed me in and I knew, in my *soul*, how true his words were. Futile as it was, though, I tried to escape. Tried to push him away. To disappear. But not even my teleportation magick worked with me in his grasp.

Not tonight.

"Thomas..." My voice barely left my lips. Thomas touched his forehead to mine and slid his hands to my waist, digging in and pulling me into him. My heart beating in sync with his. The drumming pounding relentlessly against our chests. The air waiting to breathe. The earth waiting to move... Our markings lit up brighter than the constellations—Gravity nearly vanished...I dug my fingers down his back so I wouldn't float away and when his eyes finally met mine—black and white and silver pooling together like marble—Thomas clenched his jaw and separated us.

And I swear to God, the stars stopped shining when he did.

He was Chivalrous enough to give my mouth room to breathe, but he held my body close. I am a hostage after all. "Answer me. Before I *make* you."

"Right. Why did I—Come to think of it, I'm not so certain I would be pushing daisies. I mean, it's all very complicated you know? With me being half... what are you guys *exactly*? LeMehti are the First Immortals ever to walk the earth. And 'immortal' is just an umbrella term, isn't it? I mean, you got the DeKenna that are fallen angels—ergo, demons. Though there are subcategories for these. And not to mention all the Reveries. A girl can't *possibly* know where she fits in." Silence. He's breathing too much...I'm not breathing enough. "I can try to kill myself all I like but I won't actually *die*. Unless, of course," I nervously messed with my hair with my one free hand because, well, I'm scared and trapped and disgusted and fucking *blushing* and pretending *not* to be, "I eventually find my magickal kill switch and—"

"You being half mortal has *no* relevance to death." Thomas looked away for a moment and when his eyes found mine again, "You *will* find yourself in a grave dug by your own hands for the simple truth that you choose not to face."

"Enlighten me." Thomas let out a laugh and believe me when I tell you that it was one of the most haunting sounds I've ever heard.

"*You're* the kill switch, Devi." The stars sparkled again. Thomas leaned in. His only focus my lips.

It all added up in my mind in the heaviest second. What threatens *their* existence is the same weapon that can end *me*. How that's possible seeing as how I bear no control of my Reaper ability is beyond me. But it's more than that. I'm something *else*…

How terrifying is it to know, down to the stardust inside of you, that you are a living, breathing apocalypse? It's only a matter of time until I become what we're all afraid of. I wonder if they heard the same warning Lorna and Helena's covens had. I wonder if a LeMehti from the past uttered the words in the hopes that they would fall into the minds of those who would do what needed to be done. I wonder if I should let Thomas do what needs to be done…

He shattered the silence when he did the impossible and let me go. Literally. The shards fell to the earth like a mirror crashing onto brick. "Stay here." He walked at a regular *human* pace.

"Where are you going?" I managed to spit out. "Wait." I took a few steps towards him but he whirled around and glared at me; using his ancient magick to force my body like a fucking puppet back as my feet dragged across the grass until I was back in my original form and location. I had to *stay here*.

I had no access to anything that would help me see where Thomas was going. What he's planning. But one thing's certain beyond imagining. I'm safe. With him. At least for tonight.

After the minutes trickled down my spine, impatience nipped at my hair while the memories of the two of us replayed with too much realism. His touch is Vincent's touch. His face, Vincent's face. And I am always powerless against it. "Enough," I said to no one but the trees. I tried to wiggle my toes to see how much freedom Thomas left me with. "Aren't you just a fucking knight in shining armor?" With mobility in my toes, I was able to break the spell. "Well, I'll be. I *am* stronger tonight." I walked along the edge of the clearing; it's a beautiful Fall night in London and I'm not about to spend it standing like a damn statue because some jackass *ordered* me to.

I enjoyed not five minutes of stargazing in the field when the forest spat out something vile. "That was fast."

"Get up."

"Manners work wonders, you know?"

"Now."

"Well, fuck you, too," I mumbled under my breath.

The wind grew stronger and more powerful with every passing moment. In the cool night air, the quiet of the forest etched towards frightening. Not even the ants had come up to the surface since our arrival. The zephyr pushing without relent against me, flowing my hair across my face. It wanted me away from Thomas. I didn't dare move, though.

I don't know how long we stood there, watching, anticipating. Old memories of us at The Court crept into my eyes again; blowing soft whispers on the edges of knives down my neck...I fractured my ankle to bring me back to the present. Thomas almost twitched at my cracked bones.

Almost.

"So, are we going to stand around, or do you have a plan accompanied with that fed up look on your face?"

A loud scream pierced in my ears, although it was coming from over a mile away. I had stopped breathing again. I wanted to move, but hesitated. I stood there, shaking instead. I lost time again. No.

*Thomas* lost time...and I got lost with him.

For a moment, I pried into his mind, searching his memory. We lost 30 seconds. And in that span of time, Thomas had retreated to the waterfall.

"What happened? Why did you need the water?" He knows I surveyed his memory. His focus now is on something else. Something I can't access.

"Give me your hand." He stretched out his hand to me and I couldn't help but chuckle nervously.

"After you tell me why *you* lost time and dragged me with you."

"Give me your hand, Devi." Why isn't he simply yanking it?

"This can go on for a while, so you may as well answer me. Now."

"Confound you, woman." He grabbed my hand and then, with a thought, we were at the waterfall's edge.

Thomas let me go but failed to ignore the sight of my wrists. They were now darker and bruised deeper, with Thomas' fingerprints blindingly apparent on the surface.

"Enjoying your work?"

"Take off your clothes." I laughed a little, and then a lot.

"I'm sorry. You want me to do *what* now?" My arms folded across my chest; my black bra my only attempt at decency. Our bloody clothes were burned a few pages ago.

"Take off your clothes. You can do so willingly or—"

"Or, what? You'll take them off *for* me? I'd like to see you fucking try." The closer he inched to me, the more I had to lean my head back to keep my eyes in his. The falls were pointlessly raging to fill the pool with water that could never drown us while the air made sweet attempts wrapping itself around me; grabbing hold of my hair, ready to pull me back if Thomas did anything the element deemed dangerous. "Thomas," he kept walking. My arms dropped to my sides, revealing my markings. The light of them made him flicker. The glow took us both by surprise and I crept my arm back to my bare abs. "You wouldn't *dare.*" The second I let the words fall from my lips, I saw my bra fly across the grass. The next thing I knew, we were under water. What's more confusing is the fact that he had to touch me at all. Why didn't he just *will* me naked?

I escaped from the depth of the pool and waded; turning to look for the piece of shit. I turned again and he was there. I sank in a bit more so that only my shoulders were hovering out of the water. But, I'm completely naked. I'd have to make a run for my clothes. I could will myself an outfit, but he'd only take it off again and—oh, this is pointless. Know when to stop. My eyes clenched and I turned my face away from his.

"I do apologize, little one. But, you needed a bath." His laughter was melodic as it slipped through a beautiful smile I hated to see on *his* face.

"You're an asshole. I hope you're aware of that." I didn't feel the ripples from his advances to me. He sank into the water. His eyes level to mine.

"Fatally." I dropped my gaze. "However, you needed this." His arms stretched over the glinting surface. Both our faces dripping and the moon's light apparent on our skin.

"And what makes you the authority on *my* fucking needs?"

"You're not the only Empath." I coiled my fists.

"You are devastatingly *annoying*."

"And you are *unimaginably* hardheaded." I rolled my eyes. "You needed a restart, dollface. Whatever visions you've been having—" his features settled into worry, "I need you focused, not shaking and crying." *Crying*?

"Fine. But I could've done this shock therapy with my clothes *on*, don't you think?"

He shook his head, leaning in. "You know the protocol." That fucking protocol.

"Is that what *you* did? Did you need the water to snap you back to reality?" I already knew what he did here the moment I got into the pool. It retained his energy, the memory of him. And since I can pick up on lovely things like that, me being in the water is like me being Thomas when he was in it. It was vague, though. Like recalling a dream from the night before. But Thomas, being a few steps ahead of me, enchanted the waterfall, denying me access to the full memory of him in it, or, the more likely contender…he enchanted *me.*

"Yes."

"What happened to you? I remember screaming."

"Yours or mine?" The way he focused his eyes on me. It's as if he'd never see me again if he dared blink.

"Maybe the next time you decide to lose your shit, don't take me down with you."

"With me is the safest place for you. I'd strive a bit harder to convict that to memory."

"How safe am I when you disappear into Wonderland and leave me falling—"

"What? The water isn't revealing secrets for you?"

"I wonder why?" I nearly barked back at him.

"I was losing something. The pain that came with it was the cause for the scream." I barely breathed.

"Were you worried I'd mar your ego to see you hurting?" I would know the answer to that question but Thomas has barricaded himself so much so that even *I* can't always be the best darn Empath that I can be.

"I needed the shock to my system. So, the water was key. But my ego isn't so fragile, darling." He moved without moving as he circled me. His words crashing onto my skin. Almost hot enough to burn…"I left because had I remained," Thomas circled back to me, but he let himself float away, his eyes dark and no longer in mine, "there's no telling the things I would've done to you, Devi."

Steam began to rise from the water. The chaos in him and the madness in me finally hit a fever pitch. And if I'm not mistaken, the light of the moon flickered…Thomas isn't one to lose control. His is an *organized* chaos. Why retreat? My safety shouldn't be of consequence. Not when he could control himself.

Couldn't he?

# Chapter 14

## Haunted

Moments in time always flowed with little to no cracks in them. But, *this* moment… it broke and left the seams of the fibers that held it together glittering on the waters' surface. Thomas disappeared without a sound.

Someone's here.

I peered at anything that came into my view; my body sinking deeper into the pool. I saw Thomas. Fists coiled ready for our surprise guest. There was only one, this much I knew. Another LeMehti Paladin.

In the same second it took me to decide to leave the water and fight the soldier at Thomas's side, my bodyguard whispered a demand, never turning around.

"Don't move. Go under if it comes to that." The liquid rested in-between my lips. It didn't matter that the water reverted to its original 10 below temperature. I'm still burning inside. Thomas's heart was steady but it beat against our chests like the feet of a thousand soldiers marching to enemy territory. Whoever this other Paladin is, he's capable of frightening Thomas. A rarity, believe you me.

I could hear him now, shuffling through the trees, at least 20 miles out. He's taking his time…

Thomas took a step *back*. "Shit," I muttered. My voice barely a whisper. That means one thing: Thomas turned around and jumped. Mid-air, he pierced his arm through the icy water and pulled me out, casting me against his chest. It took what you could only understand as the blink of an eye. But trust me, he moved much quicker.

We fled. This was all fine and dandy. Escaping. Staying alive should be paramount. But, Thomas is running from a fight. From those that cannot kill him.

From those he leads.

*Again*.

I didn't notice the coat covering my body until I felt Thomas's fingers digging harder and deeper into me. The more Thomas drove himself to get us away, the quicker the other would follow.

My arms wrapped around Thomas' neck. My eyes barely above the hollow of his collar but I could see the Paladin chasing us a mile and a half out. I could only make out the color of his eyes. Black where white should be and crimson blanketed the entire iris. His mouth frozen in one too familiar sinister smile. And then I held Thomas tighter.

It's *not* a Paladin.

It's Kieran. The leader of the DeKenna Roan sent to attack me.

*How* did he find me here? The images around us slowed and cleared. Motionless. The sounds of a frenzied symphony morphed to a single melody of an instrument I'd never heard before. We, however, broke the sound barrier, going hypersonic in a fraction of a second, *without* moving. And then it happened. We broke through something precious. Something not meant to be broken…

Time.

From the moment Thomas emerged from the water to this moment, only 10 seconds had passed. Time. Thousands of miles—waves of reality itself echoed in my bones. In my blood...

I knew my feet were touching the earth. The warm grass soft and tangible beneath my skin. My eyes were alert and staring into the vast emerald clearing behind Thomas, waiting for *it* to tear through the air and rip me apart.

Thomas kept his hands firm on my body, never letting me move away from him. His body's my only true protection from that *thing*. My experience with the Knights of Hell were few and far between but Thomas...he knew them far better than he'd like.

Two more seconds droned by and his grip faded away from my body. He circled the area we landed, making certain that we weren't followed. My arms went through the arms of my coat and I fastened the buttons and tied the belt around my waist and *still* had time to stare at Thomas staring into the space around us. This place, where ever it was, had sweet warmth to it. The scent of thousands of wildflowers, only a few miles to the east, blanketed me. Thomas gazed up at the rolling hills that stretched into the horizon and the salt of the sea finally broke through the perfume of the flowers and it reminded me of Amah.

Sudden anger bashed across my face as her eyes burned in my mind. "How the fuck did he find us?! You kidnapped me and barreled us through time to hide me from Roan and her soldiers and," I found myself near tears and shoving and punching Thomas' chest.

"I don't know how he found us, Devi."

"You think I'm a fucking *child*? You're lying. I can *feel* you lying inside of me, you asshole! You're doing well concealing other shit but not *everything* you feel is locked away in that deteriorating soul of yours. You told them where I was, didn't you? Didn't you!" He allowed me to continue to hit him. "Then why run? What the hell is wrong with you?!

Why are you doing this to me?" Why hasn't he beaten me to the ground?

I kept pushing and shoving and punching and when I broke his ribs, I felt the pain in my own chest. We both ignored the thunderstorm brewing over the sea...But that's when he grabbed me by my shoulders and nothing moved around us...

Not my heart.

Not his lungs.

Not the wind...

"Enough," was all the disgrace to the Paladin title said to me. After an anguished second of glaring at my now very wet eyes, Thomas let go of my surprisingly unfractured shoulders and tore his gaze from mine. Running his near-shaking hands through his hair, Thomas stood a few feet from me, breathing heavily, eyes in the calming sky.

I shut my eyes for longer than I intended but was happy for the wind's return as it dried my angry tears away. Pretending you're ok only lasts for so long. Living such an intricate, perpetual lie takes a toll and you inevitably break. Little by little. Creating storms. Making immortals erase entire elements...

"You must learn to control your emotions," he said too coolly.

"Because I'm a woman?" I retorted. Thomas turned to me so quickly, I nearly fell backwards. The look of disgust on him from my flinching at his advance—it left the oddest taste of charcoal in my mouth.

"Because you're a creature capable of ending us in ways we cannot begin to fathom."

"As are you." Thomas smoothed an ache in his chest. His eyes in mine. Voice low and warm on my skin.

"Am I?" A lock of my hair curled around his finger.

"Yes." He almost smiled, his gaze on my lips. I batted his hand away, fighting every instinct to run. I felt him fight the urge to impale me. Thomas walked away, not bothering to magickally will himself a shirt.

We stood in silence, letting the minutes fall away from us as we both tried taking in the Autumn air. The sun glinted against my rings and I remembered we traveled through time. A few minutes ago it had been night. Now, it's the middle of the day. I looked over my shoulder, Thomas was only a couple of feet from me, surveying the solemn land. There's a forest two miles from us and so I assumed that would be our next destination. I barely pressed my feet harder into the ground to begin my first step when Thomas held me by the elbow.

"We're not going there." His voice was surprisingly detached and when I looked up into his eyes, they were battling again. I knew the DeKenna Knight wanted to have his way with me. But the way Thomas reacted, and his eyes now, I don't know if he'd rather have killed me himself or if he wanted to kill the Knight. I'm not certain what war raged inside Thomas.

The breeze blew a breath of relief when Thomas looked to the sky and the grass in between my toes danced with glee when his body distanced itself from mine and went toward a hill. I fiddled nervously with my current mode of dress for a moment before I grew a large enough spine to confront him about our black-eyed devil.

Anticipating my words, his head fell; his profile framed by the emerald hills.

"Why was he able to find us?" And without skipping a beat...

"I let him."

"You're—you're fucking kidding." I knew he had lied before but actually *hearing* the confession...He didn't move and now that he's laughing, I had to try with all that I had not to cry.

"As satisfying as it would be to watch that thing rape you until you rip your own skin off...." he breathed in, cracking his knuckles as he turned on his heel to face me, "we don't want you with Roan." The grass trembled beneath my feet with his every advance. Thomas saw a tear trail down my cheek and his jaw clenched. His hands too steady at his sides. "Devi, you can't understand how much it takes for me to *not* hurt you." I clenched my fists and when he took another step, I broke my hands. Thomas almost cared to flinch. "When I lost it before—"

"Which time?" Shut up, Devi. Don't make him angry. He didn't feel angry. Not yet...

"The first time, Devi. The first." He put his hands in his pockets and turned his attention to the trees. "They found an opening to our trail. I didn't realize it until the waterfall. Rahm—the DeKenna Knight chasing us—he was sent by another Breaker to take you." With a heavy breath, Thomas ran his hands through his hair. The tired bones locked themselves to the back of his neck as his eyes focused on nothing but mine.

"How—the DeKenna *cannot* Break though time. Another order had to have sent him." Helena's coven isn't capable of this. The only witch that had anything close to a spell that would even *touch* time is—*was* Keres...

"Lucifer has his own agenda for you. Beyond what he wants you to do to my kind." Of course. The one being other than Thomas and Vincent—other than Thomas that can manipulate time is the King of fucking Hell himself. "He granted Rahm the ability." That's another plausible theory.

"How did Rahm find us?" I dared.

"I'm fighting *every* instinct to ruin you, Devi..." I couldn't tear my eyes away from him. The Paladin wrung his hands and adjusted his stance. "It's a tug of war. He'll pull you close to him but I..." my body shook and it distracted him. He took a step to me. I took a step back, "I'll pull you back." Thomas shortened the gap between us and my ankle cracked again from the pressure of keeping my body from doing what it has learned to do around this man... "He won't take you, Devi. I won't let him." If only I would survive running away from him.

I shut my eyes and nearly lost my balance. When he held me from keeling over, I opened my eyes and gasped.

"You need to sit." His hold on me was too gentle and it disgusted me and he knew it. Thomas released me and walked a few paces away. "Stay here." His gaze vanished into the forest. Flashes of the desires he was keeping at bay blasted against my eyes. Pieces of my bloody corpse sprawled across this field. Whether those pieces would be torn by *his* hands or the hands of Rahm wasn't clear. There's one thing that was *crystal* clear though; I'd still be alive while scattered across the earth…

I tried following his path, to scan for what he scanned for. I can't follow another immortal's scan that well or all the time, but sometimes it works to my advantage, especially if I know what they're looking for. But he was too fast. As soon as I knelt down to sit and maybe enjoy the warmth, enjoy my heart beating again, his eyes opened.

"This should do." I stood up and looked at him first and then the dark object he held. My face scrunched. I didn't waste time on what poor girl he stole this from. From the looks of it, she wouldn't notice. I took the dark blue Celtic dress. With sleeves. *Long* ones that would keep at bay the silky breeze of the wind. Not only is this not practical for battle, it's full of memories of this woman's life. A life I'm never going to be able to live…

"Thanks," I managed. "But why didn't you just create one? Why'd you resort to thievery?" He gave me a pleading look and I grabbed the dress. No sooner did I turn on my heel to go change did Thomas take hold of me; his hands curling too easily around my arms. A thousand memories burned with his touch and it took everything I had *not* to scream…

"What? I am *not* changing here, Now let me—"

His eyes drowned in black marble, taking the moonlight with them. "I think you *are*." His voice trickled hot down my neck as he turned to face me. "I've done what I can to keep us hidden, but we need to find shelter. We may be breathing now, but I can't keep track of *them*. They move differently than we do, you *know* that. If Rahm finds us again—Get dressed."

"You're...*not* lying." Thomas' silver eyes came up for air, bringing the moon back to life with them. But he backed away, ignoring my disbelief.

"I won't look. Be quick. I need to feed you and get you a proper night's rest before you light up the whole of England. I don't have time to correct history."

"Isn't us being here disrupting—"

"Now." Without knowing any invisibility or cloaking spells that were strong enough to withstand a Paladin, I breathed a breath of defeat. "Do you need a hand?"

"No." The disgust writhing in me rattled a spell free from my memory. I inhaled and upon exhaling, I was behind a two-way wall. I could see Thomas but he couldn't see me. I didn't waste a second. I phased through the dress. The fabric thinned out, the seams giving off a shimmer. I tailored it to fit perfectly.

There's only one problem: When I took a step to phase into the dress, I bumped into Thomas. His chest bare but warm. I was certain he'd strike me when he opened his eyes.

"Took you long enough." He brushed some hair from his face and turned on his heel. "There's a town we can reach in about twenty seconds. We should be able to find a place for the night."

"You want to *run*? Why not teleport?" We teleport at the speed of *thought*. All this energy he's putting into *not* beating me to my proverbial death is draining him—*That's* why I'm off. If *he's* drained and weak, so am *I*. And it's impacting my powers far more than it should.

"Why must you question everything?" He muttered to himself.

"We have this entire forest. If you're tired, we can stay here. It shouldn't be hard to find a nice patch under a tree."

"What is this obsession with the woods? Would you not prefer to rest above ground? In a bed, perhaps?"

"I don't mind sleeping on grass."

"No. You're *used* to sleeping on the ground, in the open. Alone."

"I—the hell are you shrinking me for?" I nearly tripped over the long fabric as I stormed over to him. He poorly suppressed a chuckle. "I *love* the forest. And me sleeping alone is—" Terrifying. Heartbreaking. Lonely... "Preemptive."

"It's lonely." Damn him...

"I'm trying to keep down my body count. We all know what touching me can do to someone."

"I'm aware." A pause fell through us, leaving a moment to hear the woods. "Try and keep up." He wore my coat. It fit him perfectly. Of course I bought a man's coat. Thomas darted off and I went running after, keeping up with his 'take pity on the half breed' 75 mile-per-hour jog. But this is slow, even for me.

As we tried without thought to keep the weight of our bodies and the force of our feet on the ground from creating an earthquake, I noticed how every single living thing was nowhere near us. They burrowed into the ground, flew away, ran until they were out of breath...

"What is this place?" I asked. We had stopped in a large clearing with a tiny and modest castle a hundred yards from us. If castles can be tiny and modest. "Didn't you hear a small village or something? Where is everyone?"

"Must you ask so many questions all the fucking time? Let me answer you once before you bombard me with a God-damned inquisition." I don't think anything but the word 'fucking' mattered in all that bitching.

"Bite me." I realized what I said a second too late.

"Be careful what you wish for." Regret was thick in the air. Both his and mine bleeding into each other. "I did hear a town. It must've been the past echoing. Or, the travelers haven't arrived yet. Either way, there's an empty castle with soft furniture calling our names. Let us away." He should know *exactly* why no one is here. It hit me then. Keeping *me* alive is, in a way, killing *him*...

When he realized I wasn't following him, he stopped.

"What are you doing?" He knew precisely what I was asking and that is why he walked *so* slowly to me that the wind stopped mid-howl, the grass drowned and gravity....it, it's screaming. Begging me to breathe...

Thomas is *livid*.

"What I do is *none* of your concern, do you hear me? *You* do not question my resolve." His words burned the first few layers of my skin. He leaned in close, chest heavy with the beast he won't unleash. "The others *will* have you," he grinned. "As soon as I'm through with you." He walked away, taking my fear with him. I waited until the air was breathable and the earth wasn't under water. And when the fury inside him didn't make my heart cave in anymore, I followed him.

It wasn't until right before we reached the castle that I knew for certain that Thomas wouldn't bring me, or the world, to our knees.

"What are we going to eat, *dollface*?" He threw me a look over his shoulder. "Perhaps obtaining some water for your hostage?" Thomas took off the coat, revealing a thin, charcoal grey sweater underneath. The coat, now a makeshift basket, had fresh fruit and bread along with a big flask of water inside.

"Thanks. Now we can go inside." I grabbed an apple from the pile and chomped down as I walked ahead, too cheery from the juicy snack to run inhumanly or acknowledge, well, anything. I strolled and he followed suit.

When we came through the massive wooden doors, inside the castle was equal parts cozy and beautiful.

"I know what you're doing and I need you to know that it won't work."

"Well, shit. There goes my brilliant plan of making you use your powers, weakening you so that I can make my great escape. Whatever shall I do now?"

"You're impossible."

"So you've said." I exhaled as I ran my hand through my hair.

The castle reminded me of something. The light from the extremely ornate floor to ceiling stained glass window across the doors poured in the moonlight, I grabbed a pear from Thomas's pile and munched on, I knew where we were and the fear this beauty brought to my mind. The thought was accompanied by Thomas's chewing and chomping of an apple.

I stayed stationary, a piece of grated pear still in my mouth. Thomas set our food on a long wooden table on the right side of the entrance. He began to feel the table and then the stonewalls. His muscles stretching and tightening while his massive wrought iron markings covering his entire back glowed. That's when he took off the sweater, burning it to ember and ash in his hands. It pains him to breathe with the feather weight of a top. My eyelids fluttered a few times as my stupidity smacked me in the face. I felt like that every single second of every day. My *own* skin was reminiscent of a too-small, overstuffed, rusted, cage...

I can only imagine what it's like for Thomas, for *all* the poisoned immortals with their burning, maddened souls hanging by a thread...

I focused on him as he worked his way to the giant, curved stone staircase on the opposite side of the room trying to see, or hear, any memories of people that have been here. Usually, he'd be able to do this *without* touch, but Thomas is not well....

"As far as fairy tales go darling, I didn't figure you for Snow White." He stopped short and turned around before walking up the rest of the stairs, his hand graceful on the banister. I gave him a weird stare but finally made the connection and swallowed my food.

"Snow White choked on an apple and it was poisoned. *I* was eating a pear and the only poison here—" I made my way towards him, painfully aware of the air in this majestic setting.

"Is you." I stopped dead in my tracks. He recoiled his face, almost ashamed. I found it flustering at how difficult it was for me to ascertain his emotions. I'm beginning to think I'm too connected to his wavering state.

Thomas shifted his mood. "Find yourself a room." He disappeared like smoke from a dying flame. Despite his absence, I made the decision to search the castle in a matter of seconds.

I'll need much longer than that to filter out the cold stabbing in my heart from the pure truth of his words. *I'm* the only reason his blood is evil.

For a moment, I wanted to jump face first through the glass window before me. The shards kissing my skin and breathing in my blood...But, I sensed Thomas staring at me. So, I slid my hand away from the window and waited for him to do the honors instead. His feet brought his infected body slowly to my contagious one. Every moment he drew closer. When his body stood beside mine, I could've sworn that starlight itself trembled from the terror. I didn't move, nor did I look up at him. The Paladin simply went past me. And as he stared at the constellations, they burned brighter...almost as if he commanded it. Then, he vanished.

I looked up at the sky for a long time. Memories of a night with Vincent etched into my skin. But I can't feel a damn thing... I was going to find a room for myself when Thomas's laughter dared me to go to the room across the hall. With him in this state... He is losing what little of his mind remains...what I've taken away from him by existing.

In the entrance hall, I hopped up on the dark wooden dresser. My feet didn't reach the ground so I swung them like a little kid. When Thomas came down he stopped dead in his tracks. He took one step to me and stopped again.

"What's wrong?" He asked truly bewildered.

"I'm fine."

"You're *smiling*. What did you see?" He studied me then put his gaze at the stained glass framing a sea of constellations. Rubbing his shoulders, he made his way to me.

"I've seen as much as you. No one's here. Not even Lucifer's minions are going to find us. We're *safe*, ergo I'm happy. And I smile when I'm happy. Is that a problem?" I'm smiling because I have a memory of the love of my life you murdered swimming across my soul. That's one thing you *can't* take away from me. Not my memories...

"Never." He took a bite of an apple and a few gulps of water from the flask found their way down his throat. What I'd give to tear that foolishly exposed skin to shreds. Thomas sat beside me, the food gloriously buffering the space between us.

After a few moments of silence, I dared to glance at him. The moon bright with the kiss of the sun. Thomas was staring off into a space I was frankly too terrified to envision. And all this *quiet*...

"So, what fairy tale fool *do* you peg me for?" My words barely registered to him. His mind not quite shaking away from the vibrations inside.

"Why do you care?"

"I don't," I said, sipping some water. "Just curious," I said, shrugging. He parted his lips to say something about curiosity and a cat dying, but only silence came out.

"There is no fairy tale you would ever fall into."

"And why's that?"

"Because, Devi—" He breathed in a deep, painful breath, "you cannot belong to something that doesn't exist. Fairy tales are decorated nightmares. That's not you."

"And you're privy to what I am?" He laughed breathlessly. Hopelessly.

"Isn't it obvious?"

"Humor me."

"You're *me*." I could've never been prepared for the ache of that irrefutable truth. Thomas bit his lip. Hard.

"Can you not do that, please? You know I feel everything that happens to you as if it's happening to me." I licked my lips. No blood, but I'll be damned cause I can still taste *his* in my fucking mouth.

"Not everything." He leaned forward, playing with the starlight between his fingers. A smile hooked up in his cheeks and then he leaned back. His head rested against the brick as he turned to look at me; his silver eyes slightly brighter than usual.

His breathing made me lightheaded as he leaned forward, his fingers intertwined, trying their best *not* to form into fists. Trying *not* to fill my mouth with violence.

I couldn't take the silence, so I fucking broke it.

"I can take the hits. Stop resisting, it's dizzying." He looked at me, numb, but said nothing. His hands rubbed his eerily tired face, ran through his limp hair and rested at the back of his neck. Staring at absolutely nothing and everything in front of him. For that moment, I contemplated running. I contemplated crying. And when I contemplated taking out my daggers and piercing them through me, severing my spine, Thomas' hands remerged, resting in his lap... along with my weapons. I couldn't think.

A minute trickled down to the ground and ran as far away from us as possible. And though it was beginning to be extremely difficult to breathe the frantic air, and keep visions of Thomas attacking me separate from what I actually saw in front of my eyes, I tried pushing out whatever memory was stuck on 'repeat' in his mind.

"I'd worry more about the clockwork in *your* mind, Devi." And it was then that Thomas raised my blades, turned the points towards himself and pierced them straight through himself, severing his spine.

"No!" I jumped to stop him, or I thought I did... His hands gripped my wrists. His face not as shocked as mine.

"That was a vision, Devi. This..." He pulled me closer to him, pressing my hands against his chest. "*This* is real." I couldn't answer him because I wasn't sure if it was him I was even seeing. He freed my hands and I felt my daggers in their holster again. A shake of disappointment came about in his skull as I sat there, slightly trembling and trying with all that I had to make sure that this was truly *happening*.

"I thought All Hallow's Eve was supposed to make us stronger," I repeated. Thomas shut his eyes and faced the moon, which, I swear to God, flickered.

"Indeed it is."

"Then why are we losing it?"

"Because, Devi. You want to kill me and I want—" The light of the night sky reflected a prism of color off his white hair. It gnawed at me to see the colors and sparks of life amidst the man who showed me the meaning of madness.

"What do you want?" He hopped off the table, a steel smile across his face.

"*You.*" His eyes flickered to my lips then found my eyes. "I chose this night because you'd be able to survive me, Devi, and because I'd be less likely to do the one thing I want to do to you."

"Let me go?" I replied with a poor excuse of a grin. Thomas walked back to me, his fingers grazing my cheek before they laced around my neck, his knees pushing against mine, spreading them open. He leaned in until his poisoned breath crashed hot into my mouth.

"Make you scream..." He leaned in closer and I grabbed him by his belt to keep the bastard from moving another inch. Memories stung in both our eyes. One we shared, one that was all my own. But Thomas looked as though someone cooked his puppy. "Tonight makes me less likely to kill you." And he backed away like a man that saw his true reflection in a mirror. Except, whatever rattled his soul he witnessed in *my* eyes...

"A *Surrah* Binding?" I whispered in shock. He couldn't look at me and started for the stairs. "Thomas?"

"What?" He stopped at the banister, never turning back.

"What happens tomorrow?" There was hesitation in his heartbeats and silence filled the hall when he slowly disappeared up the steps.

"I have no idea..." His too-empty words fell heavy into the air, another handful of silent moments filled the space in between us. The entire castle stood motionless as the sound of his voice did what it did best; crippled me.

I swallowed hard and set my sights to the window. Still full of the moon. Still full of stars... I shut my eyes and wrapped my arms around myself and allowed the old memory of the last time Vincent and I made love fill me. But at the edges of that vision was what Thomas had done to me.

What he'd *always* do to me…

# Chapter 16

## Crescendo

The splintering of bone woke me. When I realized it was part of Thomas's skeleton, I relaxed my hold on my dagger and calmed my heart.

"Normal people use alarm clocks," I said from my cozy canopy bed, making sure my voice carried downstairs. He ignored me as he placed a dead doe on the table in the kitchen downstairs

I washed up and opened the locked trunk at the foot of the bed with ease; phasing the metal lock from its hinge. Inside were dresses upon dresses—that were *recently* worn. I put them back and looked at my room again. Writing desk with feather and fresh ink in the inkwell. Books with barely a layer of dust...the entire castle was filled with evidence of life.

How did I not register any of this last night?

A creepy thought burrowed its way into my mind; Thomas didn't want me to know who lived here. This was beautiful evidence of a much more vibrant painting. Thomas was hiding something from me and went to insane measures to make sure I don't find it.

That's a mystery I don't feel like drowning in quite yet.

It was early yet so I laid back in bed. Mainly to try and glean a vision from it but also to grant myself some peace. For all his maladies, he was right. When was the last time I even came in contact with a blanket let alone a bed? I'd been homeless for half a decade...

The protection from my favorite holiday came and went. Thomas will kill me. It's only a matter of time. That truth has to live at the tip of my tongue, reminding me that my hours are numbered. Thomas *is* the villain and I am his *prisoner*, not his charge.

My eyes started to drift when he walked in, filling the space, and my chest, with nothing but ice. I thought he would speak, but his weight shifted from the door to the windows at the foot of the bed.

"So I take it we're going to ignore the fact that you just self-mutilated yourself for reasons unknown?" He stood there for scanning; listening to the past and present and future. Completely ignoring me. "Great talk." I turned to my side and wrapped the navy blanket all around me. Thomas took a guard dog position sitting on top of the trunk. When he rested his head against one of the posts of the bed, a surge of pain filled me.

Heartbreak?

Channel some human emotion from this place, you dick. It'll do you some good. "Did you get bored, or something? No one's coming for us. I don't need a watch dog." No response. The question still burned my throat: why is he *protecting* me? Sometimes, I wasn't sure whether to be terrified of the poisoning rage inside him, or to be *beyond* fear of the *true* reason he's keeping me alive.

I sat up and he took in a breath. He hadn't been taking in air since he left the castle to hunt the deer. I wanted to speak then; to let the sounds of my soul echo in this space. I wanted something, anything, to fill this emptiness between us, this emptiness that was too reminiscent of oblivion.

I didn't say a word.

With my knees curled up against my chest, I held myself as tight as I could. If I didn't make myself heavy enough, as heavy as Thomas, I'd float away into the void. We were still for a long time. Watched the shadows and light dance through the room. The sun blanketing the cracks and folds of the space; gracing everything except us. At one point I thought Thomas fell asleep. His chest moving up and down with an ache that bruised my ribs. I'm the vice tightening around his lungs.

He had conjured a top for the times but had it split down the middle. It was too big on him and left his chest bare. And it dawned on me then that these fabrics, or lack thereof, were safety blankets. Tethers of sorts that kept one foot on the ground. We had different anchors but we shared the same reason for holding on for dear life; neither of us wanted to be lost.

A choir of leaves kissed outside. My fingertips found themselves on my lips for a moment. When was the last time *I* was kissed? How many years has it been now? Why does it even matter? My eyes blurred with tears. I blinked them away and Thomas rubbed his tattooed neck.

Thomas was going to speak. The vibrations of his thoughts reverberated on my tongue but I didn't know what they would manifest into. I didn't...I couldn't *hear* them. Whatever he was going to say, I couldn't listen to his voice. I couldn't bear it. I rested my head back on the pillow and stared at the desk. I the warmth of the sun faded behind clouds and I decided to do something dangerous then. Not because of what Thomas may do but because of what I would see.

I closed my eyes.

My body twisted slightly and I felt his eyes flicker towards me, checking me. I curled myself into a ball and a few seconds later, I dreamt. My dream was blank. Quiet. Soft images of a place I'd been long ago; a place that matched the cold in this room. Despite the violence of this memory, there was something comforting in the thick silence.

Vincent.

The quiet lasted longer than I had thought. When my eyes fluttered open, the light in the room had dimmed to a muted glow. I must've fallen asleep for a couple of hours because it was noon and Thomas had left his post, roasting our dinner. I cringed. I flung my legs over the side of the bed and held on to the edges for a minute; bracing myself for what was to come. I stood up, took a step and—

"Thomas, I'm up. *back off.*" Thomas was in my face while I tried not to reveal what I've been trying to mask this whole time; trembling fear. I took a step to go around him when his arm snaked around my waist. I glared at him while I decided if it was worth touching him to push his filth off of me. However, the second my gaze hit his, my heart broke, beating without mercy against my ribs. He was covered in sweat and barely breathing and it shocked me more than it ever should've. Thomas's held me tight with one hand while the other trailed from my waist to my chest and lacing around my neck, grazing my cheek with his thumb.

His chest heaved against mine, his breath hot and labored, scaring the life out of me...

"Why can I feel you?" Everything he felt—it radiated in me. He was warm. Strong. Scared. Out of control. *Why let me in?* Our pulses raced, the beads of his sweat dripping on to my lips, my own soaking through my dress.

"Devi—" He moved closer, the strands of his white hair framing his face and tickling my forehead. His hips hard against mine...

"Thomas, let me *go.*" I tried and failed in the same second to hear him inside his mind. I tried shoving him away. Tried blinking out of his hold. Nothing worked. There was a drop of water that fell onto my nose. And as it trickled down, I realized it wasn't sweat. It was a teardrop. Thomas doesn't *cry*. This is another trick. Another *mindfuck*. I'm asleep. I'm back in that chamber, shackled to the wall with nothing but *him*. This *isn't* real.

His eyes were pale...almost transparent. I had to look away. Thomas dug his hands in my hair and breathed in my breath, fighting off every urge to break my neck. He grit his teeth, his heart pounding inside me.

"Do it. End it, Thomas." I dropped my arms in surrender. "It's ok..." The moment my tears touched his hands, Thomas pulled me in and kissed me with a fever that made us forget who we were... His mouth lingered. The weight of his pain. The poison. My terror. It left me powerless. Let him kill me however he wants to. Just *kill* me...

It was *minutes* before I noticed the bed underneath us. Before I heard the leaves falling. Gradually, my senses returned. The light in the room faded in and out against my lids and when gravity disappeared...When the drowning sadness inside both of us gasped for air, my eyes flung open and I coughed, choking for air.

I had opened my eyes to the open door and nothing more. The light in the room was the same; Dim but still with a slight sparkle reaching the room from the sleeping star. I was panting. Sweat nearly drenching me. I ignored the tears...

My captor's post was empty. Plates and goblets clattered about in the kitchen; the smell of his kill nauseating me. I sat up and scanned, touching the blankets, pillows....myself. Nothing.

You're awake. It was a dream. The bastard got in your head again. Halloween is over. The Surrah Binding gone. He can do with me whatever he pleases. And pretending to be Vincent...it's his favorite war game.

"Get down here." I jumped where I sat. His voice full of static, scratching at the corners of my mind. I moved without moving, from the bed to the top of the stairs. The hesitation and confusion...the *repulsion* in my body had to be contained.

The encounter, though quite possibly a mind fuck, could also be one other thing: a new possible future; a very near, and grim, future, but *new* all the same.

You're *awake*.

I tripped and missed a few steps. I caught myself, but when my entire body drowned in an undertow, I lost my grip on gravity and fell. Maybe I can keep myself from healing. Maybe I can di—

"What the hell's *wrong* with you?" My eyes were foggy but I saw his wide, pissed black eyes and his chest against mine nearly made me vomit right there. He had caught me right before my skull met with the stone stairs.

"Let—let *go* of me." He wouldn't budge. "Vin—Thomas, let me go!" He held me tight and leaned in to where I had his fucking face in mine again…

"*Stop*." I know he meant my latest suicide attempt. Truth is, as dizzy and twisted as I was; I could've turned the stair case into sand. Thomas shook his head and stormed back to the kitchen, leaving me there at the foot of the stairs.

I didn't mean to. I really didn't. It was the *last* thing I thought would be possible at this moment but I let myself crumble to a step, held my face in my hands and cried. Not giving a damn that Thomas heard me sob.

I stood in the doorway of the kitchen, the fire warming my feet. Our eyes met; paralyzing me. I took in a breath. Is the sun setting? Perhaps that's his endgame: disorient me, exhaust me to the point where I lose grip of time. Where I can't tell what's real…. The fading light in the sky tried with everything it had to keep the room lit. But the only thing that reached these walls, reached Thomas, was a foggy afterglow of a star that could be erased by the man watching me.

His hair was a mess and brighter than anything in the room. His poet's shirt from before is gone. He sat at the table topless and in pain. If he couldn't breathe before, he was utterly *suffocating* now. My chest caved in as he looked away from me to take in a labored breath. And when he exhaled, I tried to walk to the table…I tried not to fall, but I lost my mind all over again and….

My eyes opened with the ceiling in them. I was on the ground, twisting in pain. The pressure of no oxygen...too much. I thought I moved. I thought I traveled away from him. But Thomas kept me suspended in the air. The lack of oxygen in my lungs wasn't because Thomas couldn't breathe; it was because Thomas didn't allow my lungs to work.

Then, when the strain to catch a small breath of life crushed Thomas' chest, mine fractured. And as I defied gravity like a puppet hung from a string, its feet never touching the ground, something far worse than my entire ribcage puncturing my lungs happened.

Thomas shattered.

He kept me frozen in space. The table flipped across the room. My heart stopped and started as my brain shocked with electricity trying to keep it beating. But it was *his* heart inside of me.

The only thing inside of me was the only thing inside of Thomas and it *raged…*

Oblivion.

The smoke didn't register until I saw the flames eating the ceiling. But they never came to have a taste of me... I followed the fire. The sparks engulfing the entire castle. It was then that I saw Thomas burning himself alive. I shut my eyes as everything burned but me. And when I began to choke from Thomas's blood filling inside of me, I knew that the only thing that kept him from me was thin air.

The castle was on the verge of collapse. Thomas' steps to me fractured the stone ground beneath. The screaming of the flames no match the one echoing from my body. And I *hated* it. I hated that my god forsaken body's survival instinct was to call out for someone who's dead.

I opened my mouth to yell. To snap him back to reality, but instead saw my breath painted in the smoke-filled room covered in red ash. Or…or is it snow? And when his charred flesh met with my unmarred skin, everything…everything *burned.*

"You need to eat." Was all the infected piece of eternity said. I stood in the doorway…doe eyed and petrified. The same crushing weight inside my chest but now, somehow it wasn't as devastating as before…was it *before*? I didn't bother to breathe and took one step when the immortal waiting, patiently. When I made it to the table and didn't notice the temperature rise, I finally took a breath.

The table was set with two plates and two goblets filled with water. There was a bowl with diced apples and pears, and more bread and berries. He motioned for me to sit, noticing effortlessly, the expression on my face.

The closeness between us was dangerous. It took almost all that I had not to tremble and even *more* to be able to *look* at him. Look at him and not register the ash under his fingernails. Look at him and not remember the kiss…

I sipped my water. He squeezed his fork.

This house was set on fire…he set *himself* on fire but it wasn't enough. But something stayed his hand. Something gave Thomas control of his nature again. What though? Because right before he dug his fingers into my eyes, he recoiled his hands and covered his ears…in *absolute* pain.

As we were finishing the last pieces of our food, he finally talked to me.

"If I had known you'd eat this much..." He rubbed the back of his neck and I could have sworn his heart skipped a beat. "I should've known how hungry you were." A tiny smirk, though fractured, crept up the side of his mouth, revealing some of his teeth. I had to remind myself how many necks he'd snapped and tore open with those very teeth. Including mine…

"I'm full. Thank you." I was only hungry because events like that drain me. This one in particular, more so. But he wants to pretend nothing happened. He wants to make believe that he didn't literally lose his mind and try to murder me. That's fine. I've gotten make believe down to a god damned *art*.

I took our empty plates and goblets and put them in the sink. I stood over it pondering whether or not to snap my fingers and have them cleaned or to leave them. And the longer I thought about it, the more aggravated Thomas became.

"We don't need to do chores, dollface. Let's—"

"Why didn't you finish me?" He stood, pushing his chair in, and simply stared at me. "You missed a spot." I motioned my fingers, and his ash covered nails coiled their fingers in to fists. "Why did you stop?"

"Did I, Devi?" He shook his asshole head and turned his back to me; walking toward the back door. I faced the sink, holding on for dear life. Blink, Devi. I had to force myself to hear the air and feel the sounds of the castle, the forest...of my heart. Fucking force myself to believe that I *exist* and this—this bullshit world is real. That I am real. I can't be dead...

"Is it true?" The words spilled from my lips without thought.

"What?" I turned around to answer his not so surprised question.

"You *know* what. Is it true?" I motioned to my bedroom where I felt his heart break across a hundred thousand realities. He turned on his heel to face me and was in front of my face in the same move. I clutched to the edge of the sink, breaking it.

"You felt that, did you?" He looked disappointed. "What's it to you?" Thomas leaned his head near my forehead and then his hands went over mine. I didn't dare to move.

"What can I say? Hopeless romantic." Thomas moved in closer and even though I wanted nothing to do with his eyes, I had to keep watch. If they swirled....

"You *are* hopeless." He laughed a breath on to my skin all the while pulling out my fingers that I apparently dug into the sink. "Let's go." He towards the door.

"Answer me." He turned around with his fists coiled. Thomas looked broken. Ragged.

"I'm not capable of heartache, Devi. *You* saw to that." He made his exit leaving me behind. Maybe he's right. Maybe he was channeling the life of someone here, or even *my* broken heart. This poison—my curse—what my mere *existence* has done to these beings...

He's right. Whatever soul they have left has twisted beyond recognition. Bled dry of life.

I saw to that...

I followed the Paladin absentmindedly. I found him brooding in the clearing behind the castle. I drew my weapons and pointlessly sharpened my daggers against one another waiting for him to do whatever it is he dragged me out here to do. I'm too tired to tune in to the future. The past is keeping me plenty busy anyway. There's a king's coronation, a hunting party, and the king's heir sparring with the knights—son of a bitch.

"Come at me."

"What?" I said, partly pissed and partly irritated; fully numb...

"You heard me. Let's go." His face was calm but no sign of bluffing anywhere. He unsheathed his sword from the pocket of space beside him.

"Yeah, well, sounds great to *go* and kick your ass and all, but, I think I'd like to go bake. Coconut crème pie sound good to you?" I holstered my weapons on my back and made my way back to the castle. Thomas didn't waste a second to block me.

The moment he stabbed his eyes into mine, I knew there was no way around this itty bitty sparring match. It wasn't until the earth quivered beneath our feet that I realized the magnitude within his demand.

He vanished, going back to his previous position.

"The Surrah is done. You need to be able to withstand me *and* them; be able to buy enough time."

"Enough time for what? What—" He cut me off as this entire thing simply cut me....It was a cruel, burning reminder of something sweetly cold. Cold and dead.

"Roan will beat you to death, but she can't *kill* you. She's not a Reaper. But she will take you to someone who *will* murder you, Devi. Without thought, without remorse and without touch."

"You *literally* described yourself." The air grew thick between us. "Why so gloomy about the whole thing? Being murdered by Lucifer should get your panties all wet."

"He'll not have mercy, Devi. And before you spout off—If you refuse to help Lucifer, you cannot imagine the fate that awaits you with him. You've never been to *his* circle, Devi. I—"

"And *you've* been *so* kind to me? You're fucking joking, right?"

"I would kill you dead, and be done. She—"

"Would torture me? Mindfuck me? *Molest* me? Murder me? Let me be *raped*? Over and over again? Oh, wait. That was *you*."

"I never raped you, Devi." The night with me, Thomas, and Ophelia burned in my irises.

"Yes, you did." There's more than one way to do it.

"You think *I'm* a beast? You think what you know *now* is fear? If Roan gets a hold of you, the only person you'll beg for is *me*, so shut up and listen." I swallowed my tears but not the irrefutable sting of his words. "I need you to stay alive long enough for me to get to you if we're separated." His hypnotic silver eyes bordered on white fire. He didn't wait for me to object, bitch or otherwise, make this more difficult.

"Do you remember the DeKenna?"

"They're like the LeMehti. Poisoned and everything. Like twinsies. You can hurt them with your weapons. Blah blah... We send each other Christmas cards." Thomas inhaled. Deeply.

"Who they used to be does not matter to them so do not let it matter to *you*."

"Wow. *Riveting* lesson in 'Shit Devi Already Knew'. Thanks." He crossed his arms, his sword over his back. The wind picked up and my hair caressed my face as the trees swayed as far away from the two immortal beings in their midst. "Yeah. Sorry. Keep my Empath powers with the hollow demons in the 'off' position as much as possible. Got it." I would've altered my dress to be more battle-appropriate but I've been trained to fight in anything. Because chaos can happen to you no matter what. Adapt or die.

"I need you to know how to kill them if I don't get to you in time."

"But why would we—"

"You're not listening." He looked to the giant trees and in that moment, their rustling screams quieted to a whisper. Thomas turned his attention to me again and I took a step back instinctively. My action made him purse his lips. He took a step to me and while shaking his head, he spoke. "They know no mercy, therefore give them none."

"When did you fight Roan?"

"A few months back," was all he said. "Once I teach you how to heal from their touch, you'll be more than capable of fighting Roan and her army, but there's one thing Vincent failed to teach you." Pictures of Istanbul flashed across my eyes. Every training session I had with the man I loved to death—I couldn't control my balance so I tried to control something that would keep my feet on the ground, but... "If you're not going to pay attention, I may as well end you now." He walked furiously to me, closing the 15 feet between us. I took a leap back.

"I'm *listening*." After an intense glare, he began again.

"If you had completed your training, this would not be necessary." I grimaced and he breathed loudly and spoke again. "Use the principle of phasing in combat. What will happen?"

"Things would be a little transparent." I laughed. He didn't.

"Your opponent will go right through you. Try it."

"You want me to *phase* you?" I knew what he was telling

me but I couldn't picture thinning out Roan's body and having her go right through me like a ghost. I'd done this only *once* before under extreme duress.

"Yes. Or you can phase yourself. The same principle as the dress. Now concentrate." Thomas Ported back a few yards and started marching to me, giving me about 4 seconds to concentrate on the task. Then, he ran at full force. I tried to thin him out, or thin *myself* out? Shit!

We slid 30 feet, breaking up the earth beneath us, before Thomas held me by the waist and jumped up from the ground; keeping a 40 foot tree from being uprooted. His eyes fell into mine but they lacked the ire I was expecting. Instead, he steadied me on the earth, leapt back the length of the 30 feet to our original positions and spoke a word that broke me.

"Again." I did phase here and there. But, I only managed an arm or leg. Mine or his. A downed log at one point

We slammed into each other; he broke his arm as I broke my shoulder, popping it out of its socket on top of it. Thomas helped me off the ground, his injury long healed. "Why aren't I healing?" Broken bones heal instantaneously. Popped ones generally need a little encouragement.

"Hold still and—Devi? Pay attention." Thomas grabbed my shoulder, waited half a second, and popped the limp limb back into place. His hands lingered on me as I heard the bones fuse back together. A surge of ice and static spread through them. The intricate mechanics of it all bleeding from Thomas' mind into mine.

"You know you did more than just show me how to heal from the touch of a DeKenna, right?" he didn't respond. "Can I heal *others* now, too?"

"I doubt you'll need to be able to heal your enemies when in the midst of their murder." He had a point. "Try again and this time, concentrate on phasing only me." He would appear and disappear. I could see where he'd be but he moved far too fast. I saw him thin out as his fist approached. Then, where there should've been a broken skull missing a mandible,

Thomas' fist and whole upper body flowed right through me and out the other end.

I felt nothing but a slight tingle from the energy of his body phasing through mine. I smiled and turned to receive his appraise but he charged at me again and again. Moving too fast for me to follow each time. But I caught him each time.

He came up behind me, one of my blades coming at my throat in slow motion as he moved as fast as light. But *I* phased into him and out the other end.

"Finally." He threw my blade to me and smiled. "Now, would you like to know how to kill a demon?" The tone of his voice was full of vengeance he didn't bother to mask.

"I don't have a choice, Thomas. Kill or be killed, right? Show me."

"There's a choice in everything. Free will doesn't vanish into thin air."

"You know better than most how fragile free will is." He swallowed hard, gripping the holster of his sword. It was too heavy now. "The LeMehti and The DeKenna are at war over *me*. If there is a chance to stop that, I have to take it. Killing Roan won't stop the war, but it will at least provide a cease fire."

"What would you do with that cease fire?"

"Netflix and chill."

"Devi."

"What? You want a *real* answer? I'd spend every waking minute finding a way to end myself to save *you*. Note: Sending myself to Hell—and other underworlds? Utter fucking failure."

"Is that what you believe?"

"That the ritual failed?"

"That you need to die to save me—the LeMehti. To save all our souls."

"Yes," I choked on the word as his bubbled in my throat; stupid, but full of temptation.

"There's another choice. They'd still hunt you. But, it *is* another way."

"You wanna go AWOL?" Vincent *never* shared his contingency plan with Thomas. What is this?

"I can keep you hidden. It would take Roan and my kind a *decades*, maybe more, to follow whatever small trail we leave." I took in a breath and gleaned a tiny bit of his plan.

"You want to hide me in *time*." His plan was a variation of one of Vincent's. *This* plan, however, is—dare I say it—a fucking *marvelous* second choice. Hiding me away in different times throughout history... "Why the fuck would you do that?" I took him by absolutely no surprise. The sun was going to set but it flickered and then...then the glimmering bronze and violet sky fell and immersed every single thing in a shroud of gray.

Thomas finally terrified the sun to death.

And that is *exactly* why I shut the fuck up. That, and the fact that I somehow channeled a sample of his power. A surge of his strength crashed through me, breaking every bone in its path. It tore at my lungs, twisted my insides until all I breathed was blood...

Crescendo.

Karma's a *bitch*.

My brain caved in on itself, dropping me to my knees. I wiped the blood and ooze from my eyes but it still didn't look right. Were there *two* of him? His scream vibrated in my chest but I heard nothing... One of them picked up his sword and lunged at me but the other grabbed it and hurled it into the woods. They held on to one another, laughing to no end. Tears streaming down their broken faces... And when death heaved in their eyes, when the rain fell, washing away our sins, Thomas pulled himself together.

"You need to stay out of my fucking head." I stood, completely healed. Only ten seconds had passed.

"And *you* need to control your shit. Not drag me down with it." I gasped. "Go on then. Show me how to be the best damn Reaper I can be." Thomas was about to teach me how to use the very power that threatened his existence.

"This isn't a joke—" before he continued, he ran tired hands through his hair and adjusted his stance, "The DeKenna, the LeMehti—we're not human. Never were. DeKenna are fallen angels."

"The smaller Officers, they used to be humans who've been sent to Hell."

"Some of them are humans, yes. They were given a choice to punish or be punished."

"They upgraded their prison sentence and changed their species along their way."

"Something like that."

"I got you. Watch out for their memories. This won't be my first time running into this order."

"You've only ever been in the midst of a few dozen. A hundred at the most. If Roan catches up to us, she will bring with her a *legion* of Officers. Newborn and veterans alike. That amount of history running through you will—"

"I'll be fine."

"Will you?"

"I made it for quite some time in Hell and Company all by my lonesome." I sat and crossed my legs. "Or did you forget?" Thomas needed to sit and it coursed through me.

"No, Devi. Not one moment of your time at The Court has ever escaped my mind..." Sick fuck.

"Gotta keep those trophies somewhere," I muttered, playing with the frightened grass. Thomas leaned against a tree, his hands finding refuge in his pockets.

"You need only to kill Roan and her army should fall back, giving us our cease fire."

"Should?" I realized then, far later than I should, that the sky was utterly drenched in black. A few constellations speckled across. When I was under the avalanche of his power, when I witnessed his breakdown, it wasn't for a few seconds. It took him *hours* to bring me out from that broken state...

"If the others see one of us bring the General of Hell's army to her knees, they would be fools not to retreat. Entire *armies* have been raised to fight *you*. Or have you forgotten?"

"I try to repress any and all memories from The Court. Not quite the Greatest Hits it was for me as it was for you." We couldn't look at one another. Truth is, though I don't remember everything, I remember enough. And so did he...

"You are a force beyond imagining, Devi. There's a reason no one's captured you all these years."

"I'm good at hide and seek." He chuckled, I think.

"Not *that* good."

"Yeah. *You* found me." The wind picked up and Thomas went silent for a while.

"That I did." My eyes flicked up to him but he fiddled with some light show in the palms of his hands.

"Why did you never bother to catch me before now?" I walked over to him, despite the heaving heart in my rib cage, and got a better look at the glittering specter in his palms.

"I've been a *bit* preoccupied fighting a war. Keeping all manner of devils away from you." he clasped his hands shut and gave me an irritated look. "Besides, I—"

"Don't chase what's already yours? Yeah, so you've said." The air around us was cool. The perfume of wildflowers swam across our skin. I was calmer than I should be despite the bitterness that scratched at our throats.

"Enough procrastination."

"Yup." I rolled my neck. Thomas worked a knot in his shoulder. "Thomas?"

"What?" He replied, his attention on the moon.

"Why are you going to show me how to kill you?" A deep breath took shelter within his lungs and then realized where it had foolishly ventured off to and escaped loudly out of his mouth.

"If we're separated, you need to be equipped to handle matters alone."

"Why will we be separated?" Thomas ignored me.

"Without our souls, DeKenna and LeMehti, we're no

more than human; mortal. You and I are the only Reapers here and before you open that pretty little mouth of yours, Death and the Grimm Reapers—as the humans call them—do not have hands in this war. We are alone in this, Devi."

"Yeah, I know. No Gods, deities, or Revs from *any* Realm or denomination want part of this no matter the side. They're all too afraid of me to pick up a sword."

"They fear for their *souls,* Devi. If gods and titans broke through the Veil and joined us—the damage to the earth alone would be nearly irreparable for one."

"And two?" I crossed my arms across my chest. Holding my seams in place lest I fall apart.

"We wouldn't have immortals murdering children for pleasure. Death would send Reapers across the realms taking souls before their time. We'd have *thousands* of gods *eating* the world because—"

"I drove them mad..." I rubbed my face. The stinging of his truth beneath my skin. "If anyone helps either of us or the DeKenna—" I looked to the stars, hoping to find warmth in their light, "it'll be the end of the fucking world. *Every* world..."

"Devi, it won't come to that." I dropped my gaze from the cold sky and found Thomas.

"Why? Because we're going to kill Roan? How does executing *one* general spark a cease fire *that* powerful, Thomas?"

"No. *You* Reaping the soul of one of *us* will. The game will change once everyone learns that you have full faculty of your abilities."

"Abilities. What a funny word for something that can *annihilate...*" I scratched my chin. Thomas pressed his lips together. "Is that why you want me to kill her? Send a message? Get this cease fire and give your lot more time to find a way to win?"

"No."

"Oh, right. You're going to tuck me away in *time* and keep me safe from all the big baddies. Including your own empire." I scoffed. He started the lesson.

"If I'm not there, you'll be able to pull out Roan's soul—rendering her human—and Mark the soul, sending it where ever you like or destroy it where you stand. This applies to *anyone, anything.* If it has a soul, it's yours to take." He spoke the words as though he read instructions off a baking recipe.

"Maim. Mark. Murder. Just another Tuesday."

"It's not Tuesday, Devi." My forehead met my palm. Thomas only had a crooked grin on his lips. "When we do this, it's going to trigger *all* of your memories. Will you—"

"Like I said, I'll be fine." I lied through my teeth. He wouldn't know for a while.

He removed his holster. "You'll practice on me. Lay down."

"I'll practice on *who,* now?" I stumbled on my words.

"You heard me, Devi."

"Did *you* hear you?" Now, I *know* what you're all thinking. But if I off this madman, I'm royally fucked. I cannot afford to execute my only protection. Running through time may be a pain in the ass but it *is* a solid backup plan. "You're about to show me the *exact* manner in which you murdered the love of my life. Your own flesh and blood." My muscles tensed so quickly, his tore off his bones. Neither of us flinched. "How are you certain I won't kill you the moment I know how?"

"I'm not." My eyes flickered in disbelief. He looked at me, silver eyes too bright in mine. Too honest. Too full of everything he'd ever done to me... "Lie down, Devi." I did as he demanded. The grass was cold on my back. I kept my focus on the constellations.

"How am I sending Roan's soul on its merry way?"

"You truly don't remember what Azrael taught you, do you?" He said, leaning on his elbow. I knew the box I kept those memories in.

"Dissociation has been quite the survival mechanism for me if you haven't noticed," I said, not tearing my eyes from the sky. We're *not* opening that box.

"I've noticed." Thomas said in nearly a whisper. "You choose where a soul belongs. Heaven, Hell, Purgatory, or if it is to be reincarnated back to Earth. Let's begin." He took his position back on the ground and exhaled. In the cover of darkness, I saw the poison on his breath singing the air as it left his mouth. "I need you to listen to my breathing and heartbeat. That's when you'll hear it.

"In that order?"

"Yes. Heartbeat, breath, soul. Hear them individually, tuning out everything else." I listened to his heart, beating insanely peacefully inside his chest. His breath, slow, steady and too familiar… And then I felt it. Static shock in my chest and it came from Thomas.

The world around me blurred into a watercolor painting and that's when I pulled out his soul. It hovered above us like a tiny star. I reached for it but it was still tethered to him and shot back into Thomas' chest. The world gained its dimensions again and we both stood up. But the damage was done.

"What was that? I—I saw—"

"Me." As much of him as Thomas would allow in that state.

"Not *just* you. Reaping a soul, I can see—I can *feel* everything you've *ever* done."

"I didn't allow you access to everything."

"You allowed access to *enough*, Thomas."

"Devi—*focus*."

"It's hard to focus when all I feel is you murdering Vincent!" I was Thomas killing Vincent…I was Vincent dying. Over and over. "Why do you need me to kill Roan when *you* can do it your fucking damn self?! Why won't you kill me and *end* this?" I fell to my knees, sobbing into the earth…

"Devi—"

"What the *fuck* will you be *so* preoccupied with that you might not get to me in time? Why will we be separated?! You're supposed to *protect* me! *Why* are you protecting me?! Why are you showing me how to *kill* you?!" Thomas said nothing. *Moved* nothing. Breathed *nothing*. We were suspended in time. The space between us shattered.

Before Thomas imploded, I darted for the trees. I barely

made it ten miles before Thomas blocked my path. I didn't think, not for a second. I grabbed his arm and twisted it clean off. I watched his eyes flash into white glaring flames as his arm reattached itself. I lunged at him, punching, slicing, tearing. He grabbed my neck to rip it from my body, but I blinked out of his hold. When he tracked me down on the other end of the forest, I created a light brighter and hotter than the sun from my eyes to his. When he keeled over vomiting, his bloody eye sockets hollowed, I ran. But the ground beneath us quivered, cracked and rose up, bringing me back to him.

He's not the only one who can control the elements.

With his hand tight around my throat, he lifted me off the mounds of broken dirt. I laughed. Laughed because as I choked on the blood filling my lung from Thomas stabbing me, *his* lips blistered as I boiled his insides. The scent of his cooked flesh glazing over the woods and driving the meat eating animals at its fringes insane. But they would not dare move.

I willed my blades to my hands and as I wrapped them in fire, I sliced Thomas in half and I teleported. But the moment my feet touched the ground 20 miles out, his upper half had already reattached to his lower half. And now, now he's *gone*.

I wiped the blood from my mouth, jacking up the heat in my blades. I could've sworn the sky darkened. That the stars faded into perpetual shadow. Despite my night-vision eyes, it was getting impossible to see.

"I didn't think you'd hide from me, Thomas. Come out, come out wherever you are you piece of shit." Time to Hunt.

My eyes went transparent, piercing through the Veil to see between worlds. I found him. A thousand yards to the East. And the moment I pressed my foot harder on the ground, I stopped. Thomas was behind me. His breath literally froze the hollow of my neck solid. When his fingertips grazed my flesh the terror in me broke free. I wanted to breathe but I couldn't. I wanted to Blink but I had no control. The world drowned.

In that moment, where the lament of gravity resonated and the motion of time had no direction, something cracked. Thomas took my wrists, twisting me around. But he cringed and clenched his jaw; hunching into my chest. I tried freeing myself, but he only tightened his grip. He wouldn't let himself scream and I couldn't take his pain anymore so I let out his caged howl.

The force of it broke the sound barrier ten times over; along with everything within a hundred miles of us. I kept the living creatures protected from the shock wave but the pressure of it made the both of us keel over, falling to our knees...both our throats bleeding.

"Let me go!" Then, my soul screamed for Vincent in a way it hadn't for *years* and it made Thomas tremble. Air was too heavy for us to breathe. Our bodies too hot and wet with blood. Hearts pounding against one another like armies on a battlefield until—until only two soldiers remained. One calming the other. I ceased my struggles to run and dared to smile when his gentle eyes met with mine.

"Don't cry..." I whispered sweetly.

"Devi—Devi, no!" I came to when my face met with a the bark of a hundred year old tree. And as I fused the pieces of muscle back to my jaw—that I tore out *myself*—I realized how far down into oblivion my mind had fallen...

I thought Thomas was Vincent. Again.

"Do you not grow tired of the same trick, Thomas?!" Thomas looked at me in horror.

"That was *not* of my doing, Devi." He did not lie...The stars brought light to the night as the green of the earth displayed the crimson we sprayed from our bodies. I'm losing my mind...and control of the winds. They'll rage into a tornado if I don't—Thomas wrapped his arms around me but I phased through him and grabbed him from behind; breaking his shoulder blades and spine...*after* I turned every vein in his body to *metal*. He fell stiff to the ground and I made a run for it.

There's nowhere to run...Where are you going? Let him kill you.

I stopped running.

Thomas found me, wrapping his arms around me. "How many times do I have to kill you, Devi?"

"Until I *stay* dead, I would imagine, Thomas." He gripped me tighter, his thumb rubbing my busted lip; bleeding all over him.

"Fair enough. You're lucky I enjoy the taste of your blood. It's—insatiable."

"Enough foreplay."

"With you, Devi, it's never enough..." Before we completely leveled the woods, Thomas stopped toying with me and blinked me into his arms. "Do you really wish to fall?" He was full of disappointment. The sting of evil in his words literally scraped against my skin. "Answer me." His grip around my throat cut off my air supply. I managed to nod. He slid his hand around my waist, the edge of his sword sliding in between my thighs...

"What are you waiting for?" I spat, breathless. Then something splintered inside him and he transformed my skin to glass.

My wrists shattered and his hold on my neck tore the muscles apart within.

"I'm preparing you to fight *alone* because there will be *thousands* of them and *one* of me; because I might be fighting *with* Roan, not *against* her." The glass fractured and fell from my body. Thomas spoke in a fever. "Will you be a good little girl if I let you go? I am in *no* state to baby-sit your temporary losses of sanity."

"*My* temporary losses of sanity?!" He squeezed me, his hand pushing my hip deeper into his. "Yes," I answered through gritted teeth. Thomas loosened his grip but held me close. Dare I say, gentle. Almost goddamn *apologetic*. Then he healed my wounds and let me drop to my hands and knees.

My heart grasped the reins of its pace. Quiet took my mind. A shudder crawled across the earth beneath me. I turned to Thomas and wished with more desperation than you could ever fathom, that I wasn't able to see through my inhuman eyes. Fuck, to see at all. An immortal beyond understanding stood before me but, I swear to you, he did not move; yet, believe you me, the planet shook from the quakes that raged within him.

His scream vibrated against my hands, rattling inside me in attempts to break out. Thomas battled something again and I think tonight—tonight, he'd fight it for the *last* time...

As suddenly as the planet moved, it jerked to a stop. Thomas was in front of me in a blurred motion so fast, I nearly vomited. He wrapped me in his arms but—I'll be damned because when he ran us off, he wasn't running with me as his prisoner. He ran with me as his *lifeline*.

Thomas broke the sound barrier multiple times over. Speed does not dictate time travel. No. Thomas made the earth gasp because he had in him the all too familiar urge to simply *run*.

Run when you have nowhere left to go...

The air thickened, submitting to the force of Thomas breaking through the fabric of time. It cracked and we fell in with a silence that shattered anything in its path that was not the Breaker and his passenger. The threads of time found each other again and sealed the opening; leaving a bright blue bruise behind for those who knew what to look for... A Rev would know if someone from a different era walked among them. A *smart* Rev would know to cover up that scar so that no other Breaker could follow the trail.

But then there's Thomas.

I slammed up against a red brick wall when we landed. The blue shimmering bruise almost a halo behind Thomas. He panted. His chest heaving against mine. Each breath slowly fracturing every single rib in my cage. Thomas finally looked at me. The gunmetal of his eyes drowned in white fire. Desperation dripped down from the strands of his snow white hair, so potent it singed off my cheeks. Thomas lost his balance, nearly falling over. He punched into the wall above my head and gripped on to my skirt for support, pushing his hips into mine with such force, he broke our bones.

I dared my touch on Thomas. His sweat boiled and it steamed when it hit my fingertips. When I wrapped my palms around his shoulders, he shivered. Thomas gasped for air…*we* don't *need* air. This isn't normal. This *isn't* the poison. Thomas is *dying*… All this time trying to keep me alive, trying to go *against* the blood in his veins…

"It's not the poison. Not killing me—it's killing *you*." I thought I saw tears in his eyes. I have *never* seen him cry.

As the atoms around us stood perfectly still; not daring to near the creatures in their midst. As the air frosted over our mouths, I realized the oxygen around us, the light from the windows... They *knew*. I gleaned a vision from them. I didn't think it would be so soon…I thought—it's okay. This is where Thomas will finally murder me.

And this was where I let him…

# Chapter 16

## Genesis

No air seeped from his lips. Thomas lost the war inside. I wanted him to speak, to say *anything.* But I was only answered by the eerily dulling tempo of his heart. His chest heaved for oxygen. His bones shook beneath my hands. He didn't simply lose control.

Thomas was *chaos*...

"You're scaring me." The quiver of my voice actually shocked him. His hand slipped away from my waist. I watched, horrified, as he backed away from me. Gravity held more authority over him than his own *soul*...A hurricane of silver crashed into white and black in his eyes. I'd never seen one of them move in slow motion...or is time screaming again? I held out my hand to him. Sure he'd fall at any moment. But when I took step, his eyes stopped changing. The hollows of his skull housed white flames and they hungered for nothing but me.

We coiled our fists. Blood rushing, pumping to our hearts the singular sound in the castle. I grit my teeth, getting in position. *No weapons, Devi. This is it...*

Thomas shut his eyes and took one more calculated step away from me. But when his markings lit up, he grinned, baring his teeth; his white flames all my pale desert storm eyes could see... I *knew* I had to fight back.

I willed my daggers to my hands but not before his hand shot up to my throat. Twisting me around, he pummeled my face into the brick. The castle whimpered with every blow. I phased into him, coming out his back. But I wasn't fast enough. He grabbed my daggers and pierced them down into my lungs. Cracking his head into mine, our blood left no place clean.

I burned him alive.

Struck lightning into his heart.

Turned his bones to sand.

We were equals in combat. But the harder I fought, the stronger he became. My efforts futile.

I was the fuel to his fire and there was only one way to douse the flame.

He threw me across the hall. I crashed through six rooms before I could stop. Before I pushed myself off the ground, I had to make sure the castle didn't crumble, but I threw up blood and bile instead. My wounds are healing as slowly as if I were hit from a demon. But it's Thomas. He's delaying my healing. Ten-fold it looks like. He wants to make this last.

His footsteps echoed until he came into view at the mouth of the hall. He tore off his shirt...is that *my* blood he's wringing from it? I looked down at my chest and saw the stab wounds, the shredded throat. The missing piece of skull from the back of my head... Thomas pulled me up by my soaked hair like a shot-down bird. He leaned into me, his eyes burning my eyelashes off.

Thomas raised a trembling hand to my sternum and a devilish light of black and blue bled out of his palm. The light grew. Brighter and hotter and then when he pushed it into me—

The birds were at least ten miles out. Their chirps were still too fucking loud. I opened my eyes to red brick and black shadow. I was beneath the rubble of the castle...*alive*. Lungs collapsed. Spine severed. Paralyzed from the neck down. Eye dislodged. My jaw in pieces... The tons of castle remnants would leave me nothing but a headache. These injuries are courtesy of Thomas...

Thomas cleared the bricks off of my face. *Use your magick*, I thought. *Control his mind,* I thought again. But what good would that do? Save my life? Free me from him? Put me back in the run for *another* six years? And now stuck in the past? I *could* use my magick. I *could* overpower him. All of his magick and psychic power is being used to protect him from something but it's left him completely weak and defenseless elsewhere. I could fight back...

But we all know what has to happen.

*I'm* the villain of the story. And the villains *never* get a happy ending.

Thomas crushed my neck again but this time, a few of the vertebrae unhinged. He decapitated me without slicing my head off. I'm *still* alive. Where's my kill switch?

He picked me out of the ruins of the castle and examined me. I tried to speak, but it was no use. He dropped me to his feet like a ragdoll and took a step back.

Blood cradled my head like a halo The sun shining too brightly in the liquid. When he crouched down to me, I saw something glinting in between his fingers. But, as he stood to leave, as he set the ruins of the castle on fire, his fist opened to reveal nothing. He Reaped my soul. I knew as much. But where is it? I'm still here. I can *feel* the hold on my healing powers that Thomas has. I'm still *immortal*. Aren't I?

Or...or is Thomas keeping my newly human body alive while he decides which realm to Mark my soul for?

It took Thomas one *minute* to murder me and rip my soul from my chest. He should have spent an *hour*.

"Where are you going? Finish it!" Thomas was gone and I was left to bleed out beneath the rubble.

Losing my soul—it being severed from my body—I'd experienced pain like that once in my existence. *Once*.

Vincent's death.

My body was paralyzed but I retained mobility in my face and neck. I dared open my eyes, but all I saw through the haze of shadow and moonlight were the furnishings of a bedroom in a castle.

Wait.

I channeled the bed I was in. I can *channel* but can I scan? Am I still immortal? *One insanity at a time, Devi.* I'm in a room of the castle that Thomas burnt to ash. I checked the timelines and this is *after* Thomas Reaped my soul. *Breathe, Devi. Don't try to move again. Just breathe...*

I woke up screaming. Something was at the foot of my bed. I could hear it breathing. *Aching* to climb into bed with me.

"What are you?" I dribbled blood with my words. "How long have I been unconscious?" Its bones twitched in mine. When it licked its lips, I had no choice but to lick my own. The thing wanted to explode. It wanted to peel its skin off. It wanted to burn me. Eat me. Keep me.

Why didn't Thomas kill me? My death was to end the war. It was meant to cleanse the poison from The LeMehti and The DeKenna. Me dying was meant to put an end to the end of *everything*.

*You're. Not. Dead. Scan. Look for Thomas. Look for someone to help you.*

I tried to scan but something wasn't right. This *wasn't* Ireland and this *isn't* the bedroom in the castle. You're too weak. In too much pain. Ignore him climbing beside you. *Scan, Devi. Scan and look for—no*. This can't be right. I shut my eyes and prayed to God. Prayed with every pathetic fiber in my being that what I had witnessed during my scan *wasn't* real. Because it would be sheer *mercy* for me to have been executed only to return to there, with them; with *him.*

Thomas murdered me dead.

He Reaped my soul and Marked it for Hell.

This room my prison.

This demon my watcher.

And *this*...it's simply a beautifully crushing *weapon*. One that will end me for eternity.

And God help me, I will let it.

**De Capo**
**The First Night**
**Friday August 8th 2014—Chicago**
**9:00 p.m.**

My lips curved into a smile; music finding its way into my mind, sparking fledgling storylines, and fueling old tales that never tire of being spun. Though my mind wandered with the stories I write and my boots were meeting with the sidewalk, I knew. Weathered to near perfection, my leather jacket snug against the skin of my arms, while renaissance fair rings curled around my fingers, I held on to the worn out strap of my leather messenger bag; extra credit forensic linguistic theories making love to the personality disorder notes inside. But I knew...

I was happy to be wearing my scarf. Though my summer classes were nearing their end, and the Fall semester doesn't start for three weeks, you can feel the Autumn air. I looked up at a starry-night sky lighting my path towards the EL, and as my smile faded, I *knew.* I'm not here. There. I'm not anywhere except whatever place Thomas sent me.

I've lived this all before. My body is lying beneath the rubble of the castle. But my *soul*—Thomas sent that broken piece of me in a secret circle of Hell Dante knew nothing about.

And his Inferno was all the colder for it.

I'm trapped reliving my life from the exact moment it all went to shit. This is the night Vincent and I met. The night that damned us both. There is one other possibility: I'm not in Hell. But if I'm right about that, it means I'm alive under that rubble. And God help you all if I am...

So, we're going to forego the coma theory and go with the dead and in Hell theory. There's no escape hatch. No brightly lighted exit sign. There is no way out. There is only going back. Back to the beginning.

But, what if it's *not* because I'm in Hell? Unfortunately, logic did tear its way into my skull and plant a seed. If this *isn't* the Devil's handiwork then I'm in the midst of the Kuma, and these flashbacks are meant to do what the Kuma are *born* to do; inflict every pain imaginable. And in my case...

If the Kuma have me, then that has to mean that Thomas has taken my corpse back to The Court. I'm their favorite toy... Whatever is happening to me, I'm staying. Here, in *this* time, in *this* place. Because reliving—to consider reliving all of *this* as an *escape...*

A Fool's Paradise indeed...

As the train rumbled by above, I muttered a curse under my breath. "Shit. I thought I was going to make it. Ah well." With a shrug, I switched songs on my phone until I found one that fit my mood. I tucked the cell back in my jacket pocket and began to dig through the zipper of my bag in search of my CTA pass. "Where the hell did I put it? I knew I should've taken it out before I left class." Finally finding it, I shoved both hands in my pockets and made my way to the station when I had the sudden and uncontrollable urge to cry.

My heart pounded.

I grit my teeth.

Someone's following me.

I sensed a change in the air. Enough of an alteration for someone like *me* to take note. The wind, up until now, had gently swayed the trees and my hair. Except now, *now* you could taste static in it. As if lightning were to strike yet not one cloud could be seen in the sky.

My steps hastened as my hand gripped the switchblade in my pocket tighter. A bead of sweat slid down my temple, but my speed didn't bring it to life. The stress response came from the sensation of being followed. From the energy of whoever is coming for me...Oh, my God.

There's *two* of them.

"Shit." The whisper spilled from my mouth too quickly for me to stop it. I'm still half a block from the stations' entrance. Thirty feet separated me and the man that followed me. The second man followed across the street almost exactly parallel to me. A few more feet and I'd be in view of the security cameras; both the station's and the apartment of a highly paranoid Shapeshifter.

A car drove by over the speed limit.

A murder of crows flew overhead.

A hand touched my neck.

I never heard him run to me.

I took out my knife, but one of them grabbed me and ran but it was as though we fell off a building.

I don't know how we ended up where we did nor how much time had passed. I stood up against a wall with a hand covering my screams and another defending my punches and kicks. Where's my knife?! We were covered in pitch black in an alley and the only light available were this man's *eyes*. They were bluer than the sky and brighter than the stars and more terrifying than anything I had ever witnessed because a man's eyes are *not* supposed to glow.

A crack of thunder and then another. When the third bolt of lightning struck at the mouth of our alley, I trembled from the shock and stopped fighting. I stopped because the light from the bolt lit up his face long enough for me to see two things: bleeding from his forehead and nose and those very wounds healing as quickly as the hundreds of millions of volts flashed. This is no man. He's a Reverie, like me. But no Rev can heal that quickly or run as fast as he did.

He was more interested in the brewing storm than in me. I took as deep a breath as I could through his giant hand covering my mouth and readied a punch to his throat. At least, that was my plan. He grabbed my wrist midair and pinned it against the brick building with the rest of me. I didn't realize I had been crying until this very moment. With another strike from the heavens, even closer and louder than before, I started to fight violently to get out of his hold.

But I swear, it didn't make a damn difference.

He would not be moved.

"Listen to me! Please, listen to me. I'm not going to hurt you. Stop it! Stop kicking me!" I wouldn't stop. This, this *thing* brought us from one part of the city to the other in mere *seconds*. There were *two* people after me. I have no way of knowing if he's the good guy or if there was a good guy at all.

I have to get out of here.

Though he let go of my arm and his hand slipped away from my mouth, both his arms flanked my body. If I made a run for it, he'd catch me.

"Please, let me go." The quiver in my voice surprised me but it *gutted* him.

"Listen to me, please. Just...listen. You were going to die back there." The tears dancing down my cheeks were cold. I started to shake and his hands, as if by instinct, gravitated toward my trembling shoulders. "I know you have no reason to, but I need you to believe me. Believe me when I say that everything I do, everything I will *ever* do, will be to protect you, no matter the cost." The rain started then. It's not supposed to rain for another week...

His hand reached out for mine and, after a moment of hesitation, after a moment of understanding that *everything* would change if I reached back, I took it. The man in black held my hand with slight tension, yet an energy that neither of us could deny surged through us. Taking a few steps back, he pulled down the fire escape of the apartment complex behind us.

"Trust me." He said the words but they were more of a question. And till the day I die, I don't think I will *ever* know why my mind screamed the words 'with my soul'.

I looked at the dripping metal and then at my supposed savior. The rain, it seemed, took a long time to seep through the fabric of the too-long military coat he wore. I followed its length all the way down to his too-clean boots. If this man is not who he says he is, and I survive, committing these details to memory will help me when I speak to police. Yet, in the darkness, in the storm, in the inhumanity of his face, safe is all I was.

I climbed.

By the tenth story, right before reaching the landing, I turned to ask how much further when only metal greeted me. Soaked and with a tempest raging with no end in sight, I turned again, stepping on to the landing when the window in front of me opened with a loud *crack*. The puzzling Rev on the other side. I looked behind me reactively. How did he get in? *When* did he get in?

Once inside the dimly lit bedroom, I found myself cleaving on to the strap of my messenger bag. *What are you doing, Devi? Where are you? Find the bathroom and call*—the window shut with another migraine-inducing crack. I shook. I wanted to move but I found myself frozen with *him* right behind me.

"You'll be safe here." The words floated across my cheek as he walked around to face me. His fingers ran through his drenched black hair, clearing the strands painted on to his skin. A breath entered heavily through his mouth as he readied himself to speak when he changed his mind and took off his coat instead. He threw it over a chair across the room. Finally, he braced himself to talk, though it seemed to be not something he'd much enjoy.

"My name's Vincent." He stood there a moment with his hands in his jean pockets. Oh…

"De—Devi. My name's Devi." A smile came alive through him, but it died just as quickly.

"You have to get out of those clothes, Devi. You'll need to give me everything, actually."

"What do you mean *everything*?" My fingers tightened around my bag as I took a step back; my toes curling in my boots.

"Every single thing that is on your person."

"I'm sorry. I—I don't understand. The wet clothes I get, but why do you need my—"

"Everything that you've touched—they're a beacon; A guiding light for them to track. To find you." I looked out the window, the storm raging, the lightning striking closer and closer to our building.

"The water doesn't dull anything? Wash the trace away? The smell, at least?"

"Not for them." Being what I am, I had an idea of what *would* kill the trace. But, I had to ask.

"What *does* get rid of the trace, or scent, or whatever it is I leave behind?" His hands left his pockets and he crossed his arms. The wet sweater clinging on to his body and revealing the source of all the strength I witnessed earlier.

"Fire." I hate being right.

I swallowed.

Another lightning strike. Another quasi-human only *slightly* jumping out of her skin.

"What's up with this storm?" The mumbled words spilled out of me too quickly.

"It's us." I turned my attention from the draped window to Vincent. My question had been rhetorical. But his answer…

"Can you expand on that or is enigmatic and terrifying your thing?" He laughed. I think you could call it laughter.

"Neither you nor I are meant to be here."

"Wow. Excellent observation. *Elegant* articulation. Totally answers my question." My heart raced...

"Do you always revert to sarcasm when you're nervous or is that your default?"

"Not when I'm nervous. Afraid, on the other hand, yes. I'll throw in a hex to spice things up a bit, too." He grabbed some clothes for me from the closet of whosever apartment we broke into. "How on earth are you and I affecting the weather?" The clothes were set neatly on the foot of the bed.

"The storm—it's a byproduct of our interaction." Those words had their own gravity and I *swear* it nearly brought me to my knees. It did not go unnoticed. "You need to change. I'll be outside." Turning on his heel, he made his way to the door.

"Wait. How, I mean... how are you going to burn my things?" The too-tall man in black started toward me. "Do you have to burn yours too? Do *you* leave a trace? The fire will get rid of the smell but what about the *aura?* Our auras are going to be harder to erase. Their light is powerful. How do you burn away *light?*" I'm silently crying. When did I start?

Vincent took a few more steps and with each one, I had to lean my head back to make eye contact. That didn't last long. I ended up staring at his sternum but then his fingers laced across my cheeks; tears falling from my skin to his. This touch, however sweet, bore a sense of pain. For *him*. I could channel this and he knew it.

"Light cannot burn. You're right." Vincent took one step back, rubbing his chest.

"You can't use *mortal* fire, can you?" Vincent shook his head. Why would I think that natural fire would be in the equation here? *There is nothing natural about any of this.*

"We're not of anything *natural*, therefore natural approaches are rendered useless." Off came his shirt and I nearly stopped breathing.

"Naturally." There's a black marking on his sternum; a perfect circle with silver writing I've never seen before etched into it.

The sweater in his hand sparked and flames ate away at every thread and in seconds, the fire devoured the garment leaving embers in its wake. Then, even the embers caved in on themselves like supernovae and vanished. His coat went up on the chair, yet the chair remained unscathed. I could only see a tiny flicker of his aura. And his eyes...

"Hence the fire." I said, but the words came out as a whisper. This inhuman fire doesn't simply burn the aura. It scorches it from *existence*.

"Hence the fire," he repeated. "Towels are in the bathroom there." Vincent pointed to the door in the corner of the room that flanked the chair and walked out, ducking the doorframe on his exit as he closed the door behind him with a caution I couldn't understand. Before he went out of view, however, a replica of the burnt sweater enveloped his body. I stood there more intrigued with the markings on the length of each shoulder blade than the fact that this man is unlike *any* Rev I've ever known.

The part of me that is capable of knowing things I shouldn't, couldn't help but be fixated on his markings. Recently I learned that, if I touch something, I can know more about it. The psychic in me desperately wanted to use my new psychometry power to investigate the tattoos. They could possibly translate the writing for me, tell me if he is the good guy he says he is, and even what kind of supernatural being he is. In order for all this to happen, though, my bare hand has to touch his bare chest. Truthfully, this is new and I can't control it. Exactly why nothing triggered from our contact thus far. And enough nervous chatter. *Where did he say the bathroom was?*

A gust of wind blasted rain against the window pane and the clang of it made me whirl around. The drapes had been closed shut, erasing the outside world from me. My first instinct was to open the drapes. Watch the weather that always brought me comfort. Yet, on some level, I knew that this connection would have to remain severed. Vincent had enchanted the entire apartment; I sensed it the moment I stepped inside. And once something is marked with magick, magick *this* archaic, you'll do well to leave the spells be.

Rubbing the ache from my temples, I decided I couldn't wait any longer. I put my bag on the bed and took off my scarf, folding it neatly atop my messenger bag. My hands went into my jacket pockets and took the CTA pass in one hand and in the other, my cell phone with headphones still miraculously plugged in. The tingling in my noses caught me off guard. And when my lips quivered...

The last song I listened to, the last song I will have ever heard on this little extension of me, had been playing on repeat. *Cathedrals* by Jump Little Children. And, though I didn't know much yet, I knew Vincent had heard the song playing this entire time.

Every piece of clothing I removed from my body equaled a piece of me that I had to let go of. Every piece, a shield I had to lower. Every piece, a memory I'd *never* get back. And if I focused, I could see the small waves of opal lights around each item. My aura. The evidence of the very breath of my soul... And believe you me, air *can* catch fire. It was then, standing there in someone else's yoga pants and Nirvana t-shirt living across my skin, that I truly understood the trace Vincent had to spark out of existence. It's literally pieces of *me*.

And I had to burn.

# INTER SOMNIA
# DAY 1

**Saturday**
**August 9th 2014**
**Apartment-Undisclosed Location**
**Chicago**

My eyes fluttered, catching moonlight giving way to the morning sun. I cleaved to my blanket the same way I did the *first* time I realized Vincent's arms were wrapped around me. *You're repeating the past. You're in a dream.*

No.

*You're dead. Thomas finally killed you. He Reaped your soul and this is Hell...*

Vincent's heart thrummed against my back with power that shouldn't be this gentle. But a breeze swayed in from the closed windows and took Vincent with it. I don't know what woke me. It could've been the scent of breakfast filling the apartment or the emptiness Vincent left behind filling me. Whatever it was, it kept me in this time, in this place...

Reliving the beginning of the end.

I brushed my teeth, debating on a shower. My eyes wandered across the old black and white penny tiles, the clawfoot tub that smelled of lavender and radiator that hummed with warmth. My efforts of distraction failed, however. The mirror was too large. Too bright. Too full of a reality I had to face.

I can't brush my teeth forever.

I ran my fingers through my hair and took a deep breath. There I was. Alive, but trapped. I had a beating heart, but it could stop at any given second if whatever tried to kill me last night found me again. 'The police can't help you' Vincent had said.

"Dear God..." the shallow prayer too quiet to have any impact. I rubbed the inevitable, inescapable truth of my life from my eyes to no avail. A shower didn't seem too bad of an idea after all.

I made sure to be quick; scrubbing away whatever it is that's put a target on my back and allowing the lavender to sink into my pores; calming my energy. It didn't last...

Letting my hair air dry, I changed into new clothes and as I put the old set in the hamper, they went up in flames and ash; disappearing as fast as they had sparked.

"Holy shit!" I jumped back and my ass hit the brass door handle. "God damn it." The least Vincent can do is warn me before he does that.

I made the bed and then contemplated, for too long, if I should answer the knocking from the window. I walked over to the draped glass; jaw clenched; fists tight. "These things are happening too close together. If that's not a red flag...."

Shaking the warning from my lips, I went to the kitchen where, last night, Vincent and I had tea in the world's most silent tea-drinking extravaganza. Whatever is on the other side of that window would have to stay put; not here, not there.

Simply somewhere in between...

Vincent leaned against the wall of cabinets, the massive granite island separating us. He gazed out the window above the sink, practically burning two holes in the glass. After my belongings went up in smoke last night, we had chamomile tea here and discussed logistics. You know, cause that's what you do after creating storms and running from a supernatural murderer. Vincent told me there were other immortal soldiers like him. Paladins that were to protect me. Kindness was evident in his every word and action. But now, his tension and poorly hidden abhorrence vibrated from across the fucking room, barreling into my core.

Figuring the easiest course of action would be to take none, I followed his silent and brooding lead. I wanted to ask him about the knocking, though. Maybe he knew about my inexorable ability to draw the attention of anything without a pulse, because, to date, no ancient book, or the countless mediums I've had running me out of their shops have been able to figure it out. I'm a beacon for the dead and demons alike but no psychic or witch has ever made sense of it. And no, the demons don't have tails or horns. They look like you and me....

If you and me have lived in the Circles of Hell...

My stomach grumbled and I realized I'd been standing in the doorway like a psycho. I shuffled past the island and sat down to my scrambled eggs in the breakfast nook. Only a vintage chandelier rustically spray-painted white illuminated the space and with both of us in our separate corners, white knuckling our minds, a little light can go a long way.

He seemed comfortable in his black sweater. I was the opposite. Whoever the Enya t-shirt and yoga pants I was wearing belonged to had good taste in music, but do they not believe in denim? Or proper bras? I don't mind bralettes but—*you* try shoving grapefruits in a space meant for oranges. Do *not* adjust your boobs, Devi. I don't care if he's not looking, he could *feel* it with that strange connection we have. Don't you fucking—you did it...I took in a deep breath and from the corner of my eye, I saw Vincent adjust his sweater... I'm going to conclude that it was due to him connecting to my deep breathing and not, you know, my boobs.

Son of a bitch.

After a few minutes of mechanical consumption, the creature of questionable origin sped over to the kitchen doorway, gripping the doorframe. I dropped my fork onto my plate. The crash of silver to porcelain pierced my ears and sent a tremor in my bones. Vincent's back ignited with a bright blue glow. The light pierced through his sweater and reflected off the stainless-steel appliances...and my skin.

Something found us.

As the panic melted away, Vincent turned on his heel and locked eyes with mine. He rubbed his chest, and I was compelled to mimic his actions. It did not go unnoticed. When he sat down *beside* me, Vincent met my blank expression with a smile and though I knew it was forced, it wasn't false. There's nothing to worry about. For now.

I reached for my Earl Grey and Vincent's chair creaked, inching away from me. You see, my cup was beside Vincent's hand. *Too* close, evidently. I focused on drinking while he focused on anything that *wasn't* me. After three whole minutes of a hammering tick-tock of the clock, Vincent stood and sought refuge within that mighty arch of the doorway again. Despite the hero antics of last night, my literal shining knight wants *nothing* to do with his deplorable damsel. The hurricane drowning the butterflies in my stomach rose to my chest, winged corpses in tow. The temperature elevated and bit at my skin. Vincent doesn't want to be around me. Whatever he is, he cannot *stand* me. And that aversion is coursing in every inch of me.

The artificial light immersing itself in the kitchen gave me a lovely little migraine. Or is it the incessant finger tapping on my cup? My nervous tick transitioned from tapping fingers to tapping feet, to folded hands on my lap and finally, to cleaving to my shirt for dear life. I couldn't take the silence between us. I cleared the table and made my way to the exit. But my arm brushed against his stomach and Vincent backed up against the frame. We stood there, chests heaving, lips breathless, eyes utterly lost in each other.

I moved too fast so I could escape the moment, but my fingers made contact with his leg and Vincent flinched *so* badly he nearly buried himself into the frame, cracking the structure. I whipped around, watching as the fissures reached the ceiling. The anger in his eyes when they found mine... I opened my mouth to apologize, but the sight of the violence in the wall quickly disappearing threw me. I retreated to the bedroom; retreated to the memory of last night; our first night where Vincent held me tight as I slept. Remembered his warmth. Making me laugh with poorly crafted jokes ... At least then, though the extent of his skin on mine was for my protection, it didn't birth hate inside him. And if it did, he never let me witness it.

Until now.

I sat on the edge of the alien bed; heavy head barely cradled in my too shaky hands. I searched for words of comfort but found none. What could possibly ease the pain of *this*? My head shook to warn the tears from seeping. No good will come from crying. The act of it won't erase my attempted murder. It won't render the chaos creeping circles around me powerless. It won't stop that dead *thing* from pounding at the window over and over...

A deep breath carved its path into my chest, and I shut my eyes. When I opened my eyes, the gift of oxygen turned into a curse, lodging itself in my lungs. Vincent crossed the threshold to the bedroom. Whether due to my human behavior class or the resonating truth that in under 24 hours I'd familiarized myself with this creature without knowing it...I knew he wanted to say something, but he had no idea how to say it.

Every step he took calmed me, and it made my skin crawl. Or is that *his* skin prickling beneath my flesh? My eyes darted away and latched onto the white drapes in front of me, ignoring the shadow dancing behind it. But I sensed something I shouldn't. Vincent blocked my view of the ghoul in the window and knelt before me.

Wildfire spread across his eyes. The midnight blue burning into my mine. I looked away, not able to maintain his gaze. But Vincent's fingers traced my cheek, cupping my face and returning my sight to him. His heart raced. A single bead of sweat trickled down his neck. Neither of us took a breath of air. Not while it crackled... I couldn't have him touch me. Not when it came at the cost of broken things. It took everything I had to grab his wrist, pushing it away. A hushed word fell from my lips, but it hit Vincent like a slap in the face, "Don't."

The blinking of the seconds in the alarm clock flashed away time as if it were something that appeared and disappeared in existence on a whim. I coiled my fists, making myself ready to jump ship when his hands, shifting with a slight tremor, found themselves on mine. The hesitation. The sheer *caution* he took placing his touch on my skin...I think it broke us both.

None of this changed the fact that Vincent counted the goddamned seconds until our contact severed. I wanted to deck him in the face. To deck the asshole out of him. To scream every profanity imaginable until his ears bled because he didn't *have* to save me. He didn't *have* to hole me up in this safe house. He could've avoided it *all* and kept himself from the pure *agony* that I caused him.

But, goddamn it... he *didn't*.

He saved my life and now he's paying for it in a way I don't think I'll *ever* understand.

I didn't say a word and his lips were wise to cage whatever poison seethed within. With gritted teeth, I stood to leave because, unlike him, I couldn't lock away my emotions. I took not two steps when he took hold of my hand. I needed a moment to register his absolute gall. I met with his sternum. I had to lean my head back to see his eyes. Vincent looked—quite frankly, he looked like *me*; like someone who's spent every waking hour of every day trying, with *everything* they had, *not* to fall apart...

He bit his lip.

I let myself breathe.

Our fingers tangled, and I don't think anyone could've separated the bones. His mouth parted and let out a sigh I tasted on my tongue. Leaning into me, his words were going to fall. Their vibrations echoing on my lips before he even spoke. But he clasped his jaw shut and pried himself free of me with too much ease. I curled my fingers into tight balls; too aware of the fucking three-times-too-big shirt and yoga pants that didn't have pockets for me to shove my hands in to.

I closed my eyes, ready to tell him off, but when I opened

them, I stood there, doe-eyed, exhausted, and completely alone in a dark room. At home in that moment with the sting of nothingness biting at my edges and the hot tongue of the demon sliding across the window...

"Story of my life..." I barely heard my own words fumbling off my lips like afterthoughts. With as much energy as I could manage, I strode to the door and slammed it fucking shut.

Vincent wasn't here and I was not going out there. Climbing down the fire escape is starting to become quite the enticing option. But I knew I wouldn't be able to use it as an exit. I peeled back the drapes enough to see, with my head out of any sightlines mind you—I'm curious, not suicidal—glowing markings in the glass and on the windowsill. The language the same as the one I saw on Vincent's tattoos, so I had no clue what it said. They shared a resemblance to Aramaic and Latin that the markings could be nothing else but entrance seals; spells to keep whatever is out, out and whatever is in, in. I couldn't leave even if I dared. Couldn't even break the window.

I sat on the floor, the old oak creaking. The drapes agape enough for me to enjoy some warm summer sunlight in peace for a while. But peace is never lasting. With a long, defeated sigh, I dragged myself off the hardwoods. I got in bed and balled myself up with the teal blanket. I'd only slept a couple of hours. A little nap wouldn't hurt.

I went to reach for my cellphone on the nightstand to listen to music when my stomach dropped in water like a body with cement feet. A vision of my belongings burning to nothing flashed across my wet eyes... I curled the blanket tighter.

Indistinct whispers crept into my ears. Scratching in the walls followed with shallow footsteps not far behind. Each sound pounding from the outside, trying to get in. I sat up when something crashed against the door, trying and failing to break inside. In that moment, I realized that our location had been compromised, and Vincent was fighting the enemy on his own. Screams grew closer together. Bodies cracked like thunder. Feet marched like a hundred soldiers to my door.

And then a thundering fall of silence...

That's when the doorknob twisted. The door opened. I got out of bed and grabbed the lamp. A blood-drenched hand clasped over the wood that separated us. Before he could get in, before I could think, Vincent pulled him back, the door slamming shut behind them. I dropped the lamp and ran to open the door. But I was trapped on this side of the wall.

"Vincent! What's happening?! Open the fucking door!" The building shook. Glass shattered. Bones cracked *so* violently, mine nearly broke. The door wouldn't budge. I tried three different chants to undo whatever spell had been cast to lock me inside. And when all the lights flickered, when Vincent's pain was all I could taste, I did the next best thing; I looked through the keyhole.

*Never* look through the keyhole...

I couldn't tell how many bodies there were, but enough to form a pool of blood beneath my feet. I did what anyone in my position would do. I stuck my fingers in the warm liquid. I've never done this—to an object let alone myself, and I'll most likely vomit from the force, especially since the blood source is questionable at best, but what choice do I have? I lifted my shirt and painted the sigils. I put one hand on the door and the other on my stomach and...

Luckily, I only spat up bile. The breakfast bar wasn't the worst landing spot. Fucking orbing. I'm supposed to be on the other side of the locked *door*, not the other side of the *apartment*. I wiped my mouth and dodged the broken glass and corpses until I saw Vincent sunken on the ground; head down, blood-dripped arms resting on his knees...

"Vincent?" I knelt beside him; no clue which stained body part to begin with. "It's ok. I'm here." Where is all the blood coming from? I brushed the hair from his face. Scratch marks, cut lips, bruising around his neck. A gash on his forehead dripped red down the side of his temple. "Aren't you like, magick, or something? You should be healing, shouldn't you?" I don't have healing spells that work on fucking immortals...

No blinking. No movement. Eyes locked at something in front of him... His stomach sustained the worst injury. A massive gash from his side to his belly button...they have belly buttons. I took off my top and I jammed over-sized Nirvana shirt on his wound. With all my weight on it, I said the only incantation I knew to help at least *stop* the bleeding. A glimmer of a prism flashed between my hands and his wound. The bleeding slowed but didn't stop. How could it? My spell was designed for humans, not whatever *he* is.

"Vincent, I need you to lie back. Healing wouldn't be a bad addition, either." He's in shock. "Ok listen. Put both your hands on here and push down as hard as you can—well, not *really* as hard as *you* can—you- you know what I mean. Keep pressure. I'm going to get something to try and stop the bleeding. At least long enough until we figure something out. Hands right here. There you go. Ok, I'll be right—" He grabbed my wrist the second I rose up.

"Don't." The rasp in his voice scratched my throat.

"It'll be ok. This isn't my first time cauterizing a wound with a knife." He pulled me down and I became too aware of the fact that the tiny black bralette was the only thing keeping me from being topless.

"It *will* be ok, Devi." And with my name resting on his tongue, and a slight rumble in the apartment, everything was *ok*. The bodies—and their insides—vanished. All the broken things were put back together again. Vincent healed in the literal blink of an eye. My t-shirt burnt to ash and embers and a black shirt materialized in his hand for me.

"This should fit you better," he said with a weak smile. I grabbed the *Say Anything* top absent-mindedly and pointlessly helped him to his feet. We walked towards the bedroom. Wait.

I yanked my hand out of his. His eyes widened.

"What the *hell* just happened?" I was trembling and it distracted it far more than it should.

"We had a breach. I took care of it." If my eyebrow rose any higher...

"Liar," I spat the crime in his face. "I thought you said we'd be safe here. I thought you said no one would find us."

"I never said *any* of that, Devi." For only a moment, his eyes fell to my stomach; still free of the conjured top; still covered in blood magick. "I said *you* would be safe here." He took a shallow breath, strands of his obsidian hair cascading too heavily across his eyes despite his attempts to the contrary, "I said that no one would find *you* here."

"Then who were those people?" I answered my own question the second I asked it. They weren't after *me*. "They were after *you*." Familiar dread washed cold over me.

"Devi, I handled the breach." Vincent wrung his hands together and took in a pointless gulp of air that I nearly choked on. He looked at my throat. I studied him smoothing an ache from his chest that I mirrored too deeply into mine. "Devi, can you feel—"

"It sounded like a damn grenade went off in here, Vincent. And all those *bodies* sure as hell say otherwise." I couldn't stop shaking. I think I'm shaking. Did Vincent just tremble?

"Wait." Vincent's hands went up. I'd never seen anyone more puzzled.

"Why were they after you? How—"

"Devi, stop. *What* bodies?" His hands clasped over my shoulders. Eyes bright in mine. What bodies.

What bodies?

Not again. *Not* again. Not *again*....

"Breathe Devi. Start from the beginning. Devi—stop shaking." Vincent's words warmed me from the inside out. He cupped my face in his palms and took us to the living room so I could sit.

"There—" I pointed to the couch which, only a few minutes ago, had three corpses in LeMehti suits of armor on it. "There were dead men. Soldiers wearing *your* armor. Everywhere. We—*you* were attacked. Then you Samantha Stevensed this whole place and poof..."

"Listen to me. There were *no* bodies. Dead or otherwise." His head shook and it looked as though his neck wouldn't be able to stand the weight of it much longer. "What you saw, it had every intention of murdering you." A tear escaped my eye and slipped away with a finger that was attached to an immensely skilled deceiver that did not need to hone his craft. "And it's gone now."

"Liar," the word tripped from my quivering lips.

"Which part are you accusing me of falsifying? The part where what you saw had intent to murder you, or the part where it's gone?" We were both ready to punch something. Maybe that's why the walls practically howled...

"Both." He didn't blink. I didn't move.

"We need rest. Especially you. When the others arrive, your training starts." He held his hand out for mine and I gave it. We were too defeated to do anything but accept the cease fire.

Peace never lasts, though. Not when I'm around. Before he opened my bedroom door, I opened my mouth. "Please tell me what happened." An exhale managed to catch the space across his lips while I slid my fingers from his hand.

"I can't." That's all he said. Yet, for some insane reason, I could not find fault in his words. Because it's not a simple fact of him admitting to me that he couldn't give me details of the attack. The quietest shake in his voice, the exhaustion from his bones, and his eyes... His *eyes*. They all conveyed that whatever *it* was that he fought to keep from killing me, the truth of it would murder me more than its hands ever could.

Vincent saved my life. Again and instead of thanking him...

"If you'll walk away knowing anything of me, Devi, anything at all," The desperation in his face... "-let it be this:" he walked over to me. His hands finding my hips before they trailed up to the sigils I painted on my stomach. The magick drawn in blood floated into the void as embers. "Everything I do, everything I will *ever* do, will be to protect you, no matter the cost." Cradling my face in his palms, taking away every atom of fear housed inside me, I held on to his wrists...God help me, I didn't want him to let me go. These were the words he said to me last night. He held me closer, tighter, the relentless ache in both our bones now. "Please, trust me."

Don't do it, Devi. Don't ask questions he won't be able to answer. For *once*, keep your damn mouth *shut.*

"It." I opened my eyes, then he opened his; his despair quickly transformed to guilt. "You called what I saw 'it'. What I saw were dozens of *faceless* Paladins, broken and bleeding all over this sorry excuse of a safe house. The only way using the word 'it' would make any sort of sense is if I were to have seen the fight. I only saw the battlefield." His hands slipped away as he took a step back. And yes. It tore me. More than I thought humanly possible. "All those ancient spells etched on every *inch* of this place and what? A small supernatural *infantry* had *no* trouble walking right in and beating the ever-living hell out of you?"

"No one walked in."

"Right. 'Cause I *willed* into existence all the blood I used for my spell out of thin air. You know? The blood you burned off my skin that couldn't *possibly* exist because there was no one here to bleed it."

"Devi—"

"I can tell a flesh and blood corpse from a ghost. I'm psychic not blind. What aren't you telling me?"

"This isn't going to end the way you want it to."

"Newsflash! *None* of this is going to end the way I want it to!" I had to breathe because the reality of those words stabbed us both. "Why did you wait so long to heal yourself?"

"Why do you think I'd heal instantaneously?"

"Because there's no way you would've taken on *that* many goons if you couldn't Wolverine your way out of it."

"Who?" Oh my God.

"Stop answering questions with more questions and answer me." The tears couldn't be held back and it somehow destabilized his footing.

"What do you remember about the men?" I wiped my eyes and picked up the top from the floor and put it on.

"Other than the fact that they were dead and Paladins, like you?" My smart mouth left a bad taste in his. Good.

"Yes," Vincent said curtly. I couldn't stand being in the same space with him.

"Like I said, they had no faces. Their bones were protruding. They were stabbed and beaten... You're quite the one-man-army." Don't let him see how scared you are of him. There were words trapped behind his teeth; yearning to come out. Clenching his jaw almost as tight as his fists, Vincent swallowed and drowned whatever truth that tried to escape. "They had no faces." I whispered, massaging my mandible. "They weren't torn off or bashed in. They were simply...not there." He stared at nothing but saw...everything. "Vincent?"

"Devi-"

"Why even bother asking me what I remember?"

"I can't."

"Why?" The lights flickered. The wind howled, leaving its growl in our bones. We felt each other...what happened to one, happened to the other...and we could do nothing but witness it all in quiet horror. "What *is* this? What's happening to us?"

"If I tell you, every word out of my mouth will be a lie."

"Then *don't* lie." I tried to smile through a trail of tears. I could be imagining it, but I could swear I saw a layer of mist over his eyes, nearly filling to the brim, ready to spill over. He shook his head and I wanted to rip it off. I never walked so fast to escape someone before in my life.

I shut the bedroom door in his face, but the wood didn't infringe on our enigmatic empathic connection. "You wanna explain why I can feel your heart pounding in my chest, Vincent?" His silence nearly deafened me. "I know you felt *that,* too."

"I didn't mean to—" What if he's right? What if what I saw wasn't there? I could've seen the past. Maybe the future. That would explain why he didn't see them. But it doesn't explain the violence, the blood. It doesn't explain what attacked Vincent. It doesn't explain why he took so long to heal. I had found Vincent at least 10 feet away from the bedroom and one person, supernatural or not, could *not* have bled enough to paint the *entire* apartment red. "I'm sorry, Devi."

"Yeah. You and me both," I muttered. My words barely audible. I stormed to the bed and crawled in. Vincent sat outside my door listening to me crying until neither of us had any tears left to shed...

When I bothered to notice anything in the room other than the man with the revolver in his jaw in the bathroom or whatever is giggling at the foot of the bed, I saw the clock. It's nearly six. I cried myself to sleep, losing the entire afternoon. I don't need him to save me. I can send these ghosts away with my own two hands. But Vincent leaving me in a room full...*this*...that's not like him. Neither is he choosing to put me in a house so full of paranormal activity knowing I'm a medium.

"Devi?" He knocked and waited for my permission. The second he entered, he and I were the only souls in the room.

"I think you scared them away."

"The phantoms?" I sat up leaning against the metal headboard.

"No. The Ramones." That went right over his pretty head. "Yeah, the ghosts, Vincent. You walked in and they vanished." He was about to speak but—"You know I'm a magnet to practically *all* things ghoulish, that I can see the dead and you *still* brought me to one of the *most*—"

"Devi—" he held his hand up and took his time walking to my bedside, "I would never *knowingly* bring you somewhere that would endanger you."

"Then—I don't understand. This apartment is—"

"The apartment *isn't* haunted, Devi. *You* are." That truth carved far deeper than I thought possible. "You're a Medium, yes, but you're capable of *more*. My people call those with your gifts Morseas. Dead ones. You can see and commune with the dead like your human Medium counterparts, but as a Morsea, the beings you can see and commune with—alive or dead—are not confined to this Realm alone. They cross *every* Realm."

"Great. I'm literally a universal Ouija board."

"A what?" You've gotta be kidding me?

"It's—don't worry about." I tried to rid the dead off my face, but it didn't budge.

"You're a powerful psychic, Devi. With proper training, you can control this ability."

"And that's what we'll do when the other Paladins arrive?" He nodded, his hands finding refuge in his pockets. "Why train me to perfect my psychic powers and witchcraft at all? That can take *months*. I need to go home. We need to get to a safer location. I—"

"Can I sit with you?" Vincent's question filled the room. I played with my hair, deciding whether to put it in a ponytail or leave the curly mess as is. When I realized my hair ties burnt to ash, I stared at my empty palms.

"Sure."

"Is this—your hand in mine—is this ok?" I nodded, completely taken aback. Vincent's energy radiated through my body the second he wrapped our fingers together. "Learning to hone your craft, to command your abilities at will, this will combat your fear. You cannot be afraid of the dark when you know how to fight what lives within it. As for time, we're going to give you a condensed crash course in as many arenas as possible."

"What would take months—you'll teach me in weeks?"

"No. What would take years to learn, we will help you conquer in *days*."

"I know I have a head start with already being a Rev and all, but Vincent, I don't—"

"It's a matter of awakening what already lies dormant within you, Devi." Vincent drew closer, his hand tangled in my hair. "I wish I could tell you that what's to come won't terrify you. I wish I could tell you that I can take you *home*, but—"

"You'd only be lying." A sigh fell from his lips, and it hung heavy in the space between us.

"Devi, I'm trying to protect you from m—" a twist in his face, the way his brows tried to reach each other— "I don't know all the pieces of the puzzle, but please believe me when I say I'll try to keep *our* pieces together for as long as I can."

"Why are you helping me, Vincent?" Brushing my overgrown bangs from my eyes, he pulled me to his chest, half smiling, half driving me out of my mind. Completely enraging the storm no one predicted outside.

"Because *not* helping you is the same as putting my gun to your head and pulling the trigger. Repeatedly." His words bit at me. Teeth digging in and not letting go. Vincent's eyes settled into mine, clearly sensing the proverbial damage of the irrevocable truth... Our foreheads locked, and he breathlessly breathed me in. "I'll not leave you to die, Devi." And *that* truth... Vincent wrapped me in his arms and pulled the blanket over our tightly tethered bodies. Yet, somehow, it *wasn't* enough. *I* wasn't close enough. It was as if I'd be snatched away if he loosened his grip on me. I reciprocated every touch. I couldn't remember the last time I had been embraced with conviction. I couldn't remember the last time I was held with such *wanting*...

We were like that for a long time. In the quiet, the dark. The sun shifting its small rays from one corner of the room to the other. My eyes gave way to a dream, but I didn't want to sleep. I didn't want to fall away from this moment. Tomorrow would bring the other Paladins and my training. Tomorrow would bring the reality of my situation front and center. I wasn't ready for the madness... Vincent planted a couple of kisses on my forehead before sinking down the pillow to meet my wavering eyes. "Sleep, little one. Dream. I will be where you are..."

# DAY 2

Vincent's distant voice woke me. His spot beside me, empty. I sat up, listening. Three a.m. had brought with it The Paladins.. Their words tangled in a hushed, intricate language spun from a time we've no record of. Vincent and his Paladins, the lot of them together…If you look close enough, you could see the glitter in the electrified atoms around you.

My curiosity danced with fear, but logic took control of the choreography and I stayed in the room. I stood behind the shut bedroom door; palm foolishly wavering over the handle. *Should I go out there? Should I check what's crying under the bed?*

"May I come in, Devi?" I registered the woman's Cockney voice from the other side of the door. *Don't let her in, Devi.* From the crippling crack behind me, I knew a demon found its way into my room and it broke its wrist trying to pull itself out from under the bed… *Don't turn around. Drown out its wet body dragging across the floor to you. Don't flinch at its breath on your neck...*

*Get out!*

I ran blindly out of the bedroom and—back *into* the bedroom? The door slammed shut behind me. The stench of the demon's blood nauseated me.

"Please God. *Please* let this be a dream." *Wake up, Devi. Find your exit.* Find—the demon's wrangled body climbed over the bed and made her way to me; grey skin bruised and scarred. A strange glowing marking on her forehead. She opened her mouth to smile and a steady stream of red bile and loose tissue dribbled over her freshly bit lips. She never severed her glinting eyes from mine. I couldn't get the Aramaic chant out fast enough—

"Devi?" Vincent took a step to me but everyone else—they

looked at me the way you look at someone who's got a bomb strapped to their chest.

And all the numbers were about to disappear.

"Why did she cast that spell, Vincent?" the British woman spoke again. We were all *outside* of the bedroom. The others stood in the hallway. Their armor was thin and malleable like leather but glinted like onyx stone and steel, embossed in ancient silver markings. I whipped around and pushed the bedroom door open. No low-level demon. Blankets free of stains. Floors perfect and smooth without a scratch…

"Devi, you were in between Realm, but you're safe now." Vincent's voice would've calmed me if it hadn't been for the lightning crashing in his chest, and consequently, mine.

"How did I—how'd I come back?"

"I found you." Vincent grabbed hold of my hand, gently prying my fingers from the metal bedframe. "Does this happen often? Encounters with lower-class demons? Porting between Realms?" Genuine curiosity was in him.

"I—I don't know." I answered too honestly. "I can't always control where I go when I'm asleep. If I Port or whatever to another Realm, it's just another nightmare to me. I don't always know the difference." The way Vincent swallowed—it made my mouth dry. "What's Porting, exactly?"

"Teleporting. We move in the blink of an eye from one place on earth to another or between realms." Why not call it Blinking, then?

"I've teleported once but no more than about 40 feet and it didn't come without a price. But, I've never Shifted—Ported, Blinked—" I took a breath, "to another realm. Consciously, at least."

"I'll show you how to navigate those planes." He somehow managed to center me. But the way everyone else gawked. Like I held a butcher knife to my throat.

"Devi?"

"Yeah, Vincent?"

"Can I have that, please?" he held out his hand to me, his eyes gently pleading.

"Have what—oh, my God." I held a fucking butcher knife to my throat...

"You're alright, love." The too cautious Cockney voice belonged to the blonde Paladin. "You know your way around magick and orbing. However, I think it'd be more suitable to obtain the blood for your spells from a less *fatal* area next time 'round." I agreed blankly.

"Orbing what now?" We were the same height so she bore her gray eyes into mine with ease. And maybe excitement...

"You willed that butcher knife to you from *this* side of the mortal Veil to where you were trapped on the *other* side. That's a gift not many in your world have."

"I—I don't think I've ever orbed anything let alone done *that*." A deep man's voice from the corner sent a shiver up my spine.

"Give a forest enough reason and it will swallow you whole." The Paladin nearly matched Vincent in height, his rich burnt whiskey beard completing his knight in shining black armor appearance. The way he looked at me, it was as if he was tired of my face, of all my bullshit already.

"It's true, then." The blonde woman spoke again. "You've truly no inclination of the full spectrum of your abilities." I shook my head, tearing my eyes from the heavy-hearted soldier. She dissipated the awkward air with proper introductions as only the British can. "I'm Amah." She put her armored hand to her chest. "The sweet one there is my husband Gavin, and the rude bearded brooding one in the corner is Melot. The redheaded Amazon is Andra. His wife." Amah never dropped her storm gray gaze from mine. She simply knew where each elite soldier of the LeMehti army was positioned. She took my hands from Vincent's and sat us in the living room. "I trust our leader, Vincent, has debriefed you of us?" He never went into detail, but I nodded. "Our kind, the LeMehti, we're the First Immortals. Literally what that moniker implies." The first immortals to walk the earth... Sure. I can totally process that. "Our people rule over The Court. It's a neutral territory with access to every Realm's underworld.

You would know it as Purgatory."

"So, you—"

"We are charged with ensuring souls are sent to their proper destinations. May it be their Heaven or Hell or reincarnation."

"But some still remain in Purgatory." No one spoke.

"Yes. You're quite clever, Devi."

"I'm really not. I've only read a lot over the years." Trying to figure out why I'm a magnet for the dead...

"There are those that we imprison in our Court for a time." Amah squeezed my hand. "Vincent, put the kettle on, please. We've a bit of a tale in store for this early morning hour, and as for the days ahead..." Amah wrapped her pauldron-covered arm around me while the others tried to get comfortable, armor glinting off artificial light and weapons at the ready. "Devi, there are those that wish you dead for what magick you have lying dormant within you."

"I've hardly any magick in me. What I know I've learned from *books*."

"And how long did it take you to learn those spells?" I looked at Amah then at the other Paladins and didn't know what to do with my hands...

"Not long."

"You are a natural born witch, Devi. One from a powerful and rare line. Add to that everything within you waiting to break free..."

"Who wants to kill me?"

"There's a sickness spreading across our empire." Vincent's words stunned everyone. Even the tea stopped steaming for a moment. And, I could have *sworn* Vincent clenched his jaw because I, uncontrollably, clenched mine. "Across Hell."

"*Hell* is after me?" Amah turned her full lips up in a smile for me. It almost reached her eyes...

"The soldier who meant to end you was LeMehti. Our empire and yes, Hell, want you dead for what you are. For what you will be able to do to us." Melot's words, they were distant and each one burned him to speak. Amah squeezed my hand and took my attention.

"Once fully infected—both sides will stop at *nothing* to have you, Devi. We are here to ensure they do not succeed."

"Amah, you're talking about *war...*" No one dared say a word. "*I'm* poisoning the LeMehti and DeKenna because I can-what? *Kill* you? How is that even possible?" No knife sharp enough could cut the tension in the room.

"How did you come to know the name of the demons, Devi? How did you know the reason for the war?"

"I don't know, Andra. My oh so fancy psychic powers?" I curled myself on the couch, wanting, more than anything, to have Vincent beside me and not Amah.

"Gotta give credit where credit is due. The lady, she's *not* wrong." Gavin answered with a sadness I don't think anyone expected out loud. He played with a dagger, Andra smiled at me, one leg crossed over the other, her hand tight around the rim of her breastplate.

"I'm sorry. This is *mad*. I'm not some immortal killing machine. I—I don't have anything worth starting a *war* over." I searched for Vincent in the crowd when the couch sunk in beside me. I looked over my shoulder to see Vincent. One hand wrapped around my waist, the other wiped away a rogue tear from my cheek.

"That is where you are gravely mistaken." Amah's voice twisted something inside Vincent. I looked to the others, but I was only met with darting eyes and silence. Static sparked at the edge of their barely exposed skin.

And as the atmosphere shifted, as the enchantments strengthened to protect me, to protect *all* of us, I knew—I *knew* there was *no* coming back from this.

Not *this.*

# DAY 4

I sat up, rubbing sleep from my eyes. When a tornado wreaked havoc inside my core, I realized who sat in the chair behind me. I looked to the slightly ajar door to see four bodies move about. The fifth, who'd been missing for hours, found his way into my room. A shadow...*staring* at me.

Somewhere off in his never-ending mind, Vincent sat silent. Hands in fists, eyes closed. Every muscle tight and ready for war. *What are you thinking about?*

He slowly opened his eyes, and it sent a shiver so harsh vibrating through my ribs, I had to hold my chest.

"You should eat quickly. You have another training session with Andra and then with—" Melot walked in with a plate of food for me.

"You and Amah. I remember the schedule. The three of us only spent the *all* of last night hacking my brain to perfect my memory and recall." I gestured to Vincent, myself and Melot.

"It's not been perfected, yet, Devi."

"My migraine and I are *painfully* aware," I said with a yawn. Melot set my breakfast on the nightstand and parted his lips to speak but decided whatever he was going to say would be better left unsaid. "Shift change, Vincent?" The Paladin leader shook his head and his second in command left without another word, gently shutting the door behind him.

"Why'd you refuse the break?" I said, far too bravely.

"It doesn't concern you." And we're back to *this*... To bite his head off or *not* to bite his head off? One look at the weakness clawing at his eyes, though, and I knew, beyond what my Empathic powers connected me with, to leave this burdened man be.

Half way through my meal, a thousand butterflies trembled in the pit of my stomach, rising an ache in my bones. The door opened; the handle cradled by Vincent's palm, and as it shut, it took Vincent away with it. And thanks to last night, I'll always remember him leaving me alone in a room where my reflection in the mirror sitting in the corner didn't quite...match.

"I'm sorry, Andra. I thought you said today's lesson of Devi's Psychic Gauntlet training involves the use of sound," I bowed for dramatic flair, "as a *weapon*." The nervous laughter couldn't be avoided. We curled up on the big couch with our tea, resting from combat training. A week ago I tripped over my own feet and fell into my dresser. Today, I learned Krav Mage. Yeah, no really. *All* of Krav Mage. Thank you perfect memory training.

Andra looked strange without her full suit of armor. They didn't even remove it when they shielded me as I slept. So, seeing them dressed as civilians... They did it to put me at ease but, for whatever reason, it distressed me further. Like something inhuman trying its *damndest* to appear just the *right* amount of human...

"Those were my words, Devi darling."

"Of course, they were." I took a gulp of my creamy spiced chai. "Next you'll tell me we'll materialize objects out of thin air." I gave her jazz hands as my eyes sought refuge in the tiny gap between the curtains; catching the afternoon sun on the tips of my fingers... it was awful quiet for a lesson on sound. When I turned my gaze to Andra, she tucked her wild crimson curls behind her silver-studded ear. My shoulders slumped. "We're going to materialize objects out of thin air..." she tried not to beam.

"Your work with Vincent is proving bountiful. Your connection to the future—and your empathic connection to *us*—is nearly at full force."

"We only had the *one* crash course. He—the training called for physical contact and, well," I set my mug down, "there were about 237 *thousand* different things he would have rather done than *touch* me."

"Devi, that's not—" her eyebrows danced, "that's unbelievably accurate."

"He may be an asshole," I muttered, tearing into my buttered croissant and carefully stretching my bruised legs, "but he's a good fucking teacher. Alas, he was one step ahead of me because I couldn't see what those many alternatives were."

"He did you a kindness."

"Did he now?"

"For all the magick within you, my wicked little witch, you are still *human*. Had you seen *that* many versions of reality all at once—"

"Right. Seizure. Stroke.—"

"Severed spinal cord."

"Well…" I scratched my chin, "nothing your lot couldn't heal me from." She raised a fed up brow. "Not—not that I *want* to be… internally dismembered." *apologize before she tasers you again with her damn mind like last time.* "I only meant—Sorry, Andra. Which do we start with?" Her grin. They love seeing me squirm.

"One of the most dangerous weapons any woman possess, dear." Andra leaned in, her cowl-neck top revealing her black immortal markings spiraling down the sides of her neck, across her shoulders. "Her *voice*."

"Well done, Devi." Melot leaned against the front door, arms crossed across his chest with a barely-there smile.

"Thanks, Melot. I—" His walnut eyes were hard, too hard even for him.

"Now, do *better*." And here I thought Vincent was the only one capable of stunning me into silence.

"Better?" I took off my oversized t-shirt and adjusted my tank top until it wasn't stuck to my sweaty skin anymore. "I found a *dozen* different species of animals, some *nasty* ass bugs in three different buildings across the street and *far* too many questionable *corpses* on *this* block alone. Given that I've never tracked—excuse me— *Hunted*—anything other than the occasional fuck to give, I think I did a rather splendidly." He rolled up his sleeves, the black cotton sweater nearly foreign on his body. Without their haunting onyx armor, the Paladins were too human. Mundane. Fragile.

"Your psychic abilities are rare. Profound, even. But ours, Devi, are *unimaginable*. We can see the past and present. Thousands of possible futures of every creature from any point on this planet. In nearly any Dominion. All we need do is choose."

"Ah. So, you're *not* all knowing." He did not appreciate my mouth.

"LeMehti are selectively omniscient."

"Are you *selectively* choosing not to tell me where Vincent keeps running off to? One minute the man won't leave my side and the next, he's nowhere to be found. It's been 2 *days* now, Mel."

"We can only find—and know—a number of pieces simultaneously, not *every* piece."

"So, we're just going to *completely* ignore my question about your antisocial leader. Okay." I muttered, putting my hair in a bun, getting ready for what was coming.

"We're not all gods or Fate." Say what now?

"Gods?" the intensity of his regret nearly made me put a bullet in my head...

"When you live as long as us, evolution is inevitable." The knot in my chest told me not to ask a follow-up question. So, instead—

"Is that why you see so many versions of the future? Because you're not able to know everything?"

"No, Devi." Melot put his messy hair in a tight, surprisingly non-ridiculous, manbun, his black armor manifesting and slowly wrapping around his body as he made his way to me. "Because we *shouldn't*. There's a reason we smithed weapons that pierce through our own skin and delay our healing.

There's a reason our armor is only *lightly* warded against beings of this planet's many underworlds."

"Balance."

"Power like ours, Devi..." I caught the swords he threw at me and willed me in a suit of their armor in the same motion, "it should not go unchallenged."

## DAY 9

"Try again. Try *harder*, Devi."

"Amah, I—I need a break. I'm still recovering from—getting my ass *handed* to me from Mel the other day." I had to swallow. "Gavin and I sparred for 3 hours straight this morning, and you and I have been at this Hypnos business for 45 minutes." I leaned over the foot of the bed. "When exactly will I have to put people to sleep? Or *keep* them asleep? Or make them dream what I want them to dream? Fucking shit...I can barely breathe let alone cast a spell *without* any incantations. I'm *not* like you. I *need* words. I *need* talismans and rituals. I may be a witch with pure magick or whatever but it's not like *yours*." I retreated to the bed and coiled my body haphazardly in the blankets; hugging both pillows as if my life depended on it.

"Breathing will be the *least* of your concerns if the enemy takes hold of you."

"Let them. Maybe then I'll get a nap." She slapped my denim-covered ass and my eyes shot open. "Damn! I was only joking. You know that's gonna leave a giant Amah-sized hand bruise on my ass—for days?" The immortal sneered at me, holding back her laughter almost as tight as the leather stretching across her powerhouse legs. The lace top she wore didn't carry any softness to it. How could it with someone as ancient as her beneath it? "Ok, *half* joking." Amah put her ocean-scented hair into a ponytail and sat beside me, healing my sad, flat butt. The golden color somehow managed to glimmer among the bleakness of the bedroom. The color of her hair, not the bruise on my ass.

"I know you are tired, but you must learn to battle through the limitations of your humanity and require only what you believe." I sat up, failing to ignore the crack in her heart that sent me trembling. "Let's try something else. What do you *want*, Devi?"

"Devi?" Well, *this* is fucking awkward.

"Yeah, Vincent?"

"What am I doing in your bedroom?" Did I orb Vincent from the *shower*? Before I could say anything that would embarrass me for a hundred lifetimes, Amah saved me.

"I'm continuing Devi's training in Hunting. I asked her to locate you. I was too focused on her to—"

"Notice that I'm in nothing but a towel?" Vincent's smile... it could sink ships. And the rest of his body...

"A thousand apologies." Amah was not apologetic and Vincent wasn't upset.

"I'm so sorry, Vincent."

"No harm done." Before he walked out he pierced his eyes into mine and said, "Was it easy, finding me?" The third wheel in Amah turned too tight in my stomach.

"Too easy." Think before you speak.

"Good." Vincent nodded with a smirk and walked out. Amah and I spoke on top of one another.

"See, Devi? He was rather agreeable with you."

"I thought your kind didn't have to worry about things like hygiene." I ignored her and asked her what truly ate away at me. "How on earth did I do that?" I looked at her, blindsided.

"What do you mean?"

"Amah, *none* of you have taught me how to use my remote viewing abilities—I mean—how to Hunt—a high-level Rev." She looked at me blankly. "A *supernatural* creature. Especially *immortals*. And you certainly haven't taught me how to *orb* one of *you*." I grabbed my pillow—hard.

"That we have not, love." She played with my chocolate curls. The hints of caramel and auburn shining with her touch.

"There's more to me than being a Reaper. More than having some ancient magick in me that's driven two empires older than time itself to murder anything in their path to get to me. And whatever it is was able to bring Vincent to me by my sheer *will*."

"But you and Vincent are Empaths. It is only natural for beings such as yourselves to—" her pink lips tried to curve into a smile, "be *aware* of each other."

"We can be aware of each other all we want. How did I teleport him from the bathroom down the hall to *here*?" I finally broke her down.

"One acts and the other—"

"Reacts."

"It's more than that, Devi. One acts and the other *knows*."

"Why does that scare you?" Why did that *terrify* Vincent?

"I'm not afraid of you, Di." She palmed my cheek in her gentle hand. "I am afraid *for* you..."

## DAY 11

Cabin fever settled deep into my skull. Between all my supernatural training in this human apartment, I needed a fix of the mundane. I made my way to the kitchen myself a cup of tea when my bedroom door opened. I took a step back to avoid getting hit in the face only to land on my ass.

"Are you alright?" Gavin said with a humble chuckle; helping me up with one hand while the other held a cup of—yup. Hot Earl Grey tea.

"Thank you. I was actually coming to get that."

"I know. Milk and honey, right?" He smiled through the words and crouched to my level. "You didn't see me coming?"

"There's a lot going on in here, Gavin." I pointed to my head. "On top of my lessons, since Vincent is helping me with my empathic ability, I've been getting an earful—or rather—a mind, body, and soul full of—"

"Everything?" I nodded.

"People's past and present, their emotions, the ghosts... I'm connecting to it all and *their* connections—they seem to interfere with my visions of the future. Did you have to choose such a populated apartment complex?"

"We had to choose a place this full of activity to help you acclimate. But, we should be able to help alleviate that some." Gavin stood up and scratched his stomach, scanning the room for dark and creepies.

"When are you going to teach me to Scan?"

"Oh. No can do on that, Devi. Scanning is unique to immortals. Hunting, however, is more rooted in the Old Magicks, that's why you have access to it. All your training has been to bring your current abilities to full force and to unlock all that's lying dormant. Both in your craft and your psychic abilities."

"So you've all said. But you're unlocking *more* than elemental magick and telekinesis. You're looking for something."

"Nothing more than your psychic abilities that will help save your life, Devi." I hated it, but I believed him. "So, it looks like we'll be bunking tonight." I smiled yet it wasn't terribly convincing. I could do nothing but stare at the swirling liquid in my hands.

"Vincent is patrolling. He'll be back soon." My heart, unsurprisingly, fell.

"Again? He came back last *night* from running recon," I said with a little too much bite.

"Given that we're quickly moving from the strategic level to the operational level of war, Devi, having the most powerful of us—of this *unit*—keep watch..." Gavin scratched his tawny stubble of a beard, taking care of his next words, "he's doing what he must to protect you." He smoothed the cotton of his heather grey shirt and made himself comfortable on the bed. The emerald glow of his eyes failing to soothe me.

"I know my way around a fight, around magick."

"That you do."

"I'm a *Reaper.* No one will teach me how to control that part of me or tell me how I became the only human Reaper on the planet, but it's what's marked me for death and taking you down with it." Gavin couldn't look me in the eye. "But, at the very least, this training, I can protect myself now. I can help all of *you* protect me." I begrudgingly went to my side of the bed by the window and plopped down, setting my tea on the nightstand.

Gavin breathed in for comfort and not necessity, his eyes finally settling into mine. But his mouth twitched with a dozen truths he couldn't let slip and it made my insides turn. The soldier who spent the day teaching me how to orb objects and teleport myself without the use of blood spells, without the use of *words* took my hand in his. "Not from this, Devi. Not from *this*." I'm not sure which stung more; the words that gutted me or the desperation in the man who had no choice but to pierce the blade.

"Hold on!" Gavin withdrew his attack. I raised an objective finger in his direction. "Are you *sure* Vincent ordered you to teach me swordplay in—which Realm are we in?" I rested my entire body weight on the hilt of the longsword whose top met with my sternum. *I miss my daggers*. I was dressed in the Paladin's embossed obsidian and silver armor. They warded it *extra* special for the human. Making it more metal than leather to protect me from, you know, *them*.

"Now Devi, would I bring you to this dark and desolate world for my own amusement?" He rested his Claymore across his shoulders and didn't bother wiping that boyish grin off his mouth. I caught my breath and rose a sweaty eyebrow of skepticism. "Our fearless leader did, in fact, order me to train you here. This is Evenfall. The borders of it, at least."

"I've read a bit about this." Gavin was ridden with surprise. "Evenfall Bridges are used to travel between other Realms. Not a place you wanna be for too long, though." I surveyed the shadow-painted field and trees around us. The vast expanse of it all. "For a realm that's meant to be a *bridge* between worlds—isn't Evenfall, I thought it was supposed to be a *tiny* little hallway..." *Wait...oh, my God. WAIT.* I straightened myself up, pierced my sword into the terra of Evenfall and made sense of the madness of my Persian curls in the breeze.

"Devi?"

"It's *bigger* on the *inside*!" Gavin looked at my wide eyes and dirt-ridden face. I didn't care that he didn't get my geeky reference. I jumped up and down. "It's bigger on the inside!"

"That's—um, yes. The borders can expand to whatever size you require—Devi? We need to continue combat training. Your body has to acclimate to various environments and realms in the event that—*and* she's humming—"

"Is this where you store your weapons?"

"Yes, this is where we keep our weapons. We alter the size of the—"

"Hmm. Could *I* use Evenfall Bridges? My reading lacked in that regard." I unearthed my sword and adjusted my breastplate in response to a premonition I had about Gavin attacking me.

"If you want to visit Avalon. Absolutely." He walked over to me a bit too sternly.

"Why do I get the feeling my field trip would be as grim as your face."

"Look around you. These borders are devoid of life. It's perpetual twilight. Evenfall is a means to an end, Devi."

"I noticed. I can barely see you."

"Your enemies won't hand you a flashlight." I have

enemies... "There are no distractions here. You should have visions of my future attacks. You should *sense* my movements empathically."

"I totally would. However, I can't when you and your lovely obsidian armor are blocking me. Which means this is also a lesson in breaking through psychic shielding."

"Your deception skills are improving. It took me longer to tell that you were lying." Yeah, twelve seconds longer.

"What gave it away?"

"You prepped for my attack. If you want the enemy to believe your lie, you have to believe it *with* them. Then, strike when they least expect it."

"What if the lie goes against everything that I am?"

"Then you lie *harder*." A jolt of sorrow flooded my chest.

"You know what's coming, don't you?" his green eyes dulled.

"I know you'll have to put on a show—and I have to teach you to make it flawless." We sparred for ten minutes before I figured something out.

"It's a mock defense, the obsidian."

"So, then how do you attack my mind?"

"I haven't quite learned how to break through *LeMehti* psychic barriers."

"What *have* you learned?"

"That I need these Bridges to do what you can without their aid. For example, how to throw you through a Bridge to Jupiter. I think that one over there will take you to Olympus." Gavin laughed and I welcomed the sound knowing it wouldn't be something I'd hear much of the next few sessions.

"Can you do this without needing to touch me?"

"Vincent and I haven't finished that lesson in orbing yet... our sessions never last very long." I wiped my bloody lip. "So, do they know we're here? The rulers of this place, I mean? I'd rather not give Atropos a reason to cut our lives short. Get it? See what I did there—oh shit!" Gavin's sword came crashing down on mine. I barely blocked him in time.

"I'd prefer you not ask questions like that." Gavin attacked again, his sword thundering against mine. Sparks illuminating the dead space around us.

"What about a teeny, tiny, inquiry behind Vincent disappearing after every one of our training sessions—what few of them we have?" I fought back until I matched his movements, *without* the need of my supernatural abilities.

"Coincidence."

"You didn't even *try* to hide that lie."

## 11:47 P.M.

I couldn't tell you what exactly it was that woke me from my dream of the White Cottage. Whatever it is that is Vincent called to whatever it is that is me. I searched for Gavin's body, but it had long departed. Vincent sat at the foot of the bed, head in his hands. The muffled sounds of his crying quivering on my lips...

"Vincent?" I reached for his shoulder, but Vincent flinched.

"How—Devi, you're awake." How did he not know?

"How can I be asleep? You're...hurting." The drop in his face—I wasn't meant to awaken and yet, I did. "Your pain, it's a burning brick in my lungs." I rubbed my chest. Vincent's glowing blue markings from beneath his sweater were the only light in the room, but they were dimmed. Sadness will do that, I guess.

"Is that what woke you?" He slid over to me and placed his hand over my chest. Immediately, the ache, the fire, vanished.

"*You* woke me. It was—"

"A pull." His voice was a sweet murmur. I nodded. The droplets fell slowly at first, then down in a rush. We took note of the unexpected rain. "We're doing that, Devi. I haven't figured it out, but it's us. You and me. We..." I combed my fingers through his black hair. When he took my hand in his, a jolt of energy filled my veins and it warmed me to the core. "Devi, I'm scared. Scared that whatever I do *won't* be enough to save you. That I'll have to do something there's *no* coming back from." His tears flowed into my eyes. The fear in him crawling up from the tips of my toes until it wrapped itself around both our necks.

Vincent took me in his arms, the fright in us quickly melting away as lightning struck in the streets. I held him tight and the wind answered our embrace with a howl rattling the window. But it was when Vincent kissed my forehead that the atoms in the room lit up. An endless sea of stars flickering like fireflies…

"Devi," I stood up to catch the tiny sparks. He followed.

"Are we setting *atoms* on fire?" Vincent reached for the same cluster of brightly burning death, our fingers brushing. He took my hand, and I couldn't deny the calm that coursed from him to me.

"Yes." Thunder echoed behind his words. Our bodies molded together without thought. His skin was my own. My breath in his lungs.

"We have to learn to control this, Vincent." He pulled me into him, protecting me from the fires. We stood there and watched, helpless, as piece by piece, the world fell apart…

"There's no controlling this, little one. Only *surviving* it."

## DAY 12

"What the hell is going on?" Gavin grabbed me from the bed and took me to the corner of the bedroom when Amah and Andra barged in, bodies in full suits of armor.

"They're Scanning. Tracking. Scouring a few thousand possible futures until they find the true one, checking the present and past of everything for miles for any clues." Andra set her fist ablaze, matching Amah's while the other gripped tight a Claymore sword nearly as tall as her Amazonian frame.

"Right. So, like scrying, except not at all. How could I forget?" I muttered, leaning against the wall. Palm to forehead. The two women stood back to back; one scanning out the window, the other seeing beyond the walls. Both ready to annihilate *anything* that touched me. And Gavin—Gavin vanished along with Melot.

"Any word, Amah?"

"Nothing yet, Andra."

"Did you see that? Right there. Damn him."

"Yes. Shit. Probability of attack?"

"Tonight? None. But we should still—"

"Yes. We should."

"Is it the DeKenna?"

"No, Devi. Vincent wanted us to follow up on a potential threat. Everything is as it should be. You can go back sleep. We will stay with you tonight."

"Is that why Vincent left me in the middle of the night? To check on this *threat*? Why isn't he back yet? You Port at the speed of *thought*."

"Let's get you into bed, Devi." Andra grabbed my shoulder, while Amah took a quilt, covering the mirror in the room and I could not fight the urge to shut my eyes...

"What are you—where did Gavin and Melot go? I don't want—where's Vin—"

"Sleep, Devi. Vincent may have left, but he *will* come back."

# DAY 13

I stood outside the second bathroom in the hall looking at the back of Melot's head. He sat in the living room for our training session. 'Another lesson in elemental magick' he had said. But the front door was only 15 feet away. I could make it. I could run and open the door and start screaming bloody murder.

"You may not believe this now, but you are far safer *here*, with us, than out there." Mel's words crawled into my ears with an itch I had to scratch.

"Can you read minds?" He actually laughed. It wasn't clear if it was at my words or at me flinching at his.

"It doesn't take a telepath to know what you're thinking, Devi." He ran his hand through his shaggy brown hair, trying to fit his towering frame in the tiny couch. These soldiers, these *Paladins*... my hands...why am I shaking?

I balled my hands into fists and squeezed as tight as I could; my nails digging into my palms; the blue flames tickling my fingers were not intended. The voices outside amplified. Tangled. I couldn't distinguish their words. Melot walked over to me. He spoke, but I couldn't hear him over the screaming. I couldn't take it anymore.

I ran to the door and opened it. The handle melted off.

I opened it only to see the living room.

I turned around and the front door was shut. Andra stood guard at its pristine handle.

"What did you do to me?"

"Why did you run?" The words fell from Andra's lips like a ton of bricks. My mind reeled...Andra's voice brought my focus to her. Her black leggings. Knee high boots. Her fucking navy blue sweater dress that did *nothing* to conceal the outline of her gun and dagger underneath.

"Devi, you were terrified by whatever you heard outside."

"Enough to channel the flames I haven't taught you about yet." Melot's words sent a shiver down my spine.

"But you were *not* frightened enough to run directly *into* it." Andra was equal parts impressed and distressed. The flames around my fists cleared. My skin unburnt.

"Are you telling me you didn't hear the choir of horror outside? All those people *screaming*?" They had these heartbroken faces. The ones you give a small child when they've uncovered a wicked truth about life, but you want to keep their innocent minds safe a bit longer, so, you lie through your pretty little teeth to protect them. At least, until morning.

"You were brave to—"

"You need to go *help* them, Andra. Something's happening out there. Something *violent*. Why aren't you—" In that moment, with the faint sunlight of the morning star creeping in through the slits of the drapes and reflecting the dust floating in the air, it hit me...

There was *no* massacre.

I had a vision of the past... and I couldn't—for the life of me—tell the difference.

"Come along, Devi. I'll make us a cuppa." Andra's Pre-Raphaelite features softened and she disappeared into the kitchen while Melot gestured his hand to the couch. Melot sat beside me, exhaling. Disappointment—no. *Worry* ripe in his breath..

Andra came back with a tray of tea and biscuits, 'cause, you know, we're fancy like that. I had to admit, I welcomed the warmth of the drink, the sweetness of the butter cookies and the surprisingly pleasant lesson about the mechanics of the flames I conjured. For the first time, in a long time, I didn't feel out of place.

I realized how tightly I clutched my mug and decided to set it on its tray. There was something amiss in the space, though. Something resonating from my teachers and I couldn't help but—

"Where are Vincent and the others again?" I asked, not looking either of them in the eyes.

"Running recon."

"Patrolling." They both spoke in unison.

"So, which is it? Or do you need a minute to get your story straight?" Annoyed glances were thrown my way. "I need Vincent to teach me how to travel through time so I can fast forward to the less cringy parts of this—oh wait. I can't. He's conveniently disappeared. Again."

"You cannot learn that which a Breaker knows, Devi." The grimness in those words rattled us all. "Your lessons on deception with Gavin should give you a proper answer." Melot bit at me.

"He's a good teacher. I know you're both lying.

"Are we?" Melot took a bite out of a cookie. His first *ever*... "It's one thing to detect deception, Devi. It is an entirely different beast to untangle the web within."

"You are an Empath, Devi. It is in your nature to channel matters such as this. And with time, this power will strengthen and *evolve*. However," Andra adjusted her clothes and leaned toward me, "if you are to uncover the truth, you must first conquer the lie."

## DAY 15

"You're resisting."

"I'm *not*." Amah threw the pillow at me. I was to remove the stuffing from the case.

"You're literally squishing your entire bloody face to keep from using your power, you tart."

"First of all, rude. And second, I don't wanna use this *power*." Amah hopelessly shook her head in her hand, and sat beside me on the couch. "Where are Vincent and the others? After our crash course on glamour magick, he—wait for it—*left*." I was thankful for the extra-long sleeves of my black shirt. I tugged on the sleeves and balled them into my hands.

"Vincent and the rest of the team are keeping us safe, love."

"Aren't we protected from everything in *here*? Why leave?

Amah?" I reached out for her shoulder but she dodged me as gracefully as only *she* could. My touch—I'd be able to channel the truth from one of the oldest beings in existence. I'd become *that* strong already…

"Devi, we need to continue training, yeah?" She left the couch and walked about the room.

"Okay, Amah." *Don't be a brat.* "So, this power, this skill that we're to bring to the surface—object manipulation?" Her gray eyes glinted as she returned.

"It differs from telekinesis, Devi. Rather than moving matter *through* space, you Blink it—as you like to refer to it as—from one point of space to another. Like Porting."

"What will I need this for, Amah?" I hit a nerve. The Paladin took a step to me, leaning over. The storm in her eyes wild with a reality I wanted no part of.

"Disarming opponents, retrieving weapons," she took another step, her golden hair swaying over her shoulder, "extracting the skeletons of your enemies where they stand…" the truth dawned on me too easily and far too late than it should have.

"You're not training me to defend myself, are you? You're all teaching me to *kill…*"

"We're teaching you to *survive*. Never confuse the two. *Never*."

## DAY 16

I woke when the dead man in the mirror cocked back his gun and put a bullet in his head... It was as if the revolver went off in my head. I didn't shake from the crack of the gunshot. I only blinked my eyes. Blinked and saw Amah, for a second, in the mirror. Did she see? It didn't matter. Not when the dead man in the mirror cocked back his revolver and put a bullet in his head...It was as if the revolver went off inside my head....

Don't get trapped in his loop.

I grabbed the green quilt from the bed and threw it over the full-length mirror tucked in the corner of the room. I gave Amah a quick smile while I rubbed the ghost's quivering lips out of mine.

"So, we've been here a while. Shouldn't we change locations?" I hid my hands in my hoodie pouch. "Any idea when we're leaving? We can't train me forever."

"Humans constantly run to keep themselves safe." Amah crossed her legs, her ringed hand resting atop her knee, "Despite what you may—" her eyes darted to the mirror then to her gently coiling fist, "experience, we're able to protect you." She stood and took a few steps to me, her body as close to sincere as I'd ever seen it. "You don't have to run for your life, Di." Before I had the chance to run into her arms, the door opened.

"Devi, are you ready?" Melot walked in. "It's time for our lesson." Amah smiled at me and turned me over to the grumpy man in black.

"I know. Don't tell me. We're covering immortal modes of transportation today."

"Devi."

"What? Amah, I'm only curious how Porting works."

"You want to know why it will kill you." She put her hands on her hips.

"Well, damn, Amah. Yeah. That too, I guess." I shrunk into myself.

"It will tear you apart from the inside out. That's why, when the time comes, orders are to run." Melot grew impatient with every word. He held the door wide open, his markings glimmering the slightest from the sides of his neck.

"Spells have already been cast so that your body is safeguarded against—" I held up a finger.

"Spells have been what now, Amah?" she answered me with my cheek in her palm.

"You're a Reaper but you're still *human*."

"If we don't weave our magick into you, the forces of gravity at the speeds *we* run will kill you, Devi." There was the tiniest crack in Amah's perfect voice.

"And you can't slow down."

"Not when your *life* is at stake, Di." Amah nodded at Melot, sending me his way. I gathered my senses.

"Let's go, Devi."

"What's it going to be today, Mel? Synchronicity? Remote viewing? *Ballet*?" I put my hair up in a bun, chuckling, and adjusted my hoodie with a little pirouette. But what he said instead...

"Compartmentalization."

## DAY 17

I thought I heard birds chirping, but their song was too distant. "You're bleeding." Vincent's voice rivaled a whisper. I opened my eyes and wiped my nose with my sleeve. "Let me—"

"No." I recoiled from his helping hand. "I don't need magickal healing. It's only a nosebleed." He sat back in the stool beside me at the breakfast bar.

"I'm pushing you too hard."

"You're teaching me how to telekinetically lift a 50-lb Claymore off the counter. Seeing as how I never moved anything with my mind before a week ago, I'd say little epistaxis is warranted." I left to grab some paper towels.

"How did you know the weight of the Claymore?" I finished wiping my nose and took my seat, shrugging.

"You must've told me." He cocked his head, narrowing his eyes.

"You have perfect recall now. You know I didn't." There

used to be squirrels that came by the windows. They don't come by anymore... "Your psychometry—it's progressing."

"Are you telling me I don't have to touch something to know its history anymore?"

"I'm saying, with time, you'll be a force to be reckoned with." He grabbed the weapon and threw it in the small pocket of space beside him.

"Did you just fling that sword into Evenfall? The Fates are going—"

"What? No."

"That sly son of a bitch." I failed that part of the lesson with Gavin *horribly*.

"Gavin told you we use *Evenfall* to—that son of a bitch. Although, I'll give Gavin credit for his lesson on deception."

"Yes. He did such a wonderful job teaching me that." Vincent tried to be serious but I did get him to chuckle.

"Come here, Devi." We walked around the breakfast bar. "We don't cut through the Veil or through the territory of the Fates, or their borderlands, to store our weapons." He waved his hand and the space in front of us rippled and in that small circle, the image of the kitchen faded and a black hole emerged; Vincent's Claymore, and a few other munitions, resting within. "The Veil separates and protects the human realm from every other realm. We'd never tear into it."

"Vincent?"

"Yes, Devi?"

"Is that a fucking *black hole*?" His eyes darted trying to find an answer that wouldn't alarm me.

"It's a small part of one that we have access to."

"Oh, yeah. A *small* part of a *black hole* that you have full access to—yeah. Totally *nothing* profound about that sentence whatsoever." I was about to go open the curtains to look out the window when I immediately stopped myself. "Sorry. I forgot."

"Don't apologize for wanting to look at the trees, Devi..." Vincent closed the pocket of literal space and met me at the window. "I need to take you to Evenfall."

"They don't like frequent visitors. I've been there *three* times already with Gavin and Andra."

"I need to show you how to fling your foes to other dimensions."

"You can't do that from here?" before he could answer me, "That's not a psychic ability."

"It very much is." Well, shit. "You have to see the different Bridges before you can will people to them in the future."

"Vincent, the Fates—"

"The Fates are in their castle, safe and sound and far away from us. We are the *least* of their concerns at the moment. Their borders and the Bridges are neutral territory unless someone gives them reason to the contrary."

"They don't like me. Their disdain is in my *bones* every *second* I'm there." Vincent put a hand on my shoulder and it brought a wave of relief.

"Better the disdain of Fate than her *sword*." I hadn't even thought of their queen… "Is there a doorway here?" I surveyed the kitchen and spotted a doorway behind the fridge. "Good. Let's open it."

After nearly an hour of hurling and Blinking household items into various realms and planets, Vincent let me take a break. "Can we go back now?" I sat on a rock, more drained than any of my combat training.

"Not yet. Devi—" Vincent kneeled in front of me, "did you see that Bridge there?"

"The iridescent one that's barely visible between the Bridges to Tartarus and Hell? Yeah. Clocked that the *moment* we arrived. This is a different border so I know to familiarize myself with the area. If that was a test—"

"I'm not testing you, Devi. Listen to me." There was hesitation in him when took my hands in his, but the moment he touched me—he let out a breath, his eyes emitting the softest glow on our skin. "There's a future where you may be taken. Where—where I *won't* be there to help you. If that comes to pass, I need you to run *here*. To *that* Bridge."

"But, *that's* the Bridge to—"

"You'll be safe until I can get to you." His eyes trailed away from mine. This contingency plan that all the Paladins had agreed upon, apparently, was not an easy decision to come to. I couldn't glean any more than that from his touch. His mind was off into the worst case scenario that neither of us wanted to see.

"You *will* get to me, right Vince? You'll find me?" I dared take his face in my hands and my body couldn't help but slip to the ground to his. And when Vincent wrapped his arms around me, pulling me to his chest until our hearts beat as one…

"I'll find you, Devi. I *will* find you…"

## DAY 18

I hadn't seen Vincent in days. Our last training session—it left him in pieces. His presence came and went every few hours. Like a wave never too certain if it wants to crash against the shore.

Amah was missing. She guarded me last night but she was nowhere to be found. It could've been the lack of her protection that woke me, or the voices in the other room. I sat up in time to hear the fading of whispers. I rubbed the frustration from my body and swung my legs over the bed, readying myself to get up. But, before I finished stretching, I noticed something.

The mirror faced the wall. The quilt covering it.

I walked over despite my instincts to stay put. The closer I got, the quicker the temperature in the room dropped. I raced the last few steps, turned the mirror, grabbed the quilt from the looking glass, and flung it behind me.

I saw my reflection.

It was broken.

The mirror had been cracked, as if someone had punched it from the other side.

"Oh, you're up." The word fell from Amah's lips with a disappointment that barreled through me.

"Amah, what happened to the mirror?" A lovely smile painted itself across her face. *So* lovely, in fact, I knew it housed bullshit.

"Don't mind that. Come now. The others won't be back for a while. You should sleep." I sighed as my face dropped. She went over to the bed and got it ready to tuck me in all nice and cozy. I walked right up to her.

"Amah." No response. "*Amah.*" Louder. "What happened with the mirror?"

"You need to sleep." If she fluffs that pillow one more time...

"How about I don't, and you answer me."

"The quilt fell during the evening because someone, some*thing* tried to break through from the other side. Devi, I'm here to protect you and that is exactly what I've done. Now please, love, get into—"

"Do I have Briar Rose tattooed on my forehead the last three days"

"Devi—"

"No." I walked backwards a few steps. "You know, I think given *everything,* I've handled things about as well as one would imagine. Being a walking Ouija board. Having a bulls-eye on my back for soulless immortals—"

"They're not soulless. It's a *poison*—removing any shred of life—it eats away at the victim's soul until it has nothing left within it. The end result is madness."

"Excuse me. *Hollow* souls. What I'm *not* handling with quite as much decorum lately is *you* four fucking slipping me magickal roofies every two fucking minutes! And let's not even get started on how *rapey* all that is or how this just so happened to start when Vincent goes AWOL." She looked away from me as if the truth of my words slapped her in the face. I pointlessly adjusted my oversized shirt. "Now, what I want to do is have some coconut ice cream that I *know* is going to be waiting for me in that freezer. What I will *not* be doing is *counting sheep*."

I stormed through the living room making eye contact with the little girl and her broken porcelain doll for only a second before ignoring the blood pouring from her slit throat. "I'll deal with *you* later." I muttered.

I opened the freezer with a spoon in my hand, bowl be damned, and saw precisely what I thought would be in there: Coconut ice cream.

I grabbed the pint and sat at the breakfast bar and started munching like it was my fucking job; starting with the remnants that are on the lid. I heard Amah mumble something to herself in her tongue from the living room. Is she casting the ghost away? Why bother? There'll be another one soon enough. Death magnet, remember?

"I'm going to patrol the area." My spoon fumbled out of my hand, clattering on the counter from Amah's voice when she walked in the kitchen.

"Wait." The thought sprinted to my mouth. "You're leaving me *alone*?" I cried out, doe-eyed and breathless..

"I need to help the others patrol, but Vincent will no longer be AWOL. He'll be here soon." This news only left me twisting.

I put another spoonful of ice cream into my mouth. The cold of it desperately trying to influence the fire on my tongue.

She sighed and met me at the breakfast bar.

"Look, no one here is blind. We're taking measures to ensure matters remain as normal as possible for you, for all of us, Di."

"Explain to me again how holing *me* up in a *haunted* house would accomplish that? Better yet," I pushed my dessert aside, "how does me slicing into people with my shiny new toys 'ensure matters remain *normal*'?" Her jaw clenched, locking the truth inside.

"It doesn't. It keeps you *alive*." She cocked her head, as if she heard someone calling her name. "Vincent is close. I'm-"

"I'm pretty sure he wants nothing to do with me." Maybe I *should* have a date with the Sandman. At least I won't say stupid shit like that. "I mean, when he is with me, it's as if he can't breathe and now... now, he runs *away* from me."

"It may prove *difficult* for him to be in your company, but he *will* be. Take comfort in that."

"How about I don't, and we pretend I do, and you tell me the *whole* truth rather than sprinkle it in cryptic doses and talking to me like I'm five." Amah pushed herself off the counter. Her blond hair bouncing brightly against her black sleeveless turtleneck tunic.

"Eat your ice cream, Devi. There won't be anything of the sort where we're headed." She left. LeMehti armor and weaponry wrapping themselves around her limbs before she effervesced into nothing.

I stared at my spoon for a long moment before digging it into the slowly melting treat... then shoved the thing away. I sighed and leaned back in the stool, rubbing my temples; my pounding migraine demanding my attention. I closed my eyes with the hope that when they open, I'd be home.

I saw Vincent in the doorway and nearly fell off the barstool.

His face found some semblance of comfort in his palms as he took Amah's spot at the bar across from me. Vincent ran freshly bloodied knuckles through his hair and looked at me; the blues of his irises both the darkest and brightest things in the space. Why hasn't he healed?

Vincent's gaze shifted to my ice cream then back at me. He made his way to the freezer and came back with another pint of coconut ice cream and second favorite flavor that wasn't in the freezer earlier. A Snicker's bar with waffle cone bits in it.

I couldn't help but check the walls. The lids toppling onto the counter brought back my attention. He scooped out a few helpings of the Snicker's into a bowl and slid it over my way. We looked at each other; his heart pulsated in his neck. A car alarm outside broke the silence and jumpstarted us and we shamelessly ate our junk food; the moments calming him from whatever caused his fists to strike with such force that I was having trouble keeping my hands from shaking...

It did not go unnoticed.

Vincent made a beeline for the exit. He tossed his spoon into the sink and hid himself away into the bedroom next to mine. I sat there, dumbfounded.

With a defeated sigh falling to the counter, I cleaned up. When I went to wash the dishes, I nearly dropped the bowl; my spoon met with the floor and the shriek it let out was simply too loud. The sink had fractured; the fissure reaching up to the window frame above. And the spoon Vincent had used *shattered.*

I clutched on to the dishware as I fought to keep my tears at bay. I want to go home. I want to wake up. Why is he acting like this? Something is wrong. No. Maybe he simply hates me for whatever I'm doing to his people. It's not hatred though, is it? It's something *more*; something darker...

Violent.

The dishes toppled into the sink. I fell into myself onto the floor. I didn't care if he heard me crying. I didn't care if he could *taste* the salt of my tears on *his* tongue. Her hand on my shoulder was soft, but there was gravel in her voice.

"I'm sorry you're sad, miss." The little girl with the bleeding throat gifted from her drunk father. She hugged me and it was the sweetest thing I'd experienced in months. "My daddy is mean to me, too. But Momma said that, one day, when I'm done crying, I'll look up and Daddy will be gone." She smiled, not knowing that she's dead. Not realizing she'd gotten her blood all over me. That her father is creeping up behind her. So, I decided to do something I hadn't done in a while.

"Close your eyes, Cora. When you open them, your dad *will* be gone. I promise." The four-year-old shut her eyes and I touched my palm to her forehead. We hadn't covered exorcisms yet in training, so, I had to do this old school. I chanted in ancient Latin and, a moment later, she effervesced. As for her father... he'd go mad soon enough without his plaything. They always do. Yet, that didn't stop him from raising his knife and start towards me; a grin worthy of Hell and breath that filled the back of my throat with Scotch.

"Come closer. I dare you." I spat at him with a smirk getting myself off the ground. I took a steak knife from the drawer, slit my palm, and cast a spell with my blood on the counter, he disappeared... in the most painful way I've *ever* seen, but it had nothing to do with my magick.

I flung the blade into the sink and made my way to Vincent's room. *Now* he gives a shit? But not enough to be bothered to be in the same *room* as me? I stormed in, ready to rip him a new one when the gale inside of me dwindled to a breeze.

The place had been ransacked. Bed flipped over. Dressers thrown across the room. Walls fractured and curtains torn with fragments of glass trapped within their fibers. The light pouring from the windows *too* bright. The glow abnormal. As if the rays grew hotter to burn away something vicious in their path. None of my training could have prepared me for this...

Vincent held himself up against a wall. The blood on his hands replaced with ash. There was an ache in my chest. My body too heavy. Were we underwater? How did I not hear this chaos? Vincent finally faced me. And, when he did, the entire space reverted to its original state in the Blink of an eye. That's when it happened; a slight tingle in my hand. I *almost* forgot all about my cut. I checked and it was completely healed and blood-free.

It took me a long time to muster up the nerve to find his face again. When I did, he was nowhere to be found.

Shit.

The pounding, the endless burning in my mind magnified the second Vincent and I separated. I searched the entire apartment to no avail. Even dared to Hunt him but Vincent is the strongest of the Paladins. If he wants to remain hidden, even from *me*, he will be. That didn't stop me from checking outside. but the front door wouldn't open. I banged and kicked and screamed but was met with nothing. I'm trapped and bound to this apartment. And all of my supposed protectors gone.

Cue the disembodied voices.

I shook the shock from away and ran to my room. I shut the door as gently as I could. Somehow, though, I couldn't manage to loosen my grip of the handle. I couldn't peel my aching head from the wood. Come on, Devi. Deep breath. In and out. This is why you stopped using magick. Stopped performing exorcisms.

A couple started shouting at each other upstairs and that snapped me back to reality. And that's when it hit me; *this* is why Amah and the others have been casting the Hypnos spell on me. They've been trying to keep me from seeing murdered children... Why resort to magick tricks when they can banish the dead and damned with a thought? They're preserving their energy. No. They're using all their energy on something *else*. All their focus and power is elsewhere and the best way they can triage my bullshit curse is—I'm such an asshole.

I didn't bother with the lights. I crawled into the bed and wrapped myself haphazardly with the blanket; boots on and all. Though I hadn't done it in a long time, setting the little girl free and preparing my mind and body for the second exorcism for the dad took a toll. It wasn't as exhausting when I did it on a regular basis. But I had to stop. The strain went beyond my body. If it wasn't for my proclivity for bending the truth, I would've been cast away to Illinois' finest mental hospital. And now, now I almost wonder if I ever did talk my way out of being admitted...

I closed my eyes but all I could see was the writhing ghost, the dying child, and the broken guardian. When the knocking started, when the laughing literally bled through the walls, I opened my eyes.

I didn't answer the door.

I didn't answer when the voices asked the question.

And when the door creaked open…

Vincent stood in the doorway. He tried smiling through his exhaustion.. I sat up, one foot on the ground. I wonder if he heard the question. The cracking of my knuckles, that he heard for certain.

"May I come in, little one?" His towering form hunched under the entry. I nodded and he walked in, closing the door behind him, taking away all the artificial light with it and leaving us in the dark. The midnight blue of his eyes our only firelight.

He took calculated steps. His movements nearly made the room move… or is it me?

Vincent flicked on the lamp housed on the nightstand beside me and a warm glow coursed through the small prison. I ignored the ghost latched to the ceiling. I couldn't pay attention to the demon scratching at the window.

When Vincent's eyes found mine, I realized something in their large almond shape; the shine of the lamp had no effect on them. One more thing to set these people apart from me. One more thing to remind me that I'm in the presence of absolutely *nothing* human.

"They can't hurt you."

"What did you say?"

"The low class demon outside. The ghost on the ceiling. They can't hurt you." He leaned against the no longer bleeding wall beside the window. Arms crossed over his chest; the fabric of his black sweater stretching over his skin, practically suffocating him.

"If you're here to keep me safe, how did you let them—" The monsters vanished in hushed screams. Vincent willed them out of existence with mere *thought*... The laughter echoed until it, too, disappeared.

Strands of his thick black hair masked his face, hardly deterring the creature within. Leave it to the Fates to put me in a dimly lit room with *him*. I curled up my knees to my chest, wrapping my arms around them.

"Don't you see everything?" He shook his head, putting his hands in his pockets.

"We need to brush up on your memory training."

"You've told me this already?" He nodded.

"The last few weeks—you're allowed grace, Devi."

"And you?" his eyes glinted, filling the room with a faint blue haze.

"I'm here..." he held my gaze but I dropped it. Vincent cleared his throat.

"When it comes to the future—we see the *true* future but it's hidden within *thousands* of possibilities of it."

"It takes time for you to find your way." he nodded, trying to smile.

"Breaker or not, the past and present become difficult to navigate. That's why it took me so long to help you with the girl's father."

"Like when I channel the past. It's as if I'm there. Living through it. There's no break from the vision and reality. But to have to dig your way through what *you* see..."

"Our visions aren't always that disorienting. But we manage." He scratched his neck and I rubbed an ache in mine.

"What if there's a situation with *more* than one future that's set in stone?"

"You're working under the presumption that the future cannot be undone. Stones can break, Devi. Time isn't a straight line. It's complicated but—"

"Manageable." We both chuckled. Vincent *laughed*.

"You're more powerful than you give yourself credit for, you know."

"I'm psychic, Vincent. The kind that makes an ancient race of immortals want to kill me dead, but, you know."

"What makes you different, what makes you *powerful* enough for the dead, the *demons,* to get through *my* defenses is because of the *kind* of psychic you are."

"A lot of italics in that sentence." He adjusted his sweater, billowing it for ventilation. "I'm the kind that can see dead people. Channel the past, glimpse the future. The demons join in when the mood strikes. And some other cool things with my training."

"You do that a lot, don't you?"

"Do what?" His smile...

"Create armor with words." My hands dug into my legs. Vincent's gaze never wavered from mine. "You take reality and push it as far away from you as possible," hesitation dwelled heavy in his mouth as he sat beside me. I played with the blanket.

I grew tired of the strands of hair in my eyes. The instant my hand moved, his found my cheek and tucked my curls behind my ear. His touch lingering...

"Madness takes no prisoners, Devi. Not with us and *especially* not with *you.*" My eyes shot up at his. Surprise and vindication filled my veins. It's one thing to know something to the very core of your being. But, having that truth, *your* truth be evident in the eyes of another... "I think—" his face twisted with something, the glow of his eyes fading, "I think you're always on the edge of peace. One wrong move. One day too many of keeping all the lies together..." he related far too well.

"Why are you saying all this to me?"

"Because," his hand gently dropped from my cheek and rubbed his chest and I had the urge to do the same. "I want you to know that we're not the monsters in your story." The question, the question kept banging in my mind over and over.

"You never told me what kind of psychic I am to put *your* defenses out."

"*All* of them." I swallowed. He white-knuckled his knees.

"We wouldn't be able to train any of your abilities if they weren't already dormant within you."

"We've already had this discussion, haven't we?"

"When Mel and I honed your memory and recall."

"How ironic." I couldn't look at him. "While we're on the subject, remind me again what we're doing with all these psychic abilities of mine again?"

"We're waking them and maturing them to their most advanced state so that you can—"

"Kill or be killed. *That* I remember..." Vincent got up and walked about the room.

"I wish there were another way around this. But if it comes down to you and someone meaning to take your life—" he faced me, sapphire eyes desperate and misty, his hands clinging to the metal railing of the footboard, "*—whoever* is at the edge of your blade, Devi, make the kill." I don't know why, but his words wrecked us from the inside out.

Vincent made a feeble attempt to smile and turned for the door.

"Are we going to forget about what you did to your room? My hand? Any of this ringing a bell? Oh, and that *spoon*. I mean," I stood, "what did that poor thing ever do to you?" I crossed my arms, surprise taking over me when a strong breeze whipped through the room. The window's closed...

The drapes flapped and our hair followed suit. What's stranger than the wind blowing in an airtight room is that it moved in slow motion. How do I know? I can see, that's how I know. Keep up, folks.

"Vince, what's happening?"

"You are." If this were a movie, it'd be the part where I'd break the fourth wall and stare directly into the camera with a very what-the-fuck expression.

"I'm standing right here, Vincent, I don't care how many witchy psychic powers I have dormant in me, I am *not* slowing down *time*—" He made his way back to me and I took a step back.

"This, Devi, is what you are doing to *me*." I Blinked and when his hands touched mine... "You're awake..." The answer to the question. Our foreheads met and his fingers trailed across my cheeks. I cleaved to his shirt, I could breathe and for once, for *once* in my God damned life, it *didn't* hurt. "You're awake..." He whispered again. I held him tight. He held me tighter. He breathed me in. I couldn't remember how lungs worked. The warmth of his mouth closing in on mine...

The pain was as shocking as the moment we shared. I was on fire but there were no flames. Vincent stood clear across the room. The wildfire in his eyes spread to mine. We tore things asunder when we touched and when our bodies separate...

I took a step to him. When I heard the fractures, saw the cracks rise to the ceiling...I clenched my fists and whipped around. I could try to break the window open. Enchanted or not, it's worth a try.

"You should rest." I whirled around.

"Right. Cause we all know what happens when I'm awake." My voice trailed off.

"Devi, please—" His voice. My name in the sound of him.

"What happened in your room? The blood on your knuckles?" He sighed. Loudly.

"There are some questions that won't have an answer."

"Except those that you conveniently hear and feel like answering, right? Those are *my* disembodied voices. They're *my* hauntings, understand? You want to help me? Great. You want to chime in and give me feedback on some of their particularly significant rantings? Be my guest. But don't you, for *one* second, use that shit to get close to me then act like *nothing* happened. Don't do *that*. Not with what's been happening between us and *especially* not with that breakdown in your room. I *know* what I saw."

"You saw me at the end of a breakdown. What you don't know is from what."

"I know something is eating away at you and you can't

control it. It's violent and draining and I know… I know *I'm* the reason. What I *don't* know is why." My throat stung, tears rushed to my eyes and the fear of this, this *thing* hating me so damn much that it made him explode like a bomb.

I stormed for the door.

His hand wrapped around my wrist

A sigh escaped his lips and my feet did the only thing they knew to do in this situation; they took a step *back*.

"You need answers but what about what *I* need?" He closed the gap between us. His frame overpowered me. I was too small. Too human looking up into him.

"What are you talking about?" The words came out as a whisper. Instinct took over as my hand moved the strands of hair from his eyes. They shut with relief; his cheek resting in my palm. "Vincent?" He held my face in his hands and touched his forehead to mine. I thought he would kiss me at any second. I could *feel* it. As real as the touch of my own skin... I would have bet my *life* on it.

I would have died.

His lips moved; holding prisoner words he battled with himself not to say.

Our bodies slid apart, and, in that instance, a fire sparked and this time, the burn raged in every patch where his hands had been.

When I looked up, he was gone., Sitting in his beloved chair, his head against the wall; his hands white-knuckling the arms of the chair so badly I'm surprised it didn't split under the pressure.

"How do you do that?" I said, tired tears trailing silently down my face.

"Painfully..."

We were quiet for a while. I was under the covers and had my back to him. I took turns staring at the clock and out of the sliver between the drapes of the window. An hour passed as one would imagine an hour passing in a strange room, removed from sanity until I couldn't take it anymore. I did one of the things I do best.

"Are you asleep?" He may break walls but I am the queen of breaking silence.

"No, Devi." I didn't want to give him more of a reason to blow his head off. I hated that I mirrored his emotions inside of me. I suppose they're right and I am more powerful than I give myself credit for. Not many Empaths could channel an immortal. Is that why he's going to such great lengths to keep things from me? "Rest isn't my priority."

Staying away from *me* is. His hands gravitated toward the back of his neck; rubbing away an ache he concealed extremely well.

Restlessness encompassed him. His hands rested on his jeans. The pitch black of his now too large sweater made his desert-kissed skin tone stand out more. Is he Turkish? Vincent's hair draped the tips of shoulders, messy layers framing his smooth face. Too smooth because if these immortals were anything other than everlasting, they were warriors.

I opened my mouth to say something, but it clasped back shut., I sat up and curled up my legs again; nestling my head on my knees. I stared off into the blankness of the window while the soldier behind me stared off into a space I'd dare not know anything of...

"I'll be right here if you need me, Devi." What did *he* need? A haz-mat suit? Would he be able to stand being around me then? The longest record's been 18 minutes... Get your shit together, Devi. Whatever it is that we may be feeling for each other, it's stress-related.

"Devi?" I closed my eyes and sighed.

"Yeah, Vincent?"

"I'm here." His arm wrapped around my waist, gripping tight, turning himself into a human shield. He pulled me back, our bodies with nowhere to go but into each other. My head found a new place on his shoulder. The bed never moved. I never noticed the covers lift. With my back to his chest, I had a perfect view of the clock.

Let's start the countdo—

"I'm *not* leaving you." The clock shut off. The incredibly featherlike words brushed against my ear. Quite frankly, I didn't believe him. "You're not the only Empath here, Devi." He turned me around to face him and if it were possible, he pulled me *closer*. "Whatever this is, you and me—" Vincent ran his fingers through my curls, a hopeful lilt in his voice, "it isn't hate. It is *not* violence." We both needed a moment... "I'll *not* leave you. Sleep, little one. Dream. I'm here."

My heart calmed and my breathing mirrored the steadiness of his. Vincent smelled like a memory that coursed deep in your bones but cannot name. Eventually, from his hands caressing my hair and the thrumming of his heart against mine, I fell asleep.

His heartbeat my lullaby.

## DAY 19

Morning brought with it the inevitability of war. Of walking into the battlefield with my name carved into the earth. Once we stepped outside, anywhere I stood would be Ground Zero... But it was time to leave and the rush in every Paladin told me all I needed to know: we had to run.

Now.

The warmth of Vincent's breath on my lips sparked a newfound frenzy in me. "Vincent, don't." I cleaved to him, but our embrace would not erase our fate.

"Don't what, Devi? What's wrong?" I tried to speak, but only a whisper stumbled free.

"Don't go..."

"You heard the others?" I nodded. Melot and the team spoke in their tongue, but it was mostly their poorly veiled panic bubbling in the pit of my stomach that woke me. "I'm not going anywhere without you, Devi."

"Your brother found us, didn't he?" Vincent's eyebrows raised.

"I never told you about Thomas."

"No. But you're thinking about him."

"We had *one* lesson in telepathy. You—"

"It's not—you're *worried* about him. About what he might do to me. It's not so much that I know what you're thinking—" understanding washed over his face.

"You can *feel* it." Empathy for the confusing win. Vincent pressed his cheek to mine, breathing me in. Our bodies curled into each other beneath the safety of our blanket. A few minutes weaved themselves into our veins. Those seconds holding the power of infinity within.

But forever would not be long enough.

How could it?

Vincent leaned on his shoulder. The disconnect rattled the window. "There's no more time, Devi. My brother's infected but not wholly. We *have* to get you out of here before it's too late."

The Paladins were in their flexible LeMehti armor. Pitch black winged pauldrons, chain mail, vambraces and greaves. The protective metal was etched with decorative silver constellations and filigree. Each breastplate softly aglow with their LeMehti wardings.

"Where's *my* suit of armor?" I tugged at Andra's blue tunic hand-me-down I wore. Melot answered, to everyone's surprise.

"*We* are your armor, Devi." His words stung my eyes; the lump in my throat too large… He tipped his head to me and led the Paladins outside. The afternoon sun too bright as fell between the curtain slits. Between Vincent and I…

Vincent closed the gap between us. "Devi?" I knew, far too vividly now, that if I stepped out that door, I'd light up… "Look at me, Devi." The lines of his face, each curve, every freckle had ingrained itself into my memory.... His fingers stretched across the back of my neck and tilted my head up until my eyes had nothing within them but his. Vincent took a desperate breath and pulled me against his chest; his leather-soft metal and stone armor a too-familiar solace. "Your fear is in every cell of me... I'm scared, too. But, you *will* make it out of this, Devi. I *swear* it." He didn't say I'd be safe. He didn't say it would all be ok. He simply said the truth...

"And what about all of *you*?

"We're stubborn when it comes to death." He smiled. I didn't.

"But it's not out of the realm of possibility." His mouth fell. "Life isn't always contingent upon a beating heart, Vincent. You can be alive all you want, but what is that worth if your mind's gone to Hell?" I freed myself of his embrace and walked across the room despite our tether tugging us together. *Commanding* me to return to him. He ran a frustrated hand through his hair. "Helping me—it's going to cost you, *more* than your life. I—I can *feel* it, digging, heaving inside my chest. Just like I felt your hand through your hair in my own. Like we can *both* feel this—this link that's—"

"*Screaming* my name the further away you are from me?"

"What?"

"Whatever this tether between our souls is, it lets me hear you. *Beyond* words. Beyond my Empathic abilities, I can channel your emotions but I can *hear* them, too. And your fear... Devi, please, come back."

"Not until we figure out a plan that doesn't render you as good as dead."

"Devi, we need to *leave*. All of this—I don't know what to tell you."

"You can start with the truth. All of it."

"You want the truth?" with the entire living room separating us, Vincent—he was small. Human...

"If you're all going to lay your *lives* down for *mine*, yes!" the lights flickered, electrical sparks arced around our bodies. Desperately trying to reach for one another...

"You are going to be hunted until the day you die. Until the end of *time*. By Lucifer, by the LeMehti. By anyone and everyone who thinks you shouldn't *exist*. That you're too dangerous because you're the *only* human Reaper. Because you have in you something that can bring *my* kind to their knees. And the only *truth* I know—" Vincent swept across the room taking me in his arms. The moment he did, everything pacified except the silver arcs of electricity crashing into themselves around us… "is *you*. And if losing myself means you live, that you'll be *safe*…. so be it."

Vincent carried me as the Paladins ran until we came to a full stop atop of a train platform in downtown Chicago, outside the Merchandise Mart in all but a few seconds. Vincent stumbled with his landing, his fingers digging deeper into me. We were not meant to stop here…

"Vincent." No one uttered a sound. "Odd. I don't see the word 'fragile' tattooed across her forehead." Thomas was Vincent's asshole identical *twin* brother.

"What are you doing here, Thomas?" Vincent took a step back, his arms locked around me. The trains rattling beneath us echoed inside me. All those people with no clue about us…

"You think I'd allow my little brother to lead a *rebellion* alone? Tisk Tisk Vince. Now, how's about a proper introduction?" Vincent set me down and stood in front of me. I tightened my grip around his waist, not daring to be released from his shield. Thomas's voice carried a slight hint of something. Something so *wrong* it had to be the poison I birthed in him.

"He's infected." Andra interrupted the brothers' death gaze when Melot stepped in.

"Yes. Almost *entirely*." Melot's finger kissed his gun's trigger. Begging Thomas for a reason to put a bullet in his head.

"Please, have *some* faith. I want to help stop this war from reaching the point of no return. I think that's a goal we can all agree upon. Yes?" There was a pause and the atmosphere compounded. "If this lovely lady is capable of what we believe, she's in as much danger as us. No amount of training will protect her from that. I come in peace." His grey wool trench flapped in the wind revealing his sword sheathed at his back and breastplate. The only piece of armor he wore.

"The poison *is* in you and it *will* spread. When it does—"

"When it does, Melot, Vincent will do what's necessary." Andra and Melot flanked Thomas slowly. "Until then, Vincent, I'll *not* stand by and watch your suicide mission from the sidelines. This *Reaper*—she's *already* torn the Empire apart. Hell's best and brightest have assembled their forces, and, my God..." Vincent's doppelganger crossed his arms and his eyes widened in mock shock. "The change in you—"

"Do you have a point to all this, Thomas?" Andra held her baldric tightly, resting her weight on one leg. Examining the edge of her Claymore in the bright summer sun.

"Andra this *human* will be the end of everything." Thomas shot his eyes at me. "That supernatural ability of yours, Devi—it's going to bring about an Armageddon the likes of which this world has never known. If you don't kill *us*, we'll end up killing *you*. And that's the *best* case scenario. And if Roan gets her filthy hands on you and takes you to Lucifer..." he ran one hand through his long hair, the other tugged at his coat. "We're in quite the shit storm and you deserve to know the truth, wouldn't you agree? Has anyone even told her *what* she is? Why any of this is happening?" When his eyes met Vincent's, an understanding washed over his face. "You haven't told her..." Thomas scoffed and kicked a pebble over the roof. It landed next to a pigeon below. It picked at the stone for far too long...

"Thomas, that's *enough*." I've never heard Vincent speak with such command before. It's hot—I mean, *scary*. "You are fading, brother."

"And you, brother, are *blinded*. After *everything*, how could you *not* tell her?"

"Thomas." Amah's voice was doused with careful malice. "You'd do well to mind yourself, dear." Thomas bowed to Amah and then locked his gaze on me. Amah and Gavin flanked Vincent and I.

"I didn't come to quarrel. Let's start over. Devi, my name is Thomas." He was about to take a step to me when one look from Vincent and Thomas took a step back. "I'm a fellow Reaper and Empath, such as yourself and Vincent. I am the emperor's royal advisor as well as his personal guard. Up until I betrayed him, my empress, my soldiers and entire empire to help *you*."

"You sure we can't shoot him, Vince?" Gavin cocked his gun, Melot following suit. Just in case...

"I'm sure, Gavin." The disappointment in the men—it tasted like oatmeal cookies...when you expected them to be chocolate chip. I stifled a laugh.

"I didn't say anything that any of you have not already done." The wind picked up and he adjusted his breastplate; the constellations on it lighting up in white rather than silver like his fellow Paladins. "Now, then. Where are we off to with the world's most powerful weapon of mass destruction?" Andra smacked the back of his head.

"Seriously, Thomas? You're going to speak to her that way? With my *wife* arm's length away?" Melot said. He shook his head, face in palm.

"Vince, *one* shot. Between the eyes." Gavin unholstered his *second* gun.

"That was rude, Andra." Thomas rubbed the back of his head.

"Are you going to help or simply make foolish remarks the entire time?"

"I don't know, Amah. But at least I'm not threatening to *assault* anyone."

"Are—are they doing this right now?" I didn't know if I wanted to laugh or cry. Neither Vincent or I could look away from the train wreck of bickering soldiers.

"Come on." Vincent scooped me up and ran us off until

we arrived at a beach a couple of minutes later. It could have been Lake Michigan. It could have been the Gulf of Mexico.

"You told them we were coming here, right?"

"Everyone but Thomas."

"I'll never get used to this." I found a leaf in my hair. Then another.

"Running?"

"Yeah, that, the telepathic orders, and the constant spells you cast on me so that my body doesn't, you know, break in *two* from the g-forces. I think you nearly broke the sound barrier at one point." I brushed a twig out of my hair and caught a glimpse of his face. "You nearly broke the sound barrier at one point, didn't you?"

"I—you know—I wanted to get you out of there." He smiled, resting his hands on the rim of his breastplate. I leaned against a wooden fence, eyeing a pelican that made it its mission to steer clear of the two of us.

"Do they always fight like that?" Vincent looked over his shoulder, scanning back to Chicago. Witnessing in perfect clarity everything that was happening back at that train station.

"Like a bunch of new recruits, you mean?" He took my hand and we walked over to the grassy shore. "We grew up together, the six of us. That's nothing."

"Vincent, if I'm going to end the world—"

He stopped us in our tracks. "You *won't.*" I couldn't help but lose myself in his touch.

"What Thomas said... What haven't you told me?"

"There's a lot I'm figuring out, Devi. I—" You have *got* to be kidding me. "I'm not kidding you." He finally took his attention from the sunny sky and gave it to me; a puzzled wrinkle forming across his forehead. "Do I not sound serious?" No. He *didn't* hear my thoughts. There is *no* way.

"Uh, no. You were *immensely* serious." I just...

"You just what, Devi?" Stop it! "I'm not doing—" His expression resolved. "Devi, say something."

"Hello." How creative.

"No, it wasn't very creative at all." I cradled myself tight and took a cautionary step back; eyes too wide for his liking. "Ask me a question, Devi."

"Okay—how old are you?"

*Thirty-five. Can you hear me, Devi?*

I leaned in, focusing my eyes directly at his lips, but they were motionless. Our solitary lesson on telepathy involved tapping into people's minds not communicating with them. We never trained for *this*. What is happening?

*I think, well, I think we're having a bit of a chat.*

"A *chat*?" I don't think so. No more telepathy today, please.

"It's gone. Strange." He laughed but I could put a stoic to shame.

"Vincent, what happened?"

*Let me show you. Devi, talk to me. Like this.*

Nope. I think *not*, sir.

*Devi. I think we can only communicate telepathically if we **want** to. Remember your training.*

"We had one lesson and it didn't cover *this*." I sighed and tried not to overreact. "How do I *want* to?"

"The same way you *want* to walk, breathe, cast a spell." Intention.

*Like this, Vince?*

*Yes. Hi there, little one.*

*Hi.*

*Hah. This is actually fun, Devi.*

*It kind of is.*

*You've not done had this occur before?*

*Nope. I mean, not to this scale.*

*I can communicate with my kind telepathically, but never a human.*

*We never trained for **this**. How is this happening?*

*You're a force to be reckoned with, Devi.*

*That's not an answer.*

*I know... my best shot in the dark? Our tether. We'll need to practice.*

"Can we do that later?"

"Of course." Vincent took my hand and we strolled in simple silence to the beach.

We sat in the grassy sand and stared at the glittering waves for a long time. My head rested on his shoulder, linking my arm through his and the smile that caught fire across his lips tingled on mine. Vincent, consequently, felt the intense tickling on his skin and couldn't help but chuckle.

"Sorry about that."

"I don't mind.

"Why'd you say you're 35?" What a *brilliant* conversation starter.

"Physically, I resemble that age." He found it incredibly difficult to smile. Spiders crawled beneath my skin. "My soul, however..." His eyes never left the water. "My soul is as old as yours."

"I haven't lived that many lives."

"Haven't you though?" The way his eyes flicked over his shoulder to me... "We're all stardust, aren't we? You think you're only as old as the first life you remember living?" His hands tried to find something in the sand but they always came out empty. "This body your soul is housed within—in this life it may be 27, but your soul, Devi—" Vincent took my hand and drank in my eyes, "your *soul* rivals my own... Devi? Devi!" Gravity took hold of my blood pressure. Vincent *screamed* my name again and again but my mind fell too quickly in time.

In the future.

Thomas threw me across the woods, cracking my skull on a tree stump. He gripped my neck, lifting me to my feet, slowly suffocating me. When he locked his silver eyes in mine, I found nothing but hate. His hair was white, bled of all its color. Thomas dug his fingers into my chest and ripped out a bright, white burning opal stone... and when he crushed it, I died...

Thomas threw me across the woods, cracking my skull on a tree stump. Thomas gripped my neck, lifting me to—No! The vision is repeating.

Vincent!

*Devi, I'm here. Follow my voice and run!*

"You're awake. Breathe." Everyone circled around us. Including Thomas. Vincent held me, keeping my trembles from turning into convulsions. His eyes—the blues nearly painted black.

Are you scared?

*No, Devi. I'm **terrified**. Tell me what you saw.*

I don't know how I did it, but I showed him my premonition, and believe me, if I wasn't in his arms, Vincent would have broken the whole world... Instead, the ground beneath us shook and lightning storms raged across the water. But when the Veil started to tear—

"Vincent, I'm ok. I'm ok." Ignoring me, he spat out an order to his soldiers in their ancient tongue and, with heavy reluctance, everyone obeyed. Even Thomas.

"Do you always see the future like that, Devi?" I swallowed and he held me snug against him. The storm quietly passing. The rumbles beneath us stirring to a halt.

"*Visceral*? Where I'm *living* them rather than observing them like you trained me to?" Vincent took in a heavy breath. "I hardly ever had premonitions before I met you. During training it was only the anticipation of attacks or what someone was going to say or choose. We were going to harness proper visions of the future but—" But Thomas found us, and we had to leave...

"He's going to kill you."

"I'm so sorry." Vincent smoothed his thumb across my lips. If he bore his eyes any deeper in to mine—

"*You* did not do this. Do you hear me?"

"Then *who* did?"

"I—I d—we have to wait and see when he tries."

"The future of Thomas killing me is concrete, but not the *when* part."

"Yes." Vincent couldn't maintain eye contact.

"What do we do until then?" His mouth lifted into a small smile. He took my hand and we lied back in the grassy sand.

“We take what we can get.” Vincent pulled me gently to his shoulder..

I wanted to stay here, in the quiet. There was sanity here on the beach. No immortal war. No murderous threads spun, waiting to be cut. But Vincent—his anger coursed through me, shaking my bones. He wanted to leave . To tear his brother limb from limb…

“Vincent?”

“Yes, Devi?”

*I don’t want you to leave..*

*Then I won’t.*

# Chapter 17

## DEATH OF ME

The setting sun glinted off the water's surface, filling the waves with a prism of gem stones. Something hid within those stones. Something beneath the water that held a secret it wanted to share with me. Something *familiar*…

The walk from the beach to the Paladins held an air of execution. Any one of us could die if the gods willed it. If I turned into the monster Hell had to protect itself against. The monster *Heaven* would not dare fight… And when my gaze locked in the five immortals in full battle armor in the clearing of a forest I couldn't name, my heart sank.

"Finally. Can we leave now?" Thomas had the unwavering ability to take any moment and morph it into shit. He had his hands in his coat pockets, a smirk on his face I had the unwavering urge to slap right off. "We *are* running to a safe house, are we not?" Vincent's fever burned in my chest. I squeezed his hand and he thought twice about attacking his brother. Vincent glanced down at me with a slight nod.

"We go westward." Vincent's voice overpowered the entire forest.

"Alaska." Melot added. Vincent agreed on his second commander's choice and gave the go-ahead for everyone to run ahead.

"Hold on tight, Devi." *To you? That won't be a problem...* Vincent picked me up in his arms, wrapping my legs around his waist; the suit of armor and stone too comfortable to be a safeguard against—*me*... "Devi?"

"Yeah?"

"Nothing. Hold on... *tighter.*" His smile echoed in mine and Vincent ran. My eyes peeked over his shoulder, barely able to see the scenery change from state to state through the blur of wilderness and concrete. After ten minutes or so, day gave way to night and everyone decelerated.

"We're here." Vincent let me down, much to *both* our chagrin, I think. In the Alaskan wilds was an old cabin covered in all manner of warding like the apartment. The warding damn near matched the brightness of the Aurora Borealis piercing through the trees. I've only ever seen it in pictures and movies.

"These wardings, they're fresh." Vincent kept his attention on Thomas as he and the others entered the cabin. "Is *this* where you were all those time you were 'patrolling'?" he raised a goofy eyebrow at my air quotes.

"This was one of my stops, yes." *One* of his stops.

"You didn't know any of this would be happening, did you? Even with your visions, this, me—"

"No vision could have ever prepared me for *you*, Devi." We locked eyes. His chest rising and falling against my own. "Would you like a better view?" He pointed towards the iridescent night sky.

"Do we have time?" Vincent laughed and I couldn't help but play with the tips of his hair resting at his collarbone.

"I've been known to steal time on occasion." With a grin and my hand in his, Vincent took a step back, gleaming brighter than the constellations in his armor. "And this night warrants thievery, my lady." Vincent navigated us through the thick woods until we came to a small clearing that drank up the Aurora Borealis in every blade of grass.

"I've never seen the Aurora before. Not like this. Thank you."

"You never have to thank me, Devi." His fingers laced into mine and held on tight as he laid us in the grass.

"Why did you—where did you keep disappearing to?" His eyes fell from the skies.

"I was protecting you."

"So, that's a no." I mumbled, sitting up.

"Devi—"

"How long is this going to last? That armor of yours, does it help you to withstand me, or—" he sat up and with one hand, gripped his pauldron and pulled, his entire suit phasing off his body; finding a new home in the pocket of space beside him. His swords, however, they remained holstered to his back...

"The armor doesn't protect me against you, Devi. What you do to me—I will last for as long as I am able." Vincent braved his hand in mine and the contact took our breath away. "Devi, whatever this is—" the warmth between our hands sparked across our skin; emanating around us in a cloudy, coruscating haze of blue. I could taste his words on my tongue, "it saved my life..." Vincent kissed my forehead, lingering his lips. He took me in his arms and back into the bed of the grass, not allowing me to question his declaration. We watched the sweeping lights for a long time when, "Would you like to touch it?" My eyes darted from the sky to his.

"You wanna be more specific." Vincent sat up straight and I followed, both of us chuckling; his collarbone in full view since that black sweater of his was about 2 times too big for him so that he could breathe... Breathe even though he didn't need air to live.

"Would you like to touch the *Aurora?*" I Blinked. A lot.

"You...you can *do* that?" he played with my curls, his focus on my mouth the entire time.

"I can do a lot of things, Devi. You only need ask it of me." Vincent brushed his thumb brushed across my lips... tension sparked in my chest and tightened; keeping me captive until blood rushed to my cheeks. Vincent found my eyes and gave me a new-moon smile and I couldn't help but mirror him. He looked over to the fire opal sky and, with a gentle flick of his wrist, a handful of the Northern Lights flashed to life in the palms of his hands. I inched closer, resting on my knees and carefully caressed the little sparkling cloud. It held the warmth of a feathery, summer wind but static took hold of the back of my neck; waiting for a reason to shock.

"I don't want to go to the house."

"You sensed that, did you?"

"You *trained* me to. Everyone's anxious. That much energy—psychic or not—is hard to dismiss."

"I'd much rather stay here," Vincent rested on his knees and pulled me against his chest, "but, there's a fireplace and a bed with far too many blankets that has our names on it." The Aurora vanished as did my ability to look human. "I'd like to wake up with you in my arms, Devi."

"What if—" I started but Vincent sighed, trailing his hands to my cheeks and leaned in. My goosebumps prickling across his arms.

"There are no 'what ifs'. Not tonight, Devi. Not tonight..."

The second we walked inside, I locked eyes with Thomas. His walked by slowly, as though his legs weighed him down. His expression twisted and dropped my gaze when he turned a corner. A sense of exile crept into my throat. It broke my heart...

*He's seen the same future, hasn't he, Vince?*

*Yes...*

*It's not his fault. Can't we help him somehow?*

*I want nothing more, but there's no way to save my brother, Devi, without—*

*Hurting me.*

***Killing** you...*

We made our way down the hall to a cozy bedroom. It took me a moment to face Vincent. The truth he'd been hiding from me… The only way to save the LeMehti, to be rid of this poison, is to end my life... I flinched when he took my hands in his.

"I won't let it come to that."

"What—what *am* I? Why are you risking everything to help me?"

"Because the alternative is letting you *die,* Devi." I leaned against a dresser, at an utter loss.

"The alternative is *war.*" I tugged at my foreign clothes. "It's your *brother* losing his *soul.* How—" The lights twitched and the fixtures vibrated, nearly shaking me off of the chest of drawers. When the fireplace lit, "Vincent?" I waited to see if the others would show but no one interrupted us. The Paladins were in their quarters, resting but on guard.

"Saving your life is a choice I made. One we *all* made."

"You made the wrong—" he shook his head before I even spoke.

"There was only ever *one* choice to make with you, Devi, and I will make it until the end of time. Remember that. If blood spills, then so be it." He rushed over to me as if he was in a race against *time.*

"How can you say that?"

"How can I *not?*" I was to start another battle when—"Devi, please." The way he said the words, the way his body hopelessly crashed against mine, his hands tangled in my hair… I gripped his shirt for fear I'd disappear. It was all he could do to breathe… all I could do to try to understand why one day he'll want *nothing* of me while the next—even *this* closeness *wasn't* close enough for him…

In that moment, my mind played an evil little trick on me; it made me think...no, *believe* that this man was going to kiss me.

"If I kiss you, Devi..." our foreheads met and the atoms of his voice brushed against my skin with a fever I've never felt. "I—I will *never* stop. I won't know how..." Vincent's heart pounded against my chest; his every breath swimming in mine.

"Do *I* get a say in this?" my hands slid from his chest to his belt, and we both held on for dear life.

"Your *say* is liable to enchant me to no end, lady." his words grazed across my lips. Tempting every fate...

"My sound manipulation sessions—" Vincent grabbed my waist, and gently dug his hips into mine. I couldn't figure out what was harder: the beating of his heart or *him*...

"Trust me, Devi," we took in a heavy breath, "you don't need magick to bring me to my knees..." he lifted me on to the dresser and when his hands slid up between my legs, spreading them apart... when he pulled me into him and leaned in—the lightbulbs burst from our electrical arcs flashing across the room; burning everything in their path. His hands reluctantly slid out from under the back of my top. And his mouth—it held a devil's tongue that I *needed* to taste..."We shouldn't—" my nails dug down his back; slipping away as he leaned back; taking his undiscovered mouth with him.

"Set the world on fire?" I said with far too much trouble. He laughed into the hollow of my neck and I nearly tore his shirt off...

"If you do *that*, Devi—" he looked into me, one hand cradling my cheek, the other—the other grabbed my thigh and pulled my hips into him, *hard*. We moaned, "the things I'd do to you..."

The sunlight played on my skin for a while before I finally gave up. Vincent ran his fingers through his hair, revealing his equally 'I just woke up' face. I giggled and so did he.

"Amuse you, do I?"

"It's nothing. Did the others opt in for recreational slumber, too? What time is it?"

"If you're laughing at *my* expense, I'd like to know why." He smirked and leaned himself up on his elbow. "Spill it."

"You look like me." I laughed. I'd never woken up with any of the Paladins before. Then again, none of them needed *sleep* until now... "I didn't think immortals would look so *human* in the mornings."

"Ah. That I do." The sound fluttered onto my cheeks, his eyes a dawn all their own. "But you..." he tucked a wayward curl behind my ear, "you're breathtaking. There's *nothing* human about that."

I sat up and started brushing my hair with my fingers, twisting it over my shoulder, desperately trying not to blush. He noticed, though. Vincent always noticed me...

I watched him for a while as he patrolled the perimeter with his mind. The light of the sun warmed my skin and, for a while, it gave Vincent the same comfort.

"Let's get you something to wear." *And you too, I hope.* If I have to stare at his naked chest after what *didn't* happen last night—"Come here." I hopped out of bed. "Jeans?"

"Yes, please! Do you have some in the closet?" I took a step but turned on my heal back to him. "You're gonna *will* into reality some clothes for me, aren't you?"

"Figured that'd be quicker than going to Target." I mean, the man's not wrong. I gave him the go ahead.

"Wait." I spat out.

"What's wrong?" He had both his hands at my hips. We were inches apart. Our bodies had been intertwined *all* night. Surely he must be ready to break...and then it hit me with such force, I lost my footing and Vincent had to stand me up right.

"Your breakdown at the apartment. All those men I saw you murder..."

"Devi—"

"You *literally* broke apart. Those men, they weren't enemy soldiers. They were pieces of *you.* Did I do that to you?" I shook the vibrant images from my mind, but my perfect memory will never allow me to be rid of this... I tried to break away but he wouldn't let me.

"This *wasn't* your fault. Rid yourself of any guilt." I stared out the window, his touch barely registering. "When *we* have things like mental breakdowns, sometimes, things get literal."

"And violent..." I tore my sights from the early morning sun and looked up into the eyes of a man I ruin with a simple heartbeat... "Why does being around me, touching me, why does it make you want to hurt me?" His hands guided mine to wrap around him then went back to wrap themselves around my body...*tight.*

"The thought of hurting you, Devi... nothing scares me more. But I won't." His fingers glided across my skin, the fabric swimming and twisting around his grip.

"You have to touch me on purpose to—"

"To see how much I can take."

"Before you can't take it anymore."

"I won't hurt you, Devi."

"I believe you. But why is my heart drowning in your fear of doing *exactly* that? Why can't I channel anything from you? We spent the entire night together and all my Empathic ability gleaned was—"

"That I wanted to do more than *sleep.*" His heart pumped in my veins... we hadn't even *kissed.*

"Yes—wait." Vincent licked his lips and—damn him. I stepped away. "You're hiding something from me. All of you are. What am I to you that, if we're around each other too long, you break your face to stop you from breaking mine?"

The sun blinded me for a moment. Vincent had vanished and I stood there like a fool. A fool in skinny jeans and a t-shirt of one of my favorite alternative bands.

"Freshen up. I'll be downstairs." My head turned with an ache I knew I wouldn't be rid of. He stood at the bedroom door, gesturing to the bathroom. *Pick your battles, Devi.* He's in pain...

I returned from the bathroom to a freshly made bed and my pajamas resting atop the blankets. My fingers stretched across the fibers in the hopes that I would catch a memory from Vincent but then retracted the second I realized I wasn't the only person in the room.

"It's not terribly polite to stand in dark corners and stare at people, you know?" I casually spat the words at Vincent and went straight towards the window seat, opening the windows, paying no mind to the angelic man searching for something he'd lost centuries ago.

"No. I suppose it's not." His feet gingerly led him to the bed where he looked at the clothes for far too long. No doubt happy that that my psychometry hadn't advanced to the degree of channeling *his* past. It leaves you to wonder, though, how heavy a single memory can be that he'd rather allow it to *crush* him than to let me help him carry it. "But it *is* terribly difficult to *not* fall under your spell." I averted my gaze back to the woods outside, welcoming the warm morning Fall air. "You don't believe me." I crossed my arms and tried to Hunt for woodland creatures. I found some—five miles away. "Do you—do you *not* know what you mean to me?" Vincent blinked himself in front of me and cradled my cheeks in his palms. "Devi, I—"

I saw the change from blue to black in Vincent's eyes before I heard the blast. In one breath, Vincent grabbed me and jumped out of the window and bolted through the woods. But not before I saw the cabin crumbling in flames...

*Thomas?*

*No. He's **helping** us. Hold on, Devi. I have to run faster.*

Embers flaked off our clothes in a flurry as Vincent weaved new threads across our bodies. He stopped at the edge of the woods, waiting. But when my tears burnt to ash, when the world around us stood silent and still, I clung to the sight of Vincent scanning; both his swords out, prepared to murder anyone, including his brother, if he so much as *thought* of hurting me. Vincent was something out of a dream. A living, breathing nightmare that knows no end...

He stabbed his blades into the earth, creating a forcefield around us. He walked over to me, his suit of armor manifesting around him.

"Devi, are you alright?"

"End this." Vincent nearly fell back. "Being a Reaper, whatever it is that I am—it's caused this war. It's ruining you... But there's something *else* inside of me. If I die—"

"Devi, I'm *not* hearing this! *Enough.*" Disgust dripped from his mouth.

"As long as I live, people will die! I'll be running the rest of my life. You've trained me to fight back, but Vincent, if they take me—" he leaned in close. *Too* close.

*I will* ***die*** *before they touch you....*

*I don't want you to die. Not for me.*

*You're the only thing* ***worth*** *dying for, Devi. Can't you see? Don't you see what you've done to me?*

He was full of an ache I couldn't know. He pulled my body close, shielding me from everything but him. "You'll be the death of me, Devi." The sapphire of his eyes burned into my soul. His mouth so close to mine I could taste the ache in his words before they were spoken. "And God help me, I don't care. I. Don't. Care." Vincent kissed me then. His lips *forged* to mine, taking me in a way I didn't know possible. Vincent kissed me in the only way he told me he ever could.

Without knowing how to stop...

# Chapter 18

## Mimic

A few tiny seconds imprinted themselves inside my mind. I prayed my memory would hold on to this. If I lost everything else, I would be ok...as long as I could remember *this*...

Something was happening, far away from our dream. Then, with two words, Vincent broke me.

"They're here."

I leaned against the bark; wide-eyed and trembling. Le-Mehti soldiers had found us. And they brought with them a death I could taste for miles. But I had more fear in me for what Vincent would do to *them*.

Vincent *scared* me.

"We have two minutes." he took my hand. "Sentinels were dispatched."

"But, we burned the clothes and—Vincent—" I kept my eyes locked in his, even though they drifted, scanning. Even though the ground beneath us cracked. The electricity in the air sharpened. The blow of the wind changed from one direction to the other. The direction the Sentinels approached.

Vincent's markings glowed *molten*. The light enveloping the trees, the grass, my skin… if I looked close enough, the light resembled the hallmark patterns of starlight…

"Devi, hold still." Vincent cupped my shoulders and wrapped my body in a suit of LeMehti armor tailored for me. "It's heavy, I know, but it's malleable." My daggers were holstered to my back, a .45 Magnum Winchester on my thigh, and the constellations on the breastplate lit up—"Devi?"

"Yeah. Sorry. I can move in this. Where are the others?"

"We're right here." Amah said with a whoosh of air as the Paladins popped into the safety of the forcefield.

In a flurry of archaic verses, Amah said the name 'Miarrah' and, I swear I heard the wind itself *scream*…

"Who's Miarrah?"

"She'll make it. She has to. We can't run. Not from *this*, Vincent. It's time."

"Time for what? What's going on?!" I stepped into the center of the circle and was met with bloody, ashen faces. The blood, when I took in a deep breath, I could tell was not all theirs…

"You're human, Devi. I need you to believe that." Vincent's voice was too quiet.

"As human as a Reaper, witch, and psychic can be," I said blankly.

"What Thomas referred to before…what I've ordered everyone to keep from you—" he gripped his breastplate tighter, both of us white-knuckling this, "you're a Mimic, Devi." Sounds harmless enough.

"Cliff's Notes version please." I stroked my temples trying to ease the massive migraine having babies in my head.

"Touch someone enough you gain their memories and abilities. Do it enough times, they're yours permanently." Well, shit.

"Sleeping beside me, the hand-to-hand combat—I should've copied your immortal ability to teleport?" immortal tension is equivalent to a few bricks in the pit of your stomach.... there was something more to this that Vincent's confession didn't reveal.

"Yes."

"Is *this* why everyone's so afraid of me?"

"Yes and no."

"How paradoxical of me."

"You are the calm *and* the storm." The reality of his words stung my mouth. "One human or Rev who can copy our abilities is not an imminent threat. We'd make certain of that." A pause flowed through us and to be honest, it was much needed. His gaze wandered off to something too horrific for me to follow.

"But a *Reaper*—manifesting our ancient magick within them *and* rendering us human?" Melot took over story time. "That sort of power is destined to start wars."

"Why didn't any of you tell me all this before?" I turned back to Vincent. "You're a Reaper. Why didn't you teach me how to control my power? I could Mimic you and—" the forcefield wavered and Vincent's eyes flickered to Mel and the others before finding mine again. "You won't tell me, will you?" Vincent leaned in his forehead to mine and the strands of his hair sweetly tickled my cheeks. His hands cupped my neck and melted my migraine away in one beautiful motion.

"One threat to your life at a time, little one."

"Yeah... like being a Mimic that can *become* immortal given enough groping." His hands wavered. "Does touching through clothes count or this a strictly skin-to-skin kind of deal?"

"Smart, this one." Thomas flicked off blood from his sword but no one paid him any attention.

"You're nowhere near the point where you'd be able to copy our immortality. Your Mimicry is fledgling at best." Vincent clenched his jaw. He hated this truth more than anything. And I hated thinking that every touch from Vincent was merely a means to an end.

*You **should** hate a lie that sinister, Devi...*

I'm—I know, but can you blame me, Vincent?

*No. I suppose I can't*

"I can't copy your immortality. I can't Reap souls. You know, I'm not seeming all that scary." Thomas scoffed at me. But it was Vincent who spoke.

"Give it time." I blinked. Vincent kicked himself in the ass.

"Vince. We *have* to go." Andra's words cut into me.

"Devi, we're going to Port. The DeKenna, the others, they're coming."

"But Andra, I haven't learned—" Vincent took my hand in his. The way his voice carried—I think everyone's hearts broke a little bit. Even Thomas...

"It's a risk we have to take." I looked to the panicked Paladins. No one favored this move but there was no way around it. "We can heal you and the armor will protect you, as will I. Trust me, Devi." Vincent took me in his arms and—

"Did a bomb go off?" The air was tart and it stabbed my nose. Vincent held my face and waited with a weight burdened in our hearts we'd never be rid of.

"Breathe." I gripped on to his wrists but couldn't—Vincent sent a small jolt of electricity through my veins and it grounded me; opening my eyes and lungs. "You had a few aneurisms. I took in everything else." My eyes shot up at him.

"What do you mean?" The others were in a perfect circle; scanning, protecting, warding.

"The physical damage to your body—I took it from you. Healed anything else that the armor couldn't protect you from." His eyes were the bluest I'd seen them. I had no words but he required none. A palm on my cheek told him everything he needed to know...

"No one followed." Melot's voice was barely audible, but it thundered through my body and I flinched. Vincent cradled the back of my head.

"Where to now?" Gavin asked, his attention on Thomas. I wandered from Vincent and to the edge of the railing of the building we were in. I followed the lines of the structure above. The Eiffel Tower.

We're in *Paris*...

"Sydney." Andra said next. "Will she manage it?" Andra directed her question to Vincent. I lived through teleporting from North America to France. I think I can—I teleported from *North America* to *France*. Why do I feel so cold? Is the sun rising or setting? Is that the 1889 World's Fair?

I didn't realize how tight my fingers were around the railing until Vincent pried each of them off.

"It's ok, Devi. You can let go. I'm here."

"What did you say?" my ears were full of the past. He wrapped one arm around me, pulling me close.

"I'm *here*." He whispered and it dissipated the cacophony in my head. "You saw the Fair?" I managed a nod. "The Porting of that distance will be challenging." And with the strike of his words, I finally registered remnant hurt in my bones. The ringing in my ears wasn't a result of crossing space at the speed of thought. It was a warning.

*Yes, it was. We'll need to be more careful.*

"How long would it take you?" The crack in my voice couldn't be helped.

"In your terms...a split second." Thomas answered. I whirled towards his direction, his focus over the city. Confusion took my face and it would *not* relinquish its hold.

"But it took us longer because I'm—" fragile. Human. Powerless. "Couldn't we...if the issue is not knowing how badly Porting will damage me—couldn't—"

"Can you get to your point a little *quicker*, dollface? We're kinda on the clock."

"Sure, *dollface*." I bit back at Thomas before Vincent had the chance. "You lot have magick. As do I. With our powers combined—" Not a *single* immortal caught my reference. I rolled my eyes. "We cast another spell. One strong enough to protect me from your very violent form of transportation so that I don't get hit and have Vincent take the full brunt of the beating." Everyone avoided me. Gavin checked his gun chamber. Melot crossed his arms and I stood there, hands on my hips staring at the one ancient asshole who dared to make eye contact with me.

"Devi—"

"Wow, Thomas. You know my name." Andra stifled a laugh. Thomas resembled a person who—no. Thomas actually resembled a *person.* And believe me when I say; it was unnerving.

"We've *already* cast dozens of spells on you. You're inhaling magick older than time and it is *breaking* you." Thomas let his words settle into my rapidly forming fractures. It ate away at him. Every word he spoke… "Even with your own spells—" Thomas's eyes darted to Vincent, for approval.

"I—I don't understand."

"Of course you don't. How could you?" Thomas stared down at Vincent with a force so great that it pushed *me* back. "Would you care to take over brother?" Vincent stepped forward into the circle. My hand in his.

"Our magick is failing because there is a *stronger* force fighting to make certain it does."

"To—to what end?"

"To *your* end, Devi." When Vincent answered me…in that moment, we were two people drowning. Two people trying, with everything they had, to save one another. Two people who never learned to swim. Not in these waters…

"The same force that has sent our kind mad, we believe it's also combatting anything we cast." Andra's sweet voice... "That's why every inch of the safe houses were covered in wardings when normally *one* of *our* sigils would suffice. That's why it took us *weeks* training you when all we needed was—"

"Days," I said, too aware of Vincent's instinct to scoop me up and run me off as far away from all of this as possible…

"*Moments.*"

"What?"

"We have the power to bring your abilities to the surface and mature them by *will*, Devi. But this opposing force—" she trailed off, her eyes flickering between Vincent and Melot, "you're a Mimic. The only sort of training you may need is cursory."

"Ok. Then here's what we do. I'm the one in this mess. You're all collateral. But you don't have to be."

"Enough."

"Let me finish, Vincent. I can stay here and you can all run."

"Then what, Devi?"

"Then *anything*, Vincent. Anything that isn't *this*."

"No." The word fell from him, landing on my hair. That one word, believe it or not, could sink ships...

"Those soldiers, *your* soldiers, the Sentinels. The remaining Paladins. *Hell*. They're after us because of *me*."

"The situation's more nuanced than you realize, Devi."

"It wouldn't be so *nuanced* if someone would tell me the *whole* truth, Melot." I stepped away from Vincent and into the circle. "What if I speak with your Emperor? Reason with—"

"Madness holds no council with reason." Vincent gave me goosebumps. A warrior with war at the edge of his lips.

"Vincent, if I give them what they want, it will give you all time to get away and—"

"Give them time to murder you, in ways you cannot *conceive* of. Is that what you want?" I tried with all that I had to swallow my fear.

"What I want is for none of this to be happening. But, surprise! It *is* and I am *trying* to stop things from getting worse and if the end of my existence will accomplish that—"

"You're trying to kill yourself, Devi." My eyes shot back at Vincent; his truth burying itself too deep inside us. Inside everyone... "Your death will do *nothing* but bring ruin to everyone. To *me*." No one spoke. No one moved. The wind flowed at our fringes; waiting for the fire to calm before it dared enter the ring of six furious immortals and one questionable supernatural entity capable of mass destruction...

Vincent focused on something over my shoulder, to the city, the earth.... He shook his head; fatigue and defeat falling out and newfound resolve settling in when he cupped my face in his palms "Doppelgangers as diversions. We'll need to plant them in various locations." The Paladins tightened their circle. "Then we separate. Rendezvous in Sydney."

"*Clones?*" My voice was barely a whisper. Amah chimed in. Her eyes too full of the storm coming for us all.

"They're illusions, Di. To the enemy, they'll be flesh and blood, but not living. Though possible, it is against the laws of LeMehti magick."

"Thank you, Amah. Now that we've completed our lecture on the ethics of puppeteering, can we be on our way?" Thomas, you are *this* close—

"Where to first?" Gavin took his wife's hand in his, steering her from cutting off the head of their oldest friend dying before their eyes. "How long are we to stay at each lo—" Gavin had a glint of anxiety on his lips, and, consequently, mine.

"Perhaps the details of the plan may be set *after* we've left?" Andra's words sliced through Gavin and sent a shiver down my spine. It was clear we had to move and *fast*. Then Thomas opened his mouth.

"I agree with the lady. Let's begin, shall we?" The stabbing in the pit of my stomach told me their sense of urgency was not for whatever was coming for us.

"Let's not." Thomas's smile cracked at me.

"I know you're frightened, Devi, but—" He tried to comfort me.

"Of course I am! And *you* should be, too. I'm so sorry I couldn't *Mimic* my way out of this shit. I'm sorry I'm *this* to begin with. I can't do much but I *can* end this war—let me help. I can't stand by and watch you all fight for your lives to keep *me* safe. You could all *live* happily ever after if you get it through your thick skulls that I need to be handed over."

"Handing you over will mean a fate worse than death." Gavin's eyes reflected the city lights, but our tears dared not fall.

"And?" The tower trembled. "Maybe I die. Or worse." I turned around and looked up at Vincent. "Why is it ok for *you* to sacrifice yourselves for my sake, but God forbid *I* attempt any reciprocity?" the silence bit at everyone. "If there's even the *smallest* chance I can put right what's gone wrong, shouldn't I?" The air had been afraid to touch anyone but me and it wrapped itself around my body. I rubbed a tightness from my neck.

"Enough." Vincent's voice loosened the grip around my throat. Turns out, the wind was trying to choke me...

"Vincent, I know—"

"No. You *don't*."

"Then *tell* me..." A deep stare engulfed the space between Vincent and I. Fed up, I turned on my heel toward the others, walking away from the very pissed off Paladin. "Anyone?" No words. And thus, Vincent and I were left to our own devices on a tower of metal that would collapse if either of us simply lost control.

In sounds that cracked into violent quiet like far-away thunder, Vincent uttered a sentence or two in their ancient tongue and I swear, there were no words that could describe the faces on the disturbingly catatonic bodies around me.

"You have your orders."

"You can't possibly mean to go *without* one of us." Thomas finally said, coming to life. Genuine worry around his eyes.

"What's he talking about, Vincent?" He didn't look at me.

"We're planting our doppelgangers, then splitting up—"

"I *know*. I was here for that. Tell me the bit your Paladins are *shitting* their pants about."

"We don't have time for this, Devi."

"*Make* time." A bolt of lightning struck at the edge of Paris. The Paladins flinched... My eyes never severed from Vincent's.

"I'm staying here at the tower to ensure no one's followed."

"Try again."

"Devi—"

"You're *lying* to me." A second lightning bolt; the rolling of thunder echoed towards us far too quickly. Everyone took note.

"Orders are final. Go." I clenched my jaw. He tightened his fists. Everyone vanished. Before I could process their disappearance, Vincent took hold of me. "Please don't fight me, Devi. It's settled."

"*Nothing* is settled. You may have declared an order but they're *not* ok with it. Whatever *it* is." I*gnore his arms keeping you safe, Devi. Ignore his forehead kissing yours.* "There *has* to be another way where you lot don't fight for your *lives*. For *my* life."

"Devi," Vincent cradled my head in his hands, "any other way will *end* you..." I shut my eyes. The tears burning saltwater trails down my cheeks. How many versions of the future had he seen where I died? Where the others did? Where the best choice was *this*?

*Too many...*

Vincent didn't let me go and when I cleaved to him, burying my face in his chest, his grip only tightened.

"Do you trust me, Devi?" The words hit with a gentleness that I don't think I'll ever get used to. I closed my eyes and sighed and let the truth spill out.

"With my soul."

"Then let this go." I brushed the strands of hair from his sapphire eyes. And when I saw myself reflected in them, it—it told me all I needed to know...

"Where are we planting the first doppelganger?" His heart skipped a beat.. "Vincent? Where—we aren't planting any clones, are we?"

"*We* are not. Our doppelgangers, on the other hand, *they're* planting a shitload." The truth crept its way down my throat without warning. The taste of it too bitter to be a lie.

"The orders. You've told the others to watch for Thomas because—"

"He's quickly losing his battle to the poison. He's hiding it, but his hair has gone completely white. Bled of all color."

"How did you—when did you make our doppelgangers? Won't the spell fade?"

"Our clones will last for as long as I allow them to. They need only be active enough to provide Thomas a sense of security."

"To give him our location if—*when* he comes to Reap my soul."

"I'm not going to let that happen." My eyes went blank. I think all I saw were the rain-filled clouds rushing towards us. "Do you hear me, Devi?" The brightness of his gaze shocked my system. Vincent was scared and it's my fault. "Listen to me right now. None of this is your fault. *None* of it."

"You want to know something funny? Lies, they feel pretty shitty. Like something trying to claw its way out from under your skin. And, when the lies are *especially* grand, they have a *taste*. Sweet. Like vanilla or honey. I would've thought truth would taste that way. Then again, I never thought I'd be *tasting* abstractions. So, there's that." I walked away from him. Vincent lied to my face. What's more is that—"I trust you. I know you're lying to me, but I also know you have *reason*." When I looked at him, his face, his body—"You *have* to have reason. *Good* reason to look me in dead in the eye and lie through your teeth. Why else would you have done that?"

"Devi—"

"Will you tell me?"

"No."

"Why?" Vincent carefully closed the gap between us, mindful of the storm and rattling tower. Every time he opened his mouth, he fired a bullet.

"Sometimes, when all you have to choose is death or *more* death; When you're left in between the wreckage of nothing but evils..." we breathed in and the rain poured hopelessly, pounding harder against the iron, "you choose the evil that kills you less..." For a few moments, the storm brought us peace. The sound of water against metal calming us through to our blood.

"The lesser of the two," I said, blankly.

"Less, but still evil."

"You chose to help me—I'm ev—" his kiss took my breath away. It didn't matter that Vincent was immortal. We could have forever and he'd still kiss me as if time were our greatest enemy.

"You're *not* evil. My *choice* was. Never forget that." A bolt of lightning and a wave of thunder flowed through the city. Vincent managed a smile, nestling his palms on my neck; the tips of his fingers tracing a path down my nape. His forehead found a home on mine. "I have to get you out of here." he held me as tight as he could without breaking me. "This will hurt." I nodded and the tower shifted and faded from view. I unwillingly gasped and we stopped in the middle of a pitch-black field.

"Devi?"

"I'm fine." I touched my ears. There was blood everywhere. Fucking bomb. Vincent examined my injuries then healed them in the same breath.

"This is going to be harder than I thought. I thought I took in your fatal injuries."

"You did. I—I just have a low pain threshold." He looked at me funny.

"Devi, this was equivalent to you landing on concrete from 1,000 feet and all you did was *gasp*. Your threshold for pain is anything but low."

"I'll be sure to put that on my resume." We kind of chuckled...

"Devi, your body isn't built for this. I can keep healing you, transferring your injuries but—"

"It'll be ok. We have to teleport—I mean—Port in small increments, right? What if we rip the band-aid off? Take one big leap."

"If I hadn't stopped..." he trailed off, thinking of whatever possible outcome my Porting would've brought me. A broken bone, burned flesh, bleeding organs..... "If you're lucky." Shit. "I'll have to take you a second or two at a time. It has to be small leaps. This way, at least, you should build a resistance to the force. Hopefully, Mimic my Porting."

"Sure thing, Obi Wan." An incredibly blank face met mine. I guess they don't have cable in...immortal world? Jesus, Devi. "Ok, a resistance. How would I do that since your protective magick only works on me for short bursts and in the event that my Mimicry decides not to wake up and join the party?"

"It's awake, Devi. But it's repressed. I'm hoping you're subconsciously copying everything you need to know."

"Alright." I wiped my sweaty brow. "Let's go." And off we went. The field shook and the night faded. I tried with all that I had not to let him know my pain, but my body betrayed me every time; trembling and clenching. He finally stopped after the fifth second in a church.

"Are we here? Where are we going again?"

"No." He sat me down in a pew and crouched in the aisle, brushing my messy hair from my face. He stopped moving when he tucked my hair behind my ear. Vincent's eyes swirled. His thumb moved across my neck and I shivered. "You're bleeding again." I could barely make out the words his jaw was clenched so tight.

"It's ok."

"This is the *furthest* thing from ok. If I never.. Had I...." The glow from the hundreds of candles around us couldn't bring light to this man. When his hands cupped my ears, my eyes blurred . The throbbing enhanced for a brutal moment then subsided into nothingness. The healing hurt this time around. The more fatal the injury, the more painful the healing process. Check.

Vincent touched my stomach and my eyes went black. His entire hand stretched across my center and a fire raged in every inch of me, roaring to an inferno. "What—what happened?"

"Your organs—they detached. I—"

"No, no. That's enough detail. I was dying. Gotcha."

"I couldn't take in all your injuries, Devi." Before I could get a word in—"We have to go one more time. One giant leap." A much-needed pause followed his voice, as if he needed those seconds to be certain of his control. "You *will* scream." Vincent gripped me tight against his armor. The wooden floors cracked beneath our feet. The windows shattered, melting to nothingness.

I screamed...

*I **won't** lose you....*

# Chapter 19

## Metamorphosis

My eyelids fluttered open to an alarm clock on a night stand. The glaring red light of it telling me it's 3:25 in the morning. My lungs expanded as I took in a breath and then it hit me; I'm alive. I spent a second to register all my senses when my memory high-jacked my mind. Everything that happened from our first kiss to the tower to whatever happened to me here in this room flashed behind my eyes in real time like a movie. The memories jostled me and flung me up. I nearly fell off the side of the bed.

I cleaved on to the sheet against my naked chest when the numbers on the clock struck me. It's 3:26 a.m. My memories played out in excruciating detail and real time in my head, but in the real world, only a *minute* had passed.

"Devi?" Vincent... The dark space filled with a dull blue hue. I turned around and his face fell apart. "You're bleeding. Come here." I'm bleeding? Blood dripped over my lip from my nose. I wiped it off with the sheet as Vincent helped me back into the bed. "The rush of the memories. Too much to process. It'll get easier." Our bodies interlocked; his naked body against mine.

"Vincent, what happened? I can remember everything up until Paris, but when I try to remember what happened *here*..." His eyes fell back. Body too limp beneath my hand. "Vincent?!"

"I'm here. I'll always be here."

"You scared me. I thought—"

"I'm going to be alright. Just need time to heal."

"Heal from *what*? You look—you *feel* like you're about to die."

"I'm immortal." Vincent laughed. I didn't. He played with my hair, I couldn't help but lose my mind. Our first time in bed like this and...

"What do you need to heal from? Why—why are we *naked*?"

"I couldn't heal you, Devi."

"What are you talking about? You did. See?" I showed him my blood-free nose.

"You were dying." The field. The church... But I didn't die. "Yes you *did*. Here. Your heart stopped. I brought you back, but—"

"But I kept dying."

"I couldn't keep you alive. I—" his lungs struggled for air they didn't need...

*I was wrong, Devi. You didn't have enough time to change on your own...*

His eye lids were too heavy, weighing mine down. Vincent pulled me into him. But nothing he did could get me close enough...

*I couldn't lose you again...*

"Vincent, breathe. You did *everything* you could to—" He untangled us.

"Everything *wasn't* enough." He stunned me into silence. "Death came for you, Devi. Each time I healed you, every attempt I made to save you...the easier it was for *them* to find you." It can't be… "And the *way* you were dying—" He mustered the strength to sit up, "*that* sort of violence—it does not go unnoticed." *Reapers…*

"And I was constantly on the edge." I sat up beside him.

"One moment in this world—"

"One moment in Rorrim." The world of the dead... "They're going to be after me now, too."

"No. But they're going to have questions." Vincent held his head in his hands. The burden of it, of *me* barely contained in his bones.

"They were here. You fought them off while you were trying to save my life." Fuck. Can someone throw in a damn cease-fire for five fucking minutes? "God damn it. Vincent, I'm *so* sorry."

"Don't be. I did what needed to be done. But you have to understand—I didn't know how else to—Devi, this was the only way I could bring you back. The only way I had left to protect you. From tonight. From everything that's to come." The hollow beneath his eyes faded, but a whole *new* enemy dragged this man away from me. "Do nothing and watch you die, or do *something* and have you live."

"Why do I get the feeling that, for you, both of those choices were *more* than evil?"

"Because they were." My tears were inconvenient, and at this point, I honestly couldn't tell you if I cried from my own pain, Vincent's.

"I'm alive. We're together. How *evil* can that be?" I smiled, hoping to God it would make him follow suit. It didn't.

"What I did—Devi, it cannot be undone. You're not human anymore." I think I blinked. Revs were always on the fringes of what a human is. "Devi?"

"You gave me immortality."

"I *made* you LeMehti." The *first* immortals ever to walk the earth. The most *powerful*. Rivaled only by the DeKenna. "Enough to save you from… *everything*."

"I'm *immortal…*" I'm not human anymore.

"Devi, I—there was *no* other way to—" I'm *not* human.

"It was only a matter of time, anyway, right? You saved my life. Thank you." He saved my life.

"Devi, Devi look at me. You are *not* ok with this. Stop *laughing*."

"It's ok." *It's ok.* "I don't care." *I don't care.*

"Devi, stop!"

"Vincent? What the hell are you *electrocuting* me for?!"

"You were trapped. You're in shock—"

"Yeah! Because you fucking sent a few *thousand* volts of electricity through my skull! Ouch, by the way." Rubbing my temples, the last couple of minutes hit me. "Shit. How—how did you know?" Vincent pulled me to his shoulder, entangling our bodies. I didn't know where I began or he ended.

"It's you. I'll always know when something is wrong."

"So, if this happens again..."

"Electricity should do the trick. It's pain that helps us find our way out of a trap."

"Vincent?"

"Hmmm?"

"I really don't care."

"Devi, I'm not a blessing. I'm nothing of the sort. You were meant to only channel enough of my immortality to mimic my ability to *Port*. What I did—you were never meant to be—"

"LeMehti? Maybe not, but we both know this moment *couldn't* have been avoided. You said yourself, you did this to protect me from what's coming." I may as well have spat in his face. Our lungs took in air neither of us knew we needed. "Did I have a choice in this? No. But I was dead, so it's not like I could've answered you had you asked me. My mind was gone. But know this: If I'm dying, if my life is in jeopardy and you know of a way to save me, I *want* you to save it. No DNR's here. You have my explicit consent to do *whatever* it takes to save me. To save *us*. We'll deal with the fallout, whatever it may be, together." I held him tighter hoping my truth would seep through his skin. "I *don't* care."

"Yes, yes you *will*..." My ears throbbed from the torture

in his voce, his face concentrated on something in the black sheets.

"What about what I've done to *you?*" I left the warm confines of his arms and it crippled me so quickly, I threw up bile in my mouth.

"Devi—"

"I'm ok. But, when we have a minute to catch our damn breath, we *seriously* have to figure out why this cosmic tether does this to us." I gestured to my throat as I swallowed the last bit of bile. "You said, before, that I'd done something to you. That I saved your life. Consider us even." His expression twisted, trying desperately to understand me.

"We're *not* even. The two cannot compare. Did, did you hear *anything* I've said to you, Devi? You are *not* human anymore. I changed—"

"I heard you good and well." I snapped. "I was pushing up daisies—*repeatedly,* and you literally brought me back from the dead. Are *you* hearing *me?*" He bit his lip. I grit my teeth. "You saw this coming. You *knew* there would be a future where I'd end up LeMehti. Where I *needed* to be LeMehti to survive everything that's headed our way. Where you'd have to make this choice. It happened. We can't change it." Breathe... "Vincent, I can *survive* now. I have a chance—"

"It's not that simple."

"I didn't say it was. But think for a minute. You and Amah and the others...you don't have to spend your lives *babysitting* me."

"There will *never* be a world where I'm *not* protecting you."

"You scare me when you say things like that." I couldn't look at him. "And you say things like that *a lot...*" Vincent genuinely had surprise wash over his face.

"Because you know it to be true?"

"Because I know it to be true." A moment slipped between us and before he could speak, my mouth took over. "I'm sorry I couldn't handle the Porting. I'm sorry my stupid Mimicking abilities aren't fully awake yet. I'm sorry you had to make a choice that has irrevocably intertwined our lives. I—I'm—"

"Devi, look at me, Devi. Keep your eyes on me. Slow, deep breaths. You're with me. Here. In this time, in this place. I'm here with you."

"What—what's happening to me?"

"You were lost again. Your human side went into shock."

My *human* side....

"How long was I gone?"

"Only a couple of seconds. But in your mind, it was an hour."

"Not even gonna ask how you know that." I sighed. He tucked my sweaty hair behind my ears; linked his hands around my neck and inched closer to me. "Vincent, where was I? My body was here, but my mind—"

"It wasn't only your mind. Your soul—you went to Evenfall. To our Bridge."

"What?"

"Then to Rorrim. You're processing. Your new body is reacting the only way it knows how."

"By falling apart?"

"Finding a life boat."

"The Bridge to—our Bridge makes sense, but how is *Rorrim* a life boat?"

"You're a Reaper, Devi. Why *wouldn't* you go to the world where others like us rule?" Vincent wrapped us up in the blanket and we were quiet for a moment. Laying side by side, our breaths filled the silence around us.

"Vincent, how did you find me?"

"How did I find you?" Vincent mustered the strength to lean on his arm. His gaze never breaking from mine. "I would find you *blind*. In every world scattered among the stars. Across time. I found you, Devi, because I *know* you. Because you know *me*. In ways no other ever has. In ways I didn't think possible. How did I find you?" he smiled and it brought some life back into the cobalt of his eyes. "How could I *not*?" When our foreheads met, the strands of his hair tickled my lashes, his chest pushing up against mine. "Your soul is in mine..."

A kiss found its way on the tip of my nose, then my cheeks... "we're tethered..." he kissed my lips, my hands locked around his neck, every part of him on every part of me—this, this happened already. Wait.

"Wait."

"What's wrong?"

"This is familiar. Why does this feel familiar?"

"Us kissing?"

"No." I grabbed the sheet and covered myself and sat up. "Vincent, show me what happened when you changed me."

"Devi—"

"I can't remember it. Any of it."

"With good reason."

"Are you hiding my memories from me?"

"No. How can you say that?" Silence. "Your memories *are* hidden but it's not of my doing." I held myself and laughed the nerves away. "Devi, what happened to you, if you *did* remember then there would be something *critically* wrong with your mind's protective mechanism. Immortal or otherwise."

"I want you to show me." he sat up, drained from my request already.

"Devi, your mind—your *soul* is shielding you for a reason."

"Trauma and I are dear old friends. I'll be fine."

"And what about *me*?" I'm such an asshole...

"Vince, forgive me. I—I forgot you'd relive it with me." How could I not have pieced *that* together?

"Devi, listen and listen well;" I wiped away a renegade tear from my cheek when Vincent took hold of me and set fire to the dark with his markings. "Don't you *ever* think that I'd put you through something like that *alone*." My heart ached while his beat beneath my palms and it was all I could do to not— "If you're in Hell, I *will* follow you."

Vincent put his fingers on my temples and we relived *everything*. Nothing could've prepared me for it...

*Nothing.*

Vincent ran his frustrated fingers through his hair. His hands rested heavily at the back of his neck; his stone blue eyes locked at absolutely nothing before him.

The room went pitch black when he shut his eyes. They were closed for a long time. My knees curled up to my chest; the sheets gathering a tiny pool of salt water. I wiped my eyes and wrapped my arms around my legs as tight as I could. Moonlight flickered through the small space between the curtains. It danced through the trees, landing on the dewy blades of grass. And now, more than anything in the entire world, all I wanted was to be in the space between...

*Devi, I... I never should have searched for you—*

"Don't say that," I said. My voice was too loud. How could he say that to me? I turned over to him, "Vincent, you saved my life but it didn't come without a price. I *know*. But, listen—look at me." I cradled his face. His fingers traced around my wrist before they found my waist and pulled me tight against his body. Suddenly, I became too aware of the lack of barriers between our hot skin...

"The cost to save you—Devi, we're going to pay for this in ways you can't imagine. I knew that and I still—"

"You still saved my life with no regard to your own." I bore my eyes into his, showing him his reflection within... "Whatever the price, we'll pay it together." And I kissed him.

"Have you any inkling of the will power it takes for me to be this *still* with you?" It took both of us a moment to process the words. "I was never supposed to come after you that night. I defied *every* order. But none of it mattered. When I heard your name, when I saw you," Vincent played with my curls while I traced the marking on his chest. "You're all I will ever see. But, you and I, being together—Armageddon is our only end." Hearing his voice crack... I didn't know a heart could break the way ours did. "I haven't the right to love you, but... I'm here, if you'll have me."

"How long?" In addition to being a Reaper, Vincent was a Breaker. Both him and his brother cannot only travel through Time, they can *control* it. Using power like that, thought—it's only ever done under the highest command from their emperor. Wanting him to stop time so that we may have more of it—it's too selfish a wish.

"A week. Maybe two." My jaw dropped. "I don't have to bend Time itself to my will to give us *both* more of it. But, Devi," he pulled me closer, "I will. All you need do is ask it of me." The words echoed in my mind. Anxiety picked at my bones. I touched his face, his cheek burying itself into my palm. Then, I simply couldn't take it anymore.

I kissed him.

For all the fever that was in our kiss, it couldn't hide the sense of hurt in it. The familiar pang of goodbye... the painful, *inevitable,* goodbye.

"I won't go back." my words spilled out breathlessly and my lips went to find his again. He backed away. The rejection turned my stomach inside out.

"Devi," His voice was less frantic than mine. Sadness had finally taken over. "That isn't an option."

"I haven't given you my answer, yet. Officially." His head shook. It looked as though a soft breeze would blow it right off... "I will have you. *All* of you. For three days. Three years. Three lifetimes."

"We can't, Devi."

"If you know Armageddon is our end, whatever *that* means, we can change it. We can change our ending. Break the stone."

"Don't you think I've thought of that? Don't you think I've searched for a future where you and I are together? Without war. Without violence. Without death. Don't you think I've tried to find a version of reality where you're *not* ripped away from me?" my tears stung us both. I sat back, untangling myself from his embrace.

"How many versions of the future have you see?" Ten seconds fell between us. Each one fell to the earth and ran as far away from us as possible.

"Thousands."

My eyes shot up to him. "You're lying..."

"You know I'm not."

"I—I don't accept that."

"Devi—"

"You cannot say the things you've said to me, *touch* me the way you—then disappear." His hand reached out to my tears but I swatted it away. "There *has* to be a future where you and I exist together."

"There are thousands of futures, thousands of timelines where you and I exist together, Devi. But I can't find one where both of us—"

"Survive..." Vincent clenched his jaw and mine followed suit. His broken heart, mine to break...

"Devi, listen to me—"

"Vincent, I love you." I've never seen anyone's eyes drown *and* breathe before. Vincent's tears welled up in his eyes, too afraid to fall. He *doubted* my love for him. "Vincent—"

"I can make it safe enough for you to go back home—"

"But not safe enough for you to come with me..."

He sighed, the glow in the room fading. "*No one* can make it safe for you we choose this."

"I don't believe you. There's something you're not telling me." He leaned in, his eyes wild and his face, a devastating display of defeat.

"Listen to me. We—Devi, I'm a *bomb*. I don't know when I'll go off and I *refuse* to have you near me when I do. I don't know how long I could keep you alive. Understand that, please." He paused, hoping his words would settle into my mind. That his argument would derail me. Persuade me that a few days together would be enough.

"I'm half-immortal now. I'll learn to control my mimicking. Learn what you can do. I think it'd be pretty difficult for Thomas to kill me. For the others to—"

"You're death is not impossible."

"You're making no sense. How can you ensure my safety with *humans* but I'm as good as dead with *you*? And we're *both* ticking time bombs. All the big bads are gunning for you *and* me. We're going to be in each other's crossfire no matter what. Why not fight this toget—"

"That's enough, Devi."

"I don't think it is, Vincent. You're not—" If he cuts me off one more time!

"As unimaginably painful as it is to do so right now, I'm *begging* you... please, trust me." Damn him... "They'll never stop coming for us if we choose, if we try to be something no one *ever* intended *us* to be." The way his voice cracked, it sent a shiver down my spine. "I didn't think it would come to this, and this *isn't* what you deserve, but it's... this is all I have to offer you."

"And what's that, exactly?" My voice quivered as he reached for my hand and I let him take it.

"Time, my love. Time..." I turned away from him, one leg off the edge of the bed my toes skimming the wooden floor. A broken marionette on the outside; a tornado on the inside.

"Don't do this, Vincent," he was a ghost. A shadow of flesh and bone.

"I don't have a choice, Devi. This...we're not allowed. *I'm* not allowed." That word. As if a blazing blade bore right through our hearts. It *murdered* us. "Your existence alone burns the world—" his chest quaked. Firelight framed the tears in his eyes. Vincent stole me from the edge and cradled me into his arms. His heart beating against mine. "But the two of us *together*—we're breaking the universe, Devi..." the truth cut me and I couldn't bear it any longer. I shut my eyes; tears spilling cold down my flushed cheeks. Vincent held me tighter; his hands locked in mine.

"Yet here we are," I managed to say. The words fell from quivering lips; ignoring the magnitude of our lot. Vincent smiled. Calm almost washed away the hurt within us. If only for a moment.

"Here we are..." he said. His gentle words trickling down the hollow of my neck. We sealed our fate with a kiss that lit a fire in the gods that weaved our story. My heart skipped a beat, shaking against my ribs. "I love you..." When he kissed me again with that hushed vow, I knew. I *knew* with his blood in my veins, my breath in his lungs, nothing else mattered; it *couldn't*. Time is all we had and it *wasn't* on our side. This is enough.

"It has to be."

"I know, Vincent...." I didn't think it possible for immortals to be breathless, but... when Vincent climbed on top of me, his hair tickling my cheeks, his legs spreading mine apart...

"Devi?"

"Hmm?" How could I answer him when he kissed me as though nothing satiated his mouth? When his hips dug deep into mine, getting ready to slip in—

"I think we need to stop, Devi."

"Why? Are you ok?" He laughed and it filled my heart with pure joy.

"I'm fine—" he reassessed his situation, *"relatively* speaking. But, the *room*..." I lifted my head off the pillow and peeked over his shoulder. I saw the crown molding in the ceiling, a chair...and the bed floating.

"Oh my, God!" I sat up, grabbing hold of him for dear life. Vincent laughed again. Please, never stop laughing...

"I don't think you've *ever* held me this tight before."

"I'm glad you're finding humor in all of this, but despite being super immortal or *whatever*, I still, very much, do *not* like heights. Please, get us *down*!"

"It's the falling that scares you. The loss of control."

"That's implied."

"Hardly."

"Have we landed yet, Vincent?"

"Well, if you'd open your eyes. Devi, come on—Devi, you've gone head to head with *demons*. You know? From *Hell*—" we rested on our knees but I had to plop myself up higher to make my eyes level to his.

"Yes. *Low*-level demons. I used magick. I knew what I was doing. *This*, this hocus pocus—"

"Magick."

"This isn't magick I've seen in *any* Shadow Book." The chair floated freely from one end of the room to the other, passing by the fissures in the wall and the up-and-down dimming of light that didn't belong to any bulb or immortal with special glowing tattoos.

"I'm to blame for the fissures in the walls and the electrical storm in the field. We're *both* to blame for the rips in the Veil in the woods a few miles out." I saw the flashes through the flowing curtains blowing in the room despite the shut window. "You're responsible for the remaining *hocus pocus.*" He brushed my sweaty hair from my forehead.

"Do I even want to know how?" Instinctively, my hand covered my face to hide the thirteen different shades of red.

"Hey," Vincent took down my shield, "emotions are *powerful*. They can be healing, violent, *consuming*. You'll learn how to harness them. Focus them so they don't affect your surroundings and those within them, unless that is your intention. You only need more—*practice*." Attack someone with my frustration. That'll be handy.

"What do you mean by 'practice'?" the way his lips turned up in a smile when his hands trailed down my back, gripping my hips tight, pulling them into his. I palmed his chest. He found my eyes and we kissed.

"Practice..." he said, laying us back in bed, getting lost in the sheets....

"I'm—I'm new at this whole emotions manifesting into reality thing—" Vincent stopped kissing my stomach and bit his lip, stifling a laugh. He wrapped us together like a pretzel. "What's *your* excuse for—"

"Losing control?" The curtains finally calmed down but my mind raced. My eyes widened and I sat up.

"Is that it? Is *that* why you've been back and forth with me?"

"Devi—" He wore a face of disappointment. It was a very comfortable pretzel.

"Touching me for too long, too much time together, it does something to you?" He kissed me then. Not long enough for the bed to start flying but *hard* enough for the blankets to wrap around us on their own and for stars to create constellations in the dark of our room.

"When I'm with you, I never know if it's the last time. The last time I hear your voice, the last time I kiss you, touch your skin... Never knowing when the final moment is—I lose my mind. I lose control. Everything around me suffers for it. *Everything.*"

"Everything and you."

"Everything and *not* you." A moment of calm flowed through us. "I only know that our kiss brought to life thousands of stars in this room and that is all I want. I want to give you constellations in the sky of your eyes so you'll never be afraid of the dark."

I hadn't even looked at them. *Really* taken them in until he spoke his wish. My lips brushed his tired eyes and then he kissed me. Lying with him, hearing his heart. I fell asleep with that song in my soul, the light of the universe reflecting off our skin; his fingers playing through my hair.

# Chapter 20

## Byzantium

*September 15, 2014*
*Istanbul, Turkey*

The cracking of bone woke me. My eyes shot open to dark; a few freckles of light piercing through the room. I covered my ears, but the whispers filled my mind. They came from no one. They engulfed the space, sucking out all the air. I reached for Vincent, but the bed was empty. I found him on his knees, his back covered in so many stab wounds, I couldn't tell where his skin began and the slaughtering ended.

A tremor ran through him and it shook the bedroom. The battlefield ate the walls. Vincent vanished.

And that's when the bodies fell.

Broken, bleeding, butchered. Like Vincent. Save for *one* crucial difference: *Vincent* was the one exacting the violence.

Generals, Sentinels, *Paladins*. Their armor too thin, too malleable to protect them from a weapon powerful enough to incite entire armies to stop it. They wanted Vincent dead. This isn't the war that's coming.

This war had already *been*.

The sun shone too brightly, sweeping across chain mail and glinting back in my eyes. Vincent fought for his life. Limbs landed heavy in the field. Heads rolled in dripping scarlet grass. Burnt flesh wafted in sizzling grey clouds waiting to strike. LeMehti soldiers collapsed at his feet, writhing as though their immortality bled dry from their souls on his command.

And when Thomas's blade found Vincent's throat—

"Devi? Devi, wake up!" The room spun. I clutched to the sheets. "Devi?"

I couldn't help but replay everything in my mind and Vincent couldn't help but bear witness to it. "I'm sorry you channeled that. I'm—I'm still adjusting to having someone beside me when I sleep…"

"You killed your own soldiers." Without skipping a beat, he replied.

"Yes."

"They wanted you dead. *All* of them. Why? What *are* you?" His hand reached for mine. I left the bed.

"I told you."

"No." I bit my lip. "You told me you're a Reaper. You told me you—*we're* immortal. LeMehti. The First Immortals. Royal Keepers of the Dominion of Purgatory. But every species has an origin story." He took precise steps toward me. "What's ours?"

"Devi, what you saw, it was *centuries* ago. *Please...*" He moved closer and I snapped.

"Don't." My fingers dug into my arms and he clenched his fists. "Why was there an entire *war* fought against you? *What* are you? Answer me."

"You're *afraid* of me..." He swallowed back tears, the taste of the salt fresh on my tongue.

"I'm not afraid of *you*. I'm afraid of what you're capable of and that's an incredibly significant distinction. Ever since we met—I can go to sleep with my back to the room. I can close my eyes and not worry about what's on the other side because *you're* with me. But—"

"Devi, you're too far away." It broke *everything* in me to refuse his hand. The break in his eyes...

"Your *entire* empire had orders to *murder* you. Without question and you won't tell me why. I don't know what I am. I don't know *you*. I don't know *anything* about you!"

I found myself on the floor. Vincent mirrored me from across the room. We sat for a moment.

In the quiet.

In the hollow.

In the undeniable truth that love is madness and we'll be insane forever...

"You couldn't see it, but there were others fighting alongside me. It was a *civil* war. My death—it would've been a temporary solution." I finally looked at him. Vincent leaned against the side of the bed, a sheet around his waist and noose around his neck. "We had orders. *I* had orders, Devi. Neither side had the mercy of choice."

I ran my fingers across my forearm. The words etched in black ink ringing in my ears. "There's *always* a choice."

"Is there?"

"Am I not proof enough of that?" Silence... "What are you?" His eyes had shifted color to a tired crystal blue. They glimmered in the dark copper of mine. Fear *changed* my eyes from chocolate to copper...

"Not human, but that doesn't mean you have to fear me. I'm not the beast you witnessed in that nightmare. Neither are you."

"What *are* you?"

"*I* am in love with you. *That* is what I am." Vincent shook his head and stood.

"That... that's not an answer—"

"And *you*? You are magick and madness. *You're* the reason I haven't lost my mind. You're the reason I will murder *any* god who dares take you from me. I'll defy *anyone*, give everything that I am, everything that I have *ever* been, everything I will *ever* become, to protect you. To be with you..." I held myself tighter as Vincent wiped away our tears from his eyes.

"I won't stop, Devi. I'll break time *itself* until I find a life where you and I have no end." Vincent labored a breath that sinking in my lungs… "And I'll do it all again and again. In *every* life we live. I will love you, I will find you. Death be damned."

"Thomas—"

"You want to talk about my *brother*?" His jaw dropped. Go on. Take a bow, Devi. This is why we can't have nice things. Or healthy adult relationships.

"He held a knife to your neck."

"Not unlike you." He rubbed an ache in his chest. I clenched my fists. "It was necessary."

"Pain..." I finally realized.

"I was lost inside a vision. States of CaElide—" Vincent ran both hands through his hair; his eyes barely aglow, "Thomas did what he had to do to bring me back to the present."

We didn't speak. The minutes floated from our skin and into the night sky and got caught in a net of leaves and stars.

"You're keeping the truth about us—about *me* hidden."

"I need you to trust me." Vincent made his way to me cautiously. I stood up, both of us cleaving to the sheets around our bodies.

"*Trust* you?" He stopped dead in his tracks from my bite. "Vincent, how about *you* trust *me*? Believe that you can share with me *anything* and I will *still* love you in the morning. That I will love you until every star, in every sky, in every world burns out. And then, and then I will love you in the dark..." I couldn't breathe after my confession so Vincent took air for us both. "There's something you're keeping from me. Something about *us*. Please, tell me w—"

"I don't want to hurt you."

"You're *already* hurting me."

"I know." It started to rain. "Now, imagine the pain I'm protecting you from."

"Vincent—"

"Devi, *no*."

"Then keep all your heart-shaped *bullshit* to yourself." The flash of lightning lit up Vincent's desperate face. I stunned him. I've got to learn when to shut my fucking mouth. A cease-fire on the defense mechanisms would be helpful right about now, too.

"Devi... how can you say that to me? You can literally channel what I feel. Physically, emotionally—everything I am is *yours...*"

"You can *control* what I feel." He sped over to me. I had nowhere to go but up against the wall.

"Only when it comes to pain. *Not* when it comes to my love for you. *Never that.*" His anger radiated across my skin. How could I have said that to him? "Devi, you're in my *soul...* don't you *dare* think that I do not love you. I love you... Devi, look at me. You *know* me." I took the one step needed to be in his arms and the moment skin met skin, the rainstorm calmed to a whisper. I always let fear control me even when it came at the cost of hurting others. "I trust you, Devi. I trust you with my *soul.* If we do this, and we *are* doing this—" I looked up at him wide-eyed. Vincent smiled but it faded just as quickly, his hands warm as they cradled me close, "they will hunt us to no end."

"Then let's give them something worth hunting." He kissed me. His lips electrified with the truth of our words. But one word stung in our chests. One word that followed us everywhere.

"We have to leave." He took my hand and we ran down the stairs; all our belongings burning in the wind. The sheets flickered away in embers as clothes took their place. I yanked my hand from his when we reached an empty field God knows where.

"What the *fuck* is going on?"

"We're going to Istanbul." Vincent cupped my shoulders *hard* and eyed me close. "Spain first. See how you react. It'll take *two* seconds."

"We stop right *here* until you tell me why you ran us out of that place like a bat out of fucking Hell. I didn't even get to rummage through the closets."

"The *closets?*"

"I like to explore." I mumbled, shrugging.

"Devi—I had a premonition."

"You told me, didn't you? About the war? About *us?*"

"I was about to."

"And I couldn't handle it." My skin crawled.

"*Neither* of us could, little one." Vincent tangled my hands in his with a gentleness I'd never grow accustomed to. "I barely said a few words when I started to break."

"I still don't understand."

"That future I saw, Devi. That version of reality can still come to pass—"

"If we stay in that house. In the place where that reality plays out."

"The future is more likely to become reality if we give it reason."

"Let's not tempt Fate, then," I said. The glint of his eyes, even in the moonlight...

"Yet, at least." Vincent actually cracked a smile.

We arrived at the cusp of sunset in a busy park; the Blue Masque in the horizon filling the sky.

Vincent examined me, then himself. We were shoeless, coatless, and with deadly weapons holstered to our backs—completely visible.

"No one can see our weapons, but I clearly didn't think this trip through." He said and we laughed. In that moment, that tiny, innocent moment, we were two ordinary people in love. "Wait here." He disappeared and I tried not to freak out.

I looked at the humans passing by. *Did anyone notice a giant six-foot six man disappear into thin air?* I couldn't do much except sit on a bench. When it broke to pieces beneath me and I fell to the floor, cracking the brick-lain pavement, Vincent helped me to my feet.

"The bench—I sat down and—" I showed him Exhibit A.

"I felt it. Are you alright?"

"Nothing bruised but my already crippling social anxiety."

"Felt that, too." We chuckled. "Don't worry, no one saw you." I gawked at him, then gestured at the people walking cheerfully by. Our weapons were always enchanted to remain hidden from unwanted eyes, but *us*?

After a moment of processing, "Magick?"

"Mind control. But, semantics."

"Vincent, there are 34 people in the park. How—there are 34 people in the park. I never counted."

"Your LeMehti side is progressing a lot faster than I thought."

"I'm not a science experiment." I hated myself the second I said it.

"No, you're not. But I have to take note of how your immortality is coming into being. Your life depends on it, Devi."

"I know. I'm sorry. For a lot of things." My eyes darted over to the bench.

"And you need to *stop* apologizing. You're in shock and *I'm* sorry for it. Your powers, your immortality—you'll learn to control it all. Your weight, your surroundings, people's minds."

"Because it will keep me alive."

He played with my hair. "Yes, it will keep you alive..." Vincent peered down into me as though it he found something he'd lost lifetimes ago.

"You got us some clothes in that bag?"

Vincent tucked a curl behind my ear. "Yeah."

"Why didn't you, I don't know, *will* them into existence?"

"Because, little one. One should never rely on *one* skill. If you want to persevere, you need to do so using your *entire* arsenal."

"In *both* my sides. Human *and* LeMehti."

"Yes." We walked through the park as the spell lifted. Letting the others witness us in their midst. It was similar to stepping into an air-conditioned room after being out in 100-degree weather. The spell lifting, not—not the people seeing us.

"I have a place down the street." He pointed to brick building at the end of the block.

"Of course, you do."

"Come on." He kissed my fingers and I think we both did our very best not to pay attention to the increasing volume of birds screeching or the little girl and her mother rushing to get clear of us. The mother dragged her daughter quicker than her tiny feet could keep up with. The change in speed could not have been too noticeable to your eyes, but with *ours...*

"Pay them no mind." We arrived at the front of the building.

"How can I not? Did you see—*feel* how fast the mother—"

"I did. I wish I could tell you it gets better. But you get used to it."

He didn't speak after that. And after I saw his eyes, eyes that belonged to someone who has been pure death and sin in the hearts of others, I didn't speak anymore either.

We took an elevator to the 25$^{th}$ floor. The music lined the wrought iron elevator. It was particularly *uplifting*. We exchanged glances and burst out in laughter.

"Caught that pun, did you?"

"It was horrible, Devi. How could I *not* have?" Vincent nudged me, grinning.

"Thoughts keep seeping through," I said, a bit nervous.

"They shouldn't be after we *elevated* your psychic barriers."

"Oh my, God," I muttered, my free hand finding my face as we laughed.

Echoes of our sounds wrapped around the curving iron. Being cognizant of that, to see it happen... "Being LeMehti, you *see* the world."

"We do..." he said with a weary edge to his voice.

Some things, however, I knew he'd give *anything* to never to witness again. Somehow, I knew he already paid that price...

And it wasn't enough.

The elevator stopped and we began our slow walk down the hall to a giant metal door that awaited our arrival. The doorframe and the door itself had sigils etched within. They glowed brighter the closer we got.

"You asked before about our cosmic connection."

"You have a theory, Vincent?" He nodded, running a hand through his shiny black locks. The layers always managed to fall back to frame his face, though.

"Quantum Entanglement."

"Quantum Entanglement," I repeated. If it were possible, the bones of our hands held tighter. "For that to be true, you and I would've had to have had an impact. An event that took whatever it is that is *me* and whatever it is that is *you* and—"

"Tethered us, irrevocably. Because of that, I think, we can communicate telepathically even though you don't have that ability in full force, yet. No matter the place or time."

"It's not really telepathy, though, is it?"

"No. I think it's something far more profound..." A smile flashed across his mouth as he opened the door. The cling and clatter of a hundred locks opening crowded in my head.

I pointlessly sheltered my ears. "Does that always happen?!"

"You heard the locks?"

"Kinda hard *not* to. Why are you so impressed?"

"Your senses are strengthening at a quicker rate, too."

"And that's a good thing?"

He put his hand at the small of my back, directing me to walk in. "Incredibly."

When he shut the door behind him, the locks sounded off again and the powerful glow of the sigils dissipated. Their light was immediately replaced by the flames in the fireplace that lived in between the floor-to-ceiling windows across the entrance of the loft.

"Would you like a tour?" I nodded, too infatuated with the exposed red brick covering every inch of the space.

Vincent took my leather jacket and his black wool trench and hung them in the closet by the entry.

"Wait. Our bags—"

"Are in the bedroom. Don't worry. With time, you'll not only know when things like that occur, but you'll *sense* it beforehand. Even physically."

"Physically. Can't wait," I muttered facetiously.

Vincent made *scoffing* charming. "Come on." He cleared his throat and began the tour. "To the right of the magickal entryway we have a splendid kitchen with cherry cabinets and concrete slab countertops."

"Oohh! Nice. Tell me *more*." I rubbed my hands together as I passed the barstools. Vincent walked parallel to me in the galley kitchen with a smile I didn't quite know what to do with.

Vincent settled back into character. "And up the swoon-worthy iron spiral staircase, we have the mezzanine level that houses an impeccable library fit for *any* bibliophile." It consisted of two massive bookcase that were built into the entire length of the brick wall on the left and a couple *dozen* smaller ones leaning against the massive iron railing on the right, facing the windows.

"Holy shit..."

"Do you like it, Devi?"

"Do I *like* an entire *level* full of *books?*" Reading was always a safe haven for me. A book was never simply pieces of paper tattooed with patterns of ink. It was a lifeboat. A spell casting wonder, solace, and answers to questions you didn't even know you had. "Yeah, I think you could say that."

I wrapped myself in the blue paisley throw that rested on one of the leather tufted chairs in the corner and Vincent and I wandered about the library. There were books on nearly every subject and simply hovering my hand over them, I heard whispers of their tales read in Vincent's voice in my mind...

It was one of the single most calming experiences in my entire life.

I smiled gingerly and it caught his attention. I got too warm and took the blanket off. I folded it over the railing and adjusted the oversized flannel I was in. My cheeks flushed and

I tried to divert his strange focus of me elsewhere. "So, you come here often?" *What the fuck, Devi?* "That's not—I mean, do you split your time between—"

"Living in Cortem and on Earth?" Bless his soul. I nodded. "Not without reason." That was a loaded statement if there ever was one.

"Place is spotless," I said. He chuckled, but there was something different about this laugh. Something haunting...

"Is it?" Vincent ran a finger across the top of a bookshelf and examined his dust-free appendage. "Must be magick." he said with an animated grin and *ridiculous* jazz hands that sent a snort up my nose with as much grace as you'd think.

"Hold up—there's a spell that can keep matter from getting all—" I gestured with my hands to fill in the gaps my words clearly couldn't fill.

"Yes. There is a LeMehti spell that suspends matter; keeping it from deteriorating and removes any and all foreign matter."

"Yeah. That's... exactly what I said." I was astounded by the craft that now ran through me. And, to be honest, a little frightened.

We settled in the library for a while. Vincent made us tea and whenever I came across a book with a different language, Vincent helped me learn it—in seconds. Speaking and writing it, however, that would require a little practice.

Vincent's gaze warmed my back as we walked the length of the mezzanine. "Some of these books—they're supposed to be in the Vatican."

"Did your psychometry tell you that?"

"No, I—" I put DaVinci's leather-bound journal detailing how Hell *isn't* what many people believe it to be back on the shelf, "I've come across a lot of material in my studies."

"I thought you studied to be a Forensic Psychologist."

"I did. But, over the years, in between the demons and the ghosts, I conducted some *extra* research." I shrugged, picking at the hem of my shirt, looking at the setting sun through the massive floor-to-ceiling windows, "I needed answers."

"Did you find them?"

"Not quite." I flipped my hair over my shoulder and took in the immensity of Vincent's collection. "Did *you*?"

I looked to him, curious about his answer, but he scoffed with a playful grin and rubbed his neck; the gentle squeeze, warm and tight against my own.

"I found *one*..." the edges of his eyes lit up. The cobalt bright as it highlighted the messy layers of his black hair.

I forgot how to breathe. I had to do *something* to realign myself from—from *him*. I never got butterflies around Vincent. There was always a sense of nostalgia, instead.

A home I thought I'd never find my way back to.

"These books, did you steal them?" Vincent chuckled and made his way to me.

"Oh, I would *never*." The mischief dripped off every word.

I raised a bullshit eyebrow.

"Right. And I *never* jumped over cemetery walls to practice communing with the dead." I mumbled too quickly before I could stop myself. I need to leave my angsty teen years to myself.

"What?"

"What?" I shamefully stifled a grin behind my hand and wandered about to the end of the library.

There were frames with no canvases and one painting I hadn't paid attention to until now. It was set atop a locked trunk. Its wrought iron frame the only remarkable thing about it. The painting, you see, was of nothing. A canvas of black paint; the brush strokes rushed, pained...

"A failed attempt to capture a moment in time..." Vincent said over his shoulder.

"You painted over it." My blood ran cold with melancholy and fright.

"I did."

"What was it?"

"Like you said, something that frightened me."

I forced myself away from the dark memory and knelt at

the bottom of the final shelf. It housed massive volumes of mythical creatures and how they hide among us.

"I didn't know you were an artist," I said, entranced in the mythological creatures section.

"I dabble. I fare better with the writing craft than art, however."

"Me too." I found the *tiniest* armillary sphere on top of a blank journal.

"You're a writer?" Vincent perused the shelf behind me.

"Don't you know these things already? You LeMehti—your psychic abilities are *centuries* beyond what ours are."

"Be that as it may, I make it a point *not* to pry into every corner of your being. Some things I may channel by happenstance—like how you picked up on my fear from my painting—or because I *have* to in order to protect you, but I will *never* go out of my way to cross your boundaries and invade your mind, Devi."

I looked over my shoulder at him and Vincent simply radiated tenderness. I was and always would be, safe with him. That truth—it set a *balance* within and it was one of the purest energies I'd ever known.

I stood up, mindlessly tapping the top of the bookshelf. Vincent met me on my side. He picked up a book and examined it blankly. The way his fingers slid between the pages he'd read a thousand times over... "You've amassed an impressive oasis of tales."

The first edition of Dante's Inferno he had in his hand sat back on the bookcase. He straightened his posture and put his hands in his pockets; the force pulling his unbuttoned jeans down just the right amount.

"I had help in their acquisition."

"You did?" I wondered why any LeMehti would need help with *anything*, let alone a book collection. "Hey, where'd you get this? I've never seen one so small." I held the armillary sphere up in between my thumb and pointer finger. It was silver only in color, not by nature.

Vincent took a step toward me; his blood warm in my veins. "This library, its pages. They're yours to do with whatever you please. As for the sphere…" The way his eyes settled into mine, the way his heart beat inside my chest—the air let out a gasp. The lavender and cherry wine light of the setting Autumn sun enveloped every curve of our bodies. Its reflection glinting from my irises to Vincent's.

"Why are you looking at me like that?" His breathing labored in my lungs and when he inhaled, I could breathe. "Why—why do you *feel* like that?"

"Isn't it obvious?" My eyes squinted at his question. I crossed my arms, desperately trying to find the answer.

"Not quite..." Vincent's body finally met mine. His gentle hand finding its home on my cheek, his gaze intent on my lips.

It ignited *everything* in me…

"Allow me to show you, then…" Vincent uncrossed my arms and set them against his chest, the crackle of the fire below no match for the flames behind Vincent's kiss.

When his hands slid underneath my shirt, gripping me tight… "Devi, you're trembling. Do you want to stop?"

"No, I don't. But, I…" his fingers trailed my blushed face until they tangled at the nape of my neck. A hundred thoughts ran through him. The way they weighed on his soul… What if he didn't—

A lingering kiss met my forehead. I cleaved to his black sweater.

"I *want* you, Devi. From the wilds of your curls to the orchestra in your eyes, to the bite of your mouth," his thumb grazed across my lips, the pressure increasing until he parted them, "to the *madness* you burn within *every* part of me..." The gravity of his voice galloped in my heart and he pulled me closer. "I want *you*." Vincent kissed me and we crashed into the book-ridden wall. My back to the shelves, his to the sun. Our bodies lost in each other. "Do you trust me, Devi?"

"With my soul."

In the moment of silence between our heartbeats, Vincent blinked us to the bedroom. The swirling crimson and cobalt sunset flooded the entire brick-laden space.

Candles lit up, but we didn't need them when constellations sparked to life around us again.

The stars flickered. The air electric.

Vincent took off his sweater, the ancient words etched in his markings aglow in sapphire... They were warm beneath my fingertips. I kissed the one on his sternum, then rose on my tiptoes to kiss *him*... When Vincent took my shirt off, the touch of our bare skin—it was all we could do to hold on. To keep the building from falling apart...

"The world could burn and you're all my eyes will see. You're all I will *ever* see, Devi."

Abandon triggered in his midnight eyes, the blue light flashing across my naked chest.

Breathless, Vincent laced his fingers into mine. Starlight danced across our skin, but it paled in the glow of our markings. Every word he spoke vibrated with truth on my tongue. "My soul will always find yours..." I imbedded the vow in my memory. Please, don't let me forget *this*...

Vincent kissed me with a passion I didn't expect.

One I've never known...

With every kiss and every stolen article of clothing, we shifted the atmosphere. The cracks of thunder and rainstorm tore through the ancient Byzantine city. The ripples that tore through the Veil...

"Wait..." I said. Unease too cold on the tip of my tongue. Vincent stopped and I nearly floated away. He didn't have to ask me what was wrong. My answer coursed through him; knowing washing over his damp face. With a few words and a ginger kiss, he vanquished my trepidation.

"Let's set the world on fire..." I nodded with a crescent moon smile, caressing his cheeks. His sweet smirk setting the constellations alight. Vincent carried me to the bed, naked and tangled; the world outside drowning in a smoldering storm fit for omens, war, and *this*...

His mouth *never* got its fill of my body. His lips too gentle for all the *hunger* behind them. Vincent pulled me beneath him, nestling himself *deep* between my legs.

The way he stopped breathing, his forehead falling with yearning to mine...

He found my eyes, gripping my body *harder*, teasing, digging into me but *not* inside of me. "Not yet..." he whispered, his voice hot against my skin." Making me tremble wasn't enough.

"No, it isn't." Vincent mapped a path down my body with his lips until he reached what he *thirsted* for between my thighs; lighting a fire inside me *almost* as hot as his tongue...

I bent the iron bars of the headboard *beyond* recognition and it was all Vincent could do to not *level* the city.

And when his tongue could *not* be satiated, Vincent took what was *his* for the taking with his *teeth...*

Vincent found his way back to my mouth, his hands gripping every curve of my body as if I were the only thing capable of anchoring him to this earth. To himself...

He pulled me beneath him again, his hands tangled tight in mine. The cobalt glow of his eyes reflected the blazing amber in mine. He squeezed my hands, leaning in to kiss but pulling away; teasing me as he hovered his life-giving lips above mine.

"Vincent..." his name in my voice in *that* moment—it did something to him. To the *world...*

"Not yet, Devi." My name was a prayer on his lips as he dug his hips into me again and again, making me *ache* for him until neither of us could *bear* it.

His chest heaved, his mouth knew *nothing* but mine. His craving for me sparked every cell in my body. Vincent's sweat dripped cool on my tongue. I grabbed his hair, biting him. Vincent squeezed my thigh and *almost* slipped inside...

I moaned, arching my back, *sweetly* relishing in his game and it sent him *reeling*; a devilish moan of his own swept across the hollow of my neck. Vincent kissed me with the fever of a dying star. Our hearts beating in time, the weight of him the safest comfort... And when I couldn't take the pressure of him *daring* to be inside me anymore, I ran my nails down his back and Vincent *groaned*, his gasps hot in our kiss.

"I love you," he said with a break in his voice. The hushed vow kissed me with a tenderness I didn't know possible.

He wrapped me tight in his embrace and breathlessly pushed himself inside of me...

We were tethered and I knew I'd *never* know the meaning of fear again.

10

Emptiness woke me. Vincent sat at the edge of the bed, the markings on his shoulder blades a quiet light in the night.

"Vince?"

"I'm alright, Devi." I reached for him but thought twice about it. Vincent laid back beside me. "Never do that again."

"What are you talking about?" The second I asked the question, I knew the answer.

"Think twice about touching me. *Hesitate* about it." He took my hands and gently pulled them to his chest and wrapped his arms around the whole of me, his legs locking mine in his.

The blanket covering us was practically for show.

All the warmth we'd ever require came from within *us*.

"Something's bothering you."

"Enough to wake me from dreams we shared." The sting of inevitabilities took front and center in my chest.

"The clock is ticking, isn't it?" Vincent nodded. "How long do we have?" He kissed my forehead and breathed me in. He did not know when—if ever—he'd be able to come up for air.

"Not long enough..." an ache ran through us and I honestly couldn't tell you if it belonged to agony or hope, "but we'll have time. Time to create memories. Time to walk together in dreams... This is all I am able to give you, Devi, and it kills me more than you'll ever know." Vincent kissed my fingers, my nose, then me. The gentleness in him—it almost hid his fear of losing me. "Are you with me?"

The onslaught of his words twisted my stomach, and we opened our eyes; the ending of our story too clear within them. Our love—we're a bomb that'll go off without warning. There was *no* future here. No happy ending. Nothing but bodies beneath rubble. Vincent crawling out from one end of the wreckage and me from the other. But despite it all—

"I'm with you." He gave me a new-moon smile. The story behind his eyes, however…

"We will defy the stars. *Damn* the cost. Damn it back to *Hell...*"

I kissed him happily, and he nestled himself on top of me. Vincent locked my hands tight in his above my head and made love to me, defying everyone who'd dare see us dead for it.

9

Morning was hours away. I could sense things of that sort now. The passage of time. Celestial cycles and the like. If I focused enough, drowning out all other sounds, I could hear the planet *move*…

I was never without strangeness, so it was fitting that I could do such things, now. Most of my life was riddled with puzzles and oddities. The darkness in me, the crazy—it was my oldest friend.

I looked at Vincent sleeping beside me, and I couldn't imagine what awaited us on the other side of the wreckage.

Vincent stirred and woke. Dreams fresh in his eyes.

"Why are you up, Devi?" His fingers traced the lines of my face, the curls, and waves of my long hair.

"I don't want to miss you," I said too honestly. His heart thrummed beneath mine and it filled me with grace I didn't know I was allowed.

We were safe in the quiet of the crescent dark. Tangled in blankets, in one another, letting the world heal, the sweet patter of rainfall a welcome tonic.

Vincent tightened his hold on my hips and gently rolled me over to where he was back on top of me and wrapped us in our pretzel.

"Round *three*? Are you *mad*?" I sighed with a buzzing smile, cupping his arms. Vincent grinned and dug into me, careful not to slip inside. Our every desire—they ran rampant in our flesh, in our hearts.

We were mirrors...

"Maybe." He kissed my neck, the heat of his breath taking mine away. He filled his fists with my curves as we throbbed. When I let out a moan in his mouth from his playful grinding, Vincent stopped breathing... His forehead surrendered to mine. He gripped the iron bars and nestled his hips *deep* into mine. When his teeth found my lips, Vincent *pushed inside me...*

Then he pulled *out*.

"I mean, I said *maybe*," he teased with a smile and a raised brow.

"You *ass*!" I fought him off me with pillow after pillow. Vincent hugged my feathery weapons and tried to speak through his snorting. Our laughter echoed in our bones and both of us knew this would be another memory that—*if* we made it out of this alive—we'd cherish...

I grabbed him by the back of the head and pulled him to me. His devilish mouth far too ready for mine. "You're going to *pay* for that, sir." I released him and leaned against the mangled headboard, arms crossed.

Vincent only tilted his head and smiled.

He glided his hands up my thighs until they reached my hips and tugged. I fell back gently on my pillow and Vincent crawled on top of me, letting every inch of his body settle against mine.

"I intend to, my lady..." he said with a groan. "Take your pound of flesh..." His breathing quickened and mine followed suit. He lifted my hips to push into me when I stopped him.

"I intend to, sir." My new strength *effortlessly* rolled him beneath *me*. I slid myself across the long length of him and his hands went *wild*, trying to grab me. "No, no, soldier," I ordered. I sat up and he followed suit. "Hands above your head, please." He licked his lips and did as I asked, sitting back against the iron headboard, hands gripping one of the bars. He knew what I wanted to do and nodded. I wrapped the bar around his wrists. We laughed at the ridiculousness of it all, and I leaned in and kissed him.

I swayed my hips back and forth, grinding until I had him nestled in between me until I made the immortal *gasp* for air…

"Devi…" he pleaded. The spark that ran through him when I wouldn't let his hands from escaping their cuff to have me… Vincent cocked his hips up into me in *sweet* desperation, but I held them down with one hand. "Not *yet*…" I bit his lip.

When his heart pounded against my chest; when the ache of his imprisonment screamed across my skin, I set him free. Vincent tangled me in his arms and when he did, I took his mouth in mine in a fever and *finally* filled him inside me in sweet surrender.

Vincent *trembled*…

Both our jaws dropped in exquisite relief mid-kiss; birthing stars and bringing storms to new ends.

8

The clanging of a metal whisk against porcelain woke me. Eggs furiously beaten with brown sugar and a teapot gently whistling a welcome alarm clock. For a moment, in the sea of blankets and the fall of leaves and rain tickling the wall of windows, I forgot time. I forgot space. Vincent cooking breakfast in the dead of night was all I knew. His body in the kitchen, my body here, in *our* bed, sheltered… The sudden sting of saltwater that welled in my eyes was, therefore, all the more perplexing. *Why am I crying?* And then it hit me; these were *happy* tears...

"Devi?" Vincent didn't raise his voice, but I heard him as if he sat beside me.

"I'm alright." And it hit me again. They were *our* happy tears. "Vincent—" how much of *eternity* had he sentenced himself to spend alone? His bed, it was big enough for two...

"Come have breakfast with me, Devi." The humble joy in him...

I threw on some underwear and my favorite black sweater and met him in the kitchen. The fire was churchlike, peacefully playing in harmony with the drowsy drizzle. Each flame was a symphony and the rain—the prism within each droplet sparkled.

"Is it always this beautiful?" I sat at the bar and twisted my hair over my shoulder.

"I haven't noticed." I turned around and Vincent's eyes were full of nothing but *me*. I blushed with a sheepish smile as he slid my cup of tea to me.

Our fingers grazed, lingering amid the exchange. Vincent sipped his caramel cream coffee; its steam clouding in front of the immortal's blue gaze. When his eyes were in their natural state, they didn't glow. They were soft. Stonelike. Fortified enough to hide the immensity of secrets that could kill with one word, and yet... when I looked into Vincent's eyes, I was *home*...

I sipped my Earl Grey tea, the honey and milk in perfect harmony on my tongue. "I thought we could work on some magick today. What do you think?" My sights were in the city.

"I'd like that very much." I took a sip of my tea and crossed my legs up onto the stool, leaning against its back. "What's our first lesson?" Vincent took a big drink of his coffee and sat beside me to eat.

"I think, after breakfast, you should learn how to manage that LeMehti-sized Empathy." I nodded, shoveling eggs into my mouth. Vincent followed suit. "Would you like to see the city after?" I coughed mid-drink. "Are you ok?"

"Yeah. *Peachy.*" He helped me with a napkin and a laugh. "And you want to leave this safe house, why, exactly?" Vincent played with a confused brown wave of my hair and pulled my stool right up to his, cradling my cheek in his palm.

"This is a fortress, not a *prison*. I'm your *lover*, not your captor, Devi. If you wish to explore the world, then you shall."

"The others, won't we—" Vincent kissed me, the longing in him reaching depths in me I didn't know I had.

"I'm not going to let anything happen to you. We're safe here." I ran my thumb across his lips as it gave him a new-moon smile.

"I love you." My words took him aback, but Vincent smirked.

"Then you won't mind if I have the rest of your banana nut muffin." He stole the pastry off my plate and took a giant bite of it.

"You little shit!" I said after I picked my jaw up off the floor. He laughed so hard, he spat pieces of the muffin in my face.

"Yes." He swallowed. "But I'm *your* little shit." I side-eyed him and blinked us over more muffins from the pan.

"You're lucky there's a dozen of these."

"Am I now?" He cleaned us up and drank his coffee. "And if there were no more baked goods of the banana nut persuasion? What would become of me, then?"

"Unspeakable things," I said, buttering the warm muffin. Vincent put his arm around me and leaned in.

"I *love* it when you're threatening," Vincent said. I glanced down at his pants, then back at him with a raised brow. Biting off nearly the entire muffin top off, I turned to him, mumbling in mock erotic sentences. "Wow, Devi. That is, *indeed*, not something to be spoken but to be *acted* upon." My face contorted into a puzzle as his eyes narrowed into slits. Vincent turned my stool toward him, his hands gliding up my bare thighs. I drank my tea, trying to down the food.

"Vincent, what are you doing?" He picked me up in his

arms and sat me on the counter, shoving the food aside. Our laughter bounced off our skin, imprinting its memory in the walls of this place.

"Unspeakable things..."

7

Vincent and I sat on the roof of his building after our walk that was filled with bazaars, street shows, and dancing in the dark on his rooftop. I'd never been asked to dance before...

Each place we visited, Vincent taught me how to use and manage my powers, but he did it with such kindness that it *added* to the romance of our date. If I call it *anything* else, he'll have my head. He made me dress up and everything. It was adorable.

We watched the sun slowly kiss the city goodnight. We drank tea, ate coconut cashew bars we baked from scratch, and Vincent read to me from *Dracula*, one of his favorite books.

Though we didn't need it, Vincent wrapped us in a blanket. I relished in the extra warmth, thankful for the peace Vincent's chest played against my back.

He put the book away and locked his arms around me.

"Are you happy, Devi?" I looked up at him, confused.

"Of course, I am." I kissed his cheek, squeezing his shirt. He returned a lingering kiss to my forehead. But something wasn't right. "That's not what you wanted to ask me, was it? Hey, look at me. What did you *actually* want to ask me?" Vincent made a sweet effort to smile.

"When we dream together—"

"Yeah, how are we doing that? Do you walk into *my* dream? Do I walk into *yours*? Do we make our *own* dreamworld?" His heart was full of the question he longed to ask me.

"I think it depends on the situation. Depending, it could be all three scenarios. So far, we've been finding one another. Stumbling into each other's sleepy subconscious."

There was a theory for why Vincent and I could access and participate in that part of our minds. That theory—it was part of what fueled Vincent's unasked question.

"We're safe in there, right?" The way his eyes fell from the starry sky—it was as if he'd seen the thousands of nightmares I'd called home my entire life.

As if he knew what this power of ours was preparing us for.

I don't know how he did it, but Vincent pulled me closer into him, the blanket cocooning us.

"We're safe, Devi. *You* are safe..."

6

I was making pumpkin pie because, you know, Fall, when I felt the sting of something I hadn't in *weeks*. Maybe it was a false alarm—nope. I hung up the apron and went to get Vincent, who took our precious gift of time to write in his grimoire. Every letter, every line possessed the weight of something infinitely more significant than the last. He shared pieces of it with me but it's the parts that he hid that bothered me. Not because he didn't trust me, but because he knew whatever was in there would *frighten* me.

But *nothing* could frighten me more than this...

"Um, Vincent?" I clung to my favorite piece of clothing; Vincent's black sweater.

"Yes, Devi?" Vincent continued to write in his spellbook.

"I—I have to," son of a bitch, "I have to take a damn shit." He looked at me from above his book, barely keeping *his* shit together.

"Will—will you be needing *help* with that, my love?" My stomach dropped. His twisted with comedy.

"Listen! You're a boy and I'm a girl and peeing is *one* thing, but—stop *laughing* at me!" He put his grimoire on the bed and met me at our bedroom door to pinch my cheeks.

"You already know how to manipulate sound. We cut *those* particular bodily functions from our link *ages* ago, and your command of the elements knows *no* rival." He kissed my forehead and patted my head. Then, with the drama of the Globe Theatre, "Now, go forth and break the winds." He bowed and walked away, an *absolute* clown.

"Go ahead. Laugh all you like." I teleported to the bed and flung every pillow at him and when he started crying with every chuckle, I filled his underwear with fire ants.

"Fuck! Devi!" He chased me across the room but I ran and phased into the bathroom; laughing so hard I nearly pissed myself.

Teleporting small distances was getting easier, but I could not move the way they did. Phasing was only a little less challenging. It helped that training with Vincent was nothing short of magick.

When I came out, Vincent was *gone*. I rolled up my sleeves and waited.

"Come on, they didn't hurt *that* bad. I felt it too, remember?"

"I taught you to *block* minor pain." We chuckled and I found him in the living room—with a spray can of whipped cream. "What are you going to do? *Whip* me to death? Wait, that didn't sound right." He shook his head in agreement. "Let's try that again." I put my hands on my hips. "Are you going to *cream* me—no. Nope."

"No. Uh-uh."

"There's no winning this one."

"Not even a little bit." And with that, Vincent *attacked*. Whipped cream sprayed everywhere. When we fought for the can, it died valiantly in our crushing grips. "It's in my hair! My *sweater*!" We'd have everything back to pristine condition in a snap, but still.

"You're forgetting your breasts." I looked down and he pushed my chest, the cream jetting up in my face. "Vincent!" Chasing *naturally* morphed to sparring, and we were—to my surprise—equally matched. We were in each other's holds.

Pressed up against one another, arms locking the other from movement.

"Do you yield, lady?" Vincent asked, breathless. His wet back against the giant windows.

"*Never,* sir." I blinked out of his hold and sat on top of the concrete counter with his t-shirt as my trophy. I cleaned some of the cream from my hair with it.

Vincent made his way to me and bowed. His eyes in mine and his glistening chest... Damn it, woman. Keep it in your pants.

"And here I thought *I* was the only one pining for a different sort of *combat.*" I blushed, my fingers forgot how to work, and I dropped his shirt. Vincent caught it, setting it beside me. He brushed the damp hair from his eyes, licking wayward cream from his finger, then from mine. "After *everything,* you still blush." He took me down from the counter, picking up my chin so I'd have nowhere to look but up into his eyes. "You're not used to this, are you? Wanting someone who wants you in *return*... You're not used to *any* of this..." I shook my head, tracing the marking on his sternum. "You will. I promise..." A bump in the center of the marking took my attention. "It's a scar. An arrow."

"Why won't it heal? You have other scars, too."

"I don't think they're meant to, Devi. We're immortal, but we will not be without pain."

"Balance..." I said, understanding with far more ease than I care to admit.

"Yes..." His word was a whisper. I palmed his ancient wound. Vincent breathed me in.

"It's lovely.... your birthmark, not the scar." I looked up at him and his eyes drank me in.

"I'll always know your meaning, Devi. You don't have to explain yourself to me." I let my hands feel the blood pumping in his heart as he placed a gentle kiss on my forehead. "Do you want to see yours?"

"I already have—you mean my *immortal* birthmark. It's manifested?" Vincent chuckled, but worry was clear in him.

"It has."

"What's wrong?"

"Come on, Sherlock." We headed for the bathroom and a hazy blue glow filtered through my shirt. Our eyes locked on my chest then back at one another.

"I'd deduce there." He said with a smirk and a pointed finger. I gave him a no-shit look and faced the mirror. I curled up the fabric when I felt a headache come on so intensely, my nose bled.

"Devi—"

"I'm ok." Vincent took my cheek and healed me before I could wipe my nose. "Thanks." His skin on me told me what I channeled from the headache. "Something's worrying you. Enough to give me a nosebleed. What is it, Vincent?"

"It wasn't a nosebleed, Devi." He rubbed his bare chest. The air. It always stifled him. Or was *I* the one choking him? "Your brain hemorrhaged."

"Say what now?"

"I didn't heal you when I touched you. I didn't have to."

"I healed myself."

"Fatal wounds always take priority and are automatic. You'd have to willingly *choose* not to heal to stop the regeneration. Minor injuries like a bloody nose or a black eye regenerate quicker than human healing, but—"

"Are you telling me the fear I channeled from you was powerful enough to nearly *kill* me?"

"If you were completely human, yes. The small amount of my fear I wasn't able to contain, that's what—Devi, maybe you should sit down."

"No. I'm good." Rubbing my temples, though nothing but a placebo effect, helped me cope. "Let's go back to the part where your emotions—"

"The light, it's from your mark. If I'm right…"

"Nice deflection," I muttered. He curled up the edges of my shirt until the entire room filled with a blue metallic light. I looked at my chest, at Vincent's desperate face, then in the mirror.

"Vincent? Why do I have your *exact* birthmark on the same *exact* part of my body as yours?" I traced the black circle; its silver etching aglow but in blue. I would say that the similarity ended there, but I had a small scar on my sternum, too. Except, mine was from—

"Law of Contagion." Vincent's voice was distant.

"How did we not notice this earlier—" Vincent cocked his head, his eyebrows scrunched together. "Right." My cheeks blushed. "We *did* notice, but we were—"

"Otherwise *engaged...*" That fucking *smile.*

"But *you* knew about it."

"The full nature of it didn't hit me until now. I knew of it but I didn't *experience* it." Like the difference between having a vision and living the reality—blurring it to nearly nothing... I gripped the sink. "Devi—is that better?" His touch. We were both topless in each other's arms.

"Yeah." I looked up at him, the room no longer spinning. "What happened?"

"*I* happened." He clenched his jaw with guilt. "I've been alone a long time." He cleared the sweaty hair from my forehead. "I—I have to be better at controlling my emotions around you."

"But, I feel you—your emotions, when we sleep together."

"That's *different.*"

"How's that different?" Vincent chuckled softly and held me tighter.

"Because when I make love to you, I *want* you to know what you do to me." A sheepish smile dawned on my lips. "Negative affects, however, I want *nowhere* near you." I nodded, snuggling my head into his chest.

"The bare skin—it helps to accelerate healing. Transfer energy quicker?"

"Yes, though I haven't figured out why *our* bodies respond this way. Other immortals—there's only a *handful* of races that operate like us."

"And LeMehti are *not* one of them." Vincent didn't have to shake his head for me to know his answer.

We swayed in silence, trying to understand. Wading in an ocean of impossibilities. "Vincent? What is that?"

"It appears you have *another* LeMehti marking." The light of the marking engulfed the bathroom. The force of it demolished the lightbulbs. I flinched, clinging to the sexy—I mean, the not so shocked immortal who transformed the flying shards of glass and metal into flower petals. We exchanged curious glances.

"Were the lights you or me?"

"I think that was *both* of us..."

I mustered up the nerve to separate, both of us ignoring the wails of the atoms of our tether *screeching* in revolt of our disconnection. I moved my hair over my shoulder. The marking nearly spanned the entirety of my spine; spiraling down from the nape of my neck to the bottom of my ribcage with furious filigree and LeMehti script.

"Here." Vincent *dipped* his hand into the mirror and pulled the reflection out so that I could see the magick on my back without breaking my neck. Within the shining of markings blanketing us, I quickly realized that it would take more than a battered skeleton to end my life. But it had to be this way. "Yes, it does..." Vincent squeezed my hand. The inevitability of my future glossing over his eyes.

"Lightbulbs to plants. Pulling reflections *out* of mirrors..." I cleared my throat, trying to change the mood, "you're *totally* teaching me these tricks." Vincent let out a quiet laugh, stroking my cheek.

"You're a Mimic. But, I'll teach you anything you wish." Somehow, those words had a heavier sentiment, yet they warmed me to the core... I gave him a new-moon smile then became *deathly* aware that the only thing covering my breasts were my arms and out-of-control curls—or waves. Today's a day they had trouble deciding. Vincent leaned back against the doorframe, hands in his jeans, peering down at me.

"If—" I swallowed and focused on the glowing holographic marking he pulled from the mirror rather than his abs, "if the one on my chest is there because our souls are tethered, then the one on my spine is my *official* LeMehti mark?" he nodded. "Hmm. It kinda looks like a—"

"Dagger..." Every muscle around his bones tensed. He looked as though he wanted to speak; looked as though if he opened his mouth, he'd make me scream...

"Vincent?" I whispered. "What's the matter?"

I grabbed him by the belt and tugged him to me, hoping our contact would ease whatever it was that carved secrets in his flesh.

"Mmm..." He shut his eyes. "You're playing with fire, my love." His worry melted and, despite everything, it took me far too long to understand why. "I'd let go if I were you."

"I don't think I will..." I undid his belt and slid it off, pulling his hips against mine; his chest hotter than I remembered. His hands soothing every inch of me.

"Devi—"

The moment we kissed, Vincent lifted me. I instinctively wrapped my legs around him, giggling. The calm it all sparked in his heart...

He phased off what little clothes we had remaining and took me right there against the wall; cracking it to pieces. The wall dissolved behind me and I fell to our bed with Vincent finding my eyes in the starlit room; the rainstorm crashing against the windows.

Nothing mattered. Nothing *needed* to. My sweat on his tongue made him push back into me harder, and I *loved* it. He kissed me again and again, our bodies intertwined; no beginning or end. "Can you feel me, Devi?" His words spilled breathlessly into my mouth...

"I can feel you..."

"Everything I am is yours." Vincent stopped for a moment, his hair tickling my cheeks, his lips brushing against mine with his every vow. "I am yours, I am yours, I am yours."

5

I finished my tea and wondered how my giant ass feet were smaller than Vincent's. I lined them up against him and almost fell off the back of the bed. Vincent caught me with his magick.

"Telekinesis, Devi."

"Semantics," I said. Vincent smiled and blinked me beside him. "What spell are you inscribing today?"

"One that will sway you to start writing in *your* grimoire." He gave me a side-eye, and I lovingly elbowed him in the side. "You have to write in it, Devi. And name it."

"I don't really know where to start." I rested my head on his shoulder.

"You're a writer. Start with a story." A kiss met the top of my head. I let his words settle in my mind. "So, no spells in your scribbles?" I asked again, looping my arms through his.

Vincent opened his grimoire to the pages he'd just completed. The left was filled with LeMehti script—a journal entry by the aura of it. The right page, however, was a sketch of a beautiful woman sitting under the cover of trees.

"Is that... *me*?"

"It will *always* be you..."

"What are you doing, Devi?" I sat on the stool five feet in the air.

"Playing a game of Light as a Feather?"

"*That's* not a game and you're not levitating, neither is the barstool."

"*That* reference you get?"

"It's loosely related to witchcraft."

"So is the movie *The Craft*." He crossed his arms across his chest, his black sweater clinging to his every curve. "We are the weirdos, mister. No? Nothing? Good grief. Ok, tonight, we're marathoning the 90's." The way his face lit up...

"That we will. But, what about game night?" I crossed my legs, keeping the barstool perfectly still.

"With our consciousness, I think we can manage both." Vincent laughed under his breath in agreement and walked over to me.

"Now, what are you doing, Devi?" Vincent held the edges of the stool with his hands while he looked up at me, his eyes keeping me safe inside their sapphire light.

"Falling in love..." I tucked locks of his black hair behind his ears and Vincent—he was as happy to hear the sentiment as I was to profess it. But, it was as if—it was as if he remembered something he thought stolen from him long ago. The familiarity of a song you can't recall the name of.

"You're defying gravity." He cleared his throat and took a step back, cheeks—and heart—flushed. "Why?"

"You're asking me the *why* before the *how?*" Vincent waited patiently. "I defy gravity because I'm not human." Vincent smiled, but not quite in appraisal.

"We defy gravity because it *cannot* defy *us*. Half of you is still human, Devi. But you're the *only* human capable of—"

"Controlling gravity," I said, the dawning of my powers itching beneath my skin... Vincent shook his head.

"No, Devi. *Creating* it..."

4

"Is that *it?*" I muttered to myself from deep within the walk-in closets in the living room. I took off the royal jewels and put aside the stack of first edition Marvel comics, "I'm saving *you* for later," and went to our bedroom. "Hey, Vince?" I stood at the doorway wearing one of his old kilts over his grey sweats and a bored face.

"Did you find the comics?" I couldn't see his face but I knew he was smiling.

"You've quite the poker face."

"Not quite. A couple of thousand tabs open on a dozen computers... Also, they don't all belong to *me*."

"Who the hell do they belong to? Never mind. Do you have—"

"I've no more closets or trunks or *shoeboxes* for you to investigate, Devi," Vincent said between laughs after he registered my get-up—and pout. "But I've just about finished *this*." My disappointment turned into pure surprise.

"Is that a *dresser*?"

"You liked mine so much, I figured—Do you not—"

"No, I *love* it." I walked over, smoothing a hand over the top. "Why are you making me a dresser, though? By *hand*, no less."

"What do you mean? It's for *you*. Where else will you put all your clothes? Is it not big enough?" He scratched his head with the hammer, reexamining the piece of furniture.

"It's perfect, thank you. I think it'll fit in my room. I'll have to swap out my old dresser but—" Vincent set the hammer on the unfinished wood and metal box and took my hands in his.

"Devi, this dresser lives *here*."

"Oh. Well then, how can I use it?" Vincent was at a loss.

"I didn't think *this* needed saying, but I was wrong. Devi," he leaned into me, my face in his hands, his heart beating in mine, "every house I have is now yours. They're *ours*." The seconds ticked by faster than my thoughts.

"I—but, what happens when you take me back to Chicago?" He inhaled deeply, his hands locking at the small of my back.

"Did you truly think, after *everything*, I'd say *goodbye*? You are my *home*... I have been lost the whole of my existence, but when I'm with *you*—Devi, you *found* me..."

3

"See? Manipulating reality isn't as daunting as you thought it would be." The mouse eating a wedge of cheese in between us on the concrete floor was as real as Vincent and me.

"Yeah. It's not unlike mind control in certain aspects. It helps that we started there first."

"He's not alive, Devi. He's an illusion, like our doppelgängers. When you let go of reality, he'll disappear. Fall back into the atoms you stitched him together from." I petted the grey mouse as he chomped on the piece of cheddar from my hand. None of it, down to the smell of the cheese and the electrical patterns of his brain, were real. I controlled them all. And with a *thought*, I ended them.

"Bending reality, creating it… Messing with people's minds. Making them believe a lie *that* profound. How are we capable of something like that, Vincent? That kind of *power*—what on earth happened to your people that you evolved to need the likes of *this*?"

Vincent went silent for a moment. The gravity of my words too full of a past he tried diligently to forget.

"We've all evolved with traits we'd rather not have." He took my hand. "Come on. The rest of this week we'll spend combat training and put your Empathy and Mimicry to the test."

"Didn't we do that a few chapters back?" Vincent helped me up with a confused look.

"We're going to go in a little deeper this time."

"That's what *he* said."

"Who's *he*?" The snorting couldn't be avoided. Vincent stood there, chuckling along in blissful ignorance. I composed myself and explained the joke to him. He was rather delighted.

I adjusted my boobs in my sports bra and tightened my French braid. "So, us sparring—since you taught me how to control my Empathy—mostly at least—"

"You should be able to attack me without having my major pain mirror in you." I could hurt him now... "You have to, Devi. The others are protecting your family and following orders. There are only so many vault doors and concrete walls you can hit. Don't worry."

"Me? Worry?" He chuckled.

"The residents? Can you register them?" Vincent took off his shirt and threw my daggers to me. I caught them without looking.

"Um—they're a soft buzzing. All 248 of them. Like white noise. I know they're there. Most bodily functions on this scale are a whisper. A good chunk are shut off, though. But I think I'll need a few more sessions before I can control this completely."

"Good." He materialized identical blades for himself and got into position. "And visions?"

"Past, present, or future?"

"All of the above."

"Like three-day-old dreams. Only coming to the surface if I focus. But there's too many of them. Too many people to have total control over." Vincent took note of my expression. "I don't want to turn it off, Vincent."

"We need to do this *without* armor, Devi. Both physical and psychic. You need to learn to fight with the onslaught of humans and Revs in your mind. I've dulled the blades. We *won't* hurt each other the way you think." Vincent closed the gap between us, holstering his weapons in the air at his sides. He cradled my face in his hands. "Turn it off, Devi. I'm *here*. I'll keep watch." I nodded. "Turn it off and kick my *ass*." He gave me a reassuring smile, grabbed his blades, and I followed my leader's order, but he stopped me mid-strike. "I'm *not* your leader, Devi. You're *not* my soldier." Our faces twist with confusion; the lives of the humans creeping into me. We looked at one another through our clashed blades. "You are a *Paladin*, Devi. You lead *with* me..."

2

The autumn sunset from the library always fell differently. The pool of violets and turquoise swirled electric from this angle. Each passing day had been an unforgettable gift, but it came with the unnerving twinge of a timer too quickly reaching *zero*.

I looked up from a book on armillary spheres and found Vincent headed my way. He leaned against the bookshelf across from me; the sunset framing him. I set the book down beside me on the shelf I was sitting on and preened my hair; admiring the legs I hadn't had to shave since my transformation. I was constantly in shorts—*his* shorts.

"I have a safe house in Chicago. We can meet Amah and the others soon and head there. What do you think?" His abs filled and emptied with a heavy breath. The muscles cut and taught in every curve. "We can figure out living arrangements once we're—Devi?" Why is he *topless*? Why is he so far away? "Have you heard a word I said, Devi?"

My eyes shot up from his grey sweatpants and the deep V-shape at his waist, and to his eyes.

"You expect me to listen to *anything* coming out of your mouth when you *insist* on walking around like that?" I laughed nervously, pointing my finger at his enticing form. He grinned. A slight blush in both our cheeks.

With his hands in his pockets, he took a step toward me. "Alright then. Give me back my sweater and I'll happily conceal the distraction." Another step and a mischievous grin.

"This warm and cozy one I'm wearing? The one you so *gallantly* relinquished ownership of?" I sat up straight on top of the shelf, running my hands up and down my arms, knowing the touch would mirror on his limbs. "Yeah, no. I think I prefer you half-naked." Vincent examined me from head to toe, his eyes lingering on my legs.

"I didn't think you'd take such a liking to that thing. It's very old."

"It's yours," I mumbled, the comforting fabric bunched in my hands. The familiar scent of him filling my every depth.

"It *was* mine." He reminded me, cracking his knuckles. "Besides, I prefer you—" Vincent closed the gap between us, his hands tight around my hips, his mouth not nearly close enough to mine, speaking playful half-truths that tickled in my belly, "in my clothes." Vincent's hands trailed underneath the folds of the sweater, the warmth of his skin sparking across my body.

"That's a lie." he gently parted my knees with his and nestled himself into me. The heat of him radiating to my core. He grabbed me by the back of the head, gazing down into my eyes, then kissed me, *hard*.

I wrapped my legs around his waist, running my hands through his hair, and held on *tight,* biting his lip—Vincent had to remember to take in air.

"Truth is—" He kissed me again and again, his tongue hot on mine, his fingers *electric* as they slid inside me, bringing me to the edge and back—*yearning* for more, "I want you like *this....*"

I couldn't *stand* it anymore. I reached into his sweatpants and took hold of what was mine, nearly bringing my mighty, towering soldier—to his *knees...*

Vincent phased off our clothes and dug his hands into my thighs, pulling me closer...

"Wait—" Vincent stopped *immediately*.

"What is it, Devi?" His forehead fell to mine, the calm before the storm brewing within us, aching to strike.

"We've been here nearly two weeks, right? Do we have time—you don't know?" I said, confused. Vincent laughed in a gentle whisper.

"I make it a point not to—" he glanced at my naked body; his hands gently exploring me as I let out a nervous giggle, "infringe on your every single emotion, Devi. Boundaries, remember?" He nudged my nose with his, his bare chest heaving, markings glowing brighter.

"But what about—"

"Our tether?" He patiently played with my curls and chuckled softly. "You think too much." Vincent smiled and bit his lip at the sight of the beads of sweat dripping down my neck. Immortals don't sweat, but when Vincent and I... "Our tether—that, my love, there's no escaping *that*." His mouth found mine and did not let go; an echo of a break in our hearts vibrated on our tongues that we tried to ignore within the beats. "They could cut it out of our souls and it would find a way to defy the stars. To come back—"

"To life. Like a phoenix." He throbbed with every kiss and I couldn't stand it. I moaned and it drove Vincent *mad*. He teased me, pushing, digging himself against me but not inside and I loved our game...

I dug my nails down his back and Vincent grabbed my hips, gradually grinding his way inside of me, kissing me without knowing how to stop.

"You're right. We don't have time for this." He picked me up, ensuring every part of us remained connected. "But this night warrants thievery and I'll be *damned* if I can't *take* time for *this...*" on the tip of his last word, we were back beneath the sea of blankets in the living room, the roar of the fire burning beside us. Vincent laced his hands into mine and made love to me as if it was to be the beginning of our end...

The firelight dimmed, and the light of our markings filled the loft-like a night full of stars. "We will defy the stars. Burn them from the sky, making our *own* night. And then, Devi..." Vincent lingered his kiss above mine, "And then, we will love in the dark." Vincent kissed me and took time itself and *bent* it to his will. Carving out a fragment where *nothing* dared tear us apart. "And nothing will. Not tonight, Devi. Not *yet...*"

"Vince?" I traced his marking; his chest rising and falling.

"Hmm?" His hands locked me tight against his body.

"About those living arrangements…" He opened his eyes and wiggled down a bit to where we were level.

"Yeah. As soon as Gavin and the others are through securing the properties and a few other things, you can come to visit us as often as you like. You can use Amah's keys." It took me too long to realize he was messing with me.

"You almost broke my heart, you ass." I pinched his stomach and, consequently, mine.

"How could you even think that what I said was anything other than a *joke*?" One look at me and his face fell. "I don't think I'll ever acclimate to the fact that you've never—"

"I've been loved, but I—" I sat up, shaking my head, the truth of my romantic life whirring in my chest, "you're right…" He sat up with me, his chin on my shoulder.

"I have a few safe houses in Chicago. A warehouse, in particular, I'd converted a bit already. Whenever you're ready to, I'd like us to live together." I loved that he knew it was a matter of preparation I needed that would determine *when* I'd move in—not *if*.

"The others, they'll have homes, too?" He nodded.

"We'll be a family, like Melot said."

"But, you said before—"

"That we're breaking the universe." He straightened up and cradled me to his chest. The ancient city sleeping outside our window. "We would have to be cautious. Maybe limit our interactions..." He inhaled, reluctant to speak the next words. "Limit our *intimate* interactions. But," Vincent picked up my chin and his eyes lit up and set mine aglow; the sapphire and amber lights swimming together, "we *found* each other, Devi, after—" he pursed his lips. "I'll not lose you, Devi. The universe will heal…"

1

Vincent's heart beat sweetly against my ear, our bodies ever tethered. Still warm, still breathing the air of a fire not quite burnt out...

"Hi," I said gingerly. Vincent's arm tightened around my waist, squeezing my hip.

"Hi, my love." A kiss met my forehead, but it carried trouble with it.

Vincent stared at the ceiling, bearing witness to ghosts of a world I may never understand; he may not have his soul torn apart like the others, but something is scratching at the walls of his being. And I haven't decided if me being able to access the claws is a good thing or if it's far more dangerous than I can imagine.

"If we're separated—if the others take you from me..." Vincent's voice cracked, breaking us. I held him tighter, letting my heart beat in his chest. But his eyes went *black* and full of a pain he dared not let me touch. The thought of what could happen to me... "Do *whatever* it takes to survive them." I nodded. What more could I do?

"What will *you* do?"

"I'll find you. Whatever the cost, Devi. I *will* be where you are." He hid his rage well, but not well enough.

Visions of violence creeping at the edge of his skin burned behind my eyes.

Vincent kissed me without abandon. "If Thomas—if they *take* you—"

"I know..." I kissed his palm, Vincent gave me a newmoon smile, "I'll remind them why they've gone mad..." Vincent leaned in to kiss me when the black light of his eyes sparked with a horror I thought only reserved to my rarest of nightmares.

*Do **not** move from that spot, Devi.*

Vincent leaped out of bed, armor wrapping around us in seconds. He pulled his swords from the pocket of space around him, looking out into the night sky when the swords found a holster on his back and he swooped me off the bed.

Before we vanished, I could smell the sheets, *every* memory we left behind—burn. Our *home...*

*Thomas found us...*

My eyes widened at the words, and a moment later, we were on the Great Wall of China. There was blood in my mouth, but I wasn't hit. When I finally found my footing, I saw Vincent a couple of hundred feet away, face down and drenched in blood—that's when I realized it was *his* blood in my mouth. *His* broken bones writhing beneath my skin. What happened to one of us, happened to *both* of us.

Law of Contagion...

Somehow, in that *one* second of Porting, Thomas and Vincent battled for my life.

"Vincent..." I ran to him, ripping off the gauntlet and shoving the bone piercing out of my forearm back in place. He opened his eyes in time to see Thomas yank my hair. He broke my neck, the force of my body hitting his shattered my hips and collapsed my lungs. Vincent spat out my blood, gripping his chest. And when I saw Vincent crumble back to his knees and my injuries heal—

*Vincent, stop it! I'm* ***immortal*** *now! I'll heal—*

*Devi,* ***don't*** *fight him.* ***Don't*** *fight back.*

With the laughter of the maddened immortal singing the skin off my ear, I understood. If I tried to break free of Thomas, if I tried to do *anything,* Thomas would Reap Vincent's soul. Killing him.

*It will kill us* ***both...***

That agonizing sob carved itself into our chests. The cursed word that followed us everywhere...

*This* ***isn't*** *goodbye. Go to the Bridge.*

*I—I don't know how. I don't know how to move like you...*

*It's* ***okay****, little one*

When Thomas licked a tear from my cheek, the winds picked up; bricks from the wall fracturing. Vincent stood; the devil in his eyes, both our markings, the brightest fires in the night and it did nothing less but terrify me.

Especially Thomas...

But he didn't reign in his fear like Vincent. He let it pour into me; molten and vile…

I vomited. My organs failed and detached… My skeleton rendered to pieces. My brain boiled… and I'm still *conscious…*

Vincent clenched his fists, siphoning as much of my injuries to himself, ignoring his own wounds, running a *thousand* versions of my rescue in his mind but—

*I've found **none** that will end with you alive... Devi—*

*I know... It's **okay**...*

*I **will** find you.*

# Chapter 21

## Memento Amoris

I smiled through my tears. He raged through his…

Vincent made his way to Thomas and when he did, Thomas's heart trembled and I heard a loud pop. Vincent fell to his knees. The smoke from Thomas's gun scorched my throat.

"Vincent!" The wall vibrated beneath us. The Veil tore open and a lightning storm wreaked havoc in the fields.

Pain *ends*…

I ignited my fists and burned through Thomas's armored grip, but Vincent's bullet hole dripped red down our faces. The world spun, and I fell before I took a step to him... Both of us laid there, hundreds of feet apart, eyes bearing witness to nothing but the inevitable.

Vincent used what he had left in him to heal my wounds faster. Then, the flickering cobalt starlight in his eyes, the shine of his markings—when they dimmed, when I could only manage to crawl my way to him from the weight of his, my cries were the only thing heard for miles across the earth. Across the Veil…

*I **know** you're not dead. I'm the one that will be the death of you, remember? Wake up! I can still **feel** your soul. I'm sorry I fought back. Please, **please** wake up, Vincent. Wake up!*

Thomas grabbed a tuft of my hair, but this time, I didn't react. I didn't attack. If Thomas pulls my soul from my body, it'll murder Vincent.

"Let's finish this shall we, dollface?" In the blink of an eye, my head spun. I fell to my knees, trying to no avail to stand. The grass was cold and wet between my fingers and the smell of rain heavy in the sky.

I gasped for air when Thomas took me by the throat, dragging me a few feet before flinging me across the woods. I tumbled and somehow; I stood and ran for the nearest Evenfall Bridge I could find.

The ground shook beneath my feet as I ran faster and stronger with every second. I found a door to a Bridge. I ignited my fist. All I have to do is burn through it and seal it shut from the other side. The thunder rolled with a blinding flash of lightning and that's when Thomas grabbed me and my fingertips slipped from the edge of the Bridge's shimmering door...

Thomas threw me across a field. Watched with a lustful grin as my head hit a tree stump. The Dark Paladin mounted me, his eyes white, hair whiter. His fingers laced around my neck, squeezing. "Thomas! Stop! Please, snap out of it! This *isn't* you!" He tossed me around like a rag doll, paralyzing me.

"How easily you lot give up. How easily you are broken." His iron hand tightened, breaking my windpipe. Thomas stared at the sky and shivered. The rain poured and Thomas was the vision of a beautiful death. "There was a time where peace was all we knew, Devi. Betrayal doesn't sit well with us. One act. One *tiny*, insignificant love-sick butterfly brought a world to its knees as the gods sat up in their thrones, *watching*."

He shook his head in disgust. "No punishment, no consequence matters. A human Reaper—How has he hid you for so long?" For a moment, Thomas's broken heart echoed in mine... I grit my teeth, but they didn't survive the stifled scream it birthed in me. "The two of you—you're an *abomination*. You *sicken* me." Thomas drew my limp body up to his shoulder, squeezing my throat until his fingers pierced flesh...

But there was a flicker of light behind him. It grew brighter between the sheet of rain as it neared us. And when I saw his eyes—when I saw Vincent draw his weapons—a horde of LeMehti and DeKenna soldiers descended around him. Thomas looked his brother dead in the eyes and threw me off the cliff. But not before he did one thing as Vincent watched: Thomas set me on fire.

From the inside out...

It used to be when I woke from a nightmare, I knew I had been dreaming because I never wanted to close my eyes again. The risk of falling asleep—the risk of not waking up again was far too great. This would lead to months in my life where I'd stay awake for *days*; sleeping three, maybe four hours in a week. But the exhaustion, the delay in cognition, the constant terror writhing beneath my skin was worth it because, after a while, I wasn't afraid anymore. Or maybe I simply forgot what scared me to begin with.

When I woke up in a warehouse filled with four LeMehti Paladins praying I'd live through the night, I wondered why I bothered to open my eyes...

My Paladins were the empire's *elite*. These ancient soldiers, the strongest, most intelligent, and expertly skilled military unit, unmatched by *any* realm, were reduced to broken bodyguards bunched together on a bed of concrete... *asleep*. I managed to suck the life out of them.

I dared not move. The burns had healed, but they had

killed me several times over. And, half-immortal or not, death takes a while to recover from. That kind of survival—it doesn't come without a price.

"Your fatalities are a technicality. You took in every death that would've taken you from this world." I examined the four soldiers across from me. None of them were conscious. Vincent, though, was missing.

"Who's there?" I said, my throat full of gravel.

"It's me, little one." My heart skipped a few beats.

"Why are you *speaking*? Where are you?" Then it hit me; mine wasn't the only death I've taken in... "Vincent, are you—"

"I'm alright. Nothing a little skin-to-skin contact can't cure." On the tips of his last words, Vincent teleported to my bedside. "Don't cry, Devi." He knelt and cupped my cheek. "You'll make *me* cry, then we'll *both* be crying and that's just not a good look on anyone." He accomplished his mission and made me laugh. "Can I lay with you?" I reached for his wrist.

"You *never* have to ask me that."

"I know." Vincent crawled beside me and cradled me in his arms, my head finding its home on his chest.

"Vincent, you're burning up."

"I'll be fine." He tugged on my shirt, and I nodded. Vincent undressed us and we fell deeper into one another. Our skin-to-skin contact immediately sparking restorative energy through every cell.

"You took in my injuries?"

"We *all* did, Devi. Thomas—you don't remember?" I shook my head, icy tears spilling down to his marking. "Devi... shhh. This isn't your fault. Do you hear me?"

The quiver in his voice damn near broke me. "Your immortality is fledgling. You would've regenerated but we didn't have that kind of time."

"It took—it took *all* of you to fix me. What the Hell did Thomas do? What good am I being a Paladin if I can't take care of myself?" Vincent scooched down until his cobalt eyes were level in mine.

"Listen to me. If anyone's to blame here it's *me*, understand? *I* was the one who couldn't get to you in time. And I don't care how many soldiers I was fighting, *you* come first. I should've been able to Port you to safety." Vincent rested his crown to mine, pure energy looping through us. "You did more than anyone thought possible when Thomas threw you off that cliff. You're more powerful than you know." His eyebrows scrunched together, trying to meet in the middle but failed as miserably as Vincent thought he failed me... "Thomas didn't simply burn you from the inside out. He—"

"He tore me apart—"

"Atom by atom..." I didn't notice my lips trembling until Vincent smoothed his thumb across them. "Melot and the others fought the other Paladins and Knights while I made my way to you." Vincent laughed and I had no idea why until I registered the snoring of the sleeping soldiers blanketing me in a warm haze. "Thomas and I fought until he suddenly dropped to his knees, giving me the opportunity to hurl him into Andromeda." I yawned and cozied up into him, wrapping a leg around his. "Do you want me to wake you up a bit? Devi? *And* she's snoring..."

"Huh? What?" I rubbed my eyes but it was useless. "Yes, please. Wave a wand or something. I'm feeling much stronger now that you're here, but four sleeping immortals—that's quite the supernatural tranquilizer." Vincent kissed my forehead and I was as alert and focused as him. "Thanks." He gave me a new-moon smile. "So, Andromeda. Continue. Wait. The *galaxy*?" Vincent nodded and I leaned up on my elbow; hair wild and shock too bright on my face. "Of course, the galaxy..." Vincent took me back in his arms and we pretzeled each other. Every injury we'd sustained healing quicker and more efficiently the longer we were together. "But, how were you able to fight him? If my atoms were being torn apart—"

"So were mine. However, I had a force stronger than the destructive magick of my brother." Vincent's markings illuminated and mine followed suit. "I love you, Devi. That will forever conquer any maladies against us. More than that,

Thomas was tearing you apart..." his eyes fell to the memory that so clearly traumatized him, "Gods of old couldn't stop me from saving you, let alone my brother." My soul warmed. The heat tingling at the edges of our skin. Vincent pulled me in closer after that... I looked up at him, the glow of our markings playing across our desert-toned skin in waves of silver and blue.

"I love you..." I said and kissed him. The touch reverberating throughout our bones. "Vince?"

"Hmm?"

"Where are we?"

We were in a giant warehouse. Some of it had been converted and suitable for residency but most of the building still had ivies for curtains and broken glass for rugs.

"A safehouse in Chicago." My heart stopped.

"You took me *back*?" I sat up, rigid.

"I'm not leaving you, little one." Vincent pulled me back into his chest. A moment of silence seeped through us, its calm filling our lungs.

"Vincent, what did I do to Thomas?" Vincent spared no time in responding. Vincent had my answer prepped and waiting for my question on the tip of his tongue long before I thought to ask it.

"Let me show you." He put a finger on my temple and a movie of the events played in real time when only a couple of seconds passed here.

"I—that *can't* be right."

"Oh, but it *is*, my lady."

"How?"

"I never let you fall in the water, but, when you lost consciousness, you believed that was your final destination. You knew that if *you* drowned, I would follow."

"So, I drowned Thomas instead..."

"He was especially surprised."

"How—you said you didn't let me crash in the water. Do you mean to tell me you kept me suspended in air, containing all my atoms, taking in my burns, while trying to keep *your* atoms from falling apart as you fought the others *and* catapulted your brother to a different galaxy?"

"You helped keep my atoms from falling apart, too. Mirrors, remember? And, I mean—you transferred your would-be drowning from *me* to my brother *and* every single enemy combatant on the battlefield—which included the *most* powerful soldiers in the *oldest* empires across the Realms—while *braindead* and dying *dozens* of deaths..."

"Every single enemy—" I rubbed the impossibility of the two of us from my cheek. "So, we're *both* terrifying."

"I was going to say fucking *bad ass*, but your version has an ominous ring to it, too." My eyes widened.

"You should drop f-bombs more often." Vincent laughed and wrapped us into our favorite pretzel.

"I've *quite* the mouth." He booped my nose and we burst out with laughter. The others only got more comfortable.

"That you do." The way his eyes narrowed, my lips their only focus; the way his breath deepened... even after all this time, I must have turned a hundred shades of pink.

"A hundred and *one*." I playfully smacked his arm, and the sound of his chuckle fueled my heart, pumping fresh, healing blood in both of us.

"Please tell me that speeds things up..."

"What are you in such a rush to do, Devi?" I gave him the biggest 'are you fucking kidding me?' look and— "I know, I know. I only jest. No need to birth the fear of the gods in me, lady." We laughed but levity was short-lived.

"I don't mean to—having you with me like this, I want to—" I couldn't find the damn words. But Vincent did. He always did...

"This is war. Any moment could be our last. And if we have even the *semblance* of a chance to be together," he picked up my chin, "to show the gods of old the face of love..." in the same breath, we were in different room, on a different bed, "we take that chance."

"But, we haven't completely healed. Especially you."

"This touch, Devi..." Vincent kissed me, gently resting himself on top of me; one hand wrapping my leg around his bruised waist while the other caressed my black and blue cheek, "*this* touch..." he leaned on his elbows, letting the weight of him, the weight of his chest pressing into mine, "it will *always* bring me back to life..." Vincent kissed my forehead, my eyelids then my lips, his hands tangled in my hair. We locked eyes and paid no mind to the constellations in the warehouse or howling wind. We kissed; our remaining wounds tingling, healing quicker and quicker. But it was when Vincent wrapped my other leg around his waist, when he nestled himself inside of me...

"Breathe, Devi..." Vincent left a trail of kisses down my neck, my chest; the electricity of his lips sparking madness across my soul.

"How can I when you're—" When he came back for my mouth, "Vincent..."

"Do you want me to stop?" Vincent whispered, nearly slackening to a halt, playfully slipping out of me.

"Don't you *dare...*" I grabbed his hips, lifted mine, and pushed him back inside of me, *hard*. The *burning* moan that fell from his mouth into mine...

"How can I when you're—" Vincent made love to me as if it would be the *last* chance we'd ever have. And though I sensed the fear creeping at the edge of his skin with each brush of his lips, I only kissed him back the only way I ever knew how; without knowing *anything* else...

We forgot the world. We forgot the war. We forgot that we were *weapons,* and for one last time—for one *last* time, we chose to be *love...*

The familiar patter of rain and Vincent's pen strokes roused me. I watched him for a while; his chest gently rising and falling in perfect rhythm with mine. The Veil had long healed;

the earth below, however… Déjà vu hit with more frequency, and, if you looked close enough, the shadows that move in the corners of your eyes? They *run* now…

And it was *exactly* why Vincent and I would not live together. The consequences of our love…

"What are you doing?" I murmured, still waking. Remnants of our shared dream warm in my eyes.

Vincent sat at the edge of our bed, scribbling into his book. Fledgling sunlight floating across his skin from between the curtains. "It's of last night." His sweet words trailed off into the past. Into *us*… The markings on his back illuminated. Mine followed suit. I wrapped my arms around him, resting my chin on his shoulder. "I never want to forget you, Devi. Not one moment in time." The pang in our bones, the sudden break in his voice… He put his grimoire away and took me into him, kissing me as if this were a reverie and not reality. As if our touch was the only tether that kept us from being ripped apart.

"I'll be close, Devi," Vincent said, kissing my forehead.

We fell asleep with salt in our eyes and a broken universe trying to put itself back together because Vincent and I dared to be something worth remembering…

# Chapter 22

## Eclipse

I escaped, finding peace in the bathroom. The quiet didn't reverberate as much as I thought it would. The tiny space only fed my anxiety. I noticed myself in the wooden framed mirror. My eyes briefly reflected light like a nocturnal animal, and it gave way to more evidence of my inhumanity.

I hadn't *really* noticed myself until now. My face had slimmed, blemishes nowhere to be found, and my hourglass figure—every curve was wrapped in muscle.

I was foreign.

Panic filled the pit of my stomach, the weight of it—the weight of *me* cracked the blue tile beneath my feet.

"Are you kidding me?" I rolled my eyes and when I opened the door, my new strength tore it off its hinges, knocking myself in the face with its steel. It sent me backward into the brick wall, the entire warehouse shaking. "For fuck's sake..."

Every single Paladin practically *died* laughing at my glorious folly.

Everyone but Vincent, who'd wandered off nearly an hour ago leaving me behind with only the dissonant music of my soul calling out to him, burning across my skin.

No matter our efforts in Istanbul, we couldn't understand why it happened, nor how to stop it.

I pulled myself out of the Devi-sized hole I had formed. "Very funny! Whenever someone would like to help..." I trailed off trying to put the door back on its much too broken frame. I rubbed the back of my head. You know, when it's not during *sex...*

"You'll get used to it," Gavin said softly from the living area, *after* chuckling under his breath.

"I somehow doubt that," I said with a scoff.

I wonder what everyone thought about Vincent and I's relationship. Could it even be classified as such? Is he my *boyfriend? Am I having this fucking thought process right now?*

Defeated, I set the mangled door aside, annoyed that my superstrength came in waves at times. I caught the wind before I walked back to the others. I turned on my heel, the gaping hole letting in frantic air. It weaved around my fingers and pulled. I glanced over my shoulder, but the others were conversing in their old tongue. The one language I was *not* to learn. Mimic or not.

The wind tugged again, and I followed it to the edge of the broken wall. Surveying what I could in the grassy, overgrown lots across from me, I couldn't tell why the element wanted me — "Hey!" it tugged *harder* and I fell out of the hole. "Shit. Alright. Lead the way." I found Vincent in another abandoned warehouse *crying...*

Instinct dethroned logic and I sped over to him. He spoke but I couldn't hear him. He wouldn't *let* me hear the conversation nor see who he spoke with. When I arrived, eyes downcast and heart sunk, Vincent faced me; all his woes vanquished at my sight.

Or so it seemed.

"Vincent, what happened?"

"Nothing yet." The gravity of those words buckled my knees. I nearly fell back. He reached for me, but I let the stairs save me instead. "Devi—I'm ok. *We* are ok."

"Crying in the middle of nowhere in the dead of night is the very definition of *not* ok. Trust me." He shut his eyes, breathing, though he didn't need it. He ran a frustrated hand through his hair. "You saw something. You were talking with someone. Whatever you said to one another—it fucking *broke* you. It broke *both* of you. All that pain—when you died you died inside *me,* so don't tell me nothing happened!"

I cleaved to my black sweater, still full of his scent; clinging to something tangible. Something real to anchor me because this—this *can't* be happening…

"Devi, nothing good will come of me telling you—"

"I know you had a vision. I know it revolved around our future. Whatever it is, please, tell me."

"We *can't* change this future." He could barely look at me. Guilt so heavy in him, we cracked the concrete, sinking in a few inches.

"I know." I wiped a tear. He rubbed the stubble around his mouth.

"Words, Devi, a *single* word," Vincent took a calculated step toward me, "the perfect sound, the precise vibration; the sheer *will* that brought it to existence has the power to create life or end it. Some words, Devi," Vincent adjusted himself and rubbed the bones of his hands as they braved taking mine; his eyes too dark for our liking when they reached mine. "Some words are better left unsaid." He kissed my forehead and wrapped me in his arms; both of us sighing in relief. "There's a thin line between keeping secrets from you and protecting you, I know. But sometimes, the line blurs and that's when I *especially* need you to believe that keeping you out of my mind is—"

"Keeping me *alive…*"

War is strange. It rarely starts with a scream. Most of the time, it's fought in the dark. In quiet moments behind the teeth of royal advisors or in clandestine trysts that win—or *lose*—battles at the nonnegotiable end of a revolver. At the end, war is a god without worship that exacts retribution with madness and a magnifying glass on a sunny day.

Watching the Paladins spar, practicing their magick, all that ran rampant in my mind was the crippling truth that it wasn't *war* ingrained in every atom of their immortality. It was something far more necessary. And it came at a cost I don't think I'd ever understand.

They trained me the whole day after the recent attack. The main floor of the warehouse providing the perfect dystopian terrain and ceiling height we required.

This time around, physical and empathic damages were not guarded. The Paladins and I fought at full force. If I were to withstand another assault, I had to know what it truly felt like; intimately. I trained this way with everyone but Vincent.

We struck one another, but he didn't allow us to experience the full extent of the injuries—or the pain I caused him. When he and I sparred, our guards were on. Nonetheless, five and a half immortals wailing on each other with fists, swords, and magick—had we been on unwarded land, there would be *no* land.

Thankfully, like every LeMehti hideout, the warehouse was isolated and structurally fortified to withstand the onslaught of the Revs within. My guardians tried to fully awaken my Mimicry as they had done my psychic abilities and magick. But it was an utter failure. We required one crucial piece and, though they knew what it was, no one—*especially* Vincent—dared provide it.

Even though the lack of it meant my defenses would suffer.

"Vincent, I don't get it. If you know what we need to jack up my Mimicry, to level the playing field, why won't you, you know, bippity boppity boo that shit?" I rested my weight on my spear while Vincent glimpsed something untouchable in the wings of a crow flying by the windows; its wings blinking shadow and light across the face of a man I loved but knew little of.

"Because it'll *level* you, Devi. It'll level us *both*." Vincent's voice stunned. Andra and Mel stopped mid-throw to another Realm. Gavin and Amah nearly decapitated one another. "We're running out of time. Devi and I will train. Alone."

I don't think the Paladins made any attempt to hide their qualms about the order. Nevertheless, they were not as reluctant to follow it as Vincent was to give it.

Everyone's markings lit up. The markings running up and down Melot's arms were the brightest. The ones on Amah's abs, Gavin's chest, and Andra's collar bone—they all had an ominous flare in each illuminated sigil.

Vincent and I, however, eclipsed the sun…

When the Paladins disappeared, I searched for evidence of life. The crow had been the first animal I'd seen in a long time. A radius of five miles and nothing but insects cowering beneath the earth.

"What we are, Devi, the acts we commit to ensure the battles of today don't bleed us tomorrow…"

"Vincent?"

"The things I've done—" I dropped the spear and went to him, gripping his face tight. "What I've done, I deserve *every* damnation—"

"Vincent, *stop* it." His tears burned in my eyes, trembling in our bones; the frenzy of a fury that never slept, voracious for every last drop of blood in him. He took me in his arms, the chaos waiting for a reason—*any* reason—to break free.

"Devi, you have to remember—remember, there's a cost to survival, and it's *not* what you think it is." Vincent cradled my head in his hands, hands that have killed more than they calmed. "You have to be able to survive me so that you can survive *without* me. Do you understand?" I did the only thing I could—I nodded. "Don't forget these three things, Devi: They will scare you, but you're the one who terrifies them. They will kill you, but you will not die." Vincent couldn't speak. As if the sound of his own voice set his mouth on fire...

"What's the third?" I said, a ginger smile on my lips, grazing his with my fingertips. His hands tightened around my waist, pulling me into him.

"They will guard you with an army. Tens of thousands of soldiers keeping me from you—but remember..." Vincent breathed me in, a breath so deep, for one precious moment in time, only he and I existed. He met his forehead to mine, my heart beating in his, "I will *bury* them." And when Vincent kissed me, the truth of his vow flowed in our blood. The stardust of our souls illuminating our skin, reflecting prisms on the surrounding glass.

Vincent drew his swords; the song of the metal too beautiful for all the death living in its edges. The arctic air too frightened to whip at his bare chest. The frozen air did not bother me, but my bones shook from a far more crippling reason.

"Draw your weapons, Devi." Vincent was the cause for the snow... It wasn't a part of the training. It was a part of *him*.

"Vincent, we're Empaths. We'll—" it finally dawned on me. We had to beat each other to death. Warmth comes from life and, right now, he harbored none. "You *want* us to feel it when we hurt each other." The silent horror in his eyes spread beneath my skin, the reality of what he had to prepare me for if... "I'm not fighting *you* like that. This is madness. Sparring is one thing but you—you want us to draw *true* blood." I knew his logic and—he's *not* wrong. But there was something else. There's *always* something *else*... "You're keeping secrets. Tell me what this is *really* about, Vincent."

His eyes flicked to the constellations floating around us, then fell back into mine and never let go. And when he opened his mouth, my heart sunk.

"They will murder you beyond imagining. If you're to stand a chance at Cortem, if you're to survive *them*, you have to survive *me*..." He took his position, and I took mine. "Now, fight."

When the sun bowed to the moon, when Vincent was satisfied that he turned me into him, into a *killer*—in both body *and* mind—we took a shower to wash away our violence. The amount of blood that spiraled down the drain...

I drew us a bath, knowing Vincent needed it more than he dared admit.

"How is it?" Vincent squeezed the sponge over my shoulder, the steaming water calming me as it poured down my skin.

"It's perfect. Thank you." I leaned back into him; his heart finally thrumming with peace against my back. I ran a finger across the scar from a battle axe on his thigh. Vincent played with the wrought iron and blue bearded iris tattoo on mine.

"This was your first tattoo?" I nodded, the scent of coconut and sandalwood incense and candles swirling in my head. "Do the irises have any meaning?"

"I've always equated them to love." I shrugged.

Vincent ran his fingers across the petals. The wrought iron and flowers came to life on my skin and picked an iris from my tattoo and gifted it to me, leaving the art intact. The particular flower he pulled happened to be my favorite of the bouquet. I put the blue petals to my nose and inhaled.

"What about the one on your forearm?" Vincent asked, filling the clawfoot tub with blue bearded iris flowers; their perfume mixing with ours. He sweetly nestled his chin in the hollow of my neck, holding my right hand in his. I looked at the single word inked with an Elvish style and the two arrows piercing through it; the arrows balancing one another in opposite directions.

"Always equated it with love. With choice..."

"Providence," he said the word aloud and the water, for the briefest moment, shivered.

"Inspired by a dream I had years ago. A prison centuries old, a storm, these two arrows, and—" I swept my fingers across the black ink, thankful I could now block the memory of the nightmare breaking my heart from Vincent, "this word echoing in every corner of my soul..."

"Do you recall the details of that dream?" I shook my head.

"Most dreams I can play back like a movie, I can remember them better than my own life but, others—I remember how the dream made me feel, though." I curled my body into him, my eyes forever in his. "Scared, but loved. I remember being *loved*..." Vincent kept our gaze for a long time before he kissed my forehead. An hour ago, he'd cracked it open with the hilt of his sword... An hour ago, I'd taken my daggers to him—

"I know it's hard, but try not to think about it." Vincent held me tight, and we lay in the water, silent. The bath was our shelter. Shelter from everything but each other...

Survival is strange. It rarely starts with a whisper. Most of the time, it's fought in the light. In the quiet moments behind the teeth of a smile or in clandestine trysts that win—or *lose*—battles at the nonnegotiable end of your revolver. At the end, survival is a god with worship that exacts gratitude with madness and no mercy for those who hope for one more day.

Survival takes far more than it ever gives...

# Chapter 23

## Welcome Home

*September 29, 2014*
*Chicago*

It wasn't yet dawn. Vincent didn't sleep. He spent most of the midnight hours scribbling stories into his grimoire as I fashioned my own. There was all manner of memories and spells in the pages of Vincent's spellbook. The pages I could *see*, of course.

I sat on our bed, blanket curled around me, and watched him in the thrift-store chair in the room's corner. You could see the old White City's skyline amid the autumn clouds, but Vincent, older than the steel and brick of those buildings, was lost in the words he was sentenced to write and forbidden to speak of the crimes...

"Good morning," he finally said. The book vanished into the pocket of space beside him, and Vincent took his place by my side, his hand in mine. He took note of my black book, proud.

"What's going to happen today?" I already knew.

"You're going home. The others and I, we'll be close but—" I reached for his face. The instant my fingers met his skin, he nestled his face into my palm. Vincent ran his thumbs across my wet cheeks.

"Just not close enough..." My eyes fell with understanding. "Don't do this. What *changed*? We were supposed to live together. We were supposed to be a family." I knew their plan. It coursed in my veins. They'd protect me and mine from a distance. Interfering only when needed. Fear of tempting Fate won that battle. Dynamite is less likely to detonate if it's not in a room full of candles.

"You know why I can't, Devi."

"Do I? What happened to the universe healing? What aren't you telling me? I don't care what it does to me. Blur the fucking line!"

"Everything I do is to *protect* you. You have to believe that."

"We protect *each other*." He had no words for me. "Goodbyes don't protect people, Vincent. It *kills* them." He pulled me closer, his breath desperate. Vincent nestled his forehead to mine, strands of his hair sweeping across my eyes.

"Then we know what the death of us will be." The trauma in him vibrated beneath my skin. He couldn't scratch the images of what Thomas had done to me, what he *himself* had done last night, and the terror it put him through echoed in me all too vividly. I didn't try to hide my pain, and he hated himself for being reckless with his emotions around me. "I'm sorry..."

"Vincent, don't apologize for *feeling*."

"When what I feel *breaks* you—" he cradled my face. "Devi, I don't ever want to break you."

"You won't. I'm fine."

"Devi, none of this is *fine*."

We were quiet then. Vincent stroked my arms, and I held on to his shirt as if my entire immortal life rested on my grip on his body. None of this is *fine*...

*I'm* not fine.

And the terrible truth was, *eternity* wouldn't be long enough to fix me.

Vincent held my hand tight and told me to breathe. His touch, the spark that helped anchor me to reality. *This* reality, not those of strangers. I would learn, soon enough, he had said, that I would find my own anchor. A lighthouse guiding me, always letting me know how to find my way back to my mind.

"Where are the others?" I got out of bed and found some clothes.

"Patrolling, I think." He went to the windows.

"You *think*, Vince?" I got dressed and examined him. In the early morning dark, he seemed almost magickal. Not in any other meaning than an undying creature returning your gaze as it breathed. "Vincent, where are the Paladins?"

"They're otherwise engaged." I grabbed my holster and shoved my weapons in. He smiled, and I followed suit.

"They've been doing a lot more than having sex and protecting my family and friends, haven't they? Even when they were with us, they were elsewhere. On guard. On mission. Scared to *death*..."

Though I hadn't perfected it, I scanned the past. I looked at our time together to find a pattern and, though I found a few, I could not put a name to them.

"They're following orders." I nodded my head blankly.

"I want us to live here. In the warehouse. A little sweeping, some candelabras—"

"Devi, you have no idea what you're asking."

"Yes, I do. We're supposed to give everyone something to hunt, remember?" I rushed over to him, our weapons at our backs, but our deadliest artillery lay behind our teeth... "You're the love of my life." I never saw tears well in his eyes that quickly. "I've always been lost, without a haven to call my own, that I belonged. My *entire* life. But you—Vincent, you're my *home*... I'm not afraid to sleep when I'm with you. I'm not afraid of *anything*. Talk to me. What's wrong? We're stronger together and you *know* it. Let me help you. You said I lead with you—

"Devi, please don't ask me to stay."

"Why not?" He replied the moment I asked the question. Without thinking. Without hesitation.

"Because that is *all* I want to do. Because I *won't* be able to refuse." My tears stung.

"Then *stay*, Vincent. What's so wrong with that?"

"Everything, my love, everything..."

"Don't." Vincent wrapped his arms around me, cradling my head against his chest. "Please... *don't*." My stomach twisted.

"Devi?" I gagged, choking for air and desperately clutching at Vincent. "Devi, what's happening?!" The helplessness in his eyes...

The Paladins rushed in, utterly broken, bloody, and too *late*.

Before Vincent could react, I blinked out of existence...

When I opened my eyes, Thomas had his hand latched around my throat. A gash in his forehead revealed his fractured bones, courtesy of Amah.

"Vincent's getting quite sloppy with his scanning. *How* could he have missed me taking you *again*?" Thomas leaned in and licked my lips, biting them bloody. Before I tore out his rib cage, he flung me up into the sky. I broke the sound barrier...

Twice.

I crashed into his target that carried hundreds of people. That impact was all it took to link me to every single person on board. And as I descended back to earth, the deaths of the passengers on the burning plane sprung to life inside of me, starting with the children...

I fell from the skies like a star without a wish; skin flaking off with burning embers, breaking the sound barrier. The lake swallowed me whole, shattering my skeleton. Reliving the deaths of the passengers disoriented my healing. The past, present, and future of 337 lives coursed through my veins.

My lungs fought between air and water. The pressure crushed me the deeper I sank. My body caught between dying and healing. I never learned to swim, but many of the passengers did. Now, so can I. Their memories taught me everything I needed to know.

It was pointless swimming to the surface. There were too many people inside me weighing me down. Too many timelines spiraling in my mind…

I should let myself sink…

The water bubbled and caved in on itself. In the blink of an eye, I was on my knees in the park behind the Museum of Science and Industry. The 1893 Columbian Expo buzzed beneath my bare feet.

Every inch of me surged with life that shouldn't live. I stopped coughing up blood long enough to orient my equilibrium. To rid myself of what was left of the passengers. The sirens and shouting echoing from across the water stung my ears; the air burned as I breathed it in. I tried to stand, but collapsed. The ground quivered beneath us from the force of my fall.

I knew Vincent by his presence alone, but what I couldn't discern was the reason for his silence; his distance. Between the cries of the city below and the wailing of sirens, my body wailed for the Paladin who wouldn't dare wipe my tears away.

"Vincent?" He stood motionless behind me. His heart raced within mine, my body trembling from the beats.

"Devi. I'm here." His voice cracked. The taste of the salt in our soft sobs potent on my tongue. With my bearings in order, I faced him. But he backed away from my advance. My stomach dropped, nearly buckling my knees. "Devi, *don't.*" The quiver of his bloodied lips vibrating on mine…

"You think I'll channel how you ended up this badly injured if we stand closer?" The carnage crawling on Vincent's skin… "Vincent, why can't I *feel* you? Why won't you *heal?*"

"I tried to get to you as fast as I could." He didn't look me in the eye.

"I clearly can't die by way of drowning," I replied as panic slowly built in my chest. "I think you were a little busy fighting for your *life*. Don't worry about mine."

"There will *never* be a world in which your life is of no consequence to mine."

"I know. I'm—Why are you cutting off our tether? I thought that was *impossible*."

"I suppose it's not..." Asshole. "I heard that." You were meant to..." After a staring contest that resulted in nothing but both our black stone eyes paling to grey, I tried again. "Why don't you want me to witness your battle, and why's it taking you so long to heal? Did you fight Knights?" He closed the gap between us, but our connection remained shrouded.

"Time isn't something we have, Devi. Please—" Vincent's hand reached out for mine, but I refused him, "Yes. It wasn't just Thomas and Miarrah. DeKenna Knights were present...."

"Is that supposed to clarify you shutting me out? For the love of God, Vincent. If you're paying the price with your *body*, I don't want it. I want *nothing* to do with it. My safety will *never* be worth your pain. *Never*, do you hear me?"

Nothing he could say would take away the rotting guilt in my chest.

"Yes, it *will*." My eyes fluttered in shock. "I will pay *anything* asked of me, in every world, every single time, whatever the cost." His hands found my body and pressed his chest against mine.

"Why?" I pleaded, fingers cleaving to his red-soaked shirt.

"You *know* why." I dug my face into his shoulder. Ran my hands beneath his shirt. His blood was warm on my hands but—

"Why won't you let me feel you?" He breathed in heavily and held me tighter. But when he began shaking...

Immortals *don't* shake.

"You still have the deaths of *hundreds* inside of you. Do you truly think I'm going to add myself to the mix?" I wriggled myself out of his hold.

"YES!" His eyes had never been wider. "You giant fucking fool, *yes*! I don't care if you're in pain, afraid, confused, happy, hungry—insert any and all physical and mental states—I want them *all*. The entire fucking *world* can be burning in my bones, but *you* come first. I will always, *always* make room for you. You're not sparing me from hurt when you hide—when you *separate* us. You're doing the *exact* opposite. "

"I'm sorry, Devi." He braved his forehead to mine, our hands nearly as tangled to one another as our souls. "I—it *won't* happen again. But I need you to understand, the way we're tethered—I tried to shield you from receiving my injuries, but to have endured my pain—"

"Would've *paled* in comparison to the hundreds that died on the plane. I understand." I took a deep breath, "And I *don't* care." Vincent tried to smile. His body finally healing from our contact.

"Lady, you are madness."

"And you, my lord, are chaos." Vincent kissed me. Again and again, until his body had nothing more left to give. Then, he kissed me again…

"Please, don't go..." I whispered, my throat raspy.

"I love you..." His words brushed against my lips.

In that sweetness of silence between us, we kissed. Kissed as if we'd never see each other again, and we never did…

Vincent took my breath away. His tongue tasting me with a fever I knew too well. The push of his hands pulling me into him; his lungs full of the inevitable. Goodbye was at the edge of our skin; longing to break free. We held on with *everything* we had and *more*…

And it wasn't enough.

When Vincent vanished from beneath my touch, I opened my eyes to emptiness. To the remnants of the dead seeping into the fiber of my being. My tears spilled, trailing murder in their wake. I did the only logical thing I could think of: I let their death kill me.

If only I was a thing deserving of such mercy…

The fabric against my fingertips was wrong. The fall from Thomas burned my clothes and left me naked in the lake. Vincent dressed me in what he knew I'd need for what was to come; a pair of sweats and a plain grey t-shirt.

"Devi? Come here..." Andra found me alone beneath the trees. Vincent's absence haunting more than the history of the Expo.

She took my face in her hands and the look of shame buried behind her eyes filled her with disgust. "We didn't see them in time. I'm *so* sorry."

I shook my head, too full of nothing, and wrapped my arms around the broken Paladin.

A deep breath later and she brought us among the crowds.

There were 15 survivors in the water. Fifteen out of 337 people.

"I killed them. I killed *all* of them," I finally managed.

"No, you didn't." Gavin's words were meant to comfort. They failed.

"Whatever it is that I am just *murdered* all those people and—the fallout of their families, their stolen futures—" I gripped my chest and staggered away from them. I could barely speak. "Spare me your sugar-coated bullshit about—"

"*Thomas* and the others killed those people. *Not* you. There is a difference." Andra may be right, but at this point, there's too much distance between black and white.

"The difference is that innocent souls were lost because of *me*. If I hadn't been on that plane, had I never been *born*—"

"But you *were* born and you *were* on that plane. You are what you are and we all must live with it. Including you." Andra looked at me with a pained stare as Amah and Melot encroached the masses. "Devi, this line of thinking—" she grabbed me close by the shoulders, her eyes too hot, "it will lead to nothing but *ruin*. Do you understand me, girl?"

My eyes flicked to Gavin. He stood steps from me, gun in hand, smile on lips, every inch of him painted by the soldiers of a queen too infatuated with beheading. The black of all the Paladin's armor streaked with hundreds of brush strokes.

"Yes... I understand." Melot willed people as *far* away from me as possible while Amah stood watch for any more potential attacks.

"We'll be stationed close. Say our names, Devi, and we'll be beside you." When Andra took her hands off me, it was all I could do to not crumble. "Choose any paramedic. The FBI agent we spoke of is already here." She squeezed my cheek and I held her sweet hand. Neither of us wanted to let go. But, I took control of myself. As much control expected of anyone in war, and Andra vanished with the others in a gently glinting cloud of smoke.

No one was meant to die today.

No one but *me...*

And it did *not* go unnoticed.

Though I couldn't see them, the Agents of Fate were in the midst of my crime scene. Debating on erasing my existence but also, for reasons none of them understood, knowing that they could not.

"Miss, are you hurt?" The frantic paramedic asked as he clocked in the frenzy behind me. When did I make my way to this ambulance? "Can you tell me your name?"

Speak. Say something, Devi. He sat me in the back of the bus, searching for the source of my pain. But all he found was a very dry, lost girl in pajamas, no shoes, and utter shock. All I saw were black body bags. Tiny ones. Each one a victim of *me...*

"What's your name?" He said again, pointing the flashlight in my eyes. When they reflected light back...

"I'm not hurt. I wasn't on the plane." He tried to say something but couldn't get the image of my inhumanity out of his mind.

Enter the FBI.

"Ms. DiCaprio?" The man in black called out to me as I wandered away from the ambulance. This FBI agent had more concern for his cold hands that he stuffed in his fall coat than for the kidnap victim that had been missing for nearly two months. His green eyes were hard, analytic. "Can you tell me your name?"

His voice nowhere near kind enough to strip my attention from the ground full of body bags. The ones that they could find, at least...

"Devi DiCaprio." The vibrations of the dead—of everyone—bubbled beneath my bare feet and I had to move. I walked towards the government issue black SUV, then stopped when I realized I *shouldn't* know where he parked.

I shouldn't know his fiancé left him because he spent more time on my case than with the woman who cheated on him a year ago.

"I'm Agent McAlister," the jerk said his name as though it should've borne some meaning. Other than being a Rev, Joshua McAlister was... "Ms. DiCaprio, how did you get here?" I laughed.

"I'll do you one better: How did you know where to find me?" I retorted. No answer.

Official story is a drone picked me up via facial recognition. *Unofficial* story? My family and the Feds were *so* desperate to find me, when a psychic—one that happened to work with my Paladins—came to them offering information, they accepted.

I got in the back seat of the car and stared out the window. Josh stood there and wondered how I managed to get in since he never unlocked the doors.

Once at the hospital, he decided to begin questioning me.

"While we have the chance, do you feel up to answering some questions?" Agent McAlister asked rather gingerly.

"Doesn't matter if I do or not. Ask away." I stared at the bed, my hand grazing the sheet and the hospital gown waiting for me to wear it.

"It matters—"

"Ask, Agent McAlister."

"Can you tell me what happened to you?" I sat on the bed, swallowing the vomit that rose quickly. But 14-year old Lily Klein who died on this bed three hours ago hadn't left.

*'The Good Cop act is kinda charming.'* Lily spat with a grin and I nearly laughed out loud. Her black curls still bounced as she crossed her arms across her chest. She leaned against the glass wall; eyeing Agent McAlister with her one unswollen eye. The blood dry against her copper complexion was too bright and smelled too much of the car crash her bitch Munchausen By Proxy mother caused.

Don't worry. She didn't survive either.

"I left class and headed for the 10 o'clock train. It was Friday, August—" *'You're sounding too rehearsed.'* Lily warned. "Before I could reach the train station, I was hit over the back of my head—" I had to remind myself to pause. Take a breath. Squeeze my hands together for self-soothing. *'Now you've got it...'* "I blacked out. I never saw who it was." I stopped, the creeping memory all too apparent in my trembling limbs. And Lily's...

"What happened next?" Agent McAlister asked, jotting notes.

"I woke up in a living room. Overheard one of the men say I'd been out for 16 or 17 hours?" *'Why is he looking at you like that?'* Lily was too ready to punch him in the gut. "What's with the face, Agent McAlister?"

"What are you talking about, Devi?"

"You look like you're about to question a *person of interest* and *not* a victim."

"And here I thought that Psychology degree of yours wasn't going to make an appearance. Graduated with Honors, right?"

"*Forensic* Psychology, and one has nothing to do with the other." Lily laughed.

The concerned look on Josh's face when hospital staff told him they found nothing. They'd done their job *meticulously* but were *stunned* at how I had no evidence of anything other than psychological trauma.

The interviewing at the police station didn't bode much better for Josh. I played my role the way I was trained to. Better, even. Better because the terror lacing in my answers was the most honest thing between the Agent and me.

"Can I have my phone call, now?" Josh had no response other than a pointed finger to the phone at his temporary desk just outside the room. I sat in front of the telephone sifting through a hundred different possible scenarios out in my head. "Let's hope we get scenario number 37." I whispered to myself. I picked up the phone and dialed my adoptive sister's cell.

"Let me look at you. Are you hungry? You want some chai?" The sparkle in Izumi's eyes fizzed away as they ran over my frame. I wore clothes they didn't recognize and wore slippers rather than shoes and had a blanket wrapped around me. They made horrible attempts at concealing their fear of the reality of my situation. I had been kidnapped, missing; been through Hell, and neither my best friend or sister would ever be able to fix it.

And it *broke* them.

I stepped over the threshold of my apartment and saw the glow of the protection sigils. The Paladins were here.

"You can't understand how crazy we've all been around here." If Lennon only knew that I could. That I've seen her pray to God every night to bring me back. That Izzie cried herself to sleep after endless nights conducting her own search for me. Their screaming matches raw in my throat when their efforts—mortal and supernatural—yielded nothing.

"I'm sorry." The quiet fell harder in the room than I anticipated. Lennon went to make tea while Izzie and I convened in the living room. I sat on the couch but didn't realize I sat on the remote control. The TV flashed on.

"The kidnapped 27-year-old Middle-Eastern student, Devi DiCaprio, who went missing in August, was found today." The picture they used of me was actually nice. Izumi ran over to the set and shut it off. Her straight, black hair swaying with her movements. Izzie was pale, but her fair skin dropped a few shades when they met me downstairs.

"Damn press work fast," Izzie said with nervous laughter. I couldn't hear it, but I knew Izumi chanted her mom's Japanese mantra. *Our* mom since she adopted me when I was—I glanced at my palms, the havoc they were capable of now...

"Fucking vultures, is what they are." Lennon spat from the kitchen filling up the tea kettle. Her strawberry-blonde waves were hidden in a bun. A couple of stray strands rested at her shoulders.

When warm drinks and pointless chatter settled into momentary silence had a chance to change into a heartfelt reunion, I made my move.

"I'm—I'd like to take a nap. Is that ok?" The turning of their stomachs almost made me throw up the sugar cookies and Chamomile.

"You don't need our permission, Devi." Izzie's warm, cocoa eyes rendered a calm in me. "Go. We'll be here when you wake up with Dad's lasagna waiting for you. With extra mozzarella, of course." Italian was my favorite. It was fitting, then, to be taken into a family with that heritage.

I tried to smile at Izzie's words, but left to my room instead.

Down the hall and out of sight, I stood at my door. If I walk inside, that's it; I'd spend the rest of my life as though *nothing* happened. As though I'm not human.

That Vincent and I...

I opened the door.

The vibrancy of my past crashed into my chest.. Colors were more focused, energies sharper, memories heavier.. .

The black wrought iron of my bed and the navy and bronzes of my bedding vibrated with an unfamiliar frequency. Someone *other* than the Paladins had been here. Shutting the door behind me, I took not one step when the light flowing from the peacock-colored drapes demanded attention. And as my eyes caught the illuminated dust floating across my face, I saw it.

In that single moment, the past played itself in real time. The police, Agent McAlister, and CSI crew as they combed through my room for clues. I followed Josh as he stopped and stared at my industrial shelving unit that housed my books and candles. He focused on my copy of *Paradise Lost* for a long time. Everyone looked defeated when they left. The only lead they had found came from the wooden box that held all the tools to my Craft. The text on exorcisms scared one CSI investigator so bad, we both had to sit down.

*"You think this could be some Occult-related shit, Agent?"*

*"We leave no stone unturned. Someone took her and the sooner we find out why, the sooner we find her."*

As everyone but the FBI Agent exited, I managed to stand. I realized something about Joshua. He's got a secret. He surveyed the mess of a room one last time and left. And as he shut the door behind him, the vision effervesced and I caught myself before I fell to my knees with the Dutch angle tilt of the room.

"A three-hour vision of the past experienced in—" I checked my clock, "Holy shit," Three *seconds...*

I staggered myself to my Jane Austen writing desk. I ignored the pictures of Connor and I beside my laptop as best as I could but after a moment of shallow breathing, I knocked the frames down and the plants hanging on the walls twitched. *Take a deep breath, Devi.*

I rested my head in my palms, my elbows on the wooden antique. And that's when the chair cracked loudly beneath me. The wheels rolled off everywhere. I stared at the door. *Please don't let them come in.* Lennon and Izumi didn't notice the crash and I hurried to put the chair somewhat back together.

I stood in front of my mirror.

My immortal marks—proof-positive of *everything.* I traced the perfect circle on my sternum, my fingers grazing each unknown word. Could Vincent feel this touch? I turned around, flipping my hair over my shoulder. The mark on the nape of my neck; the dagger down my spine. Spiraled and Gothic and utterly impossible...

"You're home, Devi," I muttered weakly. This isn't home.

I have no home. Not anymore...

My door rattled, waking me from my nap, but did not open. I tensed, my fingers grabbing as much torn fabric as possible; *they're* here.

My blanket dragged away from my feet. I sat frozen as the whispers scratched at my walls. Their voices hummed. One on top of the other. The tick tock of the clock creaking louder and louder.

They called my name...

"Hey, Devi? You awake?" Their knocks on the door stopped as Izumi popped her head in, her bangs bouncing. "Hi, sleepy head. Devi?" Answer her. Say *something.* "Connor's on his way." She hasn't sensed it. Can't see the creature crawling on the wall behind her, baring its teeth. *Don't* scream, Devi. Do. Not. Scream.

Remember your training.

Remember the last 14 years of your life...

"Connor. Yeah. Come sit down, Izzie." I jolted up and grabbed her by the wrist. The creature's jagged claws barely missing the back of my sister's skull.

"Whoa. Everything ok, Devi?" One look and she *knew...* "You had a nightmare, didn't you?" She sat beside me, my dull hands clammy against the soft porcelain of hers. "Why do you keep looking over my shoulder?" The *thing* peeked its wild murky eyes from the foot my bed, grinning its jagged jaw, drooling blood on the iron it could not cross. *"Devi,"* Izumi said with conviction.

The bottom-feeding demon and I cocked our heads and it *vanished*. Silent banishments... Before being immortal, banishments would take *words* to work. Now, now I can banish a lower-level demon with mere *thought* in a single second.

"Sorry. I'm tired is all." We're all psychic; Izumi, Lennon, and I. They've seen their share of evil. But, they don't see it the way I do. Not entirely.

"Should I tell Connor to stop by tomorrow?" My sister by choice and not DNA is no fool. The hairs prickling at the back of her neck alerted her that something was amiss *before* she walked to my room. It's *why* she came in the first place. I looked into her warm eyes and wanted to vomit.

The lies I'd be forced to spit into her face for the rest of her life.

*Her* life...

I managed a smile and blinked as quickly as I could, drying the tears before they swam—washed. Before they *washed* over my eyes.

"Let him come. I'm gonna hop in the shower." I left Izzie's comforting confines and grabbed some clothes from my closet.

"Devi?"

"Hmmm?"

"Whatever happened, you know you can talk to us, right?" I stared blankly in my underwear drawer. Izzie and her family—when they found me, I was half-alive in the middle of some backroad on their way home from a camping trip. I'd nothing but my name on my tongue and an unwavering sense of doom deep in my bones... I knew my birthday and my ethnicity—Middle Eastern. Assyrian, I think it was—or was it Persian? I can speak both languages so that was no help. There were no missing persons reports, no warrants for my arrest, no CCTV footage… It was as if I burst into existence in that moment. I was a ghost and they gave me life…

"I know." I closed the closet door, stubbing my toe beneath it. My daggers and gun were set atop my black boxer briefs.

"There you are. Are you sure you're ok?"

"What? I'm fine, Izzie. Stubbed my toe."

"Devi. I had to snap my fingers in front of you and *repeatedly* call your name. The pain of your toe didn't even phase you. You didn't space out. You—you were *gone*." Not gone enough.. .

"I'm sorry. I'm right here, Izzie. I'm right here." I hugged her hoping that my Paladins would work their magick and protect her from the targeting stain my aura left behind. I wanted to hold her tight and *never* let go. But, if I did, I'd kill her. I'd *kill* her… "I'm gonna take a quick shower and then, what say you, me and Lennon play Gin while we wait for that relentless dumbass to show." Hesitant and cautious as always, but ever loving, Izumi agreed and left to relay the message to Lennon.

And me?

I locked myself in my bathroom working up the nerve to deal with the burning witch in my mirror.

Welcome home…

# Chapter 24

## In The Morning

She housed the usual desperate expression smoking behind the fire. Her oozing hands palmed the mirror, slipping with each frantic reach for my throat. The witch's charred skin crackled and fell off in clumps when she smirked. Her eyes twisting with a pain I knew far too well. So, when she broke through to my world, I almost let her strangle me to death…

I hit the wall. Each squeeze of my neck cracked another vertebrae and drank the air dry from my lungs; but something was different this time. The witch couldn't drag me through the mirror and into her world.

I'm too heavy.

I'm healing.

I'm not *human*…

I put my hands on her, ignoring the fire draped across her butchered form and we locked eyes. And for the *tiniest* moment, I saw tears in drown in eyes that once housed a soul... She disappeared with a flurry of ash and flames and I hunched over the sink. I vomited bile and soot into the marble bowl. When I had a chance to breathe, I forced my gaze into the mirror, waiting—longer than one ever should—for my reflection to sync with me. "Where the fuck did you go?" I took a hold of my neck, still hot from the witch's touch. I brushed off the charcoal embers and saw minor burns and bruises. Shit. Superficial, but these won't heal for a day or so. Make-up and a turtleneck. I'm always cold anyway. It won't be suspicious that I'm wearing a sweater in a 70-degree apartment.

"Devi? Did you fall? We heard—" Izzie and Lennon.

"I tripped over the damn trolley—again. All good!" After a moment of deliberation—and my wishful thinking—they left reciting a famous line.

"For crying out loud." Lennon muttered and they both laughed at my exquisite ability to defy all logic when it comes to klutziness.

"That girl needs to be covered in bubble wrap." I almost laughed with them.

I turned on the shower and sat at the edge of the tub. "What a fucking mess..." I muttered. I'm not back *five* minutes... I could patch some of this back up myself, but I may need supernatural reinforcements of *Paladin* proportions.

I took off my shirt when a wave of energy electrified in my chest. I tripped over my feet getting to the mirror. My eyes, my chest, my back...

"I'm on fire..."

*No. It's your markings. You're safe, Devi.*

*Vincent?*

I thought I saw him in the reflection behind me. I thought I made sure to keep my eyes wide open, but I didn't. The bathroom was magically repaired, and I stood there in a half-singed bra, goosebumps despite the steam, and my face slowly—but inevitably—disappearing right before my eyes...

I left the battered lavatory, doing well to leave my battered mind in there with it. When I walked into the living room and saw Connor sitting on the leather couch—my favorite blue throw blanket smothered beneath him...

The pressure from the shocked silence crushed me. I threw up in my mouth, the dull glow of the lights flickered in my eyes. No one noticed the liquids rippling in their glasses. Too hung up on the electrical phenomena.

Lennon and Izumi had told Connor to give me my first night back to rest before coming by. But Connor n*eeded* to witness me alive. I couldn't fault him for that. We'd spent nearly the last decade of our lives together. The six shots of whiskey he had last night, however...

My tongue dripped with his fear of never seeing me again and *scorched* with one of the *very* things that had been our undoing.

They all exchanged looks as I cleared my throat, trying not to jump out of the bay window. *Focus on something else. Don't squeeze your fists. Say something. Anything.*

"Devi..." Connor stood up, smoothing his beard and khakis. He wanted to leap across the couch and vintage dresser anchoring it and sweep me into his arms. And, if I hadn't broken up with him before I went missing, if Vincent and I hadn't fallen in love—Connor and I would share more than a simple embrace tonight.

But that's not the way our story was meant to be read.

"Hi, Connor." He rushed over to me and took me in his arms. His broken heart, the dread he drank in every bottle—finding me dead at the bottom of each one... It coursed through me and I had to pretend that I experienced none of it. Not the way I truly did. "I'm ok...I promise."

"I thought—"

"I know." Take in the room and not his emotions. Lennon touched-up the white paint on the faux fireplace. Looks good. The TV hanging above it has a tiny crack in it from when Izzie battled a renegade pigeon that wandered in last week when the Amah left the window open for that very thing to occur; for me to have that distraction *now*.

The aloe-vera and orchids were well-fed. All the plants full of color; cushioned by candles on the mantle cocooned in a bed of crystals that were now nowhere near strong enough to protect us from what lurks in this house.

Connor and I sat down and I made sure to sit on the corner, my favorite spot on the couch that faced the bay windows. I curled up in my blue blanket, easily removing Connor's scent from it. The other couch was draped by a quilt that Izzie finished over the summer. The industrial coffee table in between still had my copy of Shakespeare's *Romeo and Juliet*. The girls, they didn't move it one inch...

I looked over to them, over Connor's head sitting beside me talking about work and trying not to ball. I almost smiled at them, even Connor, when something in the window seat tucked in the bay window—that I will *not* jump out of—took my attention. A heartbeat? Racing and close.

I walked to the windows and the sound became frantic. I stopped dead in my tracks before the spider went into cardiac arrest. Is—is it *afraid* of... *me*? I took another step toward it and it scurried away from me *so* quickly, one of my ribs cracked.

"Devi? Are you ok?" Connor put his arm around me and I flinched. The horror on his face when he saw my fist...

"Yeah. Totally. I'm sorry. Just need some air." I sped away but it didn't stop him.

"Air? It's what, 40 some-odd degrees outside?"

"Connor, leave her be." Izumi provided incredibly proper instructions, but, as usual, Connor didn't listen to what I needed.

I used our back door to go up to the roof. The sunset and clouds luminesced soft opalescent. I closed my eyes and held myself together. The brisk air chilled me for a moment, but then, my immortal side took over and my body became a comfortable 70 degrees. I can sense my body's temperature.

I *know* the mechanics of *how* that happened. What's more, once the birds registered my presence, their chirping muted; they're bodies sprawling in the air and away from *me*.

"Devi?" His voice was cautious trying not to startle me. No doubt he was afraid I'd take a dive. And from 6 stories, I can't say I wasn't tempted; if only to see how I'd break...

"Hey."

"Here, you're going to freeze out here." Connor pointlessly wrapped his jacket around me. I tried not to be repulsed by his scent. A week before I disappeared, I found out that Connor had started drinking again. "You're home, Devi. Everything will be ok." His whisper had a hint of calm to it, but it held more hurt than anything. He pulled me into him, his chin resting on my shoulder; both our eyes facing the setting sun. Both of us knowing far too well that I was about to fall apart.

"It's on fire," I blurted out.

"What is?" The world...

"The sky." He saw a setting sun. I saw... I dared myself not to do it. Avoid lighting a match. But when you're drenched in gasoline, it's only a matter of time before you light up.

"I can stay tonight if you want. For as *long* as you want, Devi." Want. What a funny word. It took me getting *kidnapped* for Connor to treat me this way.

"Connor, there's—I need to talk to you." As if he knew my thoughts, a drum beat in him and, for once, Connor *fought* to keep me.

"Devi, every day—every *second* you were missing, I lost pieces of myself. The chunks got bigger and bigger." He took my face in his hands and every memory we ever shared would not let me move...

"Your hands..." I whispered. The familiar heat—He paused and leaned in, a half-smile on his lips.

"You *make* them warm." No. I may be forced to live a lie, but I'll not live *that* lie.

"I—I can't do this, Connor."

"Do what? What's wrong?" One shot. One kill.

"It's over. Please accept that." The shattering of his heart... How am I still standing? Rage replaced romance. Connor wanted to break *everything* on this roof. Including himself.

"Devi—" He boiled with pain and it was all over his eyes.

"This has nothing to do with what happened to me. I can't—we can't keep riding this carousel, Connor."

"You're ending things because I had *one* drink two *months* ago?" He's had three bottles of whiskey in the last *week*. That's actually not so bad...

"No. I broke up with you because you're a recovering alcoholic and *lied* to me about using. *Repeatedly*. I ended things because I'm tired of being at the bottom of your priorities list. I ended things because," breathe Devi. Stop *crying*, "because I don't want either of us to hurt anymore." He grabbed me tight, his eyes downcast and battle-ready.

"Devi, I *love* you." The splinter in his voice crushed me... "but you don't love me back...not anymore." Despite his misgivings, when we were happy, we were fucking *happy*. And I'll never be happy with him again. The first man I ever kissed. The man I shared *every* first with...

"I will *always* love you, but we're—" toxic, shattered, out of chances... "We're not meant for one another, and I know you know that."

"You're tired. I'll let you rest." His hands dropped from my cheeks and he took a step back.

"Connor, this isn't something *sleep* will remedy."

"I know." His hands curled into mine, lingering. His bearded lips quivered, holding back his collapse as long as possible. And me? All I could do was replay the vision that would end us in every meaning of the word: I wake up in the middle of the night and follow a trail of insides left by Connor's corpse. The bones of his hands piercing out of his skin as they reached out for the tiny feet of our freshly murdered son and daughter; the red of their bodies the brightest thing in the pitch black hallway.

I cursed the vision of the future from my mind as the wind howled. Connor, and his fingers, slipped away from me. And with that, my first love walked out of my life. I've never been more thankful for our damned relationship than right here in this moment. If we stayed together, I'd only bring ruin to our family. Because whatever kills Connor and our children in that version of reality—it kills them because of *me...*

And then it hit me.

Like a crack of thunder in my chest too fast to catch and too loud to miss. If I stay *here,* with Lennon and Izumi, they succumb the same fate.

Because I *cannot* die, those around me *will.*

The only way to protect them will be to stay far away. I'll have to move out. Live alone and far away from everyone I love.

So far way...

I crawled into bed and was surprised to see the figure standing in my doorway.

"Hey."

"Hey yourself." Izumi shut the door and got comfortable under the covers. "So, Connor stormed out like a bat outta Hell. You ok?"

"I broke up with him." her face fell, the sweet cocoa of her eyes doing their best to stay above water.

"I see." She bit at her cuticles. "For good this time?" I nodded, failing miserably at swallowing the lump in my throat. "Shit doesn't stop, does it, Dev? And your birthday's next week." She held my hand. The love resonating from her—did she notice me shiver?

"It's all good." I forced the words through a weak smile.

"No, it isn't," she said too sincerely.

"It's not..." I shrugged, sitting up, letting my nervous fingers play with my dark chocolate hair, "but, it is what it is. What am I supposed to do?" My nose stung; my eyes too wet to face her.

"Eat ice cream and watch a movie?" Lennon said with a grand Southern entrance that only her vivacious self could accomplish. *Cherish these moments, Devi. There won't be many of them to come...*

"What's this chick flick we're to be entertained by?" I finally chimed in with a half-smile. *Normal. You're doing great. Everything is the same.*

"Screw the movie. What's the *ice cream*?" Lennon laughed as she plopped on the bed with a devilish grin. I named off the desserts on my fingers.

"A pint of Rocky Road for Izzie, Moose Tracks for Lennon, and—"

"Devi? Earth to Devi?"

"Yeah, and Butter Pecan for me. What's wrong?"

"You zoned out. *Again.*" Izzie practically spat the words. Anxiety at the edge of her voice.

"You sure they checked you out okay at the hospital? You're choosing Butter Pecan over *Coconut*. Maybe we should go back." Lennon's ocean blue eyes had the slightest mist in them. Mist I shouldn't be able to detect in this dim lighting, from this distance.

"No, Len. I'm good. I—I was trying to decide what flavor I wanted." Bold-faced lie but I *wanted* them to believe it and—two of the most important people in my life suddenly smiled wide and accepted the truth I conjured into their minds.

I can *make* people think what I want...

It wasn't wishful thinking in the bathroom. I *made* them want to leave...

Lennon popped in *10 Things I Hate About You* and there was so much laughter I almost forgot that, though the three of us were all always more than human, I was now irrevocably *less*.

Insomnia is a natural consequence of the supernaturally inflicted. It was around 1:30 in the morning when I went to run the trash. Heading back, a tug of nerves stopped me. There was someone walking up the stairs and despite my knowledge of him, I gasped anyway.

"Relax," Joshua said, fixing his jacket's collar.

I rolled my eyes. "Exaggerated startle response," I said, crossing my arms across my Marvel pajama shirt.

"Of course, it is." He examined me from head to toe.

"Is there a reason you're like this or do you just *enjoy* being an asshole?"

"Interesting." Joshua adjusted his military stance and I mirrored him.

"I'm really not."

"I beg to differ."

"What do you want, Agent? I've had a long fucking day." Don't grip the banister so hard, you'll pull the rails out of the concrete.

"Simply checking in, Ms. DiCaprio."

"I'm alive. Check-in complete. Goodnight." I turned to leave but he followed. "Don't you have to be a pain somewhere else?"

"Not till midnight." His cheeks were pink. He'd been outside a while before deciding to grace me with his oh-so charming presence. I should get used to it, though, shouldn't I?

"Then I'd suggest you hop to it." I shooed him away but—

"Ms. Di—"

"You know, Joshua, they're selling lives over at Walmart. Half-off, I hear."

"Ah, there you are." I nearly decked that glib grin off his face.

"What do you *want*, Agent?" Josh exhaled through his nose and took out a business card from his pocket.

"If you need to talk, don't hesitate to call. I'll always answer." He handed me his card but I didn't reach for it. He looked like a lost puppy…

"Go home, Josh. Obsession is unbecoming." I headed to my apartment, but he ran and blocked my path; his cologne danced in the air, overpowering my senses. One whiff and I knew its name and the woman he bought it from three years ago.

She lives in Manhattan now. Pregnant with baby number two.

"You're not as good of an actress as you think yourself to be, Devi. I see right through you."

"I didn't realize being transparent was one of my superpowers." He huffed. I puffed, with a giant grin.

"I know you were on that plane, Devi. What I *don't* know is how you made it without a single scratch."

I crossed my arms and scoffed. "Conspiracy theories? I *wasn't* on the plane, Agent." *Through* it, on the other hand...

"When *you're* involved, you never know."

"What's *that* supposed to mean? You know what? Whatever helps you sleep at night."

"You think I've *slept* since your case landed on my desk?" His words crashed into me without warning. He scratched his face; the sound of nails to stubble sparking new frustration in my bones. I have *wrecked* this man...

"Listen to me, Joshua. Go home. *No* good will come of this."

"Meaning?"

"It means, if you want to sleep, Agent, you'll let this go."

"Someone's after you and I won't stop until I put whoever it is behind bars." I laughed. Loudly.

"Let me save you the trouble. You *won't*. The end." I walked away and didn't stop when he called back.

"And what about you?"

"You want to chase me, Agent, go right ahead. Good luck catching me, though." I escaped into my place and as I clutched to the front door, his heart racing in my chest. We both stood on opposite side of the door for a long time before Josh finally left. His defeat fresh on my tongue.

The entire apartment was dark. Tiny glows of light coming in from the streetlights stretched across the space, illuminating the quiet home like a melancholic poem. Nights always went by the hardest. The last week, sleep—and food—barely made the list of things I needed to live. Each meal with the girls grew exponentially agonizing and the hours I'd normally spend asleep were spent reading, writing, and practicing my craft. Bathing and even using the bathroom became less of a necessity and more of a *choice*.

Though I didn't need it, I flicked on the lamp on my nightstand. My eyes adjusted accordingly; decreasing their night vision and allowing the lamp to help me see instead. I crawled into bed and grabbed the book I'd started reading a few nights ago. Luckily, I learned to control the flow of information. I could read like a human or absorb the whole of a document by *touch* at will now. I read the first sentence and placed the bookmarker back in, setting the hardcover gently beside me.

Its breath fogged up my window. The rhythm of our hearts beating in time. Izumi and Lennon would wake. *This* much negative energy—it'll wrap itself around their necks and demand to be witnessed. I muttered a spell, casting a Lullaby to keep my friends asleep and *safe*. The lower-class demon tapped its leathery fingers on my window; its slit ear-to-ear grin stretching across my lips, our heads tilting... I clasped my hand over my mouth, but I moved too quickly. I didn't *think,* and the demon jumped through the glass, its body naked and electric on top of mine.

My markings lit up something awful and blinded the beast. It covered its eyes and screeched, and I tore out its larynx, its blood spraying all over me before I could teleport myself out from under it. I ran down the hall and reinforced the warding on both Izumi and Lennon's doors as I ran by. The creature galloped behind. I had to keep it contained. If

I teleported anywhere else, it would only result hundreds of innocent people dying. If I stayed *here—*

The demon grabbed me by the hair and flung me into the living room before I could try anything. I crashed through the windows and held on to the ledge. Where are the others?! I pulled myself up, but it was too late. Joshua had been in his car and saw me...

My night vision turned on in the dark space, emitting a pale, iridescent glow across the room. The demon gurgled. A choir of wet, primordial taunting clicking from its throat. The plants started to wither, some even caught on fire. It made its way across the ceiling, twisting its head a complete 360°, boring its burning, dirty marbled gray eyes into mine. Six lives or six hundred... no one would die tonight.

"Come on, you piece of shit." I was ready to kill the demon. "I don't have all night." I willed my daggers to my hands and charged.

The claws dug in, breaking my skin and piercing into my stomach. In a desperate attempt, I set the demon on fire, burning my back along the way. But it worked. It fled and I threw up. My throat rushed with blood. Gagging led to more vomiting; acid dripping from my nose... I spat my insides and willed myself to my feet right as Joshua banged at my front door.

Any trace of the demon vanished with it. I put pressure on the gash in my stomach. I staggered to get to my room, leaving a horror show behind me. Josh kept knocking, waking Izzie and Lennon and the whole damn building. I whirled around and, as much as I hated doing it, I lulled Izumi and Lennon further. There would be no way to explain my injuries. The blood... I'd have to control their minds, and I wasn't going to do that to them. Not to *them.*

I leaned against the door. He's panting, sweating, and fueled. My head hit the door and I choked on a chunk of my intestine before I could swallow.

"Devi! Open this fucking door before I break it down!" He would.

"You really *do* need sleep, Agent."

"And miss our little trysts?" Hearing my voice calmed him. "Let me in, Devi."

"What's wrong, Agent?"

"Open the door." Coughing was a natural bridge to throwing up. Thank the stars for immortal soundproofing. One whispered spell and Josh couldn't hear anything I didn't want him to. If only I had thought to cast a vision spell earlier.

"I don't think I can do that quite yet. I'm not, uh, descent." The pain is intensified. I had to *scream—*

*I'm here.*

Vincent put his hands on my wounds. The throbbing morphed to jackhammers. I screamed into his chest. The moment my body healed Vincent wiped my tears. He's covered in ash and his swords had the weight of broken bones on them.

"You were in battle." Vincent smiled despite the action causing him to wince. My fingers stretched across his cheek and he buried his face into my palm. I never thought I'd see him again... "Who hurt you?" He pulled me closer, holding me tighter with every breath, as if I'd vanish; Slip through his fingers and float away if he loosened his grip in the slightest...

"You feel the battle." Not a question. A statement of fact. I nodded. Josh was about to break down the door when he simply didn't. Vincent froze him in time. The quiet, somehow, crawled about our skin in a blanket of frost that should not exist when the two of us wailed inside.

"I can only tell that you were in a fight." I brushed his war-torn hair. Still-burning embers spilled out with skeletal fragments. *His* skeletal fragments. "I can also sense your pain. Whatever of it you allow me to channel anymore, that is." My eyes welled up with ache far too quickly and I hated it. It blurred my vision. My sight of Vincent. But I saw the atoms. The balance of our constellations slip... "Vince?"

"I have to go." He kissed my forehead, pain in every inch of it and vanished beneath my touch...

I spared no time opening the door to Joshua but was only greeted with a white glare as I stared down into the barrel of his gun.

"Patience is a virtue, Agent." He lowered his weapon and did a once over of me as he barged in like a maniac. "Jesus. Relax and keep quiet. People are sleeping. You know, like *you* should be."

"*You're* awake." Asshole.

"I have a migraine." He stormed off to the living room and I followed. I noticed too late that Vincent cleaned everything and swallowed relief. When Joshua stood by the windows, he stared at it for a good minute. He holstered his weapon and tried to find something in his hair. "If you're ready, the door's—"

"Shut up."

"The *fuck* you just say to me?" Joshua sped over to me before I could react. I had nowhere to go but backwards into a wall. He clenched his teeth.

"Tell me what happened. N*ow.*"

"I don't have to tell you *shit,* Agent Asshole. Besides, how do you expect me to answer you when you so *kindly* told me to shut up?" Silence. "Do yourself a solid. Get the *hell* out of my sight." He laughed, leaned in closer, and then I heard it. A fracture in the wall...

"I don't know what the *fuck* you're cooking, but it smells like bullshit."

"You kiss your mother with that mouth?"

"What hap—"

"Listen," I shoved him as politely as one can shove a jerkoff, "you have *no* right barging in to my home and demanding answers. I don't know what you *think* you saw, but I'll tell you now it *wasn't* probable fucking cause. Now, *leave.*"

He sat on the edge of the sofa scratching his fledgling beard. "Tell you what, when you tell me the truth, I'll show myself out."

"Tell *you* what, I'll call your supervisor and tell her you're surveilling me off-book." We had a glaring contest. I won.

"I saw you." And I saw his memories.

"As stalkers tend to do."

"Will you stop it?"

"Sure. Soon as you leave." I gestured to my front door and then crossed my arms across my chest. I don't care if he saw the demon and I duking it out in the living room. I don't care that he's a demon hunter. An exorcist...

I *can't* drag him into this madhouse.

He rolled up his sleeves and ran his fingers through his hair and sat down. The rain began then, tiny droplets cascading over the glass, its soft hum managed to soothe me.

"So, are you going to set up camp on my couch or—" Joshua stood up and made his way to me. Me and my big mouth.

"Can I ask you something?"

"Can't you save it for my interrogation?"

"This isn't about your case." I raised a curious eyebrow. "Why do you push me away?"

"*That's* your big non-federal case question?" his lips pursed and his eyes were set. Nothing would move this man. "I don't even *know* you. It's not personal. Don't worry about it." Josh took another step toward me and a crack of thunder hit down the street.

"There's a colorful mind behind those eyes. I think, eventually, it's going to become too bright." He sighed, trying to find sanity in my fireplace. "You might not find your way back."

"I'm pretty good at this, Agent. All you should worry about is getting into therapy for this unhealthy fixation."

"You can never be serious, can you?" his head shook, exhausted and engulfed in this shit. *My* shit... "What good does it do you?"

"What? Having a sense of humor?"

"Distracting yourself from *everything* that eats away at you." He's a perceptive asshole. I'll give him that. "You know, you go through the motions. Indulge others in societal ceremonies. Say please and thank you and the like, but—"

"But, what, Agent?" I ran a hand through my frizzed curls.

"But you're a robot, Devi. A machine. Hell, I've seen *sociopaths* with more emotion."

"What's your point?" I crossed my arms.

"You smile and, fuck Devi, you smile and I want to cry. You say you're okay but you're not. You are *not* okay."

"Excellent assessment. It's *almost* like you're a cop or something."

"Goddamn it, Devi. Let me help you." He ran his hands over his stress-ridden face; his soft beard providing no buffer.

"I'm going to say this to you one last time, Joshua. There is *no* helping me."

"Eventually, you'll break down and all the things you're protecting yourself from will come for you and that will be it."

"All this from less than a week of surveillance..." I muttered, rubbing my temples. "*What* will be it?"

"Tell me what's happening." He got in my face and stared down into me. I had to keep the ghost in the kitchen from possessing Josh and wearing his body out of my apartment for me.

Esther was always sweet like that.

"Move, Agent." This is a nasty little habit he has. Always getting too close. Close enough to kiss me. Lightning struck in the street, and the power went in and out for a minute. Vincent... "*Move.*" I shoved Josh and Tate, the ghost, chuckled; the butcher knife in his hand gleaming. I signaled him with my finger to stand down and the apparition of the old gangster obliged me. "Why can't you leave me the hell alone? I *don't* need your help. Go save someone who actually *needs* saving, Joshua."

"We can't control what we feel, Devi. *You* need saving. I'll put up with your bullshit and your temper tantrums. I'll deal with your nightmares and psychopathic kidnappers. And I won't hesitate to fight when the time comes. But you *have* to work with me here, Devi." Josh ran a hand through his hair and even Tate and Esther knew that his every intention was pure. "Believe me, *whatever* it is I can help you."

"You can't exorcise the bad guys out of me, Josh." His mouth dropped but was relieved. Almost as though he *expected* those words.

"Of course. Shit, this explains a lot." He staggered a bit back towards the couch. He looked over his shoulder towards Tate, but he disappeared before he could spot him. "Witch?" I confirmed his suspicion.

"And psychic." He looked at the crystals and plants in my apartment with a renewed gaze.

"Fitting."

"Demon Hunter?" I pointlessly asked.

"And Exorcist." Laughter almost made it through our lips. Almost.

"That explains your intuition." The ceasefire lasted for as long as a ceasefire between the two of us would last. "Knowing what you know, it's not going to change the situation. If anything, it's going to be *more* dangerous."

"You think your 50 Shades of Spooky is going to scare me off?" Before I could retort, he sounded off again. "You and I both know that we—" he licked his lips, and made his way to me, standing far too close for Vincent's comfort. Staring into me with eyes I knew I'd have to get used to for the rest of my life. He took my hand and I couldn't avoid it without hurting him. He'd already been marked, like the girls, but why add salt to the wound?

Josh put his card in my hand and the visions swirled in my head. "Goodnight, Devi."

When he left, I slid down to the floor and buried my face in my hands. A warm haze came over my hands and I smelled something familiar. The sea.

"Are you all right?" Amah... "Hey, not so hard." I didn't realize I hugged her. "Are you?"

"Where were you, Amah?"

"We couldn't get to you in time." She smoothed my face and smiled, though it hurt us both to do so.

"You've been saying that an awful lot." I shook my head and left to my room. I checked on Izumi and Lennon on the way. Both slept like babies. I didn't talk to Amah until we were in my room. "Why couldn't I heal? Vincent had to—" Her eyes widened and she stepped back. "He had to heal me. What's wrong?"

"The touch of a demon—it cannot kill you, but because you're still human, it delays your regeneration much more than it does ours. More than our weapons." She was off in her mind, processing a hundred little things at once.

"How slow?"

"Hours. Days. Depends on the severity of the injury. But you *will* heal." I rubbed my stomach, my eyes intent on the patterns in my rug.

"Amah, where is your commander?" Her spiral work of markings on her abdomen were visible from her cropped breastplate. And they lit up like fireworks.

"We don't know." My heart sunk.

"He—he was just here. Fresh from *battle*. DeKenna soldiers from the smell of it. *Track* him." A part of her knew she had to follow my order, an order I didn't even mean to give. I had to control my newly birthed frenzy, and position. Amah let her fingers fidget as she found a place by my window; gazing out at something I'd never see.

"If we were meant to know his whereabouts, he'd have given the order. As for yours..." She faced me and it was the face of sorrow. "We will follow your commands, Devi, but—"

"Not the ones that directly competes with *his*."

"It does not compete. It *threatens*." My eyes lit, filling the whole space with black light. Fear and rage. They present the same way in my eyes—and Vincent's. One color for the two sides of the same coin. "Devi, calm yourself." I closed my eyes and tried to reset. "That Hunter, Joshua. Be mindful of him, Di. You may not get along, but he is *not* your enemy."

"I thought you wanted me to calm down." We almost laughed. She is genuinely trying to create a distraction. But it's more for *her* than me. "Amah, why is your heart breaking?"

"Devi—"

"*Tell* me."

"Vincent has not abandoned us, love. Vincent is doing what he has vowed to do." Her markings calmed but her words sparked an explosion inside me that trembled the entire block. "Protect you." If I hear that word one more time. "But my heart is breaking because," she took my hands in hers, her eyes glowing in mine, "because, love, yours never *stopped...*"

The sun rose with a splintering burst of Vincent's voice *screaming* in my throat.

*Devi! Get out of there!* ***Now!***

I broke through my bedroom window and jumped. I ran the second my feet hit the ground. The Paladins were all over the city keeping DeKenna soldiers away from me and I ran as fast as I could away from my home to keep Izumi and Lennon away from *me*. They were going to wake me up with cake and a song...

"Devi! Run!" Vincent flicked a demon's blood off of his swords and the splatter sizzled as it hit the pavement down the block. Every instinct told me to run to *him* but he signaled otherwise. I would not be safe in any place Vincent possessed.

"Where?!" In that moment of stillness, Vincent dressed me in LeMehti armor and answered.

*"Everywhere!"* I ran. Downtown Chicago. The Sahara Desert. The Paris Catacombs. But somewhere between Istanbul and Evenfall, I lost consciousness.

A sharp stinging woke me. Someone grabbed a tuft of my hair from behind and threw me into a stone wall. When I got to my feet, daggers in each hand, there stood a Knight of Hell.

He smiled a blinding grin beneath his hood. Charcoal and red embers burning from his eyes. I took not one step when he was in my face. He grabbed me by the neck and pulled me against his chest. I thought I stabbed him. I thought I fought back…

"What's the matter? Lost all your senses?" He—he *took* my power? The Knight unclasped his cape and pushed me to the ground, the earth beneath cold and wet… I was dizzy. I called for Vincent in my mind but—but I didn't know if he could hear me. What if I was too far away? The Knight kicked me in the face and knocked me on my back. He dropped to his knees and grabbed my thighs. It took him time, but he burned through my armor and tore at my underwear... God, please *no*.

*Vincent, where are you?!*

Minor spells worked. I cut him, burnt him, made him believe his skin was made of glass. But they didn't last. None of it lasted. "No! No, get off of me!" He took my jaw in his hand and squeezed until the bones cracked. He watched me choke on the fragments and my teeth and blood for a moment. The sight of it getting him harder. The Knight moaned, "Vincent!" This place—I'm too far away for Vincent to find me.

"Say his name *again...*"The Knight took my hand and rubbed it against his dick… I cast a spell, slitting his throat. He was hurt but he took my hand, dipped it in his blood and sucked my fingers.

"Stop!" The ground quaked and the Knight knew it was me.

"You shouldn't be able to do that. Especially *here*." He leaned into me, "Impressive. I should hurry things, I suppose."

"No!" I punched him in the face and disemboweled him with my bare hands. He fell to his side, writhing in pain but *laughing*. I—I couldn't move. I felt everything he did to me, *everything* I did to *him*, but I can't run away…

"What have you done to me?!"

The Knight grabbed my hair and jerked me back to him. He rolled back on top of me, spreading my knees apart; breaking my hips in the process. I cried out and he moaned.

He phased his armor off and unbuckled his pants, pushing his hips into me while he held my wrists over my head, licking my lips; shoving his tongue down my throat. I bit it off and spat it in his face as I choked on his blood. "In a minute you'll choke on a thing far more delicious than *that*." I couldn't see straight anymore. Whatever curse he'd cast on me, it grew more powerful with every passing moment. This *place*, it helped *him* and hurt *me*. "Are you ready for me yet?" The demon slowly slid his fingers inside me and then *shoved* them into me; his eyes rolled back as he pumped his claws inside me; cutting my flesh. "Mmmm." He pulled out his bloody fingers and sucked them dry. "I'm going to enjoy *fucking* the life out of you—" he slapped me, shattering the bones in the side of my face, "I don't like it when they cry. *Smile* for me." He grabbed my hips, but his eyes went blank and crimson from his neck poured all over me...

Vincent's hand latched inside the Knight's throat, paralyzing him.

"*Don't* touch her..." Vincent flung him off of me and the *crack* his bones made when his body hit the ground. I couldn't move my legs but I could move my arms. I turned to my side and watched in horror...

Vincent put the demon's head in the vice of his hands. "Look at me! Keep looking..." Vincent ran his thumbs across his eyes and burned them. He tore his lips off and when the Knight sat there, gurgling, Vincent took his hands and pulled the bones out of his flesh.

Then, Vincent beat the Knight into oblivion...

His insides splattered all over Vincent's face, into his mouth. The crushing of his bones, the tearing of his limbs. Vincent didn't murder the demon—he *annihilated* him...

"Vin—" I vomited. "Vincent! You're killing him! Stop!" He held the demon's limp body by the back of his head. It wasn't simply the demon's assault on me that engulfed Vincent. There's something else. There's always something *else*...

"Stop?!" Vincent's eyes were drunk with fury, with my *pain*. The way his tears fell from our eyes... "How can you want me to *stop?!*" He noticed me then. *Really* noticed me... My hands caught his attention. I followed his gaze and saw my knuckles. Dripping in red like Vincent's...

He blocked my empathy from channeling the demon, but not *himself*.

Not with our tether back...

He let the demon drop in the same breath as he drew his blades, the ancient script paling in comparison to the inferno in Vincent. Vincent Reaped the Knight's soul and sent it back to Hell. And with the demon now a mortal man, Vincent cut his head off and Ported his corpse out of existence.

The moment Vincent's skin was on mine—crying was the only natural reaction.

Vincent healed all my wounds, but we both knew there would *never* be magick strong enough to erase what the Knight had done to me, what he *almost* did... "Devi?" Vincent held me close, his hands shaking.

"I—I wanna go home. Please, Vincent, take me *home*." I shut my eyes, tears spilling down our cheeks. Vincent wrapped me in his long, black coat, gently scooped me in his arms, and he blinked us out of the First Circle of Hell...

Vincent had connected our tether again. The rush of it—our souls sparked to life.

"You and me. *We* are home, Devi. No one will *ever* take that. *No one*." We didn't move. It was as if Vincent's mind had left and only his body remained motionless in my arms.

"Vincent?" I reached my hand to his cheek. We sat on a mattress in the dimly lighted bedroom of the safe house he and I were meant to live in... The massive industrial windows of the warehouse let in nothing but darkness. It was after ten o'clock at night.

Five minutes in Hell—that circle of Hell—and 15 hours on Earth *vanished*....

He locked eyes with me.

"You're not safe anymore, Devi."

"Neither of us are. They came for *both* of us, Vince."

He couldn't deny it any longer. "We're safer together. I—I

was a fool to believe otherwise, Devi." There were sigils in the red brick and on the windowpanes. The power of the protection Vincent etched into this place reverberated through to my bones. The warmth of it, the careful strength… "Would you like a bath?" I thought for a moment and, despite Vincent cleansing me in every way imaginable, I still felt…

"Yes, please." Vincent tucked me tighter in his coat and walked across the room to the attached bath and I cleaved on to his trench and breathed it in.

He lit candles all over the room for me, drew the curtains in the large bedroom shut, and played my favorite Celtic music; making certain the volume was in its lowest setting. I didn't ask for it. I didn't know I even needed *any* of those things until he provided them.

"Devi?" Vincent waited for me to nod and he cradled me in his arms and picked me up, taking me to the brick bathroom full of plants and crystals. He sat me down on the stool and looked up into my eyes with longing, with regret, with every mistake he'd ever made paid for by my body... His eyes fell and he swallowed back a sob. "Call me if you need anything." Candles breathed lavender and coconut. He filled the bath with rosemary, rose… it truly was for purification. I loved him all the more for this. "It should—it's not—it should help."

"Thank you." I squeezed his hand.

"I'm here, Devi." He left the door ajar and sat outside the bathroom on the concrete floor. I wanted him with me, but I also knew Vincent was a haunted house with more suffering than he ever allows me to witness.

I undressed, but with each article of clothing removed, I was slapped with the Knight's face. *Get in the water, Devi*. The bath's effects were almost immediate. After a few minutes, though, my immortality proved stronger than its witchcraft and I didn't feel the clawfoot tub being set back down onto the concrete tile until I saw Vincent's eyes gently glowing in mine.

"Hey, hey. You're okay." He took my face in his hands and I held on to his wrists as though they were the only thing that kept me from falling into whatever black hole I was just in. "You had a flashback. It's over now."

"I—I don't remem—Vincent, please, *don't* go." He tried with everything he had not to cry, not to travel back in time and kill the demon again. But he didn't. Playing with time like that... Even to keep everything from happening to me, to begin with...

This was the *least* damaging consequence.

He tugged on his shirt, asking without words if it was okay to remove; if we could have skin-to-skin contact. I nodded. He got in the tub, sitting behind me, and gently held me. When I held him tight, Vincent's embrace strengthened around me; his immortal body providing the extra healing the magick in the water would never match.

In bed, I was in my favorite black sweater and pajamas. Vincent brushed my hair, braiding tiny strands here and there as he hummed along to the violins and piano. Our constellations returned, and they twinkled across our skin, gifting us with their glow.

"Devi?" Vincent made sure the fluffy blankets completely cocooned me. I made sure I was snug against his chest.

"Hmm?" Vincent presented a fist to me. I looked up at him and he gave me a smile.

"Open it." I took his fist and unfurled it. What I saw within left me puzzled. "Happy birthday..."

"The armillary sphere? I thought everything burned—thank you." I picked up the tiny trinket. My psychometry held fragments of the sphere's origin, but what it gave me was every single memory we created in our Byzantium home... I found his face and the tenderness in every curve.

We have perfect memories, but *mine...*

I kissed him without abandon and the surprise that flashed across his skin... He kissed me back, stopping *only* when I did.

"Wait. It's my birthday?" Vincent nodded and curled me in; his body my shield.

"October 6th. It's not yet midnight."

"Are birthdays still valid when you're half-immortal?"

"They count if you want them to. You can be 28 tonight or remain 27." A tender kiss met my temple. "Here." He took the sphere. "Watch." Vincent held the tiny sphere in between his fingers and pressed them together. The sphere and all its rings clasped to one, creating a single ring. "It's a thing that does *another* thing." He copied the phrasing I had used in Istanbul when I found out his couch also turned into a bed. "Multifunctional would be another way to put it." He made me laugh and the sound of it made it easier for *both* of us to breathe. "It's also a key, Devi. It will allow you access *anywhere...*"

"Do you have *any* idea what you've just done, sir?" I glanced over at him.

"I gave the love of my life a key—" he touched his forehead to mine, "that *lights up.*" Vincent's soul radiated in the corners of mine.

"I love you, Vincent..." I whispered, kissing his hands. The rain joined us, reflecting tiny prisms off of the stars in our room. I took the object, more enamored with it than before. "Isn't it supposed to light up?" I said, intently examining it.

"When it's meant to, my love. When it's meant to..."

"Vincent, I love it." I experimented with it, trying to figure out which finger it would fit best. Vincent took the sphere and my right hand and sized the silver sphere to fit my ring finger. But the LeMehti sigils and zodiac symbols *didn't* come to life.

Vincent took me in his arms and cradled me; embracing me in the iron grasp that I cherished. "I'm here, little one. I'm *always* here. No matter what happens, no matter what I say, that is the truth." I smiled, but it didn't stop me from...

"You're scaring me." There's an earthquake rumbling inside us, but I can't understand why.

"I know." He looked at my lips, and I leaned into him. He kissed me then, and I moved my mouth with him, tasting his scent and breathing his breath. And at that moment, he curled me into his arms again and my head lay on his chest; my soft hymn playing from inside his body. "Go to sleep, little one. It'll all be better in the morning..."

# Chapter 28

## Makes Me Sick

I didn't have to open my eyes to see that he was gone. The hollow in my soul told me that all by itself.

Mel was nearing. I stared blankly out the window and I couldn't move. I couldn't will my body to do anything. The hollow *hurt*.

This was all a cruel joke. Some twisted form of judgment for a crime I never knew I committed. Mel was at the door, biding his time before he walked in. My body decided it needed air, and I breathed. I remembered why it was I woke up at all.

Oxygen deprivation.

"Devi."

"Not home. Leave a message."

"We have to go."

"I—I don't want to go anywhere, Mel." I didn't want to cry, but shit happens. Mel took me in his arms and I felt if I fell apart, he'd catch all of my pieces.

"I have no words for last night." He knew... "There were too many of them. There's no excuse. We *never* should have separated. We're going to fortify your block and take shifts with you." In that breath, we were in my room.

"What was his name?" Mel grit his teeth but knew better than to refuse me.

"Ivan."

"He—Vincent—Ivan didn't have a *face* left. There's a violence in him I don't understand."

"Devi, that thing *defiled* you. Do you think Vincent would have tapped it on the wrist? Do you think *any* of us would? I can't even imagine what he must have felt knowing he could have saved you from that, but couldn't because—"

"Because what? Answer me, Melot. That's an *order*."

"I'll make you something to eat." He walked to my door, but I got up and took him by the arm and wouldn't let go.

"Stop lying to me." We were quiet then and eventually, my hand slipped away from his arm. "It's my fault, isn't it?"

"You're the perfect weapon. And in the wrong hands, in the hands of *Lucifer,* you're *the* weapon."

"How is he so sure I'm going to do what he wants?"

"He's the King of Hell, Devi. He can be *persuasive*. And now, the demons—this poison burns differently there." He played with his hands for a moment. "If Roan gets her hands on you—"

"All Hell will break loose. *Literally*."

"No, Devi." He didn't want to say the next words. His fists tightened and as he opened his mouth, my ribs cracked with each word. "Hell won't break. *You* will. And you will take the entire world down with you." We both took a moment to let my bones heal, but no amount of time would have kept Melot crumbling from the next words. "If Lucifer has you—Devi, the things he'll do to you..."

"Melot, it's alright. He won't take me."

"You will lose your mind in ways you cannot fathom. You'll be *begging* for—Once there is nothing of you left, he *will* control you and bring you back to—"

"Ok, Melot enough. I'm—I'm not going to be the end of the world." I took his hands in mine. Held them tight, and he held me tighter…

"You misunderstand. You will not bring about the destruction of everything because Lucifer will break you." I don't think I've ever had this much fear electrified in my chest before. Or is that Melot?

"Then why? What makes me—"

"Armageddon?" I bit my lip. He grit his teeth. "You're a Mimic…"

"No…" the truth of my fate drained my body of color.

"Devi—" Melot took a hand to my chin, picking it up so my lost eyes could find his. "We don't allow fear to guide our sword." I opened my mouth to speak, but his voice overpowered mine. "We don't allow guilt to fuel our actions." The Rules of War. "The more you feel responsible for what's happening, the quicker we'll lose you to your very own poison. Have faith. Nothing is written in stone. And if it is…" He wiped my tears away and steadied my too trembling body, "finish the rule, Devi."

"We break the stone." He gave me a smile, one I rarely saw in him.

"Devi?" I jumped into Andra's arms the moment she spoke my name. Her guilt—I saw in vivid detail now the battles that kept the Paladins from saving me last night. Andra has never tried so *desperately* not to weep.

"I'm ok, Andra." Lying tastes sweet but feels like swallowing glass when *you're* the liar. She cupped my face and kissed her forehead to mine.

"My dear *love*, you are *not*." She cupped my face, leaning into me, her tall frame a comfort all its own.

"No. I'm not. But I don't have time to deal with—with last night. I *have* to be ok." Melot started walking away from us.

"Andra, we have to begin." He didn't want to give Vincent's silent order any more than Andra wanted to follow it.

"She hasn't eaten. Let me take her for an hour. Let us give her a minute to *breathe*, Mel."

"Devi, we need to train you. Vincent wanted you to be prepared." He had to swallow. "There is no time to—"

"Got it. I can compartmentalize. What butchering with a side of sexual assault, right? Let's go." Mel shut his eyes for a moment too long before he took my hand and took us to the door down the hall.

"Devi," I had no idea I was shaking until his touch calmed me. "We will teach you to process trauma. More than that, you can confide in us." I looked at the two unbreakable immortals that I rendered into misty-eyed spirits. One wrong move and they'd float away had they not been holding to me.

"I know." In that second, the three of us blinked to a warehouse where Gavin and Amah awaited us. There were two stainless steel tables between stood between us. One covered in military-grade human weapons and the other…

Cue the training montage.

There was no more crash course this time around. *This* gauntlet would be in-depth, intense, impartial. If I was to know how to combat one of the most powerful creatures in the 7 Realms, enduring a crack to the skull wouldn't be enough. Knowing that pain was half the battle.

"Never start a fire unless you are willing to burn with the flames. Do you understand, Devi?" he didn't wait for an audible reply. He took my wave from the ground as enough acknowledgment. "If you're to survive them—on your *feet*, Devi." Red saliva dripped to the cement floor. I wiped the blood from my teeth and steadied my form. "If you're to survive them—say it, Devi." Melot holstered his sword; its hilt steaming and wet with a stream of my blood slowly effervescing in the air like volcanic ash—the spell worked. Leave no trace behind. Not even your past…

"I have to be better than them." Melot's eyes flicked to Andra. She tinkered with a crimson orb in her palm; too many constellations within it to be from *this* earth. "I have to be *worse* than them," I said, digging out the root of a shattered molar. Melot found my eyes; his armor covered in—*me*. "I become what they fear." Andra's orb rippled out of existence, and Melot gave me a single nod.

"Let's go over that battle again." I braided my hair quickly and adjusted my armor, taking my starting position. "No, Devi." Gavin and Amah Ported in around us. "We're going to run the same sparring session, but in reverse."

"Oh, *reverse*. And here I thought you wanted me to fight you blind." I laughed. They—however—drew their weapons. "Mel—our fight didn't entail three other immortals."

"Adapt to your surroundings. Prepare for every single possibility. Trust in your strike. Trust in your weapons." Mel snapped his fingers, and the warehouse went dark; four pairs of eyes and markings glowing for a moment. "Trust in *yourself*." With that, Melot attacked—starting with another crack in my skull. Then, the Paladins who'd sworn to protect me whatever the cost—beat the shit out of me.

"Again, Devi. Focus. You have two sides. Conquer both so that you will never be rendered helpless without the other." Amah had said. And then she detonated enough C4 to bring down a hotel... strapped to my chest.

Don't worry. It would've been a small hotel.

"A lesson is energy manipulation." I suffered a few contusions and lacerations, but I did it. I contained the explosion between my hands. And if I ever needed to, I can direct that energy to an enemy.

"Wonderful lesson," I said, picking C4 goop from my teeth. "I should teach you all something one of these days."

"What did you have in mind, Devi?" Mel said as he and Gavin cleaned their weapons.

"It's this ancient art form. Doesn't come naturally to everyone, though. It's called Taking a Fucking Break." I sat on my ass, panting, with a chuckle. They laughed with me... and at me, of course. And we did. We all took time and talked to one another. Really *talked*. I dared to ask for a movie night and they obliged me.

"Devi, we are your soldiers. We will follow you." Gavin had said.

"More than that, we're your family," Melot added. "Now, pass me the donuts."

"I love how you all think that a couple of weeks with you when we first met would be enough to prepare me for the *Paladin* Gauntlet." I pushed myself off of the concrete, digging out the better half of a broken javelin from my thigh. Amah had thrown me a hundred feet across the warehouse with that shot...just shy of breaking the sound barrier.

"The expectation was for you to *phase* through the pillar, Devi, not crash through it." Amah fiddled with the ends of her hair. "At least dodging the javelin..." She muttered as Gavin and Andra played a hand of poker.

"Thank you for that *brilliant* commentary, Amah. I never would have pieced that together." I staggered to my feet, already healed, and threw the sharp stick over my shoulder. "Tiny newsflash my all-mighty ones: I'm *half* all-mighty. Things are going to take a little—"

"You're half LeMehti but you are a natural-born *Mimic*." I have awoken the beast that is Grumpy Melot.

"Hey, good morning there," I muttered and wiped powdered cement from my chin.

"You should absorb everything that is within us without thought. Whatever is holding you back, let it go. We cannot afford to have you struggle, Devi. There is no room for failure."

"You finally watched Frozen? Nice. Who's your favorite character? Is it Olaf? It's Olaf, isn't it?" his cheeks turned at *least* three shades of pink.

"Do you enjoy wasting our time?" and he's back. "We

will fight this battle with you, to *any* end that exists, but we cannot fight it *for* you, Devi. Act like you care whether we all live or die. Act like you give a damn about the heart beating for its life inside of you."

"You wanna know what's holding me back? I barely sleep or see my friends. Every waking minute I have is spent lying through my goddamned teeth to everyone I love and I am scared out of my mind that each time I am near someone, every time my best friends hug me, it will be the last. I care *too* much, Mel. You think I don't know what's at stake because of this fucking heart beating in my chest? I'm trying to be the soldier—the *leader* you all need me to be, but—but all you're getting is this, this living death. I can't change that and I'm *not* human. You can't understand what that's like... All I want is to go *home*—where the *fuck* is Vincent?!" A wave of energy poured out of my core. All the windows shattered. bombs detonated, and with each tear dropping into my palms, a warehouse in the district *leveled.*

Gavin stepped out to rebuild my wreckage while Andra reassembled the bombs. Melot knelt in front of me with both hands on my shoulders. "*That's* more like it."

"Going bat shit?"

"No," he wiped away a tear before it destroyed something else, "using your emotions as a weapon. Now, are you ready to phase through concrete at the speed of sound?" I shot my eyes up at him and redid my bun.

I shoveled scrambled eggs in my mouth and gulped my tea. When the Paladins walked in for the evening's training, they didn't know whether to perform an exorcism or grab a mop.

"Hey, guys! There are banana nut muffins in the oven. I made *plenty*." I scribbled into my grimoire. One night after training, I figured it was time. I made it from scratch. It's missing a few elements, though.

"We—do we have an *oven?*" Gavin asked nervously to Amah.

"Mel, the book." I saw Mel give Andra a nod.

"Y'all didn't even *have* a kitchen. You do now." Melot turned the corner and behind the massive concrete wall where I was eating my breakfast on the artillery table, there was a kitchen.

"Is something wrong with my spellbook? I know it's not finished, but I wanted to get it started before I forgot—"

"Devi?" Andra met me at the table, watching me eat with one hand and skim through the blank pages of my spellbook with the other.

"You want some eggs? They have brown sugar in them. They taste—" I leaned into her, whispering, "like pancakes." My wide eyes didn't sell her on the breakfast. I shrugged and took a sip of my tea.

"You built that kitchen today? By hand?"

"Yup. Sure did, Gavin. Well, *most* of it was by hand. I wanted to finish it before you got here, so I used some magick."

"Tart, it's lovely but you know we don't eat."

"I know, Amah. But you do, occasionally. And I know you can will food into existence, but a home-cooked meal is just so much more satisfying and why are you all gawking at me like that?" I took a breath, then another. "Right…"

"Perhaps a quick kip, Di? Say, an hour?" I wiped my mouth and followed Amah as we went upstairs to my bedroom. I got into the bed and, with one touch of her finger to my forehead, I fell asleep.

I chose to move out months ago. Lennon and Izumi did not take that conversation well. Especially since I'd missed birthdays, promotions, break-ups and the like… Distancing myself—though not always intentional—did serve a purpose.

They'd hate me a lot more when I moved out and it would hurt them less.

I'd live in the loft Vincent brought me to the night he rescued me from Ivan. It was meant to be our home...

It finally satisfied me with how the loft was coming along. The upstairs wasn't big, but it had large rooms, two of which I made into bedrooms, and one gym. I built a second bathroom and Vincent had built a kitchen and library for us on...

The lower levels were massive—shit. The television in my apartment is shutting on and off.

I teleported back to my place with the girls to find Agent Asshole making his way up the stairs.

"Thanks for the heads up, Tate." The ghost chuckled. I stuck my tongue out.

I opened my front door before Josh could knock. "You know, I thought you'd be here sooner. What took you?" I went to the living room and sat down on the leather couch.

"I should ask you the same question. I've been calling you for twenty minutes." He stood coolly in the doorway, his hands in his pockets.

"I was talking to the ghost in my apartment." He narrowed his eyes. "So, do you want to cuff me *now* or at the station?" His face twisted in confusion, then realized I could see the future.

"I'm not arresting you for Obstruction, Devi."

"Gee, thanks. I'll add that to my Friendsgiving list." I got up to change out of my pajamas. When I walked by him, he grabbed me by the arm.

"Where are you going?" I tore myself away. "Sorry."

"I'm not a flight risk, Josh. I'm going to change. We're going downtown. I really don't feel like walking into a *federal* building in my X-Men sleepwear."

"I said we're not doing that today."

"Then why are you here?"

"Aren't you psychics supposed to know things?"

"Aren't exorcists supposed to *expel* shit?" he gave me a grimace, I raised him an eyebrow and a smirk.

"I wanted to make sure you were all right."

"A phone call would have sufficed. But thanks. I'm peachy." I winked at him wryly and concentrated on bending his will to mine..

"No. I had to see for myself."

"Ok. You *see*. Now, if you're *not* going to interrogate me, I think you should leave." I changed my mind. Let's see if he exits *without* my tricks. Oh, no... what is *that*?

"Do you have gas?"

"What?" Josh pointed to my face. "No. Just go away," I said, and pushed him to the door, then *out* of it.

"I'm coming back later tonight. We'll talk then."

"Um no. That's not going to work for me. I have plans tonight." Training, fixing my new place up, trying not to get killed—the usual.

"Yes, you do. With me." He saluted and walked down the stairs.

"You are infuriating!"

"I know!" He looked up at me from the landing and smiled a crooked smile that deserved a fist.

I had to figure out how to get rid of Connor. It's been a year and he still won't stop trying to get back together. As Josh left, Connor walked in and saw me. He got in the elevator and I met him in my living room.

"Devi?"

"What are you doing here, Connor?"

"Nothing. I was on my way to work and wanted to see if you were all right."

"Thanks. I'm fine. Connor, you could have called. You—this has to *stop*." The sound of his heartbreaking nearly broke my ribs. "Please."

"I guess I should get going then." He got up to leave, but then turned around. "What did that agent want? Can I ask you that as your ex?"

"Josh—Agent McAlister was checking up on me. Like you. That's all."

"I don't like the way he looks at you." He looks at me like I'm the bane of his existence.

"He looks at me like I'm a Rubik's cube." A soft chuckle. I'll take it. "He thinks I'm not telling him everything about the kidnapping."

"You're not."

"Excuse me? What on earth do you think I'm keeping from you?"

"I don't know Devi. Ever since you got back..."

"What?"

"You've been different." I'd be surprised if he *didn't* note the changes in me.

"Really? Tell me, how am I supposed to be after being kidnapped and held hostage for months?"

"I'll talk to you later, Devi."

"Get your ass back here, Connor!" I got off the couch, ready to bite his damn head off.

"It's been almost a *year*, Devi."

"*And*? The balls on you coming here telling me I should be this way or that. Telling me I should be all fucking better. *Fuck* you, Connor!" Breathe, Devi. "I'm sorry I'm not healing on your fucking schedule."

"I—I didn't mean it like that, Devi."

"The hell you didn't. Do you think if I was 'better', that I wouldn't have broken up with you?" He did. "Newsflash! We're *never* getting back together. And I'm sorry about that. I *am*. But me and you... we were *never* meant for more than the past and I know you know that.»

"You've changed. You—"

"Did what I had to do to survive." The way his stomach flipped in mine... "Get out. I never want to see you again."

Why are you crying, you *stupid* girl? I climbed into my bed, my empty, cold fucking bed, and hid beneath my covers.

If I stay with him, our future will be full of nothing but blood and body bags. The look in his eyes—like I was damaged goods. Like I was *crazy*. He's not wrong... I'm broken in ways immortal magick cannot even begin to heal.

Walking the streets after my rounds with the Paladins, letting the darkness of the city sink its teeth into me—it helps keep the maladies of my life at bay... Knowing what's out there, the horror of it. The muggings, the domestic abuse, the molestations... I turn down my Empathy guard and let it all inside of me. But it doesn't make a dent. I thought the passage of time when I walked to my apartment would distract me; blur the complexities of my wreckage enough for me to come up for air.

To *want* to come up for air...

But all I want to do is put a bullet in my head. All I want is to find each serial killer that writhed in my bones, each piece of shit human carving innocence from my chest and pull their spines from their throats.

But I *can't* feel it. *Any* of it. I can't feel a goddamn thing but myself... and it makes me *sick*.

# Chapter 26

## Labyrinth

*October 31, 2015*
*All Hallow's Eve*

The air was thick. Quiet and full. One wrong move and the sky would bleed... Something was amiss tonight. There was pressure in the Veil and it was bursting at the seams; the spillover leaving a mess that went unnoticed in the masked and costumed streets. My favorite time of year had morphed into a freak show and I was the oddity on display.

The wolves drank in my scent from five miles out. Vampires gawked and salivated from rooftop to rooftop; the young ones fighting over the best vantage point of my bedroom window. Amidst them and other manner of creatures, both living and... not, there stood the covens. Soldier witches stationed at the four corners of my block. Some local, some from Budapest, and the most curious one from New Orleans. Curious because she was a witch without a coven. A witch that every coven studying me answered to.

"Devi? You ready to go, sugar—why? I know you love Halloween, but do you have to sit in the dark?" Lennon walked in, tucking her lipstick in her purse. Given everything, we didn't celebrate last year. It made today all the more special. Especially since I hadn't moved out. Not yet, at least...

"I hadn't noticed," I said too truthfully, to her genuine concern.

"Anything interesting out there?" Lennon peered out the window with me, but she leaned in too close... I went to put on my black iridescent fairy wings, made sure my boots tightened, and tried not to laugh.

"Nothing more than the usual. Vampires, werewolves, witches," I said, doing a mental check of the weapons holstered to my back that everyone was blind to but me.

"There's literally no one out here, Devi." I was half-joking but truly surprised that she wasn't able to see them.

"You sure?" Her wide eyes caught mine in the mirror as I smoothed out the lace of my high-low romper. "I'm kidding, Lennon." I tried to laugh it off. "Let's go find Izzie and get this show on the road."

"What's your costume again? Dark Witch?"

"Just because I'm wearing all black lace and boots doesn't mean I'm a witch." She raised an eyebrow. "It means I'm a dark fairy witch. The wings give nothing away?" I shrugged in mock flight. "It's all that glitter, Lennon. It's in your eyes. Affecting your vision. Look, it's in your seashell boobs! God, you got it all over my bed, woman!"

"You're such an ass, Devi. Come on. Let's go find Wonder Woman." We chuckled, and it hurt all the more when I had to hide the pang of finality that followed. Something was coming. I couldn't tell what it was, had no vision of it, but it was an ending. That, I knew for certain...

"You sure you're not cold, Devi? Do you want my jacket?" Izzie took a sip of her drink; her full lips pressed together with too much concern.

"We'll be inside most of the night and then in your car. Besides, the dress has sleeves, and it's actually a warm 60 degrees." I was always the friend who could never get warm. No matter the season. Since I became LeMehti, if I wanted, I could raise the internal temperature of everyone in this lounge. I could set the whole place on fire without a word....

"Devi? Hey!"

"Yeah, I'm right here, Izzie. No need to snap your fingers in my face, guys."

"We wouldn't have to if you'd answered us the first 5 times we called your name." Don't break your glass. Remember to breathe, and for the love of *everything,* ignore the man planning on murdering his date when he takes her home tonight—wait. What?

My eyes shot up to the corner of the lounge. The lighting was dimmer, darker, but not for me. I could see with perfect night vision clarity—in full technicolor.

"Devi, where are you going? The others will be here soon. The costume contest—they're going to—she's not even listening to me, is she Izzie?"

The karaoke cover of Sweet Dreams hung in the air. Alcohol I didn't drink pumped in my veins. I've had visions of the future before, but never like this. Never in real-time... No. Telepathy. It finally kicked in. And the first mind I connect with is a seasoned serial killer. He will kill this woman and go on killing for another *decade* before he's ever caught.

I stood behind him. This tall, white, ordinary piece of shit. Textbook, you'd call him. My hand tickled with the materialization of my blade, but the chorus to the song dropped and I quickly orbed my weapon back into its invisible holster on my back.

Turn around, I willed. Take me, instead. Kill *me...*

Carl coughed on his drink and looked over his shoulder. And when I locked eyes with him, I snapped my fingers and his date took out her phone and called her police officer sister.

Carl smirked at me, adjusted his dick, and followed me out the back.

What are you doing, Devi? Vincent will—Vincent hasn't said a word to you or shown his face in weeks. Vincent—and my other Paladin Guardians—are here to protect me from evil. Nowhere in their vow did it say they'd protect evil from *me*...

Giggling, I took his hand, and we went out the fire exit. I suppressed the alarm before I touched the door.

"You are—wait." No wonder he's had such a successful career. He's a goddamn *Incubus*. I let him punch me. Once to get him hard, then again with my defenses down so that he broke every bone in his right arm on impact to my teeny, tiny jaw.

I spat blood on the concrete, making sure it burned into the void.

"You bitch!" I smiled. Carl swallowed his vomit.

"Touch me again. I dare you." He took a step back.

"You think I'm afraid of your kind?" He narrowed his red, glinting eyes, cradling his arm.

"No." I closed the gap between us, breathing him in. "You're *terrified*, and it's intoxicating."

"It's you, isn't it? All this shit happening with the Veil?" I squeezed his throat. "You're so wrong, Heaven itself won't even fucking interfere anymore. The Balance is *burning*." I broke his neck.

"You're *lying*." the buzz of everyone's drinking faded as quickly as it manifested.

"If you are what they say—" he spat up blood on my face. I didn't flinch, "you know I'm not."

"You seem to be president of my fan club." I let his paralyzed body flop to my feet. "What am I? What's my kind?" Carl laughed, his red eyes piercing through me.

"Immortal. But you weren't born. You were *made*."

"Who told you this?"

"Word gets around. People talk and for someone as fucked as *you*, I'd start listening." I knelt to him, my blade one thrust away from castration. "I don't care if you kill me."

"I'm not going to kill you, asshole."

"I'd worry more about yourself. You've defied the world, but you cannot defy *Fate*."

"I defy Fate with every breath I take," I slid my dagger up; cutting him open from belly to throat, "and I think she likes it."

"What—what did you do to me?! Come back! Come back! What did you do to me?!" The sirens grew louder until the police cars stopped with a jolt in the alley's mouth. I hid behind a dumpster and tried *not* to channel the dozen or so dead bodies who had made their way into it over the last few months.

The officers saw Carl laying in a pool of blood and piss, crying. What the Chicago Police *didn't* see was his power, the thing that made him an Incubus floundering in the murky red puddle. Most of it, at least.

I scanned for other Revs in the immediate area to figure out who could have ripped nearly all of Carl's magick from him. I found the same vampire from earlier. He sat on the fire escape stairs of the building across from us, legs swinging, drinking—I swirled my tongue around—is that a green tea latte? His emerald eyes flashed with familiarity, but he said nothing to me. The vampire was also not the one with the ability to render the Incubus practically human.

The millennium-old predator vanished. The Incubus—on the other hand—was to be incarcerated, and my goosebumps tingled with Izzie and Lennon's worry. I Blinked myself into the women's bathroom stall—upside down.

"Goddamn it. Really, Devi?" I muttered, taking far too long to get on my feet. "Oh yeah, such a powerful immortal. *So* scary. Can't even teleport like a normal fucking—whatever the fuck I am." I walked out of the stall and into a crowd of six Marvel cosplayers. Very *drunk* cosplayers who heard my crash and every word. "Hi there, I'm just gonna—excuse me—ope, gonna scooch past you right there. Ok. Thanks. Happy Halloween!" You are *such* an idiot, oh my God.

I didn't make it to the door. My spell froze the women in

their own time bubble—one of which was crying because some *devolved* piece of shit told her she had to use the men's bathroom. I'm going to deal with that right *after* I figure out why Black Widow's reflection called my name…

## DEATH BE DAMNED

I had not conquered this spell. It would live for a few minutes before my hold on it—and the women—died. The woman's reflection drew her gun and kissed the muzzle to the glass. In this mirror world—in that version of reality—you gain the powers of the creatures whose skin you wrap yours in. If only temporarily.

In *that* world, word of me had spread.

"Orders were to shoot on site. But a bullet between your eyes would do little more than give you a headache, wouldn't it?"

"Who are you?"

"Mercy me. It *is* true. You don't remember a lick of shit." Shock quietly settled into us. I couldn't touch the woman on my side of the mirror to glean more information without marking her for death—or worse. What little I could channel was that her name was Olivia and when we were both six, we played together in a park. Made sandcastles. But in the mirror world—

"We're sisters…" I don't know why my voice came out as a whisper.

"Scary *and* smart." Olivia swallowed back her broken heart. "Exactly the reason they want you dead."

"You have LeMehti in your world, too?" She laughed at me, her mouth wet with tears.

"They're characters in a horror story, Devi." Olivia cocked her head, understanding washing over her and leaving me parched. "A story *you* wrote…"

"Why are you trying to kill me, Olivia?"

"*Kill* you? You're like the LeMehti, like that Paladin in your story, Arthur, I think it was."

"Olivia, I don't know what you're talking about, and my spell is fading. Why does your world want *me* dead and not their *own* Devi? And what story are you—" Screaming clawed at our ears. Something was fighting its way to Olivia.

"It's too late." She said under her breath and adjusted her grip on her magnum. I rushed to the mirror but stopped myself before I touched her reflection. "You have the same powers. That touch of yours. I don't know who's more cursed: the people damned to cross your path—" my sister palmed her hand to the glass and, with a tremble, mine followed, "or *you*." Olivia's spell kept the werewolves out, but it was about to fail. "You're not something to be killed, little sister." She smiled, her lips quivering in mine. "You're something to be *survived*." She was dead before she hit the ground; the muzzle burn smoking off our temples...

Every light in the bathroom exploded, and the women ran out screaming. The wolves tore at her body. Licked the blood from her mouth... the counter cracked. The only illumination on my side of the mirror was a molten bronze singing at the edges of my eyes. A werewolf stopped chewing on Oliva's torn-off arm long enough to notice me. With his sights full of me, he lost his grip on her limb. The others took note. They stood up, wiping Olivia's insides off on their button-down shirts and jeans. One of them smiled, his fangs spilling over his bottom lip. That's it. A little closer... I pressed my palm hard against the looking glass and sent a shock wave into their world. Each of their chests split open, tearing into thousands of pieces before they met with the tile below...

I walked out of the bathroom as a bartender was about to head in with a flashlight. I put the lights back together as if I did not break them, to begin with. His gaze locked onto my back, confusion billowing in his mind. He'd seen the security tape of the women rushing out, screaming bloody murder.

Little did he know, the only massacre was in another realm of existence where *he* was the werewolf eating the remains of my sister—who blew her fucking brains out to save herself from *me*...

I met Izzie and Lennon back at our table. Half the contestants for the best Halloween costume were making their way to the stage. I was helpless against the women in the bathroom. They'd live the rest of their lives forever, wondering if they witnessed a proper witch losing her mind in their midst.

Izzie adjusted her skirt and lasso and tapped Lennon's shoulder when I came back. "Where've you been? Did you know that guy?"

"What? No, he—I thought he was someone else." Izzie didn't smile, nor did Lennon, when she was paying enough attention to us. She was preoccupied taking in the glorious booty that belonged to the pirate captain two tables over.

"Right..." Izzie rested her elbows against the checkerboard table. "Dev, tonight's not a good night to separate."

"Yeah. We can't celebrate if we're not together." Lennon said cheerfully, taking a sip of her Pina Colada. I was surprised.

"What are we celebrating?"

"Having you back home, sugar. Having you back home." Lennon reached over and cupped her hand over mine and it took all of my training not to flinch.

Or break her arm.

"Then that's what we'll do," I said sweetly. "But don't be so paranoid. Yeah, tonight's a bit more active than in previous years, but there's no boogeyman waiting in the shadows to take me away. Nothing bad will happen tonight. You'll see." The blood splattered on their faces too quickly. Droplets dripped into their drinks. A warm stream of red slid down my forehead. A Knight of Hell put a bullet in Vincent's head and, consequently, in mine. Izzie's screams—the way Lennon stopped breathing. Someone pulled the fire alarm and everyone fought their way out of the lounge. Izzie stopped screaming and met me on the sticky wooden floor. Her hands ran all over my head, trying to stop the two holes in my skull. Trying, with all that she had, to dismiss the fact that the bullet wound had begun to heal.

"Devi?" I reached out to Izzie and Lennon before the Knight appeared beside us, grabbing me by the throat and traveling to the building's rooftop.

*Devi, be ready.*

*Vincent? Where are you?*

"Let her go, Kyzza." Vincent was healing, but he needed at least another thirty seconds. The Knight whipped us around, his fingers digging into my neck. I Blinked my eyes, shaking my head hoping Vincent wouldn't unleash the rage at the fringes of his skin. There were too many innocent lives in our midst.

"Who? This child of destruction? The *anathema* no gods will touch? This *whore* of worlds?" Fifteen seconds... Vincent's eyes flickered an awful burn of blue so dark, the Revs watching us on the neighboring roofs took a step *back...* but they couldn't leave. They had to observe. Study. Gather intel and, most importantly, *not* interfere if they wished to live. "Is she *worth* it, Paladin? You'd dare to fire your weapon at me with your beloved as my shield?"

*Now.*

Vincent pulled the trigger repeatedly. I phased backward into Kyzza—moving faster than the immortal bullets that pierced through his skull. Kyzza fell to his knees, the bullets not only delaying his healing but his Porting as well. Other DeKenna sent for him; smoke wound its way around him and dragged him back to Hell.

Vincent had me wrapped up in his arms in the same breath. His body my familiar shield; he kissed me, hard and full of a word I wanted *nothing* to do with. Breathless, he cradled my cheeks, and we sensed a spark jolt through us.

Our bodies were not the only things broken, nor the only things that could heal when the two of us came into contact. It seems our souls, too, could bleed.

"I have to get you out of here."

"You're going to hide me, aren't you?" Vincent picked up my chin and brought my eyes to his.

"I have to keep you safe."

"And who's going to protect *you*? You're going to hole me up in that *Bridge—*" he said not a word, and I *knew*... "You have *back-up* plan... Vincent, you *can't* hide me *there*. Going through a Bridge is one thing but playing with tim—" A fever on his tongue reached mine and dared not let go. Vincent kissed me. Kissed me as if we'd never see each other again. And we never did...

"Vincent! No!" Thomas, Miarrah, and a gang of Paladins appeared, twisting chains tight around our bodies and pulled us apart...

When I regained consciousness, Miarrah's body was slit from her skull down. Her halves were inching together, trying to become whole. I sensed Vincent running to me a few blocks away. The world off-kilter—animals nowhere to be found. The people in a forced slumber in their apartments and cars, some asleep in the streets...

Before Vincent had his way with her, Miarrah had—she'd ripped out my *heart*. It was burnt to ashes on the sidewalk, a new one already beat with fury inside of me. I forced myself to my feet and ran towards Vincent. He was drenched in so much blood it was all I could taste. I couldn't do what he did.

*I can't take away your pain...*

*Pain Ends.*

They kept blinking him away. Each time a block away. A mile. Ten miles... "Vincent!" All the soldiers were busy fighting him. No one thought to guard *me*... They teleported too quickly for me to follow with a Hunt. Vincent can't hold them off much longer.

*Vincent, where are you?!*

*Go to the Bridge!*

*Not without **you**!*

I stopped running. I stopped breathing. Seething. Being.

When I opened my glowing copper eyes, I not only found every single immortal seven miles away, I *kept* them from teleporting. Something's wrong with Vincent. He was too weak, too busy keeping me from channeling every blow to his body to blink us to our Bridge with no one tracking us.

In one breath, I blinked myself into Vincent's arms, blocking Miarrah's attack with a burst of energy radiating from me no one saw coming.

*Devi, don't!*

When I finally got close enough to use my powers to teleport us to safety, Vincent stopped fighting. The cobalt of his eyes in the copper of mine. "Vincent!" I ripped off the face of the Paladin that slit my throat and blinked myself to Vincent but—

Thomas pierced his sword into Vincent's throat; the blood splattering on my face. Miarrah grabbed me from behind, burning me alive as five other Paladins pinned Vincent to the ground, Thomas beheading him.

*I **will** find you, Devi. Death be **damned**...*

## THE COURT

The city blurred. Gravity amplified. The voices of a thousand different memories drowned in my mind. A crack of thunder. A fall from grace. A mangled body crashing into a cold stone floor. LeMehti royals splayed across an arcane throne room unknown to history clutched one another. The immortals towered before me. I stayed on all fours, biding my time. With my connection to Vincent dulled, my healing compromised, and no escape in sight, every choice I was to make had to be exact.

The snow-white marble quickly painted red from the blood dripping like cream from my lips. A hymn floated in the air; drenched in enough frankincense to burn sin from your bones. The marble fractured beneath my hands and knees. The castle stretched for miles... I'm in the midst of *thousands* of LeMehti. And I cannot, for the life of me, see beyond the black haze outside these walls.

I tried to push myself off the ground, but the crackle of chains and glint of armor and blades gave me pause.

"Do be gentle with her now. She is to be our guest." The man's voice pierced through me. Smooth. Refined. Too reminiscent of a creature not of earth.

Nothing but raging amber light flooded my sight. The burn shining from my eyes intensified collided with the silver of theirs; the impact ricocheting off their chain mail, jewels, and weapons. An Aurora illuminated the dusk, but never found the darkness beyond the massive gothic windows open to nothingness.

The LeMehti stood stoic. Echoes of hushed voices screeched in my skull. The power of the six Paladins scattered across the steps to the crystal-crusted metal thrones where the Emperor and Empress demonstrated absolute discipline. They wanted—*needed* to tear me apart.

The soldiers yanked my shackles, forcing me up on my knees. The iron singed my wrists, the scent of my searing flesh filling the ancient cathedral-like palace.

"Devi, is it?" The emperor said. His question drew my eyes to the altar turned dais.

"She does not wish to reply," said the empress. Their white hair glinted, reflecting the candlelight with halo-shaped prisms. Eyes burning gunmetal.

"That she does not, Pandora." The emperor squeezed his wife's bejeweled hand and made his way down to me; the clink of his chain mail crashing too brightly against his breastplate. "Perhaps a little persuasion, Azrael." Pandora smoothed a finger across her markings. They coiled around her throat like a python left to starve. No different from the female Paladins that flanked her position. As for the men...

"You have quite the mouth, Devi." The men hid behind Thomas. Azrael grabbed my cheeks and dug his fingers in, spreading my lips apart. Thomas grinned. Azrael leaned closer, breathing me in. "You're to be our ruin, then?" My eyes flicked to Thomas. Vincent's twin tipped his head and contained a laugh.

The monarch of the LeMehti empire relinquished his hold of me and took a step back, examining me.

"What is this place?" The candles faltered. Every soldier gripped their weapons. The sound of their hands stretching across the hilts of their swords, bones tensing…

The Paladins that held my chains trembled, sending a shiver down my irons. One look from Pandora and my guards pulled my arms behind my back tighter. The temperature of the metal rising, singing my skin. I can't heal as quickly here…

"This is where monsters dream, Devi. This is the Kingdom of Souls." Poison was evident in Pandora's every word.

Vincent and the others, they'll come for me... I pulled against my chains; the Paladins falling to their knees. I set the jagged pieces of my ribs out of my collapsing lungs and back in place. Wiping the blood and saliva from my lips, I rose to my feet, not batting an eye to the six swords at my throat. If they want me dead, let's give them something to kill.

"There she is," Thomas said, biting his lip.

"Take our guest to her chambers." The queen's order filled her mouth. "Welcome to The Court, my lady." The Paladins wrapped my chains around my neck and pulled, jerking me up in the air. I broke my back from the fall. The palace trembled. No one moved. But as they dragged me away, I saw the Royal Paladin guards and their Monarchs lay their weapons down and breathe through the violent vibration of their bodies; each immortal, trying not to split into a hundred thousand pieces.

Their terror—their terror of *me...* I didn't know how to stop shaking.

Candlelight filled the halls. The breath of flowers and phantoms choking me more than the chains. "Does that hurt you, lady?" I opened my mouth to answer one of the assholes controlling my irons, pulling me down a flight of stone stairs. But then I remembered the words Melot had said during training.

*'Do not start fires unless you are willing to burn.'*

The soldiers threw me down the remaining steps. I slammed into the door below. It creaked open. The madness that hit me—I didn't realize I fractured my jaw until I coughed up teeth.

Wiping my mouth, I looked up the stairs to see the poor excuse of Paladins dissipate. I could run. Use these chains as weapons. *They're scared of you.* I can use that fear. *Amplify* it. Or I can go into the chamber full of dead souls trapped in between realms and wait. Study them. *Become* as they are. My mimicking ability, though dampened in this Dominion, would still be of use in the long run. It was the only other thing—aside from my immortal metamorphosis—Vincent banked on if we were ever in this situation.

The second I crawled in the chamber, the iron and oak doors sealed shut; warding powerful enough to keep the likes of me within. I'm trapped. In a small room. A broken body, the dead in my head, and *armies* of infected immortals ready to murder me repeatedly. I sat up against an armoire, my chest heaving; clenching my fists. Vincent's words played in my mind: 'Turn panic into power. *Know* where you are. Find a weapon. Find an exit.' I surveyed the wooden room. The carvings of angels and demons in the walls, the twisting vines, and swords welded through the metal framing. The diamonds in the chandelier—I can bring the effigies to life, conjure the weapons from the metal, turn the diamonds into explosives—but none of that would do anything but pass the time...

I didn't promise to *pass the time*...

The voices of the souls damned outside this chamber ate through my skull. This time, however, I managed the dissonance with slightly more grace. I built a psychic shield strong enough to keep them at bay. The souls bit at the edges of my skin, clawed at the walls of my mind, but they could not purge their insanity down my throat.

Not for a while, at least.

The canopy bed was inviting; the fireplace crackled warmth at my bare feet. "Jesus. It's like a vampire threw up in here." I shrugged. "They have good taste, I'll give them that." Bloody spit dribbled from my lips. "Fuck." Immortal or not, regrowing teeth hurts like a bitch. It's going to take ten more minutes to finish healing this shit. As for my back... can I Blink myself on the bed? No. I can blink myself *next* to the bed. "Good enough." *Your legs may not work yet, but your arms do. Pull your paralyzed ass up, Devi.*

I sat on the plump bed, leaning against the wrought iron headboard of wings and woodlands, and examined my chains. I couldn't break my way out of them. They were either warded against my strength and phasing or lessened it. So, I did the next rational thing. I wrapped the links around my fingers and breathed. "Fuck my life." I set my eyes on the fireplace and link after link, the metal melted off my limbs. It took me an hour to heal from the burns. An hour to heal the hanging flesh from my neck when, on earth, it took *seconds*...

At least I can walk again.

The massive wall of obsidian windows stole my attention time and time again. There was a pull I could not dismiss.

Whatever lived on the other side wanted me closer. I knew what I'd be risking if I touched the Victorian glass—my psychic shield wouldn't protect me if *I* were the one to initiate contact. Whispers from behind the wall would weave into wails, faint dreams into perfect realities roaring beneath my skin—but I had to learn my surroundings. 'To level the battlefield, you have to understand it.' Vincent's words wrapped themselves around me as my palm met with the too-warm pane. But, there was only emptiness. No light. No day. No night. Nothing but remnants of human and creature alike scratching relentlessly. Fragments of lives long forgotten desperate to find their lost pieces. To go home. Every part of them now forever a part of me. I wiped my nose of the blood. The hemorrhaging would stop eventually. But, the same could not be said of the screams...

Then, between the souls and smoke, I caught a glimpse of where The Court resided.

"Quite fascinating, isn't it?" I fell from my trance. "The sight of it. The *sensation* of the gateways to *dozens* of worlds licking your lips..." The way she—Ophelia pressed her fingers together. It was as if she played music; plucking strings, to her delight. "You'd do well not to gaze beyond our borders here, Devi." She checked her reflection, her fingers hovering above a white Valkyrie braid. "You may not like what you see..."

"Why? Where am I?"

"Oh, I thought you were more clever than this." She scrunched her face in mock pity. "You are, at present, in Bordarrah. The juicy realm between Heaven and Earth. Purgatory and Hell, and every *delicious* thing in between." The Borderlands. The Court *is* Bordarrah.

"You rule over more than Purgatory, don't you, Ophelia?" She raised an eyebrow, arms crossed over her black armored corset.

"There's that inquisitive brain! And you know of my name. Do you know of *me*, though, little girl?" Her smile widened, porcelain teeth gleaming in firelight. "You'll not speak? What a *pain*." She smoothed out her black armor-plated gown, adjusted her baldric, and sauntered over to me. I stumbled and fell on the bed. "With our particular expertise, it's only natural that we—" her eyes darted about the room, "you'll like it here..." she muttered under her breath and trailed off. "You certainly would not present yourself in that ghastly frock, would you? Come along." With a flick of her wrist, I flew from the massive iron canopy bed to the Victorian vanity. She caught me by the throat and sat me down. My skull in her hands, she locked her eyes into mine in our reflections. "Now, what can we do with this precious face of yours, hmmm?" A sigh seeped from her burgundy lips, her hands tangled in my dark tresses. Her fingers rubbed sweetly over my eyes, lips, and face, leaving behind pigments of color. She giggled when she set my clothes on fire. Ophelia replaced them with a charcoal satin gown. Metal corset perpetually breaking my ribs... A splintered rib pierced my lung, and I coughed up blood all over the mirror. Ophelia plucked a handkerchief from the vanity and wiped my chin.

*"Enchanting..."*

There was a knock on the door. The air tilted and I opened my mouth to vomit when Ophelia held it shut, forcing me to swallow the vomit. *Don't* fight, Devi. Not yet.

"You'll not stain this gown! Learn control of your corporeal form for it's nothing more than a vessel." Her eyes were too wide, the panic within them clawed at the corners of her lids for freedom. Or were those tears?

I looked at myself in the mirror. Ophelia relinquished her hold of me and leaned into the looking glass... The splatter of blood was a simple yet eloquent reminder of all that was to come.

She strained to see in the mirror the person she once was. She'd stare until the end of time... "Listen well now, madam. You will do as is requested of you."

"And if I refuse?" I said with labored breath, my hand gripping my side. She caught my out-of-sync reflection and smiled with such force, I unwillingly mimicked the action... and her words.

"Do *not* refuse." Ophelia took my hand in hers and walked us out of the bedroom.

"Where are you taking me?" She's taking me back to the throne room.

"Does your touch on my skin not reveal any insights, Devi? Are the voices too loud? Or is it this place? Does it stifle your abilities to such a debilitating state?" Before us stood a carved door, that lead into the cathedral where the remaining highest-ranking LeMehti awaited me.

Their strength—their magick—electricity fried me from the inside out. That door was the only thing that kept me upright.

"Find your ground. That is *our* blood burning through your veins, Devi. If you do not learn to conquer fire, you are free to bleed yourself dry of it." She flicked a dagger at my chest and grinned. Her teeth glinting from the flickering candelabras above us.

I only moved when Ophelia willed my body to hers; my gown catching beneath my bare feet. She shoved me in front of her, presenting me like a prized beast. The make-up, the attire, the *perfume*—why am I not in chains?

"Ophelia, you've outdone yourself." Azrael removed his gauntlets, but armor still wrapped around him; around every immortal. Aside from being seated at the thrones, the one distinguishing piece that identified royalty from soldiers were the massive ornate sapphire clasps that secured black embroidered capes to their pauldrons.

Azrael stepped down from his seat, the fabric of his clothes scratching at my ears the closer he got.

"I haven't the care to debate you," he allowed his voice to pound in my mind. Azrael circled me, piercing his gunmetal eyes until that was all I could bear witness to. "All you need do is provide us with your services and we will grant you a merciful death." I leaned in.

"*Fuck* your services."

My words echoed in the church-like palace.

"There's hardly any fear in this one. Her scent, it isn't right, Azrael." Pandora's lips curled. Her disgust swirling in my stomach. She smirked and left her throne to meet her husband, her infected breath wafting about my skin. "My emperor asked you a question, child. A proper response is expected."

"I have a name, Pandora."

"Oh, but of course. Where are my manners?" She snarled. "What is your answer, *Devi*?" I cleared my throat.

"*Fuck* your services, your *majesties*." Her nostrils flared as she grit her teeth. But she did not speak another word. The LeMehti Empress backed away and took a glass of wine from Ophelia, drinking it with sweet contempt in her crystal throne.

"Do you understand what awaits you if you refuse us?" I glanced at Ophelia and then at the general of the LeMehti army, Elijah.

"Yes."

"Impressive. Tell me, do you—"

"Roan is hunting you." Ophelia blinked in front of me, leaving Elijah's words caged. "Devi. You *will* aid us in destroying the others. Roan, her soldiers and *every* member of your treasonous Paladin Guard." Her dove-like words were unnerving. The tips of her fingers twitched for the slightest of moments. "If you refuse..." her hand dropped to her stomach. Metal steaming from the contact. Controlled rage in both our bones, "there will be no clemency, child. Not *there*..." She closed the gap between us, eyes glistening.

"Take her away, Ophelia."

Without a thought, she followed her emperor's order. The ice blue of her gown too bright in the fire-lit space. Her gunmetal eyes shifted color along with her mood to a pool of *white*. She took me by the neck, tearing her fingers through to my spine. Blood drenched the gown she was oh so fond of. She dragged me down the altar and when the gates opened and crashed against the cathedral, an explosion of thunder screamed in the sky.

There were no stars in the perpetual night. Ophelia threw me to the ground, and I bored through the earth. She had touched me long enough for me to channel a memory that was hidden behind her tears.

"You're Thomas's *wife.*" I managed through gurgled breaths. She unsheathed her sword and cut through the air inside the first arched gateway. Wherever we are, there are no Bridges here. Only direct doorways to endless Dominions. "He left you behind to help Vincent. To help *me.*" The second her blade settled at her side, whispers turned into howls. The Paladin took me by the throat again, breaking my neck.

"Your parlor tricks will not protect you in *there*, Devi." She forced my gaze into the doorway... "This will be your final resting place, Devi! *This* is where even *your* Paladins *cannot* follow. They'll not find you. *Vincent* will not find you." Her mouth pressed to my ears. Frantic, hushed words echoing into screams. "What say you?"

"Oh, God..." Ophelia laughed as beautifully as only one of *them* could.

"God?" She nestled her tear-stricken ivory face in the red, wet hollow of my neck. She brushed her lips against my cheek and whispered. "My dear, *sweet* Seraphim, whoever told you *that* lie?" she let the truth of her words seep deep into my bones. "Do you refuse?"

"Yes..."

"Damn you." And Ophelia threw me into the opened mouth of Hell.

I followed the piano music deep into the woods; the sky alive with twilight. The slowly waking sun burned the leaves, leaving little lanterns in its wake. Disorientation dug into me. With my powers battling to rise to the surface, I had no way to know, with any certainty, how long I had been searching for the piano.

It was hours—or was it days? I found the woman playing. Her hands swept across the keys with elegance. Her entire body was encased in melted candle wax. The silver lace of her gown singed from the sun but she continued with her melancholy melody.

It was not until I stepped on a wayward branch that her wax-crusted face whipped in my direction. She kept her gaze on me and continued to play. Before I could move, the music billowed to a fever pitch, enticing the earth to pull me down and wrap its roots around my limbs. The demon left her instrument; the keys playing in her absence. She crawled across the soil making her way in between my legs. The candle wax melted off her and dripped across my skin. More of her kind appeared. They clawed, burned, and licked while she straddled me and leaned in; grabbing my mouth and squeezed it open with one hand and cracking open her wax-covered mouth with the other.

What little of my powers I had access to finally sparked, but it was too late. She let loose the flies and death that lived behind her lips and dribbled them down my throat.

"Nasty business, those DemiMeht. All that—" Pandora gestured to her mouth, her face twisting with a mischievous smile. Is that flesh burning? "Thomas, do take care of that stench. It's been so long, I forgot the side-effect traveling between Dominions has on humans. Lucky for you, Devi, you're a *half-breed*." I opened my eyes. I'm in the Empress' chamber—and I'm *naked*. Thomas grabbed a tuft of my hair and yanked my head back.

"Are you certain? Can we not let her roast longer, Pandora?" Thomas licked my sizzling neck. I elbowed him in his dick. "Mmm, be careful, dollface. Hit me like that again and I'll *come*." Ophelia laughed, biting her finger, her cheeks blushing. Thomas adjusted himself, his eyes intently in his wife's.

"Give yourself pause, Thomas. Heal the girl and dress her. You'll have your turn soon enough." Thomas followed the command and snapped his fingers. My body stopped cooking. He put me in an oil black lace gown and stood beside me, awaiting further instruction.

"Now, since you had a week in Hell's gardens to ruminate on the matter, what say you?" I'd been gone a *week*? "Will you be our weapon? Eradicate all of Hell and execute Vincent and the other Paladins for treason?"

"Fuck," I stood, a fly crawling out of my mouth, "you."

"Thomas, disobedience does not suit you."

"I—I did *not* disobey, Pandora. I *healed* her." He went to raise his fingers when one glance from me and he lowered his hand.

"You confound me, Devi. Help us win this war and we will give you an honorable death." Pandora sat at her diamond-crusted vanity. Her silver eyes finding mine in the reflection.

"Kill me quick. Kill me slow. Kill me a hundred thousand times with all the choirs of the gods, Pandora. I will *never* help you." She stopped brushing her porcelain hair and faced me. Ophelia and Thomas exchanged glances from across the room.

"Remember that you are where even angels fear to tread. *Nothing* will save you." I dared a step towards her. The black slick lace of my gown glinting in the candlelight. A flame sparking in her eyes.

"It's not *angels* you>ve guarded yourselves against with an army of thousands." I took a few more steps. "It>s not an *angel* that>s driven you mad." I smiled, embers floating from my eyes…

"Watch your tongue. You're no Reaper *yet*."

"No. Not *yet*." I cocked my head. Her heart rate rose, pounding beautifully in my chest. Pandora motioned for guards. They hesitated, and it did not go unnoticed.

"On second thought," Pandora waved, stopping the

guards from laying a hand on me, "Thomas, she is yours for the night." I looked to Ophelia, who could not bear to return my gaze. Thomas grabbed my elbow and in one motion, we were in a darkly lit chamber. The scent of paint and sex wet in my mouth.

Thomas threw me on his bed and sat in his chair; sword in his laxed lap, his tongue licking a finger in between his lips, "Shall we begin?"

**THOMAS**

He snapped his fingers, and I was back in his arms. Thomas rammed his sword into me. "Aw, we were having *such* a good time, Devi." He was breathless and sweaty. Immortals don't sweat..." Is this not what you want?" Thomas pulled his sword from my ribcage. His fingers moist with my blood. He threw me up against the wall, wrapping my legs around his waist. Holding on to me as if his entire *existence* depended on his touch on my skin... "I look like him—" I tried fighting him off, but it only made Thomas bind my wrists tight in his grip above my head. It only made him harder... "Eyes in mine, Devi. Breathe..." he tore off my gown, "Tell me you want me inside of you."

"Get away from me, you son of a bitch!"

"Keep fighting me, Devi. Burn me, shock me, break my bones... I'm almost *there*... Do you feel me throbbing?" He *indulged* in our pain—he licked the tears from my cheeks, the blood from my mouth. His forehead touched mine, and I screamed, breaking every brick in the room.

"Thomas, stop it. Please! Don't!" Thomas laughed at my weeping pleas and slipped his fingers inside of me.

"Mmm. My God..." He sucked his fingers nearly clean. "You taste of honey and sex..." he took a moment to catch his breath. "Do you want a taste of *me*, Devi? Look at me, I have

Vincent's *face*. Don't fight it—Let me *inside* of you. Tell me you want this."

"No!" The arcs of electricity sparked from my chest to his and Thomas flew across the room and into his wall of weapons; swords and brick burying him. I fell to my knees, gasping for air, catching flecks of the silver lightning in my palm…

Thomas set me on fire as he crawled out of the rubble, bloody but healed. I didn't give him the scream he yearned for. I gave him something *else*… I shut my eyes and tightened my fists. Thomas stood motionless, watching in wonderment and lust as I snuffed the immortal fires to ash; replacing their light with my own.

"Why—why are your markings glowing?" He hadn't known I'd glow like them. I was only ever *half* LeMehti. Only ever *half* as powerful…

"It's a warning." I played with the mementos of the flames he burned me with. Their warmth too cold in my hand and the *only* thing under control.

"Of what?" Thomas spat out, taking one quiet step away from me. I couldn't help but laugh. Blood-stained teeth creeping beneath my lips.

"Me."

**OPHELIA**

"You think you can embarrass *my* husband and flee?" Ophelia examined my tattered form. Her husband's handprints brightly bruising on every inch of where they relished on my body. Their touch… whether a caress or an attack, it *brands* me, taking far too long to recover from.

"Is that jealousy I detect, Ophelia?" the air nipped at my skin in Ophelia's playroom. Wine-stained marble drenched the chamber from floor to ceiling. As I got closer, I realized how that color came to be.

"Perhaps... I'm happy your Empathic abilities are in some semblance of working order. Flushed with jealousy, however, I was not." She dragged me by the hair and tossed me onto a metal slab housed in the center of the chamber; the slab's sharp iron rods protruded from every direction and were in prime position to dig into me. Ophelia forced my head back to the vaulted ceiling open to a black sky full of oblivion.

She waved, and the candelabras brightened; the flames reflecting off her dark Paladin armor and silver chain mail skirt. One pull of a lever and the rods skewered into my flesh. I gagged on a wet scream.

"You may be LeMehti, child, but your change in species does *not* garner you my respect." Ophelia jerked the lever again, the rods tightening inside me as they raised me off the table. "All we ask is for you to kill the traitors of our empire when your reaping ability comes to being. To rid all the Realms of Hell and *every* rotten thing hidden within. Why refuse such a request? This silence of yours, Devi—" she dug her hand into my mouth and unhinged my jaw, looking inside. The cracking of her sanity and my bone echoed across the marble.

She set a rod on fire and shoved it between my legs; penetrating it until it pierced through my mouth.

"Oh! Devi, you are *divine*! I'll fetch Thomas. He's been *dying* for a new painting of you." A *new* painting?

*"The blasted girl is humming again, Mahriel. Do you think it a spell?"*

*"If it is, it is a powerful one, Favienne."*

*"Why do say you that?"*

*"Have you not heard? No one can go near her. It›s been* ***days*** *now. And when they do, they are torn to* ***shreds*** *with a simple* ***word****."*

*"She weaponizes sound and doesn't realize it."*

"You're to meet with the emperor. Make haste." The pearls draped over her armored gown shined in the fire-lit hallway.

"I forgot you're British." She didn't look at me. "I think you took me out of there too early." I looked over my shoulder, but the Sentinels pretended they didn't see us. "What year is it?" I wobbled behind her. With an exasperated sigh, she gripped my wrist tighter, her pace quickening, dragging me alongside her.

"What the devil are you on about, Devi?"

"Ionnar, what *year* is it?" She stopped us in the middle of the black stone corridor, hands gripping my raw, whipped shoulders; frightened eyes in mine.

"I'm *not* Ionnar." I leaned into her, squinting.

"Oh." I lost my balance, and she caught me. "Hey, Ophelia."

"Where did they throw you off to *this* time?" She doesn't know?

"Niflheim, Tartarus, Orion..." she squeezed my shoulders, blood oozing out. "I remember now. It was Narnia."

"Devi, focus! Did they take you to *Tartarus*?"

"I don't know. It was a dungeon. There was torture. Y'all are giving the Geneva Conventions a fucking coronary." She couldn't understand my laughter. "The prisoners there did *not* appreciate my arrival. I found a door—or was it a bridge—anyway, I found it and got out. That's when I saw *you*." I mapped out the area in my mind; making a path in the air with my finger, but Ophelia swatted it away. "Ow..."

"Why are you curious of the year?" I caught a dance between the flames of the sconces. The way they moved—it was too slow.

"Because I know I've been here a long time. In Bordarrah. The Court, whatever you lot wish to call your home. But I can't tell how *much* time. Not anymore. Not *accurately*, at least. This place, it does something to my powers, to me... I just—I want to know how old I am..." I lost my footing when I leaned in to get a better look at her necklace, but Ophelia steadied me.

"It's best you do not know, Seraphim."

"Your necklace is shiny. What is that, meteorite?" Ophelia grabbed my bruised wrist, and we entered the throne room, hushed voices tickling my ears. The Paladin left me at the altar as she took her place beside Thomas and their fellow Royal Paladins by their monarchs.

"Is it your heart, Devi? Is that where your power lies?" Azrael kissed Pandora's hand and stepped down from his throne. His sword screaming as it scratched the marble floor. The pews had immortals scattered about them. Each one on the edge of their emperor's patience running as thin as the ice in my veins. "If that tongue of yours will not answer me—" my eyes darted to Thomas. He squeezed the hilt of his sword and smiled. I swallowed. "Then this will." Azrael pierced his sword into the ground. The shock wave cracking my bones. I stared into the gunmetal of his eyes as he dug his fingers into my chest. Breaking, heaving into me until he tore out my heart. "Curious." He dropped the organ to my feet, and I fell with it into a never-ending pool of blood. And as a red river of spit and bile dripped from my lips, Azrael knelt beside me, licking his fingers; my reflection distorted but present in his boots. "You *do* taste of honey... and sex."

*"Whatever it is inside of you that's helped you to survive us, Devi—what memories you›ve bound your mind to... Do not allow them to fail for you are where even angels fear to tread and our work here has only begun."*

**THOMAS**

"So much murder in that mouth." Thomas forced my jaw open, the meat hooks rattling in the fire-lit chamber. I clasped my mouth shut. "And that you're a *biter...*" He cocked his head with a devious smirk. "Should've seen that coming."

He grabbed my jaw again and pried my lips open with his finger. I have to get out of here. Where's the door? Maybe I can orb myself out. *Portal* out? Can I even *do* those things? I'm a witch. I *don't* have LeMehti magick—I'm losing too much blood, I can't—"No, no. Wake up, Devi." Thomas snatched my corset and tore the spikes free from my lungs. I gulped for air but spat blood on his face instead. "This is a problem. Your sessions with Ionnar are having lasting effects. You're meant to remember who you are the moment you leave her presence." Thomas healed enough of me to his liking. "What? No 'thank you'?"

"Go fuck yourself, Thomas," I managed, with the meat hook curved through my voice box.

"Will you watch?" I rolled my eyes, contempt deep in my scabbed lips. "You know, in this light—" he phased my corset off, leaving me in nothing but a bloody blouse he ripped down the front. His eyes followed the beads of fresh crimson on my torso. He wrapped my legs around his waist and leaned into me, throbbing hot between my thighs, licking off my blood and sweat from my breasts... I could taste it on my tongue. His loathing of me was mine. His *need* for me...

And when...

And when he finished with me, Thomas pulled out the meat hooks from my wrists and throat, dropping me to his feet. He filled his favorite chalice with my blood and dipped a paintbrush in. "For this one, I want you on your knees..."

*"Come now, are you not the* ***least*** *curious? She talks to those souls outside her chamber wall as if—"*
*"As if they keep her sanity from flaying her alive."*
*"Don't be so dramatic, Ophelia. But, yes. One soul in particular, when it fights its way through the sea of dead and finds her, they feed off each other, don't they, Ophelia?"*
*"****Now*** *who's the one with a penchant for the spectacular, Ionnar? But, you do not speak falsely. When she channels the lost souls, Devi, it would seem, is found."*

**AZRAEL**

"Why do you smile when I cut into you?" the mighty general was perplexed, flicking my insides from his serrated instrument. I wiggled my toes in the mix of piss, vomit, and blood in the tiny pool at my feet, gently swaying from the spiked shackles hanging me from the marble ceiling.

"Because I know *all* the things he's going to do to you, Elijah."

"Vincent?" It was brief, but he shivered. "The likes of Vincent will be no savior." I splashed the tips of my toes in the shiny liquid, then looked at him, rubbing my sweaty hair from my brow with my broken shoulder.

"Then why'd you stop cutting me?" Elijah threw his cutlery across the room and ran off. The last time I freed myself from this rig, it came at the cost of flogging. No, it was flaying. Wait, no, no. It was definitely 66 lashes to my back. Elijah seethed each time my LeMehti marking healed me quicker than anyone preferred. So, he simply had to flog me again. And again.

And again...

Until one day, I simply didn't cry or flinch at the leather and chains on my skin. I counted the leaves of the strange weeping willow tree in the middle of Elijah's massive torture chamber instead. Until I smiled at the glimmer of hope I bit into with each blow. Vincent would find me and when he gets his hands on everyone who touched me... I almost pitied them. The reason for their abhorrent behavior was all me. They'd lost any sense of the people they were. These are not immortals battering me to the brink of death and back again. These are innocent people trapped in a prison of their own flesh and bone, compelled to do and say things even the cruelest of creatures would think twice about.

Why not kill me and save themselves? Why not have Thomas, their resident Reaper, annihilate Hell and its minions? When my favorite Paladins came to fetch me, the answer struck me harder than Favienne's flat note at dinner. Breakfast? I have eaten here, haven't I?

"She's at it again, Rogue."

"That mind of yours, Devi. It confounds us all. Take her by the waist. Mind her wounds, Sephora." The ceiling had a skylight. It was always black. No stars. No clouds. No evidence of time ever passing. The twins, in movement but not in flesh, cleaned me up and readied me for my audience with their emperor. "Look *in* the mirror, Devi. Pay no mind to all that splashing." Time. I've lost a chunk again. By the looks of me at the gargantuan mirror for a wall, it's been six minutes, thirty-seven seconds, and... two days. My face dropped a few shades of what little color I had left.

"The lady has realized the loss of consciousness. It's alright, Lady Devi. Your session with Elijah was taxing." Both women spoke and moved in perfect unison. One braided my hair while the other pricked my lips to stain them the 'perfect shade of red' she'd said. The lovers, no one understood their malady. How did the poison entangle them so? They were the kindest to me. Maybe because I could differentiate between the two. I knew Sephora was the wild, desert-born one, like me. Rogue was the complete opposite of her beloved. She was class and calm and petite in her porcelain frame.

"Look how beautiful you are." The words spilled from their mouths with haunting harmony. "Do you like the dress, Devi? It's black and simple. We did not think a corset would be necessary. You are constantly wearing those dreadful things." I nodded blankly and followed them out of the—I whipped around. We'd been in a spa. The splashing, however, did not belong to any woman...

"Well, do you plan on standing there awestruck for the duration of the evening, or have you the faculties to walk?" I tried to focus. Sephora and Rogue brought me to the throne room. I checked my wrists and ankles. Bound with chains. Sentinels at the ready behind me; my *leash* coiled around their fists.

I met Azrael at the base of the dais. He shared a foolish grin with Thomas and clasped his hands together, but when the candles snuffed out from a breeze that had no right being inside castle walls, Azrael rose from his seat. "You always find a new reason to give me pause."

"Pause? I was certain blinding half your personal guard would do a bit more than that?" ?" I didn't need to snuff out the candles to blind them, but it sure was theatrical. His dumbfounded face raged red. A fury of ancient words sprang between the emperor and Thomas. Ophelia was at her husband's side; the luxury of sight devoid from the hollows of her skull. Ionnar and the other blind could do nothing but wait for regeneration. "Don't worry. It's only temporary."

"You, dear lady, have a darkness within." Azrael's anger trickled down to a different sort of estimation of me.

"The stuff of nightmares, I hear." He circled me; the entire time speaking to Thomas. The recent General of the Paladins harbored a distinct taste of antipathy. I hurt his precious wife. Why? Why did I do that? You do *not* attack a nonattacking opponent.

"I'll not repeat myself, Devi." Repeat *what*? My blood steamed as it slid down Azrael's sword. The point of his blade pierced into my chin, making sure his eyes were all mine bore witness to in this wretched House of God.

"What magick have you in those broken bones of yours? You are but a witch, my lady. A Seer of things long passed and creatures thriving in shadows." I swallowed a gulp of my stomach.

"A witch who can bring empires to their knees... my, *lord*." And as the Sentinels dragged me into the third circle of Hell, I looked back at Azrael and smiled...

*"Korrae, it's been three days."*

*"And? Last time she stood at those windows for a* **week***,*

*muttering about with the dead. They can't help but be drawn to her, Bennett. She is a Morsea after all."*
*"Necromancers..."*

**DAHLIA**

"What are you doing?" I murmured, still waking. Remnants of our shared dream warm in my eyes. Vincent sat at the edge of our bed, scribbling into his book. Fledgling sunlight floating across his skin from between the curtain, "It's of last night." His sweet words trailed off into the past. Into *us*... the markings on his back illuminated. Mine followed suit. I wrapped my arms around him, resting my chin on his shoulder. "I never want to forget you, Devi. Not one moment in time." The pang in our bones, the sudden break in his voice... he put his grimoire away and took me into him, kissing me as if this were a reverie and not reality. Our touch, the only tether that kept us from being ripped apart. When I heard *her* laugh... I opened my eyes. My pillow soaked and torn. I was in the company of The Kuma and, as usual, Dahlia did *not* disappoint.

"The thing about cruelty, Devi," she leaned in, her stark white curls caressing my lips, emphasizing each word with her hands, "it is *most* beautiful when *not* perceived." She stood tall, her armored form too smooth for the Celtic warrior encased beneath. "I thought you would appreciate the art of this." Dahlia wiped my tears from her eyes, "The pain that bears violence beyond imagining—*that*, Devi—is hardly *ever* found at the edge of a blade..." Dahlia adjusted her baldric around her waist and took refuge in the pendant resting at her collar. A single black hematite crystal. She rubbed the gift between her fingers and inhaled. "Cease your tears, Devi. We experience pain. We do not fall victim to it." She tore the sheets off of me. The vision of my battered body took her a moment to acclimate to. "What do we do with pain, Devi?" I wiped my face with my torn lace sleeve and sat up. Dahlia shifted her weight from one leg to both, crossing her marking-riddled arms across her chest and waited. I stood up, my dislocated hip popping back in place.

"We survive it." We turn it into a weapon...

"*How* you do so is crucial." She looked over to the wall of windows where the souls always converged. Trying to break through to this realm. To *me*... What Dahlia found beyond the wall—for something to frighten a *Kuma*—Dahlia left in a flurry, her markings glowing something awful. Alone in my bedroom, the wall of windows drew me to the very demons and damned that made Dahlia feel fear that belonged to none but her...

*"This war will see no end, Collette. She is* ***gardening****.*
*Muttering about again to the gods know which lost soul* ***this*** *time."*
*"After all these years—do not lose hope* ***now****, Miarrah."*
*"Hope is obsolete. That* ***creature*** *must die."*
*"That creature is our only saving grace."*
*"Tell me, why is it we do not kill her and rid ourselves of this poison? Thomas can—"*
*"Thomas* ***cannot****. Not completely..."*
*"Collette, sister, we are resting the fate of our* ***entire*** *existence and that of dozens of worlds on a* ***fairytale****."*
*"Once upon a time, Miarrah, we believed that to be true of Vincent..."*

**THOMAS**

With my spine still protruding, I fell to his feet. He looked at me, almost grinning, as I spit up blood on his Persian rug. Cocking his head, he contemplated something I'll never know. Thomas removed his armor and sat at the foot of his bed. With a flick of his wrist, I healed. My eyes darted to the door. To the Claymore swords above the fireplace. His laughter… the sound of it pounding in my mind harder than his fists had… Then, with a snap of his fingers, he positioned me; freezing me in place the way that always made his mouth water… My eyes reflecting candlelight. Forced smile strung up into a pout. He rubbed his bare chest, a heavy breath filling his lungs. Biting his lips, he stroked himself… hard. But only *once*. Sweat dripped down his neck far too quickly.

"Tonight, Devi—you're going to behave… and I'm going to watch." And he kept true to his word. I lay there, paralyzed, and he watched. Watched as Ophelia walked in. Thomas watched me as he stripped his wife naked of her armor. As he dug his hands into her hips when she mounted him, filling him inside of her. And when Thomas took control, when he put Ophelia beneath him, the heat of him—her moans when he kissed her—Thomas watched me as he *fucked* his wife because the one thing he *didn't* paralyze in me was my Empathy…

*"Why do we wait for her to submit? Why does Azrael not make his case to the gods? Their existence hangs in the balance as much as ours."*

*"Perhaps. But, they were not poisoned."*

*"They can help us. They can confine the damned thing and—"*

*"Confine? Devi has sleeping within her the power to render gods to mortals. If the likes of Zeus and Bastet wish to parlay with the human Reaper..."*

*"You made your point. Then we continue to be her wardens. And when her power awakes?"*

*"Let us pray there is* ***one*** *deity willing to risk her immortality for—for everything."*

**PANDORA**

"You exhaust me. How do you manage that, Devi? Can you solve that riddle?" Pandora hung her cape on a hook and smoothed the satin of her skirt; my bleeding face reflecting on her polished, black iron breastplate.

"I'm more of a Scrabble kinda girl." She played with my hair; a damp braid taking her attention. "I'd be careful with that. Sephora took special care beading those opals in. She'll have a proper fit if you mess it up." We exchanged looks, and she let my hair slip through her fingers.

"Make yourself useful. Hop on the rack." With a wave of her emerald-crusted hand, my chained limbs attached to the mechanisms of the device and stretched me apart, preparing me for whatever the empress had in store. "What is it, hmmm? Is your plan to *bore* us all to our proverbial deaths until your Reaper abilities manifest?" admiring the marks she'd carved into me moments ago, Pandora waited patiently for my response. "Well?" she clutched my jaw in her bejeweled grip.

"Oh, sorry. That *wasn't* a rhetorical question?" Pandora sighed and retrieved her dagger.

"I admire your tenacity, Devi. It tastes of chocolate. The way it melts on my tongue..." Pandora licked her blade. My blood, thick and warm, as it trickled down her wrist. She walked about the chamber admiring the souls of humans, monsters, and everything in between as they palmed and clawed at the windows. They followed me everywhere. Some sang to me, others shared tales of their lives. Stories that saved my mind when I thought I'd lost it for the last time... "You're a witch. A psychic. A killer of gods." Pandora sauntered to the table, caressing my shackles. Running her hand between my thighs at every step, she opened her mouth, the lilt in her voice nowhere near as haunting as the life it lacked. "But tell me, which is better? The power to destroy that which cannot *be* destroyed?" the tip of her dagger met with her breastplate, "or—" she leaned over me, her armored frame reflecting the protective light of my markings, "the power to create that which was *never* meant to be?" My eyes flashed black in horror. "The things I will do to you, child..." Pandora pierced her dagger into my jaw, the point slowly meeting with my brain. "You fancy yourself a storm, Devi?" her lips quivered, unable to contain the indignation within. "I will make you a goddamn *hurricane*."

*"I don't like it when she sleeps."*
*"You don't like that Pandora has granted Devi to walk about without chains, Thanys."*
*"If you think her powers cease when she rests, Dahlia—have you not ventured into her mind? Her past?"*
*"Of course I have, my love. Of course..."*
*"One memory, Dahlia.* ***One*** *memory and we will all be at her mercy."*
*"Devi is* ***not*** *evil."*
*"No, darling. She is something* ***else****."*

**THANYS**

"You and Dahlia, you're not like the others." Thanys cracked his knuckles and scooted closer to me.

"What drew you to that conclusion?" I swallowed back tears, fighting to stay awake. I drew my knees to my chest and played with a baby crow hopping around me.

"You're not poisoned. Not purely. You've both lost your shit, but it's madness by proxy. It's as if being Empaths—the sort of Empaths the two of *you* are—shielded you from being poisoned from the inside. You have the white hair, shifting silver-to-white eyes if you get too angry, and—"

"And what, Devi?" the baby crow gave my palm a gentle peck and flew off to her mother. The LeMehti man with markings sprawled across his entire body kept his gaze on me.

"Your markings. That's why you're covered in them. They protect you."

"They couldn't protect against *you*." We locked eyes.

"No, I suppose they couldn't. Everyone else's rage, their hollowed out souls… why can't you stop from channeling it?"

"We tried to, in the beginning. But you're forgetting again, Devi." The solarium lit up with fireflies. The only stars I was to ever see…

"What are you talking about, Thanys?" He looked around his home. The giant glass dome, the trees, and the endless water fountains that were his only link to Dahlia…

"Time—as illusory as it may appear—is not without consequence." My lips parted, sorrow begging to escape.

"You're not channeling it anymore, are you?" I swallowed a lump in my throat. "The madness is *in* you."

"Dahlia and I have made peace with our lot. We fought it for as long as was we could, but the likes of your poison—once it has you—"

"It's only a matter of time…" I couldn't bear to look at him. How many years did he and Dahlia have to fight off their *entire* empire's rage? How many times did they pretend to torture me while they slowly lost their souls? "The lessons, were they—"

"All true, my lady. Do you remember them?" I wiped my tears and nodded.

"Clearly, especially since I conveniently forgot that my only allies here have been torturing me for—how long since I ruined your lives?" The Kuma's face dropped. The smile he'd forced fading quickly.

"It's best not to quantify a thing as elusive as time. Or pain…"

"Did we already have a session or are we about to have one?" I looked down at my bruised arms. The skirt to my black dress had holes in it, some from claw marks, others from moths….

"We are through for the evening, Devi." I had the spiral

staircase in my sightlines. It lead to nowhere, yet it spanned the entire height of the structure. Hundreds of yards straight into the center of the glass dome. At the opposite end, however, the stairs extended into an opening in the cobble-stone ground. What I wouldn't give to go back down there...

"Which one of my memories did you make me relive?" Thanys stood, his hands in his pockets and his chest covered in nothing but gently lit LeMehti markings. The ones on his face matched Dahlia's exactly. Like a tether...

"One that is best left unspoken..." our eyes met and the exhaustion in our bones—there was a part of him that was good. An atomic speck of light hidden in a corner of his soul that he managed to protect. But, in this world of infinity and insanity, everything will meet the darkness dripping from every pane of glass in this empire sitting atop the event horizon. I got to my feet, and we made our way to the gates. The air chilled around us, the caws of the crows, an alarm screaming in my ears. Thanys unlocked the gates and took my hand in his before ordering the Sentinels to fetch me. "It *is* only a matter of time. What Dahlia and I taught you—"

"I know. I'll do what needs to be done."

*"Let's put her back in her chamber before anyone takes note."*

*"How she manages to Port out of those wardings, Bennett... it is beyond me."*

*"Is it? I think it clear as day?"*

*"Enlighten me, sir."*

*"Those wardings, Korrae, are meant to cage the likes of a psychic, a witch, a Reaper in human form. If she broke free—"*

*"What have we brought into our house?"*

**MIARRAH**

"What—what am I supposed to do here, Miarrah?" Her fists clenched, gunmetal eyes competing with the constellations on her breastplate.

"Do you know what it is that we do here, Devi? The LeMehti, we're guardians of these gates. We ensure souls go where they are meant to. Every now and again, however," her armor clanked as she paced the gateway to Purgatory, "Souls don't appreciate their—what does your lot call it? Final resting place." She looked to the massive illuminated arch, her harsh, angular hair barely flowing in the gales that howled. Although, the howls could be the wolves...

"Do I give them a map or...?"

"That mouth." She bobbed a pointed finger at nothing in particular. "The end of the world is in that mouth, Devi." The Paladin, second in command to both the Paladins and the entire LeMehti army, gripped her claymore at her belt and stood between me and the gate.

"Is *that* what's been stuck in my teeth? I thought it was chicken from the other night?" Miarrah flung an obsidian-crusted iron staff at my chest. I caught it, the force sending me back a few steps.

"Any souls that escape, you are to send them *back*. Can you manage that?"

"What? No, I can't *manage* that." Miarrah adjusted the clasps to her cape, the glint of the constellations too white-hot as she strolled to me.

"Either you herd the souls or you come with *me*. Do you want to come with me, Devi?" we stood head to head, her wretched smile the icing to the threat she spat in my face.

"Play Shepherd or return to *Oblivion*?" I straightened my stance and properly clutched the staff in my hand. "I'll choose what's behind Door Number 1, thanks."

"Brilliant." She walked away with spring in her step when she turned on her heal. "You do remember how to perform the task, yes?" Remember? I've—I've done this *before*...

Miarrah giggled and vanished into the shadows. I gawked at the electrified gate. Hiking up the lace skirt of my dress, I plopped on the grass and waited. I should be able to channel some memories of this from the staff eventually. If not, whatever creature that just possessed me was sure to spark a flashback...

**THOMAS**

"When I tell you to come, Devi—" Thomas unbuttoned his shirt, "I expect you to *obey.*"

"Maybe you should try harder." Thomas tore into the leather of his chair, his magick pulling me across the room and onto his lap. He locked my hands behind my back, forcing me to straddle him. *Grind* him.

"Is that hard enough?" Thomas clenched his jaw. His breath labored.

"Not even *close*. What are you gonna do about it?" the dark Paladin grinned. With a snap of his fingers, we were naked. Thomas dug his fingers into my hips, *aching* beneath me, and thrust himself between my lips; sliding me across the length of him over and over... "Harder..." I whispered the wet demand in his ear. Thomas clutched me tighter, grunting.

"Is *that* better, Devi? Is this how *Vincent* did it?" I wrapped my hands around his throat, squeezing, and he let out a *deep* growl that rumbled in both our chests. When I started grinding him *without* his guidance, "Devi—you're *dripping...*" his eyes rolled back, "Let me *inside* of you. I—I can make you feel what *he* did. I can make you feel *more...*" And when his moans filled in my mouth, when I drove him to the brink of *coming*, I knew I *finally* had the bastard under my spell...

"I obey *no one*." I looked down at him, my tears *steaming* as they boiled his cheeks. Flames licked at our skin, their tongues bright in his wide eyes. "After *everything* you've done to me—you didn't think I'd find a way to *fuck* you?" My hands *slowly* broke his *disgusting* neck, "You will *never* have me." And I burned us *alive*...

I walked out of his chamber naked, charred, and blistering. Sentinels made a run for me but Thomas emerged from the smokey room and barked an order at them they could not refuse. The horror on his face—the *exhilaration* of it fueled me. Thomas truly believed I *wanted* him. That my *body* wanted him... That he could make *me* feel what *he* wanted. Thomas doesn't want me. I unraveled his lust for me ages ago. I am the cause for his pain. What better revenge than to exert power over the very thing that stole it from you? That *broke* you?

I laughed, though it cracked a rib. The spell *worked*. If only I could tell my teachers...

The effigies and statues along the corridors helped keep me upright until I found my way back to my room on the other side of the palace.

I walked for an hour...

I don't remember how I made it down the stairs that lead to my room. I only remember being in the clawfoot tub; washing away what the fires couldn't. I went underwater and when I convinced myself that drowning would far surpass... anything; I heard it.

One voice in the midst of thousands behind the walls. I could never make it out, but the comfort it brought with it... I rested my head against the edge of the tub; one candle filling the small bathroom with light.

"What happened? You've been crying. You're *hurt*."

"What needed to happen." I looked away from the wall as if it could see me, see my bruises and burns. "Are you alright? You sound—different. Are you any closer to finding—"

"I'm angry."

"It's alright. I can take care of myself. Besides, I've gotten used to it. That, believe it or not, helps." The voice didn't speak to me for a while. I thought it disappeared back into the sea of lost souls in Purgatory, waiting for their new lives or ultimate fates.

I wore a silk nightgown. It was the only thing in my armoire that wouldn't be abrasive against my still-healing skin. I staggered a bit on my way to bed and laid down. I'd either fall asleep or be taken to another session with another Paladin. Or, if my captors felt especially mischievous, they'd leave me be.

Solitary confinement eventually resulted in starvation. Cleaning up your own death—nothing prepares you. Then again, what could have possibly prepared me for consciously dying, decomposing, then regenerating?

Right. My sessions with Collette.

"Devi?" the voice. "Don't try to move. You need to rest."

"Why do you sound like that?"

"Like what?"

"Like you're about to do something foolish. What are you going to do?" There was silence and it crawled too coldly against my skin.

"What needs to be done."

**PANDORA**

"Devi, what have you *done*?" Collette's perfume couldn't overpower the scent of death in the air. Thick crimson droplets trickled down from the ceiling, staining her stark, braided hair. Both our gowns slowly soaking up his remains. Scattered flesh and bone pooling at our feet. His skull fit perfectly in my hand. Smooth and clean of meat. A rib fell beside Korrae. A pretty gasp crossed her lips. I ran my thumb across Gideon's heart, still warm, still beating in my palm. I tossed it at her armored feet. They'd put his pieces back together once my spell faded.

"Your Sentinel thought himself worthy of me."

"What did he do?" The higher ranking Paladin was cautious, breathless, and too frightened to be angry. I sat at my vanity and brushed Gideon's insides from my hair. My out-of-sync reflection grinning with me.

"He got too close..."

*"Did you hear what happened with Hades? Pandora was **seething**, what with what happened to Gideon, so she demanded Hades teach the witch a lesson."*
*"Lost Heavens, tell me Persephone **slapped** her."*
*"Better. They didn't allow our empress entry."*
*"Hah! You know what this means?"*
*"Oh, **yes...**"*

"How are you doing this?!" she screamed into my ears, fracturing my entire skull.

"Aren't you overreacting? We're both women. Your Sentinel thought he could touch me without my permission." I coughed up blood. "He'll heal up nice and quick—" her gauntlet dented as it hit me across the face. "Right. You want concise responses. You're asking how I used my powers while in your possession? If you haven't noticed, Pandora, I'm kind of a freak of nature." I chuckled, smoke puffing out of my mouth; my burnt body slowly healing from my most recent trip to the 6th Circle of Hell. Or was it GeHennam this time?

"Lock her away!" Pandora's shock gave me the warm and fuzzies in *all* the right places. "No, Bennett. She is to be kept in the dungeons from now on." No one moved. Thomas was even taken aback.

"Pan, the dungeons are for—"

"Someone throw this beast in the cell before I feed you *all* to the Kuma." The Sentinels didn't lay a hand on me. Too busy white-knuckling their swords. Thomas sped over, wrapped his fingers around my throat, and flung me into the air. At the same moment, we were all in the castle's dungeons. The cell doors slammed shut, dried blood from its former prisoner flaking off.

The place was cozy. Romantic torch lighting, black stone wet with delight. No bed, though. No matter. I don't sleep much. This part of the castle—the painfully stereotypical dungeon part—their warding and all this red *matter.* It had a similar impact that Hell and the other underworld dominions did. My powers were weaker, my movements were slower. This was more than a prison cell…

It's a *cage.*

"Why did they spit you out? When we send a soul to any circle of Hell, *we* control when it enters and leaves." Oh, Pandora is still here. Everyone is…

"True. But who has more control over the souls in Hell?"

"Lucifer may have breached the laws and played with you, but that does not explain how you returned."

"Come now. You *know.*" The bitch lost about three shades.

"That's… not possible. When we're through with you, Devi, you'll *beg* for the days—"

"You threaten me with the prospect of terror yet forget the reason *why* you've locked me in this cage." I scoffed. "You think I should be *afraid*? Honey, I'm the thing that scared the *Devil.*" My eyes gleamed in the shadows. The light reflecting off everyone's armor. "Now, walk away before I show you what made the king of Hell pray to God…" I'm so fucking tired… It took Pandora a very long four seconds to speak.

"He *never* would have released you."

"Well," I dusted off my tattered dress, smoothed the bit of my cheek that was almost healed, "*someone* with gorgeous hair and a marking right here—" I pulled down my dress to reveal my clawed clavicle, "snapped his fingers and stuck me back here so fast, it gave me whiplash. Which was a shame. We had such wonderful conversation. I mean, first off, Hell isn't what everyone thinks it is. It's more of a collective. There are *neighboring* underworlds. A *labyrinth* of them. Did you know that? And Lucifer? We went on and on about all the things the Bible got wrong about him. And the weather—"

"*No more*!" Pandora's shock wave blew through me, knocking me off my feet and into the windowless, shackled brick wall. "These games of yours—do you think you frighten us?" Thomas and Bennett pulled Pandora aside when he saw me stand up with too much ease, smiling...

"You know what's interesting?" I made my way back to the bars, spitting up fresh blood, "All your lives are in my hands and you've *no* idea what I truly am. What I›m capable of. Not completely..." Their eyes glowed with bitterness. Black shadows full of terror. My laughter echoed in the dungeon. The Sentinel's armored hands clutched the hilts of their swords. "You want to know a secret?" I gripped the bars of my cell door, my eyes—a swirl of bronze and blue—sparked with excitement. The light shining brighter than any immortal's eyes in the space. "I don't know what I'm capable of, either. And you *fools* brought me to your doorstep." No one spoke. Thomas smirked while Bennett made certain the warding and locks of my new cage held. Pandora held on to a Sentinel; her armor denting underneath her grip. "*Armies* of ancient immortals against. One. Of. *Me*... I can't *wait* to play." I banged my forehead against the bars, stones in the ceiling crumbled to the ground. "I have one rule, though: No mercy..."

*"Death is not only inevitable, it's in her blood and she's beginning to like the taste of it."*
*"When do we step in, my Queen?"*
*"I fear we cannot, my love. If we open our gates, the sickness may reach us and we will be of no help to the lady and her Paladins."*
*"Then we wait for the perfect moment and strike."*
*"Let us pray that **this** time, we do not need to..."*

**AZRAEL**

It was time to eat with the immortals, and I—again—refused. Thomas crept the edge of his dagger across my chest, blood soaking my corset. He coiled his fist around my throat, his blade gliding hot between my thighs. And as his wife watched, Thomas licked my lips and called out a familiar demand. "Open. Your. Mouth."

I tore into the fabric of space and the immortals didn't know what to do first: punish me or repair what they didn't know I was capable of... I burned the food they wanted to shove down my throat and *laughed*. And when everything went black...

"The next time you perform a stunt like that, it will be your last, Devi." Azrael and the immortals from our little dinner party were in the throne room.

"You're allowing me a *next* time, Azrael? Ill-advised, don't you think?"

"Your time with Miarrah—you do not learn, do you?" The dark... Miarrah. My eyes flicked to her. She sat atop a gargoyle, her legs crossed, eating a pomegranate. The memories flooded my mind. The hemorrhaging that followed was only natural. That many times in *Oblivion*.

That many times...

"Beyond these walls, you may be feared, but in my empire, you are no more than a peasant among gods. You would do well to remember your place, my lady." Azrael spat out the words with a vile smile. The cling and clatter of steel echoed off every soldier in the cathedral. Every immortal armed to the teeth. Their blood ran cold. I couldn't help but laugh.

"*Gods*? You?" the air crackled from their fear. My rage. Our madness. I kept Azrael's eyes in mine as I ascended to his throne. My Collette and Korrae struggling to restrain my chains. "What titans of old need entire armies to protect them from *one* woman? No one moved. «I know my place, my lord. You would do well to remember *yours*."

*"Do you think she can hear us, Hastian?"*
*"Hear us? That bitch can erase us from existence*
*with* one *word. This war needs ending, Leilahn."*
*"This war's just begun..."*

**THANYS**

Ophelia appeared in the archway and looked to Bennett. He weakly shook his head, answering her silent words, and she shut her eyes, fading into the bricks.

"The Kuma are coming for you, Devi. Accept our deal." I tip-toed in the tiny pool of blood and piss, twisting my body and the chains of light wrapped around my wrists until I could face the Paladin. I looked up at him from my one unburnt eye and as the last of the lightning he struck in me subsided, I shook my head.

His markings dripped down his eyes like tears; spilling down his skin until they stopped at his chest.

Bennett put my arm over his shoulder and walked me through arched corridor after arched corridor; stained glass windows that let in the shadow of perpetual twilight in the castle. The only source of illumination in the lower levels were scrolled wrought iron sconces housing pure blue energy at each window. When we reached a non-surprisingly spectacular staircase, Bennett carried me in his arms for our descent.

The landing revealed the dank underbelly that writhed beneath the cathedral palace. Bennett tucked a stray curl behind my ear. My flinch almost gave him pause. "Do as you are told, lady." Bennett vanished in a mist and he left me staring at a pair of iron doors that opened on their own. I walked into the empty room one step at a time. Black quartz and obsidian laced the entire ballroom. Gardens of lapis lazuli, malachite and—the energy in this place…

Am I back in Dahlia's chamber?

I made my way to the center of the grand hall to where a stone bench sat. Above, in the glass dome, was the same enigmatic light pouring reflecting off every surface...

I knew he stood behind me. His heart was steady, pulling

mine to match its rhythm. I breathed in deep and turned. The soldier bore no weapons on his person. Only a pair of white silk pants and nothing more. What was frightening, however, was the absence of scars. And for someone who had seen as much violence as *he* had, his body should be a graveyard. Instead, his deep, tawny skin was a blank canvas. Covered in their black markings from his forehead to his bare toes. Just like Dahlia... this is the other half of The Kuma.

"I hate to ask again." Again? "Will you fight for us?"

"No. Who are you?" His doe-eyes swirled; Milk, gunmetal, and oil. The moment the Kuma's hand coiled around my wrist, I gasped.

Thanys.

Only he wasn't. *Vincent* stood before me. I shut my eyes and prayed. *This isn't real. It's a trick. Look again.* Opening my eyes, there was one person and one person alone who stared back into my soul. His sapphire eyes, black hair, and new-moon smile... Vincent's heart echoed inside of my own. The touch of his skin sparked across my body, and when I breathed him in...

The room tilted; falling with ease, taking me with it when Thanys released me. What followed was too familiar. The aching. The burning. My body literally broke and burned with the lack of Vincent's touch. With the *anticipation* of it.....

Thanys is an Empath. *He's* the weapon, and the hall was the stage for my memories to come to life.

"The sooner you accept your fate, my lady, the sooner this all ends." Thanys grabbed me by the back of the head, controlled rage in his mouth.

"No." I spat back. Thanys threw me to the ground and tore me apart without laying a single hand on me...

"Is she able to speak?"

"Is there a justifiable reason for your disruption?"

"Pandora requested an update."

"I said *justifiable*, Elijah." Neither man spoke.

"What's—what's happening? Where's Vincent?" I threw up blood. Elijah grabbed me by the arm and dragged me away.

"Time for bed, Devi."

"Elijah?" the tremor Thanys' voice birthed inside Elijah trickled down his arm and into me.

"Yes?" Thanys took a step toward us, surveying his gemstone garden, then locking eyes with me.

"*Never* interrupt us again." With the last words dripped from his tongue, Thanys smiled at Elijah and that smile alone didn't allow the General of the LeMehti armies to swallow.

I looked up from my hands and I was sitting at the ever elaborate dinner table with the royal immortals. Thanys and Dahlia were at opposite ends of the long wooden table. Her eyes were soft and doe-like and filled with yearning; A yearning for the man twenty-five feet across from her at the head of the table.

"It's rude to stare." I couldn't stop myself from trembling. The vile voice burned in the hollow of my neck.

"Thomas, you'll give the poor thing a heart attack," Azrael said, sipping wine. The dining hall echoed with laughter and chatter. Silver eyes catching my gaze, then dropping it like rotted meat. The pit of my stomach burned. The void in it spreading. Filling. Disappearing. When the royals went silent, I stopped picking at the scabs on my arms.

Pandora sat with her chin resting in her palm; sections of her thick wavy dove-white hair braided with moonstone and emeralds. "Would you stop that incessant tapping? Food is *consumed,* not played with." I placed my fork on my plate and looked up at everyone adorned in lavish garb to match the likes of their rankings and meal.

Miarrah sat with an empty seat beside her. She always sat with an empty seat beside her. Elijah,

"Favienne? I am dying to hear the new concerto you and Mahriel have prepared. Play for us." The Royal Paladins did as their emperor requested. "Oh, take Devi with you. She can play the violin." No. Not again.

Favienne's mood shifted, and she swept across the room and pulled me off my chair. We sat in the corner and played.

I played until my fingers bled.

Until they broke.

I played for days…

*"I take her to the edge of nothingness. To the heart of Oblivion. I make Devi oblivion and she..."*
*"Do not tell me the child fights back, Miarrah."*
*"No. She* ***allows*** *it, Collette. She* ***enjoys*** *what I do to her. What* ***it*** *does to her."*
*"What do we do?"*
*"Pray..."*

**THOMAS**

The scent of my burnt skin wafted in the air. "Open your eyes." Thomas slapped me. My lip split open. My hand flew up and held his wrist tight before he struck me again. As I crushed his bones, I opened my eyes. The fledgling fright filling him was worth everything that was to come.

It didn't matter that Thomas broke my jaw. It didn't matter that he dragged me down three sets of stone stairs; my fractured skeleton and steps tearing at my flesh.

It didn't matter that I *liked* making him angry…

Thomas stopped and threw me to my knees, sliding his fingers across my bloodied back, sucking them off clean. I turned around and grabbed him, breaking his skull open with mine.

Thomas laughed, but beneath the poisoned lilt of his voice, there was something that intoxicated me.

"If I didn't know any better, Devi, I'd say you *enjoy* the pain." Thomas circled me in the center of the throne room. The firelight rose and fell with every breath. "You *will* bend. It>s only a matter of time." I scoffed, dusting off the ash and embers from the remnants of my corseted gown. His anger shot through my chest. Thomas grabbed my mouth, squeezing it until he broke bone. Until I spat out blood and teeth in his face... "Pay attention, dollface." The stench of the madness in his words, the heat of it singed the skin off of my lips. Blood oozed down his hand.

"I do enjoy pain. *Yours*. And you're absolutely *writhing* in it." My school-girl laugh terrified him. "I don't bend, Thomas, I break. And you're standing a little too close..."

"I'm going to enjoy tearing your soul out, Devi."

"Don't make promises you can't keep, Thomas." He pinned my hands behind my back, his hips digging into me, and lapped my blood from his lips, then licked his tongue, hard, against my mouth. Sucking my mouth to get every last *drop* of me...

I charged my body, and Thomas went flying with the arcs of lightning. I smiled. Then I fucking burst out with laughter. The scent of his charred flesh had me *salivating*. Thomas pulled out his guns and nearly emptied them into me. . I never fell. The taste of my insides on my tongue grew sweeter and sweeter. I grinned, red drenching my chin as it spilled from my lips. He stared at me with blank infernos and all I could do was chuckle...

My lips grew *wider* as the bullets, blood, and acid-filled my insides. I let out a perfect *giggle* as my knees hit the brick ground from the iron lodged in my spine and skull.

Thomas nearly put both muzzles in my eyes. I bared my crimson teeth and said with schoolgirl giddiness, "I'm going to enjoy this."

"Stop!" Colette struck both her blades in between his weapons. She spoke furiously in their language, and Thomas begrudgingly lowered his arms. He leaned into me, his brow catching a bead of sweat as his chest heaved. Without a word, he disappeared, and I was left in the clutches of Collette.

She walked around the throne room sharpening her blades on one another, waiting for me to heal. The markings on her shoulder were glowing. The lines wrapping around her neck like a hand choking the life out of her... Their markings glowed around me in preparation and protection against me *before* I even touched them...

I spat out the bile I gagged on and that's when the bullets slid out and hit the floor.

"Almost through there, Devi darling?" she sat on the arm of a pew, checking her make-up in the reflection of her sword.

"Wait your turn, Collette. Patience is a virtue and whatever the fuck." She scoffed. I noted the gargantuan theatre she blinked us into. Statues of angels, demons, gargoyles... The entire hall, a sculpture of Heaven and Hell. Love and war. Life and death...

The statues sparked with souls and cracked, coming into being. "I don't like to wait. I especially don't like being told what to do." She watched the chaos from her balcony and when I killed enough of her children, "Wonderful, Devi. Now, do it all again and this time, don't turn off your powers. It ruins the entire show. You are an Empath. What good is sending effigies of murder and sex if you don't allow yourself to *feel* any of it?" She settled back into her chair, legs dangling over the balcony, and clapped twice. "Again..."

*"She's rather beautiful—when she's not trying to tear your face off."*
*"A sleeping witch is as deadly as a waking one, Bennett."*
*"Witches do not pose a threat when unconscious, Miarrah."*
*"This one does, Bennett. Her blood—can't you* ***smell*** *it?"*

**OPHELIA**

It wasn't the breathing that woke me, but the way her fingertips trailed across my cheeks. She sat at my bedside, smile sweet, teeth glinting in the candlelight. Curls of black shadow tickling my chest. I reminded myself not to move. That the thing crawling on top of me could only hurt me on her command. The Phantom Woman's eyes rolled in the back of her head. My fear, the scent of it, driving her to ecstasy. The clock ticked in time with her heart. Moans groaning wildly beneath my bed. She only hummed my lullaby louder. Lacing her hands tight around my neck. Her leather skin shifting. Mouth dripping red. Different voices gargling in her bruised throat.

"It's not the LeMehti that will murder you, my love, it's *us*…" I think she left. I think I fell asleep. I think I'm the one slitting my own throat…

"Do you hear me, Devi? Stop it!" Ophelia's voice broke through and I Blinked.

"How can I hear you when I'm not even here?" She snatched her dagger from my shaking hands and tucked me back into bed; brushing the hair from my eyes and wiping blood from my mouth and neck with her tiny white handkerchief.

"How true." Ophelia's somber air choked me. "How true..."

**FAVIENNE**

"Trust? *Obey?*" I moved my shaking hands away from my lips and gawked at the Paladin. Her immaculate form took a hold of my bed; the dark drapes framing her silver eyes and a violet so crisp, the color of it nearly crackled like a live wire. "Do you believe think this war game will work, my *lady*?" She grinned and looked at the broken wall behind me. "I'm not the only one dreaming here."

"True. Yet, 'tis only *I* who can distinguish reality from fantasy." Her eyes saw something I couldn't, and she shook her head, almost as if she were responding to someone. She looked at me again and I never saw her move to me. Her hand rose to my face and the lines that appeared around her eyes were astonishing. "Sleep well, lady. Sleep well." As she walked away, I pretended she didn't scare me.

"What? Another concerto? A flaying, maybe?" Favienne stopped in her tracks and I swear her dress nearly caught fire. "Will you do the honors yourself?" She turned slightly to me and I could see her wicked smile.

She let out a breath and even though she was across the room, the gust of the infection burned my throat. "Mahriel merely *showed* you a future." She walked away and as she opened the door to leave, she whispered something she knew I could hear. "Why send for someone to paint the masterpieces when *you* yourself are so infallible an artist?"

"How ominous. Did you practice that line before you came in here?" Favienne crossed her arms and adjusted her stance. Her long braided tresses snaking around her arm.

"Do you still hope that your beloved will save you?"

"I don't need saving, Ophelia." What… the room hazed over in a golden, bokeh glow.

"Oh, my dear, *sweet* Seraphim. How wrong you are." I rubbed my eyes and saw Ophelia standing before me. "Mind games in all their manners, my dear, are an art you must conquer quickly lest you be left wanting." She walked out the door, shutting it tight behind her. I sat there, emptiness full in my chest and madness scratching behind my eyes…

"Clean her well, Sephora, and make certain that she feels very comfortable, Rogue. We want our darling little princess to be at ease." Another gap in time lost. Sephora and Rogue were with me but kept quiet under the presence of their empress.

Pandora walked down the white steps into the pool, drenching her incredibly ornate corset, made of nothing but raven feathers. Her silk skirt swimming like liquid fire underwater as she made her way to me.

"How are we this morning? You were rather silent at breakfast." Breakfast? The two women gently cleansed my hair and skin. Pandora smiled and her markings played as jewelry around her neck. Her hair was beautiful as it cascaded down her back; tiny hyacinths trailing from her silver Sleeping Beauty crown.

"It would be wise of you to answer me, darling."

"We're fanfuckingtastic." Her skin heated, and she lifted her hands out of the water and to my jaw.

"Is that truly how you wish to end your words?" I looked right into her eyes when all I wanted to do was go under and not resurface.

"We're fanfuckingtastic, your majesty."

"Lovely." Her eyes caught something on my naked form. One of her warm hands trailed from my chin down to my sternum. "Honestly child. He has made a fool out of you. And this... "She lingered across the ancient words only she could read. "Did he tell you his name is *Vincent*?" She scoffed, never taking her eyes off me. "Truth be told... what does Ophelia call you? Truth be told, *Seraphim...*" She paused and breathed onto my face, the first few layers of my skin singed off... "Were it not for these illuminated scriptures, that fresh immortal soul burning inside of you... you would not have survived one *second* on this ground. No doubt A—I mean, *Vincent* saw this future and planned accordingly. He was our greatest strategist."

The change from the pool to the top of the cathedral was instant. She held me from the neck and let me dangle in the sky that never saw the sun. "That tongue of yours will bring you much strife. When among royalty, when among those you are of *no* equal, you *will* offer respect." We were on the highest tower and Pandora hung me from spikes. She made sure the iron hooks had gone through my shoulder blades and that I couldn›t wiggle my way out. She welded them flat on my chest. Why won't you phase through them, Devi? Excellent question. Answer: Where would I go?

I've seen the future. Trust me. This is the G-rated version..."I hope you enjoy the view." She kissed my cheek and left me to the illuminated gateways and forest grounds. She left me to see their talons curving over the gargoyles; their eyes slick with death and mouths hungry for *me*...

**KORRAE**

"Oh, waste not thy time on thought." Her too soft fingers latched onto my face then tangled themselves in my hair. As she spoke, her tiny kisses met with my mouth. "Won't you help us? Hmmm? You may even grow to be quite fond of the tasks. After all, you *are* one of *us* now. Accepting fate is what we do best." My eyes shielded themselves from her jeweled hair and medieval garb. "Very well then."

The choir hung in the air sweeter. Their delicate melodies captured me.

Literally.

Their song trapped me. Their ancient lyrics and music swayed calm into my veins. A beautiful illusion that I anticipated with excitement each time I saw my Korrae.

In her chamber, I was happy. I smiled and laughed and cried tears of pure joy as I witnessed the glory of gore across time....

"You have war in your lungs, magick in your bones, death in your blood... You are a thing not meant to be. And yet, here you are." Korrae wiped a smudge off her pauldron and ran a hand through her stiff, white hair before she strolled across the solarium to my chair; the pond in front of me displaying the sweet visions of genocide and genital mutilation. "Embrace the *beast* within you, Devi. You cannot control her forever. She *aches* for murder, and I believe Vincent will make the perfect kill. Wouldn't you agree?"

"Yes..." I'm not—I'm not *right* here...

We walked through the labyrinths and arrived at a massive wooden and rusted brown metal door. Beyond it I knew I would find one thing; Water.

The gates opened, and I saw what I had been rotting in my nose the entire trek here. There was a waterfall spilling into a pool that took half the space of the chamber. The Kuma's chambers—they were menageries of nightmares.

I cleaved to the metal door handles. Dahlia's presence choked me. With a deep breath, I loosened my grip, ignoring the metal returning to its natural curved shape after I squeezed it beyond recognition.

"Will you help us, or shall I find another memory?"

"Stay away from me, Dahlia."

"That's impossible at the moment. Now, tell me what I need—"

"What you *need* to is Thanys." She took me by my throat and tore into it. The picture-perfect sight of grace as I uncontrollably spat blood onto her face.

"You think yourself clever? You think you *know* a soul because you've the gift to feel it?" She slammed me against the quartz boulders framing the waterfall. "The name of Empath, as *you* beings call it, it is a *mockery* upon you. Do you think this is as far as your power goes? This is only the *beginning*." Rage flooded her eyes. "Then, sweet, *innocent* Devi, you will truly know what it means to *feel*." She vanished, and I was alone.

No one came for me. I laid there in my corseted gown of sapphire and steel for a long time. Long enough to see something I'd never seen before. The night sky fade and give way to the stars... And, though it wasn't much, it was enough. Never day nor night. Never here nor there. Something in between that only exists for moments in time then vanishes.

Twilight.

I found myself in a massive cathedral with a library; its upper balconies lined with books. *Thousands* of books and maps and windows here and there that opened to only shadows. Always shadows...

How did I get here?

"I am quite certain that you grow weary in Cortem. It's no place for a human." Azrael's voice echoed from behind a bookshelf, and my heart stopped. I flinched, dropping a journal to the wooden floor. He turned the corner and tilted his head. "A live one to be more specific." He walked again, and I knew to follow. Azrael stopped to trace his eyes over some volumes as he straightened the collar of his centuries-old military coat. I thought, for a second, about taking the sword resting at his waist and decapitating him with it. But, the need to know what this man would tell me overpowered the need to murder. "These books, these... *records* are filled with every soul that has ever passed through The Court."

Two Sentinels dragged in the spirit of a woman as she begged for her life. The soldiers gently placed the lady on the steps of the altar below and made sure her face was visible to Az and me.

I saw her bare feet first. Then I saw an immortal woman kneeling on the pedestal before us. The celestial creature's body was lived within onyx and silver chain mail. Her pitch-black hair, unincumbered with the intricate metal headdress.

Madelyn screamed from below as the immortal creature leaped from the balcony down to the soul. A finger graced Madelyn's forehead, and the human went stoic. When the mysterious immortal returned, I saw her face. A single, bronze glowing mark burned in the center of her forehead. But it was her clouded, silver eyes that caught me.

How could she be *blind*?

She took her position on the stone pedestal and vanished. Taking Madelyn with her. But I knew I could feel her soul being dragged to—

"Hell." I looked at Azrael and he looked at me. This place truly was a court and Azrael was more than its emperor; he was its Judge; Sentencing souls. But it wasn't like this before the poison. Before, they simply made certain souls went to their final resting places, wherever they were meant to be. But now, they *toyed* with every soul and Heaven, Hell—*no* Realm interfered... "The Marker is immune to your disease as you may have noticed. She is not of our Order." She didn't want to murder me, but she had no intentions of saving me, either.

"What have you *done*?"

"My job."

"It's your job to Judge not to play a *God*! Why doesn't Heaven interfere? Why didn't the Marker challenge you?"

"For the same reason your precious *Heaven* has yet to put its hands in this war; it is *not* their *place*."

"You're lying..."

"Am I?" Azrael called on three other Markers. Each bore a unique symbol on their forehead for the remaining realms: Hell, Purgatory, and Earth. All were blind, and all were feminine. I sat beside his throne, helpless, reliving the life and death of the humans and Revs that passed through the gates. I watched as soul after soul was Marked and sent to whatever realm Azrael deemed worthy. And when he asked *me* to lie down Judgement...

"I do not know what to do with you, Devi." I was on my knees fighting back the execution of a woman by guillotine. It took three tries... "A part of me yearns to slice your perfect skin." He lifted my chin, the sound of his voice gentle... "The other part declares the fact that any blade I use would *never* be sharp enough to make you *truly* fear me." He smoothed the sweat from my face and took an iron grasp on my neck, dragging me behind him. "I suppose there is only one way to find out, isn›t there?"

"I do not understand why you continue to fight us. Your rebellion will only bring innocent lives crumbling at your feet."

Ophelia stopped dragging me across the cobblestone ground. She gingerly lifted me to my feet and clasped her palms tight around my shoulders. "You have within you the power to end us with one thought." My rib tapped her armored corset, distracting her. "This madness can cease." She shoved the wet bone back inside me; it would take hours to heal... "Focus, Devi. For all the violence in you, there *is* peace. There is *hope*. You can save us *all*. Death is not what you think it to be, Devi." My silence infuriated her. She wanted my submission. I let the blood pooling in my mouth dribble on her pretty little shoes. "So be it." She shook her head and gave me a push. I fell back, phasing through the wall and into a completely mirrored room on the other side.

My wound stung; the blood dripping. The droplets hammered into my mind in the soundless void. My heart raced. Each beat pumping more of me down my torn satin gown and to the glass. The red on the blue of the fabric had a lovely contrast... I labored a breath and couldn't bear my reflection any longer. I crawled to the corner of the room and curled into a ball; hiding my face in my hands.

The tapping didn't trouble me. Nor did the leather-skinned creatures writhing beneath me; their breaths steaming with every bang of their horned heads against the glass. I don't know how many worlds know of my existence. I only knew what Ophelia *wanted* me to see here; that, even in entirely different realities, I was a threat...

And I needed to be stopped.

I looked over my shoulder and locked eyes with my reflection. She was in pain. Scars shimmering across every inch of her body. *Do it,* she said. The shard lodged itself in the right side of my face, but it didn't break the mirror. The others couldn't walk through to this world to kill me. *They need to kill me;* she said. *Maybe someone from these realms has the power to,* she begged, her lips quivering with blood and tears. I rose to my feet and tried another mirror. And another.

And another...

*That one, there.* ***He*** *can help us,* she cried out, pointing to the last standing wall of glass. I walked over and saw him. He looked right into me, silently crying. His broken heart cracked in mine. The woods were cold and quiet; an iridescent light show in the night sky. The magick in him was *it*. He could kill Devi and end the war. Restore every soul and—why, why is he looking at me like that? *Break the glass! Let him in! I have to die!* Her screams reached the man in the woods; a thousand banshees wailing at him. For all the hurt in him, he would not be moved. I took a step back and readied myself to jump when he held up a hand to the mirror and when that touch burned across my palm...

"Vincent..." this was our night at the warehouse.

"Forgive me, Devi..." I rushed to the mirror, my hand against the glass, desperately trying to take his.

"You've done *nothing* wrong." He shook his head, shame slipping out of his mouth.

"Fight them. No matter what they say. What they do... *fight*." He swallowed back the lump in his throat, his eyes too pale... "I will find you, Devi. Just—wait for me. I'll come for you, I *will*."

"I'll wait. I'll—I know how to survive them." The shards of glass slid out of my body, and in moments, my every wound healed. "Vincent—"

"It'll still appear that you're hurt." I nodded, knowing the part I would have to play.

"Thank you."

"Don't—"

"Vincent, I'm scared. Thomas—" I fell to my knees, weeping. Vincent followed. The way his soul *burned* when he channeled the things his brother had done to me...

"Look at me, Devi. They don't know you're a Mimic. Devi, *look* at me." He tapped the glass, regaining my attention. "They don't *know*." A fire sparked in my chest. "Every second with them—"

"Strengthens me." He almost smiled. "Is *this* why you were out there crying that night? You saw me here?"

"And more..." Vincent gently began to fade when the Devi

from that time made her way to him. Panic erupted in my stomach and spilled into our hands, trying to take hold of one another through the mirror, but it would not break. It wasn't a doorway to another world; it was a doorway through *time*... and we had none left. "I will be where you are..."

"The garden—it leaves quite the taste in your mouth. Does it not?" I followed Azrael absently. My eyes tethered to the soil. "Can you feel them, yet? The Chrysanthemums are Pandora's favorite." My hand grazed a rose bush and my ribcage fractured, reliving its death. We're in a Garden of Souls and they were coming for me.

Azrael stopped short, revealing a hole in the earth. My eyes flickered up in horror. He grabbed me by the hair and dropped me into the iron casket, welding itself shut. And as the king buried me alive, I died the deaths of thousands, over and over.

"Let's test that immortality of yours, shall we?"

The dire wolves were more ravenous than usual. One chewed on the ankle, while the other two bickered like children over the torso. It was nice, though. Seeing the animals. I wanted to pet them, but I couldn't bring myself to do so. Especially when I saw the ravens. These birds were much larger than the ones on Earth. They went straight for the eyes. Although, one did fuss about over the mouth; picking and pecking, ignoring the maggots. But when I choked on the ones burrowing their way out through my throat...

How long had they left me here? I swatted the birds and staggered to my feet; the wolves still eating my gradually regenerating intestines. I kicked them away and put myself back together. When I caught the scent, heard one of *them* limp behind me, I knew where I was.

I held my stomach together as hard as I could and looked over my shoulder. The mess of sweaty, black hair could not deter from the contorted skin, twisting across her face, squeezing her bones. Her knees bent the wrong way. She was a woman with an uncanny valley of a smile. She was a woman with a smile.

She was a woman.

With a smile.

And I smiled back…

There was a pull. A compass in the core of my soul guiding me to the castle gates.

"He'll never make it beyond those walls and you *know* it—" Azrael said. He grabbed my head, fingers cracking my skull like a watermelon. He threw me to my knees. The shock wave of the fall sent tremors echoing for miles. "Eyes front, Devi. I don't want you to miss the show." He plucked out his fingers and licked his thumb. My blood slid warm down my back. There was suddenly no little delay in my healing.

I smiled, red-soaked saliva dripping from my lips.

"He's at the gates. Azrael, Vincent is at the gates!" Pandora's shriek vibrated across my skin, and I *lavished* in the sound…

"Thomas! Now!" Thomas Ported slowly from the thrones to me; moving through space like a hundred thousand photographs flickering in water.

"Time moves differently here. Did you know that?" Thomas jerked my head back, my hair frying in his grasp. He spat his words against my cheek. The venom spewing from his lips charring my face… "Your valiant knight has been fighting his way to you for *years*…" I bore my wide, pale amber eyes into the hollows of his. "Ah, did you not know?" He looked at everyone, displaying me like a ragdoll. "The lady did not know!" The entire cathedral rumbled with glee.

Thomas got to his knees, licking his lips; fresh motivation crackled beneath his armor. "Do you know what four years of constant battle does to a man? LeMehti were built for violence, *of course*, but not—" he rubbed his forehead hard against mine, "not *this*. We were never meant for *this*, Devi. Vincent is *powerful*, but one against tens of *thousands*..."

"If he's so weak, why are you all hiding in here—with the *one* creature that can will you out of existence?" Thomas could barely swallow. I easily freed myself and stood to my feet. "If he's so *weak*, why are all of you *glowing*?" The light of every immortal's markings in the cathedral had reached a fever pitch; engulfing the candlelight and drowning the space with an aurora. "If Vincent is to fall," I took a step to Thomas, my irons clinking, "why do you need the force of ancient *armies* to face him?" Sentinels arrived every second, widening the gap between Vincent and me. Thomas sneered, then teleported out of the palace to find Vincent.

I dragged a breath into my battered body, and my charred skin renewed. Vincent was getting closer. His running pounded in my chest. The hilts of his blades were in *my* palms. Sentinel blood splattered on *both* our faces... His every movement quickened. Striking harder. Reaping souls as though they were weeds in a garden... The closer we get to one another, the faster we *heal* one another. But I've just climbed out of God knows what Realm... my powers—I can't help him if I stand here in the palace channeling everything.

"Devi, don't you *dare*. No more disobedience, child! No more!" my lungs heaved, crystal-clear beads of sweat dripped down my temples reflecting the immortal light show ever burning with terror. I looked over my tattered lace shoulder; a broken spear still lodged inside. I smiled at the empress, her porcelain hand gripping tight her emperor's gauntlet. All their Paladins with their weapons at the ready... and when my irises caught fire, flooding their metals and skin with a gleam of copper light, their hearts stopped...

"No more," I repeated, and melted my chains. They dropped into a molten pool on their precious marble. I was too weak yet to phase out the spear, so I *pulled* it out of my shoulder. The silence was bitter on my tongue, but it crawled in the back of my throat, begging to be set free. Every immortal wanted Vincent and I dead. But the truth of what I was, of what Vincent and I were *together,* stopped them from saying a single word.

With a flick of my wrist, I transformed the broken weapon into a double-edged spear.

*Vincent, I'm on my way*

I blinked myself out of the cathedral, but the spear clattered across the marble as I slid backward across the solid slabs. Vincent pushed me away... The immortals snickered. Whispered. Their hushed laughter, nauseating.

*Devi,* ***don't***

*What?! You can't fight them* ***all****! Vincent? Vincent!*

Legions of LeMehti soldiers lay motionless, weeping and bleeding in the field. I couldn't tap into anything else. Vincent blocked my scanning and—most importantly—my Empathic channel. That much war...

But he didn't—or couldn't—block *himself* from me. Not all of him.

"Damn you." The words ripped through the surrounding space when Thomas and Vincent rammed into one another. A planetary collision destined for nothing but chaos. My ribcage rattled from their crash and I jumped to my feet, blinking myself onto the battlefield again and again. And each time, Vincent threw me back inside the cathedral palace. Because—because being with thousands of LeMehti that foamed at the mouth to kill me beyond imagining was *safer* than fighting by his side...

Fine. He wants me safe? I can be *safe*.

I tore the steel off the ends of the pews and shaped them into a breastplate; etching protection prayers in every inch. The whispers grew; slowly bubbling to the surface. My daggers were in their munitions bank. One thought and the hilts were warm and familiar in my hands. My bare feet took off toward the gates and I used the last burst of energy. I Blinked myself again and *this* time, I hit the ground running. The instant flash of the soldiers' memories and mayhem coursed through my mind as if they were my own.

So be it.

A dozen were alive enough to attack me. They had me trapped in a circle. It was a perfect shape for me to gut every Sentinel where I stood. Their blood was furiously hot on my lips. When they dropped, I found Vincent in the sea of bodies; Vincent's location was a magnet; pulling me to him without thought. I phased through the corpses, not believing my eyes.

"Vincent... Vincent! What are you doing?!"

"Devi, *enough*!" his voice took *seconds* to reach me. It wasn't instantaneous... he didn't fight back. Thomas beat him to the ground. I felt n-nothing... He's going to kill him. He's *letting* Thomas kill him...

I ran. I teleported. It was never enough. Vincent was the strongest LeMehti... even as Thomas cracked his skull, bleeding him like an animal, Vincent's ability to protect me from.... No.

"No!" I ran again. Faster. And when Vincent pushed me back, I didn't budge. The black that washed over his eyes at that moment...

It was as if I was running into the arms of someone who did not wish to be saved.

*Vincent, **fight back!** Thomas will **kill** you!*

*Devi, I said **enough**!*

***No!***

I cast a spell. The only one I had enough power in me for. I set my sights on Thomas and once I had him under; my hands coiled. I didn't orb his skeleton from his body; I fucking pulled it through his flesh. Thomas's body fell limp and wet onto his pile of bones. One more jump through space, and I'd have Vincent in my arms.

My fingertips grazed his armor. Vincent wrapped a hand over my breastplate, pulled me into him, and pushed...

"Ah! Damn you!" He threw me back into the cathedral. I ran to the gates. The immortals left their pews. My palms met with the iron forest on the doors and I used my body and my mind to break through the metal. Some soldiers regained consciousness, and they gunned for Vincent. *You have **more** inside you. Come on!* I managed enough of an opening, allowing my fists through.

I imploded the chests of the soldiers.

I scanned for Vincent. His pull barely coursed through me. The immortals grew wary of something. Some force cursing at their blessed armor. It had to be Vincent. He fought back. But why can't I find him?

"Vincent! I'm here! I'm right here! Please hold on!" The cathedral trembled. I pushed against the gates, my body bending the iron and steel, but I couldn't phase through it. I couldn't break through it... I stood there, scrambling, clawing to get free, but the ache of his nothingness *ruined* me...

*Why can't I **feel** you? Where are you?! Please, God. Please help hi—*

I opened my eyes to the vaulted ceilings. The blade of the demon spear in my throat; Thomas twisting it. I gurgled, blood gushing from my mouth, pooling around my head like a halo... Thomas kicked me in the face, nearly decapitating me.

"Tisk, tisk, dollface. Stay down." I rolled to my stomach, my wounds gaping and my mind numb. Azrael gripped his throne and his terror lodged itself in my throat; scalding as it spilled out of me.

"We're running out of time, Thomas! End this!" In one motion, Thomas flung the spear at my head and vanished. I tried to move, but all I could do was watch my reflection in the crimson mirror rippling with *slow* falling droplets...

*I'm here, Devi...*

I picked myself up, and the look in the eyes of the royals fueled me. One gate separated me from Vincent. One half-dead army. One mockery of a royal church filled with immortals that have not laid a hand on me because I can *end* them…

My blood crawled its way back inside my veins from the tiles. I unsheathed my daggers and turned on my heel, and made my way to the gate. Soldiers tried to stop me but upon their touch on my skin, the poison within amplified and they tore themselves apart.

When I took a breath to teleport myself to Vincent, I stopped dead in my tracks. My daggers slid from my hands, tumbling to the marble; the cling and clatter echoing too brightly in my eyes. And when I collapsed, Thomas tugged at Vincent's core, pulling our tether—our *souls*, carving it out of our chests. It was never a tether that connected Vincent and me. Our souls collided lifetimes ago and intertwined. No beginning. No end.

Until now…

The aftermath left me lifeless. An endless, gaping grave hollowed and cold… Cold enough to *burn*. Thomas Reaped Vincent, rendering him *human*. He broke his neck and stabbed him in the heart—Vincent's blood dripped from my lips for the last time…

I was the death of him.

What happens to one, happens to *both*. Where life goes, death *will* follow. How am I still breathing?

Thomas strolled inside, wiping his sword clean of the remains of the love of my life.

"There now. That wasn't so bad, was it?" My mind was full of Vincent's memories; his life flashed before *my* eyes. Every tear carrying with it pieces of him streaming down my cheeks. His last touch. "Would you like me to finish her, too, Azrael?"

Vincent's murder echoed in my bones. It quaked inside of me and the cracks split the supposed unbreakable structure of the palace. Thomas turned around halfway down the altar when I stood. Thomas met my gaze and had my wrists in his grip at the same moment. He pulled me tight to his chest, our armor clamoring, and his oozing wound healed instantly.

"Where is he? Where did you send his soul?"

"Vincent is no longer of any consequence to you."

"What are you waiting for?! End her!" Azrael's command singed off Thomas's face down to his skull. Pieces of muscle falling to his feet with a splash. Thomas did not flinch. Archers took their positions from the balconies and surrounded us.

"Shoot her!" Pandora's commands sent the dead residents of Purgatory and beyond *wailing*. The onyx windows splintering from the force, creeping, rising from the ground and into the lungs of everyone.

Everyone but me.

"You are outnumbered and outmatched. There is no escaping what I'm going to do to you." Thomas tied his threat around my neck. I looked over to the royals, to the stunned and desperate faces of the lambs in the pews.

"My soul is a thousand burning cathedrals. No *gods* will dare touch me." I bore my eyes into Thomas. "But, please, tell me again how *I* should fear *you*." I set myself on fire, the flames licking at Thomas, setting me free and crumbling my would-be executioner to his knees. "You want a war?!" I stormed to the thrones, Thomas spitting up bile, seeing stars. Vincent had seen me… I was the last memory emblazoned behind his eyes before I was the death of him. I willed my daggers to me and lit them up. "I'll give you a goddamn *reckoning*!" the royals drew their weapons, and every immortal descended upon me but down went the tips of my blades into the altar and *none* were spared. The blast shattered glass, wayward dead, joining the slaughter. The force of my magick cut through them; casting the battered bodies away from me. The astral selves of the living falling out of their temples of flesh before being flung back inside with a satisfying *snap*.

Azrael and Pandora and their Paladins held on to one another, struggling to recover. But when the cobalt light of my eyes reflected in the screaming black of theirs, when my markings filled the cathedral with the metallic glow, their hearts stopped.

The gods watched. I smiled, my tears steaming off my skin as they spilled.

I willed my blades back and kissed the hilts together, morphing them into a double-edged sword. I blinked Thomas to my feet and froze him in time.

"The things I'll do to you..." I leaned into him, wrath quivering in every inch of me. "You'll *beg* me to be the death of you." The crackle of my blades sizzled as they plunged into his heart.

But Thomas broke free of my spell and tripped me to the ground, rolling on top of me. Time crept to a screeching halt. The palace fractured, the immortals suspended and helpless. Thomas's power collided with mine, tearing every atom in the cathedral apart. But when our blinding violence *broke* the world, Thomas *begged*, "Enough!"

# Chapter 27

## Agent Asshole

"Holy shit!" The car shrieked to a stop, nearly crashing into a parked car. Joshua gawked at me from the rearview, panic rich in his eyes. "Devi?" He unbuckled his belt and whipped around, holding back every urge to jump in the back seat to me. I thought I answered him. I thought I reached out to him—but all I did was tremble. "Hey, it's alright. You're alright," Josh said. He parked the car and opened the back to me. "You're covered in blood..." he wanted to fall to his knees. He wanted to murder whoever did this to me with his bare hands... Joshua knelt at the edge of the backseat and tried to speak through the adrenaline pumping through our veins. "I'm going to take you to the hospital, Devi."

"No," I mumbled. Why did I say that?

"Devi, someone beat you within an inch of your life. I—I have to—"

"I don't need a hospital..." the understanding that washed over his face. It killed him a little inside—maybe more than when he thought he couldn't touch me to preserve evidence. He looked over his shoulder and back at my tattered Halloween costume. Joshua took off his coat and draped it over me and got back in the car and drove in silence until we arrived at his condo.

How did I get here? Why am I in my Halloween costume? What year is it? I gripped the coat tighter to glean information. It was still Halloween night. But there was no time travel involved.

"Josh?"

"What is it, Devi?" Josh's heart skipped a beat with my voice.

"How long have I been missing?" He examined me in the rearview for a moment before he answered me. When he saw the bruises from the skull and face fractures already fading... His eyes flicked to the clock, then back into my swollen eye that wasn't so swollen anymore.

"Four hours." I almost sat up. My mouth dropped.

"Hours?" That can't be right. I've been gone for months. Vincent must have had some sort of failsafe in place. If he were to—if both of us didn't make it out of The Court, I'd be Ported to a Rev that also happens to be law enforcement. A Rev that happened to be the one person who—

"We're here." We took the back entrance to his condo. The elevator was oddly devoid of music. I sat on the large sleeper sofa and Josh stood at the entrance, hoping his locks, salt, wards, and reinforced steel doors would be enough to keep me safe.

I didn't have the heart to tell him the truth...

He sat across from me on his vintage coffee table; hands wringing, mind racing. The scent of him overwhelmed me. I took off his coat and folded it neatly on the couch beside me. When my eyes met his, "I know I'm asking a lot. I *know*—" I haphazardly motioned to my bruised body and magickally disappeared blood and ash, "this is a lot to take in, Rev or no Rev. But, *please* don't go searching for answers. I'm alive and healing. *Everything* will be ok, Josh." It was far too evident that those words were more for me than for the FBI agent cradling me in his arms, desperate to keep my shaking under control, to keep me from falling apart…

I knew I was alive before I opened my eyes; Josh's mattress smooth against my back. My heartbeat, blood pumping, electricity sparking in each cell… Vincent gave his soul for mine. Yet, all I wanted—with every fiber of my damned being—was to throw my life away.

"Devi?" Josh…

"Hi." He brought me to his bed after I cried myself to sleep in his arms… He barely slept on a pilot on the floor, protecting me.

"Hi." He walked over and leaned against the closet across from me. "Would you like some breakfast?" I nodded and he gave me some of his college sweats. "Josh… don't, um—don't take my clothes in for evidence." His face lost a shade.

"Devi—you were kidnapped. Whether it was a Rev that did it or not, I *can't* ignore that. I'm *FBI*."

"That's *exactly* why you need to. Please ignore it. Please." I clung to the foreign clothes and clutched his wrist. Our eyes pleading, each hoping the other would lose the fight.

"Your sister called me, Devi. I got there as fast as I did because I was *already* in the neighborhood. What are the odds of that?" There were no odds. "But I didn't get to you in time. I saw—"

"What did you see?" I took my hand back. He scratched his beard.

"I saw you get dragged away—*bloody*—by some psycho bitch and disappear. There were people in *trances* in the middle of the streets for fucking *miles*." He took a step to me, his gun cool against the small of his back. "You have to let me in. I can't help you if you don't."

"You think that maybe, *just* maybe, you'd be better

off *not* helping me? That perhaps I don't ask for help because I *can't be* helped?" His anger was immediate, and it poured into me like honey.

"If I couldn't help you, our paths never would've crossed. There's a reason we met."

"Trust me Agent, it's in your best interest if you stay out of my life." I got up to go change, but he came rushing to me, grabbing my arm. I threw my hand on his wrist but stopped myself before I shattered it.

"If I could stay away from you, I would. *Believe* me. But I can't." He let go of me, breathless, but held me in his gaze.

"And why is that, Josh? You men and your *duties* and *assignments*. Is that what I am?" His face fell. There was only *one* reason he couldn't stay away from me.

"What are you talking about?"

"I am *so sick* of being someones charge. An obligation." I caught my refuge in the bedroom window; my eyes spotting that familiar vampire but, somehow, he wouldn't allow me to channel any information from him. All I knew was that I knew him...

"Devi, please. Tell me what happened to you." One of these days, I am going to deck him. I threw his sweats on the bed and leaned on the windowsill and crossed my arms. If I didn't...

"Where did she take you?" I looked him dead in the eyes.

"Hell." For a split second, he considered it as truth.

"Stop with the bullshit for *two* minutes."

"I don't know where I was. I only remember waking up in your car. How are you planning on explaining that in your report?"

"Stop lying to me."

"I'm not lying to you..." I grabbed the clothes and rushed by him to the bathroom to change. When I came back, he was staring out the window. The blood-drinker was long gone. "Didn't you promise me food?" He moved too fast and was in my face. Too fucking close for comfort. If Vincent were still... "Move *back*, Agent."

"Whatever death wish you have, it *ends* here."

"Who said I have a death wish?"

"Something's different in you. I saw it in your eyes last night. You're—" he looked me up and down, "you're out for *retribution*, Devi." Perceptive as ever.

"I am *not* going to ask you again, Joshua. Move *back*." He did it *slowly*. I left the bedroom and almost chuckled when I heard his awestruck 'what the fuck?' when he went looking for my Halloween costume in the hamper and found nothing but ash and embers...

"Can you take care of yourself, Devi?"

"Shut up, Joshua." I grabbed a glass of water. I didn't know how badly I needed. The realization hit too fucking hard; the only liquid I've had down my throat the last few months was *blood*...

"Can you protect yourself from *this*?" He'd drawn his gun at the back of my head.

"You're making this too easy for me." I faced him. "Go ahead. I'm game." Disgust rather than shock settled into the bones of his face.

"I'm not going to kill you Devi."

"You're not trying to prove a point, are you?"

"One day, you'll run out of all that sarcasm. You're aware of that, right?"

"If you're not going to shoot me, Agent, I suggest you put that gun back in your pants." It was in that moment that Joshua finally realized something. And the gravity of it lodged itself deep in his lungs.

"You *want* me to pull the trigger." His poor heart skipped a beat. "Why?' The fact that I wasn't scared terrified him. It terrified *me*...

"Why not?" He fixed his grip on the weapon and moved closer to me. "I don't have time for this." I waved my hand in dismissal and made my way back to the bedroom.

"Devi." He whispered my name, but he wanted to *scream* it. Josh grabbed me by the arm and pulled me into him. I pushed him away and punched him in the fucking jaw. I *almost* used more force.

I almost *killed* him...

"I told you to stay away..." He stood dumbfounded against the wall. His lips split open and bleeding down his neck. Remorse was scarce if existent at all in me.

"You wanna know what I think?" he spit red on the floor.

"No, not really, Josh." Stop being such a bitch, Devi...

"You push people away when you need them the most. But your reverse psychology won't work on *me*, Devi." He steadied himself and started to close the gap between us. Any closer...

"What would you have me do, Josh? Let everyone follow me around and get them caught in my crossfire?"

"Let us make our own decisions. We'll deal with the consequences."

"You're *insane* if you think I'm going to let—"

"That's it right there. Who are *you* to *let* us do anything? Who are you to make decisions for others? I've made my choice and there's nothing you can do or say to change it."

"Josh—"

"No, Devi." Before the guilt of assaulting him birthed itself, or that what he said started to make any sense, I walked away and slammed his bedroom door shut in his face. I crawled into his bed and under his covers. Everything that touched me now was *his*. Maybe one day I'll wake up and not remember any of this.

The thing about survival—to stay alive, you kill the parts of you that make you—*you*. What remains is a terror in your veins destined to splatter on to anyone who dares get too close... And I was always getting too close.

"Devi?" I have to find Thomas and absorb as much of his Reaping magick as possible. Maybe it'll jumpstart my own.

I'll force him tell me where Vincent's soul is—I can't—I can't bring him back, but I can send his soul to a heaven that's worthy of him. Then I make Thomas kill me. But what if I can't track him? What if the others come after me? Training. I need more training with my Paladins. That's it. Then I'll go after Thomas. I'll go after everyone.

Alone.

"Devi."

"Huh? Yeah, Josh?"

"Could you stop that?"

"What?"

"You've been tapping your spoon—it's driving me a little psycho." I hadn't even—Josh's condo. I'm in Josh's apartment with Josh. You're sitting in a chair at a table with food in his kitchen.

"Sorry." It's daytime. Day light is coming from the windows. The Sun…

"Can we be civil? I don't want to fight with you every time we're in the same room."

"Then maybe we shouldn't be in the same—"

"Devi."

"Ok. If you don't want to spar, then I suggest we don't speak."

"Right." He laughed unamused, shoved his plate across the table and darted out of the room. I got up to wash the dishes when Joshua came storming back in. "Tell me what's going on."

"Um, we went over that already, didn't we?" I didn't see it soon enough. He carefully took my arm and turned me into him, his eyes angrier than I'd ever seen them. "What the hell? Let go of me."

"I *refuse* to believe that you're insane because if I do that, then *I'm* the crazy person. I'm not clueless. You hardly talk and when you do, it's about bullshit. You're walking around like a hollow shell. The woman I met last year—the one who survived God knows what—I don't think you ever came back alive." He wanted to cry. He wanted to hold me. I *wanted* him to hold me because truth is, if you kiddos have been keeping up, I *did* die. And the person I've had to become— "Running away or taking a vow of silence isn't going to help anything. Something happened on Halloween. Please, tell me."

"I'm not telling you *anything*. Now let. Me. Go."

"What happened to you?" The fire inside of him twisted.

"Nothing happened. One minute I'm with my friends at a bar getting ready to see who won the best costume and the next I was in the back of your car. Get off me now, *please*." Before I knew it, before I even *felt* it, the tears spilled from my eyes. "Just let me go! I can't stay here anymore!" I have to save everyone, I—I need a bullet in my head...

"Devi, stop it!" Too tired of struggling, I let him hold me. "Tell me what to do."

"Stay away from me." He lifted my chin, and that was it. This man was going to bring my life to ruins. I got out of his hold effortlessly and walked away, but in Joshua-fashion, he followed me.

There was a knock on the door at the same time Josh's cell phone rang. He was not pleased to answer it. "Yeah—Who's coming for her? *Shit*." He pounded his way to the door, and I stood frozen in the hallway, barely keeping my stance as I held myself against the wall. It can't be. Could it? Joshua unbolted every lock and turned the handle and I didn't want to believe who I saw on the other side.

"I hope we're not interrupting." I'm dreaming.

"What are you doing here?"

"Rough around the edges, this one." He looked right at me, but it couldn't be him. "Agent McAlister, Ms. DiCaprio is *our* responsibility now." Is that Mel?

"I apologize for Mr. Smith's demeanor. We recently came off from a ten-hour flight. May we come in?"

"And you would be?" Amah grinned and revealed her badge.

"How rude of us. I thought your supervisor would have debriefed you by now. I'm Special Agent Saoirse Brennon and this is my partner Special Agent Morris Smith."

"Is there a reason the CIA wants *this* case?" Josh turned to me, genuine panic in his heart. "I never told anyone I found you last night, Devi. I swear it."

"I—I know, Josh. I know…"

"Agent, you'll know of everything if your superiors deem it so. For now, we are here for that young lady there and it would be in your best interest to move back, and perhaps get that jaw looked at."

After a long, agonizing moment, Joshua moved aside and allowed Mel to walk in. My heart nearly imploded when he took my hand. Mel walked us over to the front door and Special Agent Brennon threw her coat over me. Their memories—something happened the night Miarrah took me to The Court, and the Paladins weren't going to let me pry into their minds—or emotions, to find out what happened after I was taken.

After Vincent's head rolled across the pavement…

"Wait. Hold on a sec. Where are you taking her? Devi?" Melot hurried me down the stairs, but I couldn't help but look back to Joshua. *I* knew I'd see him again, but *he* didn't. To him, this was the end and the way his heart broke in my chest… "Devi..."

I shook away the part of me that wanted to run away from my Paladins and back to Joshua and I replaced it with something else; Something that would be damn near impossible to accomplish.

Stay alive long enough to die.

# Chapter 28

## Wonderland

The silence quivered in my veins, rattling the windows in the black SUV. Why didn't they teleport? Gavin's grip tightened around my shoulders but I was numb to his touch. Nothing he did could alter the past. Nothing Amah and Melot said in that all too familiar panic would erase the truth from the world.

I was the reason for Vincent's murder, and we were no closer to ending this war.

Vincent's death was for naught and it raged in the marrow of my bones with a vengeance I welcomed.

"The agent saw her heal. He knows—"

"He knows enough to continue to be an ally, Gavin. Frankly—"

"She should've told him everything."

"Why are we driving?" I registered the Revs. Some on rooftops, others in cars that followed blatantly behind us. All of them curious. Only a select few with prophecy on their tongues, ready to strike me dead.

"Information gathering." They're driving through the streets on purpose to channel the Revs.

"If the Reveries come for me, they'll start a second war," I said weakly.

"A civil war, yes. Between the Revs that see you as a threat and those that do not." Melot's words made my skin crawl.

"How many wars am I to start? What I am, I can't be allowed to live. Please, *end* this. The Rev war will clash with the LeMehti war and God knows what else. Please!"

Amah glared at me from the rearview, her eyes glowing. "Devi, I'll hear no more of your rubbish logic."

"Amah, you know I'm right. *All* of you know it."

"Vincent did not give his life for yours so that *we* can snuff it from existence, do you hear me, child?" Mel whipped around to face me from the passenger seat, fuming. We glared at one another, but looking into his eyes, the pain creeping beneath his grim glare....

"I—I'm so sorry I couldn't save him. I'm so sorry..." flashes of the battle, of Vincent's death—they played across my skin in real time. The convulsions were a reasonable result. I knew how to shut it off; put the past in a box and process it later. But why would I? Why would I grant clemency for myself when none was spared for the man who sacrificed himself for me?

"What's happening? Why won't she stop? Why hasn't it *stopped?*"

"I think she won't *let* it stop, Gavin." Amah pressed her foot on the pedal and the car jolted with speed.

Gavin clutched me hard against his chest, cradling me in his lap like a baby. I caught a glance of it in the window, my wretched proof of life reminding me—more so than my pounding heart—that I was alive. I closed my eyes and tried, with all that I had, *not* to break my neck...

The armored Paladins stood motionless in a broken circle in a field in the twilight of Evenfall, putting statues to shame. Rain slid down their skin, reflecting what could be starlight off their armor. Their voices, however, trembled.

"You cannot mean to go alone. This isn't a voyage of days. This is one of—"

"Years. I know, Melot. And I'll not allow any of you to follow me into it. She'll need you when I get her out. I can't guarantee your lives if you come with me."

"And what of *your* life, Vincent? You may be powerful, but to throw yourself into the belly of the beast—how can you know that—" Amah held back her tears, but the thunder rolling in the hills knew it was only a matter of time.

"That I won't lose myself to the poison and kill Devi with my own hands?" No one dared speak as Vincent let spill the truest fear housed within every Paladin heart. Vincent held onto his breastplate a little tighter. "I will get her out. No matter the cost."

"How—how long do you think you'll be able to survive?" Amah said, stepping into the eye of the circle.

"For as long as it takes." Tremors coursed through the cool air. "We're left with little choice. Time moves differently there. She's been gone from Earth not twenty *minutes* and there—she's already been *there*—"

"Twenty days..." Gavin's voice overpowered everything in the field. "And that's *if* they've kept her in Cortem for the duration of her imprisonment. If they move her *between* Realms—" the soldiers needed a moment. They adjusted their stances and armor and mumbled curses at the rain under their breaths.

Andra's tall form stepped into the circle. "Your decision to transform her into LeMehti was as wise as it was merciful—"

"Tactical."

"Vincent. Don't speak that way."

"I speak the truth, Andra. Changing her into one of us knowing the future that awaited her—it had nothing to do with clemency and everything to do with strategy."

"She caught on to this bit of truth rather quickly. Why do you allow it to haunt you?" Vincent's eyes narrowed at Melot's words. It was as if Melot asked the dumbest question in the whole of existence. Mel swallowed and ran his hand through his soaked hair; flicking his eyes to his wife standing beside him.

Amah clutched the hilts of her swords at her baldric. "Devi is resilient. Her immortality will be her saving grace until you reach her. You *will* reach her, won't you, Vincent?" Vincent looked beyond the elite soldiers with questions dripping from their tongues when there should be enemy blood. The Bridge that would lead him to me sat between a group of weeping willows; the brook beneath babbling with waters devoid of life but full of bones of creatures whose footprints could be seen for miles. Their flesh, however, was nowhere to be found.

"I'll get her out of there, and if the cost of her freedom is my soul," Vincent walked into the circle, his blue eyes the brightest light in the entire field, "then so be it."

"Vincent, there's no telling which version of reality will play out," Melot braved. "Not there, and *especially* not when it comes to the two of you. Maybe there's more than one way to save her?"

"Of course, there are more ways." Vincent's curt words punched a sigh out of Melot. "But none end with us—or the world—*alive*."

"This is *madness*, Vincent." Gavin kicked a wayward pebble while Amah and Andra took comfort together in their whispers. More than anything, my Paladins wanted to rescue me from the clutches of their former home... But if they take one step into the belly of the beast, they'll be lost to the soul-eating poison I birthed into their kind. The visions they've had of me dying, being tortured at their own hands—what it must have done to them. When they trained me, when they shielded me as I slept...

How it must terrorize their minds to know how close

they were—and could be—to murdering the person they swore their lives to protect.

"I'm thankful for madness." He didn't have to say it, he didn't even have to *think* it, but I knew, in this fever dream laced with the preamble of a horror I'd know far too late... Vincent was thankful for the madness because it fueled the chaos in his blood.

Lightning struck and wings of birds I'd never heard before flapped for miles.

"Vince, what if—couldn't we try 1997 one more time?" Andra broke the stillness. Her eyes darted around the eyes in the circle. Silence blanketed everyone and Amah—remembering a memory not familiar with reminiscence—let the salt of her tears slide down her pink cheeks.

"Once I go in, you'll have four hours to complete everything."

"Vincent—"

"Andra, enough." Their leader took in a much needed resetting breath. They all did. "You'll have four hours to set up the warehouse, the safe houses, gather the priest—"

"Please, brother, don't do this." To see the second in command, Vincent's Lieutenant General of the Paladins heart break...

"I'm doing what needs to be done. As will all of you. Am I understood?" everyone gave a singular, nearly defiant, nod. "Train Devi for—*everything*." No one knew. The Paladins—they didn't know if Vincent would make it back out alive after he saved me from The Court. No one knew which version of reality was the correct one. No one but Vincent.

Vincent made a solemn attempt to smile at his army, then made his way to the Bridge that would lead him to his end. "If," he turned around, the rain slowing to a pitter, "if I come back..." why did he choose *this* moment to speak telepathically to them? "You know what must be done. You have your orders if I'm not able to do what is necessary." The rain settled, and no one spoke after hearing Vincent force the all too frightening words out. He crossed the Bridge and looked over his shoulder and when he found my eyes—when his tears blurred my sight—when the paralyzing dawn that Vincent saw the future of me witnessing this vision of the past... I reached for a ghost walking to his grave. The grave *I* dug for him and all he said to me was,

*Death be damned*

I gasped for breath, nearly clawing at the faded red brick wall. It took a long minute to orient myself in the foreign space. I threw the colorful quilt off me and swung my bare legs to the side of the bed. I sat there, legs swinging, eyes adjusting, the bedroom harboring a warmth whose origin I couldn't pinpoint yet.

It was day, as evidenced from the window flanking the bed and the other in the sunken living area. Day? Was it tomorrow? I stood up to investigate when the room spun and I lost my footing, and fell back on the bed.

The *room*.... his scent filled this room. The warmth—it's from his skin on mine. Vincent is dead. That's not possible. I opened my eyes and touched my fingers to my temples, and pushed. A moment later, the crystals in my ears were back in place and the quarters were still a merry-go-round—upside down. "So, it's not physiological." I swallowed back some vomit and put my fingers back to my temples. "Let's find the supernatural reason for this vertigo." All signs pointed to—*me*? I opened my eyes and looked down. It wasn't the sight of the sweater that prompted the shift in my breath, but the texture of the fabric; it enveloped me, embraced me when he could not and I sat there, in Vincent's old bedroom from three hundred years ago and wept...

I used to think that a ghost was a memory. The sort that doesn't dare cross your mind until the smell of a long forgotten perfume hits. When you hear a melody that transports you back to that one precious moment in time. It's a memory

you know, deep in your bones, that existed but you cannot, for the life of you, remember *any* of it...

But it's there. In the corners of your soul, in the recesses of your eyes, waiting patiently for the next sighting. Waiting, hoping, that the next time you witness it, it will be remembered.

Every time I look in the mirror, I see it. That memory. The one that made me who I am. It's in my irises. The curves of my lips. Bumpy bridge of my nose. It's in the grooves of my teeth, the scars on my flesh. This *memory*...

A clock bled dry of time.

But can a ghost haunt you if you're *both* dead? We all know the answer.

I am the ghost in the mirror. I'm the memory I'll never be rid of. It's fuel, you see? Horror is akin to hydrogen and, my God, the wonders they conjure.

Whether bomb or beast, I think we can all agree that God has no say in any of this. What do *I* say?

I should have died when Vincent did.

I forced myself out of bed and stopped at the top of the small stairs overlooking the cozy space. The massive iron railings on the concrete floor unintentionally had become the centerpiece of the barren space. Aside from Vincent's writing desk flanking the window and couch below, there was little display of life here. If I touched the banister, I'd know—in far more detail than I'm allowing my simple presence in the room to do—when Vincent lived here last.

I raised my hand to the railing when the door opened. I stood, frozen, frantically thinking about how I would fight who entered. The realization that I could kill this man with a passing thought.... The door let in a tall, bearded man with a tray of food. I fought every urge to take him by the throat and break him to pieces, even *after* his past played in my mind.

"Oh, hey there." The priest had a kind smile, but I couldn't return the sentiment. He had earthy eyes and skin that rivaled polished Jasper.

"Hi..." I wondered, for a moment, if it was possible that I

had dreamt the entire ordeal. But as his lips parted to speak, I felt the Paladins on the other side of the wall. The priest placed the tray on the handmade coffee table and took position at the bottom of the staircase. His eyes intent on mine.

"Everyone is in the hall just outside. My name is Creed." He smiled harmlessly at me and turned away, slightly blushing. I looked down. I had no pants on.

"Wait." He stopped short of the door. "You're a priest and your name's Creed?" *This is what we're focusing on, Devi?* I grabbed the banister to follow him.

"My parents did not have the gift of foresight. Devi?" Vincent stared out the window, the ink of a freshly written letter drying on the desk beside him. The way he cleaved to himself sent my stomach twisting. The candles burned, giving light to the otherwise gray night as the wind blew vengefully against the glass. Vincent's face—he couldn't bear to look at his reflection in the window. Or was it a haunting of a different sort that sent his soul splitting into a million pieces inside me? He clenched his jaw and fell forward, cracking the window frame beneath his hands. He let his head drop to the glass and I could hear, barely, his racing, breaking heart. There was a face in his mind, in the reflection. It was all his hope and every last bit of his agony.

*My* face..

"Are you going?" Mel's voice was calm but cautious. He took one slow step through the door and Vincent looked up, his reflection pale against the glass.

"Yes." It was a whisper, but it echoed violently inside all three of us.

"And you are *certain,* Vincent? Certain that she won't know?"

Vincent hesitated, but his eyes never wavered. "I'll not allow it." His grip failed slightly from the frame and Mel took in a long-awaited breath. He closed his eyes and then opened them to speak.

"We will follow you, no matter the cost." This, this was *before* everything. Before the poison. *Before* Vincent and I met.

Mel vanished and Vincent backed away from the window, his fists curling and uncurling. I thought I saw him turn to me, to see me as I saw him, but the bright light of the sun greeted me instead.

"Devi? Can you hear me? Are you alright?" Creed came up the stairs and reached his hand to mine. I found my senses before he marked himself for death.

"I'm alright."

"You look as though you've seen Death. I'm going to fetch the others."

"If the others thought I was in need, they'd have been here ages ago. I'm ok, Father. I'll meet you all outside." My smile wasn't the purest, but it was enough to make him leave, albeit begrudgingly.

I rushed to the window, put my hands on the still broken frames, and looked outside.

There was grass and trees and nothing else. His presence was still there. Pieces of his aura, of him he didn't burn away because he *knew*—he saw *this* moment...

I tore myself away from the past as she arrived. The smell of the eggs and pancakes stung something awful. I had to force myself to eat around Joshua. Here, I could starve myself all I wanted. Starve until I died.

Then, repeat...

"Hello, friend." Andra stood in the doorway, arms crossed, ginger smile, and dressed in jeans and green button-down. Her outfit was nearly as out of place as her assessment of me.

"Hi." My sheepish greeting was pitiful. I turned, forcing myself to look at her. Allowing her to see the person responsible for her leader's demise.

"Will you not eat, Devi?" we both glanced at the steaming tray. All I saw was Vincent setting his tea on the coffee table as he read *Dracula*.

"I—I don't have much of an appetite." Andra surveyed the room, her hands rubbing her arms.

"Come with me Devi."

I followed her out of the small space and into a gargantuan hall. The raw, black quartz walls and obsidian and marble floors emitted energy that buzzed through the air. The safe house was a close sister in construction to the Cortem cathedral palace except the arched gothic windows permitted daylight to pour within; giving life to prisms on every surface. And when it hit the water in the pool… "Devi, you need pants."

"What? Right. Of course." Andra snapped her fingers and dressed me in a sports bra and yoga pants. "This isn't quite what I had in mind."

"We're a day behind schedule," Melot said, blinking into existence.

"Sorry." I had slept twenty hours straight through. Gavin and Amah materialized behind Melot, armed to the brim. That was the extent of the introductions after months of separation. There was nothing but beating, battering, and bending reality for days. I had to learn *everything*…

"You're coming into your own, Devi. A force of nature." I drank some water and gave Creed a crescent-moon smile. It was challenging with him around the first month. But, the priest, he grows on you. Like a rash...

"And what would that be, exactly?" After the third month, all Creed wanted to do was get me to confide in him. To be my friend.

"A warrior." He continued to clean his gun—right. I should explain. Creed isn't a *traditional* man of the cloth. "You hunger for retribution and it seeps into your every strike."

"That so?" I wiped the 3-day sparring sweat from my brow and gulped water.

"Devi, this place is a haven not only for its stealth and warding but—"

"But because I can let my guard down?" I redid my ballerina bun. "Listen Pops, can I call you Pops? I don't need a sounding board. I appreciate it, of course, but what I *need* is to learn how to kill *better* than those trying to kill me." The man didn't flinch.

"I understand, I do. But—"

"Who are you, Creed? What exactly do you *do* here, other than preach? I mean, not that many Clerics packing heat, you know?" He looked at his revolver and chuckled under his breath. The short twists of his hair had grown since we first met and they framed the duplicity in his eyes.

"No, I suppose not." He set down the weapon gingerly and rolled up the sleeves to his button-down, and settled into his stool. "But you, Devi, you already know what *I* do."

I pointed to my head and smirked. "Empaths have a nasty habit of knowing things they shouldn't."

"Why did you phrase it like that?" I rolled my eyes, but Creed was more interested in my words than my attitude.

"How else am I to phrase it, Creed?" We were quiet. Both our points stewing in our bellies.

"You asked me what I do here yet, as an Empath, inquiries are redundant. Why ask questions to which you already know the answers?" I focused on the prism of light coming in through the windows. The waves and particles crashing into the atoms of air and—other things...

If I concentrated hard enough, I could see back to when the dead stars the lights traveled from were still alive...

"Curiosity. Besides, asking questions seems a normal enough thing to do. And, around here, normal is few and far between."

His eyebrows furrowed, asking me something odd. "Aren't you LeMehti like the others? Aren't you immortal? Isn't this—all of this is—"

"*Not* my way of life. I›m not like them, Creed. Not entirely. I'm a Mimic, which helps—or is *supposed* to help..." I wasn't progressing as fast as I was meant to. "I›m only half LeMehti. Hence the never-ending training."

"The way you move, your power..."

"Creepy, isn't it?" Creed was one hundred percent human. But he knew secrets that the Vatican would kill for... Creed knew secrets *he's* killed for. "I'm—I know I'm wrong. But don't worry." I took another drink of water. It was cold but it never managed to douse what burned inside my chest. "I won't hurt you. You're safe here. The others, they'd never let anything happen to you and I've learned to keep my distance." I left the middle-aged priest with a false smile on my lips but honesty in my words. He sat there less frightened of me and more afraid *for* me.

I made my way to Vincent's room, which, by some cruel wave of events, became *my* room. But Creed called out after me.

"I'll spare you the sentiments of how false you are in your self-evaluation and will only say this: If ever the time comes and you could do with a hot cup of tea and a judgment-free ear, you know where to find me." The priest tipped his head to me and went up the spiral staircase to his quarters. My bedroom was the only one on the main floor. Everyone else lived upstairs.

I stood in the massive hall for a moment. Ripples in the pool singing a song of calm that I could never acclimate to. The stone rafters above curved and warped to keep the steepled structure of the building stable. At first glance, one could mistake the safe house for a cathedral. But what is a church if not a sanctuary? These LeMehti temples—their ruins could be found in mountain-sides and in the depths of woods not touched by humans in centuries. Most are shrouded, like this one, in plain sight. It may appear that we are in a house of God, but nothing holy breathes here. And if it did, I'd choke the faith out of it...

After a much needed shower, I tried dressing myself by way of LeMehti magick. Surely I had soaked up their ability to conjure fabric from thin air by now. Their magick, you don't have to *give* something when you take. This exchange—it's as if what you do once you've taken your lot from the universe matters more than giving something of equal or greater value in return. Honor is the balancer, not matter.

For most things, at least…

I managed jeans, underthings, and a t-shirt. I haven't been in the company of anyone other than my guardians and Creed for months so, at 2 in the afternoon on a lovely Saturday afternoon, I probably should've opted for pajamas.

It startled me when I walked out of my bathroom. Mel was in my room, gazing at my fractured window. He resonated calm. As though he'd made peace with whatever happened that night with Vincent.

"We're going to Port again. You need to clear 100 miles without duress as your motivation." I didn't say anything. I made a beeline to the stairs to escape to my bed when he teleported beside me and held his hand out, blocking my path. When he spoke, the words were intended for *my* ears only. "We regret nothing." My stomach sunk. "*He* regretted nothing." Melot smiled softly when I looked up at him, speechless. Before he left, I protested.

"Mel, blinking, I mean, Porting-teleporting... Whatever. I tend to—well, I tend to slam into walls, land in trees. *Literally* inside a tree. That doesn't include the time I got stuck inside the haven's gates or the pillars. I mean, last week I landed on top of a rooftop of some factory and yesterday I was a *mile* deep in Lake Superior." Mel crossed his arms and swallowed, stifling a laugh I couldn't help but set free. "Yes, it is pretty fucking hilarious—except for when I'm trapped inside a concrete wall or—" he couldn't contain himself any longer. "Mel! I'm claustrophobic. Have *some* compassion, man."

"Apologies."

"Why am I still *this* klutzy?"

"Are we talking about your teleportation skills or are we including hand-eye coordination?"

"There was only *one* time with the sword and the arrows." He looked at me. "Ok, that was *two* times—" he raised an eyebrow. "Ok, so I've had a little trouble catching and shooting. You know what? Bite me." I put my dirty clothes in the hamper. "But shouldn't my metamorphosis into all powerful Le-Mehti immortal have, like, fixed me?" I didn't have trouble doing these things with Vincent...

"And take away the comical highlight of our days? I would certainly hope not." He messed with my wet hair and met with the others outside. At the very least, I make them laugh. After what I took from them, after what I did to their lives... they deserve to smile.

"Devi, wake up!" My eyes shot open, and I saw Andra. Her cool hands took the sting of fire away from my skin. "Are you alright?"

"Yeah." The sweat dripped down my cheeks. "I had a nightmare."

"What did you see?" Andra was overtly concerned. All the Paladins were since they deemed a little bad dream worthy of them descending into my room in the middle of the night.

"A witch in Italy. She was burning at the stake. I—I guess I burnt with her..."

"I am so sorry Devi." I shrugged at Andra's words.

"It is what it is."

"It's an occupational hazard. We'll help you manage it." Mel said with too serious a tone. I looked at him with a crooked face.

"I think you meant *existence* hazard." He chuckled weakly and we all just occupied the space with the stench of truth my words had expelled.

After practically force-feeding me breakfast, Gavin instructed me to find Amah and her unknown amount of doppelgängers. Though I knew the mechanics of Hunting, I had to learn to Hunt a doppelgänger *and* differentiate between the true Amah and the many illusions of her. When I glimpsed my eyes in the mirror after I took a piss—I didn't know whether to be impressed or afraid. They morphed from honeyed chocolate to completely transparent, with a subtle silver shimmer.

"A mist in moonlight. Freaky."

"Thanks, Gavin."

"No problem. Now go track down my wife." We laughed and the sound that came out of my mouth was almost akin to sincerity.

I had learned ancient Latin, Aramaic, and Hebrew for this spell in the event that I was too hurt to do so via thought. Slurring my words was a natural side effect because it was one motherfucker of a spell. But what it does to the world around you—I can Hunt *anything*. Living or *dead*. The Haven has a small abandoned chapel behind it, along with a graveyard. I don't get to see humans, but dead people can carry on pretty good conversations.

"What are you doing?!" Right. I was Hunting Amah. She grabbed me before I crossed the highway to meet her on the other side.

"Finding you, Amah. I already neutralized the doppelgängers—why are you so upset? Wasn't that the mission?"

"Di, why were you going to the *highway*?" I got out of her grasp and straightened myself out.

"Like I said, I was *Hunting* you and your twins. Per your husband's instructions." The hesitation in her bones... It was as if every word you've ever wanted to say drowned in your throat; filling your chest with a thousand sunken ships that *almost* made it to shore...

"Yes, but Devi, you *cannot* be that close to them." The lie. Lies were like broken pieces of metal on your tongue. When you open your mouth, you speak as though there *isn't* blood dripping down your lips. And you do it with a *smile* because lies taste as sweet as honey.

"To *who?*"

"Humans." Truth. "To the public, you went missing on Halloween night last year. If anyone recognizes you and reports it..." Truth was a knife dug so deep inside of you, it *had* to have always been a part of you. Half-truths are that blade being pulled out, leaving a gaping, aching, bleeding hole that doesn't know how *not* to beg for mercy... Amah took a pained breath as the others arrived. "You haven't perfected erasing your aura or controlling your—I am sorry, but you cannot be seen. By *anyone*."

Mercy. I don't know what mercy feels like...

"Devi?"

"Yeah, Amah. Be invisible. Copy that."

"What are you doing up so late, Devi?"

"Oh, hi." The priest sat down beside me on the back steps of the haven overlooking the graveyard. The LeMehti safe house had been here since before Illinois was colonized. Immortals were not to interfere with human affairs. The LeMehti were not to, at least. But what they did was bury the dead of the families and soldiers they could not protect from a time not found in history books. What it must be to know you have the power to help others but *ordered* not to by forces beyond your control. How different this world would be if they had stepped in...

But we all know by now what interfering with a human life can bring about, don't we?

And this is only the beginning...

"It's funny how the dead bring about peace," Creed said, looking at his pocket watch.

"Rather poetic—and macabre—for a priest." He chuckled.

"Do you not find calm here, Devi?"

"I can understand why *you* do." He looked at me confused. "You feel the peace death bestows. The quiet and the calm." I threw a pebble into the centuries-old graves. "I feel everything in between. All my senses are gripped by every soul in this graveyard. Their memories and *thousands* of possibilities of their futures. The insects burrowing in the earth and into the corpses. The chisels that etched the names into each tomb..." I had to take a breath.

"Does it take much to put aside?" he rubbed the back of his neck, his shirt stretching across his muscles.

"Put aside? You mean shut it off?"

"Yes. Shut off your Empathic power."

"No. Not entirely, at least. Right now it's only a humming and stinging. I forget they're there after a while. Unless they decide to make a visual appearance." Creed almost immediately looked into the field for evidence of any spirits floating in white sheets. The ones he'd dealt with—him and Josh will get along.

"I can only imagine what you must endure in live crowds."

"Probably why they picked this nice *isolated* location." I didn't tell him that I get a hit of people driving down the highway a few hundred miles out every so often. Or the animals...

What I'd give to feed a squirrel.

"If being here hurts you, why do you not leave?"

"What brings you here, Father?" he surveyed the night sky. The stars full of constellations and secrets.

"Fresh air, I suppose." He can't smell what I'm smelling. I stifled a laugh over my shoulder. "I was worried about you, Devi. You have not slept in weeks. If Mel and the others hadn't forced you to eat today—"Creed's mind drifted to the last time I starved myself to death... I didn't do it on purpose.

At least, I don't think I did.

"I know." We were quiet then. The sweet priest whose life would forever be intertwined in mine soaked up the sweet summer air and I made goofy faces with a seven-year-old boy who'd died in the 1600s because no one knew CPR.

"Goodnight then, darling." Creed touched the top of my hand and for a moment, I felt something foreign; human touch. With it, I had to force every muscle in my body—every *instinct*—from reaching over and breaking the bones attached to the hand that came in contact with me. And in that moment I realized—I *understood* with a heaviness I'd have to carry for eternity—my *purest* reaction to being touched is *violence*.

It's come to this...

There was something in the distance, beyond the protective confines of the consecrated ground. I walked closer to the illuminated woods at the edge of the graveyard when I stopped dead in my tracks after I heard a beat. A heartbeat. I wanted to race to it but the red flag in my mind kept my pace steady.

We were in the heart of a forest. Hidden within the safe confines of wood hundreds of miles away from the nearest road. The Haven itself is shrouded in a veil so thick and powerful, not even satellites can detect it. So that begs the question:

Who's here?

I jumped on to the stone wall surrounding the graveyard and the entire perimeter of the Haven. I perched on the wall's ledge like a bird and watched in horror.

Thomas and Vincent fought to the death. Their blades thundered together. When Vincent's heart faded, when his soul drained from my mine, I jumped.

I ran to him, but they vanished.

A twig snapped from the woods. I whipped around and before I ran toward the sound, I looked over my shoulder at the safe house. Then, I charged into the forest and into everything the Paladins had been protecting me from.

The snapped twigs would start and stop at different locations. Leaves would rustle and earth would be stepped into. I was a good two miles deep into the forest when I had enough of this hide and seek shit. Shutting my eyes, I focused. When I opened them, there was a silver shimmer across the trees and forest floor. I heard its hummingbird heartbeat pounding and saw a small shape a hundred yards out beneath shrubbery glowing in a coppery aura. I blinked myself there and pulled out my dagger when I nearly fell over from shock.

It was a rabbit.

A white fucking *rabbit.*

It ran off again and.... I followed.

I stopped dead in my tracks in a tiny clearing flooded in wildflowers and moss-covered stones when the rabbit did. When I took a few steps to the rabbit and the little guy didn't move, I knelt to him and put down one of my daggers to pet him. Maybe whoever is running this show touched the rabbit and left me a glimpse of themselves.

I grabbed a tuft of his fur and smoothed my fingers across his fluffy coat. Once in my hands, I had to be careful not to hurt the pudgy little thing. The rabbit fell asleep in my arms and I cracked a smile. His heart had calmed, and I turned him over to rub his belly, but it was wet. He was slit right through from his chin to his tail, drenched. The rabbit wasn't asleep. He was dead.

My eyes filled with water faster than I expected, and my little guy slipped through my trembling hands back to the ground with loud thuds. I grabbed my weapons in time to notice the four DeKenna demons charging at me.

It was a trap.

It was a dream...

*This is not a dream. Devi, run!* I turned to run when one of them bashed my face in to a tree trunk, breaking the trunk *and* my face in half. I kicked in his kneecaps and twisted his wrist and ran for my goddamned life.

I couldn't get away. Panic took over, and I teleported myself out of their hold before their blades slit my throat any deeper. The second my feet hit the ground, I started moving north to the safe house. I had to ignore all my wounds. My guardians would heal me once I get to them. Why aren't they here?

My fractured skull; a jagged piece of mandible piercing up through my cheek... I had to hold it in place to spit out my teeth.

When I got within earshot of the Haven, I sensed the others. They were fighting the other LeMehti on the other side of the state. No one stayed behind to protect me because *no one* thought I'd leave the grounds...

I dodged an arrow and caught another one, but a third struck me in the back, piercing through my stomach and out the other end. My only goal was to run and hide. Fighting four Knights would be madness, even for *me*.

There was a fourth arrow headed for my skull, but someone grabbed me before the arrow hit.

We made it to the wall in seconds and when the man lifted me over the edge, our touch wasn't the only inevitable thing...

He was in every inch of me in a never-ending wave. He struggled to free himself from me and got me on the opposite side of the wall. But he still held my hand. And when his grip weakened, when he purposely, desperately tried to let me go...

I locked eyes with him and the cobalt blue fire spread across my skin with warmth I thought long gone...

"Vincent..." I grabbed onto his arms and pulled myself up, trying to pull him over the wall to be with me. On the safe side of the Haven, where the poisoned LeMehti and DeKenna could not enter. But he wouldn't budge. Vincent pushed my hands away, prying my fingers from his wrists.

"What are you doing?!" I dangled from the side of the wall, trying to climb up to him, but he pushed me back every time I got close to him. Each time I pulled him to me, it was as if he met with another wall I couldn't see. A wall that separated him from me. "Vincent, please!" I choked on my tears and when I opened my eyes, Vincent was crying. His tears falling on my cheeks. And as he gripped my wrist, taking away my only hold of him, he pried me off of him and I fell away on to the consecrated ground below.

The arrow pushed out of my torso from the force of the fall to the ground. The fall also generated enough energy for a tiny little earthquake. I cracked the earth for a mile until I was able to take it into myself; the sounds of my bones breaking a sweet song compared to the terrified beating heart I heard in his chest...

That *was* him, wasn't it? I'm not dreaming.

"You're awake. This isn't a dream. Feel the grass in your hands. The stars in your eyes. This is *real*. *He* was real..."

How sweet it would be... to not know I was alive.... just for a small while....

How lovely it would be to stay silent in your echo. Not feel the *wretched* thing you've put inside of me. Just for a moment, for a small while.

"Devi?" You think these monsters scare me? Go ahead then... scare me to death.

"Why won't she respond? No, Gavin, don't touch her."

"But, Amah, she's—she's—" What are you waiting for? Come on, I'll dance to your music.

"We have to wait."

"Wait for what? Her to remain in this state forever? I'm pulling her out!"

"Gavin, no!"

"Mel, what are we to do? Devi won't *move*. She won't speak. She keeps staring at the sky." Oh, is that one crying for *me*? You're not fooling anyone, dear.

"Sit down. All of you." All of you. None of you. No one's here. He's not here... "Ready? Now!"

"Let me go! Stop it!"

"Andra, do it!"

"She's *laughing*. Devi, why are you laughing? What the hell is happening?!"

# Chapter 29

## CaElide

"It was a dream. The whole thing." Amah's voice was jagged. I sat up in my bed and rubbed my eyes, the fresh tension and hesitation amongst the others hot in my bones.

"What was a dream?" I yawned and looked at all four guardians. Mel and Andra were leaning against the banister and Gavin and Amah were leaning against the dresser next to me; both couples intertwined in one another. A lotta leaning this morning. "What's with all the brooding?"

"Good morning, Devi. We're going to have breakfast in town today. Would you like that?"

"Why are you talking to me like I'm five, Andra? More importantly, why are we *leaving*? We don't leave. *I* don't leave. People, remember?" I yawned again and adjusted myself in bed. "I still can't hold glamours for long. We can eat in the hall. I don't mind." The immortals were bothered. "Ok, seriously. I know y'all are immensely stronger than I am, but you've literally trained me for this. I *know* something is wrong, and it is stifling me. What>s going on? Was I snoring or something? Why are you all in here? Also, watching someone sleep is a little psycho, by the by. More so when you make it a *group* activity." I got out of bed but caught a wave of vertigo instantly. I fell back on the bed, my heavy head in my hands. "Whoa," I chuckled, waiting for the others to join in. They didn't. Amah looked at Mel and pretty soon, the others did, too. No one was to speak unless their new General ordered them to.

"Devi, let's go for a walk."

"I don't want to go for a walk, Mel. Unless you want to see me do random gravity checks?" No one laughed at my jab about my klutziness. "I'm—" I had a knot in my chest and was sore all over. "I'm a bit too out of it for a walk. Can't we talk here?" With that, Mel squeezed Andra's hand, and she walked out of the room with the others.

"Why are they leaving?" Suspicion spilled from my lips. As soon as the door shut, Mel's mood shifted. I tried to sneak a peek at his memories, but he quickly shut me out.

"Devi," he tried not to glare at me.

"Sorry. Did I miss something last night?" Rather than answering my question, Mel looked out the window and into the rising sun, running his fingers through his hair. Mel wore *jeans* and his shirt was too loose against him.

"You had another nightmare. A bad one. We stayed and watched over you."

"I have nightmares *all the time*, Mel. And none of them have harbored enough reason to have four mighty guardians at my bedside." Complete and utter lie... "What aren't you telling me?"

"You couldn't wake up. Nothing we did worked. We were resigned to monitor your vitals throughout the night until you awoke naturally." I don't remember any bad dreams. I did dream of the cutest rabbit, though.

"Damn. I don't remember any of it." It's happened; a dream so twisted I couldn't know whether I was awake or asleep. Alive or dead. "Did you see the dream?"

"What?" His answer was forced, as if it took all he had to say the word. Actually, he was exhausted.

"Were you able to see what I saw in my nightmare?" He rubbed his beard and walked over to the dresser.

"We didn't see your dream, but you talked in your sleep. Something about your adoptive parents." His eyes were beautifully sincere, but I didn't believe a word that came out of his everlasting mouth.

"Let's try this again, shall we? Literal lie detector here," I said, pointing my thumbs at my chest. "What happened last night, Mel? And this time, do me the courtesy of telling me the truth." He hid his gaze in the palm of his hands. There was an entire world in there. Living, breathing, dying… One word from him and it would be the end of me. Instead, Melot looked at me with a new-moon smile.

"Breakfast is ready, Devi. Get dressed. We'll wait for you."

"Mel, wait up." He stopped and turned on his heel. I looked up at him, brushing the hair and sleep from my puffy eyes. Thank goodness for barely there half-immortal morning breath. "I remember *some* of my dream. I went over the wall. There was the *cutest* rabbit and—" I giggled, but he but a stoic to shame.

"Let's go Devi." He took my hand, but I pulled it back... The rabbit. I followed him for miles, deeper and deeper into the woods. "Devi." There was a rush in his voice. As if he didn't want me to remember this nightmare. Nothing was horrifying about it. The rabbit was adorable and pudgy. But why was I on the other side of the protective shield against the wall?

"Why was I over the walls, Mel? In the dream, I was following this rabbit in the woods. But, I don't know why I was there to begin with." I rubbed my temples. "I'm supposed to have perfect recall. Why can't I remember?"

"Devi, it was a dream." Mel blinked us to the kitchen with the others.

"I followed the rabbit for *miles* into the forest. Why would I do that? Dream or not. Why would I even cross the wall for a *rabbit?*"

"You've been trapped in here for months, Devi. Your subconscious wanted to see what was out there." Gavin made sense. But his answer wasn't the whole truth.

"If I want to see the outside world, I can *scan.*" I crossed my arms and the burning in my stomach and face hit me. "Who the hell shot *arrows* at me? Did I fall face first into a tree in one of our training sessions yesterday? Good lord." I rubbed my face to ease the pain to no avail. "Demons...." I said. My words trembled as they fell from my lips.

"Di?" Vincent. I left the graveyard because I saw him *dying.*

"I *saw* them over the wall. I tried to stop Thomas..."

"You were *dreaming.*" No. This wasn't a dream. Was it?

"The demons trapped me in the forest. Keeping me there in a loop following the rabbit. He was bait. They fucking killed him." My little guy...

"Devi, we can talk about this later. You need to get something in your system."

"Mel, they were *here.* In the town. Miarrah and the others. You all fought them off. You thought I was safe in the graveyard. But I left, and the Knights got to me. I'm sorry." My fingers traveled across my face, traced over the areas where it had met with the tree trunk and demon fists.... I could feel the new bone that had healed from my broken leg. "I couldn't get away. And then I did. Someone pulled me out of the way."

"Devi, maybe you should lie down." Mel took a step toward me as the others took a step back.

"Vincent was here. He was *here.* Mel, he's *alive.*" I dared to smile. "He survived. That explains why I didn't die when he did. He didn't sever our tether," I said, my lips curled with disgust, "I survived because *he* did."

"Devi..." Mel shook his head heavily as the hearts of the immortals broke a little with every word. "You survived Vincent's death because before you were taken to The Court,"

Mel took a breath, readying himself for the blow to my chest, "he severed the tether between your souls. Had he not done so, when Thomas murdered him, you too would have perished." I looked to the others for hope. For defiance. I checked myself for any inclination of deceit from them.

I found none...

"No. You're wrong. I *felt* him. I *saw* him." His hands went for mine, but I swatted them away and backed into the fridge. "I tried bringing him with me. He wouldn't let me, though. Why wouldn't he come over the wall?"

"You had a nightmare, Devi. Trapped within it for *hours*. We couldn't wake you and at one point you were practically lifeless." Amah told me what was on the tip of everyone's tongues. But Mel flashed her a snare for defying his orders.

"Sounds like I was in CaElide. Why won't you just say that? What aren't you telling me?"

"He's dead!" I trembled from Mel's thunderous voice. I held on to myself before I fell apart. The aching and the burning back again; screaming out for a soul who could no longer hear mine.

"Where is he?"

"Devi, please. Do what is asked of you."

"And what is that, exactly, Andra? Fight? Eat? What order am I to blankly obey? Or do I simply pretend that I *believe* you when you tell me Vincent is dead?" No one spoke, but oh, did they *scream* inside. "He *survived*. We're *connected*." Melot interjected with a voice you rarely dare to refute.

"You felt Vincent *die*."

"I sure as fuck did. But last night—he's *alive*. I *know* it, Mel." I dared.

"Devi, when you were in The Court," it took Amah a long moment to speak again. She took special care not to touch me. "The punishments you endured, the deaths... You were in Hell, in the other underworlds—for *years*. The consequences that has had on your psyche—even being LeMehti—Devi, you're broken in ways we did not think imaginable. In ways someone should *not* be capable of breaking." Yet I broke... "You cannot trust everything that you witness. You cannot trust *yourself...*" I wiped her tears from my eyes and rubbed Gavin's quivering lips from my mouth. Creed was at the top of the spiral staircase. He listened to our conversation in the only way one could: in utter horror...

"So, how—how am I to trust *you*? What if you're all simply hallucinations? Shit. Who's to say I'm not still at The Court?" the wind couldn't find the strength to breathe... "*Years,* Amah?" my voice cracked, the lump in my throat catching. "I was only gone for a few *months.*" The look on all their faces.

"One Earth hour is equal to one Earth *year* in Cortem. You were missing for four hours, Devi."

"How long was I in Hell? The other Realms?" I don't know which I dreaded more; asking the question, or waiting for the answer I so clearly blocked from my memory.

"Devi—"

"How *long*?" After a heavy ticking of tocks from the grandfather clock, Andra was the one to answer. Her hands cradling her arms for dear fucking life. As if that embrace held me within it.

"900 years." The room tilted..."Devi—"

"Why can't I remember?" I pulled myself off the ground; trying to find my center of gravity.

"You won't allow yourself."

"What about Vincent? He came to The Court—"

"His journey to you took a bit over four years. Any place he may have ventured beyond that, we may never know. But Devi—"

"Right..."

"A few years, that's a blink of an eye for us, Devi. It did not hinder—Devi?"

"Yeah. I'm here. So, I'm 931 years old. That's a lot of candles."

"Devi!" they all shouted at me at once.

"Jesus! What?" All the furniture came crashing down.

The frost in the room melted, and the lightning storm fighting with the ripping of the Veil outside ended. "Did I—I'm sorry." Andra walked over to me.

"You are incredibly dangerous, Devi. And when you lose yourself, the way you did now, you become *lethal*."

"Isn't that a good thing?"

"Not when you use it against *yourself*." She wrapped her fingers around my wrists and pulled. My daggers slid out of my stomach and I finally tasted the iron in my mouth, the warm liquid dripping down my lips and spilling out of my lungs. The drops splattering too loudly onto my boots.

"I—I..."

"It's ok, Devi. It'll all be ok..." Andra wiped the blood from my chin. My flinching didn't deter her. "Let's get you cleaned up, love. Take my hand."

Andra sat me down and gently cleaned me with her magick while the others continued.

"Devi, you were dreaming. If Vincent had been here, he'd be able to cross over the wall."

"It was Thomas." Gavin tore his gaze away from mine and nailed it into Melot's. "The battle with Miarrah and the others was a distraction for us so that Thomas could take you." That wasn't Thomas. "Devi, stand up." I didn't move. "That was not a request."

"No. It was an *order*." I retorted.

I saw him coming towards me from the corner of my eye as Gavin's hand squeezed mine. But he let it go and took a few cautious steps away. Melot knelt and grabbed me by the shoulders, lifting me as though I weighed nothing. I cocked my head back to look him in the eye.

"It wasn't Thomas that saved me from the Knights."

"You know it was. Denying yourself that truth will only further the pain searing in your chest." Mel's hands slipped away from me; the rest of the regiment at attention behind him. "Get inside."

"Or what?"

"Holster that tongue of yours, Devi." Melot stood nearly as tall as Vincent, his hands clasped over one another at his belt.

"Are you supposed to protect me better from *inside* that safe house? That mock cathedral? *One* diversion and I'm nearly taken back to—" the graveyard spun with flashbacks, with Thomas's *sessions*.

"Devi, please—" I swatted Andra's hands away.

"No. How could you let Thomas get to me? How did you let *me* cross the wall? Shouldn't these be textbook contingencies?" No one spoke. But the wind, it had plenty to say.

"Contingencies *are* in place, Devi."

"Then why did they fail?"

"They didn't. You had a night—you were in CaElide."

"*Fuck* that. I know what I saw."

"No, you *don't,*" Mel said with finality. We had a staring contest.

"There's something else," I said, not satiated with Mel's answer.

"There's *always* something else." I turned back to Melot. "There are forces that impede ours, Devi. We saw you in the graveyard with Creed, *safe*. What we did *not* see is the possibility of Thomas attempting to snatch you away."

"I know you're only omniscient and omnipotent, to a degree. But for a future as dangerous as one with *Thomas* in it, I doubt *any* of you would've missed it. None of this feels right."

"Of course it doesn't, Di." Amah put her hand on my shoulder and I wanted her comfort. I *did*. But I flicked her away and teleported myself inside the Haven and made my way up the spiral staircase to the attic.

It met me with a wave of dust and faded sunlight. The wooden space was ordinary and void. Not even the likes of a ghost to help pass the time. Nothing but air and memories. Nothing but a tattered journal that belonged to a former resident here. I couldn't pry the book open. But I channeled an entry dated March 25th, 1888. The journal itself, however, I didn't need my psychic powers to know that it housed a thing irrevocably stitched into every fiber of my being.

Pure *pain…*

*"… And the blood dripped from the open mouth of the sky on their skin, yet they only saw rain. How horrible a thing it must be—then—for them to be human. How horrible a thing it must be—then—she thought, for her to never be again…"*

# Chapter 30

## Exodus

Their voices tickled behind my eyes. Their faces—stark, desperate curves clinging on to a hope that bled dry so long ago, it no longer has the same name.

The same meaning…

The Paladins, my *guardians,* don't remember a time where they didn't have to fight. For their lives, for their empire, for one another. Violence breathes in the blood of a soldier. A warrior that has done the *unimaginable*, again and again, and *again,* to ensure their skin feels the warmth of the sun one more time; to open their eyes and *know*, without a shadow of a doubt, the nightmare is over. That it's locked away in the darkest hollows of their minds.

They didn't know I could hear their conversation in the armory. I could see them scattered about the room, wanting, more than anything, to go *home*.

I returned the journal to the bookcase and backed away with every word they spoke. I hit the wall and slid down, sandwiched between a broken clock and a stack of paintings. The vision played before me like a dream; their bodies moving about the attic in the exact manner they moved into the armory.

"Melot, we have to stop her. We've lost *Vincent*, we— Goddamn it, we *can't* lose Devi, too."

"We won't, Gavin." Melot rubbed the back of his neck. He only ever did that when he felt powerless. "Though she is not ready, Devi leads us now. We do not defy her wishes."

"Then we tell her the *truth*. *All* of it." My eyes flickered to Andra. "If she is to run off on her own to end this war, let her do so knowing why it began." I thought I kept that plan secret. I thought my spells were strong enough to keep them hidden from a Paladin premonition.

"The truth could break her, Andra. She—the things she did to endure The Court. To endure *Thomas...*" we all took pause from Amah's outcry. "She *deserves* to know, she does, but if we tell her *now*—"

"It may ruin her beyond repair." Melot focused his somber gaze out the window. "How did we not get to them in time?" His voice cracked at the end and I clasped my hand over my mouth, my tears as hot as the guilt boiling in Melot's chest.

"Mel," Andra went to him, a hand sweetly cupping his, "we were protecting her loved ones. We were outnumbered."

"Knights, Paladins, all manner of ranks descended upon us that night to guarantee Vincent and Devi would have no chance..." Gavin's voice was in the room, but his mind—it was in the past, fighting a timeline that could never alter.

"This was the only path with any semblance of success."

"Vincent is gone. Devi suffered horrors the Devil *himself* wouldn't dare exact." Melot's fists tightened, and he went to punch the brick wall with full force. Andra's palm took the impact. Nothing but a gust of wind as consequence.

"This was the version that provided us with the best viable future." Andra kissed her husband's knuckles and nestled herself in his arms. His muscles laxed, and he took in a breath.

"Better one than none," Mel said, his words falling gently onto Andra's red curls.

"So, we let her go?" Amah asked the question, but her words were more akin to an unavoidable matter of fact.

"The truth will find her, Amah." Gavin tucked a lock of hair behind his wife's ear. "I only hope that she is healed when it does." Amah looked up at him, worry creeping in her voice.

"Healed?" She looked at everyone. Soldiers dressed as civilians in a room that would make the best militaries in the world blush. "That woman will know no healing. Devi was murdered in ways even *we* cannot process. She is a living tragedy, and she doesn't understand why. We cannot allow her to leave. She won't talk to us about what they did to her. Instead, she screams in sleep. She's leveled this building dozens of times. Creed almost *died*. We lost Thanys and Dahlia before they could teach her the rest of the spells. Spells *we* have no access to."

"Amah—" Amah ignored Gavin and paced about the room. We wiped our tears from our flushed cheeks and set straight our quivering lips.

"If we let her go, he *will* kill her." Thomas… "Not because he can, but because she will *allow* him to. This *plan* of hers..." there's no other way to set things right. I have to find Thomas. I have to save Vincent's soul and, once he's safe, I die. No me, no poison, no war…

"The terror of her past, it *breeds* in her bones, Melot." Andra stepped away from Mel, leaving him alone to face the defiance of my regiment—*his* regiment, once I remove myself from this equation. "There is a darkness hidden in the edges of her soul. Her *will*. It frightens us, Melot."

"What Devi did, she did so to survive." Melot bit back the hurt of his own words. His broken heart, however, he could not have shielded me from *that*. Andra ran her hands through her long hair in frustration. She tied it in an unfamiliar ballerina bun and surveyed her despondent family. She adjusted her belt and smoothed her button-down and gave a proper, paralyzing meaning to a word too long without one.

"There's no such thing as survival..."

I grabbed an old backpack from under that, oddly, had no claim to Vincent and filled it with clothes and provisions. My daggers and gun holstered.

One leg was out of the broken window when I had the urge to look back. My sweater rested under my pillow for easy access to cling to when I slept. When I unknowingly destroyed the world around me... I contemplated far too long about bringing it with me. I shook my head sighed.

I'd be dead soon enough.

I ran.

Through the graveyard and over the walls. I ran through the woods and didn't stop until I came to the train station I've been hearing for months but could never locate because *they* didn't want me to.

I was at the edge of the station. The air hesitantly wrapped around my form. I could see the sun beyond its flames and knew that I could defy its strength by mere thought. But the people, some people hurried, others cried. All held one unfelt truth that was universal, however.

Everyone could now *die*.

Simply because I was where they are.

I went to buy a ticket. When I reached into my leather jacket, I realized I didn't own a wallet.

Or money.

What the fuck am I doing?

The scenarios ran rampant in my mind; which people I'd mark for death by bumping against their shoulder if I wasn't careful, how they'd tortured and possibly killed. And with those cinematic visuals, sounds, and textures of every detail of their past and every possibility of their future, my irises drowned.

I shut my eyes, let them take in air, and once they opened, I knew exactly when and where to move to avoid *everyone.* If you looked close enough, my walk from the station to the platform resembled a well-choreographed ballet of perfectly calculated movements that only someone with supernatural blood rushing through their veins would catch.

And maybe a cinematographer.

I escaped the folly that was the train station plan and ran until I came to a cornfield in southern Illinois. All those people. All those lives you were about to risk.

You *are* out of your mind.

I didn't need the conjuring of a spell to shroud myself from the Paladins. I don't know why Vincent would order them to not follow me. One thought from any of my guardians and I'd have whatever reality playing in my mind; they honed that power in me well enough. One thought and I'd be incapable of crossing the Haven walls.

Until I wasn't.

Whether on the honor of posthumous orders or because everyone, including Vincent, knew there'd be no stopping me, the Paladins let me go; hoping the pieces would fall the way Vincent saw them falling.

Right now, I have to figure out where to go. And I can't do that when I can smell Lennon's perfume and hear Izumi's music playing. I looked over my shoulder. Over three hundred miles separated us…

"I can't believe it's today." A woman in her farmhouse said with anxiousness. Today. I don't know what day it is. Or month.

I scanned across the field into her house. The pot roast—why didn't I eat? *Focus, Devi.* Samantha threw the newspaper on the counter and went over to the sink to wash a cup for her coffee. July 1st.

Truth hit with jarring accuracy. I stood at the side of a dirt road isolated from everything I've ever known. *Turn back, Devi. Go back to your Paladins. You can't do this alone.*

But what choice is there? What choice did any of us ever have? If I were found by the enemy, if the wrong Revs caught wind of me, there'd be no one to save me but *me*. Andra and the others. I didn't know the whole of it, but I knew that if they disobeyed and followed me, their end would not be far behind.

The most powerful soldiers in the LeMehti empire *had* to stay out of my life because that's the only way they'd remain *alive*. And they *needed* to be alive for the horror that was to come…

A horror that Vincent foresaw—he saw it *all*—and he loved me anyway…

When I woke, I found I was not alone. A demon had found me. He grabbed me by the ankles and spread my legs apart... no, no, not again... I took out a dagger and slashed the blade two inches into his throat. The blood sprayed all over me and the room, but I grabbed my backpack and ran out of the motel, bumping into some worker on the way out.

The demon sauntered behind me. I made it to the parking lot when I saw three more. One male on the roof and two women leaning against a truck staring right at me with their charred eyes. Saanvae was one of them…

I'm trapped.

I took out my other blade, gripped tight, and—as though it were more natural than dying—I fought for my life.

I looked up from the blood-stained cement and smiled.

3

2

1

"Crescendo," I said.

In that second, they all stopped breathing, fell to their knees, and passed out from all the blood filling their lungs....

Their organs failed. The spell tore them from the inside out. Bones fractured until they shattered, the shards tearing through flesh.

I don't enjoy this amount of violence. But priorities shift when you've been butchered in ways once thought not possible. Comfort zones diminish and when once you wouldn't hurt a fly, you now have to adopt the belief that if you don't end someone's life fast, they will end yours faster.

But no battle is without consequence, and my body did not walk away from it unmarred. They're fucking demons, after all.

How am I supposed to heal from this? I won't keel over and die, but I won't heal for a while either.

For now, all I could do about my demon-inflicted wounds was manage them. It's pretty funny. I mean, how does one *manage* multiple aneurysms and broken ribs lodged inside—*everything*?

I clenched my fists, took a deep, *deep* breath, and ran for my fucking life.

I scanned the initial path I was to take. Making sure I'd bypass pedestrians, moving vehicles, birds, and insects. But I was too hurt. My ability to focus immaculately was going through the wringer. What took me seconds was taking me a *minute*.

I eventually made it safely to an empty apartment to get cleaned up. I changed into another outfit from my pack and as I jumped out of the three-story window; I set my bloodied clothes on fire and they were soot by the time I set foot on the ground.

"Holy shit!" I gripped my chest and waited to take a breath. "Kid, what the fuck?"

"How did you do that? That was awesome!" No, no. We're not doing this.

"Go away." I walked past the nine-year-old girl and onto

the sidewalk. But something crept in the dark. A weaving, twisting thing I had no words for.

"Hey, that was *my* window you jumped out of. So, I think you should tell me how you did that and...." my heart pounded, racing with nowhere left to run.

"Practice." Her face lit up. My eyes scanned for a threat I couldn't see. "No, no. You're a little too human—young, you're too *young* to learn that stuff." My mishap only brightened her mischievous smile.

"Hey, miss? Hey, what do you keep looking at? I'm down here." Rina reached for me, tugging my jacket. I tripped over my own feet, trying to avoid marking her for death. I could only burn the atoms seeping from my breath for so long.

Rather than being upset, she was *annoyed*. A little shit after my own heart. I sighed, scattering my breath to the Four Winds and away from *her*. She had done nothing wrong. *I* was the idiot who overlooked this possibility. I couldn't let my bullshit find her. It was *my* bullshit, wasn't it? What *is* that? My inability to differentiate between *their* kind unsettled me. These creatures were not evil, nor were they good. Yet, their ambivalence may prove more vicious than either.

"Do you need a place to stay? You can live with me and my dad." I looked down at her, puzzled.

"No. I'm ok. Just need to get out of here." And as far away from *humans* as possible.

"But, you can *stay*. My dad's parking the car and he's—I know he'll think you're pretty. *I* do." Lonely guy, attractive. Sad. Today was the anniversary of his wife's death and the birthday of his daughter.

I knelt to her level and tried to make things as swift as possible. "Listen, your dad is a really sweet guy, Rina, but—"

"How'd you know my name?" her lips widened with a hopeful smile and I stood there as I watched her father get shot over his daughter's shoulder. Two in the chest and one in between the eyes. Rina's body jerked with shock. The Agents—they didn't stop it. Why didn't they stop it?! Rina saw her father fall to his knees and his murders make their way to *her*.

"Rina, don't!" *Don't touch her, Devi. You'll kill her.* I›ve only ever heard of the Agents of Fate. I've never seen them before. They—they stood there, *watching*. "Rina, stop!" The men that killed Rina's father came for her. I ran *thousands* of different futures in my mind for every human involved. There was a future where the little girl lived. Where she grew up, happy and healthy. A future where the dirty cops spent the rest of their lives in prison for killing one of their own—framing him for *their* crimes. There was a future where her father *lived...*

But, in *those* versions of reality, I never left the Haven...

I blinked myself in front of Rina and shot one cop, point-blank, in the head before he had the chance to shoot Rina. The splatter on my face was minimal. When I was through with him, I caught the bullets his partner shot at me in my hand, dropping them all at his feet before I *made* him put his gun in his head. He pissed himself, crumbled to the ground, and begged for his life. I willed his gun-wielding hand down and marched over to the drug trafficking, wife-raping, child-murdering *stain*, firing shots into his skull until fingerprints were the only viable thing left to identify him.

The Agents—Watchers and Guides. They were immortal beings of Time and Fate—and they stood there and watched as I carried out the judgment on the humans. I finally saw one of them. The Veil didn't touch these beings. Their power rivaled that of gods. The terror in the eyes of the Watcher, however, was as human as ever. I shouldn't have survived witnessing her...

"Rina..." I gathered my senses and zeroed in on the frantic police calls. Brave, confused Rina, stood beside a dumpster with an unobstructed view of my crime. She wanted to run to her father, but instinct—or fear—told her to listen to me. I looked over my shoulder at the Agents. This man, *none* of these men, were meant to die today. But, had I let Rina run, it would be *her* bloodied corpse in the street.

"Can—can I go to him now?" she wiped her nose with her scrunched-up sleeve and waited patiently for my response. I surveyed the surrounding area. There were a few drunken folks, some tweakers, and several sober individuals awake in their apartments.

"Rina, if you hug him, the forensic evidence—" what the fuck are you saying to this child? "Yes. You can go to him." She ran at the tip of my words and I couldn't bear to witness the rest...

"I'll tell them the truth. You don't have to be afraid." I whipped around, stupefied. She looked up at me from her father's arms. "I'll tell them you saved my life," she said with a smile, tears dripping down red cheeks. "The angel said you can run. She'll keep me safe."

The lights of the ambulance and squad cars flashed across the city as they made their way through the night. The city—it lived and died between every breath. Countless lives that need not meet an end if someone interfered... Two sets of Agents flanked me, their hearts beating, confusion pumping through their veins. Fate, she had *no* answer as to why I had not flickered from existence at the mere sight of her children.

But Fate—it would seem—found the blood of men dripping from my lips *curious*...

I blinked myself to the nearest plot of consecrated ground and locked it down; conjuring a force field that would allow no one to enter; human, Rev, or otherwise. The burn of candles and echoes of hymns, the only music in the empty cathedral. Except, the longer I remained within its walls, the harder it ached; trembling beneath my every step.

I sat in a pew to gather myself. I'm homeless. I'm a killer...

I'm out of my depth.

I should turn myself in. I'd already treated the crime scene, removing any and all remnants of myself. Rina's story will be about a woman who shot the man who emptied his gun into his partner and was coming for her next. That reality was projected into as many civilians—humans as possible.

In prison, I would do nothing less than channel the lives—and crimes—of everyone in a uniform.

Maybe I should break the force field. Send a flare and make it easier for Thomas to find me. Why hasn't he come for me yet? Why haven't *any* LeMehti come for my head?

I leaned into the pew in front of me, wet eyes full of religion that allowed a father to perish and *a creature* to sit in its house.

"I wish you were here..." I buried my head in my hands and cried. In the dark, I saw myself on my knees at my bedside in The Court, weeping into my blankets. I fell into the vision without mercy...

Paint and blood were fresh on my hands and feet. There it is again. I caught the glinting. It came from the obsidian windows. The souls—they spoke on top of each other to get my attention. The moment I heard the voice, I looked up from my blankets and whirled around; eyes bloodshot and bruised beyond recognition...

"Who's there?" my memory asked. She tried standing, but after what Thomas had done—she crawled to the black glass and dared a hand to the pane. When I heard the voice—when I felt his hand on mine...

I crumbled the pew beneath me. This *isn't* happening.

"Devi, dear, it's time for your bath—Sephora, what is she doing?" The Paladins spoke and moved in unison. Every breath, every micro-expression synchronized, though it was never their doing.

"She does what Morseas do; she is conversing with the dead, Rogue."

"Do you see that, Sephora? The force field about her?"

"How can that be? Bordarrah, all of our incantations, her powers should be dulled, Rogue."

"It's the *souls*. Do you believe it, Sephora? What curious chaos. Come then. She cannot perceive us in the slightest."

They left, but *you* didn't. You told me stories and kept me sane. Taught me spells and fought through hordes of dead and damned and *more* to give me peace...

You protected me across the Realms. Across *time.*

You were where I was...

# Chapter 31

## Break Me

I gasped for air and in one crippling moment, I knew something stood at the opened cathedral gates. This something was Thomas.

The house of God cracked the sound of every atom between us in *agony*. Tiny waves of starlight flickered in terror with every breath we took.

Thomas could step over the threshold, yet he *chose* not to.

"You scared of me, Thomas?" I said, daggers at my sides as I stared him down the altar.

"I'm only afraid of killing you, Devi."

"Why's that? You think you'll finish too quickly?" He smiled but bit his lip to stop himself.

"Not at all." He stepped inside. I white-knuckled my daggers. "I intend to savor every moment of this." He tugged on his vest after he unbuttoned the top of his shirt.

"What are you waiting for?"

"Do you think he heard you?" Thomas rolled up his sleeves, his face contorted in mock interest as he made his way toward me. "That was Vincent you were praying to, wasn't it?" I rattled the foundation. "And there it is." He clapped his hands together, eyes silver and wide. "That *rage...*" Thomas composed himself and leaned against a pew halfway down the altar. "How are you coping with everything, now that you're back in the real world?"

"I'm homeless and murdered two humans for—"

"You had me at *homeless*." Thomas wouldn't keep eye contact with me. My face—it *haunted* him.

"Why won't you look at me?" He put his hair in a *man-bun* and put his veiny fucking hands in his jean pockets and ignored me. I gagged at the whole sight. "You want to end the war? You want your empire restored? Here's your chance. One shot, one kill." I holstered my weapons and stood not ten feet from him. "Keep your promise." I needed him to get closer to me.

"I tore out your soul when I executed Vincent."

"Where is he?"

"Who? Vincent? He's in Hell. Or did I send his soul to Andromeda?"

"Say his name again..."

"What, Devi? What will you do to me if I say his name again? Will you hurt me?" Thomas closed the gap between us, locking me in his arms. "Will you bring this cathedral down on us? Focus your emotions. Have I taught you *nothing*?" Thomas gripped me tighter, loose strands of his hair sweeping across my cheeks.

"You taught me to kill without mercy, you piece of shit! You taught me to *enjoy* it! I fucking *hate* you!"

"Good."

"End this. What are you waiting for? Save your people. Save *yourself*. You have *one* job. You're supposed to *kill* me not—"

"*Survive* you?" Thomas stared into me. The gunmetal of his eyes too stable for the chaos within. "You should run, Devi."

"What?" Thomas let me go and took a heavy step back.

"Don't stop until you know you're safe." Thomas examined the empty pews, mind lost in visions I dared not pry into, even if I could.

"Safe from what?"

"Me." The way his eyes shot back into mine… "I'm going to kill you, Devi." He undid another button. "Just not yet."

"*That's* not foreboding at all," I muttered. I think he laughed.

"You have a knack for saving people. Rina will live because of you. You're an Empath of LeMehti proportions. I know you hear them. How many visions of serial killers have you had on this block alone?"

"Are—are *you* telling me to become a fucking *vigilante?*"

"God, no," Thomas scoffed, and the church bellowed with everything he contained in the arms he crossed. "I'm telling you it'll be near *impossible* to shut out the *filth* of this place."

"And you care because?"

"I don't, Devi. Not since you made me *this*." I didn't think I had a heart left to break… When the candles snuffed out, I realized everything Thomas had been doing to maintain the structure. My presence was enough to rattle it, but me *and* Thomas…

"Were you there that night? At the graveyard. Was it you that saved me from the Knights?"

"Can't channel that from where you're standing?" Thomas slowly closed the gap between us again.

"You conveniently *block* yourself from me, you bastard."

"*Most* of me." He glanced down at his body, then back at me, his hands reaching for my waist. I took both daggers to his throat. "That is a sure-fire way to have us *sinning* in ways God did not intend, little one." He wrapped his hands around my wrists and pushed until my blades cut into his flesh. "I told you already, Devi. I'm *not* afraid of you."

"End this. End *me*…" I begged, wrath welling up in both our eyes.

Thomas leaned into me, holding me prisoner. His lips were dangerously close to mine and when he opened his mouth, he damned me all over again... "What makes you think I haven't?"

"Stop it! Get out of my mind!"

When I opened my eyes, the night had crept back behind the horizon, the burning light of the sun taking its place. A razored breath carved itself down my throat. Thomas never Reaped my soul... I was back hundreds of years in the past, locked up in the castle, rotting inside my mind for months while he...

I tried to get out of the bed but my muscles atrophied. I mustered what electricity I could and shocked my flesh to life.

I fell to the floor, and the castle rumbled; the candelabras shaking. There was something under the bed. A protection circle. I sat up, dumbfounded. He made the circle to protect me from *himself*... I examined the rest of the room. Thomas recently warded it from top to bottom to keep me safe inside and to keep all manner of evil out. I'd never seen warding *this* potent and it, too, targeted Thomas. My feet got their bearings, and I wandered about the bed-chamber, hand wavering over the sigils visible and glowing only when in the sights of a LeMehti. There was a caveat to the spell work.

Thomas could only enter if my life was in jeopardy...

I grabbed my daggers and holstered them on my back. Thomas had them splayed out and ready for this very moment. Still too weak to will new clothes into existence, I used materials in the room to fashion new ones. I'm not going anywhere in this nightgown he wrapped my body in... The blue cotton curtains made for a new dress. Leather from the rug and iron from the bed made for a comfortable breastplate and boots. The dress is far too long. I sheared off the front with my blade and—he's at the castle gates and I need to *run*. But if I step out of this room, I'm as good as dead.

It took Thomas a long time to get to me. He stood outside my door. Breaths were shallow, heart erratic. When his forehead hit the wood, I finally blinked. *He can't come inside, Devi.* My hand wavered over the partition. The one-inch of dead tree Thomas could speak out of existence. Everything inside me wanted to run for my life.

But…

"Don't open this door, Devi," he spat out with a struggle I'd not known in him before. But it was the way his body flinched away from the door, from *me,* that gave a heart-wrenching pause.

His bare feet were too cold in my boots. The air, a vice around his naked chest. I had to take a step back to breathe… I wasn't the only one hanging between worlds. Somehow, though, I think I was dealt the *kinder* hand… I took a shot in the dark and channeled his memories, hoping that his devastating state would render him defenseless from my psychic attack.

What I saw—Thomas fought back. Propelling me from his mind as I dropped to my knees.

"Why did you keep me alive? How could—how could you do that to yourself?" Silence. Loud, shattering silence until he glanced over his shoulder in response to something I was deaf to. Whatever it was, its violent break did not bode well with the immortal.

"Do that again, Devi, and I *will* kill you."

"Bullshit." I got up and opened the door. Thomas was—he was on the floor. Head low, knuckles bloody, skin rivaling a corpse. A hollow shadow of the soul that used to shine brightly within… I wrapped my arms around myself, at an utter loss. *I* did this to him. I've done this to *all* of them… A tear fell from my eye and streamed slowly down my skin. Thomas stared at that drop of water for far too long.

"Why have you kept me with you all this time when ending my life would free you?" I let the words escape through clenched teeth. Thomas rested his sweaty, ashen head against the brick wall. The memories of him burning himself *alive* over and over to keep himself from breaking down my door flashed across my eyes again. I lost my balance. Thomas lost...

*Everything.*

"I would not find freedom in your death."

Thomas held my gaze, and it was then that I realized, "You're *disobeying* them. Azrael, the others, they have no idea where we are, do they? What are you planning?" Thomas got to his feet and met me at the threshold of the door. The sigils vibrated. Their echoes crawling across my skin. Filling the room lost in time in a frenzied haze of cobalt.

"I am going to take us someplace no one can find, but we have to leave *now* before I change my mind." He dug his hands into the brick on either side of the doorframe, his eyes fixed into mine with a hopelessness that should not be breathing inside of this man.

"You wouldn't." I moved closer to the threshold. One more step and Thomas would be free to take me. "You wouldn't *dare*."

"I already have." Poison from his lips slid down the force-field between us, igniting the blue hue in our eyes. "Step over the threshold, Devi. I *have* to get us—"

"There is no *us*. There is *no* future where I'm safe with *you*, safe from *any* of this." The sigils burned brighter. The light glimmered against our skin, giving Thomas a hint of animation.

"Seeing as how I am your *only* means of survival, 'us' is an incredibly sound and tactical move. This place is no longer secure. Step over the thresh—"

"Why are you *protecting* me?!" His chest heaved, the glow of his marking on the back of his neck burst through his overgrown hair. And when Thomas stepped over the threshold, the warding in the room intensified to protect us *both*.

"What is this?"

"I'm *not* the threat."

"Bullshit." The silver of his eyes shifted dangerously between black and white.

"Do you *want* me to return you to The Court? Would you rather I allow Roan and her Knights have their way with you? Or would you prefer I end you right here and now?" He sped over to me, and I stumbled as I banged into the window. His hands went up on either side of me and he leaned in for my answer.

"End this." My words slapped. He shut his eyes with—disappointment? The damp strands of his hair swept across my lashes. I trembled beneath the touch and it made Thomas want to vomit.

"We're leaving, Devi." I had to wrap my hands around his waist to keep him there. Nothing but confusion and shock traveled through him.

"Why can't I take *myself*? Why in any god's name should I *trust* you?" Thomas stood a moment. Sullen. Exhausted. He kept my hands on his abs, eyeing the tattoos on my arms.

"You don't remember where the house is." He slid my hands up his chest, pulling me into him, "And, you *shouldn't* trust me." It took everything I had not to scream...

"I don't."

Thomas glanced at my tattooed arm. "But you're left with little choice." He released me from his hold, and I took refuge in the window; the sunlight warmed my back. Thomas—he warded the glass to force the light of the sun *in*. To force it on my skin... I glanced out the window, waiting for the star to flicker at my presence. It was the warmest I'd been since...

"Now what? We go to this place and live happily ever after?" He laughed and I had to try *not* to. I turned my attention to him, sifting through the visions of the future; waiting to see if one existed where I wouldn't be torn apart if I blinked out of this castle now that I was strong enough to.

"You have no idea how hard it is for me to stand here and not—" Thomas ran his fingers through his hair, keeping all his madness tethered within for as long as he was able.

"Not *what*, Thomas? Violate me? Bleed me dry? Drive me insane? You've done all that and *more*." My voice cracked at the end and it broke something inside Thomas. He hunched over, containing his rage. No. It's pain. "Thomas? You're scaring me." I rushed over to him. "Why are you—*how* are you dying?" He grabbed my waist and spun me behind him.

"Who's here?"

"Roan."

"Shit. Wait, Thomas, let me go!"

"*Shut up,* Devi." He threw me over his shoulder and jumped out of the window, running as soon as our feet hit the dirt.

Near the forest's edge, Thomas balanced himself against a tree as I pulled out broken branches from my hair beside him.

"How did she find us?!" His movements only registered *after* he clasped a hand over my mouth. The fire in our eyes could put Hell to shame.

"I thought I told you to *shut up.*" He released me and I shook my head. "Lucifer sent his army for you. Do you honestly think he doesn't harbor in him the ability to control *time?*" He dragged me by my wrist, but I tore myself away from him and ignored the burning on my skin. "Devi, *enough*. I have to get you out of here."

"And *where* are you taking me, exactly?" Thomas fumed. I seethed. "Why are we running? Scratch that. Why are *you* running? You're a fucking Breaker. A *Reaper*. Can't you just, you know?" I waved my hands in the air. "Reap Roan's soul?" He is fucking *done* with me... "How about *I* do it? All that training was for *this,* remember?"

"No, Devi."

"No, Devi? Then why train me to—"

"I'll die." My heart skipped a beat, and I struggled in between words. Thomas looked at me, then up at the clouds. "If I had told you the truth, you would have never let me teach you. And you still need one more lesson, but—it'll kill me, Devi. And I'll not leave you to *them*..."

"How then? How did I not kill you during the lesson?"

"I told you, your Reaping ability has barely come to being. Azrael taught you how to Mark souls to whatever realm you wished. What he wouldn't dare show you is how to *extract* one."

"How could he? He's a Judge, not you. And why would he ever have you show me how to fucking do the *very* thing you've all lost your minds over?" I adjusted my holster, looking to the sky for answers it could never provide. "Why didn't you take my soul and send it to Hell?"

"I don't enjoy repeating mistakes." He couldn't look at me. The pang of a regret I knew nothing of, too hot in my blood. When he finally looked at me, I looked away.. "I did not… "I did not lie to you. We *are* linked to our souls. Reapers can control their souls." Maybe Vincent sent himself to Heaven. Maybe, after I finally Reap myself, I can find him...

"Ok, so do us all a favor and send yourself to Hell. *All* of the Hells. I hear Hades holds a feast this time of year." I started walking, gesturing with my hand. "Right *after* you send Roan there. Deal? Great. Let's go." For someone on the verge of death, he sure is fucking fast. "Get out of my face, Thomas."

"You hear that earthquake?" The army's footsteps... "They're closing in. I can't cloak us for much longer. I need you to come with me." He's so sick, he can't Port me with him unless he *touches* me.

"No." He sighed and in that moment, that moment between two immortals breathing, I ran.

"Devi! No!" He chased me, but I ran harder. I was miles from him, so I took my chance to teleport when Thomas tackled me to the ground, birthing our own earthquake. We rolled around until he mounted me, my hands prisoner in his over my head. I didn't struggle. I only waited for the next opportunity.

"Would you for *once* do as you're told?! I can't protect you if you keep running away from me!"

"*Protect* me?! You *killed* me, remember? How long do you think it'll be before you murder me again? Days?

Weeks? *Hours?*" His eyes fractured, and I cried tears he held at bay. He blinked us away, but I brought us back over and over and it broke him in ways I wasn't prepared for.

"Devi, stop! Please—"

*"Please? Fuck* you! Get off of me!" I couldn't run the images of Thomas killing Vincent from my heart. When his eyes wavered on silver and black... I stopped fighting to free myself from his hold; my eyes burning with far too much black opal for anyone's liking.

"I—I don't know how much longer I'll be able to hold on. *Please—*"

"Welcome to *my* world, asshole!" This is my moment. His eyes settled on silver and mine to blinked myself out of his grip. With the DeKenna army in the forest, Thomas drew his sword. Dead, defeated eyes bored into mine, pleading with a shaking head.

"Devi, don't..."

"Go to Hell." I disappeared only to tumble across the other side of the forest, stab wounds in my side. I turned around and saw the army a few miles out in between me and Thomas. There were a dozen soldiers soulless and dead at his feet, and when Thomas saw me, he pulled out three daggers from his side...

Half the legion of DeKenna went after Thomas. The remaining 3,000 soldiers bolted after me. I ran faster and faster, making the ground beneath their feet quiver and crack open, swallowing them whole, but my stomach turned in on itself; my lungs burning. Both Thomas and I threw up blood.

Roan is here.

The edge of the forest was a couple of miles ahead. *This* many DeKenna on Earth—this many near *me*—I can't teleport. I've nowhere to go. Nowhere to hide. I had to keep running, but that made Thomas fight with a fever through a barrage of fallen angels to reach me.

The General of Lucifer's armies strolled through the quickly filling red field with a wicked grin on her face. Roan knew I couldn't outrun *Fate,* and it fueled her. Even if I were to teleport back to Thomas, she'd intercept me.

If I'm to die today, I'm going to die *fighting,* not willingly accepting defeat by running away. *Especially* not to any twisted sanctuary with Thomas.

Her Knights charged me. Thomas was a thousand feet behind them. His face covered in blood and his eyes—

*Devi*

"Devi, come back..." his voice cut through the battle. "Come back!"

*Devi, come back to me!*

*No...*

*Devi, please... come back to me!*

Beyond the army and through the metal and flesh—I found Thomas's eyes. They were pitch black...

He screamed. The atoms of his words echoing across my body, forcing me nearly off the cliff.

"Devi! *Run*!"

*Vincent...*

I knew what would become of me if I ran back to him. I knew Roan and her Knights would Port me to Lucifer the *second* they get close enough to me.

I pulled out my daggers and gauged a thousand versions of reality in the breath between a heartbeat until I found it. I'd break and bleed with every step, but I'd make it back to Vincent and save the *both* of us...

I cracked the hilts of my daggers together, setting them—and my eyes—ablaze. Vincent locked my position from across the army and I felt a surge in his body. He smiled and I couldn't help but return the action.

I dug my foot into the ground, and we ran...

The forest floor was a cemetery, and Vincent and I were the executioners. Any soldier I put in the ground, Vincent took their soul and sent it back to Hell.

But we couldn't move fast enough. Vincent was dying...

Every time I tried teleporting to Vincent, Roan snapped

me back. Every time Vincent tried blinking me to *him*, he went blind; the poison within constantly battling to take back control.

Roan dispatched more soldiers and when they attacked Vincent, I let out a scream that pulled them away from him. The force of my wail tearing them apart, atom by fucking atom.

Roan laughed as I dropped to the ground. A spell of *that* conjuring... I fell to my knees, the battlefield spinning. Roan reached for my throat but stopped dead in her tracks.

The soldiers—their movements ceased. Vincent sealed the *entire* army; thousands of demons encased in a prison of time. It gave me a chance to get back on my feet and Vincent a chance to run to me with our tears marking paths down our bloodied faces.

But he stopped short and didn't dare move.

"Vincent," I called out, but my voice quivered, throat aching to breathe. And when I took a step toward him, he took a step *back*.

With his soul barely breathing in mine—the rain fell without mercy.

Please, God... Don't take him away from me again. Not again.

*Run...*

The clock struck its final hour. If Vincent came back *now*, he'd kill me...

"Run!" His eyes were the stage of the truth I'd been so blind to. They danced from blue and black to silver and white. The unimaginable coursing through us. I stood, helpless, as he tried with *everything* he had left in him to keep his soul.

I watched in horror as Vincent tried to stop himself from *murdering* me—*again*.

In that moment, I saw my midnight blue sky reflecting the amber of mine and I ran.

Ran to absolute nothingness. Vincent vanished before I could lay a hand on him. I whirled around, scanning the battlefield. Checking the dead, the frozen.

"Vincent!" I hunched over, my wail taking flight with the winds. He returned, but he came back *wrong.*

Vincent was trapped in a time loop, traveling between countless timelines. "What—what's happening?!" I stood before him, his body vibrating through reality…

*Stop it! Goddamn it! Vincent, come back to me!*

He exiled himself in the gallows because if he *didn't….*

I stopped the storms; every atom paralyzed. I ignored the aneurysms. Let the blood drip down my eyes… I raised my hands and clawed through the panicked air. When I had a tight enough grasp, my hands burst with a black galaxy of light—the light of *Time.*

*Vincent,* ***enough****! Do you hear me?!* ***Come back****!*

I balled my hands and dragged against the fabric of time and space and pulled Vincent out of the leaps. We fell, bloody, broken, and breathless, to our knees…

We were on the ground, arm's length apart. Vincent stretched his hand to mine, but the chaos in him rose in both our throats. His bruised face contorted, recoiling his touch from mine. I crawled to him, but he vanished.

"Vincent, *please*!" He unmasked our tether completely, then, allowing me audience to his memories, witnessing every moment through him from the night I thought he died at The Court to him pretending to be Thomas and *everything* in between.

Vincent became consumed by the poison when he rescued me from Bordarrah. *Centuries* in Cortem slowly going mad.

The secret orders of the Paladins, the patterns…

The things Vincent did to protect me from *him…* And he did it *repeatedly.*

I couldn't reconcile it. *Any* of it.

"Vincent! What have you done?!" I used what strength I had to will him to me. But he pushed back. "You won't hurt me. You won't hurt me. Don't—you're so far away…." I sobbed into my hands, holding myself before I split.

"Devi, please. There's no more time. You have to run!"

His choices flashed inside me again, knocking me to the ground. "How many times? How many times?!" I tried to stand but failed miserably as Vincent watched helplessly a few yards away; desperate to hold me but *terrified* to tear me apart...

"I didn't have a choice. Please, forgive me." We stopped fighting to stand and took our place amid the blood-soaked earth and bones. Vincent's tears reflected in mine—all we had to do to be in each other's arms was to stand and take one single step...

"There's *always* a choice!" I fell forward, hands digging into the wet grass. Vincent's breath touched my cheeks; his fingers daring to cross the battlefield between us.

"Not for *us*, Devi. Not *this* time..." Vincent's hand disappeared and there was a sting in my core.

"Vincent? What—what is that? What are you doing?" I clutched my chest, the ache in him choking me. "Vincent, don't..." I begged, reaching for him, but his magick gently tugged me back, pulling me away from him.

"Remember me..." Vincent choked on the words that echoed inside me with horror. His tears drowning in my eyes.

The second tug was stronger, and I clawed into the dirt when he forced me back. "I'm *begging* you, stop! We can fight this, please!"

The black of his hair and midnight blue of his eyes sank beneath the plague of white I damned him to. And as the last remnants of Vincent's soul flickered inside mine, he raised a hand to his chest and gripped tight his armor.

My eyes widened. "No, Vincent. Don't!"

*Vincent!*

***You** are my soul...*

"Goodbye..." At the edge of his last word, Vincent's hand trembled, palming his chest. His touch radiated, mirroring across my skin for one beautiful moment and then Vincent *pushed...*

The hands of Time took hold of my arms and waited for Vincent's command to strike. Vincent mouthed *I love you* and his silent words swept gently across my lips. And with the taste of salt, iron, and inevitability on our tongues, Vincent banished me from the cliff with a truth heavier than every lie I've ever known…

There was only ever one version of reality that *didn't* end with the universe broken at our feet. It had to be the one where the universe broke *us*...

The version where I was the death of him.

The version where Vincent had no choice but the one bleeding in his hands. A choice neither of us had a weapon against. A choice that was written in the stars *centuries* before our souls collided.

One where the only way I'd survive, the only way I'd survive *him,* was for Vincent to do one thing he swore he'd never do.

Break me...

# ACKNOWLEDGMENTS

There are not enough words to thank every single person involved in the birth of this book. From my incredible formatting team to my sweet editor, to my Beta and ARC readers who braved the strange curse of this book, to every teacher who saw art in my writing—Thank you.

From the friends who support me unconditionally from all corners of the world to the friends who watched Never Been Kissed with me in theatres and—during that break room scene—adamantly reminded me I was Josie Gellar. That I was a writer (and a hopelessly hopeless romantic)—Thank you.

From Ashley's voice notes and spells to Amy's '67 Chevy Impala and faith in me to everyone in BookTok—Thank you.

From the boundless love and occasional motivational threats of my coven—Veronica, Jennifer, and Sarah—there's a reason there are characters written with the ink of your souls in the books (blood would have been too messy). You are ineffable (except for when I use words to describe your characters).

To every single person who supported my writing—Thank you.

Last, I want to thank my characters. You trusted me to bring your story to this world, and I will forever be grateful for that honor. This is only the beginning. If they mean to read us, let us give them reason...

**ANORIN** was always the quiet, nerdy girl reading books and getting lost in their worlds full of magic, impossibility, and true love. When she didn't have her nose stuck in between the pages of a story, Anorin would dream up her own. And with a background in psychology, criminology, and linguistics, Anorin brings a unique perspective to complex, relatable characters.

She adores the darker side of storytelling. Of things that hide beneath the shadows and inside your own mind. She's not afraid to explore what's waiting at the edge of reality and her stories will always have one element above all others: Love.

When she isn't writing, Anorin loves reading everything from fantasy to forensics, enjoys drawing and the crafts, and lives to ignore Do Not Enter signs (particularly those on cemetery gates). And if you can't find her at a comic book convention or in the woods, check the floor. She's constantly doing random gravity checks.